I0760851

BOOKS 1 – 3

QUEENS OF THE FAE

MELISSA A. CRAVEN
M. LYNN

Edited by Cindy Ray Hale
Proofread by Caitlin Haines
Cover by Maria Spada
Interior Art by Melissa A. Craven

For our advanced readers.
You made us feel like this
story matters.

PRISON REALM

NORTHERN VATLAN

LOCH VILLANDI

FARGELSI KINGDOM

SOUTHERN VATLA

DRAGUR FOREST

VINDUR CITY

ISKALT KINGDOM
EASTERN VATLANDS
EEDFAL
SANDUR
SOL LOCH
UR KINGDOM
TEOTANN OASIS
ELDUR DESERT
H LANGT
RADUR CITY

QUEENS OF THE FAE
BOOK ONE

FAE'S
DECEPTION

MELISSA A. CRAVEN
M. LYNN

Prologue
Alona Cahill

"Your Highness, please, you must allow me to do my job." Rowena rushed to help Alona with her hair.

"Rowena, in less than a year, I'll be serving as Lady Driscoll's maid way out in Sandur. How does anyone expect me to dress and style a great lady if I can't even manage my own hair?"

Rowena leaned down behind her until Alona could see her maid's reflection in her hand mirror. "My Lady, before you leave for Sandur, I will teach you everything you need to know. Until then, I intend to treat you as the princess you are." She ran a brush through Alona's blond mane. "Whatever traditional nonsense dictates, you were born a princess of this kingdom, and it makes no sense you should ever have to be anything less than what you are."

"I am not above the law, no matter who my mother is."

"She will get you out of this. I have faith. You will rule as your mother's heir one day."

"I was born without magic, just like you. I'm almost eighteen now, soon I'll join the serving class. There's no use pretending it isn't so. Now, show me how you do my hair in that twisty thing."

"Very well, my Lady." Rowena guided Alona through the steps to secure her hair in a neat updo, perfect for traveling. "You seem nervous."

"I'm more than just nervous. I'm petrified. What if Lady Driscoll asks me to serve her tea or something else I don't know how to do yet?"

"She wouldn't dare. Not a minute before your eighteenth birthday and probably not even after."

"What do you mean, not even after?" Alona secured her traveling cloak in place with a jeweled broach her mother gave her last year.

"My Lady, I can't imagine anyone will actually make you serve."

"Then what am I to do with my life?" Alona's eyes widened in alarm. For seventeen years she'd prepared herself for a future as a lady's maid. She'd even had days when she couldn't wait to get started in her new life. But if she wasn't allowed to serve as her mother's heir, nor allowed to serve as a maid in more than just name only, then how would she fill her days?

"Don't trouble yourself, my Lady, I believe you will become more of a companion to Lady Driscoll than an actual servant. After all, you may be destined for the serving class, but you are still the queen's daughter. That will never change."

Alona couldn't imagine a more boring task than to entertain an old lady waiting around to die. Lady Driscoll was a widow friend of her mother's. She'd always believed the Lady would treat her well, and she knew her mother and Lady Driscoll had schemes to marry her into the merchant class after she'd served a few years as a maid. But Alona wanted to embrace her new life and the freedoms it brought. One of those freedoms was the right to make her own choices in a way she'd never been able to as a princess.

"Are you quite certain you don't want me to go with you, your Majesty?"

"I can manage without you for a few weeks," Alona insisted.

If the whole point of this trip was to meet her future employer, then she didn't think it made sense to travel with an entourage befitting a princess. She'd had to argue her point with her mothers, but even they saw the sense in her request eventually. She still had to travel with the queen's guard—the head of the guard no less. But Alona looked forward to spending time with Eamon Donovan, the captain of the palace guard and a man who'd been like a father to Alona. He would escort her safely north to Sandur, an exotic city along the coast of Eldur's wasteland. She'd never traveled to the northern half of their kingdom before and was looking forward to the trip.

"Are you all set, sweetheart?" The queen consort peeked into her daughter's rooms with a forced smile on her face.

"Yes, Mama, you two can come in now. I know you've been lurking in the halls for the last half hour. And I know you both have better things to do with your time."

"We have nothing so pressing that we can't wish our daughter a safe trip." The queen crossed the room, taking a moment to adjust the broach at Alona's throat. Both Queen Faolan and Queen Consort Tierney were her mothers in every sense of the word, but Faolan gave birth to her, hoping for a strong heir—something that was not in the cards for their little family.

"Lady Driscoll will take good care of you, my dear." Faolan squeezed her hands.

"I think it's supposed to be the other way around, Mother." Alona smiled.

"Not yet."

Her last year as a princess of Eldur would be filled with many 'not yets.' Her mothers wanted her to enjoy her last year at court, but Alona wanted to get it over with.

"I'll be back before you know it, Mother." She hugged the queens, leaving them behind to comfort each other.

For the first day and a half of her journey, Alona did as she should and rode in the carriage as befitting her current station. But on the afternoon of the second day, she chose to ride with Eamon and his men on horseback. She wanted to catch the first glimpse of Sol Loch's crystal clear waters and the hot springs there. The air already smelled of sulfur, and the heat of the day caused Alona to travel with a cotton veil over her head and face to shield her from the sand and the heat. Had she been born with the power of the Eldur Fae, the sun would have strengthened her the way it did for all Eldurians. They were the strongest of the Fae, yet they were limited to using their magic only during the day. At night, Alona stood among equals.

"Just a little farther, Alona, and we'll break for the evening at the hot springs," Eamon said. "Maybe we can even find one of the mud springs where you and Finn used to have good old fashioned mud fights when you thought I wasn't paying attention." His grin was infectious, and so like his son's. She'd grown up with Finn Donovan among the other children in residence at the palace.

Finn was just two years older than Alona, but most of the time he acted like he was seven—and probably still would when he was seventy.

"If we find a mud spring, I'll be taking a mud bath. I believe I've outgrown mud fights."

"You know, Lona, pigs take mud baths." Eamon flashed a mischievous smile at her.

"Oh, you know very well the Ladies of the Eldur court pay good money for that mud."

"You're all nutters. Every last one of you refined sort."

"Well, in a year I won't be quite so refined."

"You will always be a refined lady, my Lona." Eamon's handsome smile routinely melted the hearts of most of those 'refined ladies' at court. "Even covered in mud like a pig."

"Oh, you just hush now." She laughed.

"Morgan and O'Mally, ride ahead and find the lady a mud spring. And while you're at it, put up her tent so she can rest before dinner."

"Yes, sir!" The two youngest soldiers of Eamon's unit took off ahead, eager to do their commander's bidding.

"Thank you, Eamon. I shouldn't allow such luxuries, but I am tired, and I haven't enjoyed the hot springs in ages."

"We will get our first glimpse of Sol Loch just over the next rise. The waters there will be soothing this time of year. Hot, but not too hot."

"Sounds wonderful." Alona leaned forward in her saddle, eager to set her eyes on the crowning jewel of Eldur for the first time in years. She'd grown up at the palace in the capital city, Raudur, that lay along the rocky cliffs of the Dalur River. It was cooler there and beautiful in its own way. But Sol Loch was breathtaking in its wildness. She would love to spend her days here among the many lakes and hot springs, but it was far too close to Eldfal, the massive volcano in the northern wastelands. The stability of the land here was always in question.

"I would live here in a heartbeat if the land was fruitful." Eamon gazed across the rolling sandy hills to the oasis that was Loch Sol in the distance.

"And if the water was drinkable," Alona added. "We could have a little cottage near the springs and live out our days free of palace gossip and Eldur hierarchy."

"We can dream." Eamon winked. "If we ride ahead of the carriage, we'll be there in half an hour."

"Race you." Alona dug her heels into her mount's sides and flew down the hillside, laughing the whole way.

"Alona Cahill, I didn't help raise a cheater!" Eamon called behind her.

"Finn taught me!" She galloped over the desolate hills and valleys, but Eamon quickly pulled ahead of her. His men surrounded her, keeping pace with her mount until they reached the rolling green hills of Loch Sol.

"Winner, winner, doesn't have to cook dinner," Eamon taunted.

"If you expect me to cook dinner, we are in for a sorry night indeed. I can't draw my own bath, much less cook a stew over a campfire." Alona felt so useless in these moments. She hated that she needed servants to take care of her.

"It's all right, Princess. You are far too intelligent to waste your talents cooking for a bunch of raggedy soldiers."

"Talents?" She laughed.

"Sir, my Lady," Morgan interrupted their playful banter. "We've set up camp just along the trail ahead. We've found hot springs as well as a mud spring for the princess."

"Thank you, Morgan. I appreciate your fine scouting skills." Alona nodded to the soldier.

"Thank you, my Lady." Morgan's ears turned pink at her praise.

"My men will set up camp, Lona. I will take you to the mud spring and keep watch while you enjoy the rest of the afternoon. I know you must be weary from traveling all day." Donovan slid off his horse and tossed the reins to Morgan.

Alona dismounted from her horse, feeling every aching muscle in her body cry out for the soothing balm of Sol Loch's healing waters. The unforgiving Eldur sun seemed to have sapped all her strength. The mud would ease the aches and pains and leave her skin silky smooth. When she finished bathing in the hot springs, she would feel a thousand times better.

Alona stripped down to her shift and sank up to her knees in the sun-warmed mud bath. Sitting down, she made herself comfortable for a nice long soak. The magical properties of the natural spring eased the aches and pains of traveling across the unforgiving desert.

A rustling noise brought Alona out of her sleepy stupor brought on by the steam.

"It can't be time to go already." Eamon would die before he

would let any of his men near the springs where she bathed, but she wasn't certain they still wouldn't try.

Alona was about to turn when a dirty hand clamped over her mouth. A blinding pain ripped through her head, and her mind went dark.

Chapter I

TWO MONTHS EARLIER

Brea Robinson was a lie.

Okay, not in the truest sense of the word. Brea was really her name, and Amanda and Jack Robinson were her parents. Parents who would never understand her.

This life was what felt like a lie. She'd never fit in this world of high school hallways and concrete jungles. That was what her school was. A jungle. A wild place, unsafe for anyone who didn't fit.

"I can't believe I'm back here." She sighed as she hiked her backpack higher on her shoulder.

Myles, best friend extraordinaire, sported a giant grin, one she couldn't match.

"Why are you so happy today?"

He lifted his hands to the blue sky above. "It's a beautiful day, Brea." He never said her name with only one syllable like everyone else. Since they were kids, he'd called her Bree-ya.

"It's..." She lifted her eyes to the building they'd tried improving with brick columns and colorful banners flapping in the breeze touting the Southern Ohio school's many accomplishments. "A day. A freezing day."

"Don't be so glum, chum." He draped an arm over her shoulders and squeezed. "I'm just glad you're back."

Back. Because she'd been gone. How could she forget? Mentally unstable Brea Robinson missed the first month back from winter break because she was at the Clarkson Institution for Troubled Teens. It was where they put you when you had a freak out on Christmas morning.

Her ever-eloquent mother named the episodes freak outs. Brea wasn't really sure what they were. All her life, she saw... things—for lack of a better word. Sometimes when she looked at a person, she saw features that weren't there. Pointy ears, flashing eyes, bright colors.

Sometimes they were the stuff of nightmares.

The psych-dude she saw when she was young claimed she was having night terrors, but during the day.

It wasn't just seeing things though. When she got angry or sad or even happy, it was like she lost control of the emotion, and it expanded within her, overcoming every thought and even manifesting as this weird energy beneath her skin.

An energy begging for release that sometimes got her into trouble.

"Do they all know?" She climbed the front steps, walking under a banner proclaiming the school as the football state champs.

Myles hesitated before he spoke. "I mean... there were rumors." He pulled open the glass door and waited for her to enter.

But how was she supposed to do this? Face them? It wasn't the first time she'd been two-sleeves short of a straight-jacket.

If her mom had any say, they'd have lost the key to her room.

Sucking in a deep breath, she repeated her personal mantra. "I'm not crazy. I'm not crazy."

Myles reached for her hand, threading their fingers together. "No one thinks that."

He overestimated the kids in their nowhere town. The people of Grafton, Ohio loved gossip. It entertained their small minds.

He squeezed her hand tighter as if sensing she didn't believe him. She looked down at their joined hands. "You know, this is why everyone has thought we're a thing since like the fifth grade."

"And since when do we care what they think?" He never had, but as she walked down that hall, Brea couldn't think of anything else.

Maybe her mom was right. She did belong at Clarkson permanently, somewhere that could help her rid herself of the hallucinations and surges of anger and fear she couldn't control.

"If you didn't spend all your time with me, maybe you'd have more friends." She pulled her hand free, pretending to adjust the strap of her backpack.

"Why do I need other friends?" He stopped at her locker and leaned against the pale metal. "Who else is going to dissect every scene of *The Witcher* with me? Have you finished season one yet? I'm dying to tell you all the parts you missed by not reading the books."

"Myles." She shook her head in exasperation as she turned the rusted dial. It stuck on the last number—like it always did—and Myles hammered it with his fist until it popped open. She slid her coat off and shoved it in. Opening her bag, she stuffed the books for her first classes inside. "We've been over this. I'm not a reader." But she was a watcher. She watched every single fantasy movie and television show multiple times and discussed them with Myles. "I don't need to read when I have my very own walking-talking Encyclopedia of fantasy to tell me all the parts that didn't show up in the movies."

"You're missing out." Myles shook his head.

"Speaking of missing out, what did you do while I was in prison?"

"You weren't in prison."

She rolled her eyes. With how closely the staff watched her, she may as well have been. That's what happens when you shove your mom across the room and into the Christmas tree. She still couldn't explain why or how she did it, but that didn't matter.

"Okay, fine. While I was in the hospital spending all my time in therapy, did you hang out with anyone else?"

He only shrugged and propped one Converse-clad foot against the locker. Guilt gnawed at her, but that wasn't a new feeling. She appreciated how loyal Myles was to her. Throughout her life, he was the only person she'd ever been able to count on. But he deserved more than a messed-up girl who saw inhuman freaks everywhere she went.

She met Myles in fifth grade when his family moved into the farm next door to hers. It was a love-at-first-sight kind of thing. Another lie. Love. But not with Myles. It was never romantic between them, but they'd bonded over their love of horses and desire to be anywhere but on their respective farms.

He was an attractive boy, and she knew for a fact the girls in the school liked him. It was one of the reasons they hated her so much. He could have been popular. All he'd have to do was make that short walk across the cafeteria at lunch and slide onto the bench with the rest of his football teammates.

Yep, that was right. Brea Robinson's best friend was a football player.

They walked to his locker so he could grab his books.

"Are you ever going to answer my question?" She tried to ignore the students hurrying down the hall, trying to get to class like it was any normal day. For them, she supposed, it was.

They didn't have to try and re-integrate into a place of whispers and accusing glares. She hadn't missed those.

Myles slammed his locker shut, and the sound reverberated down the emptying hall. The tardy bell rang, and he grinned. "Ooh saved by the bell."

She hurried after him. "We have the same first period, doofus."

They entered English Lit and walked to their usual seats near the back.

"Hi, Myles. You can sit by me." Ellen, a senior cheerleader, sent him a wave.

Brea had never until that moment disliked Ellen. She'd always been the sweet one on the team, unlike the rest of the girls who accused Brea of being some sort of witch—ironically, of course.

Myles grinned and puffed out his chest—ew—before sliding into his usual seat and leaning back. "Sorry, El. My girl needs me."

"El," Brea whispered with a shake of her head. "For the record, I don't need you."

His smile only widened. "Sure you do. You love me."

God help her, she did. Her parents weren't big on the love word —probably because their hearts were made of stone. But Myles let his feelings loose whenever he thought she needed it.

"Are you ever going to tell me what you've been up to?" She folded her arms on top of the dark-stained wooden desk.

"Cap had her colt."

Brea sat up straighter. Captain—named for Captain America—was the pride and joy of the Merrick farm. "Why didn't you tell me the moment you picked me up this morning?"

He shrugged. "I knew you'd yell at me because I've spent the last month in the company of beautiful beasts who aren't big on the talking." He reached over and flicked her hair. "Hey, they kind of sound like you."

"I'm not a beast," she grumbled. Or beautiful. Beauty was another one of those lies she hated so much. It was just an illusion.

He threw his head back with a full-throated laugh that had more than a few heads turning their way.

Brea leaned across her desk to Myles. "They're staring at me."

"That's because they missed you."

She snorted. "Yeah, okay." Most days, she wished the kids at her school didn't know she existed. But it was hard to ignore the crazy girl. That was an awful term—one people at the institute chastised her for every time she used it. But it didn't mean it wasn't how she felt.

Mental illness, they'd told her, was not something she could control, or deserved. They said it was an illness like any other, and nothing to be ashamed of.

But some days, shame was all she felt.

Mrs. Epstein walked to the front of the room, her gray hair pulled back into a severe bun. She started talking to them about whatever boring book—oops, literary classic—they'd been assigned to read.

Brea wasn't a reader. She subscribed more to the "do as little as possible" philosophy. Unlike Myles who was already bent over his notebook scribbling notes.

His perfect grades meant he'd eventually go on to some fancy college, leaving her behind. It was inevitable.

He wanted to be a large animal vet focusing on horses and cattle.

And he'd be amazing at it.

She watched her friend as a lock of caramel-colored hair fell into his eyes, wishing she could have just an ounce of his confidence.

His life wasn't perfect by any means, but then, perfection was only an illusion.

Another lie.

Throughout the day, Brea heard many variations of the rumors about her absence. She'd met an older man and run off with him, only to be dragged home.

She'd left to have a baby. That one stung a little. Had she really looked eight months pregnant before she left?

Then there was the story of the drugs she'd gotten hooked on, thanks to the sketchy characters who worked her family's farm. She thought she seemed pretty good after only a month in rehab.

It was Riley Anders, Captain of the boys' soccer team, who hit closest to home. As she'd walked by him at lunch, she heard the words "wacko" and "asylum" thrown into the atmosphere as if they didn't hold the power of a thousand knives.

Myles waved to her from their usual table, but she stood frozen in the center of the busy cafeteria. Classmates swarmed around her, as if not seeing the girl in the middle of a major crisis.

Her feet wouldn't move, like they were stuck in mud, swirling, sucking mud.

But the white tile floor was clean—or at least as clean as a school floor could be.

Nothing held her in place except a heart-splitting fear. This was her life now. Her breath came in short gasps as she tried to calm her shaking hands.

Energy buzzed underneath her skin, growing louder as the anxiety swirled out of control. She couldn't do this, couldn't be here.

The lies she told herself ate at her. She was okay. It was just a phase. Nothing was wrong.

Nothing was okay. This would never end.

And it was all so, so wrong.

Brea Robinson was a lie.

"Brea." Myles appeared at her side, lifting a hand to grab her arm.

She twisted away from him, forcing her legs to push through the quicksand of her fear.

"Brea!" Myles called after her as she ran through the cafeteria, shoving people out of the way.

She burst through the double doors into the hall, but it wasn't enough.

"I can't breathe," she said to herself as her head whipped from side to side searching for an escape.

"Where are you going, weirdo?"

She didn't know who said it, but a crowd of people stood in the doorway watching her.

Myles pushed through them, trying to get to her, to reach her.

But he was too late.

Brea's sneakers squeaked against the tile floor, and the hall became a blur of lockers. A hall monitor tried to stop her, but she kept going until she reached the front door of the school.

A blast of winter air struck her the moment she crashed through the doors. She gulped a breath as if she'd never feel its icy chill again and ran down the steps.

Snow coated the walkway in front of her, leading to the student parking lot where a fresh dusting covered the cars.

Snow made the world look so new, but even that was a lie. It only covered up the grime underneath.

A chill raced down her spine, and she hugged her arms across her chest, wishing for the jacket that sat snug in her locker.

Wacko.

That was what they thought of her. She couldn't face this school any longer. But where could she go? Her parents thought much worse things of her. Tears froze in her lashes, and she wanted to scream. Not even her tears could thaw her.

"Where are you going?" Myles' voice behind her was soft.

She didn't turn to him. "Leave me alone, Myles."

"Brea, you have to go back in there and show them nothing they say matters."

"But it does. It all matters." She whirled on her heel, narrowly missing a patch of ice. "You can't tell me you don't think it. Just a little."

"Think what?"

"That I should never have been released from the institute."

"I'd never think something like that."

A warm tear tracked down her icy cheek. "No, you wouldn't say it, but everyone thinks it. My parents. Them." She gestured to the school. "This version of me, the one who exists inside that school instead of in a sterile room. It's not real. I finally see it now. The Brea Robinson you see is the lie."

"Don't say that?"

Anger burned through her. Why couldn't he see this?

The doors opened behind them, and a few of Myles' teammates piled out of the building. They stopped when they saw them.

"Lover's quarrel?" Carson Freemont asked.

As the quarterback, most people wished he'd speak to them. But he'd been tormenting her since middle school, and she just wished he'd go away.

"This is none of your business, Freemont." Myles drew himself up to his full height—which was about an inch taller than Carson's six feet.

Carson laughed. "Touched a nerve, did I?" He looked to his friends with a grin. "So, Brea, heard you were in the nut house. Almost killed your ma."

And it all made sense. How some of the kids at school knew. Carson's mom was in a church group with Brea's.

Her tongue stuck to the roof of her mouth, kept there by some invisible force. A tingling started in her fingertips, and she rubbed them together, trying to rid herself of the feeling. She knew what it meant.

Brea was about to lose control.

She breathed deeply, trying to push away the emotions swirling in her chest. Shame. Guilt. But most of all, anger. She was so freaking angry at this world, this school, these kids. The list was long.

"Not about to go psycho on us, are you?" Carson lifted a brow and stepped toward her. His frame loomed over her smaller one, and she stared down at her feet.

He wasn't finished. "Come on, Robinson. I want to see some of that legendary temper. You can be a grand prize winner of a lifelong stay at the Clarkson Center."

He even knew the institute they'd put her in. The Clarkson Center dealt with delinquents with mental disturbances.

Memories flashed through her mind of the first night she'd arrived there when she was just a child. They'd strapped her to a bed. She'd thrashed against the restraints and screamed about how nothing was real.

After that, everything she'd done had been monitored. Even now, she was expected to go straight to her therapist after school.

Her fists clenched at her sides, and she squeezed her eyes shut. *Don't lose control,* she told herself.

But it was no use because she'd never had control in the first place.

Carson forced her chin up. "Look at me," he growled. "You don't belong here."

Not news to her.

"You never ha—" His words cut off as Myles barreled into him, knocking him to the concrete.

Carson tried to pop up, but Myles was bigger and stronger.

Brea stepped back until she teetered on the edge of the curb. She'd never seen Myles so angry... or violent.

She needed to stop it, to help him. Carson managed to roll them over, his fist pounding into Myles' face.

"Myles," Brea whispered, desperation coursing through her.

Her friend's hand went limp, but Carson didn't stop.

"You can't do this." Her voice was so quiet no one heard her. Carson's friends only watched in fascination as blood poured from Myles' face.

He couldn't get away with this. Searing hot rage ripped through her, filling every cell with its fury. Her jaw clenched as heat pooled in her hands. Her eyes blazed as she became more than the girl on the sidelines.

She tilted her head to the side, trying to hold back whatever was happening. But this was Myles, and that only amplified every emotion in her.

"Myles is good," she bit out. He deserved only good things.

Unlike her. It was in that moment Brea realized she wasn't good, she was fire to his ocean, rage to his joy.

The way he saw the world may have been a lie, but it had to be preserved.

Light poured from her before she knew what was happening. Pain exploded in her temple as the power split her in two. She tried to call it back, to make it stop, but it kept coming.

Her knees buckled, and she fell forward. She didn't sense the impact as she hit the ground or feel whatever that power was snap back into her.

Her eyes found Myles motionless on the ground with the others nowhere to be found. She reached for his hand, struggling to grasp his icy fingers.

Whatever this was, it was just another lie. Another illusion. She'd wake up soon to find everything as it should be.

Part of her hoped it was a dream and she'd open her eyes to find the blank white walls of the Clarkson Center caging her in once again.

A hand pressed Brea to the concrete as her eyes slid open. Flashing red and blue lights reflected off the snow. They didn't belong there, but then, neither did she.

"Am I going back to the Clarkson Center?" she wheezed out.

No one answered. By now, half the school probably watched from the windows.

She lifted her head, searching for Myles and only finding splatters of blood where he'd been before.

"Myles?" Still, no answer. Any minute, he'd walk out of the school to wrap his arms around her. "Where's Myles?"

Whoever held her down took pity on her finally. "The boy who was here? They've taken him to St. Mary's."

"The hospital? Is he..." She swallowed. "Is he going to be okay?"

"I'd be surprised if he survived the ambulance ride."

She shook her head. It couldn't be real. Just another one of her delusions. Myles was fine. He had to be. He was the best person she knew, the only one who'd ever loved her.

It should be her in that ambulance.

The man hauled her up, and her legs wobbled beneath her. She turned her head, catching sight of his police officer's uniform. He nodded to where three other officers waited beside two police cruisers.

"Brea Robinson, you are under arrest for the attempted murder of Myles Merrick."

"No, I couldn't have hurt him. Not Myles." She tried to remember everything that happened, but it didn't seem real. They really thought it was her that did this?

The officer continued reading her rights, but she couldn't hear him over the ringing in her ears.

"You'll be able to call your people from the precinct."

Her people? He meant her parents, but they'd never been her people. That title had always rested solely with Myles, the boy next door.

And she'd killed him.

Brea Robinson was a lie.

A horror story.

But the truth? She wasn't sure if that even existed.

The cop shoved her into the back of his cruiser, her hands cuffed behind her back.

She leaned her head against the seat and stared at the ceiling, wishing she could see the blue sky Myles loved so much. A tear escaped, but she couldn't wipe it away. "I'm sorry, Myles."

Chapter 2

The door to Brea's cell opened. For the last twenty-four hours, the only person she'd seen was her therapist, Doctor Cochran—and his sedatives. He claimed that seeing her parents or anyone else right now would only upset her further.

"Sedation is my friend," or so he said. The doctor just didn't know how good Brea was at tricking him and the nurses into believing she'd swallowed the pills. She had a growing collection of them under her bed, just waiting for the moment when someone finally told her she had actually killed Myles. Her best friend. The promise of those pills were her only comfort now.

"Brea Robinson?" An officer she didn't recognize stepped into her pristinely white cell. "You're being transferred."

"Transferred? Where?" Brea sat up on her cot.

"Dunno." The officer scratched his head, checking the clipboard in his hand. "That fancy doctor of yours signed orders to send you to some big city prison in Columbus with a psych ward, where you'll wait for your arraignment."

"How is Myles?" Brea clutched her clothes to her chest as she followed the officer from her cell.

"Dunno." The officer hitched up his pants as they walked down the long corridor to the main office.

"Do my parents know where I'm going?"

"Your parents signed over their parental rights to your therapist. Looks like they might have washed their hands of you." The officer held open the door for her to pass through.

Brea shuffled forward, unable to make sense of the last twenty-four hours. Everything was a blur. "I need to know how Myles is doing." Her voice sounded distant to her own ears as the precinct officers filed her transfer paperwork, completely ignoring her. No one ever seemed to listen to her. "Please, is he okay?"

"Quiet," another police officer said behind her. Brea turned, startled to see him there. She looked up, and up, to find he had the most striking midnight blue eyes she'd ever seen. "We will leave in a moment, keep your mouth shut." His tone was curt, and he looked like he didn't know how to smile, but his presence sent a wave of warmth through her, calming her fears. Everything would be fine soon. Once she got settled in the psych ward, her doctor would explain everything. That was the familiarity she needed now.

Brea followed the handsome officer with the beautiful eyes and stony frown outside into the freezing night. She didn't even have her coat. Wasn't it odd to transfer prisoners so late at night?

She ducked her head into the backseat of the police cruiser, wondering why the officer hadn't handcuffed her for the transport. The ride to Columbus would be a few hours. Maybe he thought she'd be more comfortable?

Brea's thoughts whirled from one thing to the next, like she couldn't focus on any one thought long enough to question her newest circumstances.

"Myles?" She leaned forward. "Can you tell me anything about Myles? Can you call the hospital and check on him?"

"You're better off forgetting him and whatever he might have meant to you." The voice was like warm hot chocolate. She didn't like his words, but he somehow managed to make them sound like the most soothing of responses.

"What about my parents? Did they really sign me over to Dr. Cochran?"

"As far as your parents are concerned, they never had a daughter named Brea Robinson. Now just sit back and enjoy the ride."

Brea yawned. "I don't think I like you." His voice sent an unwelcome warmth racing through her, but through the fog of her confusion, she couldn't quite work out why that was a bad thing.

It was dark when Brea woke, still in the backseat of the police cruiser —still with no idea what was happening. A spark of fear curled in her gut, and she latched on to it. It was the only true emotion she'd experienced since leaving her cell.

Gazing out the window, Brea expected to see highways and cars heading for the city. Instead, she saw trees and vast stretches of farmland. They were the only car on the dark country road. Panic seeped into her bones as she watched the man behind the wheel. She caught his gaze in the rear view mirror, his dark eyes flashing like sapphire jewels in the night. She'd seen eyes like those before.

I'm not crazy. I'm not crazy. Brea squeezed her eyes shut tight before she dared to chance a second glance at the officer. His normal midnight blue eyes peered back at her through the mirror. *Exactly, I'm not crazy.* She breathed a sigh of relief. It was never a good thing for Brea Robinson to see things that weren't there.

"Where are you taking me?" She tried to keep the accusation from her tone, but Brea did not have a good feeling about this gruff man who claimed to be a police officer.

"Somewhere safe. Just relax. We'll be there soon."

Once again, his words had a mesmerizing effect on her. Part of her wanted to do something drastic to try to escape, but the other part of her wanted to sit back and relax like the officer suggested. Brea resisted that second part of her subconscious mind trying to tell her everything was fine when it clearly wasn't.

When the driver turned down a long winding dirt road, Brea knew what she had to do. Breathing deep and even, she calmed herself. After nearly a half-hour on the dirt road, the officer finally stopped in front of a small farmhouse in the middle of nowhere. Brea had seen her fair share of psych wards and rehabilitation centers. Not one of them looked like this dilapidated place.

The officer turned to peer into the backseat. Just before he spoke, Brea stuffed her fingers in her ears and rocked back and forth, banging her head against the back seat. It was her best impersonation of a crazy person, which she was *not*. Whenever that man spoke, strange things happened in her mind. The calm he exuded was deceptive.

"Enough of that, Brea. You aren't crazy."

He stepped from the driver's side and she repeated her mantra—and her fit. "I'm not crazy. I'm not crazy."

The moment he opened the back door, Brea shot out of the car like her hair was on fire. She ran down the dark and desolate road, the cloudy night sky offering little to light her path.

"Brea, get back here, now!" The stranger shouted after her, and Brea resisted the unnatural urge to do as he said. "I will drag you back by your hair if I have to, but you're coming with me, girl."

She didn't know where she was going, but she had to get away. If she ever wanted to know the truth about Myles, she had to go back and face the consequences of what she'd done to her best friend. If that meant spending the rest of her life in a padded cell, then maybe that was where she belonged. Maybe her parents were right to give up on her.

The stranger was gaining on her, so she darted into the woods, branches and briars lashing against her face as she ran harder and faster than she ever had before.

"Brea, you don't understand. You're making this harder than it has to be. Come back to the house before you hurt yourself."

Brea stuffed her fingers in her ears as she ran, stumbling from the dense forest into a wide-open field.

"Brea, you're acting like a brat," her assailant called. She darted a glance over her shoulder and ran right into something warm and solid.

"Get behind me. Brea, Lochlan is dangerous." The second stranger of the night shoved her behind him.

"What is this? Who *are* you people?"

"You can call me Griff, and when we get out of here, I'll explain everything, I promise." He put himself between her and the man chasing her. Griff smelled like springtime and fresh-mown grass.

"I'm not crazy. I'm not crazy, I'm not crazy," she murmured, darting her eyes around the field, looking for an escape.

"No, you aren't crazy. You're just the girl we've been looking for, but I need you to trust me, even though you have no reason to. I'm not going to trick you with mind games." He grabbed her hand and warmth spread through Brea's body at his touch.

"Hand her over, Griff." The not-police officer darted into the clearing. "She's coming with me." He moved like a predator, and Brea stumbled back to put some distance between herself and these strange men.

"You can't treat people like pawns, Loch."

"That's rich coming from you." The one named Griff moved to block her from Lochlan.

Brea watched the two men talking about her like she wasn't even there. She should run, but there was nowhere to hide. She didn't even know where she was or if any of this was even happening in reality.

"I'm not crazy. I'm not crazy." The clouds parted and the field flooded with moonlight.

"Griff, don't do it. You know I'll find you."

"Brace yourself, sweetheart." Griff pulled her into his arms and turned toward the moon. The air smelled of lavender and jasmine—two things one did not smell in the dead of an Ohio winter. The air rent in two, right before her eyes, like a piece of fabric cut with scissors.

"Oh, I'm definitely crazy." Brea closed her eyes and everything went dark.

Chapter 3

The man's—Griff's—hand clamped down on Brea's arm as the world twisted and bent around them. A wave of dizziness washed over her, but his grip kept her upright.

She tried to speak, to breathe out the protests and the questions swirling in her mind, but nothing came out.

Everything disappeared. The snow, the bare winter trees covered in a thin sheen of ice.

Even the police officer faded into the background before she couldn't see him at all. Loch, Griff had called him. His smooth voice echoed in her ears, calling after her with a mixture of fear and fury until even that was gone and all that remained was a heavy silence.

Warmth. It was the first thing she noticed. Gone was the dreary Ohio winter. She pried her eyes open to find the sun breaking through flowering trees overheard. It was the dead of night a moment ago.

Neither of them moved for a long moment before Brea finally lifted her eyes to her abductor.

His violet eyes flashed when they met hers, and that was how she knew.

She'd never left the Clarkson Institute. It was all in her head. The first day back to school never happened. She never attacked Myles, never went to prison. It was all just a terrible nightmare.

Ripping her arm from his grasp, she walked backward. "You're not real. None of this is real." She squeezed her eyes shut, hoping when she opened them, she'd see the sterile walls of her room and know she was safe.

Well, as safe as she could be when her own mind played tricks on her.

But it didn't go away. The fresh smell of spring permeated her nostrils, so different from the icy air that filled her lungs only moments ago.

"Come on, Brea," she whispered to herself. "Wake up. You're safe."

The man continued to stare at her and cocked his head, one corner of his mouth lifting into a half-smile. "Are you talking to yourself?"

"No," she huffed. Why did she even respond to him? He was just a figment of her imagination.

His lips parted into a full grin. "I hate traveling to your realm in the winter." He brushed the dusting of snow from the sleeves of his shirt.

Brea's eyes followed his movements, taking in the clothing that looked straight out of one of the fantasy movies she and Myles always watched together.

Myles. She choked on a sob and turned her back on the stranger. That part was too fresh in her mind not to be real. Her best friend was dead because of her. What had she done? The guilt opened up a chasm inside her, but no tears came. It was Brea's curse. Girls were supposed to cry, weren't they? To let their emotions out. At least, that was what Myles always said. But of the two of them, he'd been the crier.

She'd never wished for tears more than in that moment. Myles deserved every bit of emotion she could muster.

Her back shook as she tried to force them out.

"What are you doing?" The man put a hand on her back, and she jumped away from him with a yelp.

"You're not supposed to be able to touch me."

"What are you talking about?"

"Before... when I've... seen things..." She sucked in a breath. "You know what, I don't have to explain anything. You're not real." She walked forward, hoping she could find some way out of this nightmare.

Around her, blooms flourished among the trees. Her feet crunched through the crisp green grass, but they weren't the only ones.

The man followed her.

"Brea, wait."

"I'm ready to wake up now." She reached a clearing and lifted her face to the sky, begging for some higher power to make this all go away.

"You're not asleep, and you're not imagining things."

She turned to face the man who'd called himself Griff. He was ridiculously attractive—if you were into that kind of thing. His long auburn hair was tied back away from the flawless skin of his face. Intense green eyes—no longer flashing violet—locked on her, but she refused to meet them, focusing instead on the pointed tips of his ears.

"You're a delusion."

"I'm not." He crossed his arms over his chest.

"I just want to go home." To wake up in the twin bed she'd slept in since she was a kid and start this day all over again. "I never left the institute. Myles isn't dead."

Griff's expression softened, and he took a step toward her. "I'm sorry about your friend. But it wasn't your fault. You don't know how to control what's happening to you."

"Nothing is happening to me except my mind imagining things." But she felt it, the energy within her. There was no denying how it kicked her heart up a notch and latched onto her anger, her sadness.

Among all these lies, that felt like the only truth she had.

Something was very wrong with her.

Without thinking, she turned and started running, ducking back into the trees. Branches whipped her face, causing a trickle of blood to drip down over her parted lips as she crashed through the woods, trying to get away from the man pursuing her.

She panted as she leaped over a fallen tree and burst past the tree line, stopping dead in her tracks at the sight before her. Rolling green hills stretched into the distance like a painting of a lonely land, untouched and wild.

Clear blue skies topped off the picturesque landscape without a cloud in sight.

"Beautiful, isn't it?" Griff stopped beside her.

Her jaw clenched. "No." Lies, illusions, were never beautiful.

She could barely make out a house in the distance surrounded by pastures where horses grazed.

"That's home." Griff pointed to the house. "I tried to get the portal as close as I could without scaring the horses with the energy it emitted."

"Portal?" She shook her head. None of this made any sense. She walked back into the woods and sat down on the fallen tree she'd jumped over while trying to escape only moments before.

The events of the day played in her mind like a movie. Returning to school and facing the stares of her classmates. Myles'... death. The word sat heavy in her mind.

Then the police station and the man who took her away from there. How did it all fit together?

Griff dropped to the log beside her. "I know this is all a little much, but I promise you it's real. I just need you to come with me."

"I don't even know him," she whispered to herself. On her many stays at the institute, she'd spent hours and sometimes days with no company but herself. When she got scared or nervous, she talked to herself. At school, she worked hard to hide the habit, but now the words tumbled out. "What does he want from me?"

"I'll explain everything in time." He nudged her shoulder like they were old friends, like Myles would have done.

She scooted away so he couldn't do it again. "I'm not going anywhere with you. Where's the police officer? I want him." Policemen were supposed to keep people safe, right?

Griff's congeniality dropped away and he stood. "That was no human." His eyes narrowed. "Lochlan is not to be trusted, do you understand?"

"And you are? I don't know you. I don't know where I am or how any of this is possible if I'm not just imagining it."

"You don't have a choice, Brea."

"How do you know my name?" Back in the wintery forest, he'd said her name when he pulled her away from Lochlan.

"You'll learn in time."

Anger burned through her. In time? She deserved answers right away if he wanted her to trust him. Unable to control herself, she lunged from the log, springing toward him and taking him by surprise as she tackled him to the ground.

"I want to go home," she yelled. A home she no longer had if her parents truly had signed over their parental rights. A home that no longer included Myles.

Griff struggled beneath her before finally flipping her off and rolling them over so he pinned her to the ground. "Calm. Down."

"No." She jerked her knees up, connecting with his crotch. His face twisted in pain, but he didn't release her.

"Brea, stop."

Light exploded from her just as it had before. The pressure on top of her vanished as Griff flew across the clearing.

Unlike her mother with the Christmas tree or Myles outside the school, Griff didn't collapse to the ground. Instead, he landed in a crouch before straightening.

"Well." He grimaced. "That's something we will have to get a handle on. Get up, Brea."

She refused. Her chest heaved as she stared up at him with wide eyes. "What's happening to me? What did I do?" She buried her face in her hands.

She truly was a freak.

Griff sighed. "Cut it out with the self-pity. I want to make it home before dark."

She lifted her face to him. "I'm not going to your home." She had to find a way back to hers.

Griff shrugged. "Suit yourself. Just be careful of the wolves." He turned and started walking away.

"Wolves?" She scrambled after him.

"These woods are dangerous at night. I wouldn't want to be caught in them after dark."

"At least tell me where we are?" she pleaded.

He didn't stop walking. "The world of the fae welcomes you, Brea Robinson."

Fae? She truly had lost it.

Chapter 4

"Why am I doing this?" Brea mumbled as she followed Griff. He even had a name that sounded like one of those characters Myles used to pretend to be when they were kids.

Why hadn't she read more fantasy books? Or paid attention to her best friend's every word about the worlds he disappeared into every night? No, instead, she nagged him about all the reading he did and waited for the movies and TV shows to come out.

During the summer, they'd hang out in one of the fields with Captain America, alternating between riding the horse and sitting against the base of a giant oak tree at the edge of the property. Myles always had a book propped up in his lap while Brea busied herself picking at the blades of grass and imagining shapes in the clouds overhead.

But that was before.

Before some kind of power she couldn't explain lived inside her.

Before she told anyone about the pointed ears and flashing eyes she saw amid crowds of people.

Before she killed Myles.

"You're going too fast." She struggled to keep up with Griff.

They'd been walking for way too long, and her feet ached. "How much longer?"

"Oh, so you're talking to me now?" Griff flashed her a grin. "Your protest didn't last long."

"I just want to know how far we have to go." She tried to see the house in the distance, but as they'd descended into a valley, it disappeared from view.

"We've only been walking for half an hour."

"No way, it's been longer than that." Her foot hit a small hole in the ground, and she pitched forward.

Griff caught her before she fell. "Graceful." He laughed. "Just what I'd expect from someone raised in the human world."

Brea righted herself and pushed away from him. "What does that even mean? There's only one world."

Griff shrugged. "Maybe for those with small minds. Do you have a small mind?"

"No." She clenched her jaw. She may not have excelled at school or basically anything else, but she wasn't an idiot.

"All right, Brea Robinson, let's clear something up." His eyes locked with hers. "I will not lie to you. That is my promise. So, when I tell you something, I need you to believe it."

His voice held such sincerity she wanted to trust him, but she'd only trusted one person in her life, and he was dead.

She shifted her eyes to her ripped jeans, focusing on the patch her mom had sewn in the knee instead of buying her a new pair. Things like that reminded her who she was--a farm girl from Ohio with a history of mental instability.

Also, a girl with nothing to go back to.

"I want to believe you," she whispered. She wanted to believe there was more out there than the life she'd been living. "I just..."

His fingertips brushed her chin and tilted her face up. "Look at me, Brea Robinson. You have questions, and I will answer them in time. For now, I need you to know you're not imagining this." His touch flittered along her cheek, and she swallowed, mesmerized by his swirling eyes.

"This is real." The words released on a breath, as if breaking free of some deeper part of her.

She lived her life in lies, but as she breathed in the fresh air of a new life, a new... world?... she hoped this was anything but.

A smile tilted his lips, different from the wide grin before when he'd laughed at her. This time, there was kindness in his expression, an openness she couldn't help but be drawn to.

He reminded her so much of Myles.

"So," she swallowed as she tested the next words in her mind. "Two... worlds?"

He withdrew his hand and nodded. "You're now in the fae world. It parallels the human world you knew."

"But... how did we get here?"

"A portal." He winked. "Magic."

Her mind stuttered on that word, and Griff turned to keep walking.

She ran after him. "Magic?"

Glee shone on his face. "You have no idea."

"What is magic?"

"Why does this place look like a freaking fairytale?"

"Why is it warm here when it was so cold at home?"

"And why would you bother bringing me here? I'm nobody."

Griff grunted and turned to face her as they crossed the fields leading up to the small stone cottage that looked like it belonged in a storybook.

"I think I liked you better when you wouldn't talk to me." He pursed his lips.

She'd been peppering him with questions as they walked. It was the only thing preventing her from focusing on seeing Myles hit the ground. "Is it still the same day I was arrested?"

"No. You were arrested yesterday. You spent a day and a night in your cell before Lochlan tried to intercept my plans to get you out."

"Are you going to answer any of my other questions?" Now that she'd let herself consider he was telling the truth, she needed to know more, to know she wasn't crazy. Maybe she never had been.

He turned and gazed up at the cottage. "Have you ever wondered why they're called fairytales?"

Her eyes widened. "You're a fairy?"

"Never call me that," he growled. "I told you this was the fae world. What did you think I was?"

She shrugged. "An elf."

"An elf?" He ran a hand through his hair in agitation.

Brea barely knew this man, but she'd seen him as jovial and calm. Riling him up was fun. She crossed the stone wall encircling a small paddock in front of a barn. Hopping up, she let her legs dangle over the side. "Do you have any dwarf friends?"

"What? Dwarves don't exist."

"Sure they do. If elves are real, why can't Gimli be hanging around here somewhere?"

"I don't know who Gimli is." His eyes narrowed. "I told you this is the fae world. Why would you think I'm an elf?"

She shrugged. "No wings."

"Wings?"

"In the movies fae have wings. Like tinker bell."

He stared at her, his jaw dropping open. "Tinkerbell," he said the name slowly.

She nodded. "She's a fairy."

"I know who Tinkerbell is!"

"Wait, really? Is there a TV in that house?" A Netflix night was just what she needed to ignore the hole inside her, the guilt and doubt she'd felt since she woke up that morning.

Pushing away from the wall, she barged into the house, ignoring the thud of the wood as she let the door swing back in Griff's face.

A small room greeted her, with stone walls and a matching floor covered in sky-blue rugs. Wooden chairs faced a giant fireplace where flames lit up the room and an iron pot hung over the fire.

A door opened to her right and an older man shuffled out, stopping when he saw her.

Griff entered behind her with a chastisement she didn't hear as she stared at the new man with his pointed ears and intensely blue eyes.

She looked from him to Griff. "It's not just you. There are more." She practically fell onto a bench behind the oak table, speaking to herself. "I'm not crazy. I'm not crazy. I'm not crazy." For the first time, she started believing her mantra.

Everything she'd seen as a kid... A realization struck her. "There are more of you in the human realm." They were the reason she'd been at the institute.

The older man raised one eyebrow before moving to the fire to stir whatever he had cooking in the pot. Her mouth watered as she realized she hadn't eaten anything since breakfast.

She pointed to the pot. "Is that for me?"

"Brea, this is Leith, a loyal servant." Griff lowered himself into a chair with an exhausted sigh.

Leith offered her a kind smile before spooning the stew into a ceramic bowl and setting it in front of her. "Welcome to Fargelsi, Miss Robinson."

"Far-what-see?" And how did everyone seem to know her name?

"Fargelsi is the forest realm." Griff leaned his head back. "We just call it Gelsi." He took a bowl from Leith. "Thank you."

Brea poked at the stew with her spoon, not knowing what the chunks were. She'd never been picky, eating whatever cheap food her parents put in front of her. With a shrug, she dug in, shoveling stew into her mouth like she hadn't eaten in weeks.

It was the best thing she'd ever tasted, but that was probably the hunger speaking.

Leith sat beside Griff and the two men spoke in low tones. The older man obviously deferred to Griff, but she wanted—needed—to know why.

Her mind drifted back to the police officer, the one who'd flashed her an unnatural look just like Griff's before hiding his eyes. His hat had covered his ears, but somehow, she knew—he too was fae.

"That man..." she started, unsure of how to continue. "The one who..."

"Lochlan?" Griff's gaze darkened as he shared an indecipherable look with Leith.

She nodded. "You... I can't figure out if you saved me from him or abducted me."

"The answer to that won't change anything. You're here."

"And I'm guessing you won't let me leave?"

He smiled in apology. "It's too dangerous. And yes, one of those dangers is Lochlan. You will learn soon enough, Brea, this realm holds many perils, including the three rulers vying for power. Lochlan's master is the Queen of the fire realm—Eldur."

She pushed her bowl away, suddenly not hungry anymore as the reality of her situation struck her. "What do you want with me?"

Griff stood and crossed to the table to sit on the opposite bench from her. He reached out and brushed the back of her hand, sending a calming wave of energy straight through her. "It's okay, Brea. I won't let anything happen to you, that's why my queen sent me to find you."

Her eyes drooped as she suddenly grew sleepy, but he hadn't answered all of her questions yet. Shaking off the weariness, she sat up straighter. "I'm nobody, nothing. Why am I here with two fae trying to pull me into their world? And what could a queen possibly want with me?"

"That's where you're wrong, Brea Robinson." He said her name like a blessing, and she couldn't help but lean in, wanting to hear more, needing his words to calm her racing heart. "You're everything."

Brea woke the next morning with no recollection of how she got into the small barren room to begin with. The last thing she remembered was eating some kind of stew and listening to Griff's mesmerizing voice.

You're everything.

When he said it, she believed him. There was something about the beautiful fae that tugged on her limited trust, making her want to know him, to know his world.

A crack of thunder ripped through the air, and her head jerked up off the feather pillow. Rain hammered on the glass panes of the window overlooking the barn. A sliver of sunlight breaking through the clouds cut across the dark wool carpet spanning the room.

"Fairytale, my butt," she grumbled. If this was a fairytale world, the bed would have been as soft as clouds and she'd have been awakened by singing birds instead of a roaring storm.

Lightning flashed across the room, illuminating the tiny wooden bed, small table in the corner, and single chair.

That was it. No decorations or other comforts.

As she sat up, wild ebony hair fell across her shoulders and into her face. She searched the bed for the rubber hair tie she'd used to hold it back the day before, but it wasn't there.

That was when she noticed it.

The sleeping gown.

Her hands grabbed frantically at the silk garment covering her small frame. Where were her clothes? "He undressed me." Her cheeks flamed as she imagined Griff's smooth hands sliding the faded jeans down her legs and his intense green eyes taking her in.

She jumped from the bed and searched the room for her clothes, finding none.

The white gown only reached mid-thigh and a chill raced through her.

She was going to kill him. Was murder acceptable in this new world? Maybe if she got arrested again, a human would come save her and take her home.

A strangled laugh escaped her lips at the thought. Griff abducted her after she killed Myles. The guilt she'd tried so hard to ignore, clawed at her, ripping through the shreds of sanity she had left.

She had to get out of here.

Sprinting the short distance across the room, she yanked on the cold metal door handle.

It didn't budge.

She pulled again.

Locked.

Slamming her foot into the door, she tried to control the anger rising up in her. "Griff, you let me out of here right now." He'd taken her from her home, turned her entire world upside down, and now locked her away.

Just when she'd started thinking he might be the good guy...

"Griff!" she screamed.

The door handle rattled seconds before Leith opened it. "Good morning, Brea." He smiled kindly. "I thought you might like some breakfast."

"Where's Griff?" She crossed her arms.

"He had some business at the palace, but he'll return soon."

"The palace?" She swallowed.

He nodded. "Griffin is a loyal companion of Queen Regan of Gelsi. I'm sure you'll meet her in time."

A queen? Brea wasn't the kind of girl to meet anyone important. But she didn't say that. Her stomach growled and she pointed to the plate Leith held. "Is that mine?"

He nodded and entered the room to set it on the table. She was ready to attack the stack of perfect, fluffy pancakes covered in some kind of green berry she didn't recognize.

"Try the Gelsi berries." He winked. "You won't regret it."

He left before she had a chance to say anything else. Giving in, she slumped into the chair and took a tiny bite of a berry. A mixture of sweet and sour juices exploded in her mouth. "Oh, goodness," she groaned, taking another bite.

Before she knew it, the plate sat empty and she wished there was more.

As the storm continued to rage outside, weariness clouded her mind. If Griff was gone, she might as well crawl back into bed and pretend for just a few more hours everything was as it should be.

"Myles!" Brea screamed, shooting up in bed, her chest heaving.

He was a prominent figure in every dream she'd had since arriving in the fae world. She didn't know how long ago that was or why she just wanted to stay in bed. Dr. Cochran probably would have told her she was depressed, but she just felt so tired.

Every time she woke, she found a plate from Leith, but she hadn't seen him since he brought the first meal. None of the meals since had anything like pancakes. Instead, he seemed to think she could live on nuts and fruit. No matter how good the fruit was, it was never enough.

More than anything, she wanted a hamburger.

But something told her she couldn't just ask Leith to head over to Wendy's.

"Ughhh," she sighed. "I want a Frosty." Instead, she ate what he offered.

Each time she tried to open the door, it was locked, but the anger she'd been known for didn't come. In fact, few emotions did. It was almost like her world of vibrant colors had turned into shades of gray.

She'd even tried summoning whatever that light blast thing was so she could get out of this room and away from the people imprisoning her, but to no avail.

Each day Griff didn't return was another she hoped he never did.

He told her to trust him, that he'd never lie to her.

But this room was a prison just like her room at the Clarkson Institute and the actual prison cell she'd occupied before Lochlan showed up.

She sniffed the sleeping gown she'd been wearing since that first night and wrinkled her nose. Her hair was matted across the back of her head.

And still, the storm outside raged on, never ending, never quieting.

Lying on her bed, she rested her head on the pillow and tried to summon some kind of sadness or fear or guilt. Just... something.

It didn't come.

"I want to go home," she whispered to herself. She wanted to return to a mom who gave up on her, a dad who didn't understand her, and classmates who ridiculed her.

Yet, that desire for normalcy was an abstract feeling, not one she could grasp or hold on to. It was always just out of reach.

"I hate you, Griff whatever-your-last-name-is."

Even those words had no power behind them.

Wherever she went in life, she was a prisoner, held down by her circumstances. The world she'd known didn't exist for her anymore, yet neither did this one. It couldn't.

So, why had nothing ever felt more real?

In this world that was nothing more than a fairytale, why did her prison hurt more than it had before?

Her appetite gone after so many days in the same room, Brea knocked the plate from Leith's hands the moment he appeared.

"I can't eat any more of that stupid fruit." For the first time in days, her anger returned in small waves.

Calmly, Leith bent to clean up the mess, and Brea saw her

chance. She darted past him into the main room, searching for a way out. Lunging for the front door, Brea stumbled into a world recovering from the storms.

A spotted horse lifted its head to regard her, and she met familiar brown eyes. No, not familiar because she knew the animal, but only because horses were one of the few creatures she understood, and riding was one of the few activities she'd ever been good at.

Considering her options, she looked from the horse to the path leading away from the cottage. Making a quick decision, she climbed over the low stone wall and approached the horse.

"I'm a friend," she whispered. "Please help me get out of here."

The horse stamped its foot and neighed.

"Stop!" Leith yelled.

As if that word held power, Brea's limbs immobilized, stuck in a current that threatened to drag her under.

She tried to free herself, to get away, but the servant approached with sad eyes. "I'm sorry, Brea, but I have orders. I can't let you leave."

"You can't keep me locked away forever!" she screamed. "What does Griff want from me?"

His expression told her he wanted to answer, or maybe even that he wanted to let her go. Instead, he drew a circle in the air with his hand, and Brea's entire body turned, moving closer to the house.

"I cannot disobey orders." He lowered his gaze. "Not even for you."

What did that mean? She tried to ask, but her lips wouldn't move as the invisible force pulled her back into the room she thought she'd escaped. Leith stood looking at her as the door shut, but he didn't say another word.

The power released Brea, and she slumped against the door. Banging a fist weakly against the wood, she called out. "Please. Let me go." Her knees gave out and she sank to the hard floor. "Please."

A rattle sounded, but the door didn't open. Instead, a slot appeared at its base and a new plate of fruit slid through the opening.

Brea lowered herself to her side and picked at the fruit, knowing it wouldn't fill the emptiness inside her.

During her long nights locked up at the Clarkson Institute, she'd known there was someone waiting for her to get out, someone who cared.

Now, she was totally and utterly alone.

The only person left to save her was herself.

If this was a fairytale, Brea Robinson had to be both the damsel and the knight, because there was no one left to come for her.

Chapter 5

It was the fruit.

It had to be. That was the only thing that made sense. Over the last several days since her escape attempt, the only thing Brea looked forward to were the Gelsi berries Leith brought her at every meal. The tart fruit was good, but it wasn't *that* good. She shouldn't crave it like she did. She was never particularly hungry after those first few days, but Brea *needed* those berries. Her body trembled whenever Leith was late.

Brea had grown to like the numb feeling she'd experienced since her latest incarceration. The distant, detached feeling that made her so sleepy she didn't have the energy to contemplate her situation. Crazy. Not crazy. It didn't matter.

Brea rolled onto her side, thinking about getting up. Leith would be here soon with her breakfast. It was the highlight of her morning. After, she'd go back to sleep until lunch. Unless she didn't eat the Gelsi berries today. She'd told herself yesterday she wouldn't eat them. Or was that the day before?

"That's different." She sat up, blinking to make sure she wasn't seeing things. Not like that would be unusual for Brea Robinson, but the door appeared to be open. "Leith?" she whispered, stumbling across the room to the doorway and peeking into the hall. No one was in the hall outside her door.

Still wearing her soiled sleeping gown, Brea crept into the front room and bolted for the door when she found no one waiting to haul her back to her cell. She didn't waste a moment this time. Brea ran across the yard, not even bothering with the horse. She wasn't going to screw this up again.

The too-green grass was like a plush carpet beneath her feet. Brea, weak from her days of sleeping too much, stumbled into the cover of the forest, gasping for breath. Casting a look back at the cottage, she saw that still no one followed her. It was odd, but she wasn't sticking around long enough to find out why.

Brea's feet skimmed over moss-covered stones and massive tree roots along the pathway through the woods. She'd never seen such a forest, bursting with energy like a living, breathing thing, watching over her.

"Now, you're really losing it, Brea."

Sunlight dappled the ground through the tall, sweeping branches above. Species of trees she couldn't remember ever seeing before flourished in this fairytale forest. Exotic blooms in a riot of colors sprouted from every available surface. There was so much to see, Brea didn't know where to look first. It was breathtaking. Still, she watched over her shoulder. As beautiful as it was, the forest gave her a creepy vibe. Like if she looked under the surface, she'd find something dark and twisted waiting to strike. It was eerily quiet. It took her a while to figure it out. There were no birds singing in the trees. The only sound in the forest was the wind whistling through the branches.

After all she'd experienced in the last few days, Brea no longer trusted anything she saw. She no longer trusted anyone, least of all herself. She had no idea where she was going. She only knew she needed to get away from her jailor and his freaky fruit long enough to clear her head and make a plan.

With that thought in mind, she kept going, following the pathway through the forest. She had no doubt Leith and Griff could track her and drag her back, but she had to try.

Finally stumbling from the forest, Brea found herself in a clearing beside a beautiful lake. Beautiful was such an arbitrary word to describe what she saw. If the forest was breathtaking, then the lake was out of this world. A laugh bubbled up inside her at that thought. She clapped a hand over her mouth to keep her laughter in check. Clearly, she wasn't in Kansas anymore.

Azure water rippled in the cool breeze. As Brea peered into the lake, she realized it was deceptively deep. She could see the rocky bottom like it was only a few feet away, but her eyes played tricks on her. Brea wondered how strong the current was as she watched leaves drift and swirl a little too fast on the calm surface.

Impossibly high mountains bordered the lake on the far side, with a cascading waterfall crashing down from the snow-capped peaks. Behind her lay the forest and the prison-cottage she'd left behind, but to the south lay rolling green hills dotted with trees and Gelsi berry bushes as far as she could see. She could walk for days in either direction and not meet another living soul.

Brea walked along the edge of the lake, hopping from one moss covered boulder to the next, contemplating her next moves. Catching a whiff of herself in the breeze, she almost choked. She couldn't remember the last time she showered, and the lake called to her. The water was so clear under the sparkling sunshine, she wanted nothing more than to dive right in and not come up for air until she was clean. Edging closer to the water, Brea caught her reflection in the surface.

Gasping, she knelt, staring at herself. "I'm seeing things again," she whispered, reaching to touch the tips of her ears. Her pointed ears. Tucking her hair behind one of them, she leaned in closer.

All her life she'd caught glimpses of the people with pointed ears. They always had fathomless eyes too. And she'd convinced herself they weren't real. But now she was seeing those same features in her own reflection. She knew she should be freaking out right about now, but the only thing Brea felt was a weird sort of... relief. Finally, here was physical proof she wasn't seeing things that weren't there. If she could see it and feel it for herself, it had to be real, right?

Feeling suddenly giddy, Brea stood and lifted her foot. She wanted to see how cold the water was before she waded in.

"I wouldn't do that if I were you." The voice caught her by surprise, and she almost fell in right there. But Griff reached out and pulled her away from the water. "Loch Villandi is beautiful but dangerous."

"Dangerous?" Brea couldn't seem to break her gaze away from the water.

"Beautiful things often have a sharp bite." He lifted her chin, forcing her to meet his eyes. "The Villandi waters have claimed many lives. On the surface, she looks harmless and inviting, but underneath lies a heartless current that will sweep you into the bottomless depths never to be seen again. It is best to leave her be."

"I wish you'd leave me be." Shrugging out of his grip, she ran back to the relative safety of the forest. But she wondered how dangerous it was. If Loch Villandi was treacherous, then the forest surrounding it must be too.

"And where would you go if I left you to your own devices?"

"Home." Brea lifted her chin.

"And how would you get back to the human world?"

"I... I will find someone to help me do that portal thing you did."

"You'll be looking from now until forever if that's your plan. Only those of my clan can open a portal between realms to bring fae or humans through, and most of them are long dead."

"What do you want from me?" Brea stomped her foot in the grass. "I'm nobody."

"You have never been *nobody,* Brea Robinson. I thought I told you that already."

"Then tell me what's so special about me that you stole me away from my home at the worst possible moment?"

"I thought it was rather good timing seeing as how you were

recently arrested and in the company of a dangerous man." Griff scratched the stubble on his chin. She'd thought elves were supposed to be all smooth-skinned and hairless, but he had a handsome ruggedness about him.

"I'm tired of your games, Elf. Either take me home or leave me be."

"I told you, I am fae. I am not an elf, a fairy, or a nymph, or any other such creature the humans dreamed up."

"Fine, Fae-man-person. Whatever you are. Take me home."

"I can't do that. But I can take you back to the cottage, offer you a hot meal and a warm bath. Fresh clothes and answers to your questions. And you may call me Griff."

"What about your cage? There is no way I'm going back in there, and you can keep your freaky tranquilizer fruit for yourself. I'm done with that stuff."

"I am sorry about that, Brea, truly. I did not mean to treat you like a prisoner. My queen summoned me, and I must go to her when she has need of me. There was no time to explain everything you need to know. I only wanted to make you comfortable and safe while I was gone."

"Here's a little note for the comment card. The next time you have a guest at your little fairytale B&B, don't lock them up."

"I don't know what most of that means, but if you will remember, I told you I will never lie to you. Come with me, and I will explain everything."

"Fine." Brea crossed her arms over her chest. "You can start by explaining how I suddenly have pointy ears."

"You've always had them." He set off for the forest path, gesturing for her to follow. "You were glamoured so neither you nor anyone else could see them."

"Glamoured?" Brea walked beside him.

"It's a Fae thing. Someone didn't want you or anyone in your life to know what you are."

"Which is what? You're saying I'm Fae?"

"You are a human-Fae hybrid. That, among many other things, is what makes you special." He paused. "Yet you don't seem at all upset by this revelation."

"It explains a lot." Brea couldn't seem to stop touching her new ears. "So you're saying my mother had an affair with a Fae person? That makes zero sense. If you knew my mother, you'd agree. She's not the adventurous sort."

"I don't know how it happened, but your birth father was Fae."

"Was? So he's dead?"

"Unfortunately."

"That still doesn't explain why your queen seems to have an interest in me." Brea's stomach growled. She hadn't had anything to eat all day.

"Here, have a silver fig, I picked them fresh this morning." He pulled a handful of figs from his bag.

Brea's eyes widened in alarm when he tossed her the fruit.

"No strange side effects, I promise. I'll have one myself." He proceeded to peel back the silvery skin of the fig and made a show of eating it to prove it wasn't freaky like the berries.

"Fine." Brea was too hungry to argue with him. "But you still haven't answered my question." She peeled the shimmery skin from the fruit and tried not to moan at the taste of the fig. She swore she could taste the sun in that first bite.

"That's a complicated question with a long answer." Griff scratched his head.

"I've got nothing but time it seems. Start talking."

Griffin walked ahead of her, staring up into the clear blue sky for a moment before turning back to her. "The Fae realm is ancient. Ages older than the human world. Within it, there are three distinct realms. We are in Fargelsi now. Gelsi is an exotic realm of lush forests and wild lands. It's warm and sunny almost all year here. To the north lies the Iskalt kingdom. It is very cold there with massive mountain ranges and frozen lakes. It's a rather bleak and cruel land, but beautiful in its own way.

"The third realm to the east is Eldur, by far the largest. It's the fire realm. Desert wastelands in the north and hot springs and marshes to the south. Between each of these realms are the Vatlands. Neutral territories you never want to visit.

"Across Loch Villandi and beyond the deserts of Eldur, lie the Eastern Vatlands, also called the fire plains. The Northern Vatlands separate Iskalt and Fargelsi. Vast rocky mountain ranges where you could get lost for the rest of your life. The Southern Vatlands are the marshlands and putrid swamps filled with frightening creatures."

"Great geography lesson, but that still doesn't answer my question. Why does a Fae queen have any interest in me?"

"As you can probably imagine, the three realms have not always gotten along." Griff kept walking and talking, seemingly bent on not answering her question. But at least she was learning something. The most important being that she had never been crazy at all.

"The Eldur queens have always believed they should rule over all the realms and that Gelsi and Iskalt should serve them. Naturally, the Gelsi queen and the Iskalt king don't feel the same."

"So you're at war or something?"

"Not at the moment. But there have been wars over this issue throughout the ages. The Eldur queen wants all the power for herself, but we are determined to maintain our independence."

"What does any of this have to do with me?"

"I'm getting there." Griff shot her an impatient look. "We are a people steeped in ancient magic. Here in Gelsi, its people draw their power from the forests and nature. In Eldur, the sun fuels their power, but only during the day. Iskalt is a dark and icy realm, and it's people draw their power from the moon, but only at night."

"What does—?"

"Patience, Brea. I'm trying to explain magic to someone who just learned magic exists."

She inclined her head. "Fair enough. Go on."

"Each realm has their own strengths and weaknesses. But one

thing we all have in common is the gift of prophecy. Our histories are littered with prophecies."

"So all Fae can see the future?"

"No, not all. Only a select few true seers are born into each realm every generation, and they are greatly revered."

Brea didn't like where this was going at all. If Griff was about to tell her there was some kind of prophecy about her, she was getting the hell out of this place.

"All of the seers of the last three generations have spoken about a young girl, born of a human mother and a Fae father. Left to live in the human world, never knowing what she was until she came of age and was unable to control her power any longer. This Fae-human hybrid has the power to save Fargelsi from the encroaching fires of Eldur. She has the power to thwart the Eldur queens and bring peace to our world forever."

"And you think that's me?" Brea wanted to laugh but she also felt the hot burn of tears in her eyes and her throat constricted in panic. This was insane, and she had a lot of experience with insanity.

"You fit every single criteria of the prophecy, Brea. That the Queen of Eldur sent Lochlan after you only proves it. She will stop at nothing to get her hands on you. I almost missed it, Brea." He stopped walking at the edge of the forest. The cottage was in view now, but Brea just shook her head in disbelief. "I almost let him take you, and I will never forgive myself for it. You are far too important to fall into the hands of Eldur."

"I'm nobody, Griff." Her voice came out small and shaky. "I'm not important."

"You belong to Fargelsi. This is your home, Brea. Your father was our queen's oldest brother. She is your aunt, and she's gone to great lengths to find you and bring you home safely."

"My aunt is a queen? A magical fae queen?" Brea couldn't wrap her head around such madness. "But I don't have powers." She couldn't be this prophecy girl who was supposed to be some kind of savior.

"I beg to differ. You aren't of age yet, so your true power has not fully manifested, but it's strong already. Have you ever felt like your emotions spiral out of control without warning? Like you feel things so much stronger than others? Like if you make one wrong move, you might drown in a sea of those emotions?"

"Yes," she whispered. "It's like that all the time. Like if I let myself really feel things, there's this energy brewing just under the surface. It scares me."

"That's what happened with your friend, Myles. Unfortunately, he got in the way at a pivotal moment when you weren't in control. That is why you have to come with me, Brea. We have to teach you how to master your emotions so you never lose control like that again. And we have to do it before you come of age on your next birthday. If we wait any longer, it will be too late."

"Myles died because I lost control of something I didn't even know I had? How could she do this to me?" Brea wanted to rage at her mother. "She knew I wasn't fully human but she just let me think I was crazy!"

"Take a deep breath, Brea. You can't get upset now. It's likely your mother never knew the man that fathered her child was Fae."

"I'm so mad I could just..." She wanted to tear the world apart with her bare hands. Even now she could feel the energy buzzing just below her skin. She couldn't let her emotions get the better of her.

"We can talk more later. Right now, let's get you inside and comfortable. You can have a hot bath, and Leith will have a big meal waiting for you when you're done. And if you want, you can have some more Gelsi berries. I really wasn't trying to drug you. The berries will help keep your power dormant so you don't hurt anyone."

Brea nodded. "Perhaps that is best." The last thing she wanted was to hurt anyone like she had Myles. She was beginning to realize how lucky she was that Griff had found her when he had. She shuddered to think what might have happened if Lochlan had taken her to the Eldur Queen.

Chapter 6

Griffin O'Shea was unlike anyone Brea had ever met. In a way, he reminded her of Myles with his sneaky grin and twinkling eyes. There was a certain joy in his demeanor. He was also different from her best friend though. Myles never took anything seriously. It was one of the things Brea loved about him, even when it frustrated her.

Griff... After only a few days with him, Brea came to realize he internalized everything, never trivializing. There was a depth to every word he spoke, a meaning behind every action.

Including imprisoning her. He'd said it was for her own good, and she was starting to think he truly had wanted to keep her safe.

She sat atop the stone wall watching Griff work with one of his horses. If she discounted the leather knee pants and loose linen shirt he wore, she could almost imagine they were back home on Myles' farm.

The Robinsons hadn't kept horses since she was a kid. Her parents sold Bellamare, her horse, claiming poverty. It probably wasn't a lie, but some part of her had always thought they did it to get back at her for not being the daughter they wanted.

Had her dad known she wasn't his daughter? In the two days since her conversation by the lake with Griff, she'd gone over every memory she had of him. They'd never been close, and she blamed herself for that. He'd never known how to deal with her problems—like seeing things that weren't there. What would he say if he found out she hadn't been imagining things after all?

She laughed at the thought. He'd never believe her. Just like he hadn't believed her when she said she hadn't meant to hurt her mom on Christmas.

Was there more to it?

She lifted her face to the sun that had been a constant companion during the day ever since the storm. Heat brushed down her bare arms, and she wiped her hands on the blue sheathe-dress Griff had found for her. He'd laughed when she insisted on wearing pants under it, but he'd fetched her a pair before watching her tie the dress at her waist.

There were a lot of things about this place that didn't make sense. How did he have clothes in her size? Where did he obtain the food they ate? She doubted there were grocery stores or shopping malls nearby.

And how on earth had he gotten her into the sleeping gown she'd first woken up in? She hadn't thought about that until it was time to change into something else.

"You look like you're thinking too hard." Griff led his stallion toward her perch.

"Griff, how did I end up in a sleeping gown?"

He lifted one brow. "I did not change you if that's what you're asking." He winked. "Magic."

That word sent a shiver down her spine.

He smoothed the creases on her brow with a finger. "Stop second guessing everything."

"Just trying to figure this place out."

"Well, when you do, fill me in." He grinned. "I'd like to figure it out myself."

She raised an eyebrow. "Haven't you lived here your entire life? You're connected to the queen, of all people. I think you're fine."

He tied the horse's lead to the gate and hopped up beside her, swinging his leg over the stone wall to straddle it and face her. "Don't let us scare you."

"What?"

"I threw a lot of information at you about wars and all that jazz."

"Don't say all that jazz."

"Why not?"

"You're some fantasy creature. You should be speaking all formally or something."

His smile widened. "First of all, I'm not a creature. Just think of me as someone from another country."

"Fat chance of that."

"Second, I've picked up a few phrases from the human realm. That one is my favorite." He cocked his head. "You wouldn't happen to know what it means, would you?"

A laugh broke past her lips. "It's just... never mind. Too much for your fairy mind."

"Nothing is too much for my mind." He jumped from the wall, landing in mud. "Come on. If we have to sit around while waiting for the queen to summon us, then we can at least have some fun."

"Fun?"

"Yes. I'm going to teach you how to ride a horse. Once the queen calls us, you'll need to be comfortable on a horse."

Her lips twitched. Yes, this would be fun. She may not have had her own horse since she was little, but she'd spent more time at Myles' farm than her own, and he'd had plenty.

Her heart squeezed at the thought, but she ignored the feeling as she'd been doing since he died. Myles and high school felt like a different life now. One that belonged to someone else. If this was her new reality, she had to embrace it. She couldn't help but think that was what Myles would want her to do.

Hopping from the wall, she avoided the mud and approached the nearest horse. "What's his name?" The horse bucked up with a neigh, kicking his feet toward her.

"Mack." Griff pulled her back. "Careful, he can be a bit difficult."

Brea bit back a smile and nodded seriously. "I'm going to need help handling such a wild horse."

"Oh no, you won't be riding him. I've got the perfect mare for you." He clucked his tongue and called, "Maisie." A beautiful gray mare approached from the barn. She was on the smallish side with a white streak stretching from mane to nose. "Maisie is an easy girl. She'll take care of you."

Okay, she'd play his game to see how far she could take it. It was her first day not eating any of the Gelsi berries, and the energy within her burned for release. She had to do something.

Griff saddled both horses quickly and led them to the gate that stood open to the rolling hills beyond. "I don't want to go into the forest with a new rider, so we'll head toward the hills."

Brea looked to her hands. "I'm going to need your big strong muscles to help me get up into the saddle."

"Hey." Griff bumped her shoulder. "Don't be embarrassed about needing help. Humans are hopeless when it comes to this kind of thing. You have your steel motor things."

"You mean cars?" She laughed.

He helped her into the saddle, and she grabbed the reins, waiting for him to climb up onto Mack.

"Maisie will follow Mack," he said. "Just work on keeping your balance. Use your thighs. We'll take it slow."

"I just hope I don't fall off." She looked away as a smile came unbidden to her lips.

Griff reached toward her, patting her hand. "You won't. I promise you'll be okay."

His sincerity made her almost feel bad for taking the lie so far. Almost. For the first time since watching Myles hit the ground, she was enjoying herself, and she didn't want it to end.

Griff nudged Mack forward, and they took off slowly down into the lush valley of swaying grasses and wheat fields. If she closed her eyes, she could imagine she rode beside her best friend, enjoying summer in their small Ohio town.

She focused on the familiar feel of the horse beneath her, the fresh scent of the spring day. Only, it wasn't spring, at least, she didn't think so. Did Gelsi ever get cold, or was it just an idyllic land full of singing birds and blooming flowers?

She wondered if she could ever be content staying here. There certainly wasn't anything for her in Ohio, no family she missed, no friends to call her home.

Running a hand down Maisie's neck, she spoke to the horse. "You're lucky this is your home, girl."

She hadn't meant for Griff to hear her. "It can be yours too."

Her head snapped up, but she didn't respond.

Griff went on. "You're the queen's niece. Gelsi is just as much your home as it is mine. You've already accepted this is real."

"How do you know that?"

"When I look into your eyes, the doubt that used to cloud your every thought is gone. If you let yourself admit it, everything I've told you makes sense. Queen Regan is going to welcome you into her court, and if you choose, we can be your people."

Her people? Other than Myles, she'd never had people before. Unless you included the countless psychiatrists and institute employees.

Griff's gaze held so much hope. Why did he want her there? The question never passed her lips because as she lifted her eyes to the most beautiful landscape she'd ever seen, she realized she didn't want there to be any ulterior motives.

So, she decided to trust. In Griff. In this unknown queen. In life's karma, because she'd been through so much crap, she'd earned a little good—even if that came in the form of elves taking her away from her home. If karma did truly exist, Legolas was here somewhere ready to confess his undying love. She just hoped he truly did look like Orlando Bloom.

She laughed to herself.

"What's so funny?" Griff asked.

"You wouldn't happen to be spiriting me away to Mordor, would you?"

His brow scrunched in confusion. "No. We're just riding horses."

She swallowed another laugh. "Okay, good."

Brea didn't know when Griff packed food into his saddlebags or how she didn't see him do it, but he kept producing wrapped parcels like the bags were one of those clown cars where the creepy clowns just kept appearing.

"You spell those saddlebags or something?" She sat underneath the single tree atop the hill where Griff had brought her. Flowers spread across the valley on the other side, an explosion of yellows and reds.

Griff gave her a what-are-you-talking-about look. "We don't do spells. That's not how our magic works."

"Calm down. It was a joke."

He set a blanket down and placed a loaf of bread at the center, along with several hunks of cheese and dried meat, and a wrapped bunch of figs before plunking himself down. Brea reached forward for some cheese but jerked her hand back when grasses grew up over her lap.

Jumping to her feet, she backed away. "What the heck?"

Griff shrugged, a small smile playing on his lips.

Flowers popped up from where there had been none before, and the faint breeze turned into a wind tunnel aimed directly at Brea. She started running, but it followed her, blowing her hair across her face.

Only moments ago, she'd marveled at how amazing this place was. Now, she didn't like it one bit.

"Griff!" she yelled. "I know you're doing this. Stop!"

"Stop it yourself!" he called back.

How dare he? Dark anger fizzled down her arms, pooling in her hands. This wasn't funny. Power seeped out of her fingertips.

"Release it, Brea."

"I don't know how!"

Light shone underneath her fingernails as she flicked them toward the wind tunnel, wanting, needing it to work.

Nothing did.

So, she did the only thing she could think of, the one thing she was good at.

She ran.

Mack stood closest, and she launched herself into his saddle the way Myles taught her to without any help. Digging her heels into his sides, she urged Mack into a run and took off down into the flowering valley, thundering across the beautiful landscape, leaving trampled flowers in her wake.

Story of her life.

It took her a moment to realize the wind tunnel hadn't followed her. She pulled back on the reins, and Mack reared up as he neighed. She squeezed her thighs to keep her seat as he thudded back down and turned back to the hill where Griff stood watching her.

As she neared him, the shock on his face sent a wave of satisfaction through her. He deserved it after trying to force some kind of magic out of her, a magic she hadn't known about until a few days ago.

That was the one part of all this that still didn't feel real.

"You lied to me." His jaw clenched.

She shrugged and jumped down from Mack, landing gracefully. "It's called hustling." She bumped his shoulder as she walked past him to get to the food. "Maybe if you weren't so bent on helping the poor weak human girl learn basic things, you'd realize I'm more than you think." She sat down and ripped a hunk of bread off the loaf.

He kneeled across from her. "But... that... I don't even ride that well."

"That sounds like a you problem." She laughed at his stunned expression. "I grew up on a farm, Griff, of course I know how to ride horses."

He still hadn't taken his eyes from her. "What more don't I know about you, Brea Robinson?"

She met his gaze. "This magic—or whatever cheesy way you weirdoes describe it—I can't do it. I can't control it. The next time you try to make me, I'll throw you in that deceptively beautiful lake. And I won't cry when the mermaids eat you."

"What's a mermaid?"

"Seriously? Don't all you fairytale people know each other?" She wasn't sure what existed or didn't exist anymore, but this fae world made her realize anything was possible.

Griff smiled. "I think I like you."

She grunted. "Well, everyone has their flaws."

Waiting sucked. Brea started losing track of the days since Griff pulled her through that portal. Not much changed in the cottage she'd considered idyllic at first. Now, it was mostly boring.

She spent most of her time with Mack and Maisie, enjoying their stoic silence. Leith was like a ghost. Tasks got done, but they rarely saw him. Each evening, Brea sat at the table across from Griff to eat dinner. It was becoming her favorite time of day, the only time he wasn't busy and would sit there for hours talking to her about anything and everything.

She'd never been much of a talker with anyone other than Myles, but something about this man brought it out of her. She told him stories of the human world, though he knew the basics since he'd traveled there a few times on missions for his queen.

Even the topic of Myles came up. He assured her what happened wasn't her fault, but if she couldn't blame herself, then who? It was easier not to think about it, and Griff made that easy. His charming smiles and gregarious stories filled her with a kind of laughter she'd rarely experienced in her life.

One night, he leaned across the table, meeting her eyes. "Let's go outside."

"Why?"

One corner of his mouth curved up. "Do you have to question everything?"

"Yes." Despite her protests, she stood and gestured for him to follow her out into the warm night air. A full moon shone brightly overhead, surrounded by a scattering of stars.

"I used to watch the stars a lot at home." She sat on the ground and leaned back against the side of the cottage. "We had a barn behind the house. I'd climb into the loft and out the window to pull myself onto the roof."

She hadn't even brought Myles there. It was a place that belonged to her alone. And now Griff.

"Sounds dangerous." There was no chastisement in his tone, only curiosity.

"I know you think humans are so... breakable, but trust me, it was better than being inside my house."

"Why?"

She didn't want to explain the sordid details of her family or her parents' constant berating to a man she barely knew, no matter how much she'd started to trust him. "That's a story for a different time." She leaned forward against her knees and drew in the dirt near her feet. "So... elves... do you all like live forever and stuff?"

His lips quirked at the term elves, but he didn't correct her for once. "Not forever, but we do live longer than humans."

"Let me guess... you're over a hundred years old."

He laughed. "Thanks for that. I didn't think I looked a day over sixty. No, I'm nineteen."

She looked up. "Only two years older than me. I... didn't expect that. How come you live out here all alone then?"

"I'm not alone. I have Leith, Mack, and Maisie."

She leveled him with a stare.

He looked away, and she wondered what he was hiding.

"You don't have to tell me."

A sigh rattled through his chest. "It's just... I didn't have the best upbringing. Queen Regan saved me after my parents died. She raised me, but she also realized court life wasn't for me. I need space to think, to just be me. That probably doesn't make any sense."

"No." She reached for his hand, threading her fingers through his. "It makes perfect sense." She'd never done well around other people, preferring animals and a desolate farm to parties and class. Griff could have lived in a palace surrounded by opulent things, but he would have had to change who he was to do it.

He squeezed her hand. "You know... when my queen found out the Eldur queen's dog was going to the human realm to bring you here, I prayed she wouldn't send me after him, after you. Humans hold little interest for me, but you... you're different." Silver light reflected off his dark eyes, giving them an ethereal glow. "I'm sorry I imprisoned you."

"I understand why you did it," she whispered. This place was dangerous, and he'd known she'd try to escape. If he hadn't locked her up, she'd probably be dead.

He tapped the back of her hand with his thumb. "Don't agree with me."

"Why?"

"Because I enjoy your biting tongue."

She laughed. "Fine. You're an idiot who did an idiot thing."

"That was weak."

"If you ever try to lock me up again, I'll rip off your man-bits and feed them to Mack."

"Whoa..." He crossed his legs. "Too far."

"Sorry."

"You should be."

She bumped his shoulder, and he turned to face her. The lines of his face looked smoother in the shadows, his stubble hidden by the dark. Griff was a character from a book, not someone who should exist in real life. And yet... there he sat in front of her. Close enough to touch. Close enough to...

His fingers brushed her cheek, and she sucked in a breath. Myles once told her a kiss is a part of someone you hold forever. He romanticized everything, and she'd always laughed it off. But now, as she sat in front of the most perfect boy she'd ever met, she wanted something of him, something to keep forever even if this adventure had to end.

"What's that?" he whispered.

Brea strained to hear whatever he heard, but there was nothing save the sound of crickets in the night. Then it became clear. Hooves pounded into the dirt path, coming through the valley.

Griff stood and brushed off his pants.

"Who would be traveling after dark?" Brea asked, getting to her feet. She didn't bother brushing dirt from her pants as she strained to see the rider.

Moonlight glinted off silver hair as he rode closer.

"That's a messenger of the queen." Griff drew himself up to his full height.

As the rider neared, Brea could make out a crest of flowers and wolves on the man's uniform.

He slid from his horse and approached, bowing. "My Lord, Griffin."

"Fraser." Griff stretched out a hand, and the other man straightened and clasped it. "Good to see you. Come in."

"I'm sorry, I cannot." He reached into the saddlebag and procured a letter with a wax seal. "From her Majesty. I am due back at court and must ride through the night." He issued one more bow before pulling himself back onto his horse and riding away.

"What is it?" Brea asked.

Griff didn't answer as he went back inside and retrieved an oil lantern from the table. He scraped his thumb under the seal and broke it before unfolding the letter.

After a moment, he looked up, a faint smile on his face. "Finally. We have been summoned to the palace. We leave tomorrow."

Brea swallowed. The palace.

The outcast girl from Grafton, Ohio was going to meet the queen.

Crap.

Chapter 7

"How far is the palace?" Brea nudged Maisie to go a little bit faster. The sweet horse had two speeds. Slow and stop. Not that Brea was in a hurry to get to where they were going. She was curious about her aunt, but she was not at all confident she could do this whole meet the queen thing.

"We will be there by nightfall." Griff set an easy pace across the rolling hills just beyond the cottage.

"Is it a for real palace?" Brea chewed her bottom lip.

"As opposed to a fake one?" Griff shot her an amused smile.

Brea shrugged. "I saw this movie once where the queen and king didn't care too much for fancy things. Their palace was a cozy log cabin."

"Your aunt enjoys the finer things. Her palace is grand—and like nothing your human eyes have ever seen."

"Like how?" she pressed. Brea didn't like surprises. She needed to be prepared for whatever was coming her way.

"You will see soon enough. Queen Regan's palace lies along the Villandi River in the forest city of Vindur."

"How can a forest be a city?" Brea leaned into her saddle, hoping her fat little mare would make it to Vindur. At the rate she was stopping to eat grass, it might take them a week to get there.

"You will see soon enough."

"Anyone ever tell you you're infuriating?"

"Frequently." Griff pushed Mack into a trot and Lazy Maisie followed.

"Look at you go, girl! You do know how to run." Brea patted the gentle horse.

Brea enjoyed the warm fresh air and bright sunshine. It was invigorating to finally get away from the cottage and jump into the next phase of her new life. She liked Fargelsi. Sometimes she even thought she felt a connection to the verdant green hills.

"So... what happens when we get there?" Brea asked. "And so help me if you say 'you will see soon enough' I may sic my horse on you. She's a hungry girl, you know."

Griff's laughter was a deep, throaty sound she really liked. "When we arrive it will be late. Servants will show us to our rooms, and you'll likely meet the queen tomorrow or the next day. She's a very busy woman, though she is anxious to meet you."

"What is she like?"

"She is a kind and generous ruler. You should strive to be yourself with her, Brea. Well... perhaps save your biting sarcasm for me." He winked. "I can take it."

"Is there nothing but rolling hills between here and there?" Honestly, she'd grown quite bored with the trip so far. She'd expected to see more. People. Towns. Something.

"We will reach the Dragur Forest soon."

"Dragur? That doesn't have anything to do with dragons I hope."

"No, no dragons."

"What does Dragur mean?"

"Haunted."

"We're going to the haunted forest? Like with ghosts?"

"It's not actually haunted. At least I don't think it is anymore."

"Oh, well, that's just peachy." Brea glanced back over her shoulder.

"Why do you do that?"

"Do what?"

"You're always looking behind us like you think we're being followed." Griff shook his head, as amused with her as ever.

"I don't even know I'm doing it. There's just a vibe I get sometimes. Like not everything around me is as harmless as it seems."

"Probably just your human caution rearing its head. Gelsi is a strange new world for you. Of course you're naturally curious and suspicious of things you don't understand."

They stopped for a break around midday in a beautiful low-lying glen. To the east, the rolling green hills gave way to green mountains with rocky peaks. To the south lay the entrance to the Dragur Forest. As Griff cared for the horses, Brea explored their surroundings, taking the opportunity to stretch her legs. After hours of riding through the hills, Brea was happy to see something that wasn't green. Gorgeous purple flowers bloomed on shrubs at the lowest part of the glen. Orange wildflowers hung in clusters among the tall grass.

Brea picked some of the orange flowers and braided them into a daisy chain for her hair. She even found what looked like bubble-gum-pink strawberries growing on a vine-covered fallen log. She picked enough to go with their lunch, placing them on a napkin on the picnic blanket they'd brought with them.

"I wouldn't do that," Griff came up behind her as she was about to pick some of the purple blossoms. "You'll be dead before we reach the palace. Even more dead if you eat those berries you picked."

"What's wrong with the berries?" Brea stood up, taking a few steps away from the poisonous flowers.

"One or two would just make you sick. More, and you'd fall asleep and never wake up. Some healers make a tea from the berry leaves for a sleeping draught, but even that can be dangerous."

"What about these?" Brea's hand went to the flowers in her hair.

"Harmless. And quite charming in your dark hair."

"No purple flowers. No swimming in Lake Villandi. No pink berries and no Gelsi berries. I should start a list of all the things that might kill me or drug me."

"Don't touch anything once we reach the forest. There, the more beautiful a thing is, the more likely it is to be dangerous."

"Got it."

After they ate and packed up, they headed into the forest. She wasn't prepared for how dark it was under the thick canopy of vine-covered trees.

"I feel like we should be traveling a yellow brick road to find the flying monkeys at the witch's castle."

"What are you babbling about?"

"Nothing." She stared into the swaying branches. "It's too quiet here. There aren't any birds in this forest."

"There are some, but most here are nocturnal. You'll rarely see or hear them."

"I find that... unsettling for some reason." Like she couldn't trust a forest that didn't have birds.

"You'll get used to it."

"So, how long will we be in the forest of nightmares?" She didn't relish experiencing nightfall here.

"It's not that bad, is it?" Griff's half smile slid into place. It was her favorite smile of his.

"It's creepy."

"We will reach the Villandi River before sunset. Vindur Palace is just across the river.

"Is the river like the lake? Should I prepare to fight the urge to dive in?"

"Not at all. The river flows north to Loch Villandi. Whatever phenomenon makes the lake so treacherous is not present in the river waters."

"Good to know. How will we cross the river?"

"There's a bridge, Brea."

"Well, you all aren't very modern, so how could I know if you'd discovered bridge engineering or not?"

"We aren't imbeciles. We just prefer simpler ways of living."

"You should think about getting cell service here. It beats the heck out of relying on messengers to carry your snail mail."

"Oh, I've seen your phones and the way humans depend on them like a drug. It may provide a certain level of convenience, but I prefer to enjoy a well written letter rather than the instant gratification of emoji texts." He smirked as if proud of himself for knowing what an emoji was.

"Whatever. I'd give my right arm for an hour at Dunkin Donuts with a large iced hazelnut latte, a smartphone, and a good pair of earbuds."

"I have no idea what you just said, but I find you utterly fascinating, Brea."

"I'm not all that complicated or deep, Griff."

"I beg to differ."

Sometimes the way he looked at her made her so nervous she couldn't see straight. *Good job, Brea. Crushing on the hot fae dude.*

"So what's expected of a queen's niece? Do I get a title or something?"

Griff frowned. "I'm not sure, actually. Technically you're a princess as the daughter of the queen's brother."

"Oh gosh, I was joking!"

"They'd probably just call you Lady Brea. But as the queen's niece, you'd have certain privileges, and in time, certain duties I imagine. Nothing you can't handle of course."

"And after you deliver me to the queen, where will you go?"

"I will stay for a while, but eventually, I'll return to my cottage where it's quiet. It will be a lot quieter without all your endless questions."

"You'll miss me when I'm gone."

"Indeed I will." Griff picked up the pace, urging Mack into a trot. "Look there." He pointed in the distance where the trees grew taller and wider than anything she'd ever seen. It reminded her of pictures she'd seen of the Redwood forest back home.

The path ahead ran in a straight line for miles and miles. "It's a lot farther than it seems, but you can just see the other side of the forest. We'll reach the river before sunset."

Brea didn't know what she'd expected of her first look at the forest city of Vindur, but she wasn't prepared for how it crept up on her. They'd traveled the whole day and never once saw another living soul. Brea had become so used to their solitude that it took her by surprise when the first fae woman she'd seen since her arrival in Fargelsi seemed to appear from nowhere.

"Why are they just hanging out in the forest?" Brea looked over her shoulder to see dozens of fae going about their business.

"We're on the outskirts of the city. Open your eyes, Brea. Not everything here is mere forest."

That was when it clicked, and her eyesight shifted. Fae were coming and going from buildings, visiting businesses and returning to their homes—all sitting among the tree tops."

"How?" Brea turned around in time to see a woman leave her home, skipping down the steps wrapping around the massive tree trunk.

"The Fargelsi fae draw their power from nature," Griff reminded her. "They grow their homes this way."

"Amazing." Brea leaned forward in the saddle, and swore she caught a glimpse inside a home with moss carpet.

"Is the palace like this?"

"See for yourself. The palace is just across the bridge." Griff pointed ahead.

Brea's eyes couldn't decide what to look at first. The bridge was made of thick, green vines that grew from a massive tree trunk into a twisting pattern of knots and leaves that extended across the river.

The bridge was wide enough for the two lanes of traffic coming and going from the palace. Far below, the crystal waters of the Villandi River made their lazy way across boulders and over rocks, splashing and tinkling like a symphony of sounds.

The palace itself seemed to have grown up from the riverbed. Vine covered stone spires reached for the skies, and pointed archways rose up in tiers from the main gates to the highest point at the center of the structure. Each spire twisted into three points that wrapped around a light source that shone brightly in the fading sunlight.

"It's breathtaking," Brea murmured in awe.

"The beacons are solar powered," Griff explained. "They provide light for the whole palace."

"Beautiful, functional, and safe for the environment."

The entire scene was picturesque, the way a tributary of the river flowed around the castle on either side, cascading in twin waterfalls over the cliffside to the main river below. Stone bridges grew from the palace at dizzying heights to connect to other wings.

"I have no words. It's possible I'm back to thinking I could be hallucinating again."

Griff's laughter brought her out of her fog. "I've never known you to be short on words. And for the last time, this is real, Brea Robinson. You've finally come home."

As soon as they passed through the castle gates, the queen's men-at-arms ushered Brea and Griff into the grand hall to meet the castellan.

"Lady Einin, it's good to see you again." Griff took both of the small woman's hands in his larger ones. "The queen has summoned us. Is she available?"

"She's visiting with a diplomat from the Eldur court. She's asked me to see the Lady Brea settled in her rooms." Lady Einin turned to give Brea a nod. She was stern-faced and didn't seem to bother much with small talk. "You know where your rooms are, now off you go." She shooed Griff toward a different part of the palace.

"You'll be fine." Griff put a hand on her shoulder. "Lady Einin will take good care of you tonight, and I'll see you first thing in the morning."

Brea nodded, trying to shove back the blazing hot panic at the realization that her security blanket would be too far away to hear her if she needed help.

"This is your home, Brea. You are safe here." He squeezed her shoulder, leaving her with the allegedly capable Lady Einin.

"This way." Einin called, turning toward the massive staircase made of the most vivid green vines.

Brea followed silently as they climbed the great staircase to the third level of the palace. Einin stopped at an ornate doorway with a pointed arch covered in white vines with pink flowers and the palest green leaves streaked with gold.

"This is the queen's quarters. She has requested to have you near. Be on your best behavior, and don't go wandering about. The maids will bring your dinner and draw a hot bath for you."

Einin slipped an intricate bone key into the lock and stood back to let Brea enter the huge room—suite of rooms. It was fit for a princess, which she wasn't.

"Surely the queen would rather put me in a simple guest room."

"Queen Regan does what she likes. Make yourself at home and ring the bell if you need anything. Good night, my Lady." She dropped a slight curtsy that left Brea completely creeped out.

"I can't have people curtsying." She shivered and ran her hands over her arms. "It's too bizarre. And now I'm talking to myself again."

Brea walked around the oval-shaped sitting room, too scared to touch anything. She definitely needed that bath. Everything was so white, it shone like pearls in the moonlight. She was sure to ruin anything she sat on in her travel clothes.

A white settee occupied the center of the room. It seemed to have grown right out of the floor from the same delicate vines that adorned the doorway. The cushions of flower petals beckoned to her after hours in the saddle, but she couldn't resist checking out the rest of her rooms.

Three arched doorways led from the main room. The first led to a bathroom and dressing area with a huge walk-in closet filled with fluffy pink gowns Brea really hoped weren't meant for her.

The second door led to a bedroom. A vine-covered canopy bed stood on a dais at the center of the room. Strands of sheer white flowers grew from the canopy and fluttered in the warm breeze flowing in through the open balcony doors.

The last doorway led to a study. Rows and rows of books filled the shelves from floor to ceiling. A white wooden desk stood in front of a second pair of balcony doors, and a pair of white fur-covered chairs waited by the fireplace.

"Give me Netflix and Uber Eats and I could live here and never leave these rooms," Brea murmured.

A door opened behind her and three maids entered carrying trays and an assortment of clean nightclothes. They were identical triplets, making identical curtsies, staring at her with identical blue eyes.

"Would you like a bath first or food first, my lady?" The lead triplet asked, with another curtsy.

"Bath, please." Brea decided to go with it. She was far too tired to protest their eager little faces. She would explain to Lady Einin tomorrow that she'd rather see to herself. Servants were definitely not something she wanted to get used to.

"My lady, you must get up. The queen is ready to see you." Triplet Two pulled the warm downy covers away, and Brea wanted to scratch her face off. She'd just had the most restful sleep of her life and she wasn't ready to get up yet.

Triplets One and Three were busy pulling fancy dresses from the closet, while Triplet Two shoved a breakfast tray in her face and went to work on her nails.

"I can dress myself." Brea munched on a delicious pastry and sipped hot spiced tea. It wasn't coffee, but it was tasty. This world had to have coffee somewhere, and if they expected her to stay, someone better find it soon.

"Nonsense." Triplet One said... or maybe it was Two.

In no time they had her brushed, curled, and stuffed into a pink gown with a narrow waist and a long train. They left her to wait for Griff to arrive, and as soon as the trio was out of sight, Brea kicked off the tight slippers that pinched her heels and shoved her feet back into her boots. Under the long dress, no one would know. She felt more confident that she could actually walk without falling over her own feet.

Griff didn't give her time to get nervous. He knocked on her door just as she'd started to pace.

"What's with the terrifying triplets?" She shoved an errant curl out of her face, and snatched off the white gloves they insisted she wear. "I swear they snipped, plucked and trimmed me within an inch of my life."

"You're the queen's niece. There are certain expectations." He tried to hide his smile.

"You can say it, I look ridiculous." She tried to flatten the back of her big hair.

"You look beautiful. But the palace styles are a bit much. It's one of the main reasons I don't live here." He gestured at his own attire. A trim cut suit with tailored pants and a jaunty hat.

"Compared to this get up, you look comfortable. Want to switch outfits?"

"No, thank you." He offered his arm. "Ready to meet your aunt?"

She placed her hand in the crook of his elbow and kicked her train behind her. Blowing a dark curl out of her face, she said, "As ready as I'm going to get."

Griff led her to the hall and into the queen's apartments. "You're wearing your boots aren't you?" He chuckled.

"If you expect me to walk like a normal person, then yes, I'm wearing my boots."

"Don't be nervous, Brea. Just be yourself. She already loves you."

"That's not as comforting a thought as you seem to think it is. She has expectations, and I doubt I'll ever live up to them."

"Don't sell yourself short."

Brea gazed around the huge room filled with dainty gilt-edged furniture and breakable things. Sunlight poured in from the balcony.

"There she is!" The breathy genteel voice washed over Brea like a soothing balm. "I'm so happy to finally meet you, Brea, darling."

Queen Regan was not at all like Brea imagined. She was short and plump with soft white-blond hair that fell nearly to her knees. Her kind blue eyes sparkled with excitement.

"You look so like my brother." Her white-gloved hand rested over her heart. "It's so sad he never knew about you before he died. Come, let me get a good look at you." The queen took Brea's hands and held her at arm's length. "Such a lovely girl. Would you like some tea while we get to know each other?"

She dragged Brea out to the wide terrace where a table covered in pastries and tiny sandwiches waited for them.

"Thank you so much for having me... your Majesty."

"Come now, you may call me Auntie Regan. We are family."

"T-thank you, Auntie." The word felt ridiculous on her tongue, but she liked the bubbly little woman. "My rooms are the most beautiful I've ever seen."

"I'm so glad you're pleased." The queen sat on a tiny vine chair that looked like a throne. "Have a seat, dear." She patted the chair next to her. "And where is Griff?"

"Here, your Majesty." Griff stepped onto the balcony, flashing a brilliant smile for his queen.

"Brother, it's good to see you again." The other voice sounded familiar. Brea turned to find a blond man leaning against the terrace railing. "The last time I saw you, you were rather in a hurry."

"Lochlan, don't be such a stick in the mud," the queen chastised. "We simply couldn't allow my niece to end up in the hands of your queen."

Brea looked from Lochlan to the queen and back to Griff.

"Brothers?"

Chapter 8

Griffin's lips flattened into a thin line, and his brother didn't seem any happier to see him. Brea couldn't wrap her mind around the fact that the two men who'd tried to kidnap her from the human world were related.

"Impersonating a police officer is a crime." The words spilled out of her mouth before she could stop them, and her cheeks flamed at her stupidity. He'd been trying to abduct her and take her into this whacked out world. He didn't care about committing human crimes in a world that wasn't his own.

Neither brother spoke as they stood in a silent stand-off.

When the queen clapped her hands together, they all jumped. "That's right! I forgot you already met my dear niece." She turned to Brea. "Darling, this is Lochlan O'Shea. You may call him Loch."

"She may not," the man in question snapped.

"Oh, don't be such a bore." She rolled her eyes in the universal expression of *men!* "Don't let Lochlan scare you, niece."

"What are you doing here?" Griff spoke like his brother was the only person on the terrace.

Lochlan's jaw clenched. "My queen sent me."

His queen. Griff mentioned Lochlan worked for the fire queen of Eldur.

"Ah, yes." Griff dropped into a chair beside Brea's aunt. "How is Queen Faolan? Still bent on destroying Fargelsi?" He shook his head and turned hard eyes on his queen. "He shouldn't be here. Eldur is no ally of ours."

"Forgive Griffin." Aunt Regan folded her hands in her lap and looked to Lochlan. "Sibling relationships can be difficult." There was a sadness to her eyes Brea wondered about. Did it have to do with her mysterious fae father?

But she couldn't ask.

Lochlan pushed away from the railing, his cold gaze skittering over Brea, sending a shiver down her spine. "I told my queen this mission was a mistake. Our talks have gotten us no closer to a deal today. I will leave you to your…" His expression darkened. "Family reunion." With that, he turned away.

"The queen has not dismissed you," Griff growled. In all the time she'd spent with Griff, she couldn't remember ever seeing him so tense.

Aunt Regan held out a hand toward Griff, palm up. He placed his hand in hers. "It's okay, Griff. Lochlan, you may leave us."

With a grunt, Lochlan stormed past the guards at the door and disappeared. The tense air choking their gathering dissipated, and Griff's shoulders dropped.

"Niece." Her aunt smiled. "Please, take a seat."

Brea lowered herself into a tiny chair she worried would break if she so much as shifted. Yet, it seemed to hold the larger Griff just fine. Servants descended on them, setting silver teacups in front of them and pouring steaming tea that smelled of oranges.

Needing something to do to quell the nervousness inside her, Brea reached for a pastry only to have her hand slapped away by a servant who used silver tongs to place food on each of their white china plates.

"Ana," the queen chastised.

Ana, a slight woman with tanned skin and caramel colored hair bowed her head in apology. "I'm sorry, your Majesty. Truly. Don't... please... I didn't mean to cause offense. You always tell us no lady should serve herself. I just..."

The queen's eyes flashed green. "You may go, Ana. Do not touch my niece again, or we shall have a problem."

Ana scurried away.

Throughout the entire exchange, Griff stared down at his plate, almost as if he were willing himself not to see the cracks in his liege's kind demeanor.

Brea watched the door Ana had disappeared behind. "It's okay, A-auntie. It was my fault."

"Brea, nothing that happens in this palace is ever your fault. As a Lady of the court, you will grow used to that."

"But I'm not a Lady. I'm just a farm girl from Ohio."

The queen smiled. "I thought Griff would have explained your importance by now." There was admonishment in her voice.

"I did," Griff grumbled. "She just refuses to see herself as special."

"That's because I'm not." Brea took an abnormally large bite of her pastry to keep more words from tumbling from her mouth. Instead, crumbs fell onto the bodice of her dress, and the dry scone stuck like glue in her throat. She coughed, spraying bits of scone onto her plate and reached frantically for her cup of tea.

Guzzling it down, she spit it out when it burned her throat, coating the plate of pastries in a thin layer of regurgitated tea. The coughing fit didn't end, and she pounded on her chest, unable to breathe in the tight dress. Once it finally subsided, she built up the courage to look at her aunt—the queen—which still seemed ridiculous to her.

The queen was too slow to cover up her look of horror, and Brea couldn't blame her. It was the moment Regan realized she'd made a huge mistake, that her niece wasn't fit to clean the floors of a palace, let alone live in one.

"I'm sorry, they didn't teach etiquette at the Clarkson Institute," Brea blurted.

Griff shook in silent laughter, the grim expression he'd worn since seeing his brother gone. She had the urge to reach out and punch him, but that would probably be frowned upon—just like spitting her food all over the queen's impeccable table.

A brown stain spread over the white lace tablecloth where tea dripped from the corner of her plate. Brea couldn't take her eyes from the evidence that she didn't belong here.

A slow smile overtook the disgust on the queen's face, and before long, she joined Griff in his laughter, the sound high and vibrant like the tinkling of a waterfall.

Brea clasped and unclasped her hands in her lap, not knowing exactly what to do. She absently picked up her scone again before staring at it in accusation and setting it down. "The scone was dry." She cringed at her words. "I just mean... at Starbucks, they're more like cake. I wasn't expecting a biscuit, and I bit off too much, but then the tea was hot, and—"

Griff cut her off. "We saw it play out, Brea. We don't need another account."

Brea scooted her chair back and stood. "I'm so sorry, Auntie. I wanted to make a good impression, but this is all a little too much. I'll understand if you want to send me back—not like I have much to go back to other than a murder charge for killing my best friend and parents who think I'm insane." She clapped a hand over her mouth. "Please forget I told you about that. I'm not a murderer. I swear. I miss Myles, and it was my fault, but I didn't mean to kill him. I swear."

"Brea." Griff raised a brow. "You're rambling."

"I know!" she burst out before clapping a hand over her mouth again. "I just yelled in front of a queen. It's just, I ramble. I'm clumsy. Sometimes I even talk to myself. I've lived my entire life with people telling me the things I see aren't real. This is who I am, Aunt Regan.

I'm totally not calling you Auntie because I'm not a hundred. Do you want me to stay or not?"

The queen's keen eyes didn't stray from her face as she studied her. "Yes, dear. I knew all these things about you already." She stood. "You will stay. But I believe you could do with some rest. I will send my own personal Lady's maid to look after you."

"But I already have maids."

"The triplets are wonderful housemaids, but they can be a bit… over stimulating, and they haven't trained as Lady's maids yet. You will still see them from time to time, but I think Neeve will be a perfect fit for you, dear. Griff, please escort Brea back to her rooms."

Griff stood and bowed at the waist. "Yes, your Majesty."

The queen bustled away in a swish of skirts, her heels sounding against the floor in her retreat.

"She hates me." Brea flopped face first onto the bed, yanking at the bottom of her dress so it stopped pulling on her.

"She doesn't hate you." Griff hesitated in the doorway. "She just doesn't want to overwhelm you."

"Or overwhelm herself." Her parents never let her forget what a burden she'd been to them with her hallucinations and outbursts. "I don't want to be a burden anymore." Tears gathered in her eyes, but she blinked them away.

"Is that really what you think?" Griff stepped into the room and shut the door. His long strides brought him to the edge of the bed. "That you're a burden?"

Brea sat up and shrugged.

Griff's eyes met hers. "Brea, you're wanted here. I don't know everything you've gone through in your life, but that's over." He bent so they were eye-level. "This is your home now."

"Can you sit with me for a little while?" She patted the spot beside her.

"On your... bed?" He jumped back. "I shouldn't even be in here. It's not proper."

"Please?" She didn't care what was proper in this world. As recent as a few months ago, she'd spent the night at Myles' house sharing his double bed. They'd never questioned it. "I'm not asking you to sleep with me, Griff. This place is so different than what I'm used to. At your house, I could imagine I was on some idyllic vacation. But this, here, is real, foreign. I can't do it alone."

"You're not alone." He sat beside her.

She nodded. "Okay, talk to me about anything else to make me forget I spat tea at the queen."

He laughed. "I haven't been that entertained at a tea in... ever." He bumped her shoulder. "Okay... something different. Confession time. Seeing Lochlan here in this palace completely messed with my mind."

She swatted his arm. "I can't believe you didn't tell me he was your brother. I knew you guys were familiar from your fight in the woods over yours truly, but brothers? Talk about whoa." She paused. "Why didn't you tell me?"

He sighed. "Our family is complicated."

"I understand complicated. Try me."

"I lied to you before. Well, I don't think I actually said I'm Fargelsian... maybe just implied."

"You're not from here?"

He shook his head. "Do you remember I told you about the three kingdoms of the fae world?"

She nodded.

"The frozen kingdom is Iskalt. Lochlan and I were born at the ice palace to the king and queen."

"You're a prince?" Her jaw dropped. "A real, honest to god prince?"

"Was. Our parents died when we were children, and our uncle took the throne. He sent us away, me to be raised in the Gelsi court and Lochlan to be raised in Eldur. It was a compromise, a way for the other kingdoms to allow my uncle to remain king. We were supposed to bring the kingdoms together."

"But that didn't happen."

"No, it didn't. Lochlan hates me. Really, he hates everything. I've never been able to get through to him. When I saw him in the human realm with you in his possession, I realized the Eldur queen wanted you as well."

"Why?"

He shrugged. "We don't know. Maybe Loch being here will give us some answers. Whatever the reason, it can't be good. Queen Faolan of Eldur is born of fire. She can't be trusted, and neither can my brother. That is why I didn't tell you." He dropped his voice to a whisper. "I didn't want you to think less of me because of him."

The corner of Brea's lips twitched up. "I couldn't think less of you, Griffin O'Shea." Her eyes found his as she turned her head. "I don't claim to be the authority on genuine people, but I would bet my last horse you're one of the good ones."

His lips curved into a half-smile. "You don't have any horses."

"I just figured it was the kind of thing people say here. I'll amend it. I'd bet every last one of those frilly dresses in my too-large closet."

"You hate those dresses, so I'm not sure that has any meaning."

"How do you know I hate them?"

"Because, even though you look completely breathtaking in that preposterous mountain of tulle, I can read the discomfort on your face."

"You barely know me, Griff. You can't read my face."

He reached up to tuck an errant strand of hair behind her ear. "Now... that is a bet I'd take." His finger skimmed over her cheek. "Your cheeks redden when you think you've said something wrong." His hand moved up over the bridge of her nose. "Your nose crinkles when something annoys you."

"Usually you."

He laughed. "And these eyes... shine the most brilliant shade of blue when you're content."

"They're always blue. Eyes don't change color."

He pulled his hand away. "How can you see all there is to see in the fae world and still keep these human notions?"

"It's a talent."

"Stubbornness?"

"I was going to say idiocy."

He shook his head. "You're no idiot, Brea Robinson."

She couldn't take her eyes away from the boy saying all the right things, things she wanted to believe. There were secrets in his eyes—like the secret about Lochlan—but she shut those out, needing desperately for someone to trust in.

Leaning into him, she wrapped her arm around his waist. For the first time since Myles' death, she felt she wasn't alone after all.

Brea and Griff spent the day playing cards in her room. He'd found a deck she didn't recognize with symbols she'd never seen before. He taught her to play a game called Flash Magic.

It was designed to be used along with a fae's abilities, and Griff encouraged her to try small things like staring at the deck and using her magic to draw a card. When she finally accomplished it without setting anything on fire—don't look at her curtains—she jumped across the game and tackled Griff to the ground.

He hugged her back, only releasing her when someone cleared their throat. Brea pulled back with a grin to find a tall girl staring down at her with beautiful amber eyes. Thick chocolate brown hair was pulled back away from her youthful olive skin.

"I can come back," she squeaked in a voice that revealed her age more than her appearance did.

Brea picked herself up from the ground, wiping her hands down the pair of pants she'd made Griff fetch from his room. Her own closet was stocked with nothing but dresses. She'd have done just about anything for a pair of yoga pants with pockets.

"No, it's cool." Brea smiled, still riding a high from using her magic.

"Cool?" the girl said the word slowly. "Do you need a fire started in your hearth? It's quite warm outside, but if this room isn't to your liking, I can do that."

Brea suppressed a grin. "No, cool means... never mind. It's fine, you can stay if you tell me who you are."

"Oh." The girl's cheeks paled. "I'm Neeve. The queen sent me to wait on you."

"Well, I don't really need waited on. But do you want to play with us?"

Neeve stared down at Griff with wide eyes.

"Brea." He stood. "Neeve doesn't want to play. She's here to do a job."

"Doesn't mean the job can't be fun."

"Actually, it does." He shook his head with a sigh. "I must be on my way. I've been here most of the day, and there's a formal dinner tonight since the Eldurian negotiators are here."

"Does the queen want me to come?"

"No!" His word came so quickly, her shoulders dropped. Of course, her aunt wouldn't want her in public after what happened that morning.

"Oh, okay."

"I just mean... We don't trust Lochlan and his party. The Eldur queen wants you taken to her court, so it's best if we keep you out of sight until they're gone."

Lochlan had already seen her, but she didn't argue because she had no real desire to stuff herself into an awful dress and sit behind a big table taking rabbit bites of food. At least, that was what the movies said one did at a palace meal.

Griff ran a hand down her arm before squeezing her hand. "Neeve will take care of you. I'll see you soon."

When he left, she stared at Neeve for a long moment, unsure of what to say. She'd never been good at meeting new people. "You're tall."

Neeve bowed her head. "Yes, it is a flaw."

"No, I mean, it's cool, I mean sweet. You know what? I'll just say I like it. In the human realm, you'd be considered beautiful with your long legs and all." She smacked a palm against her forehead. "I'm totally not hitting on you. I like boys."

Neeve cocked her head. "Hitting me? That is your choice if it should happen."

"Hitting *on* you." She scoured her mind for a term that might make her understand. "Courting you. Is that right? I only want to court boys."

Her brow scrunched. "Well, that seems rather limiting." She walked past Brea to examine the burnt curtains.

"You like the ladies? That's cool. Sweet. Fine. Ugh!"

To her surprise, Neeve laughed. "Fae do not choose one type of person to love. We don't fall in love with a fae's... genitalia."

"Wait a second." Brea held up a hand. "Are you trying to tell me I've fallen through some pansexual wormhole?" A grin overtook her face. "That's freaking awesome. Has Griff ever..."

"Lady Brea." Chastisement rang in her tone. "I am a servant. We do not gossip."

"Of course you do. I've seen *Downton Abbey*."

"I won't pretend to know what that means."

"Wait, aren't you like not allowed to yell at me?"

Neeve's face paled. "I wasn't yelling. I was merely..."

"Don't stop. Please. Servants here are all Stepfordy. I like you, Neeve. We're going to be friends."

"A servant cannot be friends with a Lady of Her Majesty's Court."

"Sure they can." Brea climbed onto her bed and sat cross-legged.

"The queen would not approve."

She laughed. "The queen will not approve of about ninety-percent of me. We just won't tell her." She lowered her voice. "Please. I'd like to make friends here." She'd never had that urge back in Ohio, but Myles had been all she'd needed. The more people she distracted herself with here, the less time she'd have to miss him, to let herself wallow in guilt.

If it worked like that.

"You do not seem like the kind of lady who'd move into the palace." Neeve picked up the discarded game on the floor.

"That's because I was kidnapped."

Neeve almost dropped the cards. "You're the girl the queen has been searching for?" She stumbled back. "The one wanted by the Eldur queen?"

"Yeah, didn't I say that?" She flopped onto her stomach and kicked her legs up behind her. "Listen, I don't have any plans to leave this room until everyone forgets what an idiot I am. But I'm starving. Who do I call to get some chow around here?"

Neeve set the game on an ornate white table near the hearth. "I'll fetch you something from the kitchen." Something in her changed, and Brea couldn't figure it out. It was like news of her identity shook something within the servant.

After a long stare, she left Brea to her silence.

The Gelsi palace had the best food.

Brea never thought she was the kind of person to like coated duck in some kind of cream sauce she couldn't pronounce. Or that she'd stuff herself with seven courses of a single meal. At home, they were more the bologna and grilled cheese type of people.

She lay on her bed, her stomach almost bursting in protest. Neeve left after bringing the food, despite Brea begging her to stay and eat with her. Fear had entered her eyes at the proposition, and she went on and on about how servants didn't eat food fit for nobles. Brea tried to convince her to take a single bite, and she'd run out of there as if her dress was on fire.

The remnants of Brea's magic trials in the game with Griff were long gone, leaving behind a pristine room once more. She wondered if the people in this palace ever stopped working.

Thoughts of the fire queen entered her mind. She pictured a woman with blazing eyes and a vengeful spirit. As she'd learned from the movies, anything with fire in these fantasy worlds was bad.

That was how she imagined the Eldur queen. Long white hair, a hard expression, and dragons at her disposal. Did this world even have dragons? Griff hadn't mentioned them. He'd have told her, right? Because, seriously, dragons!

The prospect both scared and intrigued her.

She couldn't let herself fall into the hands of a dragon queen.

A scraping on her door had her jolting up in bed. She climbed off the heavenly mattress and crept across the floor on bare feet. Raising a hand, she tried to call on her magic, letting it latch on to her fear.

But when the door opened, it clogged in her veins, unable to break free as her mind went blank. Before her stood the most beautiful man she'd ever seen. It wasn't the first time she'd thought it, but it was the first time since knowing he was evil.

There was a definite family resemblance with Griffin. For one, both he and Lochlan were ridiculously good looking—but she was starting to suspect half of the fae population of the same.

"Brea," his low growl had her stepping forward not of her own accord.

"What are you doing here?" She had to force the words out.

He shut the door behind him. "We need to talk."

She only stared at him.

"You're in danger."

Chapter 9

Brea's breath released in a ragged stream as the angry fae stalked toward her. She backed away until the backs of her thighs hit the bed. "You shouldn't be in here."

"Neither should my brother."

"That's n-none of your business." Her words shook. "What do you want from me?"

He glanced back at the door as footsteps sounded out in the hall. When they passed, he released a breath. "I left the dinner early to seek my bed."

"This isn't your bed."

His eyes bore into hers like he could see through every one of her defenses. The man before her had none of the lightness of his brother. Instead, he replaced joy with a deep intensity, just as entrancing as every one of Griff's smiles.

And also terrifying.

She rounded her bed so it stood between them.

"You don't need to run from me, Brea. I won't hurt you."

"But you would abduct me—again—and take me to your queen."

His silence told her that was exactly what he wanted to do.

"Let me ask again, what the heck do you want from me?"

He studied her for a long moment. "You aren't safe here."

"Of course, I am," she scoffed. "Queen Regan is family."

"That woman..." he pointed to the door, "...is not your family."

"You think you know me because you picked me up off the floor of a jail cell. You think I owe you?"

"Brea—"

"No, you can't pull your intimidating crap on me. I have spent my life in and out of mental institutions for delinquents. You don't scare me." Okay, he kind of did. "Don't barge into my room thinking I'm going to fall at your feet."

"That's not why I—"

"Stop lying to me!"

Lochlan crossed the room, stopping in front of her. His jaw tensed as he looked down into her eyes. "I am not your enemy."

"Any enemy of my aunt's is an enemy of mine."

"You barely know your aunt." He dipped his head to look at her more closely. "My brother is the one you really trust, isn't he?"

"He has given me no reason not to."

"He's lying to you. You're not safe here, Brea."

"I don't believe you." How could a palace like this be unsafe with all its fortifications and guards? "Are you done?"

"I came to deliver a warning. It is up to you what you do with it." He tore his eyes from her with a growl and turned on his heel, pausing before he reached the door. "If you need help, trust Neeve. No one else."

"Neeve?" Was she betraying Brea's aunt? "How do you know I won't betray her?"

He was quiet for a long moment. "Because I have been watching you for a long time, Brea Robinson, and that is not who you are."

"Watching me?" *Creepy much?* "What does that even mean?"

A knock sounded on the door before Griff's voice filtered through. "Brea, you in there?"

She considered calling out, telling him to come save her from the man standing with his back to her, his muscles bunched.

Something held her back.

Lochlan glanced back over his shoulder, his eyes finding hers. "There's one more thing."

"What is it?" Brea sighed, wanting this night to end. The sooner Lochlan was gone, the better.

"Myles."

The name on his lips caused her heart to skip a beat. "Wha—"

"He's alive."

Without another word, he pulled open the door and found Griff leaning against the wall, waiting.

Griff kicked off the wall, anger overtaking his features. "What are you doing with her?" His face reddened.

Lochlan flashed him a tense smile. "Having a chat."

"You have no right."

"And you do?" Lochlan towered over Griff, using his height to intimidate his brother.

Griff didn't back down. "She belongs here."

Brea backed away from them but the vitriol poured from the two beautiful boys. Brothers, yet enemies. And they both wanted her for some reason she couldn't explain.

They continued to argue, but their angry words blurred together as her heart pounded against her ribs. She turned around, pulling at the loose shirt that suddenly felt too tight, too warm.

Alive. Alive.

Was Myles really alive or was it another trick?

Could she trust anything in this world?

Alive.

Flashes of that day she'd tried to suppress ran through her mind. Myles hitting the ground. Waking up to find him gone. What did the paramedic say to her before she was arrested? She pulled at her hair and collapsed back onto her bed, the hammering of her pulse drowning out the angry words ricocheting around the room like ping pong balls.

"I'd be surprised if he made it to the hospital."

Those were the words, and no one had refuted her thought that he was dead. Not the police or her therapist. Not Lochlan when he first abducted her or Griff since.

It didn't mean Lochlan was telling the truth. She knew that, but the hope expanded within her, pulsing like energy beneath her skin. She needed to know, for someone to be honest with her.

The tingling she recognized now as her magic built up.

"Stop!" she yelled. Glass shattered, spraying shards across the room as every window, every piece of china broke into a thousand tiny pieces.

Pain nicked her cheek, and she wiped away a bead of blood, her chest heaving.

Lifting her head, she found Lochlan and Griff on the ground where they'd dropped to avoid the glass. It settled around them like a blanket just as dangerous as they were.

"Lochlan," she growled, darkness in her voice. "Get out of my room."

He stood, examining a shard of glass sticking from his hand. Pulling it free without so much as a wince, he looked to her once more. "Remember what I've told you." Without another word, he turned and left.

Griff picked himself up. Glass crunched underneath his feet as he approached her. "Are you okay?"

"No," she sniffed. "I'm not okay at all."

The hard expression he'd saved for his brother softened. "Are you injured?"

Other than a few small cuts, she'd escaped her magical outburst unharmed. She shook her head.

"Come on. We can go to my rooms while someone cleans this up. I think we need to talk."

He held out his arms and she let herself fall into them. After carrying her across the glass-strewn floor, he set her down and reached for her hand.

Speaking quietly to a servant outside the room, he explained the situation, and within moments, the triplets rushed in to take care of the mess.

Griff didn't speak to her until they reached his rooms, which looked almost identical to hers, save where her furniture was white, his was a deep cherry wood. Aged vines with deep burgundy flowers wrapped up the walls, never once letting them forget they lived in the middle of a magical forest.

Myles would have gotten a kick out of this.

"Griff." She tugged on his hand and forced him to face her.

"What's wrong?" He released her hand and framed her face with his palms.

"Is Myles alive?"

For a moment, everything stood still, until Griff turned away from her and kicked off his boots. "You know the answer to that."

"Do I?"

His back tensed. "Is this what you and Loch were speaking of? Why you let him into your rooms?"

"First of all, I didn't let him into my rooms. Second, you're avoiding the question."

"What do you want me to say, Brea?" He twisted to face her. "Myles Merrick made it to the hospital where they hooked him up to machines we'd never subject our people to here in the fae world. He lived for two days before succumbing to his injuries."

"How do you know?" she whispered.

Griff sighed and pulled her against his firm chest, wrapping protective arms around her. "We have contacts in the human world."

"Did you keep tabs on him for me?"

He nodded, resting his chin on the top of her head. "I hoped to be able to tell you better news. Lochlan is just using your friend to make you doubt me."

Tears broke free of her eyes. She hadn't yet cried for Myles, because doing so made it real. But this… Her arms wound around his back, and she held onto him as if her world would break apart if she let go. Maybe it already had.

"Brea." His breath blew into her hair. "You can't listen to anything Lochlan says. Ever. His motives are never good."

"I'm sorry I doubted you. All you've done is help me since I arrived."

He pulled back and put a hand on each of her shoulders. "Do you trust me?"

"I do."

A smile spread across his lips.

Something still ate at her. "The fire queen—"

"Queen Faolan."

She nodded. "Sure. She wants me."

He dipped his head to look her in the eye. Sliding a finger under her chin, he tilted it up. "I will protect you from her." His eyes blazed violet as he dropped his voice. "I promise."

She couldn't have looked away if she tried. Griff was right. Lochlan wasn't the guy who'd protected her these weeks. He didn't care about her, not like Griff.

Reaching up on her toes, she pressed her lips to his before drawing back quickly, realizing what she'd done. "I'm sorry. I know you're just helping me because of my aunt, but—"

His lips cut off her next words and he drew her against him, consuming her as if she were the air he needed to breath. She slid her arms around his neck, holding on for dear life, because there was no way this made anything less complicated.

Yet, she didn't stop, couldn't stop. Griff tasted like Gelsi berries and honey, and she never wanted it to end. His hands slid down her back before gripping her waist and pulling her tighter against him.

"Griff," she whispered against his lips.

"Hmm?"

"This is a bad decision." She was at the palace to meet her aunt. Who knew what kind of future she had here? A part of her still expected them to shove her back into the human realm the moment they realized she wasn't the kind of girl who fit here.

But she wanted to fit, with her aunt, with Griff.

"Probably." He kissed her again. "So it's a good thing I have a history of bad decisions."

"I don't believe that." As far as she knew, he was the queen's most loyal follower, her ardent supporter. One didn't gain such power with bad decisions. This was the same man who'd imprisoned her for days, but even that faded to the back of her mind. Bad decision or not, she needed this, a morsel of happiness to fill the empty chasm inside her.

"Are you saying you don't want to kiss me again?"

Was she? She considered him for a long moment before fitting her lips to his once more. "Wait... you're not like related to the queen, right? I know you're from Iskalt, but if there's a reason you rose so high in the Gelsi court... I'm no Jaime Lannister."

He grinned as he pressed a kiss to her cheek. "I don't know who those people are, but we aren't related. I promise you that."

"You and your promises."

He trailed his lips over the curve of her ear. "I promise I want to kiss you again."

"Well, go on then. Can't go breaking your word."

As he kissed her fully, thoroughly, the events of the day faded away. She didn't want to stop, because that was when the questions flooded back, the insecurities and sorrow. When she kissed Griff, she didn't have to mourn her best friend or worry about some far-off fire queen who wanted her for some unknown reason.

And best of all? His lips silenced the part of her mind that waited for the perfect veneer to fade from this new life, because if her old life taught her one thing, it was that Brea Robinson didn't get easy, she didn't get a happy ending.

Chapter 10

"Festival? What festival?" Brea stared blankly at her new Lady's maid. Neeve was a thousand times better than the creepy triplets, but she still wasn't sure she'd ever get used to having servants.

"It is Beltaine, my Lady." Neeve stared back at her, equally perplexed.

"What is Beltaine?"

"It's one of our most special holidays. It's a celebration of peace and prosperity for all Faekind. It is why her Majesty invited the delegations from Iskalt and Eldur, my Lady."

"Please, Neeve, I'm begging you, enough with the 'my Lady' this and 'my Lady' that. My name is Brea, when it's just us here in my rooms, it would please me if you would call me Brea."

"Yes my—Brea." Neeve stumbled over the name.

"I think I've read something about Beltaine before." Brea scratched her head. "Isn't that a summer holiday?"

"Summer?" Neeve frowned. "It is always spring here, ma'am."

"Ha!" Brea whirled around with a smile. "Nice try, but no 'ma'ams' either. Isn't Beltaine in May?"

"Yes. It's always the first of what humans call May." Neeve couldn't seem to sit still, bustling about Brea's rooms with a duster, but there wasn't a speck of dust anywhere. Brea had looked on one of her many boring days spent in her rooms over the last week.

"But that's months away."

"It's tonight."

"It can't be." Brea's heart climbed up in her throat. She couldn't have been here four months already. "It was January when I arrived. That was just a few weeks ago."

"Are you quite well, Brea?" Neeve crossed the room to help her sit in one of those vine chairs Brea was always afraid she'd crush.

"I don't know." Brea fanned her face, blaming her too-tight corset for her dizzy spell. If she was going to be here much longer, the fae world was about to discover sports bras and yoga pants. Surely someone around here could grow her a pair with their magic.

"Are the rumors really true?" Neeve leaned close to whisper. "Did you come from the human realm?"

"There are rumors about me?" Brea groaned. That was all she needed.

"Just a few. Our people are very curious about you. I promise... Brea... I will not repeat anything you tell me. You can trust me."

That's what he'd said. Lochlan. *If you need help, trust Neeve. No one else.*

Brea nodded. "Griff brought me here from the human realm. But I'm fae," she added quickly. "I just didn't know it till recently."

"Of course you are fae. You have the look of royalty, no less. You're the Fargelsi Queen's niece. Which means everyone is curious about you."

"I get it, but I just... how have I been here four months and not noticed the time passing?"

"Oh dear, I'm sorry, I thought you knew, but of course you'd have no reason to know. Our calendars don't exactly line up with the human calendar. You arrived here when it was January where you came from, and it's been three fortnights. So for you, it's not quite

March yet. According to our calendar, for you it is only early spring, though we do not adhere to human months."

"So I didn't lose a whole bunch of weeks I don't remember living?" Brea took a deep breath.

"No, of course not." Neeve laughed. "I'm sorry, I don't mean to laugh. You are just quite funny sometimes.

"So I've been told." Brea got back on her feet and crossed the room on shaky legs. Reaching for her teacup, Brea tried to pour hot water over the tea leaves.

"I'll get that for you, my Lady." Neeve swooped in and grabbed the cup from her hands.

"I can pour myself a cup of tea." She felt like stomping her foot, but that was childish. She wasn't above it, but she needed to keep her cool and remember Neeve was only trying to do her job.

"Please relax, you have a big night ahead of you."

"And what is expected of the queen's niece tonight?" She sighed. Not looking forward to this first of many formal events.

"You will sit in a place of honor with the queen, where you will meet the delegates from all the fae courts. Beltaine is a celebration of peace, love and fertility. A night where all our differences are set aside and new friendships are formed."

"So, I just have to sit there and look like I belong? I think I can manage that. What do I have to wear?"

"You're going to love it." Neeve smiled, but then she probably remembered who she was talking to. "At least I think you will." A frown marred her face. "Are you ready for the triplets? They'll be assisting me tonight."

"Must they?"

"I couldn't manage to get you ready without help."

"You know." Brea sipped her tea. "In the human world, I managed to dress myself without any help at all. I even made my own breakfast."

"This is different, Brea." A note of annoyance crept into Neeve's voice. "Your human clothes were simple. Your costume for tonight is—"

"Costume? You didn't say anything about a costume."

"Well, yes, it's tradition on the night of Beltaine for the nobility to don costumes for the festival. Everyone will dress like flowers and creatures of the forest."

"So it's like a masked ball?"

"No masks tonight. Would you like to see your gown?"

"Call in the trio if you must." Brea sighed. "Any chance someone has a stash of mood suppressers around here?"

"Is that like... a potion? Tonight won't be that bad, Brea."

"Not for me. For the three little maids on speed."

Brea couldn't walk. Her gown was too heavy. It had to weigh more than she did.

"I've heard people talk about suffering for fashion, but this is a new one." Her knees nearly buckled.

"Just lean on me. If you fall down, at least we'll go together." Griff chuckled, tucking her arm around his. "If it helps, you look stunning. Like the first perfect white rose of spring."

"Ooh that was cheesy." Brea giggled behind her fan—an actual white lacy fan!

"Cheesy usually works for me." He straightened his tie with an arrogant smirk.

"You know they built a crazy contraption under all this tulle, you wouldn't believe it if I told you. I've got pillows stuffed around my hipbones to keep the dress foundation from stabbing me. The scaffolding under here weighs a ton and that's before they decorated me like a cake with all these fresh roses. They actually made the roses grow around the dress."

The ball gown was stunning on the dress form with its yards of white silk and the palest pink tulle, but when Brea finally got a chance to see herself in it, she thought she looked more like a marshmallow Peep.

"The triplets spent hours sewing beaded rosebuds all along the bodice and the hem. I've never seen anything like it."

"I take it you are not pleased with the weight of the gown?" Griff escorted her down the grand staircase, gripping her carefully so she wouldn't fall in her ridiculous heels.

"Ya think?"

"Maybe this will help." Warmth from his hand running along her arm spread through her body, and his green eyes shimmered violet for a moment.

"Oh," Brea almost toppled over as the massive weight of the dress lifted and she felt as light as air.

"It seems someone forgot to do that for you."

"And you let me walk down ten flights of stairs before you decided to help me out with that little trick?"

"I find your complaining amusing this evening. And it wasn't ten flights of stairs. It was two."

She studied his 'costume.' A trim cut white suit with a white fur hat shaped like a wolf's head.

"You seem to be missing a tail."

"There's only so far I'm willing to go for a costume party."

"That's what I said, so why can't I opt for the easy suit and hat *costume*?"

"I grew up as the queen's ward, but I'm not deemed part of her family. You are. And most of the people here would give anything to be in your shoes tonight."

Brea took the last few steps at his side. "It's hard for me to think of myself as anything other than plain old Brea Robinson."

"There is nothing plain or old about you, Brea." Griff laid his free hand on top of hers still clutching his arm. "Ready for a night you'll never forget?"

"As ready as I'll ever be." Brea followed him to the rear of the palace, frowning as she realized she hadn't come down from the queen's quarters since she arrived, and she hadn't even visited this part of the palace yet. "Where are we going?"

"To the park just across the queen's gardens. It's magical at Beltaine. You're going to love it." Griff pulled her through the massive rear doors of the palace and Brea gasped at the wonderland before her. Sweeping lawns with pathways and fountains, and every kind of flower she could imagine—in full bloom at night!

"It's beautiful." She breathed.

Brea and Griff followed a line of nobles along the pathways leading to the festivities at the center of the park beyond the high brick walls.

"You will enter with the queen." He whispered in her ear, his breath warm against her skin. "This way." He tugged Brea away from the crowd, skirting the garden walls to a separate gate just for the queen's use.

"Can you stay with me?" She clutched her dress to keep the hem from dragging across the wet grass.

"I will be right behind you and the queen." He squeezed her hand. "I know this is all overwhelming for you, but the people will love you if their queen does. And it's pretty clear Regan already adores you."

"She thinks my clumsy behavior is a riot." Brea laughed. "But I think she's kind of amazing," she admitted. "And so kind. I don't know what I expected, but she's just so delightfully... perfect." Brea couldn't imagine how her aunt could ever have anything resembling an enemy. But there was beef between her and the Eldur queen. Brea might be the Gelsi queen's niece, but she already knew she had no desire to get into fae politics.

"Oh my darlings, you look beautiful." Queen Regan beckoned them to join her at the east gate. "Look at us, we're just a pair of delicate roses tonight."

Where Brea's dress was all white with pale pinks, adorned with dozens of white roses in perfect bloom, Regan's was blood red, covered in red rose petals from the hem of her gown to her bodice, where it flared into a stiff high collar the shape of a rose. With her white blond hair piled on top of her head, she looked just like a fairy-tale queen.

"You look so beautiful, Aunt Regan." Brea responded to Regan's air kisses with her own. She was getting used to her aunt's larger than life personality.

"Come with me, dear, I want to introduce you to all the nobles of my realm. I hope you've rested because tonight is going to be... oh what do the human kids call it these days? I do love their marvelous expressions."

"Epic?" Brea supplied.

"No, tonight's going to be amaz... no that's not it either."

"Amazeballs?" Brea grinned. For the past few days, Regan had Brea teaching her all the slang from the human world. They always ended up laughing hysterically by the end of their afternoon tea.

"That's it. Tonight is going to be *amazeballs*, just you wait. Your Auntie Regan has stopped at nothing to make your first Festival of Beltaine a night to remember."

"Thank you, Aunt Regan, I can't wait." And to Brea's surprise, it was true. She felt more relaxed with her aunt now and with Griff right behind her, she thought she just might get through this party unscathed.

Brea fell in step with her aunt as they strolled through the gates; the queen never hurried anywhere she went. Brea could hear the gasp and roar of the crowd, but it had no effect on Regan.

"The Festival of Beltaine is all about expressing love and putting peaceful thoughts out into the world for the coming season," Regan began, lifting her hand to wave at the crowd. "It's no secret that relationships between the fae courts have seen better days. I've invited delegates from both Iskalt and Eldur to celebrate with us tonight with the hope it will foster more positive communication among the leaders of our world. You will help me charm them, won't you, dear?"

"Oh, Aunt Regan, I seriously doubt you need my help charming anyone, but I will give it my best."

"You flatter me, dear. Come sit with your auntie while we watch the festivities." Regan made her way to the raised dais where a throne waited for her. A miniature version of that throne sat to the right of the queen's chair and just slightly back. Regan made herself comfortable and gestured for Brea to take her seat beside the queen.

Brea felt like a piece of fine jewelry on display. The crowd had grown quiet at the queen's entrance, waiting for her permission for the merriment to continue.

"Ladies and gentlemen, I present my niece, daughter of my late brother, Brandon, Breanna Louise O'Rourke. You may call her Lady Brea."

"But, that's not my name," Brea tried to say, but the queen didn't seem to hear her. She felt Griff standing behind her and wished he could sit at her side.

When he leaned in to explain, his presence calmed her, and she could breathe again.

"Relax. It's just a formality. She hasn't taken your name away. She's just given you a proper title—giving you her last name, no less. This is a good thing, Brea."

"Thank you, Aunt Regan," she managed to murmur, smiling shyly for the crowd.

"Please continue the festivities," the queen said with a wave of her red-gloved hand.

Brea took a deep breath, gazing around the park at the hundreds of fae celebrating the holiday. Bonfires roared in every corner, lively music played, and people danced under the stars. Gymnasts on stilts took great lumbering steps through the crowd, wowing the children from their great height. Fire-eaters and jugglers performed, each trying to outdo the other. Beautiful women wrapped in yards of silk hung suspended from the trees, performing amazing feats high above the crowd.

The evening was perfect. The weather was beautiful, as if Regan ordered a balmy night with cool breezes just for her guests. Servants buzzed around the park offering drinks and the most sumptuous finger foods. Brea and the queen sampled their fair share of the food and wine while they gossiped about the lords and ladies of her court.

"Your Majesty, you do us a great honor introducing your beautiful niece to Fargelsi on this lovely Beltaine evening." Brea had heard a version of this speech throughout the night. This time the nobleman was young and quite handsome, if a bit stuffy.

"Lord Tadleigh Bainebridge, always lovely to see you." Reagan turned her charms on the smitten young man. "Lord Bainebridge oversees one of the largest estates in Fargelsi," the queen explained.

"At the queen's pleasure, of course." The man offered a curt bow to Brea. "It would be my honor, Lady Brea, to escort you this evening." He took her hand, placing a kiss there like all the gentlemen before him.

"Thank you, sir," Brea stuttered.

"I'm keeping her all to myself this evening, Tad." The queen batted her eyes at him. "Another time." Her tone was one of dismissal.

His expression fell, disappointment in his gaze. "Of course, your Majesty." With that, he turned on his heel and walked toward a gaggle of ladies nearby.

Regan's fan unfurled in front of her face. "He may be handsome, but he's older than he looks, that one. I'm told he uses a tonic to keep his hair like that. And he's such an incredible bore."

"With a bit of a brown nose, too." Brea giggled.

"Brown nose? What an odd phrase." The queen took a sip of her wine.

Oh crap. How was Brea going to explain such a saying? She needed to start watching what she said. "Um, well he's rather good at kissing your ... royal ... bum." Brea's cheeks flushed in the firelight. She turned begging eyes to Griff who leaned into the queen's ear and explained.

"Brown nose indeed!" The queen roared, and Brea relaxed. "Don't be so shy, Brea, dear. You can say anything to me. I don't offend easily."

"Perhaps Lady Brea would like to see the sights, your Majesty?" Griff suggested. "It is her first festival with us."

"Oh very well, Beltaine is a night for the young, you two go have fun. Just come back to watch the fireworks with me."

"Of course, I wouldn't miss it." Brea leaned down to kiss her aunt's cheek.

She took Griff's hand and followed him through the crowd, laughing and relishing the moment of freedom from the endless parade of noblemen.

"She's introduced you to every eligible Fargelsian in her inner circle."

"Eligible?" Brea giggled. "For what, like marriage?"

"Yes. It was quite irritating to watch."

"Is she mad?" Brea's mind swirled with too much wine. "I'm not getting married. I'm way too young."

"I'll talk to her." Griff smiled, looking like he might have also taken too much wine. "I'll explain how it is in the human world. She's just excited to show you off. You're all the family she has, you know. Having you here makes her happy."

"And I'm happy to be here." Brea whirled around, making her dress lift in the breeze. "It's so beautiful here, Griff. I just still can't believe this is my real home. It's like a dream come true."

For once, Brea didn't let her cautious thoughts weigh her down. Maybe it was the wine talking, but she was starting to see a future here. A future she wanted. Maybe even a future with Griff.

"A flower for your Beltaine lady?" A wizened old woman offered Griff a perfect blush-stained rose from her basket. He paid the lady for the flower and turned to Brea, tapping the rosebud against her nose.

"This rose reminds me of your blushes." He trailed the soft petals down her cheek. "The way your cheeks flush with the faintest pink when you're embarrassed about something silly and utterly human. It's one of my top ten things I love about Brea Robinson." He pressed the rose into her hands.

"Top ten?" Her voice came out breathless and shaky. "What are the other nine?" She pressed her nose against the bloom to inhale its fresh fragrance. She couldn't remember ever smelling a rose like this in the human realm. They'd always seemed overly fragrant and cloyingly sweet.

"I can't spill all my secrets now. You'll have to wait for the other nine."

She closed the distance between them to kiss him, but he moved away. "We can't here, Brea. It would cause a scandal for the queen's niece to show affection so openly. But please know, I am dying to taste those lips again." He tugged on her hand, guiding her to the tents where the courtiers feasted and drank copious amounts of wine.

They ate roasted venison, spiced vegetables and other things Brea couldn't even identify.

"I need some fresh air." Brea tried to take a deep breath, but the confines of her corset and the contents of her stomach wouldn't allow it.

"I'll meet you by the fountains in a moment, and then we will join the queen for the fireworks."

Brea didn't want to be the girl who needed a buffer, but panic slowly ebbed its way into her heart the moment he left her. She went to wait by the fountains, worried she might make a fool of herself if anyone stopped to speak with her. She watched the crowd come and go, but no one even noticed her. Something was weird about that.

Several young girls skipping around a maypole caught her attention. Their ribbons fluttered in the breeze as they wrapped them around the pole. They skipped and laughed like young girls should, but there was something forced about their merriment. They did and said all the right things, but that sincerity didn't reach their eyes.

The same with a group of young men, dancing with girls about the same age. They were everything carefree teens should be ... but somehow not quite. They lacked a certain joy.

As Brea took in all the queen's guests, a cold sense of dread lodged in her stomach. They were all just going through the motions.

Like they only wanted to do what the queen expected of them. But there was a lackluster dullness in their eyes. It gave her the creeps.

"Lady Brea." The cold voice sounded behind her. She knew it was him before she turned. "I should escort you back to your queen. It isn't safe for you to wander around the festival alone." Lochlan gazed down at her, his perfect mouth drawn into a thin line.

Her wine-addled brain wondered what it might do to his features if he truly smiled. He hadn't bothered with a costume, though it didn't surprise her he'd refused to play along. Dressed in dark leathers and a long black cloak, he would blend easily with the night if it weren't for his silvery blond hair. Her wore the top half swept back from his face and secured with a black leather band. The hair just above his pointed ears was tightly braided, but the rest fell down his back just past his shoulders. His midnight blue eyes smoldered under dark blond brows.

"I'm sorry, what?" Brea swayed on her feet, feeling a little dizzy from staring up for so long.

"You're drunk."

"No, you're just stupid-tall." She turned to leave him, but he grabbed her arm.

"I'll escort you."

"I don't need an escort. I'm perfectly capable of walking these two little feet back to my aunt, thank you very much."

She moved to pull her arm away from him and managed to trip over her own feet. She knew she was going down the moment she lost her balance. Clutching at Lochlan, she tried to stop the inevitable, but the edge of the fountain hit the back of her calves and wet hands *grabbed* her legs. Brea toppled over, dragging Lochlan down with her.

Cold water closed over her head and pulled her dress down into the depths of the pool. Immediately sober, Brea scrambled for the surface. Why was this fountain so deep? Dark things under the surface clamored for her attention, clawing at her hands and feet, pulling her down. Strong arms wrapped around her middle, dragging her up to the surface. Just as stars danced in her vision, Brea thought she saw a sea of angry creatures staring back at her.

Then she was spewing water out of her lungs, coughing and sputtering like a fool in front of her aunt's court. Something hard thudded against her back.

"This damned fool dress almost killed you." Lochlan's hand pounded on her back once more.

"Stop." She tried to wiggle out of his arms to swim to the edge of the fountain, but he stood up with her in his arms. The water barely came up to his knees. The flowers from her dress floated around his feet.

What the hell just happened?

"Are you okay, my darling?" Queen Regan rushed to the edge of the fountain.

"I'd be fine if this brute would put me down." Brea's face flamed with heat.

"Lady Brea, are you okay?" Concerned voices rang out around her.

Oh great, I'm a spectacle now.

"I'll see to the lady," Lochlan said, stepping over the edge of the fountain and back on solid ground. Brea looked over his shoulder for any signs of the creatures she'd just seen, but the shiny bottom of the fountain winked back at her.

"Griffin will see to her," the queen insisted. "Please see to yourself, Lochlan, dear, and come join me with your delegation to enjoy the fireworks."

Reluctantly, Lochlan set her down, but not before he whispered another warning in her ear. "Heed me now, silly girl. You are not safe among this court. There is only darkness here."

Back on her feet, the weight of her dress and half the water from the fountain weighed her down. Griffin pulled her into his strong arms, and she clung to him in relief.

"Our Lady Brea is a delightful klutz, is she not?" His laughter inspired the crowd to respond in kind. "Show them you're not embarrassed, Brea. Laugh with them."

Brea bent into a curtsy, flashing them her most charming smile and shrugged as if to say, I'm a lovable goof—which she'd like to think she was. She'd just rather not make a habit of falling into fountains. And she'd grown quite tired of needing to be rescued.

Chapter 11

It took Brea forever to get warm once she'd changed out of her sopping dress into a still-not-her but more comfortable sleeping gown. Her aunt told her she didn't need to rejoin the festival after the fountain mishap because the night was winding down, and soon only those bent on debauchery would remain.

Debauchery. Brea grinned into the dark. That was her aunt's fancy speak for the drunks. Though, most of the people at the festival had been pretty far into their cups already by the time she left.

As if she'd never seen drunk people before.

It would probably horrify her aunt to hear about her mom's frequent nights out or the way her dad crushed entire cases of beer sitting in front of the TV for college football Saturdays.

No, she was no stranger to debauchery.

Rolling onto her side, she stared out the window. Six weeks. That was how long Neeve told her she'd been in the fae world. Six weeks since she set foot on the dilapidated farm she'd called home.

Six weeks since Myles walked the earth.

Her life went from psych wards and high school to adventure and romance in record time. Maybe that was why it still didn't feel real.

She waited for the day the other shoe dropped. Nothing could be this perfect.

No one.

Not even Griff.

She smiled as she thought of the way he'd escorted her through the festival, past performers and scurrying children. Other than the nobles, no one looked directly at her.

Well, except the delegates from Iskalt and Eldur.

The men and women representing the frozen kingdom sat apart from the rest of the crowd, their icy eyes finding her wherever she walked.

And Eldur... She'd tried desperately to free herself from whatever danger lurked in the waters of the fountain, but only found relief in the strong hands of a man she should hate. Lochlan O'Shea couldn't be trusted. Griff told her as much. But she couldn't shake the protective look in his eyes, or the way he'd refused to let her go until the queen stepped in.

Why did he care what happened to her?

His queen wanted her, she knew that, but this was... different... more.

She strained to hear wolves howling in the woods, reminding her she was far from home.

But maybe this could be home in a way the little farmhouse in Ohio never was.

A sigh rattled through her chest as she sat up, finding sleep impossible. There were too many questions on her mind, and only one person who might give her any sort of answers.

Crawling from the bed, she slipped her feet into woolen slippers and pulled open her door, cringing when the hinges creaked. She waited for a moment to make sure no one was around. It was ridiculous she had to worry about this when she'd spent the last ten years of her life sneaking out and running across the fields to Myles' house. But she didn't want to cause any kind of scandal for the aunt who'd been nothing but kind.

She wound her way through the dark halls until she reached a room she'd been to only once before, hoping the door wouldn't be locked. Only the queen, Brea, and Griff lived in the royal residence wing at present.

Pulling on the handle, she smiled when she heard it click and slipped into the room before a wandering guard or servant found her out of bed.

Griff lay on his stomach with the sheet bunched around his waist. To her disappointment, a loose white linen shirt covered his torso. Ear-length auburn hair stuck up against the feather pillow.

He looked so different from his brother it made it hard to see how they were related. Where Lochlan was light, Griff was dark. At least in appearance. When it came to personality, they were the exact opposite. Lochlan had none of Griff's joy, only intensity.

His hard blue gaze would forever be stuck in her mind.

But he didn't matter right now.

"Are you going to just stand there or come over here?" Griff opened one eye.

Brea shrugged. "I don't know. I just figured I'd watch you like a creeper."

He lifted his head. "I have no idea what a creeper is, but I don't approve."

"Oh yeah?" One corner of her mouth curved up.

"When the most beautiful woman in all the fae realms is in my room at night, I'd much rather have her close."

"Oh, okay." She turned to the door. "I'll go find her then."

"Get over here," he growled.

"Well, if you insist." She slipped out of her shoes and launched herself onto the bed, landing on top of Griff.

"That's one way to wake me up." He gripped her waist and flipped her so her back hit the bed. "But I like this better." Hovering over her, he lowered himself onto his elbows.

"Are you going to kiss me?" she whispered.

"Was that a request?"

She shook her head. "A demand."

"You ask so much of me." He pressed his lips to hers in a slow, sweet kiss. Griff wasn't an intense man, not a passionate man. He didn't devour her or steal her breath away.

Instead, he cherished her.

He rolled off her, landing on his side and propped his head up. "Not that I'm not happy to see you, but what are you doing here?"

"I couldn't sleep."

"And that's enough reason for you to sneak into a man's room in the dead of night?"

She lifted her eyes to the canopy overhead. "I didn't really think anything of it. I've been doing this my entire life."

He reeled back, his eyes widening.

"I didn't mean this," she blurted, gesturing between them. "I used to climb out my bedroom window to get to Myles whenever my parents sent me to my room... which was often and usually after a lot of yelling."

"Have I told you yet how sorry I am about your friend?"

She went quiet for a long moment, not wanting to talk about Myles. She didn't know if it was still too fresh, or if she just wanted to keep her best friend to herself a little longer.

Resting her head on Griff's shoulder, she hesitated before asking the question on the tip of her tongue. "Were you and Lochlan ever friends?"

"He's my brother."

"Yes, but was he your friend?"

His voice went cold. "We were young when my uncle separated us." When he didn't say anything else right away, Brea thought he was done. Finally, he went on. "But before that... I have memories, small ones. Lochlan is two years older than me, and I remember the day we learned our parents had died, or at least bits of it. The only person I wanted was him." He sighed. "The court loved my parents. Everyone sank into mourning. Servants. Guards. Nobles. It was like

Iskalt lost its soul. But so did we, me and my brother. We lost so much more than our souls."

"Did you find him that day?"

"I did. I sat next to him, and he wrapped an arm around me." Griff scratched his face and blew out a breath. "I've never told anyone about that day. I don't know why I'm telling you. I don't even know if these memories are true or a child's twisted fantasies."

Guilt gnawed at her for not talking to him about Myles, but she wasn't ready for that. She turned onto her side and stretched an arm across his chest. "You don't have to tell me. But you can... you know... if you want to."

"I've seen too much of Lochlan in the past few weeks. Before I found him in the human realm, it had been four years since our last encounter. It's easier not to think of him when I'm not staring him in the face."

"Maybe thinking of him isn't a bad thing. Do you think you could make up?"

"You mean reconcile?" He shook his head. "Not while he stands at the Eldur queen's side."

"What did he say to you the day your parents died? Do you remember?"

Griff didn't answer at first, and only the sound of their breathing filled the room. "He said it was up to us to make them proud now. That we only had each other, but that he promised it would be enough."

"Your promises," she whispered. It made sense now. Griff obsessed over making promises, and it was because he believed Lochlan broke his.

He rested his chin on the top of her head. "At the time, we thought he would rule over Iskalt with my parents' advisors to help him. He was a kid, but it wasn't unheard of. My uncle had other plans. Within a fortnight those advisors were either dead or disappeared, and Lochlan and I were sent to be raised and educated in other courts under the guise of creating worldly leaders."

"Will your uncle ever abdicate?"

He shrugged. "I'm not sure it matters to me. Lochlan is the rightful king."

Brea wanted to shake him. As an only child, she always dreamed of having a sibling to go through life with, someone to share the struggles. Sure, she didn't know how the fae world worked, but Iskalt didn't only belong to Lochlan. It had been Griff's parents' realm, their people.

How could he forsake that?

"Brea," he whispered.

"Yeah?"

"Say something funny so I can forget about all of this."

"I'm not a funny person, Griff. The sooner you realize that the better."

He pressed a kiss to her temple. "Okay, say something human because that's always funny."

"We're pretty boring. Only elves think humans are funny."

"I'm not a—" He paused. "You're making fun of me."

"Yes siree, Bob."

"There it is." His laugh shook his entire body. "I don't understand half your odd phrases, but they sure are entertaining."

"I live to please." She sat up. "Want to play a game?"

He pushed himself up so his back rested against the cherry headboard. "In the dark? Should I retrieve a lantern?"

"Nope." She popped her p and grinned. "Just give me your hand. We're going to have a thumb war."

"Brea." He frowned. "There's no such thing as a war with thumbs."

"Sure there is. I'll show you."

"I don't want to hurt you."

She laughed. "You won't."

"But it's a war."

"Shut your yap already and give me your hand." When he didn't, she reached out and grabbed his hand, locking it into the thumb war position. Scooting closer to him, she relaxed. "Okay, follow my lead. We count to eight, tapping our thumbs on opposite sides from each other. When we reach eight, try to pin my thumb."

"Brea, I'm stronger than you. How do you think you can win such a game?"

She grinned. He had no idea. She'd spent many nights having thumb wars with Myles when neither of them could sleep and they couldn't turn on the light in case his mom saw.

"Just go with it." She tapped her thumb, showing him how to do it. "One, two, three, four, I declare a thumb war. Five, six, seven, eight, try to keep your thumbs straight." She straightened her thumb, grappling with Griff's before pinning it in two seconds flat.

Griff only stared at their still-interlocked hands. "That's not how war works."

"That's why it's a game, Griff, not a battle."

"Can we try again?"

She nodded and started the count. This time, Griff lasted a bit longer before succumbing to her pin.

"Again," he demanded.

"Oh my, I've created a monster." She raised a brow.

Griff smirked. "You'd have to master your magic to create monsters."

Her jaw fell open. "You can actually make a monster?"

"No." He laughed. "I just wanted to see if you'd believe me."

"I hate you so much."

"No, you don't."

No, she didn't. She pulled her hand away and scooted up beside Griff, tucking herself into his side. Since entering this different world, he'd kept her safe and helped her navigate her new reality. She'd never be able to repay that.

"Can I sleep in here?" she asked.

"That would cause quite a stir with the servants."

"Honestly, Griff, I don't really care."

He wrapped his arm around her and kissed the side of her head.

"A lot is going to change, Brea. I don't know what's going to happen now that you've been introduced to Gelsian society. Suitors will present themselves to the queen, no doubt."

She coughed out a laugh. "Griff, there is zero chance I'm ready for marriage. I'm not even eighteen." No matter who her aunt paraded in front of her, marriage was the last thing she wanted. She had enough to get used to.

Griff sighed. "I guess I'm just saying I want to enjoy having you here while I can. Just know... no matter what happens... I'm always here for you."

That sounded suspiciously like a breakup speech, and they weren't even officially courting or whatever people called it here. She didn't know what she felt for Griff. All her emotions were tangled up in the safety he represented, the trust she had in him.

Was it more than that? Maybe. Or maybe not.

All she knew was she wanted to keep kissing him, to feel his arms around her and know she wasn't alone. Because loneliness was the most dangerous thing in the world. It bred misplaced trust and a belief in things that weren't what they seemed to be.

Brea groaned into the damp pillow beneath her face. Gross, she'd drooled in Griff's bed. Sunlight streamed across the room in strips of warm light. Footsteps echoed off the stone floor coming closer and closer.

"There better be coffee on whatever tray you're carrying." She lifted her head with a scowl, deciding right then she was never drinking wine again.

Griff lowered the silver platter to the table beside the bed, a quizzical look on his face. "What is coffee?"

"You have got to be kidding me." She pulled a pillow free and buried her head beneath it.

Griff plucked the pillow out of her grasp, an annoying grin on his face.

"Traitor." She grimaced.

"I had breakfast brought up from the kitchens. Hotcakes—"

"Smothered in coffee?"

He ignored her. "Eggs—"

"Using coffee grounds instead of pepper?"

"And fried pork."

"Fried in coffee grease." She grinned this time.

"Okay." Griff crossed his arms. "I thought I could guess what coffee is—some sort of drink—but now I'm not so sure."

"I was joking about the grease thing, but seriously, how have the fae not discovered the life-giving beverage? You have magic, and they're basically the same thing."

"First of all—" He poured tea into two way-too-small white china cups and handed her one. "If there's truly a beverage that gives life, we must take this knowledge to the queen."

She hid her grin by taking a sip of tea. "And the next thing?"

"What?"

"You said, "first thing" and that implies there's a second."

"Ah." He set his cup down and sat beside her on the bed. "You continue to refer to this world as ours. I know it'll take a while for it to truly sink in—as you humans say. But you are one of us. The magic... it belongs to you as well. This world is your home."

She set her cup on the tray and turned, pulling her feet up under her on the bed. "I forgive you."

"For what?"

She met his gaze, letting his kindness soothe her aching head. "For pulling me into a world where coffee doesn't exist." She pressed a kiss to his lips, smiling against him.

"You're ridiculous."

"That's one of the things people used to say about me when they thought I was crazy."

He frowned. "I didn't mean it like that."

She reached up, tracing the curve on his lips, letting her fingers flit over his smooth cheek—cleaned up for the festival. "I know." She pulled her hand away and reached for the tray, dragging it onto the bed.

Griff's brow furrowed. "Brea, it's not proper to eat where one sleeps."

"Then what's the point of having breakfast brought to the room?"

He gestured to the sitting area in front of the hearth.

Her brow arched. "So, you're telling me, with all these servants, you've never actually had breakfast in bed?"

He shrugged as if this wasn't one of the greatest things in life.

"Well, Mr. O'Shea, this is what we're doing. If you wish to be all formal stick-up-your-butt dude, then you can leave."

"It's my room."

"So." She shoved a forkful of pancake into her mouth. That's what it was called, she didn't care what the fae told her.

Griff only lasted a moment longer before a smile overcame the doubt on his face. He scooted closer to the tray and tentatively took a puff pastry. Biting into it, he watched in horror as a crumb landed on his shirt.

"Lean over the tray." Brea laughed.

Leaning over the tray had been a rule whenever Myles brought her breakfast in his bed. He made what he called the "Myles special." It was usually three different kinds of cereal mixed in a bowl with just the right amount of milk. Yeah, this breakfast was much different.

They ate in silence for a while, until Brea set her fork down, unable to eat another bite. "So, we have something to clear up, you and I."

He took a sip of tea and set it aside, dabbing a napkin across his lips. "Do we?"

"Last night, you told me there were ten things you loved about me. Do you know how horrible it is to do that to a girl? No one has ever loved anything about me, and you come along with ten, but then refuse to tell me nine of them."

Sadness swirled in his gaze. "Brea, I'm sure plenty of people have loved things about you."

"Don't try to ignore the important part of what I said." Getting up on her knees, she moved the tray from the bed to the small table before inching toward him. "You like that I blush."

"No, I love your blush."

"Okay, that's a super weird thing to love, but whatever floats your boat."

"I don't have a boat. As a kid, I never learned to navigate the waters because they're treacherous in Iskalt with the icebergs."

"That's interesting and all, but stop trying to change the subject. I didn't actually say you had a boat."

"Yes, you did."

"Just tell me." The words exploded out of her, and warmth flooded her cheeks. They stared at each other in tense silence before breaking out in laughter. "Please," she wheezed.

"I can't give away all my secrets."

Gripping his arm, she forced him to look her in the eye. "Just six."

"One."

"Five."

His eyes narrowed. "Four."

She nodded, sticking out her hand. "Deal."

He threaded his fingers through hers, and instead of shaking her hand, he pulled her into his lap. "You challenge me. I've never met anyone who constantly tested everything I thought I knew."

She buried her face in his chest, unable to look him in the eye as he spoke. She'd always had a shy streak that hadn't yet reared its head in the fae world.

"Keep pushing your buttons," she whispered. "Got it."

He shook his head like he'd started doing when he didn't understand her human phrases. "I love your laugh. It's like the sun breaking through in the middle of an Iskalt ice storm. The world is so cold until I hear that sound."

"That's three," she breathed, unable to form any other response as her heart stuttered in her chest.

He nuzzled his nose into her hair. "When I'm with you, I feel like I can be good too."

"You are good, Griff." She reached up and gripped his chin, tilting it down so he met her eyes. "All I see in you is good."

His eyes swirled with some unspoken emotion she couldn't decipher. Indecision, maybe? Confusion? Whatever it was lived at the core of who Griff was.

She almost forgot about the last thing he promised her until he spoke again. "And... you're fearless, Brea Robinson."

"No, I'm not."

He smiled down at her. "I took you from the human world, and now you're in the center of a fae court—and without your precious coffee. I keep waiting for everything to overwhelm you, but you sit here joking and laughing. If that's not fearlessness, I don't know what is."

"Griff, this girl you see... it's not me. I'm not all these things. One day, you're going to wake up and realize you only saw what you wanted to see."

"Impossible." He leaned her back on the bed, holding himself over her.

"If there's one thing falling into a world of fantasy and magic has taught me, it's that nothing is impossible."

The Brea Robinson in his mind didn't exist, yet when he kissed her, she let him. When he brought her closer, she held on tightly. He'd see through his own visions of her soon enough, and then all he'd find would be cracks in a ragged soul.

Griff O'Shea was too perfect, too good for the likes of her. That was how she knew the fantasy they lived in would end. She just had to make sure to get out of it intact.

Chapter 12

Brea managed to sneak back into her room without notice well before anyone else had arisen after such a late night of festivities.

"Good, you're up early." Neeve's shoulders relaxed when she stepped into the room.

"And that's a source of relief for you?" Brea liked to tease her maid. It loosened her up so she acted like a normal person.

"Normally, you're like trying to wake the dead, and then you're an ill-tempered child until I get some tea in you."

"If you could just send someone out for coffee, we wouldn't have this problem." Brea would give anything for a decent caffeine boost.

"If you could tell me what coffee looks like, it would be much easier to find it." Neeve bustled about the room readying Brea's clothes for the day.

"It's heaven in a cup." Brea threw her head back against her pillow and stretched.

"That still doesn't tell me what it looks or tastes like." Neeve set a stack of fabric at the foot of Brea's bed.

"It's dark like coffee, it tastes like coffee, and it smells like coffee."

Brea groaned as she moved to sit on the edge of the bed. "What's this?" She eyed the soft looking fabric Neeve brought with her.

"A few Beltaine gifts for you. I don't know what yoga pants and t-shirts are, but you seem to prefer men's clothing and soft things so I had these made for you."

Brea snatched the pile of fuzzy woolen clothes and squealed in delight. The pants were very yoga-like leggings, and the shirt was a long tunic in a dark blue fabric. A belt, a pair of sturdy trousers, and a jacket completed the ensemble. There was even a descent attempt at duplicating the sports bra she'd worn when she arrived at the cottage with Griff. "This is perfect, Neeve, thank you!" She gave the tiny woman a hug. "I'm sorry, I didn't get you anything."

"And you shouldn't." She gently shoved Brea back down on the bed. "It wouldn't be proper."

"Proper-schmoper."

"You say the silliest things." Neeve shook her head, a smile tugging at the corners of her mouth.

"At least I seem to be entertaining everyone. So what's on my agenda today?"

"Brunch with the queen."

"Is she mad?" Brea winced. She didn't mention she'd just eaten in Griff's room.

"Mad? Why on earth would she be upset with you?"

"For taking a dive with a delegate in the fountain?"

Neeve stood with her back turned, brushing imaginary wrinkles from Brea's dress for the day. Her shoulders shook with silent laughter.

"It's okay, you can laugh it up." Brea rolled her eyes. "It was pretty epic."

"Only you could manage to fall into a fountain at the queen's Beltaine festival." Neeve's laughter was infectious.

Brea shrugged. "Like I said, at least I'm entertaining."

"Better get ready, Brea. The queen will expect you soon." Neeve offered her a stack of fresh undergarments and shooed her behind the screen in the corner of the room. Brea had insisted she could at least put her own undergarments on without assistance. It was a compromise Neeve finally agreed with.

"Is this a fancy brunch with all the delegates?"

"Just you and the queen."

Brea breathed a sigh of relief. She loved her aunt and looked forward to the times they spent together. It was when other people were involved that she tended to stress out.

"Good morning, dear." The queen was all smiles today. Not a hint of a hangover or lack of sleep marred her beautiful face. She'd never seen her aunt *not* dressed like the fae Marie Antionette. Regan really liked to wear pink.

"Good morning, Aunt Regan." Brea bobbed a quick curtsy before she took her seat opposite the queen. "You're looking lovely this morning."

"Too much wine last night, darling. Far too much wine." Her laughter echoed across the terrace where they normally had their afternoon tea.

"Tell me about it." Brea winced.

"I just did." The queen blinked in confusion.

"Oh, that just means I'm commiserating with you." Brea laughed. "Way too much wine. But last night was wonderful."

"Was it amazeballs?" Regan leaned forward in earnest.

Brea thought about the late night spent with Griff in his rooms. "It was definitely amazeballs. But I'm so sorry about the incident with the fountain." Her face flushed with fresh humiliation.

Regan's laughter sounded like bells. "I'm just glad you're okay, dear. Don't ever apologize for your clumsy behavior. It's endearing. Don't change on my account."

"Thank you, Aunt Regan." That might have been the first time a family member ever told her to just be herself. Without thinking, Brea stood and approached the queen.

"What's this, my darling?" The queen's sweet face stared up at Brea just before she wrapped her arms around her aunt.

"Thank you, auntie."

"For what, sweet girl?" Regan awkwardly patted Brea on the back.

Brea wondered how long it had been since anyone hugged Regan. "For loving me just as I am."

"What's not to love?" Regan took Brea's hands in hers. "We have much to discuss this morning."

"Shoot." Brea returned to her seat only to realize she'd said something confusing again. "Sorry, it seems we need a translator." Brea laughed. "That just means, go on, I'm listening."

"All right then, I'll shoot."

Brea stifled a giggle behind her hand.

"I said it wrong, didn't I? Oh well, we have plenty of time for human silliness later. Did you ever wonder why I brought you here, Brea? I mean besides the obvious that I wanted to meet my only niece."

"Of course, I wondered." Brea nodded for Neeve to stop hovering and pour her tea.

"Some of my nobles thought I intended to make you my heir so they feared your arrival. I would claim you as my own if not for your human side. I love you dearly, child, but Fargelsi needs a strong fae ruler when I am gone."

"I understand," Brea rushed to say. There was nothing she wanted less than to be Regan's heir to the throne. "It wouldn't do for a half-human-half-fae klutz to take your place."

"I'm so glad you see it that way too." Regan gave a curt nod to Neeve to finish serving their brunch. "Before all of this uncertainty about what your arrival might mean, the Fargelsi court feared I would make Griffin my heir, which has always been my greatest desire. I've raised him as my own, and a more loyal son couldn't possibly exist.

But he is an Iskalt prince, and many would like to see him return to his uncle, the king."

"So, it would be dangerous for him if you publicly named him your heir?"

"It would. Unless..." Regan paused to sip her tea. "Unless he was betrothed to a Gelsian royal."

Brea's mouth went dry. Her aunt couldn't possibly be thinking about marrying her off like some kind of pawn on a chessboard? "What now?" Brea squeaked.

"You and Griff fancy each other, do you not?" Regan asked bluntly. "I saw your flirtations last night. You suit each other quite well."

"Um, well. I... um..."

Neeve saved her by sliding a plate with a slice of quiche and a side of fruit drizzled in caramel sauce in front of her. The caramel sauce danced on her plate like magic until it formed the words '*everything she says is a lie.*' Brea choked on her tea as the caramel sauce blurred and the words disappeared. She glanced at Neeve, taking a moment to breathe.

Neeve's grave look was warning enough. Brea needed to tread carefully here. But could her aunt really be lying to her? She'd gone to great lengths to make Brea feel welcomed and loved. She couldn't imagine any of that was fake.

"I do. Um. Like him, that is. Griff is a charming young man. Whom I just met and we're, ah... still getting to know each other."

"Strong marriages have been built on far less." Aunt Regan nibbled on her quiche like she hadn't just scared the pants off her niece. "We will announce your betrothal to Griffin in a fortnight. After your marriage the following month, I will name Griffin heir in the event of my death. Any children of yours shall become my blood heirs. They will continue my line. This way you will be a queen of Fargelsi one day. That would make me very proud."

"Children? Queen? A month?" Brea sputtered. She was about to tell the queen she was a lunatic when Neeve interjected.

"Perhaps Lady Brea needs some time to think, your Majesty?"

"She has time."

"May I remind your Majesty, she has also grown up in the human world where these things are quite different. By their standards Lady Brea is still a child who wouldn't be ready for marriage for several more years."

"Is that so?" The queen frowned. "This proposal seems strange to you, dear?"

Brea only nodded. She couldn't get the words out that the queen was off her rocker if she thought she was going to marry a cute boy she just met.

"Too fast." Brea finally managed to string two words together.

"Yes, that's right," Neeve continued. "Even adult humans much older than Lady Brea will court a young woman for a year or more before proposing marriage."

"I see. I suppose we could announce the betrothal in a month, and then give her a few more months to prepare for the big day. How does that sound, my darling girl?"

It sounded like it was time for Brea to get the hell out of Fargelsi.

Back in her room, Brea clawed at her clothes. She couldn't breathe under so many layers. "Get this thing off of me."

Neeve worked quickly to remove her dress and unlaced her corset with nimble fingers. "Just breathe, Brea. It will be okay. Lord Griffin is a good man."

"Yep, yeah, he's a great guy." Brea gulped air into her lungs, kicking the dress across the room. "I just don't want to marry him when I'm not even old enough to buy beer without a fake ID."

The other shoe had just dropped, and it crushed Brea.

"Was any of it real?" she asked, fanning herself. "I need air." She stumbled for the balcony.

"Brea, you can't go out there in your under clothes." Neeve

rushed to wrap a silk robe around her. Brea let Neeve fuss about her clothes as she breathed in the lavender-scented air.

"I knew it was all too good to be true." They just wanted her for her bloodline so they could make Griff a king. Did he even care for her at all? Was his *top ten things I love about Brea Robinson* just a line she'd fallen for like the stupid girl she was?

For that matter, did she mean anything to Regan but a means to an end? Tears burned her eyes. She'd cried more tears in her lifetime than was remotely fair. After years of believing she was insane, she finally found where she belonged, and that was a lie too.

"It's all a lie. Just like you said."

"What, my Lady?" Neeve patted her back.

"In the caramel sauce. You said it was all a lie."

"I don't know what you're talking about." Neeve's hesitant smile stopped her tears. "It's treason to spell out dire warnings in caramel sauce."

"He said I could trust you."

"You can, Brea. Of that, you should never doubt."

"I have to talk to Griff before I do anything stupid." Like trust something Lochlan O'Shea said. "I have to know if Griff had any part in this."

Chapter 13

Brea stumbled through the palace, forcing her way past guards wearing her aunt's colors. She sprinted down a spiral stone staircase, thankful not to have a dress tripping her up. The clothes Neeve procured for her gave her some sense of normalcy. Sure, they weren't exactly the styles she'd have worn on the farm, but close enough.

Her breath rattled in her lungs as she kept running down the long hallway. Servants scurried out of her way as she rushed out the double doors that stood open to the long bridge crossing the river to the rest of the palace grounds. The waterfall crashed to her right, sending a spray of water into the air.

The forest closed in on her as she crossed the bridge, careful not to look over the sides into the depths below. The horse stables stood shrouded in vines at the far edge of the property with a paddock out front. Riders came and went while stable boys led horses from their stalls.

It looked nothing like Myles' farm, but the smell—of horses and hay—allowed her to imagine she was back there where she'd felt safe. Any moment Captain America would walk into the paddock with her new colt by her side. She'd give Brea a look in that understanding way of hers that made her want to spill all her secrets.

Entering the bustle of the long stables, Brea inhaled deeply, her fingers twitching as if she could feel Myles' hand in hers. A familiar head appeared, snorting when it saw her.

Maisie, the sweet horse she'd ridden from Griff's house. The house she never should have left.

Everything she says is a lie.

That had to have been a message from Neeve, but then why would she deny it? And what did it mean? The kind and welcoming aunt she'd come to love was lying to her? About what?

That same aunt wanted to marry her to Griff to make him king. It was the reason she'd been brought from the human realm. Could she trust nothing that had happened since her arrival?

"Hey Maisie." She reached the stall and unlatched it before slipping inside and shutting the door.

Fresh hay was spread over the ground. "Nice digs, Mais." She approached the horse, running her hand along her smooth neck. "Looks like they're taking good care of you."

Just like her. That was the problem. She'd been well taken care of, having everything given to her on a silver platter—literally. But now she wondered if she was in a cage just like Maisie with no say in her future.

"What would Myles say about all of this?" she whispered, not sure if she was talking to the horse or herself. He'd probably tell her to do whatever it took to be free. That she didn't owe these people anything just because they took her away from a bad situation in the human realm.

But still, she felt she owed them everything. Her love. Her loyalty. Her life?

Sliding down the wall, she sat in the hay and looked up at the beautiful beast, the only thing here that could possibly remind her of home. Tears built in her eyes and a wind whipped through the stall, pulled by the magic she now knew was tied to her emotions. Would it ever go away?

She didn't want power.

The wind intensified.

She just wanted control of her own body again. Was that so much to ask?

Sniffling, she held in the tears.

"Brea?" Griff's voice sounded far off as the magic buzzed in her ears. "Brea!"

Strong hands shook her, and she looked up into Griff's worried face, a face she'd kissed only hours before. Now, she wanted him to leave her alone.

"Pull the magic back in!" he shouted.

It was only then she realized Maisie was cowered in the corner of the stall. Seeing fear in the horse, the string pulling her magic snapped and the wind died.

Brea slumped back against the wall.

Griff crouched in front of her, his arms resting on his knees. "I've been looking everywhere for you."

"Why?"

"What?"

"What do you want from me, Griff?" There was no strength to her voice, only resignation.

"Brea." He scratched the back of his head. "I—"

"Need me? Yeah, I've been told." She pushed away from the wall and got to her feet.

"Where are you going?"

"Away." She shoved open the stall door and stomped from the barn, anger burning along her skin. But if she let this magic out, she feared she wouldn't be able to pull it back in.

Griff ran after her. "Talk to me."

She reached the bridge and turned on her heel to face him. "I don't think you want to hear what I have to say!" She had to shout to be heard over the waterfall.

"What's going on? This morning, we—"

"This morning was a lie. Everything is a lie. Me. You. My aunt."

"Okay, slow down. What happened between when you left me this morning and now?"

So, he hadn't spoken to her aunt. With a grunt, she turned and stomped across the bridge. She entered the palace, the noise from the falls dying down as she walked deeper inside. This wasn't a conversation she wanted to have where they could be overheard.

By the time they reached her rooms, her anger had lessened, leaving her with the sinking feeling of being alone in a world that was not her own. She'd have given anything to have Myles with her.

Griff shut the door and approached her, his arms crossed over his chest. "Number six. When you get angry, your lip juts out stubbornly, and all I want to do is kiss the frown away." He leaned in, but Brea sidestepped him.

"Do you really want to kiss me, Griff, or is that what you're supposed to make me believe?"

"Why would you say something like that?"

She turned to the window, looking out on the realm she'd marveled at only a day before. Now, Fargelsi had lost its shine for her. She'd longed to belong here, but she wondered if she ever truly would.

Griff put a hand on her shoulder and she let him, having no more energy to push him away. She turned into his embrace, burying her face in his shirt. "Tell me the truth," she whispered. "There's no prophecy about me."

"Brea—"

"Why did you really come to the human realm for me?"

When he didn't respond, she lifted her eyes to his. "It was so you could become king, right? You needed someone with my aunt's bloodline to make you a legitimate contender."

He released her and stepped away. "You don't understand."

"I think I do."

"Regan is my queen. She has been a mother to me. That throne is rightfully mine."

"And what of me, Griff?"

"I lo—"

"Don't say it!" Her hands vibrated in anger. "I swear to God, Griffin O'Shea. If you tell me you love me right now, I'm going to punch that pretty face of yours."

"I never expected to feel this way about you."

A harsh laugh pushed past her lips. "Oh, that's rich. You don't get to be this guy. The one who says everything he did was for my own good."

"You were being arrested when I found you." He scrubbed a hand across his face.

"No." She shook her head. "I was in jail when your brother found me, not you. Was I just a game to the two of you? Some competition?" She calmed her breathing and jolts of magic leaked from her fingertips, sending sparks across the floor. "I know why you came for me, but Loch? How does he play into all of this?"

"I don't know."

Her eyes narrowed. "And I don't believe you."

"It's the truth."

"Do you even know what that is?"

A knock sounded on the door and a gruff voice filtered through. "Lord Griffin, are you okay in there?"

"Yes," Griff called back.

Brea pressed herself back against the cool window. "How did they know you were in here?"

Or that they were arguing? She thought of Neeve's odd behavior when she brought up the message or the fact that she'd resorted to covert methods instead of speaking to Brea in the ample private time they had. Lifting her eyes to the vines creeping along the ceiling, she looked for any kind of listening devices. But this wasn't like back home where they'd use cameras and recording devices.

No, here, magic could be anywhere.

She stepped toward Griff, forcing him back.

"My aunt is listening to me." Her jaw clenched.

"That's not possible."

"Yes, it is. Anything is possible here." She could see it in his expression, in the tightening of his eyes, the flattening of his lips. The truth. He'd known. "I need to be alone." If she didn't step away from him, she'd lose her minimal control over the power inside her.

"Brea—"

"Go!" The word roared out of her, a command more than a request.

Griff's shoulders dropped, and he stared at her for a moment longer. "Not everything was a lie." The words were so quiet she almost missed them.

When he was gone, she slumped onto her bed, the tension leaving her body as she sucked in a few deep breaths.

Nothing could be as perfect as this new life seemed. She should have known they didn't want her around for her. It was all a scheme.

As a little girl, she'd never dreamed of being a princess or living in a palace. She'd only wanted to be as normal as everyone else, to have a family who loved her.

But that had been too good to be true.

How much of what Griff told her was a lie? She sat up, an impossible thought coming to her. Would he really lie to her about that? Loch's words came back to her, and she had to know.

Wiping tears from her face, she left her room, holding her head high as she made her way down the now familiar hall. Only this morning she'd been so happy making her way back from Griff's rooms.

It took no time at all for that bubble to shatter.

She rapped her knuckles against his door and leaned back on her heels.

He took his time opening the door. His eyes widened in surprise when he saw her. "I thought you didn't want to see me." Hope tinged his voice.

She pushed past him into his room. "Is my aunt listening to what happens in this room too?"

Griff shut the door. "No. We can talk freely here."

Relief washed over her. It creeped her out to think of her aunt listening to everything that had gone on in this room. She hugged her arms across her chest, afraid of the question she'd come to ask.

Griff clasped his hands behind his back, nerves flitting across his face.

"I will marry you," Brea said.

A smile spread across his lips. "You will? Truly?"

"Yes, but I have one condition. There is a question I need you to answer honestly. You owe me this after all the lies. That is my bargain. A marriage for an answer. Do you agree?"

"Of course. I don't want to lie to you anymore. I want you by my side as we rule this kingdom."

"I never wanted to rule a kingdom—or get married at seventeen for that matter. You'd have known that if you bothered to ask. Instead, you plotted with my aunt to get what you want. But I'm starting to see that's how this world works. You fae are worse than humans, and I never thought that was possible."

His smile fell, replaced by a look of sorrow. Some part of her wanted to comfort him, but the fondness she'd felt only hours ago was gone, replaced with wariness.

"Ask me your question, and I will answer honestly." He reached for her, but she stepped away to gather herself.

"Is..." She closed her eyes. "Is Myles alive?"

She opened her eyes when he didn't answer right away. His jaw tensed and he took a step back, widening the space between them. "Lochlan put this notion into your head."

"Yes." She wouldn't sugar coat it for him. "But he was right, wasn't he?"

Griff sighed, his shoulders tense. "I don't know."

"What do you mean you don't know?"

He ran a hand through his auburn hair. "When we left the

human world, he'd been taken to the hospital. I do not know what happened to him after that."

She couldn't breathe. Her lungs cried out for air, and she bent over clutching her chest. Angry tears washed down her face. "You... you told me he died, and you didn't even check?"

But Lochlan had. The grumpy Eldur delegate must have gone back to the human realm to find out what happened to her best friend, the only person who'd ever truly loved her.

"Myles is alive." But could she trust Lochlan's words?

She wiped a hand across her damp cheek. Griff didn't deserve her tears, but they weren't for him anyway. Myles' smile flashed through her mind. What if she hadn't killed him?

He had to still be alive.

Straightening, she hardened her expression. "You and I are not friends, Griffin O'Shea. I will marry you and give you legitimacy, but that is all. I could have forgiven the lies about your motive in bringing me here or even the eavesdropping in my rooms. But Myles... that lie is not one I will ever move past." She walked to the door.

"Brea," Griff called, his voice thick. "Please."

She paused before opening the door. "I am not some fae girl who will fall at your feet and beg to be queen. I don't care if half my blood is of this world. I am human, and we make decisions for ourselves."

Calling on the magic she still didn't understand and still couldn't control, she blasted through the door, sending wood splintering against the wall in the hallway.

As she stepped across the broken frame, she looked back over her shoulder. "You will never control me."

The day after her fight with Griff, Brea woke with little energy. The triplets brought in her breakfast, setting it on her bed as they'd learned she liked. Their shared looks told her they must have heard what happened the day before.

They didn't dare bring it up in a room where privacy was only an illusion.

"Where is Neeve?" She pushed the food around on her plate, having no real appetite.

"The queen wanted her to help down in the kitchens," Triplet One said, her voice way too high this early in the morning. She leaned in. "She's the only servant Queen Regan really trusts, and with the farewell dinner for the Iskalt delegation tonight, she wanted Neeve overseeing preparations."

It surprised Brea that the delegation from Iskalt was still there when the Eldur people left right after the festival. They'd been meeting behind closed doors with her aunt, but Brea knew so little about the fae world relations she couldn't begin to guess why.

Triplet Two bounced on her toes as she twisted a long lock of blond hair around her finger. "There's a rumor around the palace that you're to marry Lord Griffin."

"He's perfect," the third girl sighed.

Sure, perfect if one wanted a lying, manipulative, power seeker. But she couldn't tell them he only wanted her as a means to get the crown. "We haven't announced the engagement yet."

"Don't wait too long." Brea lost track of which triplet said what. "There are plenty of noblewomen who'd gladly take your place."

Brea would happily let them. If she had her way, she'd never have to see Griff again.

Unable to take more of this inane chatter, Brea got out of bed and rummaged through her armoire. "I must go see my fiancé."

"Fiancé," one of the girls giggled. "That's a funny word."

"Oh, um, I mean betrothed."

"You won't find him at the palace." One of the girls pursed her lips. "I heard from one of the guards who heard from a servant of Lord Griffin's that he left early this morning on a mission for the crown. He won't be back for a week at least."

"He... left?" She agreed to be his wife, and he left without a word the next morning?

"Yes, the guard said it was a matter of utmost importance, but a secret mission nonetheless."

She couldn't imagine what would take Griff away from the palace. He'd told her since they arrived that one day he'd have to return to his cottage because palace life wasn't for him. But that had only been another lie.

"No matter." She abandoned the dress she'd planned to wear to speak with Griff in favor of the outfit Neeve brought for her the day before. Turning back to the triplets, she raised a brow. "I'm going to change."

They didn't budge.

"Erm... please go. If I need you later on, I'll call. I mean, I'll send someone to fetch you."

"Yes, your Highness." They each curtsied before skittering from the room.

Brea stared after them, their "your Highnesses" ringing in her ears. She wasn't meant for such a title, and if she had a say, she would never hear them utter it again.

It was time to stop lamenting her situation and act on it.

Changing into the comfortable clothes quickly, she hurried from the room and took the winding path through the palace, across an open-air bridge, and down a spiral staircase into the palace kitchens.

A cook looked up when she entered, a scowl on her plump face. "This isn't the place for you, my Lady."

"I'm sorry. I'm just looking for someone."

"Well, look elsewhere. We're quite busy this morning." She went back to her task.

Others paid her no mind as she skirted the outer edge of the grand network of rooms where cooks and bakers plied their trade. Servants rushed through with trays laden with fruits, pastries, and pots of tea, no doubt attending to the many nobles currently residing at the palace.

"The queen isn't going to like that." Neeve's strong voice cut through the bustle as she chastised one of the cooks in front of a boiling pot of sauce. "She'll want more Gelsi berries in the sauce."

Gelsi berries? The same fruit that dampens magic?

Neeve's gaze found Brea and her eyes widened. She wiped her hands on the white apron tied to her waist and rushed toward Brea. "My Lady, you should not be down here."

"I needed to talk to you, and it couldn't wait."

Neeve looked back over her shoulder at the cooks before gesturing for Brea to follow her around the corner into a storage room. She shut the door, sending them into semi-darkness.

"Are they putting Gelsi berries in the food?" It was the first question to escape her lips.

Neeve nodded, glancing at the door. "Queen Regan dampens the powers of all those staying within her walls. It is how she keeps such tight control—especially when foreign delegations are present."

Was that why Brea had only had a few outbursts here in the palace? Back in the human realm, she'd constantly felt on the brink of losing control.

"But then..."

Neeve must have sensed what she meant to ask, because she answered. "Your magic must be quite powerful with the few times you've been able to use it."

Brea shook her head to clear it. This wasn't why she'd come. "Tell me the truth. The warning in the caramel sauce was you."

Neeve nodded.

"Lochlan said I could trust you, but I don't know if I can believe what he says. Everyone is lying to me."

Neeve met her gaze. "Lochlan O'Shea does not lie. He's a lot of things, but when he speaks, you can believe him."

"And his brother?"

"That's more complicated."

"I'm supposed to marry him."

"You can't," Neeve whispered before collecting herself. "There's so much you don't know, but I can't be the one to tell you when I only know bits."

"I can't stay here, can I?" Not when they'd lied to her and tried to trap her. Her aunt seemed kind and caring, but now Brea realized she didn't know her at all.

Neeve shook her head. "It's not safe for you."

"I have nowhere else to go." She wanted to go back to Myles, but a jail cell waited for her in the human world.

"You do." Neeve gripped her arms. "There is one place in this world you'll be safe." She implored Brea to believe her with her eyes. "You need to get to Eldur."

Brea backed away from her. Eldur. The fire kingdom with an evil queen and most-probably dragons. "I can't go to Eldur."

"You must. Do not believe what you have been told. The beauty of Fargelsi is a trick meant to make the beholder trust in their safety. There is no safety to be had here for anyone. We are all trapped, but you have a chance to be free. You must take it. For all of us."

"What do you mean you're trapped? Can't you come with me?"

She shook her head, her eyes shining. "We don't have time to explain. There is a pathway through the marshes of the Southern Vatlands. I can take you only part of the way before I must return to the palace. The marshes lead across the border into Eldur where a contingent of the Fire Queen's soldiers stand guard."

"Why are they in the Vatlands? I thought those were neutral zones."

"They're there for the rare occasion I can get people out of Gelsi. Only those without full Fargelsi blood can cross the borders and the Eldurians protect them. You must navigate the marshes until you reach their camp. With them, you will be safe."

"When do we leave?"

Neeve offered her a sad smile. "Tonight. You will leave the farewell dinner for Iskalt early, claiming you are ill. I'll attend to you. Lord Griffin is away from the palace at present, so this gives us an opportunity. I'll put together some food for you and procure a horse to get you to the Vatlands. You cannot pack anything else."

Brea breathed heavily as she tried to calm her racing heart. "I'm scared, Neeve."

Neeve's expression softened, and she put a hand on each of Brea's shoulders. "You are a human girl traversing these strange fae times. If you were not scared, I would think Fargelsi is where you truly belonged."

"What does that mean?"

"That being scared will keep you safe. Here in this court of never-ending spring and beauty, we live in a perpetually emotionless state. Everything is for show. You aren't one of them, Brea. I knew that the moment I first met you."

"That doesn't make me feel any better, you know." Not on the eve of fleeing from the place she'd wanted to call home.

Neeve smiled. "Just remember—at dinner, don't eat any of the sauces. No matter how untaught your power is, you will need the full strength of it in the marshes." She opened the door, gave Brea one final encouraging look, and slipped out.

Brea leaned her head back against the wall. How had everything gotten so messed up in such a short period of time?

Oh right... the man she'd thought she was falling in love with lied to her about the death of the only true friend she'd ever had.

She glanced at the door Neeve disappeared through.

Until now.

The maid would probably deny it, but no one risked themselves for someone else unless they cared.

Lifting her eyes to the dark stone ceiling of the cool storage room, she sighed. "I will find out what happened to you, Myles," she whispered. "If it's the last thing I do."

Chapter 14

"You look lovely, darling. If a bit morose." Queen Regan looped her arm through Brea's as they made their way down to the banquet hall for the big Iskalt send off.

"Griff left without saying goodbye." Brea had decided to play the part of a lovesick teen. She'd seen enough of the girls' theatrics back home to pull it off here.

"Don't worry yourself, dear. I sent him on an important errand that just couldn't wait. He had little time to prepare, much less make time for a romantic farewell. He'll be back soon, and we can talk about wedding plans. I'm so pleased you've agreed to his proposal."

She made it all sound so normal and romantic, like he'd actually gotten down on one knee and popped the question. In the back of Brea's mind all she heard was *what would Myles say about all of this?* First, he would be stoked to find the fae realm exists, and he'd want to explore it with her. Second, he would do that side-splitting laugh thing he did at the news of her impending *betrothal*. Just the thought of his laughter brought a smile to her face.

"That's better." Regan smiled as they approached the banquet hall. "Smile for the delegates, dear. They'll be on their way back to their frozen tundra by morning, and we'll have the place to ourselves for a while."

By then, Brea would be neck deep in the marshes, if she even made it that far. She wasn't looking forward to the next few hours.

"Do you entertain often, Aunt Regan?" Brea needed to play the part of the dutiful niece.

"One of the many perks of being queen. You get to throw parties as often as you like. Don't worry, we have your betrothal and wedding celebrations to look forward to. There will be plenty more parties where you'll be the guest of honor. We'll have to start planning your wardrobe right away."

This woman didn't know Brea at all if she thought more parties and uncomfortable dresses was the way to cheer her up.

Brea followed her aunt into the banquet hall after the herald announced her and a footman guided her to the high table where she sat beside the queen. She smiled and nodded and engaged in the conversation as best she could, but her mind was elsewhere.

"None for me, thank you," Brea murmured, covering her goblet with her hand. The servers had been plying her and the queen with wine all night.

"Are you feeling well, dear?" The queen asked, eyeing her plate.

Brea had done a good job making it look like she'd eaten, but she didn't want to accidentally eat one of her aunt's magic-stifling sauces by accident.

"Actually, I am feeling a little under the weather," Brea admitted with feigned reluctance. "Just tired and a bit off from too much wine lately. I'm not used to it."

"And missing a certain handsome young man?" her aunt teased.

Anger caused her face to flush, and Brea hoped the queen would take it for a lover's blush.

"Very much," she murmured.

"Very well, dear, you may retire. Come to my rooms for a late brunch tomorrow morning and we'll get started on wedding plans."

"Thank you, Aunt Regan." Brea rose from her chair, intending to rush from the room, but every delegate at the table rose with her.

"Er, um. Excuse me, ladies and gentlemen." She bobbed her head.

"My niece is a bit tired this evening," the queen explained. "And missing a certain gentleman," she whisper-shouted behind her enormous peacock-feathered fan. Her laughter sent the Iskalt delegates into a tittering fit.

Stumbling over her train, Brea made for the door as quickly as she could and still look like the refined lady she was supposed to be. Once she hit the empty grand hallway, Brea hiked up her skirts and ran up the stairs to the queen's quarters.

"Psst, my Lady," Neeve's voice drifted down the hallway leading to Brea's rooms. "In here."

Brea turned toward the sound of her voice and found her waiting in a small servant's room. "Is this yours?" Brea looked around at the tidy room. It was nice. Nothing like her luxurious suite, but it was homey and comfortable in a way Brea's wasn't.

"The queen likes to keep me close, so I don't sleep in the servants' quarters like most palace maids. It will be safer for you to change in here. No one bothers to spy on me."

"You thought of everything." Brea kicked off her heels and turned her back so Neeve could help her out of the fancy dress. Neeve was already dressed for their trip to the Vatlands. Brea just hoped her friend wouldn't get caught helping her escape the palace.

"Relax, I've done this before. We won't get caught."

"You a mind reader?" Brea wiggled out of her bodice and tossed it on the floor with a none too gentle kick. She hoped she never had to wear such stifling clothes again.

"You're a kind young woman, Brea. In another time and place we might have been the best of friends. You care about the people around you. It doesn't take a mind reader to see that." She glanced at Brea's reflection in the mirror above her dresser. "In this world, that's a rare commodity. It would be a shame to see you lose it."

Brea dressed quickly in the sturdy travel clothes Neeve had acquired for her. Dark leather leggings, a linen tunic layered under a leather vest and jacket and a belt with a knife she didn't know how to use. Tying her long ebony hair back into a messy bun, Brea retrieved her pack.

"There's a change of clothes, food, and water in there for you. In a moment, we'll take the servants' stairs down to the kitchens. If anyone stops us, you're a new house maid. I'm giving you a tour of the palace before I take you to your new quarters."

"Got it." Brea hefted the pack up on her shoulder. "So, we'll just slip across the bridge to the stables then?"

Neeve shook her head. "The queen has eyes everywhere, Brea. We have to be smart about this. I need you to stay close and keep moving no matter what happens to me. Trust no one."

"Okay, serious faces on." Neeve's grave look shook Brea. "This is a big deal, escaping."

"A very big deal." Neeve hefted a pack onto her shoulder. "I don't know if the queen simply wants you to give Lord Griffin legitimacy through his marriage to you, or if she has something far worse up her sleeve. I only know it's important to get you out of here as soon as possible. Once we get to the kitchens, there's another stairway we'll take down to the dungeon."

"Dungeon? This place has a dungeon?"

"It will lead us out to the riverbed behind the falls where we'll make our way into the forest. A friend will meet us there with horses. From there we'll head south toward the Vatlands marshes. If we get separated, you're to head southeast and keep going until you find the Eldur camp just over the border. There's a map in your pack in case you need it."

"Thank you, Neeve. I'll never be able to repay your kindness."

Neeve peeked into the hallway, waving for Brea to follow.

Sneaking down the stairwell, they arrived in the kitchens unhindered.

"What are you doing, Neeve?" The head cook bellowed. "Shouldn't you be prepping the nobles' rooms for the evening?"

"Mistress O'Sullivan." Neeve rounded on the woman. "Just showing the new maid around. She starts in the queen's quarters tomorrow."

"What's your name, girl?"

"Ygritte," Brea blurted. "Of the Free Folk. North of the wall."

"Well, Ygritte, we don't know nothing about no free folk here. Best you finish your tour and get to bed early with you. Big day tomorrow cleaning up this mess of a palace."

"Yes ma'am." Brea and Neeve bobbed their heads and turned for the dreary halls leading to the servants' quarters.

"North of the wall?" Neeve rolled her eyes. "What human nonsense was that?"

"It just came out. I don't actually think about these things before I say them."

"If you want to survive in this world, you'd better start thinking ten steps ahead of everyone else, Brea."

"You're right." Brea followed her down the long hall but was unprepared when Neeve took a sharp left behind a bookcase in the wall. "Secret passages?" Brea stepped through the opening. Darkness engulfed them as the bookshelf slid back into place.

"This palace is a labyrinth of secrets and lies."

Neeve whispered a few unintelligible words before a fire blazed, lighting a torch she'd procured from her pack.

"Was that magic? Like a spell? Griff said our magic didn't work like that."

"Lord Griffin has been liberal with his lies, I'm afraid. He is a good man... deep down. But the queen has had him in her clutches far too long. This way."

Brea followed silently, taking the slimy stone steps carefully. They seemed to wind down into the depths of the earth with no end in sight.

"Those born of Fargelsi draw our power from nature," Neeve

explained. "But we do rely on spoken spells and words of power for much of what we do. It is different in the other realms."

"So, Griff lied about that too?" Brea frowned. *Was there no end to the lies?* The musty smells and constant dripping grated on her nerves.

"I do not know his motives."

Brea followed in silence, her thoughts a tumble of chaos. It didn't matter if Griff cared for her. He'd told her Myles was dead when that might not be true. That was unforgivable.

White noise rushed to fill Brea's ears.

"The waterfalls," Neeve called over the roaring din. "We're nearly to the river." Neeve's skirts dragged across the damp stones and muck as they began to climb.

Finally, moonlight illuminated their path as they crossed under the falls. Brea carefully followed Neeve's footsteps to avoid the deluge. Hopping from stone to boulder, they made their way past the waterfall to the river's edge just below the great palace. Sounds of the party—in full swing now—floated down to them.

"They won't notice you're gone until late morning." Neeve spoke a few odd words, and the flame of her torch died.

"You have to teach me that trick someday." Brea rushed to keep up with her friend's pace. "But something tells me it's a little more complicated than *Lumos* and *Nox*."

"There you go with your silly words." Neeve chuckled. "I will miss that."

"Then come with me," Brea begged. Truth be told she was terrified of traveling a strange land alone—through miles of swamp no less.

"I can do more good here than I can out there, Brea. I'm nobody here. The small things I do to fight the injustices in Gelsi matter to my people. In some ways, I'm all they have."

"I want to be you when I grow up." Brea huffed and puffed behind the small woman. Weeks of rich foods, wine, and too little exercise had sapped Brea's stamina.

"Hurry, we're nearly to the meeting place."

"This friend of yours is trustworthy?" Brea jogged along the rocky riverbank to catch up."

"Moira? I trust her with my life."

"Is she your girlfriend?"

"My intended you mean?"

"Why can't a woman just have a passing flirtation with a pretty girl or a cute guy and it *not* end in a walk down the aisle?" Brea muttered under her breath.

"Moira might be my wife someday. When we are free."

"Neeve?" a feminine voice called from the darkness.

"Here, Moira." She picked up her skirts and ran to the woman who'd risked a great deal to meet them in the dead of night.

Brea held back to give the two lovers a moment of reunion. She imagined they didn't get to see each other often.

"Come, Brea. We must hurry," Neeve called a moment later.

"My Lady." Moira gave a curt bow and offered her a dark cloak. "This will help shield your face and keep you warm. It can get cold in the swamps."

"Thank you, and please call me Brea." She slipped the cloak over her shoulders and lifted the hood over her head. "Thank you for the horses. I know you took a great risk in coming here."

"Anything for Neeve." Moira gave her intended a devilish wink. "She's a tough one, my girl. You're safe with her, and you'd do well to follow her instructions to the letter. She's always right. It's frustrating." She grinned, dipping into an awkward curtsy for Brea.

Brea watched them. The way they respected each other it was clear this couple was on an even footing in their relationship. Moira didn't coddle Neeve or insist she needed protecting. She was confident in her ability to help Brea flee Fargelsi.

I want that kind of relationship someday. She lifted herself into the saddle, grateful for the cloak.

"Keep to the back southern roads. Travel well, and may you

return to me quickly, my love." Moira waved as Neeve and Brea charged into the night.

They rode hard for several silent hours before Neeve took the east road toward the marshes. Brea could smell a hint of brine in the air. It reminded her of the ocean she'd once visited with her family. In the years before her *sanity* issues became a big problem, her family used to take a rare vacation every few years. Some of her fondest memories with her family were from that vacation to the beach.

Neeve slowed to a stop when the road ran out. "This is where I leave you." She slipped down from her horse. "I have to get back to the palace before sunrise, so I must hurry."

Brea stared into the darkness ahead. Fear gripped her as she dismounted her horse. She would have to travel the rest of the way on foot. The marsh was too dangerous for a horse.

"I'm afraid, Neeve," Brea whispered.

Neeve took both of her hands in hers. "Look at me."

Brea lifted her chin, meeting Neeve's cool gaze.

"You are strong, Brea Robinson. You haven't come of age yet, so I don't think you realize how strong you really are. Regan fears that kind of inner strength. She wanted to stifle it. To put you in a position with no power. As her heir's wife, you would be nothing more than a pretty face. Just another prisoner. You can do this, Brea. You have to."

"What if I get lost?"

"You won't." Neeve searched through her pack, coming up with a bottle of oil. "Keep heading east, and if you should lose your compass, look for the brightest star in the sky and keep it directly overhead." Neeve flicked the contents of the bottle, spritzing Brea from head to toe in the foul-smelling stuff.

"Ugh, what is that awful smell?"

"It will keep the creatures at bay."

"Creatures?"

"Go, Brea." She pressed a lantern into her hands, speaking the words of power to light it and gave her a gentle shove. "Head east until you reach the Eldur camps. Don't stop. Don't sleep. Keep going. You should make it there by morning."

Brea nodded, taking a deep breath before she flung herself into Neeve's arms. "Thank you. I've never had many friends, but you are one of them. I hope to see you again someday."

With that, Brea lifted her lantern and headed into the grim forest of creepy cypress trees, hanging moss, and lots of mud. It squelched under her feet as she walked. Glancing back over her shoulder, Neeve had already gone.

"It's just me and the marsh." Brea checked her compass and set her path for east.

The first mile was easy. The second mile was pretty bad, but the third mile was the stuff of nightmares. Brea stood in mud up to her knees, searching for semi-solid ground in the dim glow of the lantern. Her arm ached from holding it in front of her, but she was terrified of the dark.

Mosquito-like creatures buzzed around her face. They continued to dive-bomb her, drinking her blood until she slapped them against her skin, crushing their vile little bodies, covering her in mushed bug goo and blood.

"Oh my gosh." Brea stumbled back, putting as much distance between herself and the slithering creature she'd just encountered. "I hate snakes!" She shouted into the darkness. "Fairy land should have no snakes. That's like a rule somewhere."

Lifting her foot out of the squelching mud, she took a step forward, her knees screaming in protest from the push and pull on her joints. Her left foot found firmer ground, and she nearly sobbed in relief.

Brea pulled herself up onto the mossy bit of ground, tempted to take a rest, but she'd promised Neeve she'd keep moving, and she'd barely begun. Taking just a moment to rub some life back into her knees, Brea stood, her body protesting.

"Maybe I could sit here long enough to eat something." She reached for her pack, taking a sip of water from her canteen. Something moved in the deep water near her somewhat-dry perch. Something large. Brea fumbled to put her canteen back in her pack and searched her surroundings for the quickest path.

A snapping turtle struggled out of the water, and she sighed, slumping against the tree at her back.

"That was—" Brea's heart stopped as a pair of massive jaws appeared out of the water and closed around the turtle.

The second creature chomped on its crunchy meal and slithered out of the water. It looked like a huge lizard and an alligator had a really ugly dragon-baby. Brea stood rooted to the spot as the creature's tail stretched out behind it. It had to be twenty feet long. She almost peed herself when it lifted its head toward her, flicking its long tongue as if to taste the air around her.

"Please be full from your turtle snack," she whispered, unable to move. She had nowhere to go anyway. She eyed the trees around her, wondering if she could climb if it came to that. Not a tree branch in sight low enough for her to reach.

The creature hissed a warning, showing its massive razor sharp teeth before it ambled away. She swore it wrinkled its nose in disgust.

"Thank you, Neeve, for making me stink." Brea wasn't sure her heartbeat would ever return to normal. She stared at the creature until she couldn't see it anymore. "Get it together, Robinson." She reached for the lantern at her feet. Her hands shaking as she wondered how many of those things were out there.

Her body said, "I live here now," but her mind disagreed. Taking a careful step off the mossy perch, the tension in Brea's shoulders eased some. Solid ground.

With her compass guiding her way east, Brea moved as quickly as her feet would allow her, ever mindful of what she might step on. Nocturnal creatures were out and about, making a ruckus all around her. Insects and small furry creatures she could handle. Even the orange salamanders that scurried about didn't bother her.

Owls hooted and fish splashed in the ponds. She even heard the distant growl of a very large cat she hoped she wouldn't encounter. As the ground grew soft again, Brea searched for an alternate path. She didn't want to end up in mud up to her knees again.

Her stomach growled, and she thought of the food Neeve packed for her. Setting her lamp down, Brea rushed to retrieve the bacon sandwiches from her pack. Just a quick bite, and she'd be on her way again. Resting against a cypress tree, she ate quickly. Feeling better with something in her stomach, Brea leaned her head back against the tree, sipping from her canteen.

"No crazy swamp dragons here." She shoved off the tree and hauled her pack up on her shoulder. Leaning down for her lantern, something heavy and scaly landed on her back.

Brea screamed, throwing the huge snake across the swamp. The slithering, hissing black snake landed with a thud. It was huge and angry. Brea took a step back and stumbled over her lantern. Darkness fell all around her as her only light source went out.

"No!" Brea nearly wept.

Hissing sounded nearby, and she wasn't waiting around for the snake to find her or call his buddies in for a group attack. Clutching her compass, Brea followed the path of semi-solid ground until it ran out.

Within moments, the mud reached her calves, but she kept moving East. Without the lantern, the bugs had finally left her alone.

Thunder rumbled in the distance, and Brea laughed. "Of course it's going to rain." She threw her hands up toward the sky. "It's certainly not wet enough around here."

She trudged forward, avoiding the nocturnal growls that sounded far too close for comfort. The larger creatures seemed to want to check her out until they got close enough to smell Neeve's concoction on her, and then they probably decided she didn't smell like food.

"Thank you, Neeve. I smell so bad not even the dragon monsters want anything to do with me."

To make the time pass and to keep her mind off the creepy

crawlies, Brea kept her eyes glued to a grove of trees in the distance. When she reached it, she found a long branch to use as a walking stick. Checking her compass to ensure she was heading in the right direction, she selected a new landmark to focus on. This time it was an outcropping of rocks rising from the swamp.

She was on her fifth landmark when it started to rain. Her seventh when it started to pour. By the tenth landmark, Brea was in mud up to her thighs with no solid ground in sight.

She was exhausted and scared out of her wits. The area around her was more water than mud, and Brea's heart raced with the fear of what monsters might lurk nearby. She clutched her walking stick, using it to keep her balance in the swamp.

The magic she didn't understand thundered through her body. She had no knowledge of how to control it, only that it responded to her emotions. Griff claimed he was going to teach her how to harness her emotions so she wouldn't lose control, but that had never happened. The evidence against him continued to mount, and Brea wondered why it had taken her so long to see it.

She could feel it sizzling under her skin, begging for release. The longer she struggled to move through the swampy waters, the more the magic gathered inside her, latching on to her fear and anger like a blazing fire consuming oxygen.

Brea took another step forward, and she was up to her chest in muddy water as the rain continued to beat down on her. Lightning flashed, and something slithered against her thigh

Struggling to move faster, Brea's exhaustion overwhelmed her. Her tears mixed with the rain. "I just want to go home."

She'd gladly face the assault charges that awaited her back in the human world if it meant she could put this nightmare behind her. If she could see Myles again. Even her parents would be a welcome sight right now.

Splashing through the water, the ground began to rise, and Brea lurched forward until her knees were above water for the first time in hours. Checking her compass, she was still on the right path and the land ahead of her seemed rather solid in the moonlight.

As she moved forward, the magic pooling just under her skin seemed to reach a critical point. Stumbling, Brea's heart rattled in her chest, and her lungs seized. She clutched her walking stick like a lifeline, but she couldn't stay upright. She could feel the magic like a welling pressure in her body. With a scream of anguish, Brea tumbled forward, and a yellow light rushed from her open mouth, clashing with the lightning overhead. Sparks rained down around her illuminating the expanse of marshlands she still had to traverse.

Brea fell headfirst into the putrid mud. Rolling to her side, she tried to stand, but her vision went blurry.

I'm going to die out here all alone, and no one will even care.

Chapter 15

Thunder ripped through Brea's mind, and she jolted up in bed.

Bed?

Her chest rose and fell with rapid succession as she tried to see her surroundings, hidden by the dark.

The marsh. Creepy alligator-lizard-dragons.

She released a sigh as she gripped the thin wool blanket pooled in her lap. Had it all been a dream?

Or had her magic really almost killed her?

Her eyes darted from the bed to the sliver of moonlight appearing through a crack in the... tent door? Yeah, she was in a tent. How? Who?

A flash of lightning illuminated the sparse surroundings for just long enough to take in the small bed roll beneath her and little else. Her pack rested in the corner next to a set of saddle bags.

Brea's stomach ached with hunger, and she couldn't take her eyes off the familiar bag Neeve had given her. It took her a moment to realize the steady drumming on the canvas overhead wasn't in her mind. The rain kept coming like it had no intention of letting up.

Scrambling from the bedroll, she crawled across the mossy ground to her pack and ripped it open. Yanking every one of the few belongings she had out, she searched for the remaining food that should be there.

Nothing.

Turning her attention to the unknown saddle bags, she pulled them into her lap and dug through the stranger's provisions. Still, no food.

Warm, briny air blew into the tent, bringing with it the rain. She scooted back from the opening, dragging her bag with her. Going through it more slowly this time, she found the small knife Neeve had given her. Whoever found her must have taken it off her body.

Tucking it into the waist of pants she didn't recognize, she pulled her legs up to her chest. Weariness invaded her mind. Her limbs tingled with weakness, and it took her a moment to realize what she felt… or what she didn't feel.

No magic pooled underneath her skin. It didn't churn with her emotions and lend her strength in her greatest moment of need.

"It's gone," she whispered.

She should have felt relief. Her entire life, she'd stood on the edge of a precipice, her volatility threatening to send her into the abyss—or get her locked up in the Clarkson Institute. She now knew it had been the magic, her fae heritage, expanding everything she felt.

But now, in the absence of that, with the prospect of being just a normal human, there was an emptiness inside her, a void in her heart.

She had to figure out where she was. If whoever found her was taking her back to Gelsi, she may as well have stayed with the lizard things. A shiver wracked her body and she couldn't make it stop. Wherever they were was warmer than Gelsi, but even that couldn't still her body's shaking.

Her teeth clattered, and she pulled her tangled mass of hair over one shoulder, running her hands through it as if that could provide her the comfort she needed.

"You are Brea Robinson," she said. "You survived being pulled into a different world and living in a palace of lies. A manipulative aunt, a man who betrayed you, and... snakes." She closed her eyes, trying to make herself believe the words. "You can survive whoever is outside this tent."

A crash of thunder made her jump, sounding like it split the sky in two. If the fae world cracked open, would it let her return to the safety of Ohio corn fields, where the biggest danger was psychiatrists overanalyzing everything and mean kids at school?

At least none of them had swords.

She fingered the hilt of the knife, wondering what any of the kids she'd known would think if they saw her now.

"I need you, Myles," she whispered. She pulled the blanket around her as if it could protect her from this world. "I really hope you're alive."

And if he was, she'd see him again. In all of Griff's stupid promises, he'd never been able to give her that hope. How could he even keep all of his promises and lies straight?

She couldn't go back to Griff, not after everything.

Kicking the blanket away, she stood and crept to the tent opening, peering out into the storm.

Two guards stood nearby, seemingly impervious to the rain in their leather armor. Tents sat haphazardly around the small clearing with cypress trees looming as shadows overhead. Were they still in the marshes?

Voices came from the guards. "We can't stay here forever," one of them said.

The other didn't respond right away. "We have our orders. The girl must be awake for the journey. And we cannot leave until given the order to march."

"What if she doesn't wake up? We don't know what happened to her out there."

The second guard shrugged. "We will deliver her to the palace whether she lives or not."

Lives or not. There words were so cold, Brea realized they must mean to bring her back to her aunt. After everything, she refused to go back there. What would they do to her after she ran?

She'd made it this far. Neeve's words came back to her. "*Don't stop until you reach Eldur.*"

She couldn't give up now.

Sparing one more glance for the tent flap and the guards beyond, she pulled her knife free and scooted across the bed to the back of the tent. Gripping the thick material in her shaking fingers, she stabbed the tip of the blade into it and sawed, cutting a line down the tent.

When the slit was big enough, she stuck her head through. Water wicked into her eyes as it streamed down her hair into her face. She glanced up at the stormy sky, hoping the deluge would hide her escape.

She couldn't make out her surroundings and didn't know which way to go, but she'd figure that out once she was away from these Fargelsian soldiers. Gripping her knife tightly, she slipped through the opening and jumped to her feet. Pumping her legs, she sprinted as fast as she could for the trees.

Shouting erupted behind her, but she didn't stop no matter how much her burning legs ached for it. Weakness vibrated through her, but she didn't give into it. She couldn't.

Solid ground turned to mud underneath her feet. As more soldiers shouted for her to stop, she had to keep going, wading into the swirling goo. It rose up around her legs the deeper she got, refusing to let her go. By the time the mud reached her thighs, she couldn't move.

A cry left her lips as she tried to free herself, only managing to get deeper into the mud. A snake slithered by her legs, and she stabbed at it with her knife, flicking it away from her. It hissed and left her alone. This was it. She was going to die stuck in mud in a foreign world as soldiers chased after her during a storm.

She lifted her face to the rain as it broke through the tree cover. "I'm sorry, okay? Whatever I did to deserve this, I didn't mean it." She slapped her arm. "Brea Robinson, if there was ever a time to wake up, this is it." Some small part of her still hoped this was a nightmare, a horrid and all-too-real nightmare.

"Don't move!" a voice boomed out of the dark.

"Good thing I can't, then!" she yelled back. "You're lucky I'm stuck in mud or you'd have never caught me."

In reality, her escape was doomed from the start. She was a half-human girl who only ran when being chased, not for any sort of exercise. Yeah, she was screwed.

"Stay there."

"Already told you I have no choice." Rain pounded into the mud harder and harder as her heart rate kicked up. Whatever Gelsi held for her was better than dying right here.

"Reach out," the voice commanded. "As far as you can."

She grappled in the dark, trying to find something to hold onto as she bent toward the voice. Her hand touched flesh, and she reached her other one out, gripping the man's hand with both of hers, their fingers slick against each other.

"I'm going to pull you out."

He tugged on her hands, and another set of hands clamped down underneath her armpits, lifting her as the other man pulled.

"Don't let go!" someone yelled.

"Not planning on it." Relief flushed through her as her legs came free little by little.

An arm wrapped around her waist and hauled her the rest of the way. She almost cried when her feet hit solid ground.

"I could kiss you right now!" she yelled at one of the soldiers over the rain.

"My Lady." He jumped away from her, thoroughly scandalized.

Brea didn't have the energy to laugh. She rolled onto her stomach and pushed herself to her knees as she tried to catch her breath.

Without waiting for permission, one of the soldiers lifted her into his arms and walked back through the trees. He didn't speak until they reached the tent she'd escaped from.

He set her down, his aged face marred by a scowl. "Stay here."

Turning on his heel, he marched away.

Brea looked around the tent, thankful for its semi-safe surroundings. She sat down on the bedroll, her entire body shaking with cold. Water streamed down her back, but it didn't matter because the bed was already soaked from the rain entering through the slit she'd cut. She closed her eyes, trying to calm herself, until commotion sounded outside her tent.

A man walked in, his lips forming a smile that did not belong in this moment. "Well, my Lady, you have caused quite a stir."

She shrank away from him. "What do you want from me?"

He removed his helmet, revealing a face even younger than she'd thought. He couldn't have been much older than her. "I believe I should be the one asking questions. My men found you unconscious in the middle of the marshy Vatlands. No one travels the Vatlands alone except for one reason."

"What's that reason?"

"Tell you what, I will give you some answers, if you do the same. Let's start with a name."

"Breanne of Tarth," she blurted before she could stop herself. Something prevented her from giving her real name.

He nodded as if that was a perfectly plausible name. "Tarth, is that a Gelsi province?"

She nodded.

"Well, Breanne, you're safe here." This time, his smile reached his eyes. He had a face one wanted to trust, but then, so had Griff. "My name is Finn. The only brave souls who traverse the Vatlands on their own are those who manage to escape the Fargelsian queen."

"You're not..." She sucked in a breath. "You aren't taking me back there?"

He reeled back as if she'd slapped him. "No. Why would we do that? These men are stationed near the border to intercept those fleeing tyranny just like you. I am only here because my traveling companion has been waiting for someone." He eyed her carefully. "How did you escape Gelsi?"

"I had help." She didn't want to reveal Neeve's identity.

Finn rubbed his jaw. "Yes, well, even still... do you know of the border spell?"

He didn't wait for her to respond. "Those with full Fargelsi blood are forbidden from crossing the border by the queen. Her magic keeps them there unless she releases them."

Neeve had explained all this before, but it hadn't really hit Brea then. That was why Neeve couldn't come. Everything Brea knew about her aunt flashed through her mind. She'd known she was manipulative, but would she really go to such lengths to keep her power? To keep her people imprisoned?

Did Griff know? She wanted to believe he was just naive in all this, but she didn't know him, not like she'd thought she did.

"I'm not..." What had she meant to say? She wasn't a full Fargelsian fae? She wasn't fae at all? No matter who her father was, she didn't belong in that world.

An angry voice entered the relative calm of the tent as someone barged their way in, shaking sopping wet blond hair out of his face. Brea looked from Finn to the new intruder.

Lochlan.

He pushed his hair back, allowing her to see his blazing eyes.

"Ah, Loch." Finn grinned as he turned to the other man. "Meet our newest Gelsi escapee, Breanne of Tarth."

Lochlan's dark eyes met hers. "If this is Breanne of Tarth, then I'm Jon Snow."

Brea's jaw fell open. "How... what... I mean, what?"

Lochlan's jaw twitched, but he didn't explain how he knew about a human TV series. Instead, he turned to Finn. "This is her." He turned on his heel and marched away.

Brea scrambled from the bed, but Finn blocked her path, his face red with embarrassment. "You fooled me, Brea Robinson, but it is a pleasure to meet the woman who can vex the unshakeable Lochlan O'Shea."

"Yeah, yeah." She shoved him out of the way. "You can thank me for my service later. I need to talk to him."

Darting out into the rain, she caught sight of Lochlan's retreating back and ran toward him. "You can't just walk away from me."

He whirled to face her. "I can do whatever I please. I am the ranking officer here. These men follow my orders. I would appreciate if you no longer ran from them."

"I make no promises."

He approached her with the eyes of a predator, dark and dangerous. Griff hadn't had a lot of the traits of the fae from stories she'd seen. He was beautiful, sure, but also smiley and seemingly kind. Lochlan on the other hand fit everything from human fiction novels. Cunning. Cruel.

Achingly attractive.

"How do you know about *Game of Thrones*?" she asked.

Lochlan shook his head in exasperation and gripped her arm, pulling her into a nearby tent. "It's a deluge out there."

"I noticed." She crossed her arms over her soaking shirt. "Are you going to answer my question?"

"No." He stepped around her and stripped the blanket from his bed. Holding it out to her, he met her gaze. "Wrap this around your body so you don't catch a chill."

"I'm fine."

Lochlan's scowl deepened. "Do you know how much risk you took tonight? We are in the middle of the Vatlands. Traveling at night is nearly impossible because of the mud pits that only get deeper and deeper. They've claimed many lives. You could have died."

"But I didn't."

"Because of my men."

He was right. She'd made a rash decision trying to escape and almost paid for it with her life. "I'm sorry."

His expression softened for a beat before hardening into another scowl. "You are not to do it again. Since you so gratefully destroyed the tent we gave you, you will sleep in here tonight where I can keep an eye on you."

"How will you keep an eye on me if you need to sleep? I could slit your throat with my knife." She wouldn't, but she could.

"What knife?"

She pulled the blade free and held it up.

Lochlan reached her in a flash, knocking the blade from her hand and retrieving it off the ground. "Not anymore."

"Hey," she protested. "That's mine."

"Let me be clear, Lady Robinson. I do not trust you. I have instructed my men not to trust you. We will deliver you to the palace unharmed, but should you try to injure any of them again, you will arrive tied to the back of my saddle. Do you understand?"

Her eyes narrowed. "The palace? Which palace?" He was a prince of Iskalt but a delegate of Eldur. She wasn't sure which realm she feared more.

"Eldur."

"With the dragons?"

He turned to the door. "Don't worry, Lady Robinson. The dragons don't eat things that smell like you."

She would have sworn there was laughter in his voice as he sauntered from the tent.

She sniffed the shirt she wore and grimaced. Neeve's smelly stuff had mostly worn off, leaving behind a faint rancid scent mixed with the smell of travel.

She just hoped Lochlan was right about the dragons.

"How long was I out?" Brea asked Finn as he sat in front of her, taking the first watch. He'd brought with him a canteen of water, stale bread, and dried meat. It wasn't the gourmet meals she'd grown used to in Gelsi, but as hungry as she was, it tasted like five-star cuisine.

Finn sipped water from a tin cup, studying her over the rim. Finally, he lowered it and wiped his mouth. "Two days."

Her eyes widened. So, they definitely knew she was missing from Gelsi by now. Had Griff returned and found her gone? Were Neeve and Moira okay?

"You should get some sleep." Finn used his knife to slice through the bread and popped a piece in his mouth.

"Apparently, I've been sleeping for two days." She couldn't have relaxed if she tried.

Neeve told her she'd be safe once she reached the Eldur camp. Well, here she was, and she didn't feel any safer.

"Why is Lochlan such a jerk?" she blurted.

Finn choked on his food, wheezing for breath. "I'm going to need you to say that again when he's within earshot."

She raised a brow. She'd only just met Finn, but she felt she knew Lochlan by now. From abducting her from a human prison to warning her in Gelsi, they'd already been through a lot together. "He's your friend? You seem like nothing bothers you, yet he is kind of a douche."

Finn sighed and ran a hand through his chestnut brown hair. "Appearances can be deceiving, Lady Robinson."

"Can you stop with all the lady nonsense?"

"It's what you are."

"Because the Gelsi queen is my aunt? I'll gladly relinquish that distinction."

"No. Not because of that." He didn't elaborate, instead focusing on the meat in front of him. He offered her a piece.

She bit down. It tasted similar to beef jerky, only better. Myles used to make her gorge on Slim Jims and barbecue jerky his dad made in their smoker. She'd never liked it, but he did, so she went along with it.

"Why does the Eldur queen want me?" she asked.

Finn kept his eyes trained on his hands, but it was another voice that responded.

"That is not our business." Lochlan stood in the opening of the tent with rivulets of water dripping off his powerful frame. "We do not question our queen. We follow her orders." He gave Finn a pointed look that told Brea the two of them totally knew what the Eldur queen wanted with her. "I will take over Lady Robinson's watch."

Finn stood. "She wants to be called Brea."

Lochlan grunted as if what she wanted was of little importance to him. It probably was.

Finn offered her an encouraging smile before leaving her be.

Brea crossed her arms over the dry shirt Finn had provided her with. "I'm surprised you want to sit in here with me considering I smell too bad even for dragons."

He eyed her warily and took Finn's spot on the floor. Ripping a piece of bread, he took a bite and chewed slowly. "You can bathe once we reach the palace."

"And when will that be?"

He shrugged. "Four days? Five? Depends on this storm."

"You know what she wants with me."

"Yes." He kept eating, not looking her way.

Her eyes narrowed, and she leaned back on the bed, refusing to look at him. Rustling sounded to her right, and when she turned onto her side, she caught sight of a very naked Lochlan pulling on dry clothes.

Her face heated as she rolled back over, trying to forget the image of his corded back and firm... She shook her head. Griff drew her in with his looks and his charm, she wouldn't let that happen again. At least Lochlan had no charm to speak of.

"I trusted Neeve," she whispered. When he didn't respond, she kept talking. "Like you told me to. So... thanks."

His sigh filled the tent, and when she turned to look at him once more, he sat back in his spot with his head bowed. "I wish we could get her out of there."

So, he did care about something.

"Lochlan?"

He lifted his eyes.

She needed to know the answer to the question that could crush her. "Is he really alive?"

His eyes met hers, never wavering. "Yes."

She didn't know how, but she knew he told her the truth.

Tears built in her eyes. She blinked them away before more took their place. Shifting so Lochlan couldn't see her face, she let the tears trail over her cheeks. Myles was truly alive. Her chest expanded like she could breathe for the first time since that awful day at school when she'd thought she'd killed him.

"Lochlan?" she whispered, her voice shaking.

"Yes?"

"Thank you." When she got control of her voice, she spoke again. "Can I ask another question?"

"I'm coming to realize there's no way to stop you short of a gag."

She smiled at that. "Why do you hate me?"

As soon as she said the words, he tensed, revealing she wasn't wrong. He'd been gruff with her since the first day in the human realm.

"I don't—"

"Please, just be straight with me, I don't think I can take any more lies or half-truths."

He rubbed a hand over his face. "People have died for you, Brea. People I loved. I helped you at the request of my queen, but do not mistake anything that has happened as anything other than me following orders. You're right, I don't like you. I don't want to sit here staring into the face of the girl who has taken so much from me."

"I don't understand." What had she taken from him? Who'd died because of her? Her pulse hammered in her temples, sending waves of pain through her head. Her tears continued to fall.

"I wouldn't expect you to. You may have fae blood running through those veins, but you're just a human girl who has cost our world too much."

"I—"

"Go to sleep, Lady Robinson. Our conversation is through, and tomorrow will be a long day." He leaned his head back, closing his eyes.

Brea curled her legs up to her chest, trying to still the shaking of her body. She never thought she'd long for the solitude of the Clarkson Institute.

Maybe being delusional would have been better than being right.

The fae existed as she'd always seen, but their world wasn't meant for a girl raised on a simple human farm.

Chapter 16

"You can let me have my horse back. I won't run again." Brea slumped in the saddle in front of Lochlan. She'd banked on being better on a horse than Lochlan's men when she made a run for it. She hadn't had a plan beyond not going to the Eldur palace.

She also hadn't banked on Lochlan being the one to catch her. Of course he came crashing down on her like a blond fae-god riding Secretariat.

"You've proven I can't trust you. So, you will ride with me to the Eldur palace. You will sleep in my tent, eat my food, and remain in my sight at all times until I hand you over to the queen."

"Would you like me to wipe your butt while I'm at it?"

"That won't be necessary, unless you try to escape again. You would do well not to push me human-girl."

"The Loch-to-Brea translation there, is he will likely pop that vein in his forehead if you try to run again." Finn rode beside them, offering helpful tidbits to the conversation, much to Lochlan's irritation. He didn't seem to like that his friend enjoyed Brea's company.

"At least let me ride with Finn so it's not like riding with a boulder at my back."

"I think the lady just called you soft." Lochlan jeered at his friend.

"The lady meant the boulder comment in terms of personality." She shifted in the saddle. While that was partially true, Lochlan's bulk was like leaning against a stone wall. A cold stone wall.

"You're just jealous that the pretty lady likes me more. Honestly, it's the story of his life." Finn grinned. "Poor guy never gets the girl when I'm around."

"Why don't you go check on the rear and let them know we'll make camp soon?" Lochlan dismissed his cocky right-hand man.

"Right away, sir. Catch you later, Breanne of Tarth." Finn winked at Brea before he turned his mount and left them in an uncomfortable silence.

Lochlan snorted at his retreat. "Preening peacock."

"You're just jealous because he's charming and you aren't."

"My brother is charming. How did that work out for you?"

"I think I like you better when you don't speak."

"Hashtag same."

Brea turned in the saddle to meet his gaze. "How do you know all the human lingo?"

"I've spent a lot of time there over the years."

"Doing what?"

"Keeping you alive. Now, I've had enough of your questions, girl."

Despite her desire to continue needling him, Brea let the matter drop. She sat quietly until she couldn't take his stony silence for another second.

"So... who's your favorite *GOT* character? Tyrion Lannister was my favorite. *That's what I do. I drink and I know things.*"

"Of course you would like the talker."

"So. Who's your favorite?"

"Davos Seaworth. A quiet, loyal man."

"What season was he in?"

"I do not watch television. I read."

"Oh, you're like Myles..." Her voice caught on his name. "He was always trying to get me to read the books." With her thoughts on Myles, she didn't care about the silence anymore.

As the day wore on, Brea started to sweat. It was really hot in Eldur compared to the relative perfection of Fargelsi.

"We make camp here," Lochlan called to his men. It surprised her that he would stop when it was still light out.

"We still have hours of daylight left, sir," a young soldier gave voice to Brea's observations.

"The oasis is the last source of fresh water we will encounter before we reach the palace. We will rest here and stock up on water before we set out early tomorrow morning," Finn explained.

Lochlan lifted Brea down from the horse—like she couldn't possibly dismount a horse on her own—and instead of setting her on the ground he carried her to a small wooded area offering the only shade she'd seen all day. A small lake shimmered in the sunlight.

"What are you doing?" She gasped as he tied her hands together and wrapped the rope around a tree. "Are you even serious right now?" She kicked him hard in the shins.

"Did you just kick me?" A brow arched over his dark blue eyes.

"Come here so I can do it again," Brea growled.

"Do not ever kick me again or you will regret it." He turned to address his men.

"Lochlan, don't you dare leave me tethered to a tree like a dog!" Brea stomped her foot, itching to kick him where it really hurt. He ignored her, directing his men to make camp around her as he walked away to help.

Once the tents were ready, Lochlan finally returned.

"You're a jerk." Brea shoved her wrists in his face.

"And you stink." He tossed her pack and a cake of soap at her feet. "If I have to ride with you for the next two days, you will at least smell better." He released the knot around the tree, giving her a longer tether before he secured her to the tree again and moved her restraints from her wrists to her waist.

"Release me. Now." Brea slapped him hard across the face and immediately regretted it.

His eyes flashed with carefully controlled anger. "Go clean the swamp stink off." He pointed toward the lake, just in reach of her leash.

"I won't escape." Brea's face flamed with fury—the lack of her magic more obvious than before. "But I will not bathe in front of you and your men."

"Trust me, no one will be looking. Fae do not get caught up in the idiocy of human modesty. It's time you abandon your human tendencies."

"I'm part human, you jerk." She kicked a clot of dirt at his face. "And I'm a really good swimmer." She yanked at the knot around her waist.

"You couldn't escape even if you wanted to." Lochlan gave her an arrogant smirk. "We're surrounded by desert. You'd die of exposure before you could find help. And that knot isn't going anywhere."

"Well, if there's nothing but desert around us, then why bother tying me up at all?" Brea lifted her chin in defiance.

"To teach you a lesson in humility. Now go before I throw you in the lake and bathe you myself." He turned his back on her.

Brea snatched up her pack and the soap and stomped to the edge of the water. He was right, she couldn't even get her fingers around the magical knot at her waist. If she wasn't so incredibly dirty, she'd refuse to take a bath, but she also didn't want to see if Loch would follow through with his threat to bathe her himself.

Her face flaming with humiliation, she cast a glance over her shoulder to find not one soldier looking her way. She quickly shed her clothes and slipped into the cool, refreshing water until she was up to her neck. The water was crystal clear, and for once she didn't fear what evils might lurk beneath the surface.

Brea frowned as she worked the soap up into a lather. Everything in Fargelsi was beautiful on the surface with vile and all manner of evil things lying in wait just out of sight. Loch Villandi. The fountain. Magic-blocking Gelsi berries. Beautiful but poisonous flowers, and a vicious queen who spouted lies and played with lives. So far, Eldur seemed to be exactly what it appeared. A hot, dry desert kingdom without the first dragon sighting. Maybe they lived with the queen and guarded the palace? One could hope.

Just as she was rinsing the last of the caked mud from her hair, something tugged at her waist and she went slicing through the water like a fish on a line.

"What is your problem?" Brea sputtered, trying to shield herself in the shallow water.

"Bath time's over." Lochlan dropped a linen blanket on the ground and turned his back.

"You know, you could learn a thing or two from your brother." Brea snatched the blanket and wrapped it around herself several times. "He may have lied to me—and that is unforgivable—but at least he's a decent person."

"Griffin is many things, but decent isn't one of them." He tugged on her leash, nearly dragging her into his tent. "Get dressed."

Brea stumbled into the larger tent, grasping for her anger and the magic that normally came with it, but it was gone. And just when she really wanted to use it.

"Stupid handsome blond jerk-face." Brea let out a string of curses that would have gotten her grounded at home.

"I heard that," Lochlan called just outside the tent.

Brea stuck her head through the flaps. "I meant for you to!" She called him a few more names.

"Lady Brea!" Finn sounded shocked. "I've never heard a noble woman curse like that."

"You meant to call me handsome, Lady Brea?" Lochlan and a few of his soldiers laughed.

Brea shoved her arms through the soft tunic Neeve had made for her, grateful someone took the time to wash her things after her trip through the swamp. Slipping on her leggings and shoving her feet into her boots, Brea stomped through the tent flaps.

"Let's get one thing straight, Lochlan. Stay away from me. Don't talk to me. Don't even look at me."

"If you'll be quiet, you've got yourself a deal, my Lady." Lochlan smirked up at her from where he lounged in the shade.

"Hungry?" Finn offered her a bowl of stew and a chunk of dry bread.

"Starving." Brea accepted the meal and returned to the tent.

"It's going to be hot in there, Brea," Lochlan called. "I'd hate for you to have to take another bath."

Brea kicked the tent flaps aside and sat down under the shade beside Finn. "What did I *just* say?" She shot a glare at Lochlan before she turned away, determined to pretend he didn't exist.

Brea could feel Lochlan moving around the tent in the early hours just before dawn. She hadn't slept at all in the muggy hot space. Rolling over to face him, she regretted it instantly. Naked once again with his back to her, beads of water rolled down his lean body after a dip in the lake.

"Jeeze, Loch, put some clothes on." She rolled away.

"That is what I'm doing." She heard the rustle of his clothes as he dressed. "Most ladies find my form appealing. Do you not?"

"Does it matter?"

"Not at all. I am simply trying to understand your odd human behavior."

"I am seventeen years old, Lochlan. In the human world you could get arrested for exposing yourself to someone my age."

"I am only a few years older than you." He sounded like he didn't think any of this was odd.

"You'll have to excuse me if I find it odd to wake up to a naked fae butt in my face first thing in the morning."

"But you will be of age soon. How does a few weeks make a difference in your world?"

"It just does. And how do you know I'm almost eighteen?" She had no idea what the date was, and with the weird fae calendar added into the mix, she didn't know when her birthday was, only that it was soon.

Lochlan crouched beside her bedroll, still shirtless, his long blond hair dripping from his early morning swim, but at least he'd put on pants. "Your magic is erratic, yes?"

Brea nodded. If you could call absent erratic, then hers was a mess.

"All fae magic is tied to our emotions. Surely my brother taught you that much?"

"Yes. He was going to help me learn how to control my Fargelsi magic." Brea sat up, clutching her blanket to her chest. "But we never got around to it."

"There is a reason I goaded you all day yesterday, Brea. You magic has slipped out of your reach since your difficult journey through the Vatlands. You don't know how to use your magic, much less control it. I was trying to push it out of you through your temper, but that isn't working. When you come of age, it will return in full force, but you need to be prepared to deal with it when that happens. The last time the magic built up within you, you knocked yourself out. You can't let that happen again."

"Then what do I do?"

"I will help you." Lochlan stood up, reaching for his shirt. "Get dressed and eat something. We leave in an hour."

"Seriously? We're doing this again?" Brea stared up as Lochlan mounted on his horse, reaching down to lift her up.

"Seriously." The muscle in his jaw ticked.

"You've still got me on your leash, so just let me ride my own horse. It's not like I can go anywhere." She fumbled with the rope around her waist, but it wouldn't budge.

"Get on the damn horse, Brea." Lochlan jerked her forward by her tether.

"Rude." She climbed up in front of him, dreading another hot day riding far too close to her least favorite person.

"Take this." He handed her a thick piece of rough-cut glass.

"What is it?"

"Crystalized sand. You're going to practice while we ride today."

"Magic? How?"

"Your magic is inside you. You need to find it and funnel it into the crystal. It will glow with the color of your magic when you do it right. This exercise will help you learn to sense your magic when it is close."

"So, I just *find* my magic and use it to light up the crystal?" She turned to look up at him. "You do realize you've failed to explain *how* I'm supposed to accomplish that."

"Focus on your emotions and feelings, and you will find it. This is an internal battle no one can do for you, Brea."

"You're just trying to keep me quiet," Brea muttered.

"That is simply an added benefit of the exercise." Lochlan nudged his horse forward across the rocky desert terrain.

Brea stared at the piece of crystalized sand for the first few miles, wondering how she was supposed to find her magic when she didn't know where to look for it.

"You're not trying, Brea," Lochlan pressed.

"I'm trying to decide the best approach." Brea closed her eyes, letting her thoughts drift over the frustrating events of the past weeks. She had good memories of her time in Gelsi, but that it was all a lie just made her angry, and anger didn't seem to help her connect with her magic.

Instead, Brea focused on happier memories of Myles before all of this happened. But that just made her sad. Sadness didn't seem to be a strong enough emotion to stir her magic.

"I feel like I'm trying to cast a patronus, and I don't have enough happy memories to pull it off."

"You're not Harry Potter, Brea. This isn't make-believe nonsense. Now, focus." Lochlan pressed the glass into her hand and wrapped her fingers around it.

"Of course you've seen *Harry Potter*."

"I have *read Harry Potter*. Human books fascinate me. You should try reading sometime. It's a far better use of your time than mindless movies that never tell the whole story."

"Myles used to say the same thing."

It was the only thing they ever argued about. A smile came to Brea's lips at the memory of all their stupid fights about nothing. Just knowing he was still out there living his life made her happy. She just wondered if he hated her. A surge of fear rose up inside her at that thought. She couldn't bear it if he hated her for what she'd done to him.

"Brea, look." Lochlan nudged her. She looked down at the crystal pulsing with a vivid yellow light before it winked out.

"I did it!" A grin spread across her face. "Myles is my patronus."

"You didn't do anything because you let it go before you took control."

"That wasn't just nothing. You don't get to poop all over my success."

Finn's laughter rang out behind them. Lochlan-the-jerk-face had made him ride behind them today so he wouldn't distract her.

"I don't get to what?" Lochlan stilled behind her.

"You don't get to poop on her success," Finn supplied—for Lochlan and any of the soldiers who'd missed it the first time.

"That was not a success."

"It was," Brea insisted. "Now we know my magic is yellow."

"Yes, we do." Lochlan sighed. "What emotion filled you when the magic pulsed in the crystal?"

Brea didn't want to tell him it was fear. She could only imagine how many ways he'd try to torture the magic out of her. "Happiness," she finally said.

"Do not lie to me, Brea."

"I'm not lying."

"Yes, you are."

"So, what do I do next time when the light pulses in the crystal?"

"Take control."

"How?"

"Use your instincts, Brea."

"What if I have no instincts?"

"Just try it again. And keep your eyes open this time."

"Fine." Brea stared down at the crystal in her lap and revisited some of the scariest moments of her trip through the swamp. The image of the alligator-dragon beast filled her mind. She conjured up every last harrowing detail she could recall right down to its creepy forked tongue.

The crystal glowed with a faint yellow light, and Brea focused harder, urging the light to shine brighter. Sweat beaded on her forehead and rolled down her face. Her hands shook with the effort to keep the yellow light from winking out. When she lost it, Brea cursed and chucked the crystal as far as she could throw it.

"Brea. Don't be a child." Lochlan raised his hand and somehow summoned the crystal, catching it in his outstretched hand and stuffing it back in hers.

"Why don't you show me how to do that?"

"Because you haven't mastered the most basic mechanics of magic that even our youngest children learn through instinct alone."

"How about we do the not-talking thing again for a while?" Brea felt like crushing the stupid crystal in her bare hands.

She spent the next hour running the gamut of her emotions, searching for the right thought or feeling that would stimulate her magic. But the darn thing refused to light up again.

Looking up, Brea saw stunted trees and cactus replacing the

barren desert sands they'd traversed. "Where are we?" Brea yawned, reaching for her canteen.

Lochlan pulled her back against his chest, his arms tense. "Quiet, Brea." That was when she realized he gripped his sword in his free hand.

"What's going on?" she whispered, not liking the way Lochlan's soldiers had fanned out around them. Before he could answer, a crossbow bolt slammed into a boulder just feet from Brea and Lochlan. She nearly jumped out of her seat, but Lochlan's arm was like a vise around her waist.

Several more bolts whizzed past them, and a battle cry echoed through the sparse forest as men and women charged toward them. Brea's heart lodged somewhere in her chest as Lochlan and his men entered the fray.

"Take this." Lochlan shoved a huge round shield in front of her. Brea clutched it tight and huddled behind the barrier. His arm slid around her again, but his free sword hand hacked away at the nearby soldiers.

"My uncle's men." Lochlan snarled in her ear. "None of them leave this place alive!" He shouted to his men.

Brea had never experienced a battle up close before, and she had no desire to experience this one. Ducking her head behind the shield, she just managed to avoid an arrow to her face. The shaft stuck in the shield, and as she reached to snap it off, three others replaced it.

Adrenaline and fear shot through her system. Still clutching the crystalized sand, it blazed with the yellow light of her magic now.

Lochlan struggled with a fierce warrior Brea thought she recognized from the Iskalt delegation party in Fargelsi. Their swords clashed, and Brea screamed, clutching the shield, grateful for Lochlan's hold on her.

"You can tell Callum O'Shea he'll have to do far better than an ambush in the desert. I'm coming for him and everyone who serves him," Lochlan snarled, sending the man flying from his horse. Lochlan turned his horse around to meet another attack.

"Loch!" Brea screamed, and her magic exploded from her body in a useless wave of yellow light.

The soldiers kept coming, and Lochlan slashed his way through them with his soldiers at his sides. He was ruthless in his rage. The icy blue light of his magic tipped his sword, dropping his enemies one by one.

"There's another one." Brea pointed at a woman charging past Finn with a determined set to her jaw.

She was so focused on the woman she didn't see the man riding toward them until it was almost too late.

Lifting the heavy shield, Brea deflected his sword, saving Lochlan from a grievous injury.

"Stupid girl." The man spat, his blade coming down on her.

Brea felt the tug and rip of fabric first as the sword bit deep into her shoulder. The shock of his cold magic lit up her insides as the soldier sliced down her arm. She screamed in agony as her arm went limp, and she dropped the shield.

"Brea!" Lochlan shouted over the din of battle.

Magic churned under Brea's skin, latching onto her fear. Without a thought to what she was doing, Brea grasped hold of her magic and sent it soaring toward the man who'd tried to kill Lochlan. The last thing she saw was the horrific sight of the man's head parting ways with his body before her magic rebounded on her and darkness won.

Chapter 17

Pain seared through Brea, and she woke screaming as someone bent over her with a burning blade pressed to her shoulder. "Stop! Stop!" But he didn't. Her eyes found Lochlan over the man's shoulder, and she grit her teeth. "I hate you so much right now. What is this guy doing to me?"

Her fingers dug into the blanket beneath her as she bucked off the bed.

Hands gripped her shoulders, holding her down, and she looked up into the face of Finn. "You were supposed to be the nice one." Her body jerked again as heat flooded her.

"Relax, Brea." Lochlan's hard eyes landed on her. "It'll be over soon."

"Relax?" she screamed as another jolt of pain struck her. "Relax! You relax!" A tear slipped from her eye, and she squeezed her eyelids shut, picturing something, anything other than the crowded tent where the Eldur soldiers tortured her.

The heat abated, but the pain remained.

"Lady Brea," a hard voice said.

She shook her head, unwilling to look at the men and women surrounding her.

"Brea," Finn called, his voice softer than Lochlan's. "You can open your eyes. We're through."

Her eyes slid open, and she viewed the soldiers crowding her bed. The man with the hot blade sat back on his heels. Two women hung back, blood splattered across their armor.

Finn withdrew his hands from her shoulders.

Lochlan crossed his arms, looking as uncomfortable as he should feel.

"Why were you torturing me?" She could barely muster the energy to speak.

Finn and Lochlan shared a look before Lochlan spoke. "We do not torture. You were injured and dying. Now you're not." He turned on his heel and pushed through the tent flap without another word. The rest of the soldiers followed him, save for Finn who moved to sit beside her.

"I really need to stop losing consciousness and waking up in strange places." She lifted her head, trying to see her shoulder. They'd cut her shirt away from the wound, but she couldn't get a look.

Finn grinned at her. "I don't know, Brea. It probably makes the travel easier if you're unconscious for much of it."

She laughed, wincing at the pain it caused. "What did they do to me?"

"Lewis is our unit's unofficial healer. He's quite adept at cauterization."

"Cauterization?" She gulped.

Finn nodded. "There was no way for us to stitch up your wound before returning to the palace, and by then you may have been as dead as those Iskalt warriors we fought. So, Lewis used his magic to heat the blade and sear your wound."

The odor of burnt flesh hung in the air, and nausea welled up in Brea. She tried to roll onto her side as her chest heaved.

Finn jumped forward, helping her up.

"Get me out of this tent," she wheezed.

He lifted her into his arms and ran out into the fresh desert air.

"Down," she pleaded.

As soon as Finn set her feet on the rocky ground, she fell to her knees and the meager contents of her stomach exploded from her mouth. Her entire body shook as it emptied itself.

She lifted her arm to try to wipe her mouth, but pain paralyzed her at the movement. "Other arm, you doofus," she whispered to herself, as she lifted the arm attached to her non-injured shoulder to wipe the remaining vomit from her face.

"Feel better?" Finn asked.

She'd forgotten he was there, but she was in too much pain to feel embarrassed. Imploring him with her eyes, she begged for assistance to stand so she didn't make a bigger fool of herself than she already had.

He wrapped an arm around her waist and lent her his strength.

"No," she protested when he tried to lead her back into the tent. She couldn't stand the thought of the rancid smell for one minute longer. "Not there."

Finn pursed his lips. "You mean you're going to make me sleep in there all alone tonight?"

She gaped at him. "That's your tent? What happened to Lochlan claiming he wouldn't let me out of his sight?"

"Our dear Loch wanted some peace after that battle, and you, my dear, give him very little peace." He helped her down onto the ground outside the tent, and she leaned back against a smooth boulder.

"He's angry at me for getting injured, isn't he?"

"No." Finn chuckled as he sat beside her. "He's angry at himself that you got injured at all."

"But if I hadn't stepped in, he'd be dead."

"That would be preferable to him than having to tell Queen Faolan that you died under his watch."

She eyed the stoic man across camp. “And probably that he had to be saved by little old Lady Brea.”

“Brea, you are an odd one.”

“How is it that Lochlan knows *Game of Thrones* and *Harry Potter*, yet no one in this fracking world understands anything I say?”

“Fracking?” He grinned. “Is that a human world for f—”

“Stop! I have delicate ears.”

He laughed. “There is nothing delicate about you. We all just watched Lewis burn your shoulder purposefully, and now you lay here under the desert sun making jokes.”

She grimaced as she lifted her head, trying to avoid the pain. “Fracking is from another TV show. TV is—”

“Yes, Lochlan has explained the odd instrument that provides entertainment to small human minds.”

She was about to protest his characterization of TV nerds when a shadow crossed over them. An irritating shadow. “What do you want?”

Lochlan scowled down at her, his face never softening. “Your shoulder needs tended to.”

“Wasn’t that what the torture was for?” She narrowed her eyes.

“It wasn’t torture.” He looked away. “Finn, help her up and bring her to my tent.”

He stalked back the way he’d come.

Finn’s body shook with silent laughter.

“What?” Brea snapped.

“I just... Lochlan never gets perturbed. He controls every emotion, every impulse.”

“Are you saying I perturb him?” She almost laughed at the funny word.

Finn stood and dusted off his butt before bending and sliding his arms under her. “I’m not quite sure yet.”

She let out a squeal of surprise as he hoisted her into his arms, jostling her shoulder and sending sparks of agony curling through her. He carried her into Lochlan's tent without waiting for Lochlan to enter.

A single thin bedroll occupied the far corner next to a bucket of water and a stack of cloth strips.

Finn set her on the bed and backed away. "Well, I'll leave you to Lochlan's care."

"Traitor," she called after him. Her words died off as Lochlan entered, taking Finn's place.

He didn't speak to her as he pulled leather shoulder plates over his head and set them aside. Crimson blood coated his shirt, making it stick to the ridges of his stomach. The sight of the remnants of battle stole any remaining biting words from her.

"How many soldiers did you lose?" She pictured the Iskalt warriors and the way they overwhelmed Lochlan and his people. There was no way they came through unscathed.

His shoulders dropped just the slightest bit, and he turned away from her to view their small camp through the tent opening. "Four."

"I'm sorry." She'd never seen battle before, but they were no strangers to the cost of war in the human realm. Many young men from their small Ohio town joined the military after high school. Some never returned.

He rubbed a hand across his face and looked back over his shoulder at her. "They knew the risks of this mission. My queen is not the only ruler who wants you."

She'd spent her entire life wanted by no one, and now, suddenly three realms fought for her. It was surreal, and she didn't understand it. Which one of them was good? Could she trust any of them, or was she just a pawn to all?

With a shake of his head, Lochlan turned and lowered himself to his knees beside where she lay. His long fingers reached for the bucket of water and pulled free a small sponge.

"We must keep the area around your wound clean." With surprisingly gentle fingers, he dabbed the sponge along her skin. They'd cauterized the gash in her shoulder from the sword, but tiny cuts still stretched out from the wound. Each time the sponge made contact with a wound, her breath hissed between her teeth.

Lochlan refused to even meet her eyes as he cleaned the area.

"Are you mad at me?" She knew what Finn had said, but she still sensed a new irritation in Lochlan.

He only grunted.

"Is it because you had to be saved by a woman?"

He pulled the sponge away and dropped it back in the bucket with a splash. "Brea, we fae are not like the humans you've lived around—or even the fae of Regan's court. One's gender is of no import."

She remembered what Neeve told her about them not falling in love with a gender, but surely the army was different. "You can't tell me you value the women in your unit as much as the men."

He finally met her eyes. "Why would I not? They are as skilled as any other. You forget we have one thing humans do not. Magic. It is the great equalizer. Our fights rely little on brute strength, allowing us to put aside any human biases. Fae do not stoop to such levels."

He wrung the sponge out and cleaned the remaining blood from her wound, his touch flitting across her skin with a care she'd never imagined from him.

"You're trying to tell me this is some feminist dream world?"

His brow creased. "I know not what a feminist is."

A laugh burst out of her. "You know human fantasy books but not basic principles of human life?"

"I have been to the human realm many times, but you would be mistaken if you think your people are of any interest to me. I find humans to be cruel... vindictive. But they're also fantastic writers."

She snorted. "Yes, well, I just escaped from a fae realm where everything was a dangerous lie. Don't get up on your high horse about fae morality."

He dried her shoulder before unrolling a long strip of fabric. "I do not understand you, Lady Brea."

"Ditto, Douchey Loch. See, I can call people things they'd rather I didn't too."

"Douchey." He paused for a moment. "I like the sound of that. What does it mean?"

She choked on a laugh. "Erm... noble."

He nodded. "Then you may call me by that name if you wish."

Winding the fabric tightly around her shoulder, Lochlan looked on with honest-to-God sympathy in his eyes as she winced in pain. Who would have thought he could feel anything other than irritation?

His fingers worked nimbly to bandage her shoulder and the upper half of her arm.

"If Lewis is the healer, why isn't he doing this?" she asked, trying to distract herself from the pain.

Lochlan looked away under the pretense of trying to find something, but nothing was there. "You are my responsibility."

"But why? Your queen wants me. I get that. But everyone keeps mentioning your trips to the human realm that supposedly had to do with me. We didn't meet until that day you stole me from the police."

"They were going to send you to one of those human prisons, and I can guarantee they're not like our prison realm."

She'd ask later about there being an entire realm for a prison. That sounded... extreme. "Because I almost killed my best friend. What do you have to do with any of this?"

He sat back, not looking at her. "I cannot give you the answers you seek."

"Well, that's just peachy, isn't it? I'm stuck in this creepy world. Someone stabbed a sword through my shoulder. I have no clue what's going on or why I'm some special snowflake everyone seems to want a piece of. And you... the most frustrating man I have ever met... Just leave me alone. Please. Send Finn to watch me or something. He's much better company."

Lochlan stared at her for a long moment, his eyes icing over. "No." He seemed to shake off whatever had come over him and pushed to his feet. "There is a shirt for you on the end of the bed. I will step outside for your human modesty."

"What about you?" She gestured to his blood-stained clothes.

"I do not have another garment, but it will only be a couple days until we reach the palace." His eyes flicked from her to the remaining strips of fabric before he turned to walk out.

"Wait," she called.

He didn't stop. She felt the bandage on her shoulder, knowing where the fabric came from. Lochlan cut up his only spare shirt for bandages, leaving him with memories of the battle caked into his clothes.

He'd said many things that altered how she saw this world, but maybe it was what he didn't say that mattered more.

Lochlan O'Shea was a man of secrets and hidden thoughts. She laid her head back, staring up at the canvas ceiling. How did a man she barely knew, one who spoke in grunts and scowls, make her feel safer than his brother ever had?

Griff had been a fantasy, one that crashed down around her when she learned none of it was real. Lochlan... he didn't put on faces, he didn't lie or connive.

But just like in Fargelsi, she was still his prisoner, and she couldn't forget that one simple fact.

Chapter 18

After another day in the saddle in the dry desert heat, Brea's arm throbbed beneath the cauterized flesh. It felt tight and hot, and she was restless.

"I thought I perturbed you," Brea muttered when Lochlan carried her into his tent.

"You do that quite well, Lady Brea. I've asked Lewis to make you something to help you sleep."

"Can you ask him to make an AC unit for the window?"

"We don't have windows in tents. You're such an odd girl." She thought she heard laughter as he laid her on a bedroll for the night.

"No blanket." She shoved his hand away. "Too hot."

"Today was a hot day. It will get cooler as we approach the palace."

"She still awake?" Finn ducked into the tent.

"Unfortunately." Brea groaned at the pounding in her head.

"I have some medicine for you from Lewis." Finn crouched beside her and helped her sit up. The simple wooden cup frothed with smoke and smelled like a dead moose's butt.

"Ugh, I'm not drinking that."

"Pour it down her throat," Lochlan ordered.

"Ignore him." Finn shot him a glare. "It will make you feel better, I promise. And it doesn't taste as bad as it smells."

Brea held the cup up to her lips and winced.

"It's best if you chug it," Finn said.

Brea took a tentative sip and gagged. "Ugh, that's worse than it smells, Finn!"

"That's why I told you to chug it." He rolled his eyes. "Just pretend it's wine and don't stop till you see the bottom of the cup."

"Fine. But this better make me feel better." Brea tipped the cup back and choked down the brown smoky concoction. "That was vile."

Brea burped and smoke flew out of her mouth. She'd normally be embarrassed but a warm fuzzy cloud settled over her.

"Oh, that's nice."

Finn helped ease her back onto her bedroll. She stroked his smooth face with her good hand.

"You're a nice person, Finn. Not like Mr. Grumpy Pants over there with his grunts and scowls."

Finn chuckled, brushing the sweaty strands of hair from her face. "I know I shouldn't laugh, but this girl is hilarious."

"She's a menace," Lochlan said.

Brea hummed in satisfaction. "My complements to Mr. Lewis. He should p-put that stuff on t-ap." She yawned, belched, and fell asleep.

"No! Myles!" Brea cried out, trying to reach her friend but the police officer refused to let her near him.

"The boy probably won't survive the ride to the hospital."

Those words gutted Brea all over again.

"She's burning up," Finn's voice reached her through the fog of her fever.

"Cut her bandages off," Lochlan ordered.

"Ouch," Brea muttered as the fabric peeled away from the crusty burned flesh on her arm.

"The wound is infected," Finn announced. "The medicine should have prevented this."

"I don't think my human half liked that stuff," Brea managed.

She screamed when Lochlan came at her with a knife. He held her down as he slipped the tip under the massive scab on her arm. Infection oozed out, and her stomach churned.

"We have to cool her down." Lochlan gathered her up in his arms.

"We're in the middle of the desert, Loch. How are you going to get her temperature down?" Finn followed them out of the tent.

Lochlan handed Brea to Finn and mounted his horse. Reaching down, he took her back into his arms.

"Ugh, no more riding. Take me to see Myles. He's in the hospital. They can give me a shot of antibiotics."

"What is she saying?"

"More human nonsense," Lochlan said. "I'll ride for Loch Langt. Meet us there."

"Will she make it that far?" Finn asked.

"What?" Brea struggled to fight through the fog of her mind.

"Shh, Lady Brea," Lochlan said in a soothing voice. "You'll be better soon. The cool waters of Langt is our best chance." He gathered the reins in his hands and took off, galloping across the dusty desert plains.

"Stay with me, Brea," Lochlan refused to let her sleep. "Tell me about your favorite *Harry Potter* movie."

"*Goblet of Fire*," she groaned. "Shoulda been two movies."

"That was a great book."

"I don't feel good, Loch." She curled against him, her skin on fire.

"We're almost there. I can see the lake just over the next rise. Once we get you cooled off, we'll have to work on that infection."

"Promise you won't cut off my arm." Brea blacked out before she heard his promise.

Cool water splashed against her legs as Lochlan rode his horse straight into Loch Langt.

"That's freezing," she complained.

"It's about to get a lot colder." He slid off the horse and carried her into the deep cold waters of Langt.

"Too cold." She squirmed against him, her teeth chattering.

"Take a deep breath, Brea." Loch held her against his chest, plunging them under the surface.

The water stabbed like a thousand tiny needles. But that wasn't good enough for Lochlan. Brea gasped for breath when they broke the surface, but he only stripped away her tunic and trousers until she was down to her undergarments in the icy water.

"Why are you doing this to me?" Tears slipped down her cheeks.

"To save your life. The water is freezing because your temperature is too high. You'll die if we don't get it down. Now, take another deep breath for me."

She barely got a breath in before they plunged beneath the surface again. Brea thrashed around until Lochlan pressed his palm against her chest, right above her heart. Everything slowed with the blue glow of his magic. They sank to the bottom of the lake as she shivered in his arms.

His blond hair swirled around them like a cloud, tangling with her dark tresses. Hers black as ebony and his pale as fine silver. Her lungs were about to burst when Lochlan propelled them back to the surface.

Brea gasped for air, her mind clearer than it had been all day.

"I can't take it much longer, Loch." She shook with tremors, and her lips turned blue.

"Let's get you warm and dry and see how you feel." He carried her out of the lake and wrapped a warm dry blanket around her. "We don't have much in the way of supplies, but I'll make a fire. Sit here and drink as much water as you can stomach. Sip slowly." He handed her his water skin.

Brea shivered under the hot sun and knew she was in trouble if the fever didn't break soon.

Sweat rolled down Lochlan's face as he built a roaring fire. He even gathered a pile of huge palm leaves to build a quick shade for her to lounge under.

"I'm afraid this is going to hurt, Brea." Lochlan pulled his knife from the pot of boiling water over the fire. "But I have to clean the infection out."

Brea nodded. "Do what you have to."

"Put this between your teeth and bite down." He slipped a piece of leather between her lips. "I'll try to hurry, but if you can pass out, don't fight it."

Brea screamed as the hot knife sliced through the remaining scab over her arm. Putrid infection seeped from the wound. Lochlan wiped it away with a strip of fabric he'd boiled with the knife. Strips from his only shirt.

When he squeezed her arm, stars danced in her eyes, and she mercifully passed out.

When she woke next, she floated in Lochlan's arms in the shallow water. It was pleasantly cool this time. Her back against his chest, she glanced at her shoulder under the water. Bright red blood seeped from the fresh opening, but the cool water numbed her flesh.

"Your fever broke about an hour ago. I think the worst of it is over."

"Thank you," she murmured, weak as a kitten. She couldn't manage more than that.

"My men will be here soon, and Lewis will make you another tonic for the pain. I've made a poultice that will help with the infection. It should be ready now."

Brea nodded, draping her arms around his neck as he lifted her from the water. "I am sorry to be such a burden." Her head lolled against his shoulder.

"It is not your fault. You were hurt in battle trying to save my life. I will be here to see you through this injury, no matter what you need. I am only sorry it will likely leave a scar."

Brea shrugged her good shoulder. "Scars are badass." She eyed the few she could see marking his chest and back.

Lochlan settled Brea under the makeshift shelter, though the sun was setting along the horizon now. A vivid green poultice warmed by the fire. "That smells awful."

"I made this while you were asleep. It is similar to the human Aloe Vera plant but with more advanced healing properties. It will pull the poison of inflammation from your arm. I should have sent someone out to find the herbs when you were first injured."

"It's okay, Loch. You couldn't have known about the infection."

His jaw muscles ticked as he painted a thick layer of the green goo over her arm, layering pieces of fabric over it to hold it in place.

"Lie still and try to sleep if you can. I'll work on finding some food." Lochlan draped the blanket over her and left her to rest on her own. They'd come a long way in the few days since he'd taken to leading her around on a leash. Then again, she couldn't run even if she wanted to.

The men arrived at dusk, and Brea ate two bowls of stew before Lewis approached with a new tonic he promised would help her heal and give her a good night's rest.

She woke again later that evening, feeling like a new woman after a dip in the lake to rinse off the remains of Lochlan's life-saving poultice.

"Feeling better?" Finn crouched beside the water's edge as she emerged, wrapping herself in a dry blanket.

"Weak, but I'm feeling clear headed now and much better."

"Want to see something you'll never forget?"

"Sure." She changed back into her clothes after making him turn around.

"This is a special place for the men," Finn explained as they walked back toward camp. "But it's a bit of walk to the next ridge. We'll ride if you don't mind."

"Okay." Honestly, she'd rather go back to sleep, but Finn really wanted her to see whatever he was so excited about.

"Have you ever seen a snúa aftur?"

"Bless you." Brea chuckled. "I have no idea what you just said."

"Look just there." Finn pointed up to the sky. Swirls of green, purple, and yellow lights illuminated the night.

"An Aurora Borealis."

"Bless you." Finn cracked a smile.

"That's what we call the Northern Lights in the human realm."

"Here it's the Southern Lights called snúa aftur. To the soldiers it means we're almost home. This will be our last night at camp."

"We'll reach the palace tomorrow?" Her nerves immediately spiraled into panic mode. "What does the Eldur queen want with me, Finn?"

"I don't know, Brea, but I know you can trust her with your life. She's a good woman and a fair ruler."

"Thank you for bringing me here." She settled onto the ground to watch the lights with the soldiers. "It's beautiful."

The cluster of soldiers were all silent as they watched the colors dance across the night sky. Brea leaned against Finn's shoulder, cradling her injured arm. It was such a soothing sight. The tension in her body relaxed as she watched a riot of colors shoot across the sky.

Each of the soldiers sent a spark of color into the sky to join the phenomenon.

"What are they doing?"

"It's their magic," Finn explained. "They're making wishes. It's an Eldur tradition."

"It's beautiful." Brea wished she could send up a streak of yellow, but she barely had the energy to keep her eyes open. "What do the colors mean?"

"It's like a signature." A tiny ball of orange left his fingertips.

"Each Fae's magic has a distinct color that connects their magic back to them. Families sometimes share a similar color, but not always. It depends on the strength of their magic and their heritage from both sides."

Brea wondered if the mystery of her own heritage would ever be so clear.

Chapter 19

"The Fargelsi palace is nice, I suppose, if you're into trees and flowers everywhere." Finn chomped on a piece of desert fruit that was somewhere between a pear and a peach. "But the Eldurian palace is really something special."

"Have you always lived at the palace?" Brea had gathered Finnegan Donovan was the son of soldier and had grown up with Lochlan. She appreciated his chatter. It kept her from thinking about the pain in her arm and the unpleasant experience that waited for her when they arrived at the palace.

"We have a family house in town, but we spend most of our time in the palace when I'm home."

"Finn made himself at home so often when we were boys, the queen gave him his own apartment so he'd stop sneaking into mine and Princess Alona's rooms." Lochlan rolled his eyes at his lifelong friend.

"Who is Alona?" Brea asked.

"Queen Faolan's daughter and the Princess of Eldur," Finn explained.

"Her mother must have had a time chasing after two young boys and a girl."

"Mothers." Finn corrected. "Alona has two mothers. Queen Faolan Cahill is the ruler of Eldur and gave birth to Alona. Queen Tierney Cahill is Faolan's wife."

"Cool." She was impressed with how they never seemed to fret about sexuality like humans did. But at the moment, Brea wouldn't care if they were queens of a dung heap if she could just get off this horse and sleep in a real bed and get some real painkillers for her arm. She was much better than she was two days ago, but the fever had left her exhausted and in need of rest.

"Look there," Lochlan murmured in her ear, pointing in the distance. "Your first look at the palace."

"Oh, it's so green." Brea hadn't expected that. After days of dry desert heat and miles and miles of red dirt and sand with the occasional sparse forest of stunted trees, the Eldurian palace sat like a jewel along the horizon.

"The Dalur River flows through the south eastern corner of Eldur, creating a fertile valley, much cooler than the desert."

"It's beautiful." Brea squinted to see the many-tiered structure that rose from the green valley like a pyramid. Rich green plant life sprouted from each tier where vines crept down the walls. "It looks like the Hanging Gardens of Babylon."

"Very good assessment, Brea." Lochlan sounded impressed. "It's not the Hanging Gardens of the ancient human world, but it's close enough to make you wonder if the legend of the Babylonian gardens might have been rooted in fae lore."

Other structures rose behind the gardens. Tall towers with bulbous domes covered in brightly colored mosaic tiles.

"Where are we going?" Brea frowned when they turned away from the palace.

"There is a river and a canyon between us and the palace," Finn explained. "We'll ride up through the canyon where you'll see the great city of Raudur."

"The scenic route. Great." Any other day she would be pleased to see all the exotic city had to offer.

"We will be there soon, and you can rest. This is the most direct path home," Lochlan murmured for her benefit. "The palace entrance lies under the gardens and towers. It's a sight you won't want to miss."

Even as weary as she was, Brea couldn't help getting caught up in their excitement of homecoming. She just hoped she could truly trust Finn and Lochlan when they said she had nothing to fear from the Eldur queen.

The road began to climb and narrow as they headed into the canyon.

"Your roads could use some guardrails." Brea eyed the lazy Dalur River hundreds of feet below them. She shrank against Lochlan, suddenly grateful he insisted she ride with him. Stone bridges arched across the narrow canyon at different intervals. They were like highways, guiding the city dwellers to different parts of the city carved into the sheer sides of the canyon.

Brea gawked at the archways and partial domes emerging from the desert rock on either side of the river. Brightly painted doorways and arches broke up the monotony of the dusty red stone.

They made their way along the winding roads leading through the city to the palace gates. Exotic flowers bloomed in gardens and pots, and spicy aromas filled the marketplace, making Brea's mouth water and her stomach rumble. It was the most exciting city she'd ever seen.

As they neared the largest bridge, Brea spotted the palace entrance. Tall arched doors stood wide open, welcoming all citizens to the home of their queen. The tiered gardens sat atop the gates like the crowning jewel of Eldur's greatest city.

"What does your queen want with me?" Brea asked the question for the last time.

"I truly do not know, Lady Brea," Finn said. "But I promise she has nothing nefarious in mind. I believe she simply wanted to save you from Queen Regan's grip. To give you a chance to understand what is at stake before you make any lasting decisions."

"If that is the case, then I am grateful for the meddling. I just wish I understood why all these queens seem to think I'm so important."

"Perhaps Queen Faolan will have the answers you seek."

"Let's hope." Brea held her breath as they crossed the arched bridge—apparently the crazy Eldurians were daredevils who didn't see the sense in safety railings.

Beyond the palace gates stood an exotic courtyard complete with splashing fountains and brightly colored flowers and plants. Brea swore she saw several parrots hanging out in the trees.

Lochlan dismounted and tossed the reins to a servant before he helped Brea down. "Can you walk, or do you need help."

Brea closed her eyes, feeling a little dizzy. "I'm okay. I'd like to walk on my own if I'm about to meet any queens."

"I'm sure we'll have a chance to rest and change before she summons us."

"Lochlan? Is he here?" A beautiful raven-haired woman stood on a balcony overlooking the courtyard.

"Or not." Lochlan shrugged. "Yes, my queen."

Lochlan crossed the bricked courtyard to meet Queen Faolan as she rushed down the carved stone stairs. She was a petite woman with dark eyes and a tanned complexion. Next to Lochlan she looked like a doll. A terrified doll.

"They've taken Alona." She took his hands in hers. Her sad eyes drank him in like a long-lost son.

"Taken?" He stared at the queen, then something snapped inside him as a heartbroken look swept across his face.

"Where?" Finn rushed to the queen's side, an equal look of heartbreak on his face as well.

"More than a week ago. She was on her way to Sandur to visit Lady Driscoll when your uncle's men attacked her camp at Loch Sol. They've taken her to Fargelsi."

"We will leave at once." Lochlan released her hands.

"Eamon Donovan was with her when she was taken. He escaped with most of his men and sent word back. He's trying to get through the Gelsi border as we speak. He loves her like a daughter, he will bring her home."

"I will kill my brother for his part in this," Lochlan snarled.

"A week ago?" Brea's small voice broke the tension between them.

"Do you know something?" Finn came to her side. "Anything that might help us find the princess?"

Brea counted the days since the night she escaped Fargelsi. It felt like a lifetime ago, but it was no more than seven days ago. "Griffin left on an unexpected mission for Regan just before the farewell banquet for the Iskalt delegation. The timing would be about right."

"If he took her, she'll be in the dungeons by now." Lochlan ran a frustrated hand through his hair as he turned toward Brea. She suddenly felt like a dirty and travel-worn sloth. Wrapping her threadbare blanket around her like a shawl to cover her stained clothes she glanced at the distraught queen.

"Brea Robinson. It's lovely to meet you." Faolan took an awkward step forward. "I am sorry for everything you've been through at the Fargelsi court. That was never my intention. I had hoped to bring you here safely and avoid such confusion altogether. I'm sure you have many questions for me, but now is not the time. We must see to my daughter."

"I do." Brea gave a half-hearted curtsy. "Have questions, I mean." She was suddenly feeling lightheaded and a little woozy.

Finn reached out to catch her as she stumbled, and her shawl-blanket fell away from her arm.

"Lochlan, she's hurt." The queen gasped. "What happened?"

"We had a run in with some of my uncle's men. It seems the Fargelsi queen will stop at nothing to get her hands on both women. Brea was injured and suffered an infection."

"Finn, get her inside. I'll call the healers to see to her." Faolan ran back up the steps. "Lochlan, meet me in the throne room in twenty minutes." The tiny queen barked orders as Finn swept Brea up in his arms. "Rowena, see to the girl."

Finn carried her inside the palace residence where a servant woman waited to escort them to what would be Brea's rooms. Inside, the palace was cool and shady with fresh breezes flowing from room to room. Brea heard the splash of fountains and birds chirping throughout the great hall. It was like one big garden with walls and doors open to the outside.

"In here, Sir Finn." The servant woman rushed to open a pair of double doors. "Let's get the Lady Brea settled and comfortable." She bustled about the room, opening windows and fussing with the curtains.

Finn set her on a mahogany settee with a needlepoint cushion. Sweeping the hair back from her face, he crouched before her. "Are you feeling okay?"

She nodded, staring around the room. "Just tired and a bit overwhelmed."

"I need to speak with the queen. Rowena will take good care of you." She could sense his urgency to get rid of her so he could find out the details of Alona's situation.

"Go, I'll be fine." She hugged the blanket around her shoulders.

He didn't hesitate, and a moment later Brea found herself alone with a new servant.

"Would you like a cool bath, my Lady?"

"Please call me Brea. And yes, a bath sounds wonderful."

"Oh, I couldn't do that, my Lady. It wouldn't be proper." Rowena stared at Brea with tears in her eyes before she darted into an adjoining room to see to Brea's bath.

Suddenly she felt like she was back at square one, and she really missed Neeve. Her rooms were every bit as nice as the ones she'd had in Fargelsi, but the decor was like a different world—which she supposed was fairly accurate. Brea stood to explore her surroundings. Rich dark wood furniture filled the sitting room and silk fabrics billowed in the windows that faced the canyon. A small balcony overlooked the courtyard below. Just off the sitting room was a bedroom with the most enormous bed she'd ever seen. Big windows let the sunlight in to shine on the bed.

A small dark room occupied the back of the suite. Brea peeked into the room and was greeted with a burst of cool air. It was a grotto carved into the canyon walls. This would be the best place to retreat during the hottest part of the day. There was even a daybed there for napping.

"Lady Brea, your bath is ready," Rowena called from the sitting room.

"Thank you." She followed the servant with the round, sweet face into a garden room with open skies and leafy green plants. A sunken bathtub the size of a pool occupied the center of the bathroom. Exotic scented flower petals floated in the water.

"It's beautiful, thank you so much." Brea folded her tattered blanket, eager to sink into the bath for a nice long, quiet soak.

"I'll see to your clothes and bring you something to eat. Enjoy your bath, my Lady." She smiled and backed out of the room. "It really is lovely to meet you, Lady Brea."

Finally alone for the first time in ages, Brea heaved a deep sigh. Shedding her stained and travel-worn clothes, she sank into the deep bath trying not to feel sorry for herself.

Since the moment she escaped the palace in Gelsi, Brea had been running. Running from a bad situation into the unknown. Now that she was here—in the very place she'd once feared the most—she didn't know what to expect next.

After her bath, Brea felt blissfully clean and exhausted beyond belief. She didn't have the energy to contemplate another palace full of secrets and lies. Her arrival here in Eldur reminded her too much of her arrival in Fargelsi when everything was exciting and new and she had no reason to suspect anyone was lying.

Brea found a soft silken sleeping gown and crawled into bed. Thoughts of Myles drifted through her mind, wondering if she'd ever see him again. If he would ever forgive her. If she'd even live through this experience to find out one way or another if their friendship was broken beyond repair.

Tears rolled down Brea's face as she realized she even missed Griff and his ability to make her smile.

Despite all the luxury around her. Despite knowing she was part fae and possessed magic, that her mental illness was just another lie, Brea wanted to go home to her familiar and predictable life with her best friend, Myles.

Chapter 20

Dried tears crusted the corner of Brea's eyelids as she tried to pry them open. Footsteps sounded against the stone floor, and she froze. Someone was in her room. She'd never get used to servants constantly being around and having very little time on her own. For once, she wished everyone would just leave her to feel sorry for herself.

She rolled over to see a figure illuminated by the silver glow of the moon. The intruder stood looking out the big windows at the sprawling Eldur palace.

Another palace. A different queen. Still not the human world.

She cleared her throat and the woman turned, revealing the face of the Eldur queen who'd only given Brea a moment of attention when she first arrived.

Brea pushed herself up in bed and scooted back against the headboard. Queen Faolan had the windows open, letting in the warm night air. It blew dark hair away from her face, revealing blazing yellow eyes that cut through the darkness of the night.

"What do you want with me?" The whispered words were the

first Brea could think of. For some reason, two queens abducted her, and a king tried to kill her. None of it made any sense. She didn't know if she believed Griff's words about a prophecy any longer, not after finding out they really only wanted her to give him legitimacy.

There had to be a real reason why she—normal girl Brea Robinson—was such a hot commodity to the royals of the fae world. She cringed at the thought.

The queen's eyes swirled before settling into a more natural amber color. "You're not Alona."

Brea's brow creased. "I'm Brea Robinson."

She nodded. "Yes, yes, I know that. But I expected some... feeling that would make me believe I had my daughter back. She's been gone for months now, and we've had no request for ransom. That's why I sent Lochlan into the human realm. I had to protect my daughter no matter what. Everything has been to protect the lineage." She carved a path across the room and back again, her footsteps heavy as she paced.

Nothing she said made any sense.

Her entire body stilled, and she turned back to face Brea. "You're not her!"

Queen Faolan's fiery gaze burned yellow again, and Brea could hardly breathe. *Dragon queen. Dragon queen. Dragon queen.* The words repeated in her mind, stirring fear in Brea's gut. Her magic latched onto the emotion, refusing to let it go away. It built up, begging for release.

She tilted her head to the side, trying to hold it back, knowing blasting the queen with magic wouldn't win her any favors.

The queen's eyes widened. "Your magic... your eyes." Her voice lowered to a whisper. "Yellow."

Brea couldn't handle her scrutiny any longer. "My eyes are and have always been blue." It was one of the only traits she inherited from her mother. "You're the one with the yellow eyes." *Dragon Queen,* she called her in her head.

Lochlan and Finn trusted this woman, but Brea barely knew them, and she'd been burned before.

Queen Faolan moved closer to the bed. "My eyes turn yellow when I am controlling my magic—which I'm trying very hard to do right now despite the sun not being out at this hour."

"Right, well I won't be your prisoner. Been there, done that." She shoved the fear she felt away. There was nothing to lose anymore because everything had already been taken from her. "I am only here because your dog Lochlan tied me up, took me into battle, and said some very grumpy things. The human world sucks, but it's better than this place, and I expect you to take me back there."

The queen's eyes flashed, and she turned away, crossing her arms over her chest. "I sent Lochlan to bring you here from the human world. Do you know what that cost? My most trusted man wasn't here to protect my daughter when she was taken." She looked back over her shoulder. Tears shone in her eyes, but she blinked them away and strode from the room.

Kicking the thin sheet off her legs, Brea scrambled from the bed, half expecting her door to be locked.

When she pulled, it clicked open, revealing a long, dark hallway, deserted in the dead of night. Starlight spilled across her path under archways leading to the outside. In the still of the night, everything was quiet save for the slow trickling of fountains.

As her feet hit warm bricks, she realized she'd forgotten to put on anything other than the pale pink silk sleeping gown draped over her shoulders. She stared down at her legs peeking past the trim, remembering what Lochlan said about her human modesty. The fae didn't care if she revealed herself here at court because they wouldn't look. A body was not the fascination to them that it was for humans.

Still, she'd have killed for a razor and gigantic bottle of shaving cream so she didn't feel like a woolly mammoth in the short gown.

Archways led from courtyards to doors she hadn't yet seen behind. The Eldur palace was larger than the one in Fargelsi and even more grand. Everything seemed to be centered around the outdoors—something she hadn't expected in a desert kingdom.

Stepping into one of the many courtyards, a grand fountain depicting two male fae in a state of… erm… bliss had her face heating again. She averted her eyes from their naked bodies and lifted them to the clear sky above, wondering if they were the same stars hanging above her home in Ohio.

She expected to see dragons flying overhead, their giant wings silhouetted against the moon. Okay, expected was probably the wrong word. She'd hoped to see them, for them to be real.

"What do you think you'll find in the stars?" Finn's voice startled her out of her dream of dragons.

She looked back over her shoulder to where he stood leaning against the doorway into what looked like a library. "Dragons." It sounded stupid after she said it.

He shrugged. "I'm not sure exactly what a dragon is, but I hope you find it."

She laughed at that. "Well, there's my answer. No dragons. They're these giant winged reptiles that breathe fire and destroy cities."

"Ah, now I remember. Alona was obsessed with such creatures. She read about them in Lochlan's human books he brought back and always said a desert kingdom should have such animals."

Brea crossed the courtyard to him. As she got closer, she could make out the tired expression on his face. His lips drew down into a frown, but it was his eyes that spoke of hidden pain. "Are you okay, Finn?"

"I should be asking you that. You've arrived at yet another palace—injured I might add. Are you feeling okay? I wanted to make sure you don't take anything the queen says personally. She isn't in a good place right now, so she'll come see you soon, I'm sure."

"She already did." She'd never forget the queen's desperate words or incoherent babbling.

Not giving him a chance to respond, she walked past him into the library, her breath rushing out of her lungs at the sight before her.

Finn lifted a hand, illuminated the room, revealing bookshelves as high as she could see. Painted ceilings depicted grand adventures to preside over what must be thousands of books. Leather-bound tomes crowded the shelves in the circular room.

"This was Alona's favorite place in the entire palace." Finn ran a finger along a line of embossed spines. "She and Lochlan spent many hours together sprawled across the benches along the back wall."

He led her through the shelves to where a reading nook sat against a window overlooking a garden. Bench wasn't the right word. It was more like an extra-wide couch carved right into the wall, shielding it from view of the rest of the library. Pillows lined the surface. It was built up over a row of three-shelf bookcases.

Brea bent to examine the books. "*Harry Potter*," she whispered. "*Game of Thrones*." And on it went. *Lord of the Rings*. *His Dark Materials*. The entire collections by Robin Hobb and David Eddings.

Finn sat on the bench. "Every time Lochlan went to the human realm, he returned with stacks of books. For weeks, he'd spend every spare moment with Alona devouring the words." He picked up a book sitting on the arm of the bench and held it out to Brea. "This was what she was reading right before she left."

"*A Court of Thorns and Roses*." Brea took the book. "Myles read this, and I had to hear endlessly about it."

"Alona thought it was quite funny the humans were writing about fae as if they knew anything about us except old lore we allowed into story books many generations ago."

She offered the book back, but he shook his head and she set it on one of the shelves.

Finn lay back, his eyes focusing on the beautiful ceiling overhead. "Here in the desert, we don't get a lot of rain, but when it does come, it stays for days, sometimes weeks. In the past, if my training was cancelled, I'd join Alona. We laid here and talked of fantasy futures, so different from the ones we could have."

"You can have any future you choose." It was a stock line humans said to each other, but rarely was it true.

"Come now, Brea, do not start lying to me now. Look around. We are in a palace. Do not for one moment think any of us have a choice in our path."

This wasn't the boisterous happy man she'd traveled with from the Vatlands. "Has something happened, Finn?"

He sighed. "Just being here... Everything reminds me of Alona."

Brea climbed up next to him and lay back. "She's not just the princess to you, is she?" She looked sideways at him and watched a tear curve over his cheek.

"Have you ever loved someone so much it killed you when they were gone?"

She wanted to say no, to ignore that kind of pain. She knew now she'd never loved Griff. It had been a trick she played on herself in her desperation to not be alone in a foreign world. But Myles? He was her person, her other half. It wasn't a romantic kind of love, but it was just as strong. When she spoke, her voice was no more than a whisper.

"You feel as if you're no longer alive, like your heart refuses to beat until you see them again."

Finn's hand found hers, threading their fingers together. "We wish the pain away, but in the same breath we hold onto it as a reminder of what they were to us."

"Are."

"What?" He rolled his head to look at her.

"What they are to us. Alona was taken, but she might yet be alive." Just like Myles.

"She has to be. If she comes back to us, I'm going to lose her again, but at least she'll be safe."

"Why do you have to lose her?" Brea would never understand a world in which people could love each other and not be together.

"Because, Brea, Alona has no magic."

"I don't know what that means."

His voice shook as he explained. "Fae born without magic cannot remain among the noble or royal classes beyond coming of age. Upon her eighteenth birthday, she must join the servant class, leaving her family behind."

Brea sat up. "But that's not fair! It's cruel." She suddenly felt for this girl she'd never met, the one mourned by both the queen and this soldier beside her.

"It is our way." He sat, turning to face her. "Magic is everything to the fae."

Her respect for the fae dwindled to nothing. "It isn't right. Magic isn't more important than family." She'd never turn her back on Myles no matter what happened to her, and she refused to let this missing princess suffer her fate. "Alona will be found, Finn. And when she is, you and I will find a way to save her from such a stupid fae tradition. Maybe we can even convince douchey Lochlan to help."

One corner of his mouth curved up. "Maybe you are just what our kingdom needs. Someone to challenge what we all think we know."

"If you're telling me to be a pain in the butt, I can totally do that. It's basically my personality. But you listen to me, Finn. You and I are friends now."

He opened his mouth to speak, but she shushed him.

"I don't care if Loch tells you to leave me alone, you will not do that. I'm a bit short on friends at the moment. You can be my fairy whisperer, making sure I don't embarrass myself. And one day, we will get to see our people again—the people we love don't get to just disappear from our lives."

His eyes glistened with unshed tears as he nodded. "I'd very much like us to be friends. I just have one question first."

"Go for it."

"Lochlan told me you're calling him douchey Lochlan because you think him noble, but that isn't what the human word means, is it?"

She flashed him a grin and scooted to the edge of the bench to climb off. "Goodnight, Finn."

She turned to walk around a shelf, colliding with a giant wall of flesh. Gripping her shoulder as pain seared from the contact, she looked up into Lochlan's stormy face.

"Did you love my brother?"

Chapter 21

Lochlan's hazy eyes darted around the room before landing on Brea, a mix of anger and drunken desperation on his face.

"What?" She only breathed the word.

"Were you in love with my brother?" he slurred. "I heard you talking to Finn about loving so much it killed you to lose them." He leaned close, sneering in a very Lochlan-like way. "You didn't lose him, Lady Brea, you ran."

"Loch." Finn appeared behind Brea, resting a hand on her shoulder. "Stop this nonsense."

"I used to love him too, Brea," he went on, stumbling back as if he couldn't control his own steps. "Griff is a master manipulator. He makes you believe you're part of his family before stabbing you in the back. Don't waste your breath missing him."

Anger burned through her, but it didn't latch onto her magic, not the way fear seemed to be able to. As she looked at the pathetic excuse for Lochlan, she wasn't afraid.

He was wrong. She didn't love Griff. But maybe he wasn't so different from his brother. They both had a cruel streak a mile wide.

"I don't have to answer to you." She tried to push past him, but he grabbed her arm.

"Loch," Finn snapped. "Let her go."

"Not until I know why."

"Why what?" Her voice shook with rage. "Why I let him kiss me? Why I sought him out in the dead of night to crawl into his bed?" She narrowed her eyes. "Because I enjoyed it. Do I need more reason than that?"

His grip tightened. "Griff could have killed you."

As she studied his slack expression, she realized why he was so upset. Alona. Whether he was in love with her or not, she didn't know, but Lochlan knew the truth of why his queen wanted Brea. He'd lied to her just like his brother before him. And something about whatever knowledge he possessed made him intensely protective of her.

Finn put a hand on Lochlan's arm. "Stop this."

"Don't you see it, Finn? Brea Robinson is the reason Alona was taken." The queen had said the same thing, but she didn't understand it.

"Why? How are we connected?" What did a fae princess and a half-human girl have in common?

Lochlan released her, turning with a huff. He paced back toward them, his face a storm cloud of emotions. "Griff knew. He knew!"

"Knew what?"

"What our parents died for." He wobbled where he stood before leaning against a bookshelf to stay upright. "He knew kidnapping Queen Faolan's daughter would force the truth into the light. He tried to take you both as proof, but you ran away before he could come back with Alona."

"I still don't understand!" The words exploded out of her. She was tired, so tired, of all the half-truths and semi-lies.

Lochlan turned on her, his jaw clenched. "Alona is like my sister. You... you're nothing."

Tears built in her eyes at his words. "If I'm nothing, why did you go to such lengths to save my life?"

"I had orders." He ran a hand through his hair, tugging wildly at the ends as his breathing grew more erratic. "I can't... control..." He buried his face in his hands as his entire body shook.

"Brea," Finn yelled. "He's losing control of his magic. Get out of —" That was the last word she heard before light encompassed the room, knocking the breath from her lungs as she slammed back into a bookshelf, pain exploding from her shoulder as blackness crept across her vision. Again.

Just another day in the fae world, another time waking up in a strange place after being knocked out.

A groan reverberated from Brea's throat as she flexed her limbs, making sure everything still worked. When she finally opened her eyes, she found a tall broad-shouldered woman with cherry red hair and kind eyes staring down at her.

"Amazonian," she whispered.

"What?" A concerned look flashed across the woman's face.

"Nothing." Brea shut her eyes as pain throbbed in her temple.

"How are you feeling, dear?" Her voice was like a quiet symphony.

"Are you a healer?" She cracked one eye open. "Because if you are, I could totally do with some drugs right now."

"Ah yes, Lochlan did tell me of your strange human speak."

"Lochlan?" Her eyes shot open. "Is he okay?" The last she remembered he'd lost control of his magic.

"Yes, he sat beside your bed with Finn most of the night. He can't forgive himself for hurting you."

"It wasn't his fault. His magic... I saw it take control of him. He couldn't stop it."

"I know that, dear, and so do you. But Lochlan is a stubborn man who likes to believe everything bad is his fault."

"Where is he?" She tried to sit up. "I want to speak with him."

"He left with Finn at daybreak to follow a lead in the search for Alona. In truth, I wanted to be by myself when I met you."

"Who are you?"

"My name is Tierney. I am the queen consort of Eldur."

"You mean—"

Tierney nodded with a smile. "I am Queen Faolan's wife."

Brea already felt more comfortable in this woman's presence than the queen. "It's nice to meet you."

"Darling, I have longed to meet you since I first heard of your existence."

"Why? No one will give me any answers."

She brushed hair away from Brea's forehead. "Oh dear, I have quite the story to spin. My wife would have us wait for the right time, but you have waited long enough. And frankly, Faolan could use something good right now."

"Good?"

"You, Brea. You are good."

For the first time since learning the truth of her aunt in Eldur, Brea believed someone was finally going to be honest with her. "Why am I here?"

"Because, Brea Robinson, you were born in the fae realm."

Brea's heart stopped as her mind tried to grasp that piece of information. "That's impossible. My mom—"

"Is not your mother. You're a changeling, Brea."

"A what-ling?"

"When you were born, your fae mother wanted to protect you. But your father was of the royal line of Fargelsi. That kingdom believed you belonged to them and tried to make it so. They needed an heir after your father died and his sister took the throne. They sent many people to abduct you, but the kingdoms of Eldur and Iskalt protected you. Together, they decided you weren't safe in the fae world."

"Wait, so you're saying I'm not half-fae?"

"No, Brea, this is your world completely. You mother sent her greatest friends to exchange you with a human child. It angered Fargelsi, but they did not know of your whereabouts, and you were safe."

"Then why am I here if I was safe? Why did Lochlan and Griff come for me?"

"Because Queen Regan grows in power, and it was time to bring you home before you gain full use of your magic when you come of age. With Griffin on Regan's side, it was only a matter of time before she found you."

"Home?" Brea's gasp made Rowena come running from across the room, but Tierney waved her away. Brea recalled the bits of information she'd learned before. Princess Alona had no magic. Was she the human girl? Regan tried to keep Brea in Fargelsi through marriage, thus securing the throne.

And Queen Faolan... her rambling... the way she'd stared at Brea as if trying to see something that wasn't there.

"Queen Faolan is my mother." The words felt right, somehow, as if a piece of herself fit into place as soon as she said them. "I belong here, in Eldur," she whispered to herself. For the first time in her life, someone was saying she had a place in the world.

The Robinsons in Ohio with their drinking and cruel words didn't define her. She didn't come from them. They were Alona's parents.

Tears flowed freely down her face as she looked at the only woman brave enough to tell her. Lochlan had known, she was sure of it. Yet, she couldn't muster up the anger for him.

Not when she wanted this truth so badly.

"Can I..." She sucked in a breath. "Can I see her?"

Tierney's shining eyes met hers, and she nodded. "She will be vexed I told you, but you aren't the only one who needs something to hold onto, Brea. Just... be patient with her. Recovering one daughter does not lessen the pain of losing another."

Tierney gestured to Rowena to help Brea from the bed. Her feet hit the stone floor and she no longer felt strange about wandering the palace in a sleeping gown. Rowena helped her into the hall, but Brea shrugged off her hand and started running, having no idea where she needed to go.

Tierney caught up to her, grabbing her hand and running to match Brea's speed. She led her through the labyrinth of half-covered walkways and courtyards. They stopped outside a set of high wooden double doors.

"The throne room," Tierney whispered, gesturing to the guards to open the doors. "She will be alone at this time of day while she waits to receive her people."

The doors opened, revealing a long white carpet meandering through sandstone pillars wrapped in pale pink silks.

Queen Faolan relaxed on a gilded golden throne with purple cushions to keep her in comfort. She leaned her head back, closing her eyes, a troubled expression on her face.

Tierney prodded Brea forward.

Brea's bare feet hit the carpet, leaving indented footprints behind her as if marking this day, showing that she was there.

Her breath rattled in her lungs, drowning out the pounding of her heart. The pain in her shoulder and head seemed to fade into the background as Brea searched the woman before her for the similarities she'd never found in her mother.

"*Your eyes,*" she'd said. Did they blaze yellow with her magic? Was that a family trait?

Full fae. It made sense now. Why her Aunt Regan wanted her. Why they were attacked on the road.

Lochlan's disdain.

One day, she hoped to help him find the woman who'd been like his sister.

She stopped at the bottom of a set of stairs leading to the throne, and only one word came out. "Mom?" She cleared her throat, realizing that must be a human word. "Mother."

Queen's Faolan's eyes snapped open, settling on Brea with an intensity that should have scared her. She flicked them to her wife who stood watching with tears streaming down her face. Brea glanced back over her shoulder before facing her mom again.

"Is it true?"

Her mother covered her mouth with her hand.

Brea stepped closer. "Please, tell me it's true."

The queen, unable to speak, nodded as her eyes glassed over. Brea had longed to go back to the human realm since the moment Griff pulled her through a portal, but as she stood looking at the woman who put her there, who subjected her to a life of being named crazy and insane, she didn't know what she wanted.

"Do you have any idea what my life has been like?" She stumbled back, her emotions breaking free in a cascade of tears. "H-how..."

Her mom scrambled from her throne and ran down the steps, crushing Brea into her arms. "My dear." She wiped tears from Brea's face and looked into her eyes. "It was far better than letting the Fargelsians get their hands on you."

"And what of Alona? You ripped her from the Robinsons."

"She has had a good life here. I promise you."

Until they forced her into the servant class. But Brea didn't have the energy to argue the morals of exchanging a fae child for a human one.

"Mother." She buried her face in her mom's shoulder. "Why didn't you tell me last night?"

"I don't know. My heart is broken, child. Alona is missing, and to think of everything you've been through." She rested her chin on Brea's head. "It's over now for you. You're safe here. This is your home."

The truth in her mother's words didn't hit her until right then. This information broke her open, letting loose a million questions she feared to ask. But she could rest now because she was safe.

Tierney joined them, wrapping both her wife and new daughter in her long arms.

"They'll bring her back," Brea whispered. "Lochlan and Finn will find Alona."

They had to.

Brea finally found a place she was meant to be, a mother—two of them!—and people she cared about—even douchey Loch. But none of them were whole without their missing princess.

Brea's mom cancelled the morning sessions in the throne room and spent hours eating a way-too-large breakfast with Brea and Tierney. They smiled and laughed, but a tension ran beneath every action, a sadness.

By the time Brea finally made it back to her rooms, Rowena awaited her, chastisement in her eyes at the sight of Brea still in her sleeping gown.

After changing into a loose-fitting dress—much better than what they'd made her wear in Fargelsi—Brea returned to the courtyard with the fountain statue of naked men.

Sunlight glared off shining stones, sending light back into the atmosphere. The fountain water sparkled where it rippled. She doubted the fae had similar traditions to the humans where they made wishes in fountains, but there was always a time to start.

Thinking of the look on Rowena's face when Brea asked for a small coin, she laughed. The servant couldn't understand what she'd need with money, but she'd brought her one anyway.

Brea flipped the silver coin over in her palm, feeling the smooth surface against her palm. Everything she'd ever dreamed of and more had suddenly come true. She had a family who cared about her, despite the fact they didn't know her. A palace surrounding her that no human girl dreaming of princesses could even imagine.

And best of all... no one doubted her. She'd spent her life seeing things others said couldn't possibly exist. The Clarkson Institute was a part of her past now.

But there was one thing this world still needed, one thing that kept her from the happiness she should feel.

Lowering herself to the short stone wall surrounding the fountain, she bent over and ran her hand along the surface, watching the disturbance the action caused. That's what Brea had always been. A disturbance.

But maybe that was okay. Her life wasn't normal by any means, and she didn't want it to be.

She brought the coin to her lips, pressing a kiss to it as she held the wish in her mind and heart. After a beat of hesitation, she lifted her hand and tossed the coin into the glimmering water, watching it sink down to the depths of the fountain.

A smile spread across her lips. "That wish was for you, Myles."

She patted the stone and stood, unable to stop the laugh bubbling past her lips. Because she knew without a shadow of a doubt now. Myles was alive.

"I'm going to see you again one day."

Brea Robinson wasn't a murderer. She hadn't killed her best friend. And he'd forgive her for everything else, just like she'd finally forgiven herself.

Guilt was a human emotion, one with no purpose.

And Brea wasn't human, not even a little.

She was no longer a lie.

She was fae, and she was home.

EPILOGUE
ALONA CAHILL

The constant drip, drip, drip noise drove Alona mad. Some days she counted the drips until she fell asleep only to wake up to another day of nothing but darkness, damp walls, and the constant drip.

Alona had never thirsted for magic the way some of the serving class did. But right now, she'd give almost anything to have been born with magic just for the ability to create fire for warmth and light.

"What does Regan want with me?" she asked the walls of her cell. "I am nothing but a useless princess destined to become a maid. I have no value as a bargaining tool beyond my mothers' love for me." And they would never compromise the future of Eldur just for her. That was too high a price to pay for their daughter's freedom. Regan had to know that.

The drip, drip, drip faded at the sound of footsteps approaching her cell. Alona hadn't seen a soul since her arrival in the dungeon. Her food and water appeared once a day on the table in the far corner of the cell. That was perhaps the worst part of her captivity. The solitude and the drip, drip, drip.

"Let's go, Princess. The queen has summoned you." A Fargelsi servant scraped a key in the lock and opened the heavy wooden door of her cell.

Alona scrambled to her feet, eager to leave the dungeon behind, if only to hear Queen Regan's grand standing about her plans for Alona.

The man was silent as he escorted her up the winding stairs to the servant's quarters and past the kitchens. Alona's stomach growled at the savory aromas wafting into the halls.

The Fargelsi palace was beautiful but a far cry from the one she grew up in. There was a cold, almost sinister quality about the palace that made her uneasy. Like the very walls were watching her every move.

The servant guided her into a throne room where the queen waited for her. Alona couldn't fathom what Regan could possibly want with her. Still, she stood proudly in front of the queen, refusing to bow as befitting her station. Alona was the princess of Eldur—at least for a few more months—and she regarded the queen as a rival and not a superior.

"You wanted to speak with me?" Alona was proud her voice didn't shake at all. The Gelsi queen was known for her cruelty and her ruthless magic, and here stood Alona, powerless in front of her. Her traveling clothes stained and torn.

"Welcome to Fargelsi, *Princess*." The queen's voice held a note of amusement.

Alona noticed the man seated beside the queen. "Callum O'Shea," Alona addressed him. "It surprises me to see you here in attendance of the Gelsi queen."

"You will address me as King Callum of Iskalt." His demeanor was every bit as cold as the kingdom he stole from his nephew.

"I will call you nothing of the sort. Eldur recognizes no King of

Iskalt other than the true heir, Lochlan O'Shea. You may have allied with Fargelsi, but your nephew will never allow it."

"You do not speak for Eldur, child." Queen Regan peered down her nose at Alona. "You are nothing to Eldur or any fae realm. You have no magic. You have no voice."

"Until I come of age, I am a voice of Eldur." Alona squared her shoulders. "And you have committed a crime by taking me from my kingdom."

"What do you know of the girl, Brea Robinson?" Regan asked.

"Who?" Alona hadn't known what to expect of this summons, but this wasn't it.

"She doesn't know." Another voice joined the queen's. Alona's eyes fell to the man standing in the darkness behind the queen's throne.

"Griffin?" She'd always felt sorry for Lochlan's brother, raised in the Gelsi court. If he was anything like his brother, he wouldn't condone any of this. "You know she can't be trusted, Griffin." She begged him with her eyes to end this. To help her escape whatever the queen had in store for her, but he refused to meet her eyes.

"She raised me, Alona." Griffin stepped forward. "Queen Regan is the only mother I've ever known."

"Speaking of mothers," Regan interjected, patting Griffin's hand as if to tell him he was a good boy. "Did you know you were a changeling, dear?" Regan batted her eyelashes.

"A changeling?"

"Of course, you little fool. Your mother is a weak queen, but even she would have given birth to a child with magic. She knew I would stop at nothing to take my brother's child so she switched her with a human girl. Her daughter has lived in the human world, leaving you, a human, to stand in as her only child who could never inherit her throne. She would have me believe Brandon's child was a weakling."

"No." Alona's legs trembled beneath her.

"Brea Robinson is the true heir of Eldur. The daughter of Queen

Faolan and my late brother, King Brandon O'Rourke. She was to be betrothed to Griffin before she escaped the palace."

Alona gasped, realizing in an instant what the queen had planned. "You can't be serious?"

"You are smarter than your mother. Well, the woman who raised you." Regan smiled a cruel smile.

"I just don't get how this works in your favor." Alona stood straight. She could freak out later. "If this Brea girl is your niece and she marries your ward, Griffin, then Brea's child—a child who would share blood with you—would be your blood heir."

"Correct."

"You've gone a very long time without a blood heir, Regan." Alona smiled, crossing her arms behind her back. "This future child you've planned for would strengthen your reign and your hold on Fargelsi for years to come. But you've never been satisfied with just Fargelsi.

"If what you say is true, then Brea is my mother's blood heir. You intend to have her take Eldur and do your bidding? No, wait, that's not good enough for you. You've always wanted Eldur for yourself." Alona turned on her heel and paced across the room to pour herself a glass of wine, hoping Regan couldn't see the way her hands were shaking.

"By all means, help yourself." The queen chuckled. "I'm curious to see where you're going with your assumptions."

Alona took a sip of wine to strengthen her resolve. "With Brea and Griffin's union you get a firmer hold on Gelsi and a foothold in Eldur. But we're forgetting Iskalt." She turned to the king and a cold sense of dread swept through her. This wasn't about Gelsi and Eldur. "You have an alliance with Callum, who has no heir." If she was right, they had a deal to make Griffin Callum's heir, and by default Griffin and Brea's child would be the future ruler of Iskalt as well as Fargelsi and Eldur.

"No wonder my mother went to such lengths to hide Brea Robinson from you. What an ingenious web you've spun for the future of our world. Your grand-niece or nephew will inherit half the fae realm. But what does that give the mighty Queen Regan?"

"Your speculations are quite impressive." Regan smiled, giving nothing away. "I called you here to make a bargain with you. You are a human without magic, caught up in the fae world where you can't hope to come out on top."

"What do you think you can offer me that I would accept?" Alona crossed her arms over her chest.

"I will set you free, and in exchange for your freedom, you will bring me Brea Robinson."

"Why would I ever do that?"

"Bring my niece home and I will allow you to return to the human world where you belong."

Alona shook her head with a grimace, her heart hammering in her chest. "I visited the human world once and I didn't care for it too much. I did meet a nice girl there though. She was good to me. It would be a shame for me to betray her now."

Alona chanced a glance at Griffin. He stood silently behind his queen, looking quite grave and uncertain. He might not be a lost cause just yet.

"If Brea escaped your clutches, you can bet Lochlan has taken her to Eldur by now. She is beyond your reach, and I've grown weary of this discussion that doesn't interest me."

Without magic, Alona couldn't help her people fight against Regan's plans, but she could do one thing. She could be a prisoner. A prisoner who refused to be used as a pawn in Regan's schemes.

"Take me back to my cell." Alona turned to leave the throne room.

"Very well, show our guest to her new quarters," Regan called to Alona's escort. "We'll see how well she's ready to cooperate after she's grown accustomed to life in the bowels of Fargelsi."

The trip back to the dungeon was another silent one. But they continued down the stairs, far past the cell she'd spent her first week in. It was darker and colder. The smell of mold and rot made her gag as she slipped on the slimy stones beneath her feet. The walls closed in around her, and Alona began to panic. This would be far worse than the musty room with the constant drip, drip, drip.

The roar of the falls and the rush of the river sounded overhead. They were deep under the palace when her escort reached for his keys to unlock an iron grated door.

"I must follow my orders, you understand?" the man finally spoke, shoving the iron bars open.

"I hold no ill will for you, sir." She stepped into the larger hall on the other side of the door, and the stench of unwashed bodies assaulted her nose. Row upon row of filthy cells lined the corridor. Pitiful looking prisoners huddled in their tattered blankets and turned their dead eyes on her.

The queen's servant opened a cell door, and Alona stepped inside. The room was hardly bigger than a closet. More of a cage than a cell. A bucket sat in one corner, and moldy straw covered the muddy floor. There was barely enough room to sit, much less lay down.

Alona flinched as the iron bars clanged shut behind her. She sank to the floor, clutching her hand over her mouth to still her sobs. In one fell swoop, she'd discovered she was never fae born, and her mothers weren't her mothers after all. She would likely spend years, if not the rest of her life in this cell, paying the price for Faolan's attempt to save her true-born daughter from Regan's grasp. She was nothing more than a human stand-in daughter. But Regan couldn't take everything from her. Alona knew without a doubt in her heart that the mothers who raised her loved her every bit as much as they loved their true-born daughter.

A hand reached through the bars from the next cell and grasped hers. "Don't let them hear you cry, Alona." The filthy hand squeezed hers.

"Who are you?" She peered into the darkness, trying to make out the face of the woman beside her. She leaned against the bars, grasping the stranger's hand like a lifeline.

"My name is Neeve. I served the Lady Brea while she was here, and I helped her escape."

"She's in Eldur now?"

"I sent her through the southern Vatlands to Lochlan's camp," Neeve said. "It's only a matter of time before that girl gets her head on straight and strikes back."

"In the meantime, we need to plan our escape." Alona choked back her tears. She might be imprisoned and feeling lower than she ever had before, but Alona Cahill was a fighter and she wouldn't go down without an explosive battle.

"Fargelsi is no longer just a kingdom of the fae world, Alona. It is a prison. Those born of Fargelsi are prisoners of its queen—she holds our magic, only allowing us the faintest use of it. There is no joy here, only fake smiles and hidden agendas. For those without magic, there is no escape."

"Maybe for those born of Fargelsi and those born without magic. But I am human. I am not bound by the laws of this world, and I will find a way to fight back."

The story continues in
Fae's Defiance: Queens of the Fae Book Two
Turn the page to get started!

QUEENS OF THE FAE
BOOK TWO

FAE'S DEFIANCE

MELISSA A. CRAVEN
M. LYNN

Prologue
Alona Cahill

Alona Cahill trudged along the river's edge, eager to leave her prison cell behind for a brief taste of fresh air. The chains around her ankles chaffed, but they were better than the bars of her cage. After surviving the last weeks in the dungeons of Queen Regan's palace, she looked forward to this part of her routine.

Every week, the prisoners were escorted from the dungeon to get some fresh air and exercise in the fields beside the river. It was the only time she was able to wash the filth and grime from her body. And the only time she had to speak privately with Neeve, her fellow prisoner and co-conspirator.

"How is it coming with the chains?" Alona asked her friend.

"It's slow work. My magic is nearly useless, but every day the links grow weaker. I'll be able to start working on yours soon." They had little hope of escape, but that didn't mean either woman was ready to give up trying.

Alona was born without magic and therefore no help in terms of the power, but she had other skills. Since she was thrown into her cell, she'd worked tirelessly developing relationships with each of the guards. She knew which ones were susceptible to her charms and which ones weren't worth the effort. She knew their shifts, when they ate, when they slept, and when they weren't paying attention.

A few were a lost cause while others had a soft spot for the helpless little princess. They sometimes brought her extra food or water, which she shared with Neeve in the cell beside hers. In time, she hoped she could count on one of them looking the other way when she and Neeve made their escape.

The girls sat soaking their feet in the river, talking softly of their plans, using the rush of the water to conceal their voices.

"You're too obvious." A fair-haired man in chains sat down beside them, eying Neeve curiously. "You may as well shout your plans across the field." He eased his blistered feet into the water, breathing a sigh of relief.

"I don't know what you mean," Alona said sweetly.

"If you've found yourselves imprisoned in the lowest, darkest corners of the dungeons, it means one thing. You've angered the queen, and she will not soon forget it."

Neeve looked away, and Alona couldn't help feel sorry for her—well, she felt sorry for all of them. Everyone in the dungeons had heard of the girl executed for helping someone escape the palace. Moira, her name was. Neeve had barely been able to speak of her except to whisper her name in her sleep. Alona didn't know how, but they'd known each other.

She shifted her attention to the man before them. His eyes spoke of immense grief, but his calm façade hid it well. "You've been here a long time, haven't you?"

"Longer than you've been alive, Princess."

"You know who I am?"

"I know exactly who you are, Alona Cahill, daughter of the Eldur queens."

"If you know my mothers, then you must know I won't give up until I find a way out of this prison."

"If there was a way out, I would have found it long ago."

"Who are you, sir?" Neeve asked. Even as a prisoner she couldn't seem to drop the formality a life in service had instilled in her.

"Brandon O'Rourke." He held his hand out to her.

"You're the queen's brother?" Neeve's eyes widened with shock as she took his offered hand. "The rightful king of Fargelsi?"

"Please, call me Brandon." He held onto Neeve's hand longer than most handshakes lasted before releasing it quickly.

"You're supposed to be dead," Alona whispered.

Brandon's shoulder slumped as he swirled his aching feet in the soft mud of the riverbed. "I may as well be."

"Time to go, you three," the queen's guard called.

Alona groaned as she got to her feet, dreading the return to her cramped cell.

"Be more careful, ladies. The queen has eyes and ears everywhere."

Alona and Neeve made their way along the river's edge and back into the tunnels that led behind the falls and into the bowels of the palace dungeons.

"Get in your cages, and be quick about it," the guard called, shoving prisoners along the well-worn path.

Alona stepped inside her cell, noting the fresh layer of hay that would make her bed for the next week or more. Hers was a bit thicker than the others. Smiling at the guard, she sank to her knees, pulling her tattered blanket around her shoulders. The warmth of the afternoon outside left her quickly as the chill of the dungeon seeped into her bones.

"What's happening?" A frantic voice bounced off the stone walls. Another new prisoner trying to resist what was happening to him. "This is a mistake. I'm a nobody." The guards shoved the boy through the gates where he fell, sprawled across the floor in a tangle of long limbs and strange clothes.

"Seriously? Dude, that wasn't necessary." The boy stood up,

glancing around the room in the dim torchlight. "I definitely didn't do anything to deserve this. Where am I?"

"Shut up, human." The guard guided the boy to the empty cell beside Alona's.

"Human?" Neeve murmured, clutching the bars of her cell. "He talks like Brea."

"Brea?" The boy's eyes snapped to Neeve's.

"Where is she? Is she here? Brea!" The boy shouted, earning a blow to his head from the guard's club.

"Du-ude." He rubbed the lump on his head. "We need to get you some anger management classes. Not cool, bro, not cool."

"Get inside and shut up." The guard opened the cell door.

"I don't think so." He shook his head, taking a step back. "I'm going to need a bigger cell. I have an issue with tight spaces."

The guard shoved him inside and slammed the door closed.

"What's his problem?" The boy rubbed the top of his head, leaning back against the cold stone wall.

"Quiet. You'll only make it worse on yourself," Neeve whispered. "How do you know Brea?"

Alona leaned closer, wanting, *needing* his answer.

"How do *you* know Brea?" He turned his wide eyes on Neeve.

"I served her."

The boy stared at her. "Served her? Is she here?"

Neeve's grin was grim. "Not anymore. She escaped."

"Who are you?" Alona asked.

"Myles Merrick, best friend of Brea Robinson who I'm guessing is a lot more important in this world than the one we came from."

CHAPTER I

BREA

Why did everyone in this fracking fae world lie?

Brea still couldn't believe the fantasy life she'd fallen into. Okay, more like been dragged into kicking and screaming. She shook her head to rid it of thoughts that would inevitably lead back to the biggest liar of them all. The man who'd claimed she was the subject of a prophecy. Prophecy-schmophesy. It didn't exist.

Her hands tightened around the steaming cup on the table in front of her as she focused on this moment's lie. "And what do you call it?" She looked to the bear of a man sweeping the floor with an ancient bristly broom that looked like it belonged in a bedraggled Cinderella's hands instead of this giant. Did giants exist in Eldur? Maybe he was a half giant—like Hagrid.

"What?" She hadn't heard the answer he gave her.

"Girl." The man she'd come to know as Xander over the last few weeks leaned the broom against the stone wall and rounded the small wooden tables separating them. He folded himself into a chair that was entirely too small for him. "I wouldn't begin to guess what a girl like you was doing spending every day out here in the city without an escort."

"A girl like me?" She grimaced. "What does that mean?"

"A richie." Adamina singsonged as she bounced from the kitchen at the back of the small tavern. At this early hour, Brea was their only patron.

"Hey, Mina." Brea gave her a little wave.

Mina set a bowl of sugared oats in front of Brea and another before her father.

Brea took a bite, savoring the simple fare that was a world away from the more robust foods of the palace. "How do you know I'm a..."

"Richie?" Mina crossed her arms over her petite frame. She looked nothing like her larger father. Brea had learned weeks ago that it was just the two of them. Mina's mother died in childbirth. "It's the clothes. You won't find cloth as fine as yours here in the city except on the backs of nobles. Tell us, Brea, which family do you belong to? Is it the Wilsons? They've always been so secretive, though Viscount Wilson gets pretty chatty in here over his cups."

Brea shook her head.

Mina's eyes lit up, and she flicked them to the cup in front of Brea. "Oh, it's the Robinsons, isn't it?"

Brea almost spat oats across the table. How did they know?

Mina kept talking. "The Robinson clan is the wealthiest in the city."

Oh. Brea released a breath. There was a clan of that name in the fae world.

"That's why you enjoy Eldur beans so much. They control the Eldur bean trade."

"Eldur beans?" Brea stared down into the dark molten heaven in her cup. The lie she'd forgotten everyone seemed to be in on. "I was told there wasn't such a thing as coffee."

"I don't know what coffee is, but even as a Robinson clan member, you wouldn't drink Eldur bean brew." She leaned in, dropping her voice. "It's a commoner's drink." Her nose wrinkled.

"But if you ask me, it's much better than the tea all you richies drink."

"Adamina," Xander chastised. "That is enough. I don't smell the day's bread baking in the kitchen yet."

She held her hands in front of her chest. "I know. I know." She shot Brea a wink. "We won't tell your brothers of your taste for Eldur brew when they come in seeking ale this evening." She bounced away, her bright red hair flowing out behind her.

Xander scrubbed a hand across his face and leaned back in his chair. Now that Mina pointed it out, Brea could see the differences in how these people dressed. Instead of the colorful silks and soft linens used for clothing at the palace, they adorned themselves in worn woolen tunics with no hint of color.

"Please forgive Mina for her intrusiveness."

Brea shrugged. "I'd be curious about me too." She drained the rest of her Eldur brew. "Am I really not supposed to be drinking this stuff?"

Xander eyed her, his gaze shrewd. "If you were really of the Robinson clan, you'd know the expectations of society. Brea, you are not much older than my own daughter, and I like you."

"Um... thanks?"

"But you are here every morning by yourself. Women of an obvious higher station are targets in this part of the city and must be careful."

Brea tried to see the city as he did. In truth, she loved traversing the streets and wandering through markets full of life. It took her mind from the fact that Lochlan and Finn had been gone for three weeks without so much as a word.

Xander sighed. "Do you not have people worried about you?"

She thought of the woman she'd recently learned was her mother, but Queen Faolan had no time for her when the real people she cared about were gone.

Queen Tierney tried, but there was only so much kindness a person could take before they broke. Well, if that person was her.

"Do you want the truth, Xander?"

He nodded.

"Okay." She sucked in a breath, preparing herself. "I was a prisoner in Fargelsi for weeks. The queen wouldn't let me leave, forcing me to escape through the swampy Vatlands where I came face to face with creatures I couldn't even begin to describe. Finally, I reached Captain O'Shea's camp and saved them all from a terrible fate." A little fib never hurt anyone. "I had to fend off enemies from Iskalt and protect the soldiers, eventually taking a sword to the shoulder. It hurt, but not as much as letting the Captain suffer." She released a fake sob.

Xander stared at her, his mouth dropping open as she continued to sniffle.

"I knew it!" Mina's squeal came from the kitchen doorway. "We all heard about the girl who escaped Fargelsi, and then you turn up, a stranger in our city."

"But you thought I was a Robinson."

She laughed, the sound holding a musical quality. "I've known the Robinsons since I was a child. They are frequent visitors to the tavern. You don't carry their ghastly looks." She giggled behind her hand. "I just wanted to pull the truth out of you."

Xander looked from Brea to Mina. "I didn't hear of an escaped prisoner."

"That's because you never leave this box of a tavern, papa." She plunked herself down across from Brea. "Did you really save Lochlan?" She sighed. "Have you seen his eyes when his magic rises? They're like an icy spear straight to my heart."

Xander scowled. "Mina, that is the queen's man."

Ignoring Xander, Brea leaned across the table toward Mina. "Did you know he reads?"

Mina fanned her face. "Oh my."

Brea laughed at the younger girl, enjoying the lightness of the moment. Usually when she thought of Lochlan, it was with a mixture of annoyance and worry. It felt good to chat with Mina as if she were just a friend. Maybe she could be.

Xander pushed his chair back and stood. "Guess I'm making the bread," he grumbled.

Mina ignored him. "So, you live at the palace?"

"Only because they don't know what to do with me." Half-truths. That wasn't the reason she was there, but it didn't change how little she fit in those gilded halls with people who rarely smiled.

At least when Griff was lying to her, he made her feel like she belonged.

After telling Mina all about what the palace was truly like, Brea looked up to find patrons walking through the front door looking for their lunch.

"Crap, I've been here all morning." She jumped to her feet.

Mina stood. "Papa is going to be angry with me, but I do hope we see you tomorrow, Brea."

Brea nodded. In truth, she couldn't wait. The city and this tavern kept her heart beating when it wanted to freeze in her chest. With a wave goodbye, Brea stepped out onto the busy street. Sandstone buildings rose up before her, each more boring than the next. It wasn't the mundane architecture of the lower city that breathed life into everything around her, it was the people.

A cart rumbled past, and she jumped out of the way before following the crowd to the market square where people sold their wares. Everything from fresh fruit to home-spun clothing and ceramic dishes.

A butcher slammed a slab of meat onto a table near her, making her jump and clutch her chest. She watched him hack away at it with a cleaver before moving on. One booth caught her eyes. A handmade sign read Eldur beans. She wondered if she could get someone at the palace to make some Eldur brew from them.

Fishing a few gold coins Tierney gave her from her pocket, she approached the vender.

A young man, probably only a few years older than her met her gaze, sliding it down to take in her clothing. "You're the one who escaped Fargelsi."

How did he know?

As if sensing her question, he smiled, revealing a wide gap between his two front teeth. "We recognize strangers here."

"Oh." She held out two coins, and his eyes widened.

"Do you even know how much money that is?"

She shook her head.

"Enough for this here whole cart of Eldur beans and then some. It's only two coppers per bag, but I'mma give you one for free." He smiled again, satisfied with himself. "Anyone who defies Regan of Gelsi is a friend of Ollie's." Ollie must be him.

"You don't have to do that."

"Sure I do, miss—"

"Brea."

He nodded as he reached for a canvas sack and scooped Eldur beans into it. "All right, Brea. Though, with you living at the palace, I dunno what you want with Eldur beans." He handed her the bag.

"Thank you, Ollie."

His grin widened. "Hey, Lew," he called, looking toward one of the other carts. "A richie knows my name."

She really had to get some new clothes so everyone would stop calling her that. Her parents in Ohio had never been well-off. Compared to Myles' family, they were poor, and they dressed like it. Eyes followed her as she escaped from the market as fast as she could, uncomfortable with the attention.

If Lochlan were there, he'd bull his way through the crowd, leaving ample space for her in his wake. Finn would probably grab her elbow and make sure she was okay.

But they weren't there, leaving her alone once more.

Keeping a tight grip of the Eldur beans that would keep her sane in this place, she left the market behind, ducking into a familiar building on her right. Once inside the quiet bookstore, she released a breath and leaned against the door.

"Brea, that you, dear?"

"Fiona." Brea sighed in relief as she caught sight of the silver-haired woman walking toward her. She'd met the older woman at the palace when Fiona was tidying the library. The queen hired her to rotate the books and keep the selection fresh—with the exception of the human books. Those always stayed.

"Are you okay?" Concern etched into her every feature. "You look stressed."

She pushed away from the door. "I wonder why."

Fiona was one of the few people in the city who knew everything —well, almost everything. She didn't know Brea was the real daughter of Faolan.

"Still no word?" She set the book she was carrying on the front counter.

Brea shook her head. "Not so much as a messenger." She followed Fiona farther into the two-story store. At the back, a spiral staircase led to the upper stacks, a section Fiona called her human stories. Brea laughed the first time she found all the leather-bound tomes depicting stories about the human world.

She'd told Fiona the humans wrote about fae worlds as well, and they'd both had a good laugh at that. The first laughter Brea felt since learning the truth about her identity.

She was a changeling. Abandoned by her mother to be raised in the human realm where the things she saw and did because of her fae heritage made her an outcast, deemed a lunatic.

She still hadn't forgiven her mother for that.

And what about Alona? She grew up thinking she was one of the unfortunate fae born without powers, someone destined to join the serving class.

It wasn't fair to either of them.

"I know what you need, dear." Fiona led her up the back staircase. "I found a book I think you will enjoy greatly. It is meant for children, but..." She ran a finger over the spines until she came to a book of stories called *Humantales.* Just like the humans called them fairytales.

A smile spread Brea's lips as she flipped open the cover and thumbed through pages about princesses and kings that were obviously influenced by real human history.

Fiona put a hand on her shoulder. "Only a few fae clans have ever had the ability to open portals into the human realm, but over the centuries, many stories have filtered out and spawned fables of a world without magic."

"Why would anyone want stories about a world that didn't have magic?" She stopped on a page depicting Henry VIII as a benevolent king. It was a love story. She snorted. What would these people say if they knew the real history?

Fiona smiled softly. "We always want to imagine a world different than our own. Magic is not the great force some claim. It destroys just as much as it saves. Sometimes, I wonder if our world wouldn't be so broken without it."

"The human realm is broken too, Fiona. You don't need magic for that."

Fiona sighed. "The human world has wars and strife, yes, but magic has erased entire kingdoms from the fae world."

"What?" She snapped the book shut. "There was a fourth kingdom?"

"It serves only as a prison now." Sadness tinged her eyes. "Magic can sometimes be like dropping a nuclear bomb into a situation that calls for the delicate carving of a knife."

"Wait... how do you know about nukes?" Brea wracked her brain for anything that made sense. As far as she knew, the fae didn't have that technology. They didn't need it with their magic.

Fiona tapped her nose. "Follow me."

They walked down the stairs and crossed the store to the front counter. Fiona rounded it and reached into a compartment below, pulling free a book. She set it on the counter, and Brea's eyes widened.

"Where on earth did you get a US history book?" She ran a hand over the cover that showed a map of the country she'd called home most of her life.

"The palace library."

"You took one of Lochlan's books?" A smile slid across her face.

Fiona flipped through the pages. "He lets me borrow them as long as the queen doesn't find out. She only allows him to bring them back from the human realm if he agrees to keep them close. She does not want human books leaving her walls."

Brea understood immediately. If the people of Eldur read human books, they might make the connection to her. No one could know Lochlan travelled to the human realm.

"Fiona?"

"Yes?" She glanced up, her glasses perched on the end of her nose.

"You said only some families can create portals. How many are there now?"

"Well, that we know of in the last few decades... two. The Rifkin Clan is the nearest to the prison realm, though, so if travelers wish to pay them for passage, they must traverse those haunted lands. The Eldur courts do not recognize their noble status."

"And the other?" She already knew the answer.

"The O'Sheas." She smiled. "There was a time when they ruled Iskalt that the queen and king were great friends of ours. Eldur and Iskalt had an unbreakable bond."

She swallowed, barely able to breathe. "What happened to them?" She knew Griffin and Loch's parents died when they were boys. How old had Griff said he was? Two?

Fiona put the book away, a sad set to her shoulders. "They came to visit Queen Faolan. It was a grand visit with balls and banquets. When they left, the future looked so bright. I remember it as if it were yesterday. The rumor was they had a mission for Queen Faolan, but the queen and king of Iskalt never made it home."

"They died?" she whispered.

Fiona nodded. "Their bodies were found near the border of Fargelsi. Within months, the king's brother took the throne and sent Lochlan and Griff to be raised in foreign courts. Most people think it was a show of good faith to keep Eldur from attacking to reclaim the throne for Lochlan. But when her greatest friends died, our queen seemed to have lost her taste for war."

Tears hung in Brea's lashes. "I need to go."

Fiona called a goodbye, but Brea barely heard her as she rushed out in the blazing Eldur heat.

Sweat dripped into her eyes, but she kept going, barely registering that she'd left the Eldur beans behind. She clutched the humantale book under her arm and rushed through the busy streets, wishing she wasn't so far from the palace.

All she wanted to do was collapse onto her bed and hide in her room. Because she now knew without a doubt that Lochlan's parents were dead because of her.

Chapter 2

BREA

"Lady Brea, rushing back to the palace already? It's hardly mid-day."

Brea paused at the sound of her name, blinking at the exotic woman dressed in free-flowing silks outside the magic shop. That's what Brea called it anyway.

"Mrs. Moran. I'm sorry, I've got to get back early."

"Come by later today. I have some new herbs to show you. They arrived today from the fire plains. I can teach you all about their mystical properties."

For a moment, Brea was tempted to join her. She was fascinated with Mrs. Moran's apothecary shop. Everything she stocked held magic of one kind or another. It wasn't the kind of magic she was supposed to be learning, but it was definitely more interesting considering Brea hadn't felt her magic in weeks. Something had her blocked, and she wasn't sure how to move past it. No one seemed too concerned about it so she went along with it.

"I'll try," Brea called over her shoulder.

"Go have a nap, dear, you look a bit peaky. And have a cup of that tea I gave you yesterday. It will help you rest."

"Thank you, Mrs. Moran." Brea picked up her pace. Some of her favorite shops were closer to the palace, but they knew her as Lady Brea there. She much preferred the anonymity she had at the marketplace across the river in the lower city. It was like a different world down there. The merchants in this part of the city catered to the nobility and wouldn't dream of calling her or anyone else a 'richie', at least not to her face.

By the time Brea reached the bridge entrance to the palace, sweat poured down her back, and she was anxious for a cool, quiet afternoon in her grotto. She might actually take that nap if her mind would quit running in an endless loop of worry and regret.

Shouts and commotion interrupted her thoughts. Sneaking into the courtyard wasn't going to work this time. Both queens and half the palace swarmed the entrance, shouting and issuing orders. Soldiers and horses stood by while a distinguished looking man gave a report to the queen.

"Brea, darling." Tierney spotted her before she could creep up the stairs. "There you are."

"I was just exploring some of the shops." She inched closer to the woman who called herself one of her mothers. "Have you had news of Alona?" Brea eyed the distraught Queen Faolan, still unable to fathom her as the woman who gave birth to her. Both queens were wonderful people, but with Alona's disappearance and now no news from Lochlan and Finn, they were distracted. Most of Brea's interactions with her mothers were awkward in the extreme, none of them knowing quite how to act around each other. Brea tended to avoid them.

"We've had a disturbing report." Tierney put her arm around Brea. She was the more touchy-feely mom. "One of our scouts found the remnants of a battle. All of Lochlan's men were slaughtered."

Brea took in a sharp breath. "Loch and Finn too?" It surprised her how much it hurt to ask the question. Lochlan was a self-righteous pain in her butt and Finn was more of a stranger than a true friend—not like Myles had been. But that they both might be dead had her feeling all sorts of terror she hadn't expected. Like she couldn't possibly face this life in the fae realm without them.

"No, thank the heavens. There was no trace of them, so we must move forward hoping they made it to safety."

"But?" Brea braced for the bad news.

"It's been more than a week since the battle. Lochlan would have sent for help if he was able."

"So, they might not have made it?" She couldn't imagine Lochlan in any situation where he didn't come out on top.

"We can only hope news of their whereabouts will reach us soon." Tierney's eyes followed her wife's movements as Faolan issued orders. "But it is possible they've been taken back to Iskalt."

"His uncle will kill him." Brea's hand went to her throat.

"It's not likely Callum O'Shea would kill one of the last of his clan." Tierney squeezed her shoulder. "The O'Sheas have remarkable magic that is too precious to snuff out over something as petty as a throne."

Brea didn't think Callum O'Shea would agree with the Eldur Queen Consort.

"He is like a son to Faolan. To us both, really. He grew up right here with Alona."

"Lochlan is tough and resourceful. He can take care of himself and Finn." But Brea worried about Finn. If they got separated or were injured, would either of them have enough sense to come back home, or would they be stubborn and pigheaded and insist on looking for each other?

"Brea." Faolan gave her a curt nod as she approached. "Good. You're home. Do try to stay close to the palace, darling. We don't want to lose you too." Her words were kind and motherly, but she was utterly absent, just saying the things she thought she needed to say.

Awkward silence hung between them, and Brea just wanted to escape.

"Er—how will you look for them?" she asked.

"We've sent several scouts to scour the area surrounding the battle scene." Faolan stood, wringing her hands, refusing to look at Brea. She did that a lot. And sometimes when she did meet Brea's eyes, she could see the disappointment there. Disappointment that she wasn't Alona. "All we can do now is wait and hope they haven't fallen into Callum's hands."

"Please let me know as soon as you hear any news." Brea stepped away from the queens, feeling the awkward much more than usual. "I'm just going back to my room now."

"We will see you at dinner." Tierney turned and led her wife back to the throne room.

Brea sighed as she retreated to her room. A warm breeze swept through the open hallway, and parrots chattered in the gardens. The Eldurian palace was so beautiful. She could get used to calling it home—if there was something here to hold onto. More than just pretty rooms, exotic gardens, and strangers for mothers.

But the one thing Brea would never get used to was how boring the life of a noblewoman was. In the human world, she had school to fill her days, therapy appointments, time with Myles, and Netflix. There was always something to do. In the magical realm of the fae, her days were filled with aimless wandering and endless, uncomfortable dinners with her mothers.

If that was the life of a princess, Brea didn't want any part of it.

"Brea?" Rowena called from her closet. "Is that you?"

"Yes." Brea sighed, closing the door behind her. She supposed it was too much to ask for an afternoon to herself. Rowena was a kind servant, but she wasn't Neeve.

"I was just seeing to some new dresses Queen Tierney ordered for you. There's a lovely new day dress that will match your eyes."

"I don't suppose you've managed to find me some comfortable pants and shirts?"

"A Lady doesn't need street clothes." Rowena harrumphed as she fluffed a pillow to within an inch of its life.

"Good thing I'm not a lady." Brea collapsed on the couch in her sitting room.

"As long as you live in this palace you will dress and act like a lady."

"Maybe I should look for my own place." Brea got a kick out of riling up her maid.

"Lady Brea, your mo—the queen would not allow it." Rowena's cheeks flushed pink.

"What do you know?" Brea turned accusing eyes on the maid. No one other than the queens themselves and Lochlan—who might be dead—knew Brea was their true daughter.

"I know that this room is a mess." Rowena made to dust the spotless dresser.

"Spill it, Ro." Brea crossed the room.

"I was there." Rowena refused to meet her eyes.

"Where."

"The day you were born." Her eyes filled with tears. "Twas a happy day. For a time. Until the queen asked me to bring you to the Iskalt king." Rowena's bottom lip quivered.

"You switched us?" Brea sank down on the nearest chair.

"At the queen's order. Though I never understood why, I did as she asked. And I loved our dear Alona. Such a sweet child. And a good head on her shoulders, that one." Rowena polished the brass dresser knobs to a shine. "Always thought she and Lochlan would make a go of it one day. Knew he would raise her up from the serving class to be a proper lady if she couldn't be our princess." She dabbed at her eyes.

"And now here you are, come home to us at last. Just as ornery and full of mischief as Alona—in your own way. You could have been sisters, as alike as you are different."

"You were her lady's maid?"

"Of course. And I wouldn't hear of it, letting another care for you."

"Thank you." Brea pulled the fussy woman into a hug.

"For what, my Lady?" Rowena returned her hug with gusto, her arms a motherly embrace Brea had never known.

"For caring whether I'm here or not." Brea rested her head on Rowena's shoulder for a moment.

"Oh, sweet dearie." Rowena patted her back. "You listen to Rowena now." She held Brea at arm's length. "Your mothers rearranged the heavens to keep you and Alona safe. Give them some time. It can't be easy to gain one daughter only to lose the other. You're strangers now, but you won't always be. One day all four of you will be a family. And a strong one at that."

"We can hope." Brea forced a smile for the loyal servant.

"Go rest, my Lady." She swatted Brea with her dusting rag. "It's the hottest part of the day. No sense in trying to get anything done till it cools this evening."

Brea snorted. "Not that I have anything to do but stare at the walls anyway." She shed her lightweight overgown and retreated to the grotto for an afternoon nap. With nothing else to do, sleep was the only activity she looked forward to these days.

"Up with you, Lady Brea." Rowena pulled the blankets off the bed. "And don't give me any of your tantrums either."

Brea rolled over, clutching her pillow. "I don't throw tantrums," she muttered. "I simply protest the morning."

"The queen is bringing your breakfast herself. I suggest you get up and comb that rat's nest on your head." Rowena tossed a fluffed pillow on her head and went to make a ruckus in the closet.

"Which queen?" Brea yawned as she sat on the edge of her bed. What was the point of living in a palace if you couldn't sleep all day?

"*The queen* is always Faolan. We call her consort *Queen Tierney* to avoid confusion."

"Do I have time for a bath first?" Brea could use a cold shower to wake up, but the fae didn't believe in things like quick showers. At least not among the nobles. They believed a bath should be an event, something to enjoy—which she was all for, but a hot bath in the morning did nothing to wake Brea up.

"No. Now get dressed. She'll be here in a moment." Rowena tossed a blue day dress on her bed. She was a far cry from the triplets at the Gelsi palace. Or even Neeve.

"Yes ma'am." Brea stifled a smile for the gruff lady's maid. There wasn't anything Rowena wouldn't do for Brea, but at the same time she didn't treat her like she was made of glass. Of all the fae she'd met, Rowena had quickly become one of her favorites. Neeve was still her number one, though. She'd give anything to have her with her, not as a maid, but as a friend.

Brea dressed quickly and ran a comb through her hair.

"Do you know what she wants with me?" Brea walked into her sitting room, still brushing the tangles from her hair.

"Just a simple breakfast with my daughter." Faolan smiled from her seat at the small tea table in front of the balcony. "Please join me, darling."

"Oh." Brea forgot how to walk. Her mother made her nervous, especially when her other mother wasn't there as a buffer. She managed to set her comb on the table beside the settee and crossed the room to sit with the queen.

Too many queens in my life.

Brea swept her long hair over her shoulder. "Wait. Do I smell—?"

"I hear you enjoy Eldur Brew in the morning." Faolan poured a cup of the rich dark brew. "What do the humans call it?"

"Coffee." Brea inhaled the heavenly aroma. "Oh, this is even better than the kind they serve in the tavern."

"What was that?" Faolan poured herself a cup.

"Oh nothing. It's delicious, thank you."

"I'll share a secret with you." Faolan's eyes crinkled when she smiled—rare as it was. "The only reason I get out of bed most mornings is for a hot cup of Eldur Brew. It's popular among the commoners for a reason. I'm convinced it's the secret answer to all the world's problems."

"Your secret is safe with me as long as you share." Brea sipped from her cup, convinced her mother's fae coffee was better than the real thing.

"I owe you an apology." Faolan buttered her toast. "I owe you a good many apologies. But this morning, I'm here to say I am so sorry I've been ... such a mess since your return."

"I understand." Brea took a slice of toast for herself. "You raised Alona as your own. I can't imagine how you must feel since she was taken."

"I miss her." Faolan's eyes misted with unshed tears. "But that is no reason for me to neglect you when you probably feel like a stranger in our home."

Brea didn't know what to say to that, so she shoved toast into her mouth to keep from saying something she might regret.

"It never occurred to me that you might be bored. But why wouldn't you be? We've given you nothing to do. No wonder you prefer exploring the city to sitting here in your rooms."

"It is kind of like watching paint dry." Brea focused on the selection of jams rather than meet her mother's eyes. She didn't bother to ask how Faolan knew how she spent her days in the city.

"Alona had tutors up until last year. Perhaps you would like a tutor to teach you all about Eldur and the fae world? We can arrange that for the coming months. Though you will soon need to focus all your energies on your magic when you come of age."

Brea nodded, her mouth full of toast she didn't taste. Clearly the Eldur queen intended Brea to make the palace her permanent home. She wasn't so sure she agreed with that.

"Lochlan once told me you grew up on a farm in a small village. He said you seemed to like the horses the most."

"We had horses when I was younger, but my father had to sell them after a few bad years and failed crops. My friend Myles lived on the farm next to ours. They always had horses."

"Did you know we have stables here at the palace? And not just for transportation purposes. We raise draft horses and ponies. Landowners from all over Eldur come to our stables for the best horses in all of the fae realm."

That piqued Brea's interest. "Where are the stables? I've explored all over the city and the palace grounds, but I haven't stumbled onto it."

"Behind the palace gardens at the top of the canyon. You may visit the stables whenever you like, but I thought you might like a job there as well."

"A job?" Brea's mouth hung open.

"Not that you need a job. You're not obligated by any means," Faolan rushed to add.

"When can I start? What will I be doing?"

"You can start today." Faolan smiled. "One of the guards will escort you there and back. You'll meet with Master Arturo, and if you'd like, you may apprentice with him."

"Apprentice? With the stable master? I just figured I'd be mucking out stalls."

"Master Arturo wouldn't dare ask you to do that." Faolan smiled. "He won't treat you any different than the other hands, but he will teach you horse breeding. He's a busy man, so he won't always have much time for you. While you're there, you'll exercise horses, watch over the pregnant mares, groom and feed the ponies. They always need extra attention."

"Sounds perfect." Brea couldn't wait to get started.

"I apprenticed under Master Arturo when I was your age. The stables are still my favorite place in the whole city. You get your love of horses and Eldur Brew from me." Faolan took her hand, giving it a gentle squeeze. "And your fair share of my awkwardness too."

"Awkward?" The queen didn't have an awkward bone in her body.

"Oh, I've learned to hide it behind cool smiles and a queenly facade I've perfected over the years, but inside, I'm still the girl who spills her tea and forgets how to articulate a sentence when I'm nervous. But I don't want to hide from my daughter."

"Thank you so much for the apprenticeship. I won't let you down."

"You couldn't if you tried, darling. Wherever your future leads, learning under Master Arturo will be good experience. As your mother, I want you to be happy and make your own decisions about how you fit into our family and our kingdom. I know I am not an easy woman to know, but I hope you'll give me ... us time to work our way into a real mother-daughter relationship. And when Alona returns, I do hope you can be friends."

"I like the sound of that." Brea squeezed her hand back. It was the most unawkward moment they'd shared since Brea arrived in Eldur.

"I leave you to your morning." Faolan cleared their breakfast dishes herself and retreated to the hall. "Oh." She turned just as Brea stepped behind her, and they collided, sending the breakfast tray sailing across the room.

"Oh, darn it." Faolan stooped to pick up the broken dishes.

"Like mother, like daughter." Brea laughed and went to retrieve the silver tray. They scrambled across the floor to clean up the mess. "I'm pretty sure Rowena would yell at us for daring to clean this up."

Faolan rocked back on her heels, laughter dancing in her eyes. "I'm pretty sure we did it wrong anyway." She stood brushing crumbs from her gown. "I was just going to tell you that you can find me in the throne room most days. You are welcome to visit us there anytime, Brea dear."

"I'll do that."

Faolan paused at the door for a second time. "Not a day went by during your whole life that I didn't think about you and wish good things for you." She didn't wait for a reply before she left Brea standing there with tears in her eyes.

Chapter 3

BREA

"Finish grooming Raven, and you can call it a day, Lady Brea." Master Arturo slapped the fat pony on her ample rump. "Good work with the ponies this week. They're madly in love with you already."

"I think fae ponies are extra sweet." Brea brushed Raven's long fluffy mane until it sparkled in the sunlight.

"You spoil this one." Arturo chuckled.

"She's close to foaling. She deserves some extra attention." Brea smoothed her brush over Raven's back. "You think it'll be any day now?"

"Three or four more days yet."

"She looks ready to burst."

"I'm guessing this one is twins."

"Twins! Oh please send word as soon as she goes into labor. I want to be here with her."

"I'll send one of the boys to get you when the time comes, but I'm under strict orders to get you home before dark, so off you go, Lady Brea."

"Thank you, Master Arturo." Brea took her grooming tools back into the massive stables and went to wake her babysitter.

"Emmet." Brea shook the boy who was supposed to be her chaperone while she was working at the stables. He couldn't be more than fifteen, and she was pretty sure she could take him.

"Yes ma'am, Lady Brea." He scrambled to his feet. "You ready to leave, my Lady?"

"How many times have I told you to just call me Brea?"

"Yes, miss." Emmet trotted along behind her. She found it utterly ridiculous that she spent her days caring for horses, but when it came time to leave for the palace, she had to wait for Emmet's inept fumbling to saddle their horses for the ride back. He refused to let her help because 'a lady should never saddle her own horse.'

"I could walk there faster," Brea muttered, rolling her eyes when Emmet tried to give her a boost.

With her new job at the stables, Brea also had a new wardrobe much more to her liking. Today she wore tall black boots, comfortable trousers that could almost pass for leggings, and a linen tunic belted at the waist. With her long hair in a messy bun, she almost felt normal.

"Race you back to the palace." Brea mounted her horse and trotted across the stable yard.

"Lady Brea, I won't fall for that again. Please let me do my job and escort you home."

"Fine. But try not to ride like my eighty-year-old granny. I'd like to get home before I die of boredom."

Emmet's cheeks flushed. "I was always told when escorting a great lady I should travel at a comfortable pace so as not to tax her."

Brea snorted in a very unladylike way. "Well, I'm not a great lady, so that's your first mistake."

"Of course you are a lady, ma'am." He shook his head like he thought she might be crazy. She knew that look well.

"Well, I'm not made of glass. Do you have sisters, Emmet?"

"Four, my Lady."

"Then treat me like one of your sisters." She glanced back at him, but she'd made it worse. He looked utterly scandalized.

"I couldn't. It wouldn't be proper."

"Oh very well, Emmet. Ride ahead and make way for the Lady Brea." She waved him on like the grand marshal in a parade. There was no way this kid thought she wasn't weird.

They took the back roads to the palace. The queen insisted on it. She didn't want it to become common knowledge that a guest of the palace also worked in the stables as an apprentice. It was supposedly for Brea's own safety, but Brea thought it was more about keeping the whole switched daughter thing a secret.

Brea followed Emmet through the orchard. Large pods hung from the massive tree trunks. They looked a bit like coconuts, but the seed pods inside were more like Brazil nuts.

"Brea?" A familiar voice sounded from among the trees.

"Who's there?" Emmet put himself between her and the voice.

Brea threw her leg over the saddle and jumped to the ground. "Finn?" Her heart lurched into her throat at what she saw. "What happened?" She dropped beside him where Lochlan rested against a tree.

Finn sank down next to her, clearly exhausted.

"Talk to me, Finn." She moved to drape Lochlan's arm across her shoulders. He was injured and burning with fever.

"We were ambushed, and Loch was hurt bad. We've been trying to get home for days." Finn reached out to lean against the tree.

"Are you hurt?"

"No, but Loch needs help now. Take him and go. I'll just rest here." He sank to the ground in a faint.

"Emmet, help me get Loch on my horse." She heaved his weight, barely managing to get him to his feet. He groaned in protest. Emmet supported his other shoulder, and they moved him toward her horse.

Loch's shirt hung in tatters around his lean frame and filthy bandages covered his middle.

They finally settled his dead weight across the saddle, and Brea climbed up behind him, careful of his injuries. "Get Finn and bring him back to the palace. I'm taking Lochlan ahead."

"No my Lady, you must wait for me."

"I'm not asking for permission." Brea reared her horse around and took off through the orchard toward the palace.

"Don't die on me, you stubborn fool." She held on to Lochlan tightly as she charged down the dirt path that led into the canyon and the palace courtyard. She normally went home through the rear palace entrance where the kitchens were, but she needed help getting Lochlan to the healers.

Flying over the cobblestones, she raced for the palace entrance. "I need help!" She called ahead, not prepared for the palace guard to stop her.

"Halt!" Several soldiers crossed their spears barring her entrance. "What business do you have at the palace?"

"I live here, you fool! Stand aside."

"Lady Brea," the soldier's tone changed. "I didn't recognize you without your finery."

"Let me pass. I have Lochlan O'Shea, and he's injured."

The guards rushed out of her way, ushering her inside the courtyard and calling for assistance.

Brea jumped off her horse and stood back out of the way while the guards carried Lochlan into the palace. "Take him to the healers now! You four, go look for Finn and Emmet. They shouldn't be too far from the orchard." She ran inside and headed straight for the throne room.

"Your Majesty!" she shouted. The guards moved to stop her, but she shoved past them. "Let me through. I found Lochlan." The guards stepped aside and opened the doors for her.

"Your Majesty!" Brea stumbled into the room. The rich plush carpet at her feet tripped her up and she fell.

"Brea?" Tierney and Faolan rushed to her side. "What's wrong?" They searched her over, looking for injuries. "Where is the blood coming from, darling?"

"Not my blood." She gasped. "It's Loch. He's back and injured. Finn was with him too."

Both queens left her on the floor and raced from the throne room. Brea glanced around at the line of commoners waiting to meet with the queens. Lords and Ladies sat in the balcony above, looking down their noses at her.

"I'll just be leaving now." She cast her eyes down to her feet and followed her mothers from the room.

She found them in the healer's quarters near the queens' residence.

"Lochlan, can you hear me?" Faolan's frantic voice rose above the din. "Do you have news of Alona?"

"Your Majesty, please give us room to help him," the healer insisted.

"How is he?" Brea peeked inside the crowded room.

"We don't know yet." Tierney joined her in the hall. "Hopefully he will wake soon and have news of Alona."

"Alona, of course," Brea murmured, but she was more worried about Lochlan. He was deathly pale, and she swore she could feel the heat coming off him from across the narrow room. She'd always seen him as invincible. Nothing could shake the obstinate man with the iron will. But now, he looked weak. Broken. Like a shell of himself. Brea worried he might not make it.

She turned away when the healer bared his open wound, casting the dirty bandages aside. Blood and infection oozed from his abdomen. Someone had run him through with a sword.

Brea was reminded of her own injuries and the infection that could have killed her if it wasn't for the man lying on the table now. He'd taken her to Loch Langt to cool her fever. She just prayed the healers had everything they needed to treat him half as well as he'd cared for her.

"Finn." The Queen consort ushered her out of the way to make room for Finn who was relying heavily on Emmet to get him into the room.

"What news do you have?" Faolan demanded, turning to the second injured man who was supposed to be as good as family to her. But the queen only had ears for Alona.

"She's in Gelsi." Finn collapsed on the bed in the corner of the room. "Queen Regan holds her in the dungeons."

"The dungeons? How dare she put a princess in the dungeons!" Tierney's face turned red to match her hair.

"How are you, Finn?" Brea asked over the queens' tittering about their lost daughter. "Are you injured? What do you need?"

"Water, food, and sleep. In that order. And maybe a bath." He groaned as he laid back on the cot.

Brea moved to sit beside him, pouring a cup of water for him. His lips were cracked and bleeding from too much time under Eldur's unforgiving sun. "Sip slowly." She cautioned him. "I'll find you some food soon."

"Where in the dungeons? Can we get to her?" Faolan demanded.

"I'm afraid not, your Majesty. Regan has her held deep within the bowels of her palace. I'm told none can reach her from outside the palace."

"Well, we will have to find someone inside to help us." Faolan's shoulders stiffened with resolve. "That woman will rue the day she dared lay a hand on my daughter." Faolan swept out of the room, not bothering to ask the healers how Lochlan was doing.

"I think maybe I'll sleep now," Finn murmured. "Water, sleep, then food. I can bathe next week." He was fading quickly, but Brea knew she needed to get some more water in him first.

"Not so fast, Finny boy. Drink this." She refilled his cup and helped him sit up to drink it. "You can rest when this is empty."

"Where's Finn?" An older soldier barged into the room, his eyes zeroing in on Finn. "Tell me everything," he demanded.

"Listen, I don't know who you are, but he needs to rest. You can ask him your questions about the princess once he's had a chance to sleep. Come back in the morning." Brea glared at the man.

"I'm his father." The man moved to sit on the cot beside her. "Eamon Donovan, head of the Queen's guard."

"Oh." Brea focused on helping Finn sip from the cup. "I didn't realize."

"Don't apologize for championing my son, Lady Brea. He's lucky to have a friend like you. Can you tell me what happened? Where did you find him?"

"In the orchard." Brea recounted the details for Captain Donovan.

"And Loch?" He cast a worried glance at Lochlan's still form across the room.

"I don't know. They are still working on him."

"I'm glad you were there to help them." The captain took his son's hand.

"I'm okay, Father. Go see to the queens. They'll be worried about Lona."

"Get some rest. I'll come back tonight to check on you." The captain left, asking Brea to send word if anything changed.

Finn was asleep before Brea could set the empty cup on his bedside table.

Not knowing what else to do, Brea sat in a chair beside Finn's cot while the healers treated Lochlan's injuries. When they finally finished, Brea approached his bedside. "How is he?"

"The injury was severe, and the infection has spread beyond his wounds. The next few hours will tell us whether he will make it or not."

"You have magic. Isn't there anything more you can do?"

"We need to keep his temperature down. And keep him comfortable."

"Well, don't you have some kind of magical cooling blanket or something?"

"We do. It's called ice." The healer gave her a small smile.

"Is there anything I can do to help?"

"We have other patients to see to throughout the palace this evening. It will help if you can keep an eye on him. Keep the ice packs cold and change them the instant the ice melts."

"I can do that." Brea nodded. Taking the bowl of ice, she sat beside Lochlan's still form.

"I'm serious. You big fae brute, you better not die." Brea lifted a fresh cloth filled with ice from the bowl and draped it across his forehead. She didn't intend to move until he opened those midnight blue eyes and said something mean. Then she'd know he would be okay.

CHAPTER 4

BREA

"Dear." Someone shook Brea's shoulder.

Her eyes slid open, and for a moment, she didn't remember where she was.

The healer. Finn. *Lochlan.* Rubbing her face, she looked to the man laying still on the bed wrapped in bandages and ice.

"Lady Brea," the voice said again.

She lifted her eyes to find Captain Donovan standing next to her chair. "You should go back to your rooms."

She shook her head, her eyes finding the empty bed where Finn had been resting. "Where's Finn?"

"I had a few men help him to his rooms where he'd be more comfortable. My son was unharmed, just exhausted. We do not yet know the extent of their journey, but it took a toll on him."

She nodded, settling her eyes back on Lochlan. "Will he wake?"

"The healer said his fever broke. We need to remove the ice."

"I can do it."

He shook his head. "You need sleep, my lady."

"No." She stretched her neck to the side. Sleeping in a tiny wooden chair wasn't fun. "I can't leave him alone." She didn't know why. Lochlan wasn't her friend. Most of the time, they couldn't stand each other. But he did this for Alona, was injured searching for her. Maybe Brea felt some sort of connection to the girl she'd been switched with, or maybe she just wanted to pay Lochlan back for saving her life when she was the one injured. She didn't like owing him anything. After this, they were even.

"Lady Brea." Captain Donovan sighed. "Your mothers would be vexed with me if I let you stay here all night."

She snapped her eyes to his. He knew? This man she'd never met before this day. "How?"

He seemed to understand her question. "I have been in this palace since I was a young man at the queen's side. There is very little that goes on I am not aware of."

"Does Finn know?" About her. About Alona.

He shrugged. "I do not know. Lochlan and I have been under strict orders to share our knowledge with no one, but my son is shrewd. Alona is like a daughter to me, my lady. I was with her when she was taken, and I have to live with that. But you I can protect, even if it's just from yourself. The healer and her assistant will take care of Lochlan. I'm ordering you to go get some sleep."

She sighed and pushed to her feet. "Yeah, okay." Unable to take her eyes from Lochlan's distressed face, she released a breath. "Just..."

"I will have them inform you of any changes."

"Thanks." Turning, she made herself walk from the room and into the waking palace. Early morning sunlight streamed through archways, lighting the stone underneath her feet.

She was due at the stables soon, but she couldn't fathom being so far from Lochlan right now. Master Arturo would understand.

Sleep wasn't an option with the worry coursing through her, so she hurried to the courtyard she visited every morning to make a wish in the fountain. The wishes ranged from going back to the human realm to seeing Myles again to Lochlan returning.

This morning, there was only one.

She didn't have a coin on her, so she bent to pick up a pebble near the base of the fountain. Holding it in the palm of her hand, she closed her eyes.

Let Lochlan live.

Releasing the stone, she watched it hit the water with a satisfying plunk. This palace couldn't take another tragedy. For a month, they'd walked around in a fog of despair, trying to ignore the things they refused to talk about. Alona, gone. Finn, gone. Lochlan...

At least Finn was back with them in one piece.

But Lochlan... What would happen to her mothers if they lost another piece of themselves? The family in this palace had what Brea had always dreamed of. Two parents—three if one counted Captain Donovan—who truly cared about those under their watch. Alona grew up with Lochlan as the sibling Brea always wished she'd had.

And Finn, good, kind, Finn—the boy who could make anything better.

Alona may have been taken from her home as a baby just like Brea, but she got the better deal.

Brea trudged back to her room to find Rowena waiting for her with a too-bright smile.

"May I draw you a bath, Lady Brea?"

Brea grunted. "No."

"I'll fetch you something to eat then." She ran out the door before Brea could tell her not to come back.

Yanking off her boots, Brea took off yesterday's clothing and slipped on a comfortable sleeping gown before curling up on her bed. She slid the Humantales book toward her.

Reading stories that held some basis in human history brought tears to Brea's eyes. Would she ever see her world again? The cars and technology. People who didn't treat her as some fragile princess.

Netflix. Man, she missed Netflix.

And Amazon two-day shipping.

If she wanted to buy something she had no use for here, she'd have to make the effort of going to a shop. And everything was just so dang useful.

"Don't they know how to waste money?" she grumbled to herself.

It was probably the weariness speaking, but she hated this world of magic and kings and queens. Her magic sizzled underneath her skin, but she was too tired for it to become more than that.

She curled in on herself and hugged the book to her chest. Rowena returned with a silver tray laden with food.

"I brought you Eldur Brew." She winked, a satisfied grin on her face. "The queen's lady's maid told me you enjoyed it, so I snuck some up. We don't have to tell anyone of your lowborn tastes." She laughed as if it were some giant joke.

"I'm not hungry."

"Come now, Lady Brea. A good breakfast makes every morning brighter." She set the tray on the table next to the bed. "I'll even allow you to eat it in bed."

With a sigh, Brea rolled over and reached for the cup of Eldur Brew—coffee to her. "Is there any sugar?"

Rowena lifted a tiny silver spoon and scooped sugar into the Eldur Brew.

"More." Brea stopped herself. "Please."

Rowena nodded. "Today, I think you're going to need it."

"Lady Brea," Master Arturo snapped. "That is not your job."

She rolled her eyes and continued stabbing clumps of hay with a pitchfork. She'd planned to avoid the stables, but the longer she sat in her room with Rowena staring at her, the more restless she became.

"Chill. It's all good. We won't tell the queen."

He yanked open the stall door and crossed his arms. "A woman of your station does not muck stalls."

"Then what am I here for?" She threw the pitchfork, and it cracked against the wall. Her chest heaved. "Please, tell me why my m—the queen would allow me to work with you if there are so many freaking rules."

"My lady." Emmet jogged toward them. "Are you okay? I heard a crash."

"Wonderful. My babysitter is here." Brea was throwing a tantrum, but in her exhaustion, she didn't care. Working in the stables took her mind off the man who still hadn't woken, despite his fever breaking. It let her forget about this new crazy world she lived in where nobody left her alone.

She'd tried to sleep after breakfast, but her mind wouldn't quiet. Now, here she stood with no more than an hour of sleep in an uncomfortable chair, and Master Arturo and Emmet staring at her like she was back at the Clarkson Institute.

Magic sparked in her fingertips, but not enough to do more than tingle along her skin. Man, she needed rest.

She calmed her breathing. "I'm sorry." She ran a grimy hand over her sweaty hair. "I know I shouldn't be here doing this." Which seemed nuts to her after growing up on a farm and doing the dirty jobs her mom refused to do. She couldn't count the number of stalls she'd mucked with Myles.

Master Arturo bent to pick up the pitchfork she'd thrown. "Lady Brea, the queen allowed you this apprenticeship against the judgement of others so you'd have something to occupy your time. But she was very clear. You are to learn about our breeding programs, the pride of Eldur. I can't have you going home to the palace each day with your clothing in dirty tatters and your face streaked with grime. It isn't proper."

She didn't care what was proper, but she realized it mattered to her. "I understand."

"Emmet, show her ladyship back to the palace. I think she's done for the day."

Emmet looked to her nervously.

With a sigh, Brea walked past him. "Let's go."

By the time they rode along the now familiar road, the sun had started to sink on the horizon. She wasn't sure where this day had gone, but she clicked her tongue, nudging the horse into a trot. The quicker she got back to the palace, the sooner she could check on Lochlan.

At the back gates near the kitchen, she dismounted and ran inside, weaving through the halls until she stood on the threshold of the healer's quarters. Glancing down at her dirty boots and pants, she cringed, knowing she probably smelled as bad as she looked.

Tucking an errant lock of hair behind her ear, she approached Lochlan's bed. His face was relaxed in sleep, but it had much more color than earlier in the morning. A breath rushed out of her. He was going to be okay.

"Lady Brea." Rowena stepped up beside her. "You just missed Finn. He was here speaking with Lochlan."

Brea's eyes widened. "Lochlan was awake?"

The maid nodded. "He's been in and out of consciousness all day. The healer claims that is quite normal."

"What are you doing here, Rowena?" She wasn't aware her maid knew Lochlan well.

Rowena shrugged, red creeping up her neck. "I've stayed most of the afternoon so I could give you a full report when you returned."

"Wait... you sat here for hours... for me?"

"Of course."

Brea stared at her maid with this new knowledge. She knew the woman had been with Alona for many years, but how had she so easily developed affection for Brea too?

"I think you like me, Rowena."

Rowena frowned. "Well, yes, you are my lady. I remember holding you in my arms on the day of your birth. No amount of grumbling or childish outbursts will erase that."

"Childish outbursts," Brea grumbled. No, she didn't grumble. Rowena wasn't right. Except, she sort of was.

"Come, Lady Brea." Rowena put a hand on her arm and guided her into the hall. "You need to bathe."

"Are you telling me I stink?"

"Yes."

A laugh burst out of Brea, a foreign sound after such a lousy day, but it felt good. She followed the strange maid without another protest.

Brea jerked awake, and cool water sloshed across the floor. She'd fallen asleep in her bath after telling Rowena to give her some peace. The woman tried to bathe her. Brea would never get used to all the nudity the fae thought nothing of.

The same thud that woke her sounded at the door again. Her brow creased. She stood, letting rivulets of water stream down her weary body. Every muscle ached as she stepped from the tub onto the cold stone floor, a puddle forming at her feet. She reached for the bath sheet and dried herself before shrugging on a silk robe. Twisting her hair in the towel, she approached the door and gripped the handle.

She wished Rowena was here to tell whoever it was to go away. How long had she been asleep? Moonlight filtered through the window, casting shadows across her bed.

Pulling the door open, she jumped back as a body rolled in. Someone had been slumped against the door. It only took her a moment to realize it was Lochlan staring up at her with hazy eyes.

"Loch." She shut the door and crouched down at his side. "What on earth are you doing here?"

"Had to..." He sucked in a breath. "Talk." His eyes slid shut. "What's wrong with... hair?"

"Huh?" Oh. She touched the towel on her head, suddenly self-conscious. "Come on, douchey Loch. Let's get you up."

He let her wrap his arm around her neck. "I needed to find you."

Her lips curved up as she heaved him to his feet. "Well, you did. In my room. In the middle of the night. Good job." Stumbling under his weight, she crashed into the bed. He fell onto it, and she sighed. "Good a place as any." Noting his bare feet, she shook her head. Why would Lochlan escape from the healer and come to her rooms in the middle of the night? She highly doubted the healer let him go.

Straining, she pushed his legs onto the bed and checked his bandages to make sure they were still in place. "You shouldn't be here," she whispered.

His eyes slid open and fixed on her. "Brea." He tried to lift a hand, but it fell back to the bed. "It's Myles."

Her entire body froze. What could Myles possibly have to do with this place? With where Lochlan had been? She hovered over Lochlan, willing him not to say the words she feared more than anything.

But that was the thing about wishes. Whether they were made in a sparkling fountain with gleaming coins or in the darkness of the night with nothing but desperation, they rarely came true.

A wish was nothing more than a lie one told themselves.

Myles was okay.

He'd remain safe and alive.

She didn't need him.

All wishes. All lies.

Lochlan's voice cracked on his next words. "He's in Fargelsi. Queen Regan has him."

And all those wishes shattered, slicing through her heart like the fragile glass giving false protection to their hope.

Chapter 5

LOCHLAN

Pain was part of this life. Lochlan experienced his fair share. He'd seen queens crumble and families torn apart. He'd felt the sharp tip of a blade pierce his flesh many times.

He'd lost Alona.

But the agony he saw, the pain he caused with his words, was unlike anything he could remember.

This human girl was strong, stronger than anyone else he knew. She'd been taken from her own world and thrown into a battle between queens, yet it was this news that finally broke her.

Her shoulders hunched forward almost as if she caved in on herself. Tears hung in her long lashes but didn't fall.

"How," she whispered, her breath shaking. "How did that woman get to Myles?" Anger sparked in her eyes, and she clenched her jaw. "Griff." She slid from the bed and paced the length of the room. She yanked the towel off her head and damp hair tumbled over her shoulders.

"Brea." He forced the word out past the pain in his chest. He still wasn't quite sure what happened or how he'd ended up back at the palace, only that Finn saved him.

But he did remember the weeks before their battle with the men from Iskalt.

Brea continued pacing and talking to herself. "He's dead. Griffin O'Shea doesn't deserve to be in the same world as Myles, let alone the same palace." She froze. "It's all my fault. He's here because of me."

"Brea." Lochlan tried and failed to raise his voice as a shiver wracked his body and he started convulsing. Pain shot through him, and the room faded away until all he could hear was "No, no, no."

Warm hands touched his bare chest above the bandage, and the feel of her grounded him, keeping him from sinking into the darkness.

"You're freezing cold." She yanked the blankets from under him and folded him in a warm cocoon. Still, he continued to shake. "Oh, for freak's sake."

Lochlan didn't know what she was doing until a warm body pressed up against his under the blankets. Her arms wound around him.

He wanted to protest, to push her away, but for the first time in hours, he started to warm.

"I saw this in a movie," she whispered, her breath hot on his shoulder.

Not even her wet hair bothered him as he let himself relax in the comfort. When was the last time someone hugged him? It was probably Alona, but that would have been ages ago.

He'd forgotten how nice it felt to have a caring touch.

But Brea didn't care about him, she couldn't. How could this girl learn to trust anyone in this world when the man she'd fallen for turned out to be nothing more than a manipulative liar?

They wanted the best for her. Lochlan, Finn, the queens. Everyone in Eldur would embrace Brea if she let them. But he could see it in her eyes every time she looked at him. She wouldn't believe anyone so easily again.

"Do you feel better?" she asked.

He couldn't speak.

"I kind of hope you forget this."

Of course she did. They weren't friends. He'd imagined her worry when he first returned injured.

"When I was in Fargelsi," she went on. "I refused to talk to Griff about Myles. It irritated him, but maybe some subconscious part of me knew. Myles is good, ya know?" Her voice quivered. "He doesn't deserve to be here. His family must be so worried. They love him. Unlike..."

She stopped talking, and he wanted more than anything for her to go on. He'd learned bits and pieces of how she grew up from checking in on her over the years at the queen's request. The humans who raised her didn't deserve such a strong, resilient daughter.

"Whenever things were bad at home, I'd climb out my window and run across the fields separating our farm from Myles'. No matter what he was doing, he had this smile like he was always happy to see me, like I was never interrupting no matter what I needed. He was the only person who ever made me feel like I mattered."

Lochlan turned his head to rest his cheek on Brea's damp hair. She'd always mattered in the fae world, even after she was exchanged for Alona. The first time Queen Faolan sent him to check on her in the human realm, he was fifteen. He'd hidden behind a barn as he watched her lay in the grass gazing at the clouds with a boy by her side—probably Myles.

There'd been a simple kindness in her then, a kindness he hadn't seen since rescuing her from the swamp. But he saw it now in the way she lent him her warmth, in the way she spoke of her friend.

"It should be me," she whispered, the words barely audible. "Myles is trapped in Fargelsi, but it should be me."

Gathering his strength, Lochlan finally spoke. "It shouldn't be anyone. I need to tell you more." He sighed, knowing she wasn't going to like this. "I learned of Myles' fate from... Griff."

Her head shot up. "Explain."

Ignoring the pain speaking caused him, he went on. He owed her the words. "We spent weeks trying to find a way into Gelsi, but the magic on the border has been strengthened since your escape. Once, it only affected people of Fargelsian blood. Now, no one can cross without permission. One night, we were camped in the Vatlands and Griff came to us."

"Why would he do that?"

Lochlan sighed, remembering the letter Griff had given him for Brea. It sat at the bottom of his saddle bags that Finn had carried across his shoulder for the last part of his journey. "He said he cares for you, and you deserved to know. For what it's worth, he did look like he regretted his role in abducting Myles."

"It's worth nothing."

"I know." Giving her the letter would only cause her more pain. He'd have to wait until she had Myles back no matter how much it angered her.

She was quiet for a long moment, and pulses of warmth flooded him followed by searing heat. A cry left his lips, and he bucked up off the bed.

"What's wrong?" Brea sat up but didn't let go of him.

"How are you doing this?" His remaining strength evaporated, flowing from his mind to his body. The wound in his chest pulled together as the last of the infection oozed out, soaking the bandage. He yanked at the bandage. "Get it off me." It was suddenly too tight, and he couldn't breathe. The moon hung in the sky, it shouldn't have been possible for her Eldur magic to rise.

"I can't. You'll bleed."

"Brea," he growled.

"Fine." With deft hands, she unwound the bandage, her eyes going wide.

It took all his effort to lift his head and see that the wound was still there, though much smaller than it had been.

Brea sat back on her heels. "I don't understand."

"What were you feeling just then?"

"Sadness. Guilt. Some anger."

How was it possible she shrank his wound and pushed the infection from his body?

"I don't understand." Her voice was small.

He didn't either. Shrinking away from her, he pressed himself into the bed, wishing he had the strength to walk away. Brea Robinson had a power he'd never seen before, and he wasn't sure if the feelings rolling through him were excitement or fear.

Probably a little of both.

After the revelation, Lochlan fell into blissful darkness as his exhaustion won the battle. Brea didn't return to the bed, and he wondered if she was afraid of herself as well.

He woke gradually as one does when they have nowhere to be. Sunlight flickered across his skin, and he touched the wound to see if he'd been dreaming the night before. No, part of it had been healed.

It wasn't completely gone, and he wondered if that was only because Brea couldn't yet control the power. She turned eighteen soon and had to be taught.

As much as the girl frustrated him, he'd remember last night's kindness for a long time. He lifted his head, hoping to see her skittering about the room. A sleeping gown lay draped on the end of the bed, but other than that, there was no sign she'd ever been there.

That she'd ever laid beside him with her warm arms wrapped around him.

The door burst open and a familiar woman bustled in, a tray in her hands. "Lady Brea, I brought breakfast." Rowena circled the room before finally seeing him. Her jaw dropped open before her eyes narrowed. "Lochlan O'Shea, this entire palace has been searching for you all night."

He sighed and tried to sit up.

"No, no. You stay until we can get someone to help you. As it seems Lady Brea isn't here, you can eat her breakfast." She set the tray on the table next to the bed.

"I will not eat in bed." He finally managed to push himself up. "It isn't proper."

"Proper schmoper." She placed her hands on her hips.

He raised an eyebrow. "Is that one of Lady Brea's odd phrases?"

"Yes, and I quite enjoy it. If you get out of that bed, I'll go find the queen and tell her just where I found you this morning."

Lochlan met her gaze in a silent standoff before sighing. He'd never imagined eating in bed, but he could see he wasn't getting out of this.

Rowena handed him a cup of tea.

"Do you know where Brea would have gone before even receiving her breakfast?" he asked.

Rowena nodded. "Possibly. She could be in the stables."

"Why would she be in the stables?" A morning ride, perhaps?

"Her apprenticeship."

He coughed. The queen's daughter had an apprenticeship in the stables? Had this entire palace turned upside down while he'd been gone? "I must speak with her."

"Well, you can wait until she returns. You are in no shape to ride to the stables. I will find some guards to help you back to the healer—and we won't tell anyone where you've been." With one final eyebrow raise, she turned on her heel and left.

Lochlan groaned as he slumped out of bed. The healer would never believe what Brea's magic did to his wound.

Until he understood what it meant, no one could know.

He hadn't been able to protect Alona, but he refused to let anything happen to another Eldurian princess.

Not even when her name was Brea Robinson.

Because that girl was not going to make any of this easy.

Chapter 6

BREA

"Go away." Brea rolled over on her bed and threw her blanket over her head. Everyone in the palace had knocked on her door over the last two days, but she refused to come out or let anyone in. She was so done with this place and everyone in it. After her one trip to the stables, she realized nothing could take her mind off Myles and decided she'd rather wallow in bed.

"Regan has Myles." She whispered the words that sounded impossible. Here she was on the other side of the fae world with no way to help him. No one could get inside Fargelsi now that Regan had completely sealed the borders.

"Lady Brea, get out of bed this instant." Rowena peeled the covers away from Brea.

"Ugh, how did you even get in here?" Brea had barred the door on the inside and barricaded it with her dresser and half the furniture in her sitting room. It was all still piled in front of the door.

"I have my ways."

"You can walk through walls?" Brea's eyes widened.

"Walk through walls? You are in sore need of an education in magic." Rowena pulled her from the bed and steered her toward the bathroom. "Walk through walls, honestly."

"Then you can apparate?"

"Stop speaking nonsense words and get in the bath." Rowena already had the sunken tub filled with hot water and all manner of scented oils and flowers. "You will stop acting like a spoiled child and attend the ball this evening."

"Nope." Brea turned to retreat to her room. "I've had enough of fae parties to last me a lifetime. No thanks." She slammed the bedroom door behind her and slid the lock in place.

"You will attend this party as your mothers' guest."

Brea whirled around to find Rowena stripping her bed. "How are you *doing* this?"

"Get in the bath, Brea. You smell like one of your horses."

"Fine. But I'm not going anywhere, so you can go out however you came in." Brea stomped to the bathroom where Rowena had opened the doors and windows to let in the fresh air.

Stepping into the warm bath, Brea let out a moan as she sank up to her chin. The tub was large enough for four people and almost deep enough to be called a pool. Clearing her mind of all things Myles, she let herself relax in the bath, washing away days of sweat and tangles from her hair.

"That's enough, now. Time to get out." Rowena laid a bath sheet on the rack beside the tub and marched out of the room. "Hurry up child, we have to get you ready for the ball."

"I'm not going. Besides, isn't it still afternoon? Don't balls happen at night?"

"Not in Eldur. Here they happen at dusk. You have an hour to eat something and get dressed. The queens expect you in the courtyard at four."

"Whoever heard of a ball at four in the afternoon?" Brea slipped under the water to rinse her hair, contemplating not coming back up, if only to escape Rowena's ministrations. There was no way that woman wouldn't deliver Brea to the courtyard on time without a hair out of place if that was what Queen Faolan wanted.

"You will ride up to the gardens with the queens. Now, out with you."

Brea reluctantly left the safety of her bath and wrapped the bath sheet around her. She barely winced this time when Rowena used her magic to dry Brea's hair. Every drop of water from her hair splattered on the tile floor behind her, leaving her hair soft and dry.

"I need to learn that trick once my magic figures out what it's doing." She crossed her sitting room to the vanity that had only moments ago blocked the door. Rowena had moved everything back while she was in the tub.

"Sit."

"Yes ma'am." Brea flopped onto the chair, resigned to the fact that she was going to this ball tonight whether she wanted to or not.

"So what's this party about? We celebrating fae Flag Day now?" Brea had lived among the fae long enough to know they would use any excuse to throw themselves a party.

"I don't know what Flag Day is, but tonight we are celebrating your eighteenth birthday, and you are Queen Tierney's guest of honor."

"It's my birthday?" Brea slumped against her chair. She couldn't get out of this or ditch out early. Tierney had been nothing but nice to her. She owed it to her mothers to be there. "I've lost all track of time with the weird Fae calendar."

"Humans don't know how to keep the proper time." Rowena busied herself with Brea's hair. "I hear a rumor that they don't live long past one hundred."

"Most don't live that long."

"With all their fancy medicines and doctors, you'd think they'd be the ones to live the longest."

"How old are you, Rowena? If you don't mind me asking." She was a grandmotherly sort so Brea had always assumed she was in her seventies, but she was beginning to suspect Rowena might be the oldest person she'd ever met.

"One-hundred-and-eighteen on my last birthday."

"Wow. Will I live that long?" Brea picked at the scones on the tea tray Rowena brought for her. There was even a pot of Eldur Brew she poured for herself. She hadn't eaten anything in more than a day, and her stomach growled in angry protest.

"Oh you'll live much longer, I'm sure." Rowena tugged on her hair, twisting it into an elegant style she couldn't manage on her most patient day. "Royals always live longer than commoners."

"I'm not a royal." Brea sipped her coffee.

"You might not feel like one, love, but it doesn't change the fact that your mother is a queen, which makes you of her royal blood."

"I suppose all the nobles will be in attendance tonight?" Brea changed the subject anytime the conversation went anywhere near the word 'princess' in regards to herself.

"Birthday celebrations are a special occasion in Eldur. Tonight, commoners and nobles alike will dine with you and your mothers."

"Oh no," Brea groaned. All the commoners she'd met in the marketplace would know who she was by the end of the night. There would be no hiding her link to the palace now.

"That's right, the whole of Eldur will know you as Lady Brea after tonight." Rowena chuckled.

"And what must I wear?" Brea had visions of the ridiculous dresses she'd had to wear in Fargelsi and didn't relish the thought of donning a gown that weighed more than she did.

"It's a lovely sea foam green silk. I think you'll like it. The queen chose it for you. She said she wanted you to be comfortable."

Brea doubted that was possible, but she went through the motions, putting on her underthings, surprised when Rowena skipped the corset.

Rowena held the dress aloft as Brea slipped it over her head. A cloud of soft sea foam silk fell around her, light as a feather. Long, sheer sleeves cascaded to the floor.

"There's a slit in the sleeves for your hands." Rowena helped her adjust the fitted sleeve that hugged her arms from the base of her shoulder to her elbows, leaving the rest to flutter behind her when she walked.

With a slit up to her hip, it was a far cry from anything Regan would have put her in.

"It's beautiful." Brea gazed at herself in the mirror. The simple dress left her shoulders bare, and it was as comfortable as her sleeping gowns. "Good job, Mom." She turned to admire the gold trim along the neckline and the gold sandals she would have worn in the human world.

Rowena had threaded a string of golden beads through her hair. It reminded Brea of a tiara, which she didn't like, but the effect was perfect for the dress.

"I guess I have a birthday ball to get to." Brea heaved a sigh. It was the last thing she wanted to do when her best friend probably sat in the dungeon in Fargelsi and didn't have a clue what was happening or why he was involved.

"Now, be on your best behavior and don't embarrass your mothers." Rowena held the door open for her.

"Thank you, Ro-Ro." Brea leaned down and kissed her rosy cheek.

"Oh, be on with you." Rowena shooed her down the hall to meet her mothers.

"Brea, darling you look lovely." Tierney crossed the courtyard to greet her. "Happy birthday, dear." She folded Brea into her arms, and she had to admit, Tierney gave the best hugs.

"We are so sorry to hear about your friend, Myles." Faolan linked her arm through Brea's. Both queens wore simple silk ballgowns adorned with exotic flowers in the queen's colors. Queen Regan wouldn't have deigned to wear something so simple, but both of Brea's moms looked lovely. "We will do everything we can to bring him and Alona back to us. I give you my word, he is every bit as important as Alona."

"Thank you ... Mom." Brea decided in that moment the name didn't feel awkward at all. "He is the most important person in my life. I can't sit back and do nothing to save him."

"We will figure this out, darling." Tierney linked her arm around Brea's free arm and together they headed to the carriage awaiting them. "But please, try to enjoy your party tonight. It was supposed to be a surprise, but we decided you probably wouldn't like that."

"Good plan." Brea laughed. It warmed something inside her that her mothers really were learning who she was and what she liked.

"Your eighteenth birthday is an important milestone, Brea," Faolan explained as their carriage rolled along the cobblestone streets. "In the next few days, your magic will begin to change, and you'll have more control over it. We've arranged for you to have a tutor to help you. You'll have lessons each afternoon once you return from your apprenticeship at the stables."

"Thank you both. I hadn't even realized it was my birthday. I've lost all sense of time since I arrived in the fae world."

"We hope you will one day think of Eldur as your home, but for tonight, we just want you to have fun and know that we are working to bring Myles home."

It was a relief to hear they realized how important he was. Not that Brea would ever stop worrying about him until she laid eyes on her best friend again.

"Lady Brea." Lochlan reached to help Brea down from the carriage.

"Loch, how are you feeling? Should you be here?"

"I wouldn't miss your birthday." His lips twitched. "With your lack of control, you're liable to set the whole place on fire. Wouldn't want to miss that."

"Very funny." She took his hand, noting how pale he was. Despite the facade of his fine clothing, he was in no shape to attend a ball. She'd only ever seen him in his black leathers or soldier's gear. Even in Fargelsi, he always wore simple black clothing.

But tonight, he was in full Eldur fashion, and Brea approved. His long fitted jacket matched the dark blue of his eyes. Trimmed in silver brocade with slitted sleeves, it fit him like a second skin. His silver undershirt buttoned high, with a stiff collar, and his fitted trousers were of the same dark hue as his jacket. A pale blue and silver sash tied at his waist, accentuating his broad shoulders and narrow hips.

Following the queens, Brea walked silently beside him through the tiered garden, up to the highest level, her arm tucked tightly around Lochlan's. They passed commoners and merchants, each bowing as the queens strolled past. Cool breezes swept through the crowds as if called here by magic, which was probably the case. Fires in a rainbow of colors danced in the braziers as the sun met the horizon.

"Isn't it odd to have a ball so early in the evening?"

"Not in Eldur," Lochlan said with a frown. "Surely someone has taught you that much about Eldurian magic?"

"I still know nothing." Brea shrugged.

"I thought Griff taught you how Eldurians draw their magic from the sun."

"And in Iskalt, you draw your magic from the moon. And in Fargelsi, from nature." Brea remembered that much, though she didn't know what it meant.

"So, if your people harness magic from the sun, and mine from the moon, what would be the logical conclusion?" Lochlan pushed her to find the answer for herself.

"Oh!" She gazed around the gardens at all the obvious displays of magic, and it clicked. "They can only use their magic during the day?"

"And I can only use mine at night. But, at dawn and again at dusk, we are both powerful."

"What does that mean for Fargelsi?"

"They can use their magic anytime, which grants them a certain advantage, but they are not nearly as powerful as Iskalt and Eldur."

"I see."

"Now that you are of age, it is important that you learn to harness your magic."

"The queens have arranged for a tutor." Brea and Lochlan followed the queens to their thrones for the evening. They took up their place behind the queens on the dais. It was all so familiar. Brea fought the urge to yawn, pasting on her fake smile instead.

Nobles and commoners alike came to wish the Lady Brea a happy birthday, offering her little trinkets and baubles from the finest gold to the most common beads and stones. Brea found she preferred the simple gifts from the common folk. They were more heartfelt. A young woman shyly offered her a fuzzy white baby pigmy goat Brea refused to let out of her sight.

"You're supposed to eat that, you know." Lochlan stared at the baby goat in her lap. "It's delicious roasted with rosemary and onion."

"Shut your face, Lochlan O'Shea." Brea held her hands over the baby goat's ears. "Her name is Rosie, and she's my pet." Brea scratched the goat's head eliciting a lazy bleat.

"If you're going to keep that thing in your rooms, you need to get it a friend. There's nothing more destructive than a bored goat."

Brea leaned forward to ask her mothers if she could explore the gardens.

"Don't go far, dear," Tierney said. "We have an announcement to make soon, but take Lochlan with you."

Brea left the dais with Rosie in her arms, not overly concerned if Lochlan followed her or not. She made her way through the crowd, offering smiles and nods to those who looked like they wanted to talk, but she kept moving until she saw a familiar face near the buffet.

"Breee-anne of Tarth," Finn slurred, sipping from a flask. "How's the birthday girl?"

"I'm fine, thanks, but you're clearly drunk." She took his flask away, taking a sip of the contents for herself. "Yuck, that tastes like burnt leaves. Try the champagne.

It's delicious." Brea snagged two glasses from a passing waiter.

"Don't mind if I do." Finn poured a healthy splash of his flask into the champagne flute.

"Leave him be, Brea." Lochlan took her glass of champagne from her and drained its contents in one gulp.

"Hey, that was mine."

"I've seen what happens to you after you've had too much fae wine. I don't relish taking another swim in the fountains tonight."

"It happened one time." Brea turned toward Finn, ignoring Lochlan.

"What's wrong, Finn?"

"What's right?" He laughed, his eyes red rimmed like he hadn't slept much since his return.

"It's Alona's eighteenth birthday too, Brea," Lochlan said sadly.

"Oh, right. I'm sorry, Finn. I know you miss her. We'll get her back. Myles too, if I have anything to say about it."

"How?" Finn turned frantic eyes on Brea. "How can we get them back when they're fully out of our reach?"

"Brea, leave him alone," Lochlan moved to stand between them. "You don't know what he's lost. What any of us have. You can't possibly understand."

"I can't?" She gave him a shove. "I don't know what it's like to lose the most important person in my life? I can't understand how utterly helpless everyone feels about poor Princess Alona? Screw you, Lochlan O'Shea."

Brea stormed away, making her way back to the dais to sit with her mothers. Alona's mothers. She might have been born of Faolan's body, and they might be trying to force a family bond with her, but at the end of the day, Alona was the one everyone wanted, not her.

"May I have your attention, please?" Queen Faolan tapped her champagne flute. "Tonight is a special night. Princess Alona's eighteenth birthday. Though she isn't with us, our hearts and minds are always with her in her captivity."

"Why did I ever think this party was supposed to be about me?" Brea turned to leave. She didn't need to be here for this.

"But tonight is even more special because we have a very important guest of honor here with us."

Brea stopped long enough to catch her mother's eyes, pleading with her to stay.

"Some of you know her as Lady Brea Robinson, guest of the queens. But may I present her as Princess Brea Robinson—"

"How could she?" Brea wanted to disappear. She wasn't ready for this. She wasn't some kind of replacement for princess Alona.

"—Of Fargelsi."

Wait, what? Brea turned accusing eyes on her mother.

"Brea is the rightful heir to the Fargelsi throne. Yet the false queen has kept her prisoner there for years. Brea has recently escaped the clutches of our greatest enemy and has come to Eldur to help us fight. With Brea's help, we will bring Princess Alona home, and we will work together with our allies to bring an end to Regan's reign of terror and place the rightful heir—and ally—on the throne." Faolan lifted her glass to the cheers from the crowd.

There it was. The third shoe dropping right on her head just when she wasn't expecting it. With Faolan as her Eldurian mother and Lord Brandon as her Fargelsian father, she would always be a pawn to these people.

Noblemen and courtiers crushed around Brea, vying for her attention even more now than they had before.

"Please, excuse me." Brea hung her head. Clutching Rosie in her arms, she let the crowd sweep her away from the queen. Her mother. The woman who just betrayed her and settled one more lie on the house of cards that was Brea's life.

That house of cards crumbled around her like a pile of ashes.

Brea didn't stop until the brick path beneath her feet turned to grass. Looking up, the last rays of the sun began to fade away, and the party was in full swing behind her. Stumbling across the grassy lawn surrounding the tiered garden, Brea made her way toward the familiar building in the distance. The stables were her favorite place in the whole city. Her one refuge that made her feel normal.

"Lady Brea?" Master Arturo frowned at her dress, the tears in her eyes and the goat in her arms. "You know what? I don't want to know. Come with me."

"Sir?" Brea stumbled after him, her heels sinking into the soft dirt.

"You said you wanted to know when Raven was ready to give birth."

"Really? She's having the twins now?"

"Yes, and I could use your help. Just don't tell the queen I had you do anything beneath your station. And don't get that pretty dress dirty. You can find an apron and boots in the storage closet."

"Where can I put my goat?"

"'In the stewpot' is probably not the answer you're looking for, is it?" The stable master rolled up the sleeves of his fine tunic, and she realized he probably came from the party too.

"No." Brea put a protective hand over Rosie's head.

"Put her in the last stall with Penny. She'll take care of her." Penny was Arturo's faithful dog who liked to mother all the creatures she came upon.

"Thank you, Master Arturo. I'll be quick." Brea darted for the supply closet, eager to visit Raven and meet her twin foals who would likely share Brea's birthday with her and the great princess Alona.

CHAPTER 7

BREA

Raven paced the length of her stall, her long tail swishing back and forth. Brea stood frozen on the other side of the stall door. How did she get here? She'd ridden horses most of her life. But birthing one? Memories assaulted her of her last day with Myles. They sat in class talking about his horse, Captain, a mare who'd given birth while Brea was at the Clarkson Institute. But Myles wouldn't have stood back, frozen in fear.

No, he'd be in there comforting her.

Master Arturo busied himself laying fresh straw. "The straw has to be clean," he explained. "So it won't stick to the foals."

Brea nodded as if she took in every one of his words, but white noise invaded her mind. Myles should be there, not her. He'd have loved working in the stables and birthing horses.

Master Arturo continued talking. "We shouldn't have to do much to help her. Horses are amazing creatures and can do this pretty much on their own."

"What's happening?" a deep voice said over Brea's shoulder, a voice she'd recognize anywhere.

"What are you doing here, Loch?" He wasn't exactly the kind to hang out in barns or care whether a horse gave birth safely. In fact, she didn't know if he cared about anything at all. Well, except Alona.

"You left the party, and I..." He rubbed the back of his neck.

"You what?" She didn't have the energy for his vague words, not with the twins coming and the worry about Myles consuming everything she was.

"I don't know."

"Brea," Master Arturo called. "I need you to come tie Raven's tail."

Brea threw a look over her shoulder at Lochlan. "Maybe you should figure it out. Excuse me, I have something much more important to do than sit at another party." As if the words lent her strength, she pushed open the stall door and entered the wide space. Since getting pregnant, Raven had been kept in the front stall which was three times as large as the others.

Considering the pacing pony for a moment, Brea pulled a ribbon from her own hair and approached. "Hey, girl." She offered her a kind smile and reached out to run a hand down her velvety neck. "You're going to be just fine."

Raven stopped moving, letting Brea draw her hand down her back. "Myles used to tell me horses were much more intelligent than us. More kind. More courageous. I think he was right." She released a shaky breath as she thought of her friend. If she could believe her moms at all about Myles being just as important to rescue as Alona, she'd see him again.

The problem was she didn't know how much she trusted them. Alona was just an idea to her, some girl who got to live the life that should have been Brea's. She didn't know her. But Myles... he was a part of her.

Using the ribbon, she tied up Raven's tail, and she could imagine why Master Arturo insisted on it.

"Okay, Brea," he said. "Now, we must back away and give her space so we don't add to her stress. I am going to fetch a couple of stable boys from the party. You stay here and watch. We fae have many kinds of magic, but this here is unlike any other you'll see."

He hurried from the stall and down the long hall. Brea kept the stall door open as she stood on the threshold.

"Where is your goat?" The sound of Lochlan's voice made her jump. She hadn't realized he was still there.

"The dog is goat sitting."

"Because that doesn't sound ridiculous at all."

Brea jerked her gaze toward Raven as the pony lay down and rolled onto her side. Brea looked toward the barn door, hoping to see Master Arturo appear, but no one came.

"It's happening," she hissed. Where was Myles when she needed him?

"It can't be happening," Lochlan whispered back. "We're the only ones here."

"I don't think Raven cares about that."

The pony let out a groan.

"I think she's pushing. What do we do?" Brea bounced on her toes as magic tingled in her fingertips, latching onto her fear and excitement.

"Calm down." Lochlan gripped her arm. "Even I can feel your magic building. You don't want to scare Raven."

He was right. Brea clenched her fists at her sides, surprised when the power obeyed her and shrank away. They hadn't been lying to her. It was her eighteenth birthday, and she truly did have more control.

They continued to watch Raven until Master Arturo's voice called to them. "I'm here! I'm here!"

Brea glanced behind him but saw no stable boys. "Where's your help?"

He huffed as he reached them. "Not in any state to help with a birthing." His scowl told them everything they needed to know.

The stable boys he could find were drunk.

"It seems you two will have to assist."

Lochlan's eyes widened. "I don't—"

"Of course, we will." Brea shot Lochlan a look. He may be a prince of Iskalt and the Eldur queen's surrogate son, but that wouldn't save him tonight. "Tell us what you need us to do."

"Well, first, we wait."

Lochlan stood tense beside Brea as they watched Raven strain until two feet appeared.

"What do we do?" Brea whispered.

"Patience, my lady." A gleam shone in Master Arturo's eye.

When Brea was told she could spend her time in the stables instead of bored at the palace, she'd never imagined she'd get to witness something like this. As more of the foal's legs appeared, she leaned forward, not wanting to miss a single thing.

Master Arturo was right. This was a truer kind of magic.

Sliding the stall door open, Master Arturo entered slowly. "Push, girl." He looked back over his shoulder as if considering Brea. "All right, my lady. You can come in."

Brea almost wished he hadn't let her. What if she messed this up like she had a tendency to mess everything else up? The lantern flickered, casting shadows on the walls as she moved. If she knew how, she'd have used magic to light up the entire stall. But her magic was useless in the face of such an enormous task. Bringing a life—two lives—into the world.

"Brea, you need a cloth to grip the foal's legs."

She looked back at Lochlan and pursed her lips. "Give me your jacket."

For once, he didn't argue with her. He slid the dark jacket down his arms and held it out to her.

Master Arturo shook his head. "We have horse blankets you can use."

She smirked and dropped her voice so only he could hear. "I know."

With a shake of his head, he crouched down and gestured for her to follow suit, speaking softly the entire time. "Okay, Lady Brea, grip the foal's legs but don't pull. You need to wait for her to push, and then you apply pressure."

A slimy sack covered the legs, and Brea held back bile rising in her throat. She could do this. For Raven. But also for Myles. He'd be proud of her.

They went through cycles of Raven pushing and Brea helping the foal out before Master Arturo finally told her it was okay to pull. Once the shoulder was out, the rest came more easily until there was a new black pony in Eldur.

"It's a girl." Master Arturo grinned. "Lochlan, we need your help. There's still one more."

Lochlan reluctantly entered the stall. "W-what do I need to do?"

"Fetch a blanket from the stack I put at the other end of the stall and rub the foal down. Make sure she's completely free of the sac."

Brea didn't get the satisfaction of watching Lochlan actually do work in the stables because Raven started pushing again.

Before long, two new female ponies lay on their sides in the clean straw, one white and one black.

Brea rubbed the white one down, cleaning her black socks. She glanced up, meeting Lochlan's eyes as the black pony rested her head in his lap.

The smock Brea wore didn't protect her gown from getting filthy, but she no longer cared. It didn't matter that the woman calling herself her mom just revealed to all of Eldur that Brea was an escaped Fargelsian princess, or that she knew without a doubt they wished Alona had been sitting in her place.

Even her fear for Myles faded away for this moment, a moment she shared with Lochlan O'Shea of all people. Her cheeks burned as she remembered helping him heal, and the feel of his skin against hers.

She shifted her eyes away, not wanting to see him as more than the entitled prince she thought he was. Arrogant. Cruel.

Also protective.

The white pony—it would need a name—climbed to its feet, its legs wobbling slightly. She looked at Brea, her wide amber eyes seeing past the false smiles and sarcasm, almost like she could read the fear in Brea's heart. She nudged the side of her head, and that was it.

Brea Robinson was in love.

Brea didn't know how long she stayed at the stables, but she trudged back toward the palace with Lochlan at her side, wishing they'd decided to ride. Exhaustion from the day's events tugged at her, both good and bad.

She couldn't face anyone at the palace—not with the way she ran from her own party—least of all her moms. She was grateful Lochlan didn't insist on speaking. He was a silent presence beside her, and for once, she didn't want to argue with him. Watching him care for the foal would be the image of him she'd hold onto each time they went to battle against each other, each time he annoyed her to the point of rage.

Rowena met them at the gates, her arms crossed over her chest. "Where have you been, my lady?"

Brea sighed. "Have you been waiting for me here all night?"

"Of course not. A guard saw the two of you coming up the path. Your mothers were quite distressed."

"Rowena," Lochlan barked. "Not tonight. Lady Brea was assisting me with an important matter. You can tell that to the queen."

Brea looked to him in shock. He was... helping her?

Rowena, looking thoroughly chastised, backed down. "Yes, of course, sir."

Lochlan trudged past them, his soiled jacket draped over one arm like a badge of honor.

"I need a bath, Rowena." Brea glanced down at her ruined gown.

"And a way to destroy this without my moms taking notice."

To her maid's credit, she didn't worry over the dress. "So, where were you two, really?" She lifted a brow.

"Birthing two ponies."

Rowena stopped walking. "I was... not expecting that."

"What were you expecting?" Brea asked.

"Something sordid." Brea's face must have shown her disgust because Rowena laughed. "I found him in your bed, Brea. It's not that odd for me to think there is something betwixt you."

"Betwixt us?" Brea covered a laugh with a cough and nodded to the guards at the door before passing them. "I'm not even sure Loch has feelings, and certainly none for me."

"Your moms once held hope for him and Alona."

Brea raised a brow. "Okay."

"Without magic, Alona was—is—destined to join the serving class. She cannot take over her mother's rule as queen. But, she could marry a king and be saved her fate."

"And Loch is the rightful heir to the Iskalt throne." It made sense. "So, why did they give up that hope?"

"He changed. The queen began sending him on missions no one other than her knew the meaning of when he was fifteen. He'd be gone for weeks at a time and never came back the same. After that, he wouldn't entertain the thought of courting Alona."

They reached Brea's room, and Rowena got to work starting a bath, but Brea wanted to know more. Lochlan, the man who'd lost his parents and his throne when he was four years old only to be given to a foreign kingdom. The one who called his own brother an enemy but would do anything to save Alona.

And, of course, the man who'd held a newborn pony and looked more content than she'd ever seen him.

That guy was a contradiction, and unraveling his secrets would be the perfect distraction to keep from thinking of Myles every moment of every day.

"Lochlan O'Shea," she whispered. "Who are you really?"

CHAPTER 8

BREA

Brea could've stayed with the new ponies all day, but Master Arturo insisted she go back to the palace for lunch. She'd been there since dawn, not wanting to leave.

The stable boys—or men, she supposed since they weren't very young—worked under the harsh eye of their Master. He hadn't forgiven them for their antics three days ago.

She felt kind of sorry for them, but also thankful because their absence meant she got the coolest experience of her life.

She rode one of the horses back to the palace with Emmett trailing behind and passed the reins off to him after dismounting in the courtyard.

Her stomach rumbled, but she refused to go to the great hall for lunch. Her moms would be there, and she hadn't spoken to them since they revealed her Fargelsian heritage without her knowledge. That wasn't their secret to tell, but what did they care? She might be related to her mom by blood, but she wasn't her daughter, not truly. You couldn't force a family connection no matter how hard you tried.

She could have Rowena fetch her lunch, but found herself standing outside the library instead of her own rooms. It was her favorite place in the palace other than her wishing fountain. When she stood among the tall shelves of books, she could pretend she was back in the world she'd grown up in.

When she flipped through human books she'd never considered reading before, she could almost believe nothing had changed and that her best friend was preparing to talk her ear off about the newest story he'd soared through.

Maybe that was the real reason she loved it here. It reminded her of Myles.

She skimmed a finger along familiar spines as she wound through the stacks to reach the nook at the back, only to find she wasn't alone.

Finn lounged on the pillow-covered bench with Harry Potter and the Order of the Phoenix open on his lap. It was such an odd sight in this land, she couldn't contain the laugh that bubbled up.

Finn jerked his head up. "Oh, it's you."

She hadn't seen him since he was drunk at her party, and she suspected he was avoiding the world just like her. "Don't you work?" She hopped up onto the end of the bench. "You're part of the queen's guard, right? The troops your father leads?"

He nodded and snapped his book shut. "They do give us time off occasionally."

"Oh." She pursed her lips, unsure what more to say to him. A strange sense of déjà vu struck her, and she realized it was because they'd been in this predicament once before, both seeking solitude in the library and finding each other instead. Maybe it meant they were... friends. She so desperately needed a friend right now. She'd cling to just about any thread of kindness.

A sigh rattled from his lips. "Brea... I haven't gotten the chance to tell you how sorry I am about your friend."

She looked away. "Yeah... thanks." Her eyes glassed over, but she blinked away the tears. "I'm sorry Alona wasn't here for her birthday." *Their* birthday.

He stared down at the book in his lap. "This was her favorite."

Brea scooted closer. "Why?"

"She thought it was hilarious humans thought magic worked this way."

Brea laughed. "But we—I mean they—don't. It's just a story, fiction. Humans don't believe magic exists at all."

"Like the muggles."

She bit back a grin. "Yes, like the muggles."

"When Lochlan brought human books back from their world, it was almost like he wanted to see how humans thought. I always wondered if the gifts meant more, if he..."

"Loved Alona?"

Finn nodded. "Even when Loch and I were sort of together—"

"Wait." She put a hand up. "Hold on. You cannot just drop this bomb and keep talking."

"Bomb?"

So many questions rolled through her mind. "So, you and Loch, like... dated?"

"I don't know what dating is, but we were young boys. You forget, Brea, that fae are—"

"Pansexual dreamboats? Yeah, I've been told. I'm just trying to picture it. Lochlan is so... Lochlan. And you're basically perfect."

He shook his head. "Lochlan is more than you think he is. When we were trying to find a way into Fargelsi, we were attacked."

"And you saved him by getting him back to Eldur."

He nodded. "After he took a sword for me."

She didn't know what to say to that.

"Lochlan and I never had real feelings for each other, but he is one of the few people I want beside me as long as I live."

"And Alona is the other." By the way people talk in this palace, she was a saint everyone loved. Brea tried not to resent her.

Finn rubbed a hand over his face. "Have you ever felt like your soul had been ripped from your chest? It's a hopelessness, a knowledge that you can't do a thing to save the most important fae in your life." A tear trickled down his cheek, and Brea remembered a similar question he'd asked her the first time they sat here.

Have you ever loved someone so much it killed you when they were gone?

You feel as if you're no longer alive, like your heart refuses to beat until you see them again.

We wish the pain away in the same breath we hold on to it as a reminder of what they were to us.

And yet, nothing had changed since then. Finn and Lochlan's mission to the border only ended in more pain.

Brea scooted closer and wrapped an arm around his shaking shoulders. "I know exactly what that feels like, Finn," she whispered.

He lifted his eyes to hers, and she saw herself staring back. Her fear. Her guilt.

"This Myles," he started. "You love him as much as I love her, don't you?"

She nodded. "Not romantically, but it's just as strong. Finn, he's my only family."

He leaned his head against hers. "Not your only family."

"If you mean the moms I don't know, don't say it. They just want Alona back. This isn't my home, Finn."

He held out his hand palm up. "Take my hand."

She threaded her fingers through his.

He squeezed her hand. "We can be each other's family. You and I... we'll get them back, Brea."

"We have to. I thought I killed Myles once, and it was unbearable. But now, I will do anything to save him."

"When the time comes, Brea, I'll help you. That's my promise. No matter what, I'll make sure you get him back."

She sniffled. "And I'll do whatever I have to do to bring Alona home to you."

Finn wasn't the first person in this world to make a promise to her.

But he was the first person she knew in her heart wouldn't break it.

Rowena eventually found Brea in the library and brought lunch to her and Finn. They stayed there flipping through books and sharing stories of Alona and Myles. It was better than any kind of therapy.

For the first time, she felt like someone truly had her back.

Not her aunt or her moms. Not the boy she'd started falling for in Gelsi or the one who drove her insane in Eldur.

Finn was nothing more than a soldier, a friend.

He was what she needed.

"When Alona comes back," she started. "I want to convince the queen she should get one of the new ponies as a welcome home present."

Finn smiled. "She loved being around the horses."

"Loves. We aren't allowed to talk in past tense. I've told you this before." It was the first inkling that Brea and Alona had anything in common. "I hope she likes me."

"She will. Alona is kind. She can make you feel like the most important fae in Eldur."

The door to the library opened, and footsteps sounded on the other side of the stacks before Lochlan came into view, a scowl on his face.

"I looked for you two at lunch."

Brea shrugged and gestured to the tray of half-eaten food on the table. "We're not exactly in the mood for palace goings on."

Lochlan looked from Finn to Brea, his frown deepening. "Both of you have been avoiding me as well as the queens."

"Not in the mood for a lecture." Finn stood, leaving his book behind. "Brea, I won't forget that promise." He walked off, leaving Brea and Lochlan staring at each other while his steps faded away.

"What promise?" Lochlan asked after another beat of silence.

Brea got to her feet. "It's not important." For some reason, she wanted to keep the deal she'd made with Finn secret. Lochlan would probably call such a promise reckless, but he didn't know how empty either of them felt. Brea understood Finn on a level she'd never expected. "Why were you looking for me? Want news on our girls?"

"They're not our girls," he scoffed. "Those ponies belong to the kingdom until they're sold."

"I will not allow them to be sold." Her jaw clenched. "If you can just forget how it felt holding them in your lap when they came into the world, you're colder than I thought."

"I never claimed to be anything other than cold. I'm not your friend, Brea."

"Noted." She looked away, trying not to think of him coming to her room injured or seeking her out in the barn. When she met his gaze again, a storm brewed in his eyes.

"Your mother has asked me to help with your magic."

"You're my tutor?" She brushed by him. "Hard pass."

"You don't have a choice in this."

She twisted on her heel, coming face to face with him. "Right, I forgot. I don't have choice in anything."

His gaze hardened. "You are eighteen now, of an age to control your powers. Powers we know nothing about. You did a partial healing on me, something I haven't ever seen. Your blood is half Fargelsian and half Eldurian. The rarest of mixtures when Gelsi does not allow its citizens to cross borders." He leaned down so their faces were closer. "We. Do. Not. Know. What. You. Can. Do." He bit out each word. "Do you understand how dangerous that is?"

She shrank away from him and his blazing eyes. "It's daytime. Can't you only use magic at night?"

"I do not need to use magic to test yours or to teach you further control. You do not control magic, Brea. That is impossible. But magic is fed by emotions, amplifying them. And those, our *feelings*, can be controlled."

Her entire life, she'd felt the power whenever she was angry or scared or sad. Her shoulders slumped as she realized Lochlan was right. She didn't want to feel like this any longer.

She couldn't.

Because it wasn't going away.

Brea was fae, and she had magic. Two truths she could no longer ignore.

Heaving a sigh, she met Lochlan's gaze once more. "I need help." She couldn't admit he was right, but this was as far as she went.

He nodded, his expression softening. "We start now." He moved to walk away but stopped and turned back to her. "We will understand your power, Brea. I won't let it overwhelm you." He opened his mouth to say more but shut it and nodded before walking to the door.

"Thank you," she whispered, too quiet for him to hear.

Chapter 9

BREA

"Where are we going?" Brea jogged to catch up with Lochlan's long stride.

"The orchard. No one will bother us there."

"Ohh, let's go visit the ponies." Brea skipped ahead of him along the dirt path.

"Focus, Brea. This is important. You can go visit your ponies after training.

"You're no fun, Douchey Loch."

"I feel that word is more of an insult than you've led me to believe."

"I promise, among humans it is a great compliment. You might not be much fun, but I greatly appreciate your dedication to my training, oh great douchey one." She could barely keep a straight face, but the way his shoulders drew back and his big head swelled even more, he bought it. He made it too easy sometimes.

"It is my pleasure to help you, Brea."

She really wasn't looking forward to this. Her magic scared her. It was too unpredictable, and Lochlan was about to push her into using her magic on purpose.

Lochlan ignored her, coming to stop among the massive fire-nut trees. She'd recently learned the Brazil-nut-like trees had started to smolder and burn as the fire-nut pods began to ripen. In the coming weeks, the pods would burn away, leaving just the seeds behind.

"It's cooler in the courtyard." Brea fanned her face with her hands. The sun was just beginning to meet the horizon, but it was still hotter than Death Valley up there without the breezes that rushed through the canyon.

"Do you really want an audience to see you try to hone your magic?" Lochlan smirked at her.

"No, not particularly." She leaned against a tree trunk and yelped, jumping away from the hot surface.

"There's a reason they call them fire-trees."

"Noted." Brea brushed at her back to make sure she hadn't singed her clothes. "So how does this work when I have zero control over my magic?"

"That is lesson number one." Lochlan stood across the clearing from her. "You don't control the magic. Forget everything you think you know about magic. It's all human nonsense."

"Okay, so how do I make it do what I want?"

"Your magic is linked to your emotions. You will learn to guide your magic by controlling your emotions, which is not going to be easy for you."

"Why me specifically?" He was already irritating her with his know-it-all attitude, like she should just know this stuff when no one had ever bothered to teach her.

"Humans let their emotions rule them. It's their biggest fault and our biggest challenge to break you of their bad habits."

"Well, I'm sorry." Brea crossed her arms over her chest. "We can't all be emotionless robots like the great *douchey* Lochlan O'Shea." Magic sizzled at her fingertips, itching to get out.

"Control your anger, Brea." Lochlan circled her. "Feel it. Experience the emotion. But don't let it rule your actions."

"And exactly *how* am I supposed to do that?" She could feel the difference in her magic now. Before, it was always a flash of awareness, a tingle just beneath her skin. This was more. This was big.

"Take a deep breath." Lochlan stood in front of her. "Close your eyes and focus." He moved in even closer to whisper in her ear. "And admit you find me handsome."

"What?" Brea's eyes snapped open, and the magic blazed hot within her, like a fire. For the first time, she realized that was probably why they called Eldur the fire realm. It wasn't about the hot temperatures, desert terrain, or even the fire plains and the dormant volcano. It was the fire that burned within its people.

"Admit it." Lochlan moved to sit on the ground, lounging back like they were at a picnic.

"You're infuriating. I'll admit that." Brea's head throbbed with the heat of her magic.

"Focus, Brea. Control the emotion. Your magic is linked with your anger. It's different for everyone. Different emotions drive our magic. Some more than others. I'm not sure anger is the right emotion, but your magic responds to it quickly ... and it's more fun for me." He propped up on his elbow.

"You're a jerk." A burst of energy left her body, slamming into the tree trunk behind Lochlan. An avalanche of smoking fire-pods rained down on his head, bouncing like coconuts off his skull.

Lochlan cursed, slapping a hand over his head where his blond hair singed.

"You're right, this is fun." Brea sat down pretzel style in the thick green grass, dragging one of the pods closer to her. "Thanks for the snack." She cracked open the pod and shook out the warm toasted nuts.

"They aren't ripe yet." Lochlan massaged his head.

"Tastes good to me." Brea popped another nut in her mouth.

"Yeah, they do, but they'll give you rancid bad breath for days when they aren't ripe."

"Of course." Brea dropped the pod, already tired of this game.

"When you've felt your magic before, what other emotion really seems to respond? And be honest. Remember, I am trying to help you."

Brea knew the answer, but she didn't want to tell him.

"I don't know, anger seems to work pretty well." Brea got to her feet. "Why don't we try that one again since you're so good at pissing me off."

"But you aren't capable of reeling that emotion back in. We should try something else." Lochlan rose to stand in front of her. "We need to find something easier to work with now, and then we can work up to anger. That's always the hardest emotion to control."

"Fine." Brea took a step back. "Fear. It always gets me."

"We can work with fear." Lochlan nodded, pacing back across the clearing. "Is it fear in general or more like fear for your life?"

"Fear in general usually has the magic buzzing under my skin pretty quickly. It's a little different than anger. It's intense, but not as … sharp. Anger is more of a quick flash."

"Fear holds more promise," Lochlan said. "What do you fear the most?"

"Do you really have to ask?" Brea shot him a glare.

"Myles. Right."

"And don't you dare think of using him as some sort of training tool."

"You really do think the worst of me, don't you?"

"The fire-nut doesn't fall far from the tree."

"I am not my brother. Or my uncle. And neither of them are half the man my father was." Lochlan took a step toward her. "I wouldn't dare use your best friend just to push your magic to the surface. I know what he means to you."

"You couldn't possibly know."

"Right, I don't know what it's like to lose the most important fae in my life." He gave her words from the previous night right back to her. "Alona is my Myles, Brea. Trust me, I know."

"And we're back at anger." The sharp edge of her magic prickled under her skin, and she tried to control the emotion, but it was like trying to catch smoke.

"Look at me, Brea." His voice sounded in her ear, and she looked up into his dark blue eyes. His arm slid around her waist, and he pulled her close. "We're working on fear," he reminded her as his mouth claimed hers. The warm kiss was brief, but it did the job. Fear pulsed in her veins, and her magic bubbled up to the surface like a pot boiling over.

Brea gasped as she stepped back and her palm—flashing with the yellow light of her magic—struck his face.

"Lochlan!" He went down like a dead weight.

"Yes. Fear is definitely the right emotion." He groaned as he rolled over in the grass, her bright red palm print on his face. "Take a few deep breaths and focus on the reason for your fear. Try to contain it. Understand it. You can control it better when you understand the source of the emotion."

Lochlan just kissed her. It ignited her anger, but more than that, it terrified her. *Why?* Her magic continued to simmer, and yellow sparks danced around her fingertips. The heat of her magic surprised her, but she was part Eldur—part fire itself, or so it seemed.

"Why does my kiss frighten you?" Lochlan pushed her to explore the emotion.

"I don't know. It was a shock." She brushed her still-tingling lips. She could almost taste his magic—like cinnamon and cloves. Warm and spicy. A second wave of fear spread through her, heightening her magic and fanning the flames.

"Do you truly fear me?" Lochlan sounded almost hurt by the idea.

"No I—" But she did. At least on some level. She didn't believe for a second that he would intentionally hurt her. "I trusted your brother, and look where that got me." The magic moved from just under her skin to deep within her core, simmering there, waiting for her guidance.

Lochlan approached her, taking her hands in his. "For the last time, Brea Robinson, I am not my brother."

"You make me nervous." Brea pulled away from his grasp. "That's all." She didn't like the honesty of her words. She knew in her heart that Lochlan was nothing like Griff.

"I think you fear what Finn would say if he knew I kissed you."

"Uh, confusion much? That's the emotion I'm feeling right now. What are you even talking about?"

"You like Finn."

"Sure, we're friends. Besides, from what I hear, you're the one who likes Finn that way." Her nerves spiked at that admission. Her chest ached with the intensity of her magic as it seeped into her palms.

"That was ages ago."

"How long were you boyfriends?"

"Such a human thing to say." He chuckled.

"We're heading back toward anger and irritation again."

"We weren't exactly together. We were just boys. We cared a great deal for each other—still do—and we experimented with those feelings. He was my first kiss. Kind of like yours with Myles."

"Wait, what?" How did he know anything about her first kiss?

"Well, I just assumed." Lochlan refused to meet her gaze.

"But how did you know my first kiss was an experiment?" She was nearly fourteen when it happened. She and Myles were out riding his horses and stopped at their favorite spot where their farms met along a babbling brook right beside the tree they always said was theirs. That was the day they decided they wanted to know what all the fuss was about. So they shared a kiss. It was sweet and one of her favorite memories of Myles, but it was also the day they both knew they were a hundred percent just friends.

"Lochlan O'Shea, how long have you been watching me?"

"Years." He turned to meet her gaze, his face revealing nothing.

"Years?"

"At first it was for your mothers. They wanted to know how you were doing. I was fifteen the first time I visited you. You were just a kid then. But you were always with Myles. Your relationship then reminded me of what I'd never had with Griff. It made me miss him."

"And then, what? You kept spying on me?"

"Not spying." He finally met her eyes. "Never spying. I was watching over you, making sure you were safe. Making sure your mothers had news of you—that they could get to know you through me."

"How often?"

"Every few months. Since you were eleven. I mostly saw you at school or just after. I was fascinated with the human education system."

"You watched me for seven years? And you saw our first kiss? Our only kiss?"

"It was then that I realized your relationship with Myles no longer reminded me of what I didn't have with Griff, but what I'd found with Finn. Our first kiss was similar. Just an experiment between the best of friends. Innocent, but no less important."

She should be mad. She should be furious. Brea wiped away the scalding hot tear trailing down her face. Her magic still churned inside her, waiting for an outlet.

"I know you better than you think I do, Brea. You're strong. Look at you. It's your first day, and already you're holding your magic like a natural."

"It's night." Darkness had fallen around them and the orchard glowed under the simmering light of the branches. "Is this normal?" She needed to focus on the lesson and not on the violation of her privacy Lochlan just admitted to. He might not call it spying, but she did.

"No, but you are not normal, Brea. I've suspected it for a long time, but now I know for certain. Please come sit with me." He sank to the ground, patting the grass beside him. Brea reluctantly joined him

"I'm not happy about this news. Just so you know."

"We have bigger things to discuss. It is nightfall, and you still hold your magic. I need to know how it feels. Is it as strong as it was before sunset?"

"No, it has calmed. It's because I dealt with the emotions, right?"

"Partly. Though the moment my magic surfaced at nightfall, yours should have vanished."

"What does that mean?"

"We know your father was of Fargelsi. A royal."

"Regan's brother."

"Did you know he was the rightful king of Gelsi before Regan killed him?"

Brea took a deep breath, the magic still churning in her core, but the heat had cooled in the absence of the sun. "No. I did not know that. It seems there will never be an end to the things people keep from me."

"Most fae in your circumstance would take after their mother's magic. As far as your magic is concerned, you should be Eldurian. But you have your father's magic too."

"I have Eldur magic during the day and Gelsi at night?"

"No. I think you have both at the same time. During the day, your fire magic is present, but it is bolstered by your earth magic, making you incredibly strong."

"Great. So now I'm a magic freak?"

"You're also a royal, whether you like it or not. I know that is not something you're willing to recognize yet.

"My mother is a queen. My crazy aunt is a queen. I am not."

"Royal bloodlines are strong. And you have two of the strongest coursing through your veins."

"So I'm an extra-supersized fae freak?"

Lochlan ignored her. "Between your dual magic, your father's royal blood, and your mothers, you are likely the most powerful fae our world has ever seen. If that ever becomes common knowledge, our people will look to you as a savior. And our enemies..." He didn't need to finish that sentence because they both knew.

Chapter 10

BREA

Savior.
Fae freak.
Royal.

The labels this world threw at Brea were too much. She couldn't handle the constant expectations, the gobs of information she still didn't know.

And the kiss.

She lay in her bed, staring at the canopy overhead. Too many emotions to decipher rolled through her like waves, bringing her magic to a crest before it tumbled into her stomach, crashing in on itself.

Lochlan tricked her. The kiss was nothing more than him trying to stir up her emotions and get her power to explode out of her. He hadn't done it again in the week they'd been training, but he used other tactics, talking about her family in Ohio and some of the things he'd witnessed. Embarrassment burned through her.

How many times had she told her mom there was someone

watching her? On some level, she'd felt it and even seen him, claiming there was a boy with pointed ears and flashing eyes.

All that got her were multiple stays at the Clarkson Institute.

And he'd seen it all. Had he watched them strap her to a bed as she screamed she wasn't lying?

Did he watch when her dad called her every name his drink-addled brain could conjure?

He thought he knew her because he spent all these years watching over her, but she wasn't even sure she knew herself. She knew she should feel creeped out that her mom would send someone to spy on her, a teenager no less, but instead, she took an odd comfort in it. Even when she'd been locked away, she hadn't been alone.

Lochlan wasn't Griff, and maybe it was time for her to stop treating him like they had the same motives. One wanted to manipulate her while the other had devoted his life to keeping her safe.

Kicking off her covers, she sat up as Rowena entered the room carrying a tray that no doubt held Brea's breakfast.

"Morning, Ro."

Rowena set the tray on the table and placed her hands on her hips. "Ro? What have I told you about that silly nickname?"

"You know you love it." Brea's lips curled into a smile. "Or would you prefer Wena? Rowy? Lady Wen?"

"My name is Rowena, my lady."

"Okay, no nicknames for you. Got it." Brea snagged a pastry off the tray and wrapped Rowena in a hug. "Thanks for breakfast."

Rowena stiffened. "My lady, this isn't proper."

Brea laughed. "So?" She released the uncomfortable maid and bounced toward her wardrobe. "I think I'll get my Eldur Brew in the city this morning." She hadn't been into the city in the weeks since Lochlan and Finn returned. Maybe it was finally starting to master her magic or starting to trust this place, but she felt better than she had any day since coming to this world, and probably before.

She flung open the wardrobe doors and flipped through the

dresses, wanting something simple. "Rowena, just for today, I'd like to forget about every bad thing that has happened."

"Forgetting does not make it disappear, my Lady."

"Yes, I know that. But I need to smile. Maybe even laugh. I want to have fun." She looked back over her shoulder. "Does fun exist in the fae world?"

Rowena's expression softened. "Yes, Lady Brea, though, it's rare for royals in Eldur."

"Ah, but I'm not an Eldur royal. This city only knows me as a Fargelsian princess."

Rowena stepped to her side and pulled a simple yellow dress free. "This one."

Brea smiled. "You're right. It's perfect." Knowing Rowena wouldn't care because of the odd fae lack of modesty, Brea shed her sleeping gown and slid the sheath dress over her head.

"Sit," Rowena ordered, pointing to the stool in front of the vanity. "Now that you are a known princess, I cannot have you wandering into the city looking like any old commoner." She ran a jeweled brush through Brea's long hair before twisting it into a braid and wrapping it around the crown of her head. "And you are not to go alone. I don't know how your mothers allowed it before."

"They were a little preoccupied, Rowena."

"Yes, well, we all miss Alona, but you're their daughter too, and you deserve their full attention."

Brea turned her smile on Rowena. She was the first person to voice what Brea had been feeling since arriving. Alona being abducted was a tragedy, but she wanted a place in this family too.

She thought back on Lochlan's revelations, and her smile widened. "I have had their attention. My entire life they have cared." That knowledge lifted a weight from her, freeing her from the abandonment she hadn't even realized she'd felt.

Yes, Myles and Alona were still prisoners. Aunt Regan would still come after her if she ever left the safety of Raudur City.

Lochlan was still a frustrating enigma of a man.

But, just once, she wanted to be a young woman exploring a new world she'd found herself in. No worries, nothing to push her magic out of control.

It was her birthday present to herself, even though that day was past.

She belted the waist of the dress, much to Rowena's dismay, and tied the pouch of coins her mom gave her to the belt. Slipping into her boots, she waved goodbye to Rowena and darted into the hall.

Getting into the city was about more than just having fun. She'd made friends there and was anxious to see them. But Rowena would have a fit if she didn't find an escort.

Maybe Tierney would go with her. Changing direction, she headed toward the throne room. Her two moms were never far from each other's sides. She figured the queen would have duties to attend to, but her wife might enjoy a trip.

The door stood partially open and arguing voices filtered out. Brea recognized Lochlan and Eamon Donovan immediately. She slipped into the back of the room.

"There is nothing we can do about it," the queen stated calmly.

Lochlan ran a hand through his hair. "So, my uncle is allowed to just welcome the prisoners into Iskalt?"

Prisoners?

Eamon held up a hand. "Your Majesty, we have company. Maybe this is a discussion for another time."

All eyes fell on Brea, and she wished she'd just gone into the city on her own.

"Dear." Tierney rushed toward her. "Good morning." Her kind smile relaxed Brea's nerves. "What brings you to the throne room so early?"

"Um... I wanted to see if you'd like to go into the city today."

"Oh, darling, I would love to, but I have appointments most of the day."

"Oh. Okay." Brea's good mood plummeted. "I can just go by myself then. That's not a problem."

"Nonsense." Her face brightened. "Lochlan will take you." She clapped her hands together like it was a grand idea.

Brea looked to Lochlan, who'd jerked his gaze their way upon hearing his name. She'd avoided him outside of training, and his dark look told her he had no interest in going into the city today.

"That's okay. He doesn't have to."

"Nonsense, Brea." She looked to her wife across the room. "Faolan, can you spare Loch for the day?"

Faolan slumped on her throne, looking exhausted despite it being early in the day. "Well, there is little we can do on this matter. Lochlan is all yours."

They traded him like he had no say, but he probably didn't. As a ward of this palace, he probably obeyed the queen in anything.

Lochlan grumbled something under his breath and walked toward the door. "All right, Brea, let's go."

Brea ran after him, struggling to match his pace. "Really, you don't have to. I know spending time with me isn't high on your priority list."

He stopped walking, not turning to her. "Why would you say such a silly thing?"

She shrugged.

"Brea, we train every afternoon and evening. I'm not the one who has been avoiding you outside of that."

"I haven't—okay, I have. I just feel super weird that you know all these things about me, but also I—"

"Like it."

"Yeah. I mean no. I mean... I don't know. I feel...protected? That's probably not the right word. I know you were only there on orders from the queen, but I like thinking I wasn't alone at some of the worst times."

Lochlan started walking again, still not looking at her. "I was ordered to go to the human world once a year, Brea, but I was there much more than that." His voice was low as if he couldn't believe the words he said.

A smile spread across her face, bringing back the happiness she'd felt in her room earlier. "Okay."

Opting not to have any of the guards fetch horses, they walked down the long road from the palace to the great city beyond. Brea buzzed with excitement the closer they got.

"I know you do not read," Lochlan started. "But I'd like to visit the bookshop while we're here."

"Oh good. I want to see Fiona anyway."

"How do you know Fiona?" He looked sideways at her.

"She's my friend."

His brow creased. "Oh, right. She comes to the palace to take care of the library. Stay close to me today. This city can be dangerous and is very crowded the closer we get to the market." As they entered the city streets, he pointed out shops and landmarks as if she'd never been there before.

It took her a while to realize he didn't think she had. She bit back a grin and nodded along with his explanations for everything they saw.

Outside his tavern, Xander swept the walkway, his large shoulders hunched forward.

Forgetting Lochlan by her side, Brea shouted, "Xander!"

The burly man looked up, a grin spread across his face. "Well, if it isn't our Fargelsian princess."

She ran across the road, narrowly missing being hit by a cart carrying casks. She threw her arms around Xander, realizing how much she'd missed being with anyone who didn't treat her like a royal.

He laughed and patted her back.

A cough cleared behind them, but Brea ignored Lochlan as someone appeared in the doorway of the tavern.

Adamina squealed when she saw her, and the two girls ran into each other's arms. "It's been weeks." Adamina squeezed her.

"Can't breathe, Mina." Brea laughed as she stepped back from the girl.

"Sir Lochlan." Xander's eyes widened as he finally took notice of Lochlan. "Welcome."

"Xander." Lochlan inclined his head. Of course he'd know the tavern owner.

Leaving the men outside, Adamina pulled Brea through the door. "I just made some Eldur Brew. It's like I knew I'd get a visit from a princess today."

"Please don't call me that."

Adamina giggled. "Why didn't you tell us? We just thought you were an escaped Fargelsian noble, not the princess."

Brea shrugged and dropped into a chair. "Reasons."

Adamina shook her head and walked back into the kitchen. Xander and Lochlan walked in, both stiff with discomfort. Lochlan had that effect on people.

Brea patted the chair beside her. "Relax. It'll be good for you."

He sat beside her, his eyes traveling over her face. "How is it that the people in this city are so infatuated with you?" He leaned forward, putting his elbows on the table. "I'm not sure you even noticed how many Eldurians waved to us on the way here. They love you. Why?"

"They don't love me," she scoffed. She'd never been the lovable type. In school, the kids made fun of her, despised her.

He sat back, his eyes never leaving her. "What am I missing?"

Adamina returned with two steaming mugs. She set them on the table. "Eldur Brew, coming up."

Brea brought the cup to her lips and inhaled with a sigh. The brew burned her tongue, but she didn't care.

"Eldur Brew?" Lochlan stared at his cup in disgust. "Put it down, Brea. That's not a drink suitable for a princess."

"Don't be such a snob."

He looked to Adamina. "You serve her a commoner's drink?"

Brea set her mug down and stared daggers at him. "Don't be a douche."

"See, I knew it was an insult!"

"Fine. Yes, douchey means obnoxious." She raised a brow. "Offensive."

He met her gaze, his voice dropping. "That is how you see me?"

"Sometimes, yes." She stood, sending an apologetic smile to Adamina and Xander who watched on in fascination.

"What are you doing?" Lochlan asked.

She rounded his chair and put her hands on his shoulders. "Relax, Loch. No one here is watching you or judging you. We aren't surrounded by gilded palace halls. No one here wears a crown." Her hands slid down his arms, and she squeezed. "Now, pick up the drink that Xander and Mina have graciously provided. Take a sip, because drinks do not have class distinctions."

She released him, fully expecting him to shove the mug away like the petulant child he could be. Instead, he lifted it, staring into the dark liquid before tilting the cup against his lips.

Brea moved to stand beside Adamina and they waited in anticipation.

Lochlan set the mug down, a crease between his brows. "That tasted pleasing."

"Pleasing?" Brea yelled. "Seriously? At least tell me I was right?"

He smirked. "I do not think you can handle that."

She laughed. "Well, for your information, my mother enjoys Eldur Brew. Take that for it being a commoner's drink."

His brows shot toward his hairline. "The q—" He caught himself, throwing a look toward the tavern owner and his daughter. "That is quite strange—even for a Fargelsian."

Xander and Adamina joined them at their table until they needed to finish preparations to open for the noonday meal.

By the time Lochlan led Brea back into the street, he'd had three cups of Eldur Brew, but she wouldn't point that out. A small smile played on her lips as she greeted shopkeepers by name. They smiled when they saw her, and a few tried to bow.

Brea spent a lot of time among these people to distract herself from worrying about Lochlan and Finn when they were gone. Now, with Lochlan by her side, it felt more complete. She was still using the city to forget her constant fears, but in that, she and Lochlan were together.

They sauntered through the market, bumping shoulders as the crowd jostled them. "Myles would love this place." She grinned. "So full of life, so vibrant."

"I've never thought of Raudur City in such a way. My duties at the palace and abroad kept me too busy to spend much time dwelling on it."

"Well, maybe you should start. I know you're an Iskalt prince or whatever, but Loch, you grew up here. These people are yours."

"And yours."

She looked away, concealing a smile at the thought. The people of Eldur had a fierce pride in their kingdom, and she was a part of that.

They left the market behind, still walking in step with each other. Brea had waited to ask about what she'd heard, but she couldn't any longer. "What were you arguing about in the throne room this morning?"

"It's not important." He rubbed the back of his neck.

"It sounded important. Something about prisoners."

A sigh pushed past his lips. "Have you been told of the fourth realm of the fae?"

She nodded.

"It is the prison realm, spelled to protect the rest of the fae from its dangers. No one ever escaped... until now. There are now prisoners living in Iskalt, and my uncle has given them places in the army, an army that was an honor to serve when my parents ruled the kingdom. It was the most noble fighting force in all of faedom. Now, it is another in a long line of Iskalt traditions I have to watch my uncle burn to the ground."

Brea glanced down to where his fists clenched at his sides and reached for one of them. She pried his hand open and held onto it for just a moment before releasing him. "I'm sorry. I can't imagine how difficult it is to lose your parents and then your kingdom."

He stopped walking and stared down at her. "My parents died for a noble cause, Brea. I will not take that from them by wishing it was not so." She wanted to ask if that noble cause was her, but held the question back, unsure if the answer would hurt her more or help her understand.

Lochlan continued. "One day, I will reclaim what is rightfully mine. And then you and I can repair the damage that has been wrought on our world." He turned to walk into the bookshop.

Brea ran after him. "Me? What do I have to do with it?"

He froze inside the door. "You, Brea Robinson, will be the queen of Eldur."

Her jaw dropped open, and the magic froze in her veins, threatening to shatter her like an icicle crashing into the ground. Queen? No. That wasn't the deal. "But I don't even want to be a princess," she whispered.

Before she got a chance to ask any questions, Fiona swept in, brushing right by Lochlan to wrap Brea in a hug. "Lochlan O'Shea, what did you do to the girl? She looks as white as an Iskalt winter."

He shrugged as if he truly had no idea why she suddenly couldn't speak. Fear, but also anger, curled inside her, but she breathed deeply, using the mental exercises Lochlan taught her to control the emotions—and therefor control the magic. It did no one any good if she wrecked Fiona's shop.

"You're okay, dear." Fiona rubbed her back as she guided her farther into the store.

She should have known Eldur wanted her for the same reason as Fargelsi. They needed an heir, one with magic. It made so much sense. Alona couldn't inherit the throne because she had no power, hadn't they told her that a few times already? How had she not put it together?

Faolan didn't want to bring her daughter back to get to know her. She needed Brea the same way Regan had.

Brea's breaths came in short gasps as she did everything she could to control her magic.

"Lochlan," Fiona hissed. "What happened?"

"I told her something she didn't want to hear." He sounded so nonchalant as if he hadn't just pulled a "you're a wizard, Harry" on her. Only, she already knew about the magic. She wasn't just a wizard. More like a wizard-queen.

How ridiculous was that?

Her magic snapped inside her as she gained full control and marched toward where Lochlan thumbed through books on a shelf.

Pushing her hand out in front of her, she forced Lochlan against the shelf. It rattled from the impact, and a book teetered before falling on him. He tried to pick it up.

"Don't move," she growled.

"Calm down, Brea. Rein in the magic. Control the emotions."

Her jaw clenched. "I am controlling it, and I don't want to rein it in. You listen to me, Lochlan O'Shea. I am no one's pawn. You fae-people watch me my entire life after abandoning me to a world I didn't belong in. You trade me between kingdoms like a prize. I might have Fargelsian royal blood and Eldurian royal blood, but I am still Brea Robinson of Ohio. And I will make my own blasted choices."

He nodded, his eyes never leaving hers. "You're going to make an amazing fire queen."

Pulling her magic back in, she released him and turned before striding out the door. It wasn't Lochlan's fault people kept things from her, or that she was in this situation in the first place. If it wasn't for him, she doubted anyone would be honest with her.

No, there was someone else who needed to hear what she had to say.

CHAPTER II

BREA

"I am not a queen." Brea crashed into the throne room, holding her magic back and using her brute strength instead. Okay, she ordered a guard to use his strength and stared him down until he obeyed.

Now, said guard stood cowering near the door while Brea stomped down the long aisle to her mother's gilded throne. A throne she refused to sit on at any point in the future.

Her mother looked up from the Eldurian citizen she'd been speaking to--an older woman who set a basket of eggs at the queen's feet. It was an image straight out of a novel where some fantasy queen accepted gifts from her people as they entreated her to settle land disputes and other issues.

Somehow, it seemed almost beneath the great Queen Faolan. Brea only saw her interact with the people at her birthday party, but this was... different.

"Princess Brea of Fargelsi." Her mother's voice was a cold reminder to keep her mouth shut as she gestured to the citizens waiting along the far wall. "Please, tell me what has happened that is more important than this woman's missing child."

Brea's anger simmered and faded as she took in the haggard faces around the room. To the queen's right stood Captain Donovan, his warm gaze setting her at ease.

The doors to the throne room opened again, and Lochlan rushed in with Finn following close behind.

"I'm sorry, your Majesty." Lochlan bowed. "I could not stop her."

Queen Faolan—because she was a queen at the moment and not a mother—studied Brea, her eyes narrowed. "Captain Donovan, take the Gelsian princess to my rooms. She can await me there while I finish my service to these fine people."

How could she all at once sound like a dragon queen and a fair and noble ruler? A shiver raced down Brea's spine, and she pushed out a breath. She was better than barging into throne rooms and stomping through palaces. That wasn't the girl she wanted to be—a spoiled princess, upset when she didn't get her way. The true Brea Robinson knew what hard work felt like, how it was when she had to stand tall when the whole world was against her.

Turning on her heel, she lifted her chin and followed the captain, not sparing a glance for Lochlan or Finn who tried to follow.

"Lochlan, Finn," the queen's voice rang out behind her. "You two must stay here. The princess will survive without your yammering."

By the time they reached the queen's rooms, a deep weariness replaced the anger inside Brea. She smiled a thank you at the captain before he left her in the queen's sitting room.

Silence surrounded her, and she walked to the floor to ceiling windows that looked out over the city, a city she wanted to call her own. She loved the people, the shops, the life. But it wasn't hers.

Eldur wanted her for the same reason Fargelsi had, the crown. How could she be an heir to two kingdoms when she didn't want one? All she wished for was a family who cared about her and a home that felt like hers.

What had she gotten instead?

Parents who abandoned her in another world. A palace she'd never truly belong in. And people who wanted her for nothing more than the royal blood in her veins.

Just perfect.

Glancing down at her long dress, she tried to brush the dirt from the bottom of it. That's what she got for running through the city streets to confront the queen.

Her eyes flicked from her mother's pristine white couch to the dirty dress. No, she couldn't sit there no matter how tired she was.

Instead, she slid to the floor in front of the window, remembering how she'd once imagined Eldur as a cruel place full of dragons and other creatures. Other than her mother's sometimes coldness, it was more than she could have imagined. If she refused the crown, would she be sent away?

She didn't know how long she'd been sitting there when the door opened, revealing the immaculate queen, her eyes sweeping the room.

"Brea?" She craned her neck to see into the other room.

"Here." Brea lifted a hand to get her mother's attention.

"What on earth are you doing on the floor?"

Brea climbed to her feet. "I didn't want to dirty your couch."

"Couch? Oh, you mean the settee? Darling, you are a princess. My people might not know the truth of which kingdom you call your own, but an Eldurian princess never sits on the floor." She lowered herself to the couch, er, settee and patted the spot beside her. "Come now. I know you think us very primitive, but do you honestly think this has never been dirtied? We have magic, Brea."

"You... Clean with your magic?"

"Heavens no." She put a hand to her chest. "But the palace maids do. Lochlan and Alona used to have quite the fondness for mud, so it was a good thing."

Brea smiled at the image of a little boy and girl running to her stiff mother caked with mud. She sat next to her mother and tapped one finger against her knee.

"So," Faolan began. "Lochlan has told you."

"That I'm... That I'm..." She couldn't say it.

"Going to be queen?"

Brea nodded. "That."

"Well, what did you think would happen? We've already told you of Alona's inability to inherit due to her lack of magic."

"What about Lochlan?"

"He is not my son. And besides, he has his own kingdom to rule once he is strong enough to deal with that wretched uncle of his." She pursed her lips. "Why does this distress you?"

Brea looked away. "I don't know how long I've been in the Fae world, but it can't have been more than six months. Until then, I thought I was a human farm girl. I'm not..." What was she going to say? She wasn't good enough? That she'd fail and let everyone down? "Don't fae live longer than humans? You will be queen for a long time."

She smiled sadly. "Brea, I have been the queen of Eldur for one hundred and forty seven years."

Brea's mouth fell open, but she had no words.

"I was eight when my mother died, leaving me the crown. Do you think I was ready for it then? The truth is I am tired. I have seen many wars and political battles."

"Is that why you sent Loch to find me in the human realm?"

She shook her head. "I have wanted to bring you home every day since I handed you over to my greatest friends."

"Loch's parents?"

"Yes. They took you to the human realm and lost their lives for it. You need to understand something about this world, Brea. Nothing is done without a reason, a purpose. In the noble households, every child is conceived to fill a role. A royal line is only as strong as it's succession."

"So, you're saying you found someone to have a child with in hopes that child could rule one day?"

She nodded. "But that is not all. Regan of Fargelsi had begun to rise in power. Her magic was much stronger than mine—which is not supposed to be possible. Eldur is always the stronger power of the two, evened only by Fargelsians' ability to use magic without the sun. We were scared of her, to be honest."

"We?" Brea froze. "You mean you and Regan's brother, my father."

"Your father..." A smile tilted her lips. "He was a great man, a great king of Fargelsi. We could see the future unfolding. Regan's power would only grow, so we needed a weapon, someone who could use their power both night and day, but hold all the strength of Eldurian blood."

Brea leaned forward, resting her elbows on her knees as she hung her head. "Me." She was a weapon of mass destruction, only brought to life for that purpose.

"Yes." Her mother's voice was no more than a whisper now. "Brandon and I conceived a child. It was our duty to this world. Regan killed him before you were born. She knew what we'd done, but she couldn't get to me here in Eldur. It was clear to her right away Alona was not the child of our union, but you were gone, safely kept in the most nondescript place we could find in the human world."

A laugh burst free of Brea. "You could say that about Ohio." She rubbed her face before lifting her eyes to her mother's. "So, you're saying I have no choice, that I never have. I still don't know who I am or who I trust. How am I supposed to be a queen?"

Her mother reached out and took her hand. "I will teach you, dear. I'm not relinquishing the crown tomorrow. And as for who you are—you're my daughter, and I'm so very glad you are finally home."

Tears blurred Brea's vision, and she tried to wipe them away, but her mother wouldn't let go of her hand. "But I'm not Alona. You don't even know me."

"A mother does not have to know her child to love them. Alona is in my heart. She might not be of my blood, but I love her no differently from you. Not a second goes by where she is not in my thoughts, my fears. Sometimes I can't breathe when I think how far away she is, how in danger." She wiped a thumb under Brea's eye.

"But I have experienced that same fear every day for eighteen years as I've been missing you. Alona never replaced you, the same as you cannot replace her. There is room for both of you in here." She placed a hand over her heart.

Brea shot to her feet as tears continued to cascade down her cheeks. "I need some space." She pulled her hand free, not watching to see if her mother's expression fell.

"Yes." The queen stood and flattened the crease out of her dress. "I expect you do. Take your time, Brea. Just remember, you are fae. You have as much responsibility to this world as I did when I made my decisions."

Rushing toward the door, Brea pulled it open and sprinted past the guards. Tears clogged in her throat, and the only sound was her footsteps echoing against the stone floors.

She reached the courtyard with the naked-man fountain and collapsed against the low stone wall circling it. Digging in the pouch at her waist, she pulled out every coin she had and started tossing them in one by one.

"I wish this was all a dream."

"I wish I could just have one more day on Myles' farm under our tree."

"I wish this stupid magic didn't threaten to boil over every time I got emotional."

"I wish I was normal."

That's what she'd wanted her entire life, wasn't it? To be normal? For the hallucinations and energy underneath her skin to just go away. And now... She was born for one specific purpose: to be a weapon against her aunt.

She wanted to kill Regan for bringing Myles into this, for taking Alona from Finn and their mothers. But could she?

If she allowed herself to become this... magical bullet or whatever it was they wanted her to be, would she ever be anything else?

CHAPTER 12

LOCHLAN

Lochlan was probably never going to sleep again.

Not with Brea Robinson's voice in his head.

"I wish this was all a dream."

She hadn't known he'd followed her to the courtyard or that he'd watched her just like so many times before. Not talking or revealing his presence. Only listening, seeing.

And what he'd seen was a girl who didn't want to be here. She didn't see how much she truly belonged, how the people reacted to her.

How Lochlan reacted to her.

The first time he'd wanted to reach out to her instead of just watching in the human realm was when he was seventeen years old. He'd walked across the barren fields stretching in front of the Robinson's house. Paint curled and peeled from the worn wooden walls. A tire swing hung from the large oak in the yard, but it looked like the rope would break with the tiniest weight.

And there stood a girl in the barn entrance, her hair streaming out behind her. He'd seen her a hundred times before as he kept watch for the Eldurian queen. This girl in ripped pants and a shirt so old the colors had faded from the fabric... She was a princess.

Most of the time he saw her with Myles, but not this time. He'd watched much closer than the queen would have allowed because he had to know what she was doing.

Music had filtered from their dilapidated barn, and he'd peered through a broken window to find Brea dancing as if she'd never heard a beat in her life. He'd shrank back into the shadows when Myles finally joined her.

"What are you doing?" Myles had yelled over the music.

A grin lit up the sad girl's face, reaching all the way to her eyes. "It's my birthday, Myles, and I'm throwing myself a party."

Lochlan hadn't stayed long enough to see if Myles brought a gift. He'd run back across the fields, using the night to hide him as he forced open a portal into Eldur and barreled through, landing right in the middle of a royal celebration. Time was different in the fae realm —the seasons here never aligned with the human realm. Alona's birthday was more than two months ago for them, but there was always a royal celebration on this day every year.

He'd gone from a lonely girl the world seemed to have ignored and her joyful party for two to a ball fit for a princess. He only now realized that yearly ball was meant for the absent Eldurian Princess.

He'd never been the same after that day. Nothing had. He told the queen what he always did, that Brea was safe and healthy, never mentioning the other h word that would have been a lie. She smiled sometimes, but Brea was never truly happy.

And he certainly didn't mention he'd become fascinated with a girl he'd never spoken to, one who didn't know their world existed. As Brea grew older, he realized somewhere through the years, he'd fallen in love with her.

Lochlan sighed as he rolled over in bed, the blankets twisting about his legs. She drove him crazy, but he'd thought he'd gotten over his teenage crush a long time ago.

Then he heard her say she wished none of this was real, and it sent a spear right through his heart. He was real. His world wasn't a dream. She had to get used to that.

He rubbed his face, remembering her horror at the thought of being queen. Hadn't he had those same fears about one day ruling Iskalt? Maybe they had more in common than he'd thought, but he could never admit to the terror thrumming through him at the mention of finally taking the crown from his uncle.

Lochlan might never be able to tell Brea how he felt those years ago. There might be no hope for them, but they'd rule this world together one day as allies and maybe even friends.

A knock sounded on his door, and he glanced to the window. The world outside was still dark, and he couldn't fathom who would be calling at such an hour.

"Just a moment," he called. Slipping from his bed, he reached for the silk robe on a peg by the armoire and shrugged it on, tying it at the waist.

The knock echoed through the room once more before the door burst open, revealing a heaving Finn.

"What's wrong?" Lochlan had always been able to read every emotion in his best friend's face.

"You must come. I was on duty tonight, and we've received a messenger."

"That seems like information for the queen." He raised an eyebrow.

Finn shook his head. "This man... He comes from Iskalt."

Ice shot through Lochlan's veins, and he was sure his eyes frosted over as his magic thrummed to life. Nothing good came out of Iskalt. Not anymore. He stepped into his boots, not bothering to lace them up or get dressed. "Has the queen been informed?"

"Yes. My father went to fetch her."

Lochlan grunted. "Don't let Faolan hear you say anyone fetched her. Come, I must see this messenger."

Finn's brow creased. "You're not going to change?"

"No." Where Iskalt was involved, Lochlan wanted to be the first to know. It might have been a selfish need, being that the queen deserved that right in her own palace, but Lochlan had never been able to shake the guilt over letting his cruel uncle rule Iskalt for so many years.

Finn led him to the great hall where they'd let the messenger warm himself with an ale by the fire. "He rode for many days, only stopping to change horses. I don't think he has slept since leaving Iskalt."

Lochlan gripped Finn's shoulder. "Thank you. Can you send for Brea? I have a hunch I'm going to need her to hear this."

Finn nodded and sent someone to wake Brea while Lochlan crossed the hall to where the hearth breathed life into the cold room. The orange glow reflected off the face of an older man with gray hair tied into a knot on top of his head. His haggard face basked in the warmth as icy eyes stared into the flames.

He wrapped both hands around his mug and lifted it to his lips.

"What is your name, sir?" Lochlan stopped beside the man's chair and looked down at him.

The old man lifted his tired eyes. "Duff O'Dell, your Highness."

"I'm not—"

"I know who you are. I'd recognize those eyes anywhere, sire."

Lochlan turned a wooden chair and sat facing the man. "You are from Iskalt?"

He took another sip of ale before setting the empty mug on the table next to him. "You do not remember me."

"Should I?"

"No. You were a child when I served your parents. I was one of their personal guards."

"Do you serve my uncle?"

Duff sighed. "We all serve your uncle, sire. I no longer guard the king, but my son does. We've expected our princes to come home for many years, and you never have."

"I—"

"No need to explain it to me, boyo. Most of Iskalt is under the thrall of Callum O'Shea. They will follow him to death, but only because they think they have no other option."

Lochlan clenched his jaw. "And you?"

"I have had the truth of the man revealed. It is why I have come, risking my family back in Iskalt."

Lochlan was about to tell him to speak when commotion sounded behind them. The queen's arrival. Faolan breezed into the room with no care of who her retinue disturbed. Few others lingered besides Lochlan and Duff, but the queen's guards and maids turned the quiet conversation into a crowded state report. He breathed a sigh of relief when Brea slipped in at the back of the group, doing her best to go unseen.

"Lochlan." Faolan held chastisement in her eyes. "You are not to speak to messengers without me."

"Dear." Tierney put a hand on her arm. "If this has to do with his kingdom, he has the right."

Faolan's gaze softened when she looked at her wife. "Yes. It is late, so let's see what has gotten us all out of our beds." One of her guards dragged a wingback chair to them, and the queen sat.

"Your Majesty." Lochlan dipped his head. "This is Duff O'Dell. He has come with news from Iskalt."

"If you'll excuse me, my Lady." Those nearby sucked in their breath at the term. Lochlan closed his eyes for a brief moment, but the queen didn't correct her title. "Lochlan O'Shea is my ruler, not an Eldurian queen. I came to speak with him."

"And here we both sit." Faolan looked wholly unaffected. "Tell us why you have come."

"There are too many ears," Duff hissed.

The queen sighed. "Leave us," she ordered. "Eamon, Finn, Brea, you stay." The guards and servants hurried out, leaving the cavernous room empty except their small group.

Duff focused his gaze on Lochlan, ignoring the queen and the rest. "I live in a village about a day's ride from the Vatlands between

Iskalt and Eldur. We are a quiet village, peaceful. Until now. We've been finding friends and neighbors dead. At first, we thought a sickness had come, but there are marks on the bodies, burns. They have rings of charred flesh crossing their torsos."

"A barrier spell," Lochlan whispered. He'd seen those kinds of burns before while stationed along the Fargelsian border. Anyone with full Fargelsian blood died if they tried to cross.

"A barrier spell, your Majesty?" Duff looked to him in confusion.

Lochlan leaned forward. "Tell me, Mr. O'Dell, do people still travel to your village? For trade and other purposes?"

Duff nodded. "Yes. Though, the flow of traders to the markets has slowed."

"Then it is not complete yet."

"Lochlan," Queen Faolan snapped. "What you speak of is not possible. Callum O'Shea does not have the power for a barrier spell."

"Don't you see, your Majesty? He's crafting it, or at least trying to, using one of his own villages as the test before expanding it to all of Iskalt, turning the people into prisoners just like those in Fargelsi."

"But how? It would take more than Iskalt magic for a spell of such magnitude. And it doesn't explain how trade has not stopped."

"But it does." Lochlan tried to remember everything he'd learned studying the Fargelsi barrier. "It takes an enormous amount of power to sustain even a small barrier around a village. More power than Callum can wield on his own. My uncle has never been a great magician. As he tries to complete the barrier, his magic seeps into the village. It's not complete yet, but it is killing people all the same."

Queen Faolan covered her mouth with her hand. "He doesn't have that kind of power."

"Regan does." Brea's voice surprised Lochlan, and he sat up straighter.

He met Brea's eyes. "Speak."

Brea bit her lip. "Fargelsi and Iskalt have an... understanding. I don't know if that's the right word. To them, Eldur is the common enemy. A horrific spell such as this has to come from my aunt. She'd help your uncle. I'm sure of it."

"Even so," Queen Faolan started. "There is nothing we can do. Iskalt problems are not our own."

Lochlan hardly heard her. He barely noticed her bidding goodnight to the messenger, or Duff looking to him helplessly as a maid led him to a room for the night.

All Lochlan could see was Brea, and the secrets she'd kept.

A secret that could end them all.

Chapter 13

LOCHLAN

Lochlan needed to find his bed again to try to obtain the elusive sleep. Maybe then he'd receive some clarity.

Some answers.

But he'd never claimed to do the smart thing.

"Loch," Finn called him back, but Lochlan brushed past him on his way out the door.

He needed to speak to Brea. He only planned to ask questions, to find out the whole truth. Her mother refused to help Iskalt, but it was his kingdom and he'd do what he could.

But that was logical Lochlan, and all logic left him the moment he learned what his uncle was doing to their people.

Brea reached her rooms and stopped with her hand on the door. "I know you're following me."

"We need to talk," he growled.

"Fine." She pushed open her door. "By all means come berate me in the middle of the night. I haven't had enough people lecturing me lately."

He didn't miss the sarcasm in her voice, but he also didn't care. There were two Lochlan O'Sheas. One was stuck as a teenage boy wanting to protect the princess and experience just one of her smiles.

The other, the cold Iskalt prince, he'd do anything necessary to get answers.

The latter won out as he kicked the door shut and advanced on Brea. Her eyes flashed yellow as she stood her ground, refusing to move.

"My uncle." His jaw clenched. "Tell me everything."

She crossed her arms. "Only if you back up."

With a sigh, he did as she asked.

She nodded in approval. "I really don't know much. It's not like my aunt let me into important meetings, and everything Griff told me was a lie."

A growl rumbled low in his throat at the mention of his brother and the thought of them together. "Tell me what the Iskalt delegation did after I left Fargelsi."

She shrugged. "Honestly, I don't know. I was kept away from many of the state dinners because I'm a bumbling fool, and my aunt was embarrassed of me."

He took a step toward her, wanting to erase the self-conscious flicker of doubt across her face. "You are no fool, Brea Robinson."

She stepped back, pressing her back against the wall. "I—"

"Is it true?" His voice lowered. "Regan and Callum have formed an alliance?"

"Yes."

"You should have told us the moment we brought you to the palace."

She pushed at his chest. "Oh, you mean when you were all mourning Alona? Or when you left for weeks with no word, leaving us scared out of our minds that something happened to you too?"

She was scared for him? He lifted a hand, planning to cup her cheek. Instead, he gripped her chin and forced it up as he hovered over her. "This was important, Brea."

She hit his hand away. "How was I to know? I've lived my life in the human realm, not this messed up fantasy sideshow. I. Am. Not. One. Of. You."

He leaned down to look into her eyes, his power meeting hers. "You are. You always have been."

"Maybe I don't want to be," she whispered.

He wanted to kiss her. More than anything else in the world, he wanted to feel her lips against his again. But the next time he kissed her, it would be real. He wouldn't be trying to enrage her to fuel her magic. And it wouldn't be a result of this heated anger between them either.

When he kissed her, she would feel in one moment everything he'd bottled up over the years of watching her in the human realm. All the sadness and the pride. Even the tiny bits of joy he'd watch her capture. She'd feel dancing in an abandoned barn and sitting under a gorgeous tree with blue skies overhead.

That was how he once saw her.

And now? The princess of two kingdoms who'd escaped an impenetrable palace and made the population of the entire capital fall in love with her.

"You infuriate me," she said, staring into his eyes, unflinching.

"Not as much as you infuriate me." He stayed where he was, his chest pressed against hers, for a moment longer before reminding himself why he'd come.

Something was happening in Iskalt, something terrible and dangerous.

He took a step back, giving them both space to breathe. "It's time I help my people." All these years he'd been safe in Eldur while they suffered under Callum. "I've abandoned them long enough."

"My mother won't allow it if she thinks it's not Eldur's problem." Brea pushed away from the wall, the yellow fading from her eyes.

Lochlan rubbed the back of his neck. Brea wasn't wrong, but maybe that didn't matter. "I love Faolan like she is my own mother, but she is the queen of Eldur. Iskalt blood runs through my veins, and it's time I let that guide me."

Brea's lips twitched into a smile. "I feel like I'm watching a little boy become a man right before my eyes."

The scowl he unleashed on her had no venom behind it. "I know it must be a foreign concept in the human world, Brea, but you do not need to voice every thought that comes into your mind."

"So, I guess I shouldn't tell you I'm proud of you for choosing your people over my mother's wishes?"

He turned away from her to hide his smile. "Pride is a useless emotion." In three strides, he reached the door and opened it. As he stepped into the hall, he heard Brea calling behind him.

"I'm proud of my little silk-robe wearing princeling, and I don't care how useless that is."

He shut the door and shook his head with a laugh, his chest expanding with Brea's pride. It may have served no purpose, but he felt her words in every bone of his body.

He glanced down at the robe he'd forgotten he was wearing, and a flush crept up his neck.

Even in his embarrassment, the moment he lay down and set his head against his soft pillow, he fell fast asleep, Brea's pride like a blanket protecting him from the troubles the next days would bring.

Chapter 14

BREA

"I won't allow it, Lochlan." Queen Faolan perched on her throne in the empty throne room. It was barely light out, but Lochlan had called them all here to discuss the threat on Iskalt.

Brea wasn't sure why she was there. Yawning, she perused the morning buffet, sad to see the absence of Eldur Brew. No matter the time of day, the throne room spread offered the best food to be had in all of Eldur. "Ooh jelly popovers." She helped herself to several of her favorite pastries, wondering if she just went back to bed if anyone would miss her.

"It is none of our business." Shocked, Brea's attention turned to the queen. How could she say such a thing to Loch, knowing how he felt about his people and his absence all these years? It occurred to her that her mother might not know him as well as she thought if she expected him to sit back and watch his uncle turn Iskalt into another Gelsi prison.

"It is my business, your Majesty. I cannot allow my people to suffer any more than I could stand by idly while the people of Eldur suffered. I will leave for Iskalt today, with or without your help. I have nothing but the deepest of respect for you. You have been the mother I've needed all these years—and you always will be—but I can no longer turn a blind eye on my kingdom."

"And what about Alona?" Faolan asked. "Our forces are working hard to bring the Gelsi barrier down. We have to focus on bringing her home, Lochlan. I would have you and Finn stay close to act the moment we receive word the barrier is breaking."

"That's not fair," Brea interjected, a popover halfway to her mouth. "You can't ... take the Iskalt blood from his veins any more than you can give him fire magic. So how can you sit there and tell Lochlan to ignore the suffering of those he feels responsible for?"

"You overstep, Brea." Faolan frowned. "This does not concern you. I don't even know why you were summoned at this early hour. Go back to bed, darling."

"No." Brea met Lochlan's pleading gaze. This was why he'd asked Rowena to send her to the throne room. Only Brea with her human nonsense would have the gall to speak to the queen in such a way. "I mean no disrespect, your Majesty, but if you were a guest in Iskalt and learned your people were being slaughtered here in Eldur, would you ignore it?"

"Of course not, I am queen."

"And Lochlan is their rightful king. He isn't a child anymore, as much as you might like to think of him as the son you never had. Please, don't ask him to choose between you and Alona who are his family, and his people who are his duty. It's cruel." Brea took a step back, thinking she'd pushed her mother too far. "I mean, respectfully, your Majesty." She bobbed a curtsy for added measure.

"She is right," Lochlan said. "I will leave for Iskalt today, but I would prefer if I had your blessing, if not your help."

"I would sooner see you safe at home, here in the palace." Faolan sighed. "But I know the weight of the responsibility you shoulder, Lochlan. I cannot become directly involved in the unrest within Iskalt. I will not require my troops to join you, but you may ask for volunteers. That is the best I can do for you, my son. Please do what you must and return home to us safely." Faolan stood to dismiss them.

"I volunteer as tribute!" Brea stepped toward her mother's throne.

"What?" Faolan looked at her like she might never understand her daughter.

"No." Lochlan looked at her like he might throttle her on the spot.

"You need me." Brea lifted her chin in defiance. "I have fire magic. You'll need me during the day when your magic is dormant."

"I have Finn for that." Lochlan crossed his arms over his chest. A fleeting emotion showed in his dark blue eyes, but it was gone before Brea could decipher it.

"So, you're going to march into Iskalt—a land where everyone uses magic at night, with a bunch of useless troops—and Finn—who can only use magic during the day?

"Hey." Finn scowled at her. "I think that was an insult."

"If you have to think about it, it was." Brea left her half-eaten popovers on the table. "You need me, Lochlan. I don't have a time limit on my magic."

"You know, she's probably right." Finn shrugged. "She's not trained, but she's better than nothing."

"Hey! I can do stuff." At the very least she could scare people with her erratic magic.

Finn raised a brow as if to say he could give as good as he got.

"No. End of discussion." Lochlan turned toward the queen and gave a curt bow. "Thank you, your Majesty. I will keep you updated with our findings in Iskalt. Finn, we leave before noon."

"I'll be ready." Finn gave Brea a half-hearted shrug, snagging one of her popovers on his way out.

"Try to get some sleep, Brea, darling," her mother said. "It's still much too early to have bothered you with this unfortunate business."

"It's okay. I prefer it when people keep me in the loop with what's happening around us." Brea loaded up her plate with pastries and headed back to her room. She had some packing to do.

"If you are going to steal one of her Majesty's horses, at least steal a good one."

Brea whirled around, cursing herself for making too much noise. "Master Arturo, I uh—didn't want to er—take a horse you might miss."

"I take it you've a mind to follow Master Lochlan and his troops?" Arturo moved to unfasten the saddle she'd just settled onto her mount. An aging mare with a feisty temper if not much speed. "You'll need to move faster than old Red here can manage. You'll take Sassa. She'll get you where you need to go in a hurry."

"Thank you, Master Arturo." She helped move her saddle bags to the young white mare, eager to put as much distance between her and the palace as possible. Brea couldn't put a name to the feeling. She just knew she had do something to help, something that wouldn't make her feel so useless all the time.

"Take the north road, and you should catch them before nightfall. They'll make camp at the plains just south of Loch Sol."

"Don't tell—"

"I never saw you." Arturo smiled, slapping Sassa's rump and setting Brea off along the trail up to the orchard where she'd find the north road. "Don't get lost, my Lady."

"Thank you!" Brea called over her shoulder. It felt good to let Sassa set the pace as they raced through the orchard. Lochlan and Finn left more than an hour ago, and she had a lot of ground to cover if she was going to catch up to them.

Lochlan spent the morning asking for volunteers and managed to gather a troop of three hundred Eldurian soldiers to accompany him into Iskalt. If he'd taken an extra day or two to plan, he probably could have left with twice that. It made Brea nervous to think of what might lay in wait for him in Iskalt. For all they knew, this whole thing with the dead villagers might be a trap, and he was walking right into it.

"Come on, girl. Let's see what you can do." Brea urged her mount into a full gallop once she reached the north road. A column of dust rose into the sky along the horizon. That cloud was her destination.

An hour into her trip, Brea was convinced the sun was going to kill her. The dry dessert air parched her throat, but she had precious little water with her. Just enough to get her to Loch Sol.

At the top of the rocky rise, Brea hoped she'd find some sign of shade where she could rest and give Sassa a drink of water.

"What are you doing, woman? Are you trying to make me crazy?"

Brea closed her eyes at the sound of his voice. "How did you know I was following you?"

"You kicked up more dust than three hundred soldiers. I figured it was you, or Faolan found some more volunteers for me." Lochlan stood from his seat among a scattering of boulders at the bottom of the hill she'd just crested.

"And which one of those is your preference?" She guided her horse over to his.

"A few hundred soldiers, or one inept girl with erratic magic? Hard choice."

"I won't go back." Brea took a sip from her canteen. "You might as well face it, I'm coming with.

"Just try to stay out of trouble."

"Who me? Contrary to what you might think, I am not a trouble magnet."

Lochlan guided his horse away from hers.

"What are you doing?"

"Moving away from the lightning that is sure to strike you at any second."

Chapter 15

LOCHLAN

"Oh my gosh, this is heaven. Loch, you gotta try this." Brea's voice drifted to him in the darkness. They'd ridden hard all afternoon and reached the hot springs near Loch Sol just as the sun began to set.

He'd sent scouts ahead with orders to make camp near the mud springs Loch Sol was famous for. Judging by the sounds Brea was making, it was worth the extra effort to find the springs. But his mind wasn't on Loch Sol or even Brea who occupied his thoughts often of late. It was with his people.

"Seriously. This is like heaven."

Something warm splattered across his back. "Did you just fling mud at me?"

"Yes. You should try relaxing. Brooding about your people now when you can't help them yet isn't doing you any good."

"Are you suggesting I join you?"

"Are you suggesting there is something improper about that? I have clothes on in here you know."

"That's not how you're supposed to do it, Brea." He chuckled at her modesty.

"Well, that's how I do it. I don't relish getting mud all up in my lady bits."

Lochlan snorted as he stood and shed his travel stained shirt and trousers, leaving his underthings on. She was right—in her way—worrying wouldn't get him there any faster. Sinking down into the hot mud, Lochlan stifled a groan.

"You could make a fortune selling this stuff to humans." Brea slathered the mud over her shoulders, rubbing it into her tired muscles.

"Eldurians pay a handsome price for this mud. It has healing properties that keep the effects of aging at bay for a time."

"Humans would kill for this stuff."

"Humans are vain creatures." Lochlan settled back into the mud, feeling the tension ease from his shoulders.

"Not all of us are caught up in our looks."

"You aren't human, Brea," he said softly, watching her profile in the darkness.

"Maybe not in body. But in spirit, I think I always will be."

Lochlan moved closer to her, unable to keep his distance. She had a way of making him feel better even when it seemed his world was falling down around him.

"It's part of your charm. Don't ever lose it, Brea."

"My mother expects me to."

"Give her time. Faolan is a good mother, but she is also very stubborn. I imagine that is where you get it from."

"What kinds of things did you tell my mothers about me after your spying visits?"

Lochlan frowned. He didn't like to think about Brea's life before. The parents who should have adored her, treated her like trash. Alona's biological parents. He could never see much of her in them. They didn't deserve either daughter. "Lots of things. I told them about your school. About Myles. How you loved your horses when you were young and were sad when your parents had to sell them."

"What about all the other stuff?" Her voice was small in the darkness. It stirred something inside him, knowing all she went through in the human world. So many times he'd wanted to bring her home, but it wasn't safe for her then and probably never would be.

"I told your mothers you had nice parents who cared for you as best they could given their limited means."

"Thank you." She stood, letting the mud slide down her body.

"For what?" He joined her, resisting the urge to pull her close.

"For keeping my secrets."

"If I could have changed anything for you, I would have." He took her hand, helping her out of the mud spring.

"Wait, now what?" Brea looked down at herself with a frown.

"Now we walk to the hot springs." He pointed across the sparse forest of stunted trees to the clear waters of one of the many hot springs surrounding Loch Sol. Still holding her hand, he led the way.

"There should be a spa hotel here. I'd never leave." Brea sighed into the cool evening breeze.

"The area around Loch Sol isn't a suitable habitat. It's much too hot during the day, and nothing grows here. But I'm sure if you ask your mother, she would bring wagonloads of the mud into the palace and build a mud spring just for you."

"Here we are. Be careful, Brea, it's very hot." Lochlan reluctantly released her hand as she stepped into the natural sulfur spring to rinse the volcanic mud off.

"It can never be too hot." She tiptoed into the deeper side of the pool, the steam curling the stray locks of her hair falling from the messy knot on top of her head. "I loved taking bubble baths when I was a kid, but my mom rarely let me indulge. Said I made too much of a mess and it cost too much to fill the tub. It was never hot enough or deep enough. And now I have a swimming-pool-sized tub in my bathroom and servants to fill it."

She sounded so sad, like maybe she missed the drunken fools who were supposed to be her parents.

"Do you miss your home?"

"I don't have a home, Loch." She shrugged, dipping her shoulders under the water, rinsing the mud from her underclothes she'd insisted on wearing into the spring.

"Eldur is your home."

"Maybe some day. It still doesn't feel like it though. I love the city and the people. I'm just not so sure about the palace or those who reside there."

He knew she was still upset about the prospect of becoming queen someday, but that day was likely a distant future where Brea had found her role within her family and the people who already adored her.

"Make yourself useful." He turned his back to her, changing the subject. "Help me wash the mud off where I can't reach."

Her hands felt nice against his hot skin as she rinsed the last of the mud away. "There, that's better." She turned him toward her, running her hands along his arms. "See, relaxing isn't so hard. Even you can do it when you try." She looked up at him with her crooked half smile.

For once, not overthinking his actions, Loch, pulled her close, his hands settling around her as his lips brushed hers. A gasp of surprise escaped her as she tilted her head back to look at him, her body warm against his. He pulled her closer, and she pressed her lips against his, her fingers dancing through his hair as she deepened their kiss. Lochlan growled as her fingertips traced the shape of his pointed ears. A shiver shot through him at the simple touch.

"Do me." She broke away, turning her back to him with a nervous laugh.

"What?" His kiss addled brain couldn't grasp what she was saying.

"Rinse the mud off my back."

"I can do that." He murmured in her ear, scooping up a handful of water he let his hands slide down her back until the tension left her shoulders and the last of the mud rinsed away.

"Thank you, Brea."

"For what?" She murmured in a sleepy voice.

"For keeping my mind off things I can't fix right now." He pressed a kiss against her throat and took her hand to lead her back to camp.

Traveling over the mountain pass, through the Northern Vatlands and into Iskalt took longer than expected after a fresh snowfall left them seeking a different path—and warm clothes for Brea. She hadn't thought that far ahead when she packed her things to follow.

It felt good to be home—doubly so having Brea with him. Part of him wanted to show her his home, but he wasn't here for sightseeing. He had a village to inspect.

"Are we there yet?" Brea asked.

"Almost. The village lies in the valley below. You can just make out the buildings on main street."

"Oh, I see it." Brea leaned over her saddle. "It's bigger than I thought."

"It's a milling town. They have a thriving economy and are remarkably self sustaining this far from the capital city.

"It's like a little Alpine village." Brea smiled. "It's adorable."

"There's a nice inn where we'll stay tonight. The men can make camp just outside the village while we investigate these strange deaths."

"I'm looking forward to a warm bed and a hot meal."

"We used to come here often when I was a kid. I still remember the candy shop and the bakery." Lochlan realized he was more eager to show Brea around the village than finding out what his uncle was up to. He needed to get his head on straight before he let himself get too caught up in Brea and her infectious smiles.

"It's awfully quiet," Brea murmured as they entered the outskirts of town.

Something wasn't right. The village always thrived with activity.

"Loch." Finn slipped off his horse, waving several of Loch's men to fan out behind them with their weapons drawn. Lochlan gave his friend a nod, he could feel it too. Something was very wrong.

"Oh," Brea whispered a moment later as they made their way past the mill. It had snowed recently, but just a light dusting to cover the bodies that lay strewn about. They were all dead.

Dread filled Lochlan's mind as he walked ahead to find villagers laying on the sidewalk and in front of store windows. All dead.

"What happened?" Brea's voice broke with the anguish Lochlan felt at the sight of so much death.

Lochlan stopped at the center of the town square. Children had played here while their parents went about their business in town. He fell to his knees beside a child no more than six, his cold frozen body seemingly unharmed. The boy's lips were blue, and his cold dead eyes stared back at Lochlan with an accusing glare. He should have been here for his people. He should have challenged his uncle for the throne years ago. He was a man now. No longer a boy hiding behind Faolan's skirts. But he'd stood by and let this happen.

"This was powerful magic," Finn whispered. "Callum lost control of it. He's not powerful enough to complete the boundary spell on his own."

"They're burned. Just like the others." Brea bent to examine a little girl with winter flowers in her hair. She didn't deserve this. None of them deserved to have their lives cut short because his uncle was a madman.

Lochlan couldn't breathe. Everywhere he looked he saw dead children. Mothers with their daughters, come to town to sell their ribbons and eggs. Father's stocking up on supplies for the coming winter storm. Shopkeepers and townsfolk just going about their day, all struck down by some kind of insane magical boundary spell his uncle couldn't hope to pull off. Yet he'd sacrificed an entire village just to see if he could do it.

"Finn, send a messenger back to the troops. Tell them to come down from the pass. We have work to do." Brea turned toward the hardware store. "You three." She pointed to the soldiers who'd accompanied them into the village. "Round up all the supplies we'll need."

"For what, my Lady?" the soldier asked.

"These people deserve a final resting place, and we're going to give it to them. We'll need shovels and carts and lots of manpower."

"The ground is frozen, my Lady. In Iskalt they burn their dead and scatter the ashes in the mountain pass."

"Then we'll need to visit the mill for wood for a few pyres. We will not leave these poor people to rot in the sun when the weather warms."

"Yes, my Lady." The soldiers went to do her bidding.

"We'll start with the children." Brea grabbed another group of soldiers and set them to work gathering up the children from the town square and laying them carefully on a wagon bed.

As she issued orders, Lochlan sat in the snow, his heart shattering into a thousand pieces over the unnecessary deaths of his people. People he should have protected.

Before long, Brea had soldiers clearing each building, one by one. She was a natural leader. She led by inspiring others to join her. She never asked them to do anything she wasn't willing to do herself. His men leapt to do her bidding, and Lochlan only hoped that one day he could inspire such loyalty in his people. But he had to protect them first.

Chapter 16

BREA

"Loch, you're shivering." Brea crouched down at his side. Smoke from the pyres curled into the air, remnants of the people who once gave this village life. They burned the bodies hours ago, but now, as the sun disappeared behind ice-covered trees, Lochlan remained.

"Go away, Brea." He sat on the snowy ground with his knees bent and shoulders hunched forward, watching the smoke drift through the dusk to cover the village in a thick cloud.

Had it really only been the day before she sat next to Lochlan in a mud bath and felt his lips on hers?

That moment and this one didn't belong in the same world.

Lowering herself to the snow beside him, Brea focused on the breath releasing from her mouth in long streams of steam. She was no stranger to harsh winters, having grown up in Ohio, but this was different, more pronounced. She couldn't remember ever feeling so cold, like ice invaded her veins.

But that had little to do with the temperatures, so different from the heat of Eldur. The first leg of their journey into the Northern Vatlands, the temperatures grew progressively colder, but once they crossed the border into Iskalt, the sudden shift to epic freezing took Brea by surprise.

She'd never understand the fae world, or the magic it possessed.

Lochlan hung his head as darkness invaded the sky, and still, they remained silently side by side. He didn't need a pep talk, or for someone to tell him to rise and return to the men camped outside the now empty village.

Wrapping her cloak tighter around herself, she leaned on her knees. Snow seeped into her riding pants, but she was past caring.

"I was four when I left Iskalt." Lochlan's voice carried with it all the pain of this day. "Four when my parents died, when this kingdom became nothing more than a dream to me, a some-day possibility. I always told myself I'd reclaim it one day, but while I had one-days and maybes and a warm palace in Eldur to keep me safe, real people have suffered."

"It's not your fault," Brea whispered.

"Isn't it?" He turned tortured eyes on her, shining with power as the moon rose overhead. "I should be their king, Brea. You wouldn't understand what that means."

"I know it means you feel guilty."

"Guilty? That doesn't begin to describe what I'm feeling. You are heir to the Eldurian throne, yet you do not want it. Nothing stands in your way of taking that crown once your mother relinquishes it. I am a prince with little hope of ever wearing the crown I've dreamed of my entire life."

"It's not fair. You should get to rule a kingdom, not me."

He lifted his eyes to the smoke once more. "Fair does not matter in this world. I want to do what is right. And I've failed. I was too late to save them."

"So, what are you going to do about it?"

He met her gaze. "It is done, Brea. There is nothing I can do."

"I call bullcrap."

"What?"

"You heard me. Sure, you can't save this village, but how many are there in Iskalt?"

"One hundred and eleven—now ten."

"Wow, I did not expect you to know that." She pushed herself to her feet and looked down at him. "Then we have work to do."

"I do not understand."

She sighed. "You fae need everything spelled out, don't you?"

"You're—"

"One of you, I know. You're like a broken record, Loch—and no I won't explain that because we have more important things to do."

"I already told you, this village is lost to us."

"And it's all your fault. Yes, I've heard. But there are a hundred and eight—"

"Ten."

She waved his correction off. "—Villages in this freeze-your-butt-off kingdom. I might not be the most reliable person to say this, being that I'm an heir to two kingdoms and want to go hide in a cave, but maybe it's time."

"Time for what?"

"For you to do what I know you're dying to do. Take back your kingdom."

His mouth opened, but no words came out.

She continued. "I know. You kind of want to kiss me again right now, don't you?"

He cleared his throat. "Brea, now isn't the time, but I need you to know, that was a moment of desperation. I've been terrified since the moment the messenger arrived in Eldur telling us what was happening in Iskalt. You were just kind of—"

"There? Yeah, I get it. Two fae royals get into a mud bath. There has to be a joke in there somewhere. But Loch, this isn't about us right now. I know you're hurting. I know what it feels like to let people down. But just because something shakes your faith and makes you feel like the worst human being on the planet doesn't mean it's time to stop fighting. Maybe it's a signal to start."

Lochlan rose to stand in front of her, the moonlight shining off his pale hair streaked with soot. "I'm not a human being, Brea." He turned on his heel and marched away, the snow crunching underneath his boots.

Brea stayed frozen in place, wondering how she'd failed so spectacularly in her pep talk.

Lochlan didn't need her. It didn't matter how good his lips felt against hers or how much she wanted to kiss him again, she wasn't the person who should be at his side.

"Alona should be here," she whispered. Brea didn't know the human girl she'd been exchanged with, but what she did know was that this life belonged to her. Faolan, Tierney, the crown, Lochlan... Brea was living Alona's life and doing it poorly.

She trudged back to camp where soldiers sat around fledgling fires barely speaking. The day had been filled with horrors, and the Eldurian warriors had to use their magic to light pyres for dead women and children.

None of them would forget what happened here.

Soldiers nodded to Brea as she passed. If they wondered why the Fargelsian princess had come, they didn't voice the thought. One day, when she was revealed to be Eldurian, they'd know she belonged among them.

Lochlan was nowhere in sight, but Finn sat near the far edge of camp on his own in front of sputtering flames. Once night had fallen, the Eldurians could no longer use their magic to keep their fires alive.

Finn looked up as she approached, but the usual smile didn't tilt his lips. "Dóiteán."

"What?" She sat beside him on the blanket he perched on and leaned into him for warmth.

"It's the Fargelsian word for fire. I know no one has taught you how to use that side of your magic, but they use words to control it."

"Like spells."

He shrugged. "I figured your Fargelsi power would be easy to control without the Eldurian magic tainting it at night. Worth a shot because I'm freezing my bum off here."

Brea pursed her lips and studied the tiny flame that looked like it would die with one more big gust of wind. He was right. She might as well try. If she burned down the camp, at least they'd all be able to warm themselves near the fire.

Reaching one hand out, she let the weaker Fargelsian power pool in her fingertips. It didn't carry the explosiveness of her Eldurian magic. "Dóiteán," she whispered.

Nothing happened.

"Dóiteán," she said, louder this time.

A pop cracked through the air before flames spread over the sticks. Brea and Finn scooted back to avoid being burned, but a triumphant feeling surged through Brea.

She'd done it.

Lochlan ran out of a nearby tent as the other soldiers searched for the source of the sound. When they found Finn and Brea's fire, they rushed over, crowding around the warmth.

"I'll be right back." Brea went to each of the other fires, repeating that single word. By the time she'd finished, weariness overcame her. She stumbled back to where Lochlan stood across the fire from Finn.

"You shouldn't be using your magic." He crossed his arms. "You can't control it."

"I believe I just did." She didn't appreciate the harshness of his tone—even if he was hurting. "You could have made those fires, and you didn't. So, somebody had to."

He pointed to Finn. "You shouldn't encourage her."

"You're right." Finn ducked his head. "I'm sorry."

Lochlan grunted and retreated to his tent.

"You can't honestly believe he was right." Brea fell to her knees and held her hands toward the flames.

Finn sighed. "He does not need me to argue with him right now."

She settled in beside him once more. "Loch thinks this was his fault."

He rubbed his face but didn't respond.

"I think..." Brea sucked in a breath. "I know this is a totally illogical thought, but I can't help thinking part of the blame for the state of Iskalt rests with me."

Finn snorted. "Brea—"

"No, hear me out. I think... Lochlan's parents died saving me from my aunt. They left their kingdom to bring me to the human realm, and somehow, Regan had them killed before they returned. Lochlan and Griff lost their parents, but Iskalt lost its royals. Because of me, Iskalt is now under the rule of a cruel man. And for what? So I can be some sort of weapon against my aunt? That's why I was born, right? But I can barely control this magic." Her voice lowered. "All this death, the horrors from this village that I will never forget, what if it was all for nothing?"

"You are not nothing, Brea. Some would say you're everything."

She remembered Griff telling her that same thing, but it had been another one of his devious lies.

"What would Alona do?" She bumped his shoulder. "If she were here, what would she say to Loch?"

"Alona had a much quieter strength than you." A sad smile curved his lips.

"Are you saying I'm loud? Or pushy?"

He shook his head. "Alona and Lochlan had a friendship few could interpret. Sometimes it was like they spoke their own language, that of siblings."

"Myles and I had that." She smiled at the memory. They could communicate what they were feeling with a single touch or nod.

"Lochlan will always do what is right, Brea. He doesn't need someone to tell him he must fight for his people or what his next move should be. He's not an Eldurian villager that must be convinced to join the next campaign. Alona would have known that. Lochlan would tell her to leave him alone, but she'd join him anyway."

"And then what?"

"She'd just be there. No speeches. No arguing." He smirked at her.

"I don't argue."

He only stared at her. "Lochlan is fully capable of shouldering his own pain and that of everyone else. He's a stubborn brute like that. But Alona wouldn't have let him, because pain like his—a lifelong struggle with duty and power—it's enough to harden even the most joyful fae. And Alona refused to let Loch become a man of stone."

"It sounds like she's a good friend."

Finn looked away. "He needs you, Brea. He will never admit it, but I've known from the moment I met you why."

"Are you going to enlighten me?"

"No." He leaned back, stretching out beside the fire and closing his eyes. "I don't think I will."

Brea didn't know how long she stared into the flickering flames, her damp cloak finally drying as she scooted closer to the warmth.

Finn's words ran on a constant loop through her mind. He was wrong. Lochlan needed Alona, his best friend, not her. He needed Alona like she needed Myles. Completely and without reservation.

Yet, as they camped beside a village of the dead, Alona and Myles were prisoners of the queen who made this possible. Callum O'Shea tried using Regan's spell to create a barrier, but Iskalt magic didn't work like Fargelsian. There were bound to be repercussions.

Brea knew hardly anything about the power, and even she knew that.

What was Callum playing at?

Had he wanted Lochlan to see this? Maybe it was a test... or a signal of more to come.

Brea sat up straighter as a thought came to her. He couldn't have believed it would work. Iskalt was trying to draw Eldur into a war.

It was the only thing that made sense. If he performed enough atrocities on his people, Callum knew Lochlan would have to respond—probably with the might of the Eldurian army.

But there was one thing Callum didn't know. Queen Faolan had grown into an isolationist, not wanting to send her people to fight another's war.

Brea jumped to her feet and paced in front of the fire. She had to tell someone, but why would they listen to a girl who knew nothing of war? Back in the human world, the closest she got to battle was watching some of the men in her town join the military.

Glancing toward Lochlan's tent nearby, she knew he'd at least hear her out. Her long strides took her to the tent, and she considered knocking, but the fae cared nothing for privacy, and she was half-convinced he wouldn't let her in.

Pushing the tent flap aside, her eyes widened when a wave of warm air hit her. The tent was... heated?

Lochlan sat on the edge of his bed roll, his legs stretched out in front of him and his head in his hands. He didn't move as she entered.

A light glowed from somewhere in the tent, but she couldn't figure out the source. Its glow reflected off Lochlan's bare chest. The man loved to be half naked—a fact Brea was not the least bit upset about.

"Loch." Her voice was small, tentative. "How is it warm in here?"

He didn't lift his head. "I am of Iskalt, Lady Brea."

"Right." His magic worked at night. She didn't appreciate his sudden formality, but this moment wasn't about her.

All thoughts of telling him about her suspicions flew from her mind as she stared down at him. Instead, she thought of what Finn had said. Brea would give anything to feel like Myles was with her. Maybe Lochlan felt the same about Alona.

Holding her usual word-vomit in, Brea channeled the quiet princess she'd heard so much about. Lowering herself to her knees at his side, she leaned forward and wrapped her arms around him in an awkward hug.

His body stiffened, and he tried to pull away.

Brea held on tighter. "I'm here," she whispered. "You don't have to say anything. Today was horrible, and I get the feeling the days coming will only get worse. It's okay to let yourself feel the pain, Loch." She rested her chin on the heated skin of his shoulder.

His stubble scratched against her, but she didn't move. Tonight wasn't about the kiss they'd shared or the anger that seemed to always stand between them. This moment was an acknowledgement of two facts: nothing coming would be easy, and they were in this together as friends and allies.

His body relaxed into hers, and he buried his face in her hair. They stayed in their embrace, both taking comfort in not being alone.

The images from that day would never leave their minds, but the false Iskalt king would pay.

Just as Regan would pay for taking Alona and Myles.

"Brea," Lochlan whispered, lifting his head.

She leaned back and met his gaze.

"It wasn't all for nothing."

She sucked in a breath. He'd heard what she'd said to Finn about Loch's parents. "I—"

He pulled her back into their hug. "No. Don't refute it. You're the key. I've known it since the very first time I saw you in the human realm."

"I may be a key, but what door do I unlock?" The one that gets her friends kidnapped by an evil queen, or the one leading to an incompetent practically-human girl sitting on the throne of Eldur?

"I guess we'll see."

Yes, they would. She wouldn't have believed this a few months ago, but she and Lochlan might be on the same side. It wasn't the side of Fargelsi or the Eldurian crown. Not the side of Iskalt or this magic they both possessed.

They would do what was right for the people they cared about—whether that was Alona and Myles or nameless villagers in a distant kingdom.

As Brea sat beside Lochlan and let him feel his pain, she no longer had to channel Alona, because she wasn't her, and she'd made herself believe the people in this new life of hers needed Brea Robinson just as much.

CHAPTER 17

BREA

Traveling back through the mountain pass into the Northern Vatlands, Lochlan set an urgent pace. If he was eager to reach Iskalt on the trip coming, returning, he was like a man possessed, never letting them make camp for more than a few hours before they moved on.

Brea just hoped her mother would have the heart and the sense to help Lochlan protect his people. It didn't matter if it led to a war Faolan didn't want. With the death of an entire Iskalt village, this was about common decency and respect for all life—not just Eldurian life.

"Will you help me convince the queen that Callum needs to be stopped?" Lochlan rode beside her along the Southern road that would lead them into Raudur City in less than an hour.

"I don't know how much help I'll be, but I will try."

"She listens to you, Brea. You're the reason I had help on this trip. She wasn't going to allow it until you spoke your mind."

"Hopefully, my mother will see the sense in coming to Iskalt's aid before it's too late." Brea urged her horse to keep up with Lochlan's. She could just make out the tiered gardens in the fading sunlight. She was eager for a nice hot bath and her own bed, but she imagined they all had a long night ahead of them first.

Lochlan leaped off his horse the moment they passed through the palace gates into the courtyard. "Meet me in the throne room in ten minutes."

"Which one of us was he talking to?" Brea glanced at Finn, looking exhausted after their mad dash across the Eldur desert.

"Unfortunately, I think he means both of us." Finn tossed his reins to a servant and followed Lochlan into the palace.

Brea slipped off Sassa's back, patting her long white mane. "Thanks for the ride, girl. Master Arturo will be happy to have you back." She handed the reins off to another servant, heading inside the cool interior of the palace, stopping only long enough to splash water on her face at the fountain and take a long gulp of the refreshing basil and berry infused water the servants made ready for visitors to the palace.

"Brea, darling, we were so worried." Tierney crept up behind her on her way to the throne room.

"I'm sorry, Mom, I just couldn't let him do this alone." Brea wiped a hand over her tired eyes. "I didn't mean to worry you."

Tierney stifled a gasp, taking Brea's hand as she fell in step beside her.

"What?" Brea asked.

"It's nothing, dear." Tierney patted her hand. "That was just the first time you've called me Mom without forcing it."

"Oh, well, that's not nothing then, is it?" Brea smiled at the sweetest of her mothers. It was so easy to love Tierney. Faolan was harder, but Brea suspected that was because they were both so stubborn.

"I fear this report will be worse than the last." Tierney led Brea into the throne room where Lochlan and Faolan were already at odds with each other. "Oh, dear." She gasped at the look on Lochlan's face. "Our poor boy has had a shock, hasn't he?"

Brea gripped her mother's hand. "You've no idea."

"Please, your Majesty," Lochlan said. "If you could have seen it with your own eyes. Helpless children lying dead in the town square, covered in snow. Men and women going about their business one moment and dead the next—the whole village sacrificed for a magical experiment that had no hope of succeeding. It can't be ignored."

"I understand your anger and frustration, Lochlan, I do. But this is not a matter for Eldur. If you took a step back from the horror of it all, you would see that is exactly what your uncle wants."

"That's what I thought too." Brea stepped forward. "Callum O'Shea knew his experiment wouldn't work, but he slaughtered all those people anyway. He wants to lure you into a conflict."

Lochlan's face paled at her remarks, like he thought she'd just betrayed him by agreeing with her mother.

Faolan gave her daughter a nod of approval. "We cannot allow such a distraction at this time. We must keep our focus on Regan. Our troops at the Fargelsian border are working to bring the barrier down, and then we are going to bring my daughter home. And I will speak to you later about your disobedience, running off to join the troops like a common woman. It is not for a princess of Eldur to get involved with the dealings of Iskalt."

"But I am not a princess of Eldur, am I, mother? You've made me a princess of Fargelsi, escaped from the realm to come to Eldur's aid. But according to your politics, why would I get involved in Eldur's issues with Gelsi if you can't be bothered to help with Iskalt?"

"Do not twist my words, child."

"You forget I come from the human world where we help those in need no matter where their loyalties lie. When a disaster happens, it doesn't matter if they're American, Chinese, or British. Rich or poor. They're all people, and when it comes to the loss of life, politics don't matter. And I'm eighteen. In *my* world that means I don't need your permission to make my own decisions."

"What would you have me do? Divide my army and invade Iskalt and Gelsi at the same time? Abandon my efforts to bring Alona home? Or your friend, Myles? Regan and Callum want to divide us, and so far it's working." Faolan stepped down from her throne, taking Lochlan's hands in hers.

"I know how much this hurts. How you feel torn in two, but one day you will rule Iskalt, of that I have no doubt." The queen reached for Brea's hand. "And one day you will rule Eldur. That bright future is the one I fight for every day. You will be the greatest of allies, but we must be strong and stay focused on the direct threat, which is Regan."

"He will strike again," Lochlan said. "And next time it will be closer to home. Callum O'Shea will draw you into this conflict. How many lives must be lost for you to see that? Will it take Eldurian spilled blood?"

"That's not fair, Lochlan. I care for your people, I do, but my priority will always be Eldur first. Once we deal with Regan's direct threat to Eldur and bring Alona and Myles home, Callum will back down. Let's cut off the head of the dragon and the rest will fall into place."

"I cannot wait while more innocent people are slaughtered. I must return to Iskalt." Lochlan stood with his head held high. "It is time I put my people first the way you have always put Eldur first. I will leave tomorrow."

"Please stay a few days before you leave us again," Tierney interjected. "We understand your need to be with your people, Lochlan. You are their rightful ruler, and it was only a matter of time before you were ready to challenge your uncle. We support that." Tierney met her wife's dark gaze with one of her own. A battle of wills happened in that single instant, but whatever it was, Tierney won.

"We do support you, Lochlan. But we are sad to see you go. Please, give your troop of volunteers a few days to rest. If they are still willing, they may accompany you into Iskalt. I won't have you leaving entirely on your own."

Brea watched the subtle way her parents communicated, and she realized Tierney was the Faolan whisperer. She needed to take lessons from her mom to learn how to communicate with her formidable mother.

"I will go with Lochlan," Brea announced. "Just long enough to help you gather your countrymen and those who would support your claim for the Iskalt throne. You're not very good with the talking. I'd like to help you, if you'll have me."

"You should stay here where it's safe," Lochlan muttered.

"That wasn't a no, so I'll take it as a yes." Brea turned to her parents. "Mothers, I will be careful and will return in a few weeks. I'd just like the opportunity to do what I can to help Lochlan. I could use the time away to wrap my mind around the idea that one day I may rule Eldur. At the moment, that is simply not something I can even consider for my future."

"I cannot allow you to leave, Brea," Faolan insisted.

"Good thing I'm not asking." Brea turned to leave without the queen's dismissal. It didn't matter what her mother wanted, Brea refused to let Lochlan walk out that door not knowing he had the assistance he needed to take his throne. If her mother couldn't give him that, then the only thing Brea knew to do was go with him to help in whatever ways she could.

Chapter 18

BREA

"I thought I might find you here."

Brea looked up from her spot on the grass to find Finn sitting on the paddock fence, watching her with the young ponies.

"I tried to get back to work today, but Master Arturo said there was no point if I'm just leaving again in a few days. Apparently, the man knows everything."

"He'll outfit Loch's unit with fresh mounts. The stables master always knows what's going on before the rest of us do." Finn came to sit with her while the young foals tested out their gangly legs in a wobbly game of tag. "What are their names?"

"Dawn and Dusk." Brea smiled at their innocence. "I thought when they're full grown, Dusk could be mine, and Dawn could be Alona's."

"She would love that." Finn's voice sounded far away. About as far away as the Gelsi dungeons.

"You're as torn as I am, aren't you?" Brea picked a wildflower and wrapped the stem around her finger like a ring. For a moment it reminded her of that time with Griff when she'd almost picked a poisonous flower. Everything in Gelsi was poisonous, but she never had to worry about that in Eldur. Here, nature was always exactly what it seemed. The people, sometimes less so.

"I feel trapped. Like I can't possibly split myself in half to help the two most important people in my life when they need it most. The moment I heard the queen sent her army to the Fargelsi border, I wanted to go. I need to do my part. I need to be there when Alona is freed. But Loch needs me too. I can't abandon him now."

"Loch will understand, Finn. Alona needs you. Let me be your other half. I'll be with Loch."

"You're right." Finn rubbed a tired hand over his eyes. "The queen is sending fresh troops to the border in two days. I will leave with them after I talk to Loch."

"Milord?"

Brea and Finn turned toward the weak voice. They saw her just as she collapsed.

"Who is she?" Brea asked as they raced toward the young girl.

"By the looks of her she's from Eldfal."

"Isn't that north of Loch Sol?" Brea was proud of her growing knowledge of fae geography.

"Yes."

"Did this kid just walk across the desert by herself?"

"Barefoot by the looks of it." Finn examined her blistered feet. "She needs water." Finn grabbed his canteen and propped the girl's head up.

"Need to see the queen, milord," the girl murmured.

"We'll take you to the queen soon. Drink a bit of water for me first, and then we'll go." Finn tipped a trickle of water into her mouth, coaxing her to drink slowly.

"How could she survive such a journey? She can't be more than ten." Brea checked her pulse. It was strong but much too fast.

"Sheer willpower." Finn picked her up. "Let's get her to the healers."

"I need to see the queen," the girl insisted. "I have an important message for her."

"How about you tell me your message, and I'll deliver it to the queen myself while you get some rest?"

"No. None but the queen herself should hear this news."

"She has every right to bring her grievances and concerns to the queen like everyone else who comes to the palace." Brea examined the girl's feet as they made their way back down to the palace. It was a miracle she was still walking when she found them in the paddock.

"Then let's get some more water into her so she can speak to her queen."

They paused every few minutes so the girl could take slow sips of water.

"What's your name, sweetheart?" Brea asked.

"Bailee." With each sip, she seemed to grow stronger. "I think I can walk now."

"Not on those poor feet, you can't." Finn refused to set her down.

"Are you sure you won't let us take you to the palace healers first? Some mud from Loch Sol would give you instant relief for your feet."

Bailie's eyes misted with tears. "No, milady, I must see the queen. Even if I have to wait in line all day."

"Well, you're in luck. We have a move-to-the-front-of-the-line card with your name on it. And when you're done giving your message to the queen, you can have all the pastries you want from the table in the throne room.

"And then you're going straight to the healer's, young lady."

"Oh, I'm no lady, milord. Just a village girl from Eldfal." Her lower lip trembled, and her face filled with a soul-crushing grief. This poor girl had been through something awful.

As they entered the palace courtyard, Brea jogged ahead to retrieve a bundle of cooling towels and berry-infused water for Bailee.

"Drink this," she ordered while mopping the girl's dirty face with a cool towel.

"Oh thank you, milady. That feels nice."

Brea wrapped the other cloths around Bailee's feet.

Making their way into the throne room, Brea groaned at the line of villagers come to seek audience with their queen. She hated to steamroll over them, but Bailee needed rest.

"Your Majesty." Finn approached the throne. "Pardon the interruption, but Princess Brea and I found this child up near the North Road. She's come from Eldfal with a message for your ears alone.

"She walked all that way on her own?" Faolan stepped from her throne to greet the girl. "She should go straight to the healers this instant."

"She won't hear of it, your Majesty," Brea said, hoping for once her mother would act like a genuine person with a conscious rather than the queen.

"Set her down, Finn." Faolan guided them to a chair meant for the nobles.

"Her name is Bailee," Brea whispered.

"Bailee." Faolan crouched down so she was on a level with the girl. "What message have you brought for me from Eldfal?"

"Oh, Majesty, it was awful." Bailee's eyes filled with tears. "It was Mount Eldfal, madame. It erupted four nights ago. I came as quickly as I could."

"And you were such a brave girl to do that all on your own. Mount Eldfal hasn't erupted in centuries. We've had no reports of any sign that it might no longer be dormant."

"It was the soldiers, Majesty," Bailee said. "They came, just a few of them. They did it at night so we couldn't protect ourselves with our magic, ma'am. We've all been taught since we was young how to shield ourselves against the mountain if it should erupt. I've never seen it happen in all mi life, ma'am. I was with the flock when it happened. I have a pregnant ewe about to give birth, so I've been staying the night out on the plains in case she needs help in the night."

"These soldiers, where did they come from, Bailee?" The queen asked. "Did you recognize them?"

Bailee nodded. "They came from across the sea. I seen their ship when they came from Iskalt. They headed straight for the mountain at dusk, ma'am. They made the mountain rumble with their magic."

"What happened when Eldfal erupted?"

"It happened so fast, mi Majesty." Bailee dropped her head, great big tears splashing on her hand. "The lava moved quick as a flash, ma'am. It destroyed everything and everyone in its path."

"What of the village?"

"There's nothing left, mi Majesty," Bailee said in a choked whisper. "Nothing at all. Just me."

"Oh, my darling girl." Queen Faolan swept the girl up into her arms ran a comforting hand over her hair. "You are so very brave and smart to come straight here. Don't you worry about it anymore. I will take care of it from here. I want you to go with my good friend, Finn and see the healers and get some rest. I will come visit you soon."

"Yes. Thank you." Bailee tried to stand, but Finn picked her up and headed for the exit.

"Loch was right," Brea said, turning her attention on her mother. "This is Callum's doing. He's destroyed an Eldurian village."

"Is it true?" Lochlan stormed into the throne room, scattering the citizens waiting in line to speak with the queen. "Eldfal is no more?"

"We don't yet know the extent of it," Faolan said, returning to her throne. "At this time, I will ask our citizens to please return tomorrow. We must clear the throne room immediately so we may discuss this threat on Eldur and decide our next moves."

Lochlan waited impatiently for the commoners to leave. As he paced like a caged lion, Brea knew he was at his breaking point.

The moment the double doors closed, Lochlan turned on the queen. "I told you it would come to this, but even I didn't realize it would happen so soon. Callum must be stopped, your Majesty."

"I did not think he would have the gall to make such a blatant move against me." Faolan sat back against her throne, unable to meet

Lochlan's beseeching gaze. "I stand by my decisions, Lochlan. I believe Callum and Regan mean to distract me and divide my forces, knowing I cannot sit by while Eldur burns."

"Then *do* something," Brea begged.

"I will not recall my army from the border. Regan still poses the greatest threat against us—and by us, I mean Eldur and our Iskalt brothers and sisters."

"We must do something for Iskalt and for all those Eldurians who died." Brea shared a desperate look with Lochlan.

"And we shall." Faolan stood from her throne, crossing the room to a desk against the wall. "I will call in our militia on a voluntary basis. Give me two days to gather what forces I can, and you may lead them against Callum along with your seasoned unit of three hundred volunteers. That is the best I can do."

"It will have to be enough." Lochlan nodded. "I will gather Iskalt soldiers and militia along the way."

"Where will you attack?" Brea asked.

"This is not a mission that will lead to battle right away," Lochlan said. "This is a campaign to gain the support of my people and grow my army before I seize the throne from my uncle once and for all."

CHAPTER 19

BREA

The militias weren't coming. Well, some of them were, but not the force that could have made up the greatest part of Lochlan's army, not the Raudur city militia.

Warriors from outlying villages trickled into the capital, and more would come as Lochlan led his force toward Iskalt.

But the people right here in the largest city in Eldur? They sat in their homes, closing their doors against the thought of helping a foreign kingdom.

Brea walked the streets at dusk against her mother's wishes. Sure, there were dangers in any city, but as the sun disappeared, Brea was one of the few in Eldur with magic still coursing through her veins.

Magic she couldn't control without the words she didn't know, but that didn't matter. The people of Eldur still thought her the Fargelsian princess. They didn't know how inexperienced she really was.

As she stared up at the squat buildings, stretching as far as she could see, she couldn't help thinking about another city in another place. Back in the human world, Myles' dad occasionally let her and Myles tag along when he went to Columbus for supplies. It was a two-hour drive north into the city. There were few similarities between those tall towers that reached toward the sky with glass windows reflecting sunlight back into the atmosphere and these heavily adorned sandstone buildings. In place of paved roads, there were cobblestone cart paths.

But the people, they weren't so different. They went about their days working and shopping at the market. Taverns lined the road, not unlike the bars of human cities—serving as a place for people to unwind and let their rowdy out, as Myles would say.

There were mothers and fathers, children chasing each other in games of tag. The poor relied on the charity of strangers, and the wealthy lived in grand homes among the upper city, close to the top of the canyon.

Lord knows, Lochlan would never admit it, but the fae weren't so different from humans. They desired love and comfort.

Brea stopped outside Xander's tavern in the lower city market. At this time of day, the fae inside would be drinking mead instead of Eldur brew. The door opened and a young couple stumbled out, almost falling down in laughter as they headed up the road.

Loud chatter filtered out of the tavern, and Brea propped the door open with her foot, peering in. She was an outsider getting a glimpse at a simple fae life. Most of the time, she still thought of herself as human, different from the fae around her. But staring into the crowded room, Brea wanted to be one of them, just once. She wanted to know what it was to belong, not simply because she was supposedly a princess and future queen, but because these fae seemed to take such pleasure in just being together.

Her eyes followed Adamina as she wound around tables, two mugs of mead in hand. She set them on a table in the back corner where two familiar fae took them gratefully.

Brea entered the tavern, letting the door swing shut behind her. Her dress caught between her legs, and she stepped forward, wishing she'd worn something different into the city. The leather bodice suddenly felt too constricting, cutting off her breath. The room started spinning and didn't stop until a hand landed on her shoulder.

"Princess." Xander's gruff voice calmed her. She hated the title he used, but at least he didn't try to bow. "Are you okay?"

She nodded. "I'm good, Xander. Thank you. The last few days have been trying, and I'm just a little tired." She'd been working herself to the bone getting all the arriving militias accounted for and equipped. She'd convinced Lochlan to stay longer than he'd planned, but as the day of their departure neared, the doubts entered her mind.

How could she expect to be any help to him?

What if they failed?

Shouldn't she go with Finn to Fargelsi?

But what would Myles do? What was right? He'd tell her there was nothing she could do for him. If there was a way to free him, she'd go to any length, but there wasn't. So, Iskalt it was.

She forced a smile and looked to Xander. "Yes. I wish to speak with Lochlan."

"Would you like some mead?"

Her face screwed up in disgust. "Um, no. An Eldur Brew will be fine."

One side of his mouth curved up. "I'll have Mina bring it to you."

This time, her smile was genuine. "Thank you."

Tables quieted as she passed, and she wasn't sure she'd ever get used to that. What would happen when they learned she was the Eldurian heir?

Lochlan and Finn didn't see her until she practically collapsed into the booth across from them. They looked up from where they'd been huddled in conversation on the same side of table. Brea could see it as she looked at them, how they were once drawn to each other when they were younger.

Lochlan with his light looks and dark countenance. Finn with his sparkling eyes and the way he could find joy even when his heart had been ripped from his body.

"Shouldn't you be up at the palace?" Lochlan lifted a brow, but there was no scolding in his voice.

He'd seemed to have forgotten all about their kiss, but that was fine with Brea when he said things that infuriated her so much. "Shouldn't you?" she challenged.

Finn chortled as he sipped his mead.

Brea held Loch's gaze until Adamina set a mug of Eldur Brew in front of her. "Thank you, Mina. I know you probably had to make this special at this time of day."

Adamina smiled down at her. "Anything for you, Brea. Let me know when you need another." She shot a look at Lochlan. "Something tells me you might need it with this kind of company."

Brea hid her smile behind her mug as Adamina flounced away.

"I don't think Mina likes you, Loch." Finn shoved his shoulder with a laugh.

"That's because few in this city like the foreign prince who thinks he's better than them." Brea shrugged.

It wasn't a lie. She'd spent a lot of time among these people, and they held no loyalty for Lochlan. In their opinion, he was a pushy brute. They weren't wrong.

"I don't need people to love me." Lochlan drained his mug and held it in the air, a silent call to Adamina for more. He waved it impatiently.

As Adamina set another in front of him and took the empty mug, she muttered something like "fool of a man."

Brea shook her head. "It's a wonder they don't like you. You're very courteous."

"Was that supposed to be human sarcasm?" Lochlan scowled. "It does not become you."

"Then it's a good thing your opinion is of little import—as you'd say in your haughty way."

"Children." Finn leaned forward with his elbows on the table. "You were playing so nice on our jaunt into Iskalt."

"Jaunt." Lochlan snorted with a shake of his head.

He was right. There was nothing jaunt-like about the trip. Only death. Fear and grief overcame the loathing for a few short days, but now she was pretty sure Lochlan was back to hating her.

She didn't hate him, that much she'd realized, but she wasn't quite sure how to stop arguing with him when he was such a disagreeable fae. As tensions rose in the palace with the militias preparing to march into Iskalt, the tensions between Lochlan and Brea grew more strained.

"I don't need people to like me," Lochlan grumbled as he sipped his mead. "Their respect is enough."

There was something sad in that statement, and for a moment Brea wanted to reach across the table and put her hand over his. The pain had never left Lochlan's eyes, no matter how hard he tried to cover it up.

She lowered her voice. "Wouldn't you rather they respect you out of love instead of fear?"

"They will never love me, Brea. You need to understand... those in the fae realms are hesitant about outsiders. Eldur is not my kingdom. I may have grown up here, but they are not my people. And for that reason, they will not trust me."

"But they like me." At least she thought they did. "And they think I'm a Fargelsian princess."

"Fargelsi has kidnapped their beloved princess, and you show up having escaped Queen Regan. Don't you see, Brea? You give them hope for Alona."

"Hope," she whispered to herself. It was the most honest thing anyone had ever said to her. She'd spent her life being told she was crazy and that no one other than Myles ever loved her. But now...

Finn spoke as if reading the thought out loud. "I see it too. They barely know you, yet you have their love. If you can escape Gelsi, why can't Alona?"

They all knew the reasons it would be harder for Alona. She was a human with no magic, and Regan was no doubt keeping her in more secure holdings. But Brea saw what Finn and Lochlan meant.

She sipped her Eldur Brew in silence, wondering if this hope they claimed she gave the people actually meant anything at all.

Eldur Brew was the devil.

Brea lay awake in her bed, unable to sleep. She'd returned from the tavern hours ago, leaving Lochlan and Finn to their cups, but it seemed this sleepless night would only add to her weariness.

Her mother convinced Lochlan to wait three more days for more militia to arrive. Most brought their own horses, but the palace armory had been busy arming them with adequate weapons rather than the more rudimentary ones they'd brought.

Everything was moving as it should. Wagons of supplies were loaded and ready to accompany the force. It wouldn't be easy. Most of these fae hadn't seen a battle in their lifetimes, and others not for many years. They weren't the seasoned warriors making up the Eldurian army that now sat on the Fargelsi border.

But they were all Lochlan had.

Brea rolled over, burying her face in her pillow. How did she get here? In three days, she'd ride away from her mother's palace in fighting leathers, armed with a sword she didn't know how to use and magic she had a tenuous control over.

Yep, this probably wouldn't end well for Brea.

But she had no other choice. With Finn leaving for Fargelsi soon, she had to be by Lochlan's side. Despite their arguing and constant insults, if anything happened to him, she... a groan rattled in her throat. It would be so much easier if she could hate him, if he'd shown himself to be the snake his brother was.

Thoughts of Griff sent warring emotions through her. She'd

thought he was the first person other than Myles to ever truly see her, but it was all a beautiful lie.

A thud sounded against her door, and she lifted her head, sighing as she kicked the sheets from her legs. If she could be sure she wouldn't destroy the entire palace by doing it, she'd reach out with her magic and pull the door open.

But alas, she had to use her legs.

Yanking the door open, she prepared to unleash her rage on whoever stood on the other side. Instead, she rolled her eyes. "You've made quite the habit of showing up at my room in the middle of the night." She held her arm across the doorway so Lochlan couldn't enter.

But when he lifted his icy blue eyes to hers, magic swirled in their depths, and it was so beautiful she dropped her arm. "I need your help."

There was no scorn in his voice, only desperation, so Brea gestured for him to enter.

He walked in, his eyes skimming over the discarded clothes strewn over the floor and other possessions out of place. Brea hadn't let Rowena in to tidy up once she'd gotten back from the city. The maid needed sleep too.

"Want some tea?" Brea asked.

"I'm okay."

"Good, because it's cold, anyway." She scooped clothes off the floor and set them on the end of her bed before leading Lochlan to the sitting area. They hadn't been alone together since she comforted him outside the village of the dead, and the silence stretched like a vast sea, seemingly insurmountable.

Crouching in front of the hearth, Brea whispered "Dóiteán" and flames licked up over the logs, casting a glow across the room.

Lochlan sat down and scrubbed a hand through his hair and down over the long tail.

Brea straightened and walked toward him, taking a seat next to him on the couch—settee as those in the palace called it—so close their legs touched. Lochlan didn't move away from her.

She nudged his shoulder. "You said you needed my help."

He nodded. "I don't really know where to start."

"Hey." She took his hand between both of hers. "You can say anything to me. I know your world is bleak right now, but you can do this. You know that, right? You are the rightful king of Iskalt, and the moment you let people see that, see the real you, they won't be able to hold themselves back from supporting you."

He turned to look at her, his eyes holding some emotion she couldn't decipher. "You haven't changed. All these years I've watched you and marveled at your human optimism. No matter what you went through, your strength never wavered. How can you believe there is good in this world when so much bad happens?"

"Because I've seen it. My life has been hell, Loch. There were no palaces or doting parents for me." She paused, not knowing how exactly much he knew of her life, how much he'd seen. But there was no use hiding the darker parts of her, not from him. "The first time they locked me away, I was nine. For three months, I spent all my time with people whose jobs were to figure out what was wrong with me—mentally—why I was having delusions and telling lies. I was institutionalized four more times before my arrest for almost killing Myles."

"I don't see the good in any of that."

"That's because you're not looking. Griff kidnapped me and trapped me in Fargelsi, but everything I went through, every trial and abuse, it brought me here. Loch, Eldur is the good. You say the people love me, but I love them too. There's a kindness here. I see it every day as more Eldurian fae travel to the palace to join a fight for a kingdom that is not their own."

"I haven't considered any of that."

"Of course, you haven't. You were raised a prince, told that commoners must obey your every command. But they don't have to, not this time. The warriors about to make this journey with us are not here out of obligation. They're here because it's the right thing to do. Only the light can defeat the dark, Lochlan O'Shea."

He flipped his palm over to intertwine their fingers. "Maybe your human traits aren't the burden I thought they were."

"Optimism and faith doesn't have to be just for humans."

"I need you, Brea."

Her breath hitched at the admission.

When he continued, the feeling inside her deflated. "I need the Raudur City militia, but they do not come."

"What can I do about that?"

He released her hand and skimmed his thumb under her chin, tilting it up so she met his gaze. His mouth curved into a half smile. "I need you to make a speech, a call to arms. Say whatever you must. They will come for you in a way they won't for me. You inspire them." He stood, ready to leave once she gave her consent.

"I..." What could she say to his request? She'd never dreamed of being a princess and didn't want to be a queen. The people of Eldur shouldn't follow her. Who was she but an inadequate fae girl who knew little of their world?

A fae who may as well have been human for all the good she did them.

But there was this man, the one who lost his parents when they saved her life, the very same fae she'd argued with since the day he stole her from the human police station.

For him, she'd do it. For him, she'd do just about anything. Make a speech, go to war, wear the crown.

"How do you know?" she whispered. "That I inspire them?"

His face softened as he realized what her question meant. She'd agreed to help. "Because, Brea..." His voice lowered as he turned away and walked to the door. "Even in my darkest night, you inspire me."

CHAPTER 20

LOCHLAN

"Where are you going in such a hurry?" Finn jogged to catch up to Lochlan and Brea in the courtyard.

"I have a speech to give." Brea didn't break her stride as she headed toward the lower part of the city where most of the commoners dwelled. Lochlan tried to get her to set out for the queen's market near the palace. It was a lot nicer and more crowded this time of day, but she insisted the people she needed to reach wouldn't be there.

"Wait, you have a what now?"

"A speech. Just call me Greta."

"You're speaking nonsense again, Brea. That's not your name."

"How is that different from most days?" Lochlan said, feeling uncertain about this call to arms. He should do it himself, but he had more faith in Brea's ability to inspire her people to come to his aid.

"Greta Thunberg... she's a human who gives lots of speeches and gets people to act..." Brea paused as if waiting for either of them to react to some joke they didn't understand. "Loch has no personality, but he needs soldiers. Those villagers needed soldiers to protect them in Iskalt and Eldfal. So we're going to get some."

"Where?" Finn fell in step beside her.

"The free market near the docks."

"Do you ... think they sell soldiers at the market?" Finn's smirk would normally make Lochlan laugh, but this was too important. He had too much riding on Brea's ability to win the people of Eldur over to his side.

"Of course not, but that's where the militia will be going about their lives."

"It smells down there." Finn sighed.

"It smells like hard work. We're courting the city's militia today. We have to go where they go. These men and women have jobs that keep them busy. It's likely they don't even know the militia has been called in for volunteers."

"It's not entirely voluntary," Lochlan said. "It's their choice to serve, but the militia is paid handsomely for their service. Many will join for the compensation—if they're moved to fight for the cause."

"Then let's go find a soapbox for me to climb up on."

"The things she says..." Finn shook his head. "You think we'll ever understand her?"

"I doubt it." Lochlan enjoyed the way his best friend and his—whatever Brea was to him—sparred with words. He couldn't help but think of Alona and the way the four of them would fit together. Someday.

"Neither of you are funny." Brea led them through the upper levels of Raudur city down to the lower regions near the river and the open marketplace where the "normal" people, as she described them, carried out their business.

"Princess Brea," one of the shopkeepers called to her. "I have some new tunics you might like. Nothing as fine as your lovely dresses, but they're perfect for wearing to your apprenticeship with Master Arturo."

"Thank you for thinking of me, Mrs. Milton. I will come by later today. You know how I prefer simple clothes, and I'm in need of some new tunics. My lady's maid has a habit of losing them in the wash."

As they made their way into the heart of the lower city, more people came out to see Brea. Not just to sell her things, but to genuinely connect with her. They followed her without hesitation when she told them why she was here.

"They love her," Finn said, as mesmerized as Lochlan by their response to the unusual princess they still didn't realize was their own.

"See how you make things happen?" Lochlan murmured when they reached the market square to find a crowd waiting for them near the trader's guild.

"Yeah, it takes loads of magic and charisma to ask a bunch of people to come listen to what I have to say when they're already here." Brea shook her head like it was nothing when to him it was everything. That she would do this for him and his people when she had no reason to. Did she not know how rare a person she was?

Brea smiled as she stood at the center of the growing crowd, completely at ease with herself and the relationships she'd built with these people.

"Hi, everyone." She gave a nervous little wave. "I was never good at delivering speeches in school, so I'll just jump right in and say what I came to say. We need your help." She gestured to Lochlan and Finn, not realizing the disdain some of the commoners had for Lochlan and much of the Eldur nobility.

"Little more than a week ago, a village in Iskalt was slaughtered. The usurper king, Callum O'Shea is responsible. He tried to create a magical barrier around an innocent village, replicating the barrier around Fargelsi. His magic failed and killed every man, woman, and child within its borders."

Several gasps echoed through her captive audience. Lochlan couldn't breathe, he was so desperate for this to work. He needed the people to understand what was at stake. That is wasn't just about some foreign village they didn't know or care anything about. It was about them and their families. This was just the beginning of Callum and Regan's potential reign of terror, and it was up to him and Brea to stop it.

"But that's a long way away, right? The problems of another realm. It shouldn't concern us here in Eldur." Several heads nodded in agreement, and Lochlan clenched his fists at his sides. He needed to trust her. Brea had a natural charm and an effortless way of speaking to people. It wasn't his way, but it worked for her.

"But I'm afraid it does. Just a few days ago, several soldiers from Iskalt came into Eldur on King Callum's orders. They visited Eldfal late one night. Using their magic, they caused the mountain to erupt, wiping out the entire village except for one brave girl who traveled across the desert all on her own to warn the queen of this attack. She's just ten years old and a hero. I can't imagine what that poor girl suffered.

"Suffering sucks, doesn't it?" She peered into the crowd. "We all have our burdens to bear. Some suffering is worse than others. But at the end of the day, we're all just fae, right? It doesn't matter if you're from Fargelsi like me, or Eldur, or Iskalt, or even the human realm. We're all people, and when there is needless suffering in the world, it is our responsibility to stand up for those who can't stand up for themselves. It's our job to help them when they just don't have the will or the energy to do it on their own.

"You all know how I escaped from Fargelsi. I couldn't have done it without a very dear friend who helped me—at great risk to her own safety. She didn't have to step up, but if she hadn't, I wouldn't be here. I would still be Queen Regan's pawn.

"Regan O'Rourke is the real enemy. She would like us all slaves to her will—and she'll have it too, if we don't stand up for what is right. Right now, Eldur is surrounded by threats. Regan holds your princess, yet she's in league with Callum, pulling strings to distract our focus so we fail on both fronts.

"But a king stands among us. The rightful king of Iskalt needs your help. With your busy lives, you may not have realized the queen has called in volunteers from the city militia. No one is required to join us, but I beseech you all. Before long, Regan's touch will reach us here in the safety of Raudur as it already has in Eldfal ... unless we stop her now. I've been her prisoner. I know how ruthless she is. She will stop at nothing to claim the power she feels she deserves, and she will use Callum as a weapon until she no longer needs him—until Iskalt belongs to her. Don't let her do to this city what she's done in Iskalt and now Eldfal, which stands no more. Put the call out to your friends and family. Let everyone know the time has come for the Raudur militia to take up arms to aid the future king of Iskalt. That man right there." Brea pointed at Lochlan. "He is the greatest ally Eldur will ever have, and he needs us to stand with him.

"I am just a simple girl from humble roots, despite my royal title. I understand you all have families and livelihoods you cannot abandon so easily. I stand with Lord Lochlan O'Shea, and I will fight by his side for the safety of all fae, no matter what kind of magic they possess, no matter what realm they call home. I ask you all to do the same. Send out the call to all of Eldur as your queen has requested. Join us, and together with Iskalt under King Lochlan's rule, Regan will never stand a chance." Brea shuffled her feet in the silence that followed. "That's all I had to say, so ... uh, thank you for listening." Her cheeks flushed pink as the crowed cheered for her.

Lochlan was ready to follow Brea to the ends of the world and back again. He couldn't imagine anyone who listened to her heartfelt pleas wouldn't feel the same. She thought she was an inept human. She didn't see the inner strength that called out to her people. She was a natural, and he owed her a debt he wasn't sure he could ever repay.

It took Lochlan and the queen two days to rally four-hundred volunteer militia from all across Eldur. It took Brea four hours to call in a thousand from the city's militia in their own backyard. He could kiss the ground she walked on.

"She did it." Finn shook his head in disbelief, staring down at the latest lists. "In one afternoon, she handed you an army."

"She'll make an excellent queen someday," Lochlan agreed.

"You know what this means, don't you?" Finn gave him a hard look. "You don't need to spend the next six months campaigning across Iskalt, calling for soldiers to join you. With nearly two thousand soldiers at your back now, you can make a move against Callum."

"I'd like to double that number with some of my own countrymen, but that can be done along the way." Lochlan was grateful for his friend's support. No matter what happened in Iskalt, Finn would have his back the whole way. He couldn't face this without the man who'd become more of a brother to him than his own flesh and blood.

"Pardon, Lord Lochlan," a page murmured behind them in the throne room. The queen was busy handing out orders to prepare for such a huge response to Brea's rally cry. Lochlan suspected she was more than just proud of her daughter. She was speechless from the outpouring of support she'd garnered for Lochlan. "I've a message for you and Princess Brea. Could you see she gets it?" The boy gave a curt bow and handed over a letter sealed with the unmistakable twisted branches of Queen Regan's seal—addressed to Lochlan O'Shea and Brea Robinson.

"What could she possibly have to say to you or Brea?" Finn frowned as Lochlan broke the seal.

Lochlan muttered a string of curses as he read the queen's missive. Part of him wanted to burn the letter and pretend he'd never seen it. But she deserved to know the truth. He'd seen what happened when Brea was kept in the dark, and he wouldn't be another attempting to manipulate her. "She needs to see this." He folded the letter and tucked it into his pocket. "Keep working on readying the campaign. I'll be back as soon as I can."

Lochlan knew where to find Brea during the hottest part of the day. She'd spent her morning at the stables before delivering her speech. No doubt she was exhausted. Heading to her rooms, he debated how to break the news.

He knocked on her door, but she didn't answer. Peeking in, he didn't see her. If he didn't know her as well as he did, he'd think someone had ransacked her room. Clothes lay scattered about, and half-empty teacups held the dregs of her morning and afternoon tea. She'd refused to let Rowena clean her room everyday, only letting her in at the end of the week to 'tidy up.' From what Lochlan had heard, Rowena crept into her rooms while the princess was busy with her horses. Otherwise, Lochlan wasn't sure Brea would have been able to find her bed.

"Brea?" He tapped on the door to the grotto. He didn't want to wake her if she was napping, but this was urgent. She lay sprawled on the chaise lounge in the cool darkness of the room. Her brown hair fanned out around her, and her cheeks flushed pink with sleep. She looked so peaceful he didn't want to bother her. She wore one of her simple tunics she'd no doubt purchased in the free marketplace—and nothing else. Her bare legs curled up as she lay on her side.

Sitting beside her, Lochlan called her name again, gently shaking her shoulder.

"What's happening? Who's there? I'm up." She tried to sit up but knocked her head against Lochlan's.

"Ouch." He rubbed his forehead, a smile tugging at his lips. She was a bewildered mess, not quite awake yet.

"Loch?" She scowled up at him. "It's the middle of the night. What do you want?"

"It's afternoon, and I spoke to you not four hours ago. Have you been asleep all this time?"

"It appears I don't know how to nap." Brea rubbed the sleep from her eyes. "I don't do quick little power naps. If I lay down, I'm out for a few hours at least. I don't usually fall asleep when I come in here."

"Listen to your body, Brea. Rest when you need it. We have a long campaign ahead of us."

"How's it going with the volunteers? Has my speech helped? It's probably too early to tell."

"You've performed a miracle, Brea." Lochlan brushed his fingertips along the edge of her face, wishing he could just focus on the success of her speech and not the news he brought with him. "A thousand city militia have volunteered since this afternoon."

"Shut up!" A smile unlike any he'd ever seen lit her face. "That's incredible."

"You're incredible." He tucked a stray curl behind her ear.

"Is that what you came to tell me? We should celebrate."

"I have news from Regan." He reluctantly pulled the envelope from his pocket.

"Myles?" She sat up and snatched the letter from his hands.

"She's offering a trade. She will free Myles if you give yourself over to her."

Brea's eyes moved rapidly as she scanned the short missive. Her tears ran freely, each one a stab in the gut for Lochlan.

"You can't give her what she wants, Brea. I know you love Myles and you'd do anything to free him, but if you give yourself to her, you will never leave Gelsi again. You will be her creature forever, a plaything she will manipulate to get what she wants."

"It's Myles." The helpless tone of her voice nearly broke him. Brea was anything but helpless, though he knew exactly how she felt. He'd felt the same when he'd heard of Alona's capture.

"And she is using him against you in the worst possible way."

"Why did you even tell me?" She dropped the parchment, letting it flutter to the floor.

"Because you deserve the truth. I won't be another royal who uses you as a pawn, keeping you in the dark. This is your choice. I won't insult you by making it for you."

"She's torturing him." Brea threw her arms around Lochlan, her shoulders shaking with sobs.

He pulled her onto his lap, letting her rest her head on his shoulder as she cried for the boy who'd once been her whole world.

In so many ways he was jealous of Myles. He had her heart in a way no one else ever would.

"I know you don't want to hear this, Brea, but sometimes as a royal, we have to make hard decisions. Decisions that will benefit our people at great cost to ourselves. If Regan gets you within her grasp again, it won't end well for any of us. Least of all you."

"You think I care what she does to me? When I can free Myles in an instant? I don't care if she tosses me in the dungeon and throws away the key. I don't care if she marries me off to Griff so my children can be her blood heirs. Not if it means I can send Myles back home to his family where he can be safe."

The thought of Griffin married to Brea made Lochlan physically ill. He tightened his arms around her, wishing he could just hold onto her and keep her safe. But Brea didn't need or want anyone to protect her. She would see it as the ultimate betrayal. He would have to be true to his word and let her make this choice on her own. He just hoped she made the right one.

"You are too important to lose, Brea. Too important to Eldur. Too important to Fargelsi. And far too important to me."

Chapter 21

BREA

Too important.

Brea didn't want to be important.

She wanted to be an impetuous teenager who didn't have to concern herself with the consequences of her actions. Well, she had the teenager thing down, considering she'd stomped from her own room leaving Lochlan calling after her.

She hadn't even been able to muster up the pride she should have felt when she managed to throw up a barrier across her doorway, locking him in.

Ha! He wouldn't be able to get out until his magic returned with the moon.

Sometimes there were benefits to this magic business. Other times, she wished she could flush it all away.

The full force of the Eldurian afternoon sun struck her in the face as she stepped out from under the covered walkway to reach the fountain she now claimed as her own.

The coins representing every unfulfilled wish she'd cast since arriving glittered in the crystal-clear water.

"I'm not making a wish," she mumbled to herself. They only provided a false hope that any of this would ever get better.

While she was inspiring the people of Eldur and living in a grand palace, Myles was being tortured, and it was all her fault.

Yes, yes, she knew guilt was a useless emotion, but she clung to the desperation choking her, and she couldn't breathe.

She bent over, trying to catch her breath and rested a hand on the fountain. These waters weren't like those of Gelsi where creatures threatened to pull her under, but they held dangers all the same because they made her believe in something, even if it was a false belief.

Ripping her hand free, she slammed her foot against the stone. When it didn't hurt, she did it again.

"These stupid boots," she screamed, needing something, anything, to take the brunt of her anger. They wouldn't even let her stub her toe.

She slid to the ground and pressed her back up against the stone as hot tears burned her eyes. Myles' smiling face filled every space in her mind. He'd once been all she had. How could she let Regan keep him in her clutches?

Her mother might have been family by blood, but Myles was family by experience. He'd been there for everything.

Lochlan was cracked if he thought being a royal and making hard decisions meant anything to her compared to Myles.

She didn't know how long she sat there alone before the light faded away. "Dusk," she whispered.

And that meant... she felt his presence before she saw him.

Lochlan was like a single life raft in a crashing sea. Even if they disagreed on this, even if he'd never understand, she needed someone to see her, Brea Robinson, not the princess for just one moment.

Because the princess wanted to ride by Lochlan's side as he fought for his kingdom. She wanted to sit atop a beautiful horse at the head of the army that came for love and honor, not obligation. Tomorrow, when the gates of the Eldurian palace closed behind the last soldier, the princess of both Eldur and Fargelsi should be with them.

But Brea? The changeling girl raised as a human with a single friend to call her own knew what she needed to do.

Lochlan walked forward and slid down to sit at her side, his shoulder brushed hers as he leaned back against the raised wall of the fountain.

"How'd you find me?" she asked.

Lochlan's entire body was still, and he didn't answer her question. "Three years ago I went into the human realm of my own accord. Your mother didn't send me that time, but it had been months since I'd laid eyes on you. In the time I was away, you'd turned fifteen, but you were so much older than that. I saw it in your eyes."

He scrubbed a hand over his face, and Brea couldn't look at him. It had stopped feeling strange, knowing he'd watched over her for so many years. He was like a guardian angel, someone who'd been there when she thought she'd had few who cared.

Lochlan blew out a breath before continuing. "I went to the usual places to search for you. Your farm, your school. I didn't find you, and I started to panic."

"You were worried about me? Loch, you didn't know me. We'd never even spoken."

"Part of it was because I never wanted to have to tell your mothers anything happened to you, but there was more. I needed you to be okay. Me. Not your mothers."

"So, what happened?" she whispered, drying her tears with the sleeve of her tunic. "Was I okay?"

"No. I didn't see you at your farm, but there was a boy there. He was sitting under the tree where I'd seen you and him a hundred times before."

"Myles." A fresh batch of tears drifted down over her cheeks.

"Fae are not allowed to reveal themselves to humans. I didn't have any glamour magic to cover my features because it was daylight, but I couldn't help myself. I broke one of the most sacred laws of our world because I needed to know where you were."

"Wait." Brea turned her entire body toward him. "Are you saying you met Myles?"

"To his credit, he didn't seem scared of me. I think he was too distraught for that. I asked where the owners of that farm were, and he told me they were taking their daughter to an institution for the mentally unstable."

Brea shifted away from him, shame filling her.

"Don't hide from me, Brea." He lifted her chin so she met his gaze. "That boy... I mean... he was waiting to confront your parents. That's why he was there. He was ready to go to battle for you, do whatever was necessary. He's the only human I've ever actually liked."

"Hey." She pinched his side.

"You aren't human, Brea. And Alona was raised fae."

Brea couldn't wrap her head around everything he was saying. "So, Myles knew? About fae?"

"Not completely. He knew I was something other than human."

"That's why..." The breath rushed out of her as everything made sense. Myles never questioned what everyone else called her hallucinations. "He knew I wasn't crazy." She'd always thought he just didn't care if his best friend had delusions, that he was too kind to hold it against her. This changed everything. "Why are you telling me this?"

"Because, Brea, tomorrow I leave to fight for my throne, and I want you with me."

"But I'm a crap fighter."

"I know."

"I can't control my magic."

"Everyone knows that."

"Then why does it matter what I do? If I accept Regan's deal, it will have no impact on your campaign."

He pinned her with a look, his icy eyes swirling with magic. "You do not know your worth, Brea. You will have an impact on me." He leaned closer, his voice dropping to a whisper. "You've always had an impact on me."

Brea closed the remaining distance, sealing her lips to his, reveling in the way his cold magic mingled with the heat of hers.

This kiss wasn't the first they'd shared. The first was nothing more than a ploy to make her angry.

The second only a moment born out of fear for what they were to discover the next day in Iskalt.

But this... she poured everything into the moment, wishing it didn't have to end. She'd known so many lies in the fae world that it was hard to determine fact from fiction.

Brea Robinson is a lie.

The old feeling crept up in her, because for once, she had no doubt Lochlan gave her all his truths. This time, she was the liar.

Desperation clung to them as Brea pushed Lochlan back into her room. A smile curved his lips, but smiles didn't belong to a night like this.

The night before the heir to the Iskalt throne left to reclaim his home.

The night before a princess of two kingdoms became a prisoner once again.

"Brea." Lochlan tried to stop her, but she cut off his words with another kiss, and his strength waned as he pulled her tighter against him, his large hands gripped her back as if she'd disappear the moment he let her go.

Brea hadn't given him the answer he wanted about leaving, not yet. But she'd made up her mind. Tears clouded her visions, and she squeezed her eyes shut, kissing Lochlan with everything she had.

His legs hit the bed, and he sat on the edge.

Brea hovered over him, opening her eyes to gaze into the depths of the man before her. He was beautiful in a way she'd never seen before. Also stubborn and kind of a jerk.

But there was nothing she wished for more than to stay in this spot in time forever.

Her heart hammered in her chest as she blinked tears away.

Lochlan reached up, brushing his thumb under her eye. "I'm going to make you a promise, Brea."

She shook her head, remembering Griff and his broken promises. "Don't, Loch. If you promise nothing, you break nothing."

A crease formed between his brows. "We will save Myles and Alona. I refuse to let you tell me to hold that promise back. Come with me into Iskalt where we will defeat my uncle. Then, with the might of Eldur and Iskalt combined, we will help them. I'll do anything to bring them back, Brea. Anything except losing you. If you go into that palace in Fargelsi, you will never walk out again. That isn't the way."

She pressed a finger to his lips, not wanting him to say another word. Myles might not be able to wait for them to conquer Iskalt, and if she lost him, she'd no longer be whole.

"Kiss me," she whispered. "Kiss me like tomorrow might never come. Make me think of nothing else. Please."

Sliding a hand around her back, he pulled her onto his lap, his eyes never leaving hers. "Don't be afraid of tomorrow, Brea. The dawn always follows the darkness."

"I didn't ask you to speak." She pushed him down onto the bed. "I told you to make me forget." Not waiting for him, she pressed her lips to his, sinking into him.

The fire that had burned between them since the day they met, the anger and defiance, expanded into an inferno as they both tried to take everything from the other.

When Lochlan slid a hand under her tunic, grazing the smooth skin of her stomach, his touch seared into her, and she needed more.

Sliding the shirt off over her head, she gazed down at him and cut off his protest with another kiss. It wasn't the time for proprieties he wouldn't have considered with any other fae woman.

She no longer wanted to be put on a pedestal while the fae world around her turned in a haze of immodesty and passion.

"Lochlan." She brought her lips to his ears. "We go to battle soon. Act like it."

His expression was hard as stone, and Brea waited for him to reject her, to tell her this wasn't right.

But it was. She just needed him to see it. They were both hurting and desperate, but out of all the decisions she second guessed and doubted, this one was as clear as the waters of her fountain.

She'd fought it, fought him, not willing to trust another O'Shea brother, but she couldn't deny it any longer.

"I want you." She skimmed her lips up over his cheek. "Tell me you want me too."

Lochlan gripped her hips and flipped her off him. She yelped as her back hit the bed. He held himself above her and dipped his head, capturing her lips. "We leave for battle tomorrow." He repeated her own words. He just didn't know they'd be headed toward two separate battles.

But he would, and she couldn't help but wonder if he'd ever forgive her.

Probably not.

This night might be all they ever had, and she was going to hold onto it, letting it be what she remembered as she became a prisoner once more.

CHAPTER 22

BREA

Brea stared up into the canopy overhead as she let herself live in this dream world for a moment longer. As soon as she scooted out from under Lochlan's arm and left the bed behind, this reality would crack, never to be the same again.

Even if she somehow ended up back here at the Eldur palace, it would be after she'd betrayed them. She was supposedly some magical weapon that could be used against Regan, but underneath all of this fae mumbo-jumbo, everything in her still felt very much human.

And humans fought for those they loved.

He knew.

How had Myles known that her hallucinations were real and never told her? As they lay awake talking through most of the night, Lochlan explained how he'd told Myles Brea's life would be in danger if she learned the truth.

Which was just more proof of what she needed to do. Myles had done all he could to keep her safe. Now it was her turn.

Turning her head to the side, she studied the man beside her, the one she'd tried so hard to hate. Blond hair lay skewed across his forehead. She'd give anything to see those icy blue eyes once more, but if he woke, he'd never let her go.

And she had to do this.

There were no more tears, not anymore. Now was a time for decision, not emotion.

Lochlan grumbled as Brea rolled his arm off her and climbed out of the bed. Padding across the room, she pulled on the leather-patched riding pants Rowena never let her wear and a long tunic-shirt she belted at the waist. After slipping into her boots and packing a few supplies in a drawstring linen bag, she gripped the door handle.

Glancing back over her shoulder one final time, she hardened her resolve and hiked the bag onto her shoulder.

One day, she hoped he'd understand.

The door creaked when she opened it, and she slipped into the hall. The sun hadn't yet risen on Eldur, so most of the palace slept still. The sound of boots on stone echoed down the hall, and she ducked into an alcove to avoid being seen by the guard. Once he turned down another hall, she darted out and ran through the royal residence, not slowing until she was out in the main palace. A few servants prepared the main rooms for a new day. She passed the kitchens where the palace cooks had begun their morning routines.

Slipping into the front courtyard, Brea nodded to the guards on duty. They acknowledged her, but didn't speak. In these clothes with a hat on her head, they probably mistook her for a servant boy.

She wedged open a door to the palace rooms across the courtyard where the guard slept in shoebox rooms that were smaller than her bathtub.

By the time she reached her destination, she was already panting. Lifting her hand to the cracked wood, she knocked as quietly as she could.

No one came.

She knocked again and still, he didn't answer. Trying the door, she found the room empty, and something inside her deflated.

Only one person would help her get to Fargelsi, and he'd already left.

Turning on her heel, she headed back to the main palace, ready to slink back into her rooms, defeated. She'd barely made it out of Gelsi alive the first time. If she tried the journey on her own, she'd surely die, and what good would that do Myles?

She passed the small courtyard near her rooms where the fountain had been her constant companion and froze. Pivoting toward the fountain, she took in the man standing in front of it with his sword belt on and a bag at his feet.

"Finn?"

He turned toward her. "I've been waiting out here. I didn't want to miss you."

She choked back a sob. When she'd knocked on his door and found him gone, she thought she'd lost before she began. "How did you know?"

He stepped toward her. "I was with Loch when he received the message." His eyes found hers. "If it was Alona, I'd go."

That was her answer. This was the right thing. "And you what? Packed me some supplies?" She grinned

"Don't be a fool, Brea. Without control of your magic, you'd never make it back through the Vatlands. Have you forgotten the state we found you in last time?"

She couldn't let herself hope. "You're—"

"Coming with you. Yes. I'll get you to Fargelsi."

"I could kiss you right now." The fear inside her receded and for the first time, she truly thought she could save Myles.

"Please don't. I'm already betraying Loch. I won't make it worse by kissing the woman he loves."

"He doesn't love me," she scoffed, trying to ignore the other part of what he'd said. Finn was right. Lochlan would see this as a betrayal. In one night, he'd lose both her and his best friend.

"Brea." He held her gaze. "He has been in love with you since before you knew he existed."

It was too much information for her already-overloaded brain. Lochlan loved her now, but that love would shatter into a million pieces when he woke to find her gone.

"I cannot handle anything more than this mission." She released a sigh as her eyes memorized every stone of her favorite place in the palace. Would she ever see them again?

Finn wrapped an arm around her shoulders. "You'll come back, Brea. We'll make sure of it."

She wished she had so much faith. Fishing a copper coin from the pouch at her waist, she stepped up to the fountain one final time.

When the sun rose, Lochlan would ride into Iskalt with nothing more than militia at his back.

Maybe they were both doing what they'd always been meant for. Brea was a Fargelsian princess just as much as an Eldurian one. She only had to accept that.

Pressing her lips to the coin, she let it fly toward the water, closing her eyes as it disappeared under the ripples.

"Keep him safe," she whispered. "Keep them all safe."

With one last sweep of her eyes, she followed Finn through the palace to the path that would take them to the stables.

Finn saddled two horses as Brea looked back at the shining palace, standing like a beacon of the goodness she'd experienced for the first time in her life. She'd hold it in her heart to keep the dark away.

She mounted Sassa, the same horse that had taken her to catch Lochlan on the way to Iskalt.

Leaning forward, she patted her neck. "Ready for another adventure?"

The twin ponies stood in their stall, watching Brea leave them behind. She'd never forget everything she'd experienced here.

"Here." Finn held a knife and scabbard toward her. "You're going to need this."

She nodded and took the blade, strapping it to her leg. Shifting in the saddle, she sat up straighter. "For Myles."

He nodded. "And Alona."

Brea hesitated. "I will try to help her too. You know that, right?"

"Yes, Brea. I know." He clicked his tongue, nudging the horse forward. The only stable boy awake ran after them as soon as he noticed them, but there was no stopping Brea now.

When the dawn finally appeared, the palace that had finally started to feel like home was nothing more than a structure in the distance, indistinguishable and unremarkable.

Brea knew differently. Eldur and the people she'd come to love would carry the hope for this realm, but it was time for her to leave hope behind.

Chapter 23

LOCHLAN

Lochlan knew Brea was gone the moment he woke. It was like he felt it in his soul.

Everything in him screamed to race after her, knowing she couldn't have gotten far, but she'd made this choice. Who was he to unmake it?

Lochlan tore through his room under the guise of preparing for his journey. Really, he just wanted to throw things. A teacup shattered against the wall, sending a spray of tiny glass shards cascading down the stone.

Someone knocked on his door, but he couldn't see anyone, not until he got his emotions under control. At least it was daylight so his magic couldn't spin out of control.

"Lochlan O'Shea." The voice reverberated around the room, and he closed his eyes, knowing that tone all too well.

"She's gone, Tierney." Everyone knew Tierney as the sweet foil to the harder Faolan, but Lochlan knew better. Growing up, she'd been the one punishing him and Alona for their constant schemes while her wife was embroiled in affairs of the kingdom.

Both the Eldurian women loved him like their own son, but it was Tierney who raised him.

"Loch, we've heard reports of crashes coming from this room. The guards are afraid to enter." Her eyes drifted around the disheveled room. "Hmm... Whatever has happened cannot warrant a tantrum on the morning you leave for Iskalt."

"I'm not throwing a tantrum," he grumbled.

"Aren't you?" One eyebrow raised, she approached him and reached her slender arms out to pull him into a hug just as she'd done a thousand times over the years.

He let her hold him only a moment before pulling away. Not only had Brea left on the eve of their departure, she hadn't told her mothers, the two women who'd be crushed by her willingness to disappear into Regan's household once more.

"Now," Tierney said calmly. "Tell me what has ruffled the feathers of the inscrutable Iskalt king." She'd always called him the king instead of simply a prince despite the fact that he didn't wear the crown.

"Brea." Call him a coward, but he couldn't meet her eyes as he told her the news. "She has left for Fargelsi."

Tierney stepped back, her face impassive as she took in the news. She sucked in a breath and turned to the door. "Guard, please inform the queen she is needed in the throne room and then fetch Finnegan Donovan. He will have had something to do with this."

Lochlan didn't know how she could be so calm when he'd just told her Brea was on her way to the enemy.

"Get mad," he said. "Come on, Tierney. I know this calm facade is only for show. I've seen your temper. Throw something. Curse the human world that made Brea so self-righteous."

Tierney turned back toward him. "You have done enough of that for the both of us, wouldn't you say? Now, I must walk to the throne room to tell my wife another daughter of ours will soon be in the hands of her enemy. I know you, and I know her. One of the three of us must keep our heads. Come. You have a lot of explaining to do, boy."

Lochlan took in the mess he'd made, knowing it would be cleaned by the time he returned. And then, when the sun rose directly over Eldur, he'd lead his makeshift army away from the only home he could remember in any detail.

Brea leaving didn't change his duty to his people.

Faolan paced the length of the throne room when they arrived, tears already staining her cheeks.

She knew.

When she saw them, she rushed forward. "Where is my daughter?"

Lochlan let them yell at him, he let Faolan rant. He deserved it, after all.

"When a messenger from a foreign queen comes to this palace, Lochlan, no one sees them before me." Faolan was practically growling now. "How dare you make decisions about my kingdom, my daughter."

"She deserved—"

Faolan cut him off. "That isn't for you to decide! The Iskalt throne might rightfully be yours, but I am the Queen of Eldur. My word in this palace must be obeyed." Her lips formed a sneer. "She never should have seen that message or had that choice before her."

Lochlan couldn't take this any longer. He'd never known Faolan to be particularly kind, but this went too far, even for her. "You would have me lie to your daughter?" As much as he hated the choice she'd made, he never questioned if showing Brea the message was the right thing to do.

"Yes!" Faolan's screech grated on his nerves. "We are fae, Lochlan. I don't care if we aren't the tricksters of Fargelsi, lies are still currency here. We aren't ruled by human morality. Maybe you've spent too much time in the human world or trapped in those human books over the years."

A throat cleared from the doorway, and a young guard stepped in. "Your Majesty." He bowed.

"What is it?" she snapped.

"Finnegan Donovan could not be found. His room is empty, and no one has seen him yet this morning."

Lochlan closed his eyes for a brief moment, knowing exactly where his best friend had gone. "He took Brea to Fargelsi."

Tierney looked to the guard. "You can go. Please inform the militia generals to prepare their men for departure." It was an order Lochlan should have given, but as he stood in his stand-off with Faolan, he couldn't think of his next moves.

The guard left them alone once again.

"Finn." Faolan cursed. "That boy has always been trouble."

"Trouble," Lochlan scoffed. "Was he trouble when he helped save Brea from the Vatlands all those months ago? Or when he saved my life along the Fargelsi border? What about when he rode by my side to investigate the village in Iskalt—something you were against."

He pictured Brea traveling the swampy Vatlands with all number of creatures keeping her company, not to mention the mud pits. "She's going to live because of Finn." It didn't make the betrayal sting any less. Would Brea have stayed if she didn't have someone to lead her on the treacherous journey? Not likely.

"Watch what you say next, young man." Faolan's face held a storm Lochlan no longer cared if he unleashed. If she had her way, he'd be no better than Griff was to Brea, a lying, conniving fae—not unlike those in the human storybooks.

"I won't let you turn me in to her enemy." He didn't agree with her choice and wouldn't get past the betrayal any time soon, but he would always choose Brea's side.

"She wanted this." Faolan's ranting started to make less and less sense. "To return to Regan."

"What are you talking about?" Lochlan burned with anger.

"Faolan." Tierney put a hand on her back, and the queen instantly relaxed. "Brea did what she thought right."

"Yes, Yes." Faolan covered her face in her hands, her back shaking. "I know." She sniffed. "I'm sorry."

Lochlan couldn't remember ever seeing Faolan cry. If Finn were here, he'd hug the queen, despite it being wildly inappropriate for a mere soldier. He wouldn't have cared.

How was Lochlan supposed to ride to reclaim his kingdom without the two people who got him to this point? He wouldn't have the courage without Finn or the army and the inspiration without Brea.

"I couldn't protect either of them," Faolan cried as her wife rubbed her back.

Lochlan glanced from the queen to the door. The only thing that would fill the Brea-sized hole in his chest was looking out on the men and women volunteering to ride into Iskalt.

Tierney's glassy eyes met his, and she nodded, giving him permission to leave. There'd be no regal goodbyes, no tearful moments for him.

When he stepped into the hall, a voice called him back. "Lochlan." Faolan ran after him. "Go with the best wishes of Eldur. But come back to us. Please."

He couldn't promise his return, so he dipped into a bow. It wasn't out of obligation, it never had been. A king didn't bow to other royals. But she'd taken him in when he had nothing. There were few people he loved or respected as much as Faolan and Tierney Cahill.

Clearing his throat, he turned and walked away from the throne room and the people in it.

He reached the armory where a servant met him with the bag he'd left in his rooms. If he succeeded, they may never be his rooms again. And if he failed, they might still not belong to him.

After all, dead men needed no beds.

He refused to stop fighting for his people while there was breath in his lungs.

In that way, he understood Brea's sacrifice. To her, Myles was her world, just like Iskalt was his.

He strapped a sword belt around his waist and drew the sword, peering at his reflection in the gleaming blade. The man staring back at him wasn't the boy who'd come to Eldur as a ward of the crown, an orphan kid whose own brother would grow to hate him.

No, the hard eyes meeting his were those of someone who had nothing left to lose.

He slid the blade into its scabbard and wrapped his fingers around the smooth wood of his bow. Slinging a quiver of arrows over one shoulder, he left to meet his soldiers.

Some gathered in the courtyard just inside the gates. Others congregated in the streets between the palace and the stables.

Master Arturo himself brought Lochlan's horse forward and held him steady as Lochlan mounted the great warbeast. He'd always thought the world looked different from atop a horse, smaller somehow.

And with a sword at one's waist, it became a crueler place.

Maybe Faolan was right. Being cruel was in a fae's nature, lying a part of who they were.

He'd told Brea the truth, and it might get her killed—if she were lucky.

Finn knew the truth and had betrayed Lochlan for it.

It was time for him to erase silly human notions and give in to what he'd always been meant to be.

An ice king.

CHAPTER 24

BREA

Brea never wanted to see the southern Vatlands marshes again. She never wanted to feel the squish of mud under her boots, see a snake or hear the croak of a frog for the rest of her life, no matter how long that might be.

With solid ground beneath her once more, she gazed at the long winding road that would lead to the palace where her aunt reigned. A troop of guards awaited her, having already informed her Regan reinforced the border so none could cross without permission, not just those with Fargelsian blood anymore.

"This is where I have to leave you." Finn stood in the mud up to his knees.

"I wish you could cross the border with me." Regan would never let him cross.

"I'd give anything to get inside that dungeon to see Alona again."

"I have a feeling I'll be right there with her in a few hours."

"Give her a message for me?" Finn asked.

"Of course."

"Tell her I've never stopped thinking of her."

"I'll do everything I can for her." Brea gave him a last farewell before they headed in opposite directions. Finn would travel along the Gelsi border until he found Faolan's army, and he would do his part to bring down the barrier that kept him out.

Brea traveled this road once before with Neeve. It felt like another lifetime—something that happened to another version of herself.

It took her and the guards all night to reach the outskirts of the forest city that surrounded the palace. Her companions refused to speak to her, but they didn't let her out of their sight. Regan knew she would come. She'd had her people waiting.

Months ago, Brea was on horseback making this journey. This time, she relied on her own two feet to follow the guards' horses. They didn't offer her a ride. She'd been terrified escaping Fargelsi, but there'd also been hope of something good at the end of the road.

Now, only darkness and imprisonment awaited her.

Her time in Eldur had changed her. She was stronger. More confident, and so very angry with her aunt. She wished she could walk into the palace and toss her aunt in the dungeon she was so fond of. Brea might possess the power to defeat her ... someday, but Myles didn't have time to wait around for someday to arrive. He needed her now.

Brea followed the guards down the high road to the main bridge that would lead them directly to the palace. They made it as far as the front gate before the palace guards stopped them.

"What do you bring us?" one of them asked the men on horseback.

He started to speak, but Brea cut him off. "I'm here to see the queen."

"What do you think this is? Eldur? The guard snorted. "Go back where you came from, peasant."

"She's requested my presence." Brea stood firmly.

"Has she, now?" The man barked out a laugh and spit at Brea's feet. He looked to the guards and they nodded, confirming Brea's words.

"She won't like it if you turn her niece away. I've had a long trip from Eldur, and I'd like to retire to my rooms."

"Brea?"

His voice shouldn't still affect her. Not after all this time and the gravity of his betrayal.

"Griffin." Brea was proud of her calm tone, not betraying her feelings.

"I will escort the queen's niece to her rooms." Griff shouldered past the guards, taking her hand in his like it was old times.

Brea tugged her hand away, and without another word, followed him into the palace.

"I would see her now to get this over with," Brea said, hesitating at the foot of the stairs. "I won't be spending the night in my old rooms. I'm here to trade myself for Myles. I'm sure you're aware of your queen's offer. It was likely your idea to bring him here. You'd know I'd do anything for him, and you used it against me."

"Brea." He looked haggard and so very tired. "Nothing is as it seems here."

"You're the one who taught me that." Brea took the steps up to the queen's quarters, not waiting for Griff to show her the way.

"You should wait to see her in the morning. Give her a chance to call for you when she's ready."

"I'm over it. I'm so over Regan and the intimidation she exudes, her endless parties and her syrupy sweet facade. We do this my way. She made me an offer, and I'm here to accept it on my terms."

Griff rushed up the stairs behind her.

She found her aunt on the terrace, just like any other day. She was lingering over her breakfast, reading reports of the goings on in Gelsi. Somewhere in that stack of papers there was likely a form briefing the queen of the Eldur troops working tirelessly to bring down her border spell. Another one detailing the movements of the young Iskalt king, and probably another one telling her Brea had arrived.

Brea slammed the missive she'd received from Regan on the table in front of the queen.

"Brea, darling." Regan beamed her beautiful, perfect white smile at her. "You've been a naughty girl." She eyed the mud-stained clothes she still wore from her trek across the Vatlands.

"Cut the crap, Regan." Brea collapsed on the delicate vine chair opposite her aunt. She used to be afraid she'd break her aunt's chairs, but she understood magic better now. "You made me an offer. I'm here to accept it on a few conditions."

"Oh, come now. Let's catch up before we discuss unpleasant things."

"I don't have it in me." Brea wiped a tired hand over her eyes. "Just drop the pretense, and let's get down to brass tacks."

"Oh, I missed your charming human phrases, dear. It's been so quiet here without you. Would you like some tea?" She rang for her maid.

Brea turned, hoping to see Neeve again, but frowned when one of the triplets dropped into a curtsy before the queen.

"Where is Neeve?" Brea frowned.

"She's been ... detained. Punishment for helping you escape, I'm afraid." Regan had the triplet pour her a cup of hot herbal tea, but Brea didn't trust anything her aunt had a hand in making. "She's faring much better than that friend of hers from the village."

Brea's eyes widened. "Moria?"

"Yes, that was her name. A nasty business, executions."

Her blood froze in her veins. Moira was dead. Guilt and sadness warred inside her. And Neeve was suffering her grief in the dungeons.

"Drink up, dear, and tell me all about your time in Eldur. Wasn't it just dreadful under that hot and unforgiving sun?" Regan leaned forward as if preparing for a grand story.

Brea's gaze narrowed. "Fine, I'll make you a counter offer if you're just going to simper at me all morning." She sucked in a breath. She had to get Neeve out of there. After Moira, she owed it to her. "I'm here. Release Myles and Alona … Neeve too. Let them go, and I will stay." She threw a look to Griff. "Release them and I will..." Pausing, she knew she'd regret the next words. "Marry Griff. Willingly. He can be the king, and I'll be your ornamental queen. If I ever have children, they will be your blood heirs." The prospect of such a life sickened her. She couldn't imagine a world where she would ever let Griffin touch her, much less father her children. Her mind instantly went to thoughts of Lochlan and of all the things they would never have together, and it took every bit of strength she possessed to keep the tears at bay.

"But if I do all of that, you have to take the barrier down and free your people.

"Well, now, I see someone's been doing their homework since she ran away. But that's not going to happen. You will have to amend your terms, dear."

"Let's get to the part where you free my friends." She had to remind herself that was why she was here.

"Alona is your friend now?" Regan cocked her head at Brea. "A girl you've never even met."

"We have mutual friends we both care a great deal about." Brea leaned back in her seat, weary down to her bones.

"I'm afraid I can't release Alona. She is too important. Myles, even your little traitor friend, Neeve are nothing to me. Though clearly, they mean a great deal to you. You've come such a long way for them. Why not take the night to relax and enjoy your old rooms, and we can discuss this tomorrow when you're in a better mood."

"We'll discuss it now."

"Blast, you really are my brother's child. Just as stubborn and needlessly noble."

"That might be the best thing I've ever heard about my fae father." Though Brea knew precious little about the man Faolan agreed to have a weapon-child with. "Release Myles and Neeve today. Myles will go back to the human realm unharmed, and Neeve will be sent to the palace at Eldur."

"Fine." Regan waved a delicate hand. "Go to your rooms and get cleaned up. Your clothes are still in your wardrobe. We will have a party to celebrate your return tomorrow evening."

"No." Brea slammed her fist down on the table causing Regan to flinch. "I will not be your plaything or your paper doll to dress up when you're bored. And I sure as hell won't spend my life suffering through your parties. I am here to trade places with Myles. Period."

"You expect me to throw you in the dungeon like a useless human when you are to be queen one day?" Regan threw her head back and laughed. "No, darling, you are my prisoner, but I don't need iron bars and cells to keep you under control. You've proven just how malleable you can be. Myles will be freed from the dungeons, but he won't return to the human realm. He will take up residence at Griffin's cottage where Leith will serve as his warden. We'll even send Neeve there to keep house. They'll be safe and happy while you take up your role as my doting niece who has come home at last."

"I will agree to your terms, but I have terms of my own." Brea leaned forward. "I get to see Myles and Neeve before you send them to the cottage, *today*. And I get to visit them once a month."

"Absolutely not. I will not have my niece cavorting with prisoners. If you wish for them to be free, you will not speak to them. You will not see them. Those are the terms, dear. It is the best you will do."

"I will attend your parties, wear your ridiculous dresses and play whatever simpering idiot role you want of me. But every other day of my captivity, I don't see you, I don't talk to you, I don't even hear your voice. I will stay in my rooms, only visiting the gardens or the stables so I have something to do. I will wear whatever I want, and I will prepare my own food."

"You will eat a steady diet of Gelsi berries to subdue your magic."

"No." Brea refused to give her that much power. "I will honor our deal if you keep up your side of the bargain. If Myles is your leverage over me, then my magic is my leverage over you. This is about trust, Regan. You should give it a try. I'll give you everything you want, but you will not subdue my magic."

CHAPTER 25

LOCHLAN

Lochlan gazed across the sprawling camp that grew in numbers everyday. A mishmash of Eldurians and his own countrymen and women. More than two thousand soldiers and militia had joined him in his march for the Iskalt palace. The Eldurians came because their princess asked them to, though they still didn't know Brea was theirs. The connection between her and her people was evident in the way they followed her lead.

He'd never had any doubt Brea could inspire people to greatness. But what astounded him were the sheer numbers of Iskalt men and women who joined them along their journey.

"Your Majesty." A young man several years younger than Lochlan approached his tent with a formal bow.

"Captain Walsh." Lochlan returned his bow with a nod. It was strange the way his countrymen treated him with such respect and reverence. It reminded him of the way his father's men behaved around the king. "How are your men faring this morning?"

"Very well, sire. We've scouted the roads around the palace and discovered a way around Callum's men."

"Show me on the map." Lochlan bent over the large map covering the makeshift table in his tent. Captain Walsh was the first man Lochlan met when he led his soldiers through the pass along the Northern Vatlands and into Iskalt near the village Callum slaughtered. The young man led a contingent of soldiers—boys mostly—who had heard Lochlan was coming. They claimed they wanted to join their rightful king and help him take his throne. Lochlan was speechless. Walsh led more than four hundred young soldiers, all eager to do their part.

"Excellent job, Walsh." Lochlan clapped him on the back, placing a marker on the map where he planned for his army to make a move on the palace.

"Thank you, sire." The captain bowed and took his leave, seeking out a hot meal and a warm bed after a long night of scouting.

A sense of pride swept through Lochlan. He was finally making a move to claim his throne. He had a capable army at his back, with day and night magic wielders. He'd never felt more certain of his path. Never felt so like the King of Iskalt he was born to be. And he'd never felt so alone.

Deep down, Lochlan understood why Finn left to put his efforts into freeing the woman he loved. He had no doubt, if given a chance to swap places with Alona, Finn would do it without a second thought. But Lochlan needed his best friend. Here among his soldiers, captains and lieutenants, Lochlan had no one he could trust the way he trusted Finn. He second guessed every decision he made, asking himself what Finn would say if he were here. He didn't want to resent his best friend for abandoning him at the worst possible time. He didn't want to resent him for doing what he had to for Alona. But he still felt the sting of betrayal every morning when he woke up in his tent alone without the one person he trusted above all others to advise him. Without Finn ... without his brother, Lochlan was lost.

"Your Highness?" An older man approached the tent.

Lochlan frowned. The man looked oddly familiar, but he couldn't place him. "You were one of my father's men?"

The man smiled, his eyes crinkling with amusement. "You used to call me uncle when you were just a boy." He held his hand out, and Lochlan took it, shaking his hand, but his name escaped him.

"Brennan Cormac," the man supplied.

"Of course." A genuine smile spread across Lochlan's face. "Uncle Bren." Lochlan remembered playing with Brennan's sons not long before his parents' deaths.

"I once served as a general in your father's army. I'm an old man now. Retired for twenty years since the wrong O'Shea thought to sit on your father's throne and send his boys off to grow up in foreign courts. I've waited for this day for a long time, your Majesty. I'd be proud to help Nial O'Shea's son take what belongs to him."

"I find myself surrounded by inexperienced soldiers and militia. I am in dire need of a seasoned advisor. I would be honored to work with the man my father called brother."

"He'd be damned proud of you, Lochlan."

"Thank you, sir." Lochlan stepped back, offering Brennan a seat by the table.

"Now, how can I help?"

It felt strange, trusting a man he barely remembered, but if his father trusted Brennan with his life, then Lochlan could too.

Nephew,

Go back to your Eldur queen and hide behind her skirts like you've been doing all your life. Your rag-tag unit of boys and farmers with pitchforks don't stand a chance against a king's army. Go home before you hurt yourself and get those good Iskalt boys killed playing war games you can't hope to win.

Your uncle,
Callum O'Shea, King of Iskalt

Lochlan crumpled the letter in his hand.

"You might as well wipe your rear with that. Nothing Callum has to say is worth the parchment it's written on." Brennan studied the map of Iskalt in the growing darkness. Another day gone, and they hadn't made a move yet. Lochlan had spent the day with Brennan surveying his troops and making plans, but Lochlan still didn't feel confident about his chances against Callum's forces. His magic wielders alone could level Loch's army.

"You know what you have to do, Loch. It's the only clear path to victory."

Lochlan stared at the map, hoping to see whatever Brennan saw, but he just saw the makings of a bloody battle and terrible odds. "And what's that? Go home like my uncle told me to?"

Brennan snorted. "Of course not. Callum and all his advisors are as predictable as a textbook. They will not expect you to think outside the box."

"Make your suggestions." Lochlan gave him a curt nod to go on.

"Callum underestimates you. He sees you as a spoiled young prince. A boy with a streak of entitlement a mile wide. He doesn't know you, so let's catch him off guard."

"How?"

"You have something he doesn't. A thousand Eldurians with day magic. We attack at noon tomorrow. Your friends' fire magic will send Callum's soldiers running for cover. They'll never expect it."

"But with only a fraction of his numbers, all the fire magic in the world isn't going to help if we can't overcome his thousands. We would stand a better chance if we attack at dusk when my soldiers have both fire magic and ice magic."

"And Callum's thousands will also have their ice magic at the ready. But if we attack at noon, that puts all of Callum's men and your Iskalt soldiers on an even footing. At noon, they're all just men. Your fire magic wielders will give you the edge you need to get inside and overthrow that spineless coward once and for all. He's so arrogant and close-minded, he'll never see it coming. He would never consider not fighting with magic, and he will expect the same of you.

Lochlan studied the map and the numbers, pitting his army against Callum's larger one. It could be a suicide mission, but if Callum made certain assumptions and relied too heavily on his magic wielders, then pure brawn could work.

What would Finn say? He could practically hear Finn's excitement for this plan. He would appreciate the simplicity of it. Pitting soldiers against soldiers at a time when their ice magic lay dormant, leaving them with nothing but their swords and their wit. It would come down to who were the better fighters, and who wanted it more. He could feel the anticipation of his soldiers. They wanted this. Even the Eldurians were passionate about removing Callum O'Shea from his throne after what he did in Eldfal.

"We march at noon." He was ready for this. Lochlan O'Shea was borne to take this throne and repair the damage his uncle had wrought over the last two decades. It was time, and he was ready. As ready as he would be without the two most important people in his life who should be standing at his side.

"The men are in place, your Highness." Captain Walsh approached Lochlan and Brennan where they stood overlooking his army surrounding the Isklat palace. "Trebuchets and catapults are at the ready. We'll breach those high walls in no time, sire."

Lochlan frowned. Something wasn't right. Callum would never sit inside his castle while an army surrounded him. Siege wasn't his style. "He's not taking me seriously," Lochlan muttered.

"He doesn't believe we have a chance of defeating him during the day," Brennan said. "That mistake will lead to his demise."

"Walsh, have your men lay waste to those walls," Lochlan gave the order. "Brennan, call the longbowmen to cover them. This will be a long day, and we're up against more experienced men. We need to be smarter and faster."

"You can count on us, sire. We will have you on your throne by evening" Walsh gave a curt bow before he set off to give the order to begin the siege of Lochlan's ancestral home.

Within the first few hours, Lochlan knew this would not be a quick afternoon battle. He charged down the line on his black warhorse, calling out orders for his archers to engage the moment Callum's men made an appearance. As of yet, Callum hadn't even acknowledged Lochlan's siege. He threw everything they had at the palace walls, which were finally crumbling, but it would take most of the night to bring them down. His men were tired and tense from their one-sided battle. Soot streaked their faces as the ground shook from the catapults launching their burning missiles.

"He's toying with me." Lochlan rode beside one of his father's greatest friends, wondering if he'd made a mistake trusting in him.

"He thinks he will tire you out waiting for sunset."

"And he's right. Our soldiers have already had a long day. They cannot withstand a full night of this."

"The Eldurians will be our secret weapon," Brennan insisted. "They wait just over the next rise."

"Waiting for night? When they'll be as useless as we are right now?" Lochlan was losing patience after so many monotonous hours of the same activity.

"Waiting for the right moment to turn the tide in your favor, your Majesty. Callum has little mind for battle strategy. He will not make a move against you tonight. He's prepared to let us throw ourselves at this wall all night and maybe even the next until we are so exhausted we can't even think straight. That is when he will make his move. And that is when the Eldurians will defeat him."

"I see the sense of your plan." Lochlan gripped the reins of his horse tightly. "It is the waiting that is killing me. Waiting and worrying about my soldiers."

"We will rest the soldiers in shifts so they will be ready when the time is right. You are young, lad." Brennan laughed, slapping him on the back. "Too young to know how boring and miserable war can be. The heat of battle isn't always the hardest part. When it's just you and the blade in your hand, time flies. Nothing matters beyond the death of your immediate opponent and where the next one lies in wait. But siege? Siege is a different beast all together. Callum's advisors are making you wait just for that reason. They're not hiding behind these walls because they're scared. Callum is showing patience I didn't think he had. We will wait patiently, and when we lure him out, we will be ready."

"I appreciate your advice, Brennan." Lochlan nodded, watching as a fresh unit came to relieve the weary soldiers manning the trebuchets.

"I would have thought the Eldurian Queen would have sent you with some of her own advisors." Brennan glanced at Lochlan, trying to gauge his reaction to the prying question.

"She is supportive, but her attention is on Fargelsi. Until her daughter returns, Queen Faolan will not have much to offer Iskalt." It felt odd, explaining Lochlan's lack of support in the way of seasoned officers and commanders. His soldiers were green, and he had precious little experience himself.

"I imagine Eamon Donovan is banging at the Gelsi border much like we're doing with this wall. He will see Princess Alona home or die trying." Brennan sat up taller in his saddle. "It does my heart good to see a light at the end of the tunnel, my boy. You will make a king your father would be proud of. You'll restore the relationships between Iskalt and Eldur, and then we can focus on the real threat—bringing that Fargelsian witch down once and for all."

"That's the goal." Lochlan sighed. "Though I'm not sure I see the light yet."

"We've come a long way since you were a child, your Majesty. Just you wait. Your reign will be magnificent."

Lochlan wished he had Brennan's optimism. Without Finn, Alona and Brea, he felt like he was missing an arm. His confidence was gone, and he was lost in a sea of indecision and second-guessing himself.

CHAPTER 26

BREA

Every morning that Brea woke in the extravagance of the Fargelsi palace was like fighting a new battle. Forcing herself to rise.

Facing the servants and guards acting as if she'd never left.

And Griff.

With a sigh, she eyed him where he sat across the room. "Are you watching me sleep? Again?" Every time she opened her eyes, the beautiful man she'd once thought she could love stared back at her.

"Just afraid you'll disappear on me." He stood and moved closer, his eyes never leaving her face.

Brea sat up and scooted back until she hit the headboard. "You're creepy. You shouldn't sneak into my room this early in the morning."

"Because you never crept into mine in the middle of the night?" One eyebrow arched, and Brea was hit with a wave of emotions and feelings, cutting the air off from her lungs.

She'd been happy. None of it was real, but it was the first time in her life she hadn't just had to accept her life. She'd enjoyed it. "Griff," she breathed.

"Number seven." He stepped closer to the bed. "That you don't fix your hair at every possible moment." He took a seat on the edge of the bed and reached out to tuck an errant strand behind her ear. "The other ladies of the court worry over their appearances, never leaving a single lock out of place. But you... Even after waking up with the most ridiculously messy hair... It doesn't bother you."

She gripped his wrist and forced it down, wanting to push him away, to tell him nothing he said had any effect on her. In a way, it didn't. She didn't love Griffin O'Shea, she knew that now. But his ten things he loved about her still made her heart skip a beat when most people couldn't even find one. "You missed seven."

He frowned. "I did not. Did you not receive my message?"

"What message?"

"Regan sent me to examine a rift in the barrier near the Northern Vatlands, but instead of a tear, I found Loch and his men."

She nodded, already knowing where this was going. "You were the one who told him Myles was here."

"I also gave him a sealed letter for you. In it was number seven."

Lochlan never mentioned a letter, but she couldn't muster the anger or indignation for him, not when he might be fighting for his life while she sat here with his brother. "What did it say?"

He slid from the bed. "I can't tell you now." He put a finger to his lips.

Brea followed his gaze around the room. She almost forgot her aunt could listen to any conversation that happened in here.

"I've missed you, Brea."

As she stared into his entrancing gaze, she realized she'd missed him too, but not the Griff who'd lied to her or allowed her to be her aunt's pawn.

She missed the guy racing horses across the open land near his cottage, the one with a smile in his eyes and laughter in his voice.

The man who'd made her feel safe when her entire world had been turned upside down.

That version of Griffin O'Shea didn't exist.

"Come here." His eyes pleaded with her.

Against her better judgement, she stood and approached him, letting him pull her into his familiar hug. She breathed in his scent, letting it calm her.

"Meet me in the stables in one hour," he whispered into her hair. "Please."

She nodded against him, not wanting to let go. No matter what Griff had done in the past or his loyalty to her aunt, when he walked out that door, she couldn't help feeling she'd be very much alone in this dangerous palace.

But she'd known from the moment she decided to take Regan's deal, she'd have to do this on her own. Save Myles. Marry Griff. Live her life as a prisoner.

He dropped his arms and stepped back, giving her one final imploring look before leaving her to the silence of her solitude. She flopped back onto her bed, staring into the vines creeping up the walls of the room.

If only Lochlan could see her now.

A few weeks ago, she'd laid beside him, knowing that their one night was the end of something that never really started. Where was he now? She had no doubt the people of Iskalt rose as their true king returned, but would it be enough?

It had to be.

If she was going to spend her life behind the walls of this palace, she had to believe he was out there conquering the world. That was who he was.

A tear raced down her cheek, but she wiped it away. There was no room in her heart for sadness, not when all she wanted was for it to harden into stone. Maybe then, none of this would hurt so much.

Heaving herself out of bed once more, she dressed in her faded leathers and tunic she'd arrived in that one of the triplets had washed. She refused to wear anything in her closet from before.

The guards on the bridge had taken her knife and never returned it. They couldn't have an angry armed princess running around the palace grounds. She kicked the empty sheath across the floor before stomping from the room, the clack of her Eldurian boots against the gleaming floors gave her some sense of satisfaction.

Guards and servants smiled at her as she passed, but just like everything in Fargelsi, there was a forced cheer behind it.

Her stomach rumbled, but she'd barely eaten in the days since she arrived, choosing to hole herself up in her room, sleeping the days away rather than make her way down to the kitchens to fend for herself. The first night at the celebration Regan ordered her to attend, she'd pilfered an unopen bottle of wine from the cellar and gotten sloppy drunk out of spite.

Since then, her aunt hadn't come to see her, which was fine with Brea.

No one stopped her on the way across the falls to the stables, and as she entered, a familiar scent struck her, reminding her of Master Arturo and the ponies. She'd grown to love her life in Eldur, and then it was all torn away.

But she didn't regret it. Not now that Myles and Neeve were safe.

"Brea," Griff hissed, poking his head out from one of the stalls.

She jumped, slapping a hand to her chest. "Are you trying to kill me? Oh wait, do that again. Death might be preferable to being your prisoner."

He opened the stall door and ushered her in before shutting it again. A large white mare Brea didn't recognize stood at the back. "You're not my prisoner."

"Oh really? Then what would you call forced marriage?"

"The deal you made."

"Only because I wanted Neeve released with Myles. I don't want to be your wife, Griffin. Sorry if that hurts your massive ego."

Pain flashed across his face, but it was gone as quickly as it appeared. "Contrary to what you believe, I don't want a wife who hates me. But neither of us have any choice, Brea. All we can do is live with this."

"If that's all you have to say, I have a ceiling to go stare at." She put a hand on the stall door, but Griff's voice held her back.

"Myles got away."

"What?" She twisted to face him once again. "Explain."

"On the way to the cottage, he and Neeve escaped the soldiers guarding them."

Brea slumped against the wall. "You mean Myles is out wandering Fargelsi?" This kingdom was dangerous, deadly. Myles may have been better off as a prisoner.

Griff gripped her shoulders and dipped his head to peer into her face. "He's okay."

"You don't know that."

"I do, actually. Brea, look at me."

She sniffed and lifted her eyes to his.

"He reached the border where the Eldurian scouts found him and Neeve and took them back to camp."

Her breath came in short gasps. "Eldur has them?" Relief flooded through her, but she didn't know if she could trust any of his words. “But how did they get across the border?”

He released her. "Call it an early wedding present."

"You..." She pushed out a breath. "You did this? You opened the border for them?"

"I placed one of my men among their guards. He had orders to look the other way. Regan never would have let you visit them, Brea. The cottage... it wouldn’t be much better than the dungeons. I hate myself for abducting that boy from the human world and dragging him into this. I was only following orders, but maybe this helps make it right."

"Why do you do the awful things you do, Griff?"

Griff peeked out of the stall, eyeing the stable boys shoveling hay into barrels and feeding horses. None of them were close enough to hear. "I have to."

"But you don't."

"There are things you do not understand."

"Then explain them to me."

"I can't." He paused. "I came to her when I was two years old, Brea. I love Fargelsi. For all her faults, Regan raised me. She protected me and wants to make me her heir. I'm going to be the king of Fargelsi. And when that day comes, everything will change."

Brea sighed. "Power attracts the corruptible. Suspect any who seek it." If anyone asked her how she remembered that quote, she wouldn't know. Myles went through a Dune phase and repeated basically anything Frank Herbet ever said in his life. But those words had never seemed truer than in this moment as she stared at a man who could have been good. Griffin O'Shea was sweet and kind and noble.

But he wanted to be king, and that was where each one of those traits ended. He wasn't entitled to a crown or becoming heir for the good of the people. Regan convinced him it would make his life worthy.

"Brea—"

She cut him off with a look. "I'm sad for myself, Griff, but mostly I'm just sad for you." Now that Myles and Neeve were out of harm's way, it no longer mattered what happened to her.

"We have no choice in any of this." He leaned close, dropping his voice. "Brea, we have to make your aunt believe in our happy union."

Brea nodded. He was right. Regan had to think she'd gotten her way--which she had.

And then one day, Brea would get hers.

"Okay, where do we start?"

"A betrothal ceremony."

"Where are those triplets when you need them?" Brea grumbled as she pulled her hair free of the braid she'd been trying to wrap around the crown of her head. For most of her life, she'd thrown her hair into a ponytail and called it a day, but that didn't cut it in this fancy-pants world.

"Ugh!" She launched her jeweled comb across the room, and it flew out the door, landing with a crack in the hall.

Brea turned in her seat to find a slender woman standing in the doorway. Her blond hair was pulled back into a low braid worn by many of the servants. A green woolen dress hung off her too-skinny frame like a sack.

"Hello." Brea eyed the scared girl, realizing she knew her.

"It's you." Brea stood, her mouth hanging open. The last time she'd see her was years ago in the human world. She'd met her at a coffee shop and they'd really hit it off and spent the day together. Brea remembered falling asleep watching Netflix with her, but when she woke up the girl was gone and Brea was convinced it was all a hallucination. She'd forgotten all about that day until she laid eyes on her now. But she couldn't remember her name.

"I remem—"

"Hello, my Lady," she interrupted, dipping into a curtsy.

"I thought I made you up." Brea rushed across the room to hug her, but something in the girl's eyes reminded her they weren't alone.

"I have been sent to assist you, my Lady."

"Oh." Brea stopped short, her eyes scanning the room for any sign that Regan was listening. "Thank heavens you're here. I am completely hopeless with these whacked out fae hair styles."

The maid smiled, but there was something wrong behind it, something broken. Gone was the feisty girl Brea had once hoped to call friend.

The maid turned into the hall and picked up the comb with delicate fingers. Not saying a word, she walked toward Brea and began dragging the comb through her hair.

"Are you my new maid?" Brea stared at her in the looking glass.

"Yes, Lady Brea. The queen would like me to attend you from now on."

Brea almost smiled. Her aunt knew how much the triplets bothered her. But Regan didn't do anything for no reason.

"Please, just call me Brea."

The girl nodded as her deft hands wound Brea's hair into an intricate design over the crown of her head. By the time she was done, Brea was speechless. "How did you--"

Not even Neeve or Rowena would have been able to accomplish such a feat.

"I grew up in a fae court, my Lady." The girl walked toward the white dress that lay spread out on the end of the bed. "We must get you dressed for the ceremony."

Brea stood. "Are you going to tell me your name?" She wracked her brain, trying to remember the girl's name she met years ago.

"That has been forbidden." Her eyes tightened. "You must speak to me as little as possible."

"But why?"

"Please, let's get you dressed."

"I can get myself dressed. I'd like to know your name, please."

A knock sounded on the door, and Brea yanked it open before the maid could. Griff peered past her into the room with a grim expression. "I was in the hall and heard yelling."

"I wasn't yelling, and shouldn't you be getting ready for the ceremony?" Brea didn't have any more energy to hate him.

His eyes never left the maid as he wrapped an arm around Brea's back and pulled her close.

She pushed at his chest before remembering what he said about pretending. If she had to shove Lochlan from her mind and play love with Griff to stay alive, she could. This was a dangerous game, and the only way she could win was if she managed to keep her life.

Relaxing into him, she hugged him back.

"I can't wait to make you my fiancé today," Griff said, his voice loud for anyone listening in. Bringing his lips to her ear, he whispered. "Any secret you make your maid confess will cost her. Do not ask her questions."

"Why? What's going on, Griff?"

He released her and stepped back. "I must prepare myself." He put a hand on the door to close it behind him and stopped, turning to face her one last time. His lips formed a single, silent word. One that changed everything.

Alona.

The girl Regan sent to wait on Brea was the missing Eldurian princess, the human raised as fae. The one who had come to visit her in the human world when they were sixteen years old.

Brea turned to stare at her, knowing she'd been living her life for the last few months.

But not anymore. As their eyes met, understanding passed between them. Because they'd been in this together since the moment one baby was exchanged for another.

A betrothal ceremony had no real meaning other than a promise—ironic considering all of Griff's broken promises.

There would be no magic binding them together until they were truly wed, but now the people of the three kingdoms would know their intent. Over the next months citizens would trickle into Fargelsi to witness the Iskalt prince marrying the Fargelsian princess. It was a union blessed, and one Regan claimed was unbreakable.

She was probably right.

As Brea stood beside the doors to the garden where the ceremony would take place, she knew there was no going back. She'd made her choice, and it was time to live with it.

Cracks spidered through her heart as she pictured a different O'Shea brother waiting for her among the flowering trees and vine-covered benches. Lochlan would have hated every moment of this elaborate gathering.

Griff reveled in it.

Two brothers, so different in many ways, yet both stubborn and arrogant in the way of princes.

Alona stood behind Brea, a single ally in a sea of enemies. No others crowded the small space. Brea dropped her voice and turned to Alona. "I tried to free you too."

Alona's expression didn't change. She was resigned to her fate, and it broke Brea a little more. "Finn wanted me to tell you you're in his thoughts."

Tears welled in her eyes, and she blinked them away. "I wish he'd forget about me completely."

"He loves you."

Alona glanced behind them. "We must not speak of such things, Brea. Not ever."

Brea was about to argue when the heavy garden doors swung open, her cue to enter. No music played as she walked through the gardens, reminding her that this was not a wedding.

She reached the large oak tree shielding Griff from the sun. His auburn hair was combed back away from his face, revealing smooth, clean-shaved skin and sparkling eyes.

His smile lit up his entire face when he saw her, but all she could manage was a nervous twitch of her lips.

Regan stood next to Griff, her beaming smile a contradiction to her duplicitous nature.

No crowds awaited them, only the queen and a single maid. Brea searched for others before her aunt drew her attention.

"The kingdom will bless your marriage with extravagant parties, Brea. But a betrothal is for the earth, the very ground we walk on. Fargelsi receives its magic as a blessing from the land. It is now time for the land to bless your union as well. Come here." She held out a hand, and Brea took it, wondering how she'd once felt comfort in her aunt's touch.

Regan pulled her to stand in front of Griff, and as Brea gazed into his eyes, her heart pounded against her ribs. Because this wasn't right.

It wasn't fair or just. People like Regan couldn't win. Guys like Griff shouldn't get the girl.

She wanted so desperately for it to be someone else standing in front of her. Tears built in her eyes as Regan began the blessing. When Griff clasped their hands together, the tears spilled down Brea's cheeks.

Regan wound a lacy bolt of silk over their hands, and Brea couldn't breathe.

For Myles, she told herself. She did this for her best friend, and she'd do it again. But that didn't stop the pain ripping through her heart or the hatred seething in her mind.

Griff acted as if he didn't notice her tears, as if they were the happy tears of a hopeful bride-to-be. His denial would never change the outcome. A part of her would always hate him for not being Lochlan O'Shea.

As Regan finished the blessing, all Brea could think of was that she shouldn't be here. She belonged by Lochlan's side, fighting with the army she'd helped assemble.

Instead, she was a puppet, a pawn.

She met Alona's sad eyes, and it took everything she had to keep from falling to the stone pathway in a garden that wasn't hers. Her garden, her courtyard had a naked man fountain and coins representing every wish she'd tried to force into being.

Now, she had nowhere to put her wishes.

She stumbled back to her room to change before going to the main hall for the lunch celebrating the betrothal. As she crossed the threshold into her room, her legs gave out beneath her, and she fell to the floor, not feeling the impact.

Sobs wracked her body, and Alona's arms came around her, keeping her from collapsing onto her side and curling into a ball like she wanted to do.

"Shhh," Alona whispered. Maybe she was reminding her they were being listened to, or maybe it was just comfort, but Brea didn't want to be quiet. She wanted to rage against Fargelsi and rebel against her aunt. She wanted to ride into battle with the Eldur crest on her chest.

And most of all, she wanted to see Lochlan again. Just once.

They'd had no news out of Iskalt, but he had to be alive. This world wouldn't be right without Lochlan O'Shea barking orders and being his general douchey self.

She wouldn't be right.

"I love him," she whispered as more tears clogged her throat.

"Me too," Alona answered.

They were speaking of different men they might never see again, but in that, they were together.

Two girls trapped in a foreign palace with no light to guide them home.

Epilogue
Lochlan O'Shea

The plan was doomed from the start.

Lure the Iskalt soldiers from the castle into a fight. Sounded simple. The miscalculation? It took them two days to leave the safety of their high walls, two days for Lochlan to taunt his uncle.

Now Callum wanted him dead.

"Retreat!" he yelled. "Everyone, fall back!" He kicked his horse around and thundered into the valley beyond the Iskalt palace. "Retreat!"

The Iskalt citizens who'd joined his side followed the command as they used their magic to combat that of the people behind them.

The sun rose on the horizon, and with each passing moment, Lochlan's magic faded like the stars in the sky.

Pain ripped up his leg as an arrow struck him, and he screamed. His horse reared back before picking up speed. Another arrow sailed toward him, and he yanked on the reins. The horse threw him from his back and kept running.

Lochlan stumbled to his feet and stared down at the arrow

shaft lodged in his thigh. Grabbing it with two hands, he broke it, leaving the head still in his leg. There would be time to remove it later.

Dizziness overcame him for just a moment as horses galloped past him followed by foot soldiers. He joined the steady stream of Iskalt warriors fighting against his uncle. They had to make it over the next hill before Callum's men caught up with them.

This was where the plan was doomed.

As the dawn came, Iskalt magic lessened, but they had a force of Eldur soldiers Callum knew nothing about.

If they made it to them.

Lochlan hadn't counted on the size of Callum's force tripling his. He didn't think it would take this long to goad his uncle into a real battle. Callum was rash, not one to abide a siege.

But battles over open ground—those he reveled in.

And now he'd have one.

Lochlan held his sword tightly as he ran, even as the strength in his hands lessened. He could see their destination on the other side of the valley, a hill of snow and ice, behind which the Eldurian forces hid.

Pain enveloped him with every step he took, but he couldn't stop now, not when so many people were counting on him.

The only thing that kept him moving was picturing Brea in his mind. A messenger from Finn told him they had Myles and Brea's friend, Neeve. She'd done it. She'd saved her friends. But what was happening to her now?

The only way to save her was to win this fight, this crown, and take his kingdom back. Only then could Iskalt and Eldur march on Fargelsi. Only then could they stop the pain and strife throwing their world into human-like chaos.

And it started here, with this pain he overcame every time his boot hit the snow.

Every time he wobbled and didn't fall.

Every time he saw his people risk their lives for their kingdom.

Being king wasn't about power or luxury. He only wanted to do what was right.

His strength waned as he crested the final hill among the thundering horses and Iskaltians running for their lives.

But with the dawn came a new strength. As his power and that of his people faded away, the Eldurians' power grew.

And they were ready.

By the time Callum's men pounded over the hill to find fresh troops full of fire magic awaiting them, it was too late.

A new day had dawned in Iskalt.

And with it came a man who was finally worthy of wearing the crown.

The story continues in
Fae's Destruction: Queens of the Fae Book Three
Turn the page to keep reading!

QUEENS OF THE FAE
BOOK THREE

FAE'S DESTRUCTION

MELISSA A. CRAVEN
M. LYNN

Prologue
Myles Merrick

"Have you ever seen anything so beautiful?" Myles stared up at the arched entrance to the Eldurian palace that opened into a courtyard of fountains and tiered gardens. After weeks of traveling through swamps and deserts, it was a welcome sight.

Neeve shifted atop her horse. "I do not trust beautiful things." On their journey, she'd gained color in her skin, pale from months kept in the Fargelsi dungeons with only brief trips above ground.

Myles watched her carefully for any sign of joy or happiness that they were free. Being a prisoner was no picnic for him, but that was in the past now, and he was about to be reunited with his best friend in the entire world.

A girl who was apparently a fae princess.

"Neeve." He shook his head. "If you let them take the beauty from your world, they win."

Neeve's frail body hunched forward, and she no longer looked like the tall, strong girl he'd met when he first became a prisoner. Instead, she seemed... lost.

She heaved a sigh and nudged her horse forward. "What was the cost of our freedom, Myles? Regan of Fargelsi does nothing she doesn't wish to do. You and I... we are worth nothing in this fight, and yet, I can't help feeling everything has been given up for us."

Myles glanced to Finn, their escort from Fargelsi. He'd barely spoken on the journey except to tell him the only reason he was leaving the Fargelsian border was for Brea.

It seemed the outcast he'd known before had changed quite a bit if she instilled loyalty in such men. He smiled at the thought, half expecting Brea to come sprinting from the palace doors to throw her arms around him.

He didn't know how the two of them had arrived in this strange world. One moment, he was defending his best friend from the bullies at school, and the next, he was waking up from a coma to find a strange man with pointed ears hovering over him.

Queen Regan told him Brea had tried to kill him, but he didn't believe that for a second.

Finn slid down from his horse as a servant rushed forward. "Take our horses up to the stables. Tell Master Arturo I will require a fresh mount in a few hours' time." He handed off the reins before turning to help Neeve down.

The two of them walked toward the entrance where a line of guards stood against the wall.

"Oh sure." Myles grimaced. "I'll be fine on my own." Riding horses was nothing new to him, but he'd never regained his strength from the captivity. The journey only made it worse. He tried to dismount as he'd done a million times before at his farm, but his legs wobbled when he landed, and he pitched forward, falling to his hands and knees.

A tired sigh rushed out of him. "Anyone have a stretcher?" They were the last words he remembered before his head hit the stone.

Voices entered Myles' peaceful slumber.

"These two have been through a lot."

"Finn didn't tell them."

"What do we do?"

Myles groaned as his eyes slid open, and he took in the people surrounding him. "Where am I?"

"The healer's rooms." A broad woman with the brightest red hair smiled at him. "You have been through much trauma and a long journey. Go back to sleep, young man."

He shook his head and tried to sit up.

The woman put a hand on his shoulder. "Do not tax yourself."

Rows of identical cots lined both walls, most unoccupied. A few beds over, Neeve slept.

"Where's Finn?" The fae man hadn't said much, but Myles had sensed it was out of sadness more than stubbornness.

"He rested for a few hours before leaving again for the border."

Myles' brows drew together. "Why?"

"Because both my daughters are prisoners there." The woman's lips turned down.

This time, Myles managed to sit up, his eyes wide. "You're Alona's mom."

She nodded. "I am queen-consort Tierney Cahill. We've all been worried about you, Myles." Tears gathered in her eyes. "Excuse me." She turned away, wiping her face. "Rowena, let me know when he is capable of visiting my wife." With those final words, she rushed away, leaving three men and one woman behind.

"Can I get you anything, sir?" The woman asked.

"Who are you?"

"Rowena. I was—am—lady's maid to Alona and Brea."

"Brea." He straightened. "Where is she? Has she been by to see me?" After everything that happened, he just needed to hold her, to see for himself that she was okay.

Rowena shook her head, a tear coursing down her face. "I must...

I'll bring you something to eat." She followed in the tracks of the queen-consort.

Something didn't feel right. This entire place was... wrong. Without Brea, everything was wrong.

One of the men bent to look into Myles' eyes as if examining him. He must have been a healer. He straightened and nodded. "Exhaustion. Nothing a little sleep and food won't cure. You must regain your strength."

Myles didn't know why so many people were concerned about him. He was a stranger here, not someone who mattered. He wasn't a lost princess like Brea. He almost snorted at the idea. What would the Robinsons say to that?

"I'm Master Arturo." The bearded man to his left put a hand to his chest and cleared his throat. "I am glad you are alive. For Brea." His lips quivered, and he looked to the other man. "This is Captain Donovan. We care about your friend, Myles, and she cares a great deal for you. If you need anything, ask us."

Donovan... He must have been Finn's father. "Thank you."

The two men nodded and left. Myles breathed out a giant sigh of relief. He didn't realize Neeve had woken until she spoke.

"They love Brea here, don't they?"

Myles nodded. He was beyond happy for his friend. He'd always had his parents—who he was trying not to think about—but she'd only had him. Now, she found a world that embraced her, loved her. "I need to see her."

Neeve shook her head. "You need to rest. She will come."

"I can't wait." He slid from the bed, wincing as his bare feet hit the cold stone floor. Seeing Brea here would make everything real, it would dislodge the rock sitting on his heart making him crazy with worry. Because the girl he knew would have been the first person to greet him when he arrived.

So, why hadn't she come?

The healer was nowhere to be found as he crept from the room into a stone hallway.

Neeve nudged him out of the way as she stepped into the hall.

Myles raised a brow. "I thought you wanted to wait."

"We're in this together, human. Through our captivity, the journey into Eldur, and now a foreign palace where we could end up lost in one of these hallways, it's the two of us."

He paused, turning to her with a smile. "That is the nicest thing a fae has ever said to me."

"Most fae have only abducted and imprisoned you, so I'm not surprised."

"Was that a joke?" Over the months he'd known Neeve, she'd never even laughed at his jokes, let alone cracked one of her own.

"No." She started down the hall, crossing to where it opened into a courtyard with a circular fountain.

"They sure like their fountains here, don't they?"

Neeve shrugged. "Eldur is a hot kingdom, human. They enjoy water."

"Stop calling me that."

"What?"

"Human." He crossed his arms. "It's mean."

"But it is what you are." She cocked her head, considering his request.

"Well, yes, but you say it with such... derision."

"Hu—Myles." She peered down a hall before entering it. "Humans are lesser beings than fae. That is fact. Any derision in my words is the correct way to address inferiority."

Myles released a frustrated breath and turned the opposite way of Neeve. "I'll find Brea on my own."

As soon as he'd separated from her, a line of guards stopped him. "Why are you wandering the palace?" one of them asked.

Myles looked back the way he'd come, but he'd made so many turns there was no way he could backtrack to the healer's rooms on his own. "I'm looking for the princess."

Another guard rushed past them, shouting, "There has been news from Iskalt."

"Sorry, he looked like he knows where he's going, so I'll follow him." Myles ducked away from the guards and followed the other one as fast as his weak legs could take him.

The guard rushed through two ornate double doors that stood open with a guard on each side.

Myles entered and stood at the back.

"Your Majesty." The guard kneeled before a woman who sat on an ornate golden throne, her hands folded in her lap. "We have word from Iskalt."

The queen gestured to him. "Rise, sir. Tell us what has happened."

He got to his feet. "There was a battle, your Majesty. Many people died, and the day was almost lost when Lochlan O'Shea suffered an injury."

It was like the entire room held their collective breath. Myles didn't know the importance of these words, but he could feel the monumental moment.

"Go on." The queen leaned forward, her stoic mask slipping to reveal the fear underneath. "Is Lochlan dead?"

The guard shook his head. "No, your Majesty. He is now king of Iskalt."

No one spoke for a long moment as silence hung heavy over the room.

"King," the queen whispered, her voice growing louder. "Lochlan has taken the Iskalt throne?" Hope replaced the fear in her eyes.

The guard nodded. "Yes, your Majesty. Callum O'Shea is now his prisoner, and the people of Iskalt rejoice."

She sat back against her throne, her entire body relaxing. "We can get them back."

Myles got the impression those words were only meant for her.

She straightened. "This is a great day. Our ally has regained the throne that was rightfully his. With the might of Eldur and Iskalt together, we can defeat Fargelsi and recover our princesses."

Princesses. Myles blood went cold. She meant more than one.

His jaw tensed as he walked forward, each step taking him to a truth that would crush him.

Neeve appeared at his side, having found the throne room on her own.

Her eyes told him she too understood. Her hand slipped into his. Myles knew fantasy customs from his books. He needed to kneel or at least bow, but at that moment, nothing mattered except the truth.

At the healer's, why were there tears in the eyes of the people who'd cared about Brea?

Why hadn't she already come to him?

How did they secure his release?

His long stride took him to the first step leading up to the throne. Someone leaned over to whisper to the queen, and her eyes widened, probably realizing who he was.

He met her gaze. He'd been Brea's family before any of these people appeared, before her mother decided she was worth coming for.

Queen Regan made sure he knew all about how Faolan of Eldur abandoned Brea as a baby in the human realm, and Myles hated her for it.

When he spoke, he kept his voice low. "Where is she?"

A guard stepped forward. "Bow to your queen."

"She's not my queen." He scowled. "I am human, and we bow to no one." His jaw clenched. "Brea is the most important person in my life. Tell me where she is."

A single tear tracked down her cheek, and for the first time, Myles noticed how haggard she looked, like she hadn't slept in weeks. "My girls... She's taken both of them."

"Who?" But Myles already knew the answer.

"Regan offered a trade. I couldn't stop her."

"No." Myles stumbled back, his hand slipping out of Neeve's. She reached for him again, but he didn't want comfort.

He wanted Brea.

And she'd given herself to save him.

All the time spent sitting under their tree on her farm or walking the halls at school flashed through his mind.

Someone was speaking, but he barely registered their words as they spoke of traveling to Iskalt for a treaty signing. Only Myles and the queen seemed to be stuck in this sequence of events where Brea left them. Their gazes connected.

"How could you let her do it?" he asked, cutting off the man who was speaking.

The queen shook her head. "Brea has a mind of her own. Now, it is up to us to save her this time."

And he would. Because Brea Robinson was his person, his best friend, and she was worth fighting for.

CHAPTER I

LOCHLAN
TWO MONTHS LATER

A treaty was a promise, a vow, binding in magic. Those who broke the ancient agreements would see themselves lose something they held dear.

Power.

Lochlan had seen it before. His parents were good rulers, faithful rulers, but they'd also been tied to Fargelsi in a treaty. When Brandon O'Rourke ruled the eternally beautiful kingdom, it worked. Fargelsi, Iskalt, and Eldur lived in harmony with queens and kings who didn't only respect each other, they were friends. There was love in the fae realm back then, back before everything fell apart.

Lochlan stood on a stone balcony with one hand on the sculpted half wall surrounding it. From his vantage point, he could look out across the fields of Iskalt, untamed and wild, frozen.

He glanced behind him at the tall double wooden doors that led back into the bedroom once occupied by his parents.

If they hadn't broken faith with Fargelsi, would they be there still?

His hand shook, and he curled his fingers into a fist to keep the freezing temperatures from making him weak.

After Regan came to power on the death of her brother, Lochlan's parents and Faolan broke the treaty by taking the only Fargelsian heir and hiding her in the human realm.

And his parents died on the journey, cut down by Fargelsian soldiers who shouldn't have been able to find them.

But the magic of a fae treaty was absolute.

There was a cost to being unfaithful to the words.

"Your Majesty." A young page boy opened the balcony door.

Lochlan turned, eyeing the kid who'd called him Majesty. It had been over two months since he took the crown from his uncle's head, yet the title was foreign to him. It belonged to his father, not the boy left behind, the one who hadn't even been raised within these borders.

Ice raced through his veins, but he didn't pull his cloak in tighter. After living in the kingdom of fire and heat, he wasn't used to the snow and ice. But he was born of Iskalt, so the ice belonged to him. He let himself feel it, revel in it.

He was home.

"Speak, boy."

The page flinched at his harsh tone, but Lochlan didn't have the patience to worry about every palace worker's reaction to him. "S-sire, the Eldurian delegation has arrived."

Faolan. He hated how he longed to see the Eldurian queen, how he felt she'd put more right in Iskalt than he could hope to. He'd seen the woman lose two daughters and hold her head high. Nothing could defeat her, and Iskalt needed a calming presence like that.

"I'm sure they want to rest after the long journey." He entered his rooms, and the page followed. "Tell Iain to make sure they have everything they require. Rooms have been prepared for them." He reached the door and opened it, gesturing the page through. "It is late. I will meet with the delegation over breakfast in the morning."

It was a sign of respect. Iskalt was a kingdom of night. Only when the moon appeared did they have magic. Eldur's magic thrived in the day. Starting the meetings when they had the upper hand showed honor.

The page disappeared around the corner, and Loch stepped into the hall, shutting the door behind him. There was someone he had to see.

The Iskalt dungeons lay below the palace, their halls damp as water seeped into their walls. Veins of ice crept down the rough stone, a far cry from the wood-paneled walls just two floors above.

Lochlan glanced each way to make sure no one followed him. He'd broken his guards' habit of watching him wherever he went. His footsteps echoed off the low ceilings.

Only two guards sat at the entrance to the deeper cells, both bundled up in furs. Lochlan nodded to them as he passed.

They mumbled shaky "your Majestys."

Lochlan didn't remember much of his time in Iskalt as a kid, but he could see himself running through these halls, daring friends to enter the small cells. During his father's reign, they'd gone unused. Once Callum came to power, he'd filled them with those loyal to the old king.

The first thing Lochlan had done as king was free the many men and women who'd been down here for years. He'd also kept many of Callum's loyal men locked away before transporting them to the prison realm.

Now, the long line of dark cells held only one prisoner.

"Nephew." Callum's hoarse voice rose out of the dark. "It's kind of you to visit."

Lochlan lifted a hand, calling on his magic to create a ball of blue light in his palm. It illuminated Callum's sneering face, pale from two months underground.

"I'm not here for you." Lochlan met the gaze of one of the few family members he had left. Only two people in this world shared his blood, and both were on the opposite side of the coming war.

Lochlan was very much alone.

"Do enlighten me." Callum bent over as a cough wracked through him. He put a hand on the wall to steady himself.

Lochlan glanced at the pile of ratty blankets in the corner. "Do you need another blanket?" He didn't want to kill his uncle. Every time he considered it, he remembered how much his father had loved Callum once.

"You can't assuage your guilt with blankets, nephew."

Lochlan's jaw clenched. "I have no guilt." He leaned toward the bars. "I am not your nephew. In this kingdom, I am the king. You'd do well to remember that." He stepped back, letting the light dim. "I came down here to tell you tomorrow is a great day for Iskalt. Faolan of Eldur is in this palace."

Callum growled. "That witch."

"I will bring Iskalt back from the destruction you led it to. We are going to destroy Queen Regan, and you'll be here to watch it happen." His smiled. "You've lost, uncle." He turned to walk away.

"I should have had you killed when you were nothing but an orphaned pup," Callum growled.

Lochlan paused. "Yes. That would have been smart."

"When will I be heading to the prison realm?"

"You won't." Lochlan turned without another look at the man who'd stolen his throne and hurt his people, making a promise to himself that he'd never look upon the man again. "I will not let your crimes fade in our memories, uncle."

Callum O'Shea was now a part of Iskalt's past.

As he emerged from the dungeons, he wondered what the kingdom's future would be? What about his future?

A few short months ago, he'd thought he knew.

Brea.

Her eyes haunted his sleep, fathomless blue eyes that flashed yellow with her magic. What was happening to her now? She'd been a prisoner in Fargelsi for too long, and there'd been no word of her.

He wasn't watching where he was going when he slammed into someone, sending them sprawling to the velvet carpet of the hall.

"Ouch," the man groaned, rubbing his head. "Do you have to be so big and bull-like?" He still hadn't looked up. "It's like getting trampled by Hagrid."

Lochlan's eyes widened. "What do you know of Hagrid?"

"Only that he's a half-giant with a heart of gold." The man picked himself up off the floor and froze. "Wait... what do you know of Hagrid?"

"Human," Lochlan growled, his finger's closing around the man's arm. "Come with me."

"Ow, dude, all you had to do was ask!" The man whined the entire time Lochlan dragged him down the hall past curious servants.

Lochlan shoved him through a doorway and stared at everyone in the room until they scurried away.

The man pushed away from him and blew messy hair out of his eyes. "Whoa." He turned in a circle, taking in the domed ceilings of the library. High shelves lined the walls with ornate golden carvings. It was a beautiful room, but Lochlan missed the cozier library in Eldur where he'd spent so much time with Alona and Finn.

The man ran a finger over spines. "These are all fae books, aren't they?" He turned to face Lochlan. "The Eldurian library has a better collection. You can't say you're a book collector without the full Harry Potter series."

Lochlan cleared his throat. "What are you after, human?"

"After?" The man shrugged. "I got lost on the way back to my room."

"There are no humans in the Iskalt court." Lochlan advanced on him. "I would know."

"How?" The man crossed his arms over his chest, lifting his chin in defiance. There was something familiar that had Lochlan stepping back.

"What?"

"Do you know every single fae in your court? Who are you? The king?" He cracked a smile like it was a ridiculous notion.

Lochlan's brows drew together. "What is a human doing in Iskalt?" He only knew of one human in all the fae world—Alona.

The man's jaw dropped open. "Oh wow, you are, aren't you?" He laughed. "Hard eyes, all blue-flashy and crap. Ridiculously long Legolas hair. They spoke of you at the Eldur court." He dropped into an elaborate bow, throwing his arms out to the side in mockery. "Shall I kiss your feet, your Majesty?"

"Stand up, fool, and tell me who you are."

"Man." He straightened. "Rowena said you were a grump, but that doesn't begin to cover it."

Rowena? Human.

The library started spinning, and Lochlan reached out for something, anything to hold on to as the world came crashing to a halt. "Myles?" he croaked out. The boy Brea loved more than herself, the one she'd surrendered to Regan for.

"At your service." He stuck out his hand.

Lochlan only stared at it. "You expect me to shake that?"

Myles dropped it with a shrug. "Guess not, grumpy king."

"Brea preferred douchey Loch." The words slipped out before he could stop them. He pressed his lips together.

Myles smile dropped. "She also preferred sacrificing herself for people without giving them a choice in the matter." There was no bitterness in his voice, only sadness.

Lochlan sighed, hearing his own desperation reflected in this stranger's voice. But Myles didn't feel like a stranger. In an odd way, he was connected to Brea, like a part of her. "Brea is stubborn."

"You can say that again." Myles' shoulders dropped, and he sat down on a wooden settee. "This is very uncomfortable, by the way."

"I know." After growing up in the opulent palace of Eldur, he'd grown used to a level of comfort not seen in Iskalt. Everything here felt stiff, cold.

It wasn't yet his home.

But it had to be.

He studied the young man who was so far from home, the one Lochlan's own brother had abducted and forced through a portal. Yet the fear in his eyes wasn't for himself. Lochlan knew because he recognized it. They both loved the same girl—in different ways—and didn't know if they'd ever get her back.

When Regan abducted Alona, Lochlan's heart broke.

When Brea returned to Fargelsi and Regan, his heart stopped beating completely, turning to ice inside his chest.

Maybe that was how he was able to lead his men into a seemingly unwinnable battle... and win.

Myles hunched forward, burying his face in his hands. "It's been two months since I arrived in Eldur, a freed prisoner who still felt very much locked away. I won't be truly free until she is." He shook his head. "I don't know why I'm telling you this. I don't even know you."

"Because some part of you knows I'm the only person who can understand." Not the only person. This was what Finn had been going through since the day they found out Alona was gone. Lochlan had been sympathetic then, but he hadn't quite understood the gut-wrenching pain. Not like he did now.

"I want her back, your Majesty." Myles lifted his face, tears hanging in his lashes. "I need—"

"Listen, this isn't the end for her. Brea is strong." Lochlan pushed away from the shelf and crossed to stand in front of Myles. "She's tougher than anyone I've ever known. We'll get her back."

He nodded. "We will."

Lochlan ran a hand through his hair. "And look, when we're alone, call me Loch. It's what she would have wanted." He'd spent months keeping people in the palace at arm's length, wanting them to respect him as king, but not as a friend.

But now... with this human... connecting with him was like having Brea by his side.

Myles' smile was weak. "Yeah, okay. And I promise only to call you Legolas in my head."

Lochlan quirked a brow.

"You know who that is, right? I saw the library full of human books in Eldur, and Rowena told me they were yours."

"Do I know who Legolas is?" Lochlan scoffed. "I am the king. Don't ask disrespectful questions."

Myles laughed, but there was little joy in it. He got to his feet. "I think we're going to be friends, Loch."

"I don't make friends." Lochlan had only ever had three friends in his life, but Finn and Alona were more like family. And Brea was... special. She'd refused to leave him alone until he craved her company.

Myles smirked. "Always time to start."

The ink dried as the magic drew it into the parchment before both Lochlan and Faolan. They stood side by side behind a table on the dais in the cavernous Iskalt throne room.

A crowd of onlookers, both from Iskalt and Eldur, watched as their leaders tied their kingdoms together.

There were two kinds of binding magic a fae could enter in to. The first was the most sacred. A marriage. When two fae performed the marriage ceremony, they were tied for eternity, unable to love another.

The second was a treaty. It could be signed between kingdoms or simply neighbors.

Once Faolan scrawled her signature at the bottom of the page, she slid it to Lochlan. He dipped his quill in the ink pot before etching his name into the document.

After he was finished, he looked out at the crowd, finding many faces, some familiar, others foreign. Tierney stood with Myles and a tall girl he recognized at once.

Neeve.

There was no time for him to dwell on the Fargelsian's presence or how she too was released. Iain walked forward to stand at Lochlan's side. He was one of the few men who'd served Callum that Lochlan didn't send to the prison realm. As the head of the palace household, he was needed to keep things in running order.

He'd also served Lochlan's parents faithfully.

"Sire," he whispered. "Dusk has fallen."

After a day of meeting with his old family who were now foreign dignitaries, he'd waited until this very moment. A treaty between the kingdoms could only be magicked at dawn or dusk when both Iskalt and Eldur held magic in their veins.

"Thank you, Iain." Lochlan nodded to Faolan, and they turned to the crowd, standing side by side.

Faolan spoke first. "I, Queen Faolan Mordha Duin Cahill enter into a promise with Iskalt willingly. Eldur will honor this treaty and obey its demands. Eldur will come to Iskalt's aid should the need arise. We will work together to defeat evil in this world and to protect our shared people." She pressed her open hand to the center of the parchment, and golden power flowed down her arm, setting her hand alight. The power faded from her skin, soaking into the document. When she removed her hand, the print faded.

An awed silence hung over the room as Lochlan stepped up to repeat Faolan's words, making only necessary changes. By the time his ice blue magic faded from the page, no one would question Iskalt or Eldur's commitment to peace.

But there would be no peace while Regan ruled Fargelsi. Of that, he was sure.

Tierney walked forward and put an arm around her wife before taking Lochlan's hand. "Today was a good day." She smiled and pressed a kiss to Faolan's cheek.

Lochlan nodded, gazing at the mass of fae who had started wandering from the room to find positions outside among the crowd waiting for their king's speech. It wasn't just a good day, it was needed as the first step toward a better future for all of them.

So, why couldn't Lochlan feel any of it? Since the day he'd left Eldur to regain his throne, he'd been a walking man of stone, unaffected by anyone or anything.

"I have a speech to make." He hurried toward the door, but Tierney sped up and looped her arm through his.

"Smile, Lochlan. You just did right by your people."

"I know." He sighed.

"I think about her too, you know. Both of them. We all do." Tierney offered him a kind smile, one that had always made him feel loved, wanted.

But now, it only set him further adrift in a sea of icebergs.

"I wish I didn't."

"Don't say that. One day, when they return, it will help them to know they weren't forgotten even on our best days. And make no mistake, boyo, this is one of the best. It has been a long time since Eldur had an ally. Much will change now, and it is because of you."

"I didn't do anything other than get injured in a battle. You give me credit that is due to my men."

Tierney pulled him to a stop outside a set of double doors. "Warriors need someone to lead them, Loch. Something they believe in, and they believe in you. Don't forget that. Your people... they believe in you. That is more powerful than any fear Callum instilled in them."

He pulled her into a hug, needing to feel like the kid she'd raised once more. Faolan was the queen who took him in, but when Tierney entered their lives, everything changed. She was just as important to Eldur as their queen because of how she changed the people around her with kindness. As one of the most powerful magicians in the Eldur court, she could have had anything.

And all she'd wanted was a family.

"I love you, boyo." She pressed a kiss to his cheek. "Now, go make the Iskalt citizens fall for the Lochlan charm." Her lips curved up at her own joke. They both knew he had no charm, but he had passion, and maybe that was more important.

A guard opened the doors that led out onto one of the palace's many balconies. This particular one wrapped around the front of the palace, sitting high above the arched doors.

He walked across the red-tiled floor to reach the carved golden rail. Guards in steel armor and blue threaded overcoats stood at intervals. On each end, an archer prepared their arrows for any sign of attack.

And below... that was what caught Lochlan's eye. A crowd stretched through the square and out into the fields beyond the palace—numbering in the thousands. Iskalt citizens had come from their villages to hear their king say their troubles were ending.

Lochlan touched his throat, amplifying his voice. "Greetings, Iskalt!"

The crowd cheered, their flags flapping in the night winds. Most of them held lights in their hands, and it made the field dance with what looked like a thousand tiny multi-colored stars.

It was beautiful.

For the first time since taking the crown, Lochlan felt like he was where he was meant to be.

He remembered Tierney's words and channeled her optimism. "Today is a good day for Iskalt. We have entered into a binding agreement with Eldur."

They roared their approval.

"I will not promise the troubles are over. Our kingdom has long been a harsh one where crops struggle to produce enough to feed our villages, and raids are common. No more! Shipments of food from Eldur's bountiful fields will begin to arrive. Hunger will not defeat us!"

The applause was deafening.

He went on. "Our army has grown since my uncle's imprisonment as more loyal Iskaltians come forward to protect the kingdom.

We will now protect the trade routes and make routine stops at the villages. Criminals will not defeat us!"

More cheering.

"And finally, it is time to bring peace to the fae world. We will soon devise plans to help all the kingdoms. Fargelsi will not defeat us!"

Lochlan smiled as he watched his people cheer for the future he so desperately wanted.

Once the sounds died down, he swept his gaze across the clearing and dropped his voice. "We have all lost people. Many of you mourn loved ones." His eyes found Myles at the other side of the balcony. "I too have suffered, but their losses will not be in vain. Our sorrow will not defeat us. We are Iskalt." He pounded his chest. "*We* are Iskalt."

Their cheering rose toward the night sky as if telling the moon who they were.

And who Lochlan had just become.

A king.

No matter what happened to Brea and Alona, that was something he couldn't escape, so he had to step into it and let it become him.

Once inside, Faolan greeted him with tears in her eyes. "I never thought I'd see the day when Niall and Enid O'Shea's son took the crown. They'd be proud of you, Lochlan."

Tierney wrapped her arms around him. "Brea would be proud too."

He almost laughed at that. Brea would probably have found his speech ridiculous, and she'd have let him know. But he'd give anything to hear her criticism, to watch her eyes spark as he angered her time and again.

While he ruled a kingdom, she sat as a prisoner of another.

Whatever torture Regan was subjecting her to, he only hoped Brea could come back from it, that she wouldn't lose the fire in her soul.

CHAPTER 2

BREA

"Do you like the dahlias or the orchids?" Regan examined the beautiful flowers selected from her own gardens.

"Does it matter?" Brea refused to play along with the wedding preparations. She tried not to think about the wedding at all. Now that Myles and Neeve were safe and beyond Regan's reach, that was all she cared about.

Regan stood with her hands on her hips, her long hair falling in a mass of white-blond curls to her waist. "Of course, it matters, darling. The wrong flower could throw the whole event off, and your wedding, my dear, will be the event of the century if your Auntie Reagan has anything to say about it."

Brea would never understand her aunt. She was a madwoman with a queen's thirst for power and glory, and the mind of a deranged party planner. She was determined to make Brea agree with all her decisions for the wedding, while Brea was determined to disagree on principle and petty revenge.

"What about those pretty purple flowers that grow in the forest?"

"The violet anemone is frightfully poisonous, my Lady." The head gardener said, utterly scandalized.

"Yeah, let's go with those." Brea leaned back in her chair and put her boot-clad feet up on the table. If Regan was going to make her go through with marrying the wrong O'Shea, then Brea was going to wear whatever she wanted outside of Regan's parties. The messier the better.

"Feet on the floor, darling." Regan shoved her feet off the table, using a dainty hankie to keep her hands from touching Brea's boots. "And I'll not have poisonous flowers grace your wedding. It's bad luck."

Brea snorted her disgust. "Fine then go with the black dahlias."

"The black dahlia is a cursed flower, my Lady." The gardener was possibly more irritated with Brea than Regan was.

"The orchids are quite beautiful, don't you think?" Regan shoved the flower cuttings in her hands.

"Meh, I still like the dahlias. Maybe the big orange ones."

"Orange is a hideous color for weddings." Regan tapped her foot, but Brea had nothing else better to do than make sure her aunt didn't get her way on everything. Brea didn't care what the wedding looked like in the end. She would show up and keep her end of the bargain, but if this was the only wedding she'd ever have, then so be it. It wouldn't be one she planned.

"Then how about the peachy-pink ones?" Brea sighed. She'd go through all the colors until Regan agreed on one, but Brea would boil and eat her own shoes before she'd agree on orchids for this farce of a wedding.

"Those are lovely too, I suppose." Regan's shoulders slumped before she handed the cuttings to the gardener and ordered a bazillion peach and white dahlias for her niece's 'big day'.

"Can I go now?" Brea folded her arms across her chest.

"Absolutely not. We still have to pick the invitations and plan the menu, and the kitchen will bring up the cakes for us to taste this afternoon."

"Cakes?"

"Yes, you have to pick a cake, dear. Don't tell me you don't want to spend the afternoon tasting cakes? I promise I wouldn't allow Gelsi berries anywhere near my own food."

Brea's stomach growled at the prospect. Regan had kept her promise, allowing Brea to make her own meals, but she wasn't allowed to leave the queen's quarters and that meant Brea couldn't visit the kitchens whenever she was hungry. She was limited to the few unprepared items Alona brought to her each morning and afternoon. She existed on things like raw fruits, vegetables and nuts, cheese and dried meats—whole foods that wouldn't mix well with Gelsi berries. The food wasn't filling, and there was rarely much left for her evening meals after Alona had returned to her cell in the dungeon. Which meant Brea was hungry most of the time. She'd lost weight during her time here, and the prospect of gorging herself on wedding cakes was sheer torture. She'd have to take the tiniest bites possible or pretend to eat when Regan wasn't looking.

"Fine, let's do the invitations and get it over with." If she played her cards right, she could waste enough time disagreeing with her aunt that there would be no time for cake tasting today. "Not that I know a single person in Fargelsi I want to invite."

"You are going to be our princess, darling. The whole kingdom will come for your big day. You'll meet everyone, and in no time, you'll have new friends."

"Yeah, friends who're prisoners and forced to like me," Brea muttered.

"What's that, dear?" Regan hummed as she sorted through paper samples. Freaking *paper*. How could there be so many kinds? As far as she was concerned, they could write it on toilet paper because that was all this wedding was worth.

"Where is that accursed maid with the calligraphy samples?" Regan cast a menacing look at the nearest maid.

"I-I'll go check on her, your Majesty." One of the triplets curtsied and fled the room like her hair was on fire.

"Good help is so hard to find." Regan shook her head, focusing on a dozen white pieces of paper that looked the same to Brea. "Come look at these, Brea."

"Huh?" Her attention was a million miles away. Somewhere in Iskalt with a certain man with midnight blue eyes.

"We don't speak with noises, Brea O'Rourke. A lady speaks with distinction and enunciation."

"Don't call me that." Brea's throat burned, and she couldn't swallow.

"Why not? It's your name, dear."

"You may call me Brea Robinson or Brea Cahill."

"Nonsense. It will be O'Rourke when you marry Griffin."

"His name is O'Shea." It hurt to speak the name or to think that someday soon it would belong to her in the worst sort of way.

"He took my name ages ago, sweetheart. I don't think you realize how strong the mother-son bond is between us. He came to me hardly more than a babe. He remembers little of his life before I saved him from that cold, miserable place."

"You mean after you killed his parents?"

"I did no such thing, Brea. Now it is time to pick your invitations, and I won't hear another protest. This is a happy day." She slammed her fist on the table, rattling the china samples they'd narrowed down to four patterns earlier.

"Apologies, your Majesty." Alona sank into a perfect curtsy at the door. "I won't be late again."

"Enter." Regan stood stiffly at the center of the room.

Brea locked eyes with Alona and noted her subtle nod. She'd spent several weeks trying to get a message out of Fargelsi whenever Brea was occupied with the queen. Brea desperately wanted to let her mothers know she was okay, but judging by Alona's expression, it wasn't looking good.

Regan could never know she and Alona were friends. She could never know they shared a deep abiding love for the same people and that love had bonded them in the weeks since Alona became her maid.

"Here are the samples, your Majesty." Alona handed her a thick roll of parchment.

"Spread it out on the table."

Alona rushed to do her bidding, her hands trembling as she rolled out the scroll filled with calligraphy samples. They all said the same thing in different styles.

Breanna and Griffin O'Rourke. A thousand times across the scroll. It made her head pound and her heart race, seeing it in black and white.

"May I be excused?" Brea could barely get the words out.

"No, you may not." Regan studied the intricate lettering with a practiced eye, crossing out the ones she didn't like. "Maid, you are dismissed."

"Yes, your Majesty." Alona gave Brea another nod, their signal for Brea to meet her in the vacant guest suite below Brea's rooms. It was the only room they could find where they were certain Regan couldn't listen in. They had to be careful sneaking into that part of the palace since it was seldom used.

"Choose one." Regan passed four white sheets of paper across the table.

"Not to sound facetious, but does it matter? I can't see a difference."

"This one is thicker. This one has silver edges. This one gold. And the last one is textured. You can feel the difference if you'll just pay attention." The biting edge of Regan's tone told Brea she'd pushed her too far.

"I like the silver edges, but does it have to be white-white? Could it be like, eggshell? That's a color, right?"

Regan nodded, making note of her choice. "I grow weary of your procrastination, Brea."

"You know, you could just pick everything, and it will be beautiful. I really don't care." Brea decided to play nice so she could go meet Alona. "You have much better taste than I do. I—"

"Your Majesty," Lady Einin, the castellan entered the room. "An important message from Iskalt has just arrived for you."

"Iskalt?" Brea gripped the arms of her chair, hoping for news of Lochlan.

Regan marched across the room to the silver platter the castellan held. Regan broke the wax seal, and her eyes darted across the page.

Brea could see it in her aunt's face. It wasn't good news, but bad news for Regan typically meant good news for Brea.

Regan flung the foreign missive across the room with a piercing shriek that scared the bejesus out of Brea. Every single servant in the room ran out like the place was about to blow.

"The gall of that... that *boy*!" Regan snatched up a china plate—one Brea actually liked—and sent it crashing into the fireplace.

Brea scooted her chair back just in time as the rest of the china sailed across the room to join the first. Regan's magic filled her gaze as she lifted her hands, and the table toppled over and slammed against the wall. Her face grew scarlet with rage, and her eyes blazed with green fire.

Brea watched in awe as her aunt threw an epic magical temper tantrum, trashing the room, screaming her head off like a spoiled child who didn't get her way.

Brea wondered if she could escape without notice like all the servants had, or if she should try hiding under a table Regan hadn't destroyed yet.

The queen's shrieking stopped as suddenly as it began. Clearing her throat and straightening her dress, she turned to Brea, her eyes calm now. "Brea, darling, your wedding will be such a happy day." She sniffed as if overcome with emotion.

That was it. Her aunt was a certifiable whack-job. And utterly terrifying.

"Come, dear. Choose one of these lovely calligraphy styles for your invitations, and then you may go. Auntie has some things to attend to this afternoon so our cake-testing party will have to wait for tomorrow." She rested her hand on Brea's shoulder, and Brea couldn't help her violent flinch.

"Um, I like that one. It's pretty." Brea pointed to one of three samples Regan circled, not caring which one it was as long as it got her out of this room.

"Yes, that's my favorite too." Regan giggled like they were best girlfriends. "Run along, dearie. I'll see you at dinner."

"Bye." Brea shot out of her chair and down the hall as fast as her legs would carry her. She wanted to grab the message on her way out, but she didn't dare. She just hoped Alona had good news.

"You're here. I didn't think you'd get out of there anytime soon." Alona paced across the half-charred bedroom that had never been repaired. The castellan had magically sealed the room off, but Alona found a way around the magic, picking the lock with a hairpin. They'd tested the room for over a week before they decided it was safe, and no one was listening in.

"She received a message from Iskalt," Brea blurted. "Loch was headed for Iskalt when I left Eldur." Panic made her chest tight, and she couldn't breathe.

"Focus, Brea. What was her reaction to the news?"

"An epic fit that scared the life out of me. That woman is insane, Lona."

"That sounds like good news for Loch. I'll do some digging and see what I can find out."

"Were you able to get the message sent?" Brea asked her the same question every day, and it was always the same answer. Not yet.

"I'm afraid it's not possible to get a message out anymore." Alona dropped into a dusty chair by the window. "No one but the queen's trusted guards can get anything through the barrier. I found out today she's strengthened the border. Before, no one born in Fargelsi could get in or out. Now, no one of any kingdom can cross without the queen's permission. I'm afraid we might be stuck for a while, Brea."

"We'll keep trying. I need to master my Gelsi magic while I'm here, anyway. Maybe one day I can grow strong enough to break us both out of this mess."

"I just don't know why you don't refuse to marry him." Alona gave her a pleading look, like she was trying to tell her something important.

"I have to keep my end of the bargain or she will make your life miserable and she'll go after Myles and Neeve again."

"But they are safe in Eldur. Mother will never let her touch them. You cannot marry Griffin. You don't know what it m—"

"I can't be responsible for starting a war, Lona." Brea sank down to the floor, feeling weak from too little food, too much stress, and not enough sleep.

Alona leaned forward to meet her gaze. "She is responsible for all of this. If a war comes our way, it won't be because you backed out of a wedding or broke a promise you made under duress. It will be because she is hell bent on having one. We can't stop her in here, so you might as well break off this engagement."

"We'll never get out of here if I'm locked up right beside you in the dungeon."

"If you marry him, you will never be free, Brea."

"Then we will have to rely on our family to do their part out there, and when that happens, we will be ready to strike from the inside.

CHAPTER 3

LOCHLAN

The paper scrunched into a ball as Lochlan wrapped his fingers around it, holding it in his fist. Anger welled up in him, and for once, it was probably a good thing the sun was in the sky at this hour. No telling what kind of magic he'd release otherwise.

The Fargelsian messenger stood in front of the throne, shifting from foot to foot and glancing toward the door as if he wanted to make his escape.

Lochlan hadn't said a word as a chasm opened inside him, creating emptiness where he'd been so full only a few months before as he lay in bed beside the best woman he knew.

Brea Robinson was supposed to save them all. That was her purpose, wasn't it? To be some kind of weapon none of them understood.

But she hadn't needed to be a weapon to save him, to make him believe it was possible to reclaim the throne underneath his butt. She'd given him hope and then ripped it all away.

"Lochlan." Faolan looked sideways at him from the seat next to his throne. They'd been holding court together during her stay in Iskalt. "Loch, what is it?"

He barely heard her as he opened his fist and smoothed out the wrinkled paper.

Queen Regan of Fargelsi invites the king of Iskalt to celebrate the binding of her niece, Princess Breanna O'Rourke and Griffin O'Rourke.

He stopped reading, having already seen he had two months. Binding, that was what Fargelsi called it. He supposed it wasn't wrong. A fae marriage did bind them together. He stared at the names as the letters swam in his vision.

"Breanna and Griffin O'Rourke," he whispered. Neither name sounded right. Brea would forever be a Robinson, not even a Cahill. And Griff...

The threads of his anger unspooled, and his chest deflated. "She chose this." A fae marriage had to be entered in to willingly for the magic to take hold. Brea couldn't be forced into the ceremony.

He wasn't sure what would have been worse, knowing Brea had to marry his brother against her will, or knowing she wanted to.

"Chose what, Loch?" Faolan's words were tinged with fear as she looked from the messenger to Lochlan. "Is it about Brea or Alona?"

He closed his eyes and passed the letter to her, knowing it would crush her in a different way. Once Brea married Griffin, she'd never be free. Was this her giving up?

Getting to his feet, he sent a scowl toward the Fargelsian messenger. "Go."

The wiry man fled from the throne room as Lochlan descended the steps.

"Loch." Faolan covered her mouth. "She can't."

"And yet, she is." Without looking back to see if her sadness matched his own, he walked down the long velvet carpet. Parishioners parted to let their king through, bowing as they did. It was enough to make any man feel powerful, but Lochlan had never wanted power. He didn't want to watch people bow and scrape and bend to his every whim.

The only reason he'd wanted to be king was to protect the people of Iskalt, to defeat his uncle. That mission had filled him even after Brea left him for Fargelsi, even after she made him love her and then took it away.

But duty filled the mind, not the heart.

Lochlan stopped at the arched doorway leading out into the snowy courtyard. A handful of guards were preparing to mount their horses nearby.

Without thinking, Lochlan stepped from the doorway, and they all froze. He cleared his throat. "I need a horse." He had to get some space from the palace, from all the people inside who'd share his hurt over Brea's decision.

One of the guards handed him the reins to his mount, and as Lochlan stepped into the stirrup, the last person he wanted to see appeared. Myles sprinted from the palace, a fur-lined cloak draped over his arm.

It was only then Lochlan remembered he wore nothing but his long-sleeved tunic and trousers.

Myles bent over, panting, and held up a hand. "Dude, I am out of shape. It's been ages since I had to train for football, and then after all that time in the dungeons and—"

"Myles." Lochlan cut him off. "What do you want?"

He held up the cloak. "Tierney thought you'd want this. And me."

"You?"

"Sure, Lochlan. I'd love to go for a ride. Thanks for asking." He grinned as Lochlan bent down to take the cloak and draped it over his shoulders.

Lochlan sighed. There was no escaping this human. "Guard." He gestured to one of the other guards nearby. "Give the human your horse."

Myles mounted his horse and looked down at the guard. "Your

king thanks you. He's just too much of a grumpy gus to say it." He nudged his horse forward, flashing one more smile at Lochlan.

Lochlan followed him. "I have a right to be grumpy today." He hated using Myles' odd term, but he couldn't think of anything else to say.

"Loch, I don't know what's happened now or why you just walked out of the throne room, but there is never a reason to be a jerk to the people who serve you."

Lochlan's brow scrunched. "It's called being commanding. I'm king."

"Potato, potahto. The end result is still the same. No one will like you."

"And yet, I can't seem to get rid of you."

Myles seemed unbothered by the insult. He shifted his gaze to look out over the field in front of them. "That's because I have to watch out for you. It's my duty as her best friend."

How was he supposed to do that when the one causing so much pain was the best friend he spoke of? Lochlan would never admit what he felt for Brea. He wouldn't let anyone see how news of her marriage stole the breath from his lungs.

Instead, he dug his heels into the horse's sides and took off. Faolan would chastise him from venturing far from the palace without guards when there could still be people loyal to his uncle in the villages. But Lochlan was tired of sitting in the palace and making his people come to him.

"Where are we going?" Myles' horse trotted alongside his.

"There's a village about an hour's ride from here." Despite the biting chill, he knew this was what he had to do. Push Brea to the back of his mind and focus on his people.

They reached the small village in good time, and Lochlan was pleased to see the amount of new construction taking place. Homes that had been destroyed in raids by Callum's men were being mended, and the market bustled with activity. Villagers stopped moving as he passed, and he nodded to them.

"We should dismount," Myles said.

"Why?" It was harder to protect one's self on foot.

Myles didn't wait for Lochlan as he slid down. "Because you should walk among your people, not ride above them."

The human had a point. "Maybe you were meant to be a king." His feet hit the dirt road, and he wrapped his fingers around the reins.

"Nah." Myles laughed, his cheeks red from the cold. "I just read a lot."

It was one of the few things Lochlan already knew about Brea's friend. He was possibly the first person Lochlan met who read as much as he did.

Myles said hello to every villager they passed, and Lochlan tried to follow his lead, pasting on a smile. It was still difficult to think of this kingdom as belonging to him. For so long, he'd been the ward of the Eldur queen, only relied upon to venture into the human realm. But now, tens of thousands of people counted on him for their most basic needs.

And he owed them. The villagers rose up against Callum, coming to the aid of a king they didn't know, one who was rightfully theirs.

"Your smile is kind of scary." Myles chuckled.

Lochlan let the false smile drop. "Excuse me for not being cheery on the day I found out Brea is marrying my brother."

Myles stopped walking, his jaw clenching. "Brea is marrying Griff? She can't. He... They must be forcing her."

"That's not how fae marriages work. No one can force her into it."

"Then she must have a reason. Maybe Alona is being hurt. When we save her, she'll be free of him."

Lochlan's shoulders rose as he sighed. "This isn't the human world, Myles. There is magic involved. A fae marriage is irreversible. She will be tied to him until one of them dies." His voice lowered. "She will love him."

"No, she wouldn't. He abducted us, ripping us away from our lives for this jacked-up world. She could never love him."

"Once the ceremony is performed, she will be able to love no one but him." The words hurt to say. Marriage magic was simple. It prevented those involved from ever loving another.

Myles went quiet for a long moment as they continued walking through the village. Lochlan used the respite from his constant chatter to distract himself with his people. At this time of day, many of the villagers went about their daily work, never straying from their tasks. Some hammered on the sides of buildings, repairing what had fallen into disrepair.

Others sold their wares in crowded stalls.

One of the first things Lochlan did as king was open the palace coffers and send gold to the villages to rebuild and plant the few crops that could grow in the hard, frozen ground. It wouldn't be enough to feed the kingdom, but with the new treaty with Eldur, that was less of a worry.

"I remember the day Brea stopped believing in fairytales." Myles' voice held a somber note. "Her favorite used to be Cinderella, but you might not know what that is. Basically, a girl who is nothing more than a servant to her family falls in love with a prince. When we were younger, she kept this Cinderella book under her pillow. We were thirteen when Mrs. Robinson found the book. Do you want to know what she did?"

Lochlan didn't respond because he feared what happened next.

"She laughed." Myles stared down at his feet. "I'll never forget that moment. I was sitting in their living room, but I could hear the words Mrs. Robinson said. She told Brea there was no escaping the life they were given. That children's stories had no place in the mind of a girl like her." He closed his eyes and sighed. "She told Brea she'd never be worth anything. That no prince was coming for a girl who belonged in a mental institution."

Lochlan's heart ached for that young girl. He'd known things were rough for her every time he visited the human realm, but

Myles had a window into her pain Lochlan hadn't. "What did Brea say?"

"Nothing. At least, not to her mom. But that night, she ripped up the book. If anyone deserves a good ending to their story, it's her. Brea no longer believes in fairytales, and maybe she's right. Because in this world where anything should be possible, she still has no choices, no options. The prince at the end of her wedding aisle is the wrong one."

Lochlan shook his head. "Maybe he's not. Maybe she's chosen a side." As he said the words, he hated himself for them.

Myles jerked to a stop and twisted on his heel. His fist flew out so quickly, Lochlan didn't see the punch coming before he stumbled back, pain spidering out from his eye socket.

Myles' chest heaved, but there was no apology in his eyes. "You don't know her at all, do you?"

Lochlan held a hand to his eye as villagers rushed toward them, having seen the scuffle. He could have Myles thrown in the dungeon for laying a hand on the king, but he wouldn't because he deserved the bruise that would form, the reminder that he'd doubted the girl who'd only ever protected the people she loved. She wasn't in Fargelsi because she'd chosen Regan.

She'd chosen her friends and their freedom instead of her own.

Myles rubbed his knuckles. "Your face is like a brick, a big ugly brick."

Lochlan waved off the people trying to help him. "I'm fine." But he wasn't, not by half.

Myles started walking again, not looking back to see if Lochlan followed. A king led, he didn't trail after some human boy, yet, Lochlan followed him. "I watched Brea for years, but you're right. Maybe I don't truly know her. Can you tell me about her?"

Myles slowed to walk in step with Lochlan as they both led their horses along the dirt roads. "She's stubborn."

He snorted. "No kidding."

"She used to tell me I shouldn't be her friend, that I was too good for her."

"No one is too good for her."

"I know, but she didn't. Brea was... a bit of an outcast. The kids at school didn't understand her, and she didn't let them see who she truly was. I was on the football team—that's a popular human sport—and she thought that meant I could be popular if it wasn't for her." Myles laughed. "Once, when we were fifteen, she refused to talk to me at school for an entire week as an experiment. Even hid in the library at lunch. I spent the week trying to change her mind while ignoring everyone who suddenly noticed me. Because she'd been right. Without her, other people wanted to be my friend."

An immeasurable sadness wound through Lochlan for everything Brea had gone through. "What did you do?"

"I wore her down. I didn't care about anyone else. I just wanted my best friend. One night, I found her outside her house chasing fireflies. They're these flying bugs with tails that light up. Brea loved them, but they did not love her. She was terrible at catching them." He laughed. "I caught one for her but refused to give it to her until she told me she missed me."

"Did she tell you?" Lochlan pictured the kind of life Brea and Myles lived in the human world, so different from his.

"No." Myles' lips curved up. "But later that night, she climbed into my window and curled into my bed. She didn't tell me she needed me, but I knew. Just like I needed her. We didn't speak of that week again and everything went back to normal."

They reached the end of the village and Lochlan nodded to a woman ushering her children across the road. "We should head back to the palace."

"Always somewhere for a king to be." Myles shook his head and mounted his horse.

They didn't go back through the village. Instead, they wound through the fields surrounding it until they found the road back to the palace. A troop of guards rode by them, bowing their heads.

They rode in silence for a while until Lochlan couldn't take it anymore. "What does Regan do to her prisoners?" He had to know what would make Brea think marrying Griff was a better option than remaining a prisoner.

Myles's fingers flexed around the reins, and his gaze hardened. "She kept us locked in dark cells below the palace. Alona told me before I arrived they were let out once a week to clean in the river, but that stopped."

"You spoke with Alona?" Lochlan sat up straighter. "And she's—"

"Alive? Yeah. Living? Heck no. They kept us in the dark and fed us scraps. A few guards were sympathetic, like they didn't like the situation any more than us. I mean, Regan had imprisoned her own brother and—"

"Wait! Stop." Lochlan pulled back on the reins. "Repeat." His heart thundered against his ribs. He couldn't have heard Myles right.

"It was dark and—"

"Not that. The part about Regan's brother."

"Oh yeah, Brandon. He's been down there for ages. You can just tell, and—"

Lochlan didn't wait to hear the rest. He snapped the reins and urged the horse into a gallop. Freezing wind whipped him in the face, but he couldn't stop, not now, not when this was the first thread of hope they'd found that Fargelsi could be defeated.

It took him half the time to reach the palace at this speed, and he jumped off the horse, throwing the reins to a guard before storming into the palace and breaking into a run. Faolan was no longer in the throne room, so he sprinted through the dark halls to the guest wing where the Eldurian party was staying.

He could barely think as he hammered his fist on Faolan's door.

It felt like an eternity before Tierney opened the door, giving him the sad look he'd wanted to avoid. But this moment wasn't about Brea's upcoming wedding. It was more, bigger, world-changing.

"Is Faolan here?" His chest heaved.

Footsteps sounded behind him, and he assumed it was Myles, but didn't turn to look.

"Lochlan." Faolan appeared from another room, her eyes rimmed red. "You've returned. Come in."

Lochlan moved to shut the door behind himself, but both Myles and Neeve were there. It didn't matter. This was something everyone had to know.

"What's wrong?" Tierney was the first to catch on that something else had happened.

Faolan lowered herself to a settee, one hand on her chest. "More news of Brea?"

He nodded and stepped forward. "Faolan, Brandon O'Rourke is alive."

Her eyes widened, and she gasped. "H-he died. Eighteen years ago."

"Actually." Myles and Neeve shared a look. "He's been in the Fargelsi dungeons."

Faolan's hands shook as she clasped them in her lap. Tears gathered in her eyes. "Brandon," she whispered.

Lochlan nodded. "The rightful king of Fargelsi."

Faolan's words were no more than a whisper on her lips. "Brea's father."

Chapter 4

BREA

"Good morning, my Lady." Alona let herself into Brea's bedroom the day of her wedding. In a fit of paranoia and distrust, Regan had taken to locking Brea in her rooms for the last week just to keep tabs on her.

"There is nothing good about this morning, Maid-Girl." She still wasn't supposed to know Alona's name.

"Where are you, my Lady?" Alona whisper-shouted.

"Under the bed."

"Why?"

"Seemed like a good hiding place."

"Are you always so strange?" Alona peeked under the bed.

"Pretty much." Brea tucked her blanket around her, wishing she could just stay in her cocoon.

"We have a busy day ahead, best to get on your feet." Translation: *I'm sorry you have to go through with this, but I'm here for you.* Over the last few months, Alona and Brea had learned to communicate their true sentiments without destroying the illusion that they were just a Lady and her maid.

"You're right." Brea sighed as she scooted out of her hiding place. "Did you bring food? I'm starving, and there's no way I'll ever make it through the day without caving in and stuffing my face with wedding food full of Gelsi berry sauces."

"I brought you a fortifying wedding breakfast. I cooked it myself." Alona stood with a proud look on her face.

"You... um... cooked? Again?" Brea was amazed she had it in her to try again. Alona was a disaster in the kitchen.

"I am learning to cook, my Lady. I hope you enjoy what I've prepared."

Brea gave her a look that said she shouldn't trust anyone. It was too dangerous.

Alona rolled a dining cart beside Brea's bed and removed the lid to a small silver dish.

A message—in butter—scrawled across the plate. *A friend of Neeve's is helping me.*

Brea blinked up at Alona and used her fork to wipe away the message. "Is that the real stuff?"

"Yes, my Lady."

Brea's stomach growled. "That's the most beautiful thing I've ever seen, but what am I putting it on?"

"I baked bread!" Alona removed the lid from another dish, revealing slices of hot fresh bread.

"Oh." Brea pulled the cart forward and shoved half a slice in her mouth, picking up a second slice in her free hand and slathering it in butter. "Wh-at else?"

"Scrambled eggs and bacon."

"I heart you so much, Maid-Girl." Brea almost cried as she swallowed the fresh bread and grabbed a fork to dig into the fluffy eggs. It was the first hot meal she'd had in ages.

"I heart you too, my Lady." Alona busied herself tidying up the room while Brea stuffed her face.

"So what events must I attend this morning?" She was certain Regan had every moment of her day planned to perfection.

"None." Alona wrestled with a pile of Brea's dirty clothes, kicking her boots into the closet.

"Seriously?" Brea breathed a sigh of relief.

"Her Majesty doesn't want anyone to see you until the main event." Which meant Regan didn't want to let Brea out of her room until the last possible moment.

"So I have a free morning?"

"Yes, my Lady. Unless... you'd like to go for a long walk on the grounds?" Alona's gaze bore a hole right through her. She still wanted Brea to call the wedding off.

Brea ignored her silent protests. "A whole morning to agonize over what I have to do this afternoon." Brea collapsed back on the bed with a loud belch. "At least my belly is full for once."

"Well then, I have another surprise for you." Alona pressed a finger against her lips to keep Brea quiet.

Lifting the linen cloth on the dining cart she revealed three bottles of fae wine.

Brea sat up and silently clapped her hands. "Where did you get it?"

"From the pantry just before the Gelsi berry juice was added. They haven't been opened yet, so they're safe."

"Well, let's crack one open. It's my wedding day, after all."

"How much has she had to drink?" Regan frowned at the hiccupping bride as the seamstress worked on the final fitting of Brea's gown. She'd lost more weight since the last fitting, and the dress needed to be taken in again.

"I'm *right* here," Brea shouted. "I can *hear* you." She pointed to her fae ears and swayed on unsteady feet.

"I'm not sure, your Majesty," Alona said, trying to hide her own inebriation. "You know how nervous brides can be on their wedding day. I thought it might calm her, but I'm not sure she can tolerate fae wine."

"Clearly not." Regan frowned again.

Brea leaned forward and pointed to herself. "Coffee!"

"Get her some strong tea," Regan snapped at one of the triplets.

"No. That's not what I said," Brea whined.

"Keep her in this room." Regan scowled. "She's not to come out until she can walk in a straight line without falling over and making a fool of herself."

"Yes, your Majesty." Alona bobbed an unsteady curtsy, and Regan slammed the door closed behind her.

Brea collapsed into a fit of giggles on the platform where she'd stood. A cloud of pink and white silk and tulle billowed out around her, and her giggles turned to tears.

"Oh, what's wrong, my Lady?" Alona rushed forward to help her up.

"Everything. I hate my dress." Fat tears rolled down her cheeks. "I look like Little Bo Peep. And I don't know if I can do this. I'm not ready to get married. And Griff... it's not right." She pressed her face into her hands and sobbed.

"I'm so sorry, my Lady." The seamstress helped Alona get her back on her feet. "I wish I could give you the dress of your dreams, dearie." She patted Brea's bare shoulder. Even she knew this was the last thing Brea wanted. But in Fargelsi, they were all prisoners to their queen's wishes.

"Come drink some tea, my Lady," one of the triplets curtsied, somehow managing not to spill a drop of the sweet dark hot tea. It almost looked like coffee. Almost.

"I miss Rowena." Brea slumped into a chair by the fireplace. Not that it was ever cold enough here to warrant a fire. It was always perfect weather in Gelsi. Regan wouldn't have it any other way.

"I miss her too," Alona whispered. "She was the best."

"Ro-Ro." Brea blubbered into her tea.

"You didn't call her that to her face, did you?" Alona glanced over her shoulder to make sure they were alone.

"She didn't care for my nicknames." Brea managed a watery smile.

"I bet not." Alona chuckled.

"I think she can walk through walls."

"What? No she can't."

"Then how does she get into my rooms when I barricade the door?"

"Oh my, you turned my home into an uproar, didn't you?" Alona crouched beside her. "Rowena has access to the secret passageways so she can come and go without disturbing you."

"Secret passageways?" Brea's jaw dropped. "Why didn't anyone tell me about those?" Brea sipped her tea as another tear slipped down her cheek. "No one ever tells me the cool stuff."

Alona and the seamstress shared a look.

"How is she doing?" The seamstress asked.

"Better, I think."

"I'm sorry I wrinkled your beautiful dress." Brea flatted her palms against the wide ball gown skirt. "I didn't mean to call it ugly. It's not."

"It's just not you." The elderly lady smiled.

"Right."

"I think we have what we need for the final alterations. You can take it off while the girls finish your hair and clean up your face."

"Thank you, ma'am." Brea stood, eager to get the dress off. She felt like it was wearing her.

The triplets took over, curling and brushing her hair until her scalp tingled and she was sure it would all fall out. With a few twists and braids, they secured her hair into an elaborate fae style complete with sweet pea blossoms that matched her dress to perfection.

Looking in the mirror, Brea couldn't see the first sign of her puffy eyes and tear-stained cheeks. "It's like magic." She examined her face, smooth as porcelain and flawless.

"Of course, it's magic," one of the triplets said. "But you have such pretty skin to work with all we had to do was bring out your eyes.

They were the best makeup artists ever. They didn't even need makeup to make her look like her cheeks blushed just the right way, and her eyes were highlighted with sweeping subtle shades of purple.

"You have to teach me how to do that." She tested her thick dark lashes.

"Is she ready?" Regan swept through the door in a stunning ivory dress that outshone Brea's silly poof-princess-prom dress by a mile.

"Ready, no." Brea felt like vomiting. "Dressed, nearly."

"And sober?"

"Eh, I don't think we want me sober today, Regan."

The room went deadly silent.

"Niece. You will address me as Aunt Regan, your Majesty, or Madame."

"Those are all titles of respect, and particularly for today, I don't have an ounce of that for you. But I will be ready in a moment, if you will excuse me." Brea ducked behind the dressing screen to don her finished wedding gown.

"Leave the room," Regan ordered. The maids and seamstresses made a beeline for the door.

"Zip me up, will ya?" Brea turned toward her aunt.

"You are either very, very drunk or brave." Regan moved the zipper up to secure the dress in place.

"Or long past caring about what happens to me. You won, Regan. I have nothing left to lose, so this is what you get. A snarky, not sober niece."

Regan's eyes flashed green with her magic. "Don't be so sure you have nothing, darling." Her voice sounded creepy, making Brea shiver with the touch of Regan's power. "I can make your married life easier, or harder, but that is up to you. I'll give you today to act like a petulant child, but come tomorrow, once your fate is sealed, you would do well to remember your place."

Brea backed up against the vanity table just as calm washed over Regan's face. "Sit down, my darling, Auntie Regan has a gift for you." She shoved Brea down onto the stool, turning her to face the mirror.

"This was my favorite crown when I was a young queen not much older than you. I would be honored if you would wear it today." She placed the glittering circlet of diamonds across Brea's forehead. A large pink teardrop diamond dangled at the center of a cluster of diamonds.

"It's beautiful, but I'm not sure I'm the crown-wearing type."

"After today, you will be a princess and eventually mother to the future king or queen of Fargelsi. You are royalty. I would have you look the part."

"It is time." Alona announced.

"Girls," Regan called, and the triplets came running. "See that Brea makes her way over to the ceremony. I shall join you all momentarily." Regan left the room.

She wanted to make her own grand entrance after Brea. Everything that happened in Fargelsi was all about Regan. Even this farce of a wedding.

"Leave me be." Brea begged the triplets to back off with their giggling and simpering.

"Come girls, fall back and give our Lady some space," Alona said, shoving a fresh glass of wine in Brea's hands.

"But her Majesty insisted we escort her."

"Then follow her at ten paces behind and give her a few moments' peace."

"Thank you." Brea's lips trembled as she walked down the long corridor to the gardens, taking great gulps of the fae wine that would get her through this ceremony. The one where she would tie herself to a man she did not love. No matter what happened next, the only man who would ever hold her heart was Lochlan O'Shea.

Someone took Brea's wine glass and shoved a bouquet of flowers into her hands as she moved in a foggy cloud—thanks to copious amounts of fae wine. It always went straight to her head. The last time she drank her fill of fae wine was the night she fell into the fountain here at the palace, and Lochlan had to go in and fish her out. That was the night he'd warned her that nothing was as it seemed here in Regan's court. She hadn't believed him then, but it didn't take her much longer to figure out he was right.

But here she was again. Completely hammered, walking across a thick carpet of sweet pea blossoms, grown for her wedding. Soft murmurs of appreciation rose up around her, but she was lost in a sea of memories of another man.

She couldn't even look at Griffin, standing at the end of the world's longest aisle. The sun shone brightly overhead, and a pleasant breeze flowed through the garden. Butterflies danced, and flowers bloomed on every surface. It was a perfect wedding, and if the right man stood at the end of this aisle, she would be the happiest woman in all the fae realms. But Brea Robinson was never that lucky. She didn't win the day, and she didn't get the guy.

As she moved to stand in front of Griffin, Brea had to remind herself why she was doing this. To protect those she loved.

"Are you okay?" Griffin whispered, and Brea snorted, coughing to cover up her laughter.

"No, I'm not okay," she slurred.

"You're drunk?" A frown fell across his face.

"Just get on with it." Brea retreated into herself, preferring her wine-soaked memories to the present. She went through the motions, saying whatever was required of her, offering her hand when it was time to bind hers with Griffin's. She could feel the magic snaking around her hand like a creeping vine, but she ignored it. Thinking of her time with Lochlan. All the fighting and bickering. The way he'd saved her when she was out of her mind with fever. Training with him, realizing he believed she could take care of herself when no one else had ever thought her capable. His quiet strength and desire to protect his people. The first time he kissed her just to make her angry. Their last night together. She would have to rely on her memories, making sure they never faded from her mind. She would cling to them when she had nothing else to hold on to.

Someone said her name along with Griffin's, and a blazing white-hot flash of magic seared through her.

"I give you the Prince and Princess of Fargelsi."

Applause rang out around them as Griff led her back down the aisle, his face grim and his hand firm over hers where it rested in the crook of his arm. She didn't recall placing it there and tried to pull away, but her new husband refused to let her put distance between them.

It was finished. She was married.

Griffin steered her toward the palace until they stood in a room alone.

"Talk to me, Brea." He cupped her face with his palms. "Are you okay? Are you even in there?"

"Don't touch me." She stepped out of his grasp, unsteady on her feet. She leaned over a chair, taking a great gasping breath into her lungs.

"Did you really have to get drunk to muster up the strength to marry me? Am I really that awful?"

"Yes." Something warm burned in her chest, and she thought for a moment she was having a heart attack.

"Now that we're married, you won't feel that way. Just relax, Brea. It will all be okay soon. Trust in the magic."

"Magic? What magic?" The burning intensified. She wanted to hate him. She wanted to rage at him for not having the courage to stand up to Regan and refuse to marry a woman who would never love him.

Love? The burning sensation in her heart eased. "What is this?"

"Didn't anyone tell you?" Griffin's face paled, and he stumbled back.

"Tell me what? Griff, what's happening?" She was trying to hold on to her hate, but she could feel it drifting away along with the emotions attached to memories she held so dear. Memories of another man she would always love. But he wasn't her husband.

"Did you pay attention to the ceremony at all?"

"I wasn't exactly happy about attending it, so no."

"Brea, we are married. What does that mean to you?"

"Honestly, not much. We're bound by law as husband and wife." She shrugged. "That's about as deep as it goes for me."

"Law? I thought you knew. I thought Regan explained it all to you before you agreed to marry me."

"Just cut to the chase and tell me what you're babbling about."

"We are magically bound, Brea. Fae marriages last forever. When two fae willingly come together in marriage and speak the solemn vows as we did today, they will never love another."

"What are you saying? We can't get divorced? I kinda figured that."

"You gave your solemn vow to never love another, Brea. That means the magical bond of our vows will..."

"Will what?"

"Because you agreed to the marriage, it will make you love me. Even if you don't want to. I-I thought you knew. I would never have forced this on you if I realized you didn't know. The only way to break this magic is death."

Rage had her magic sizzling at her fingertips. If the only way out was death, in that moment, Brea had a mind to kill him. But it wasn't his fault. Not really. Griffin's only real fault was that he was weak. The burning in her chest intensified with every ill thought she had about her husband.

"They will come looking for us soon. We should return to our guests." Brea fled the room. She needed to find Alona and that second bottle of wine.

The banquet was torture. Not because Brea was hungry, which she was. Not because she was tired, which she was. It was torture because it seemed as if it would never end.

Regan made toast after toast, and all the nobles honored the happy couple. It was odd how no one seemed to notice neither of them were actually happy. Griffin spent the evening apologizing every chance he could get, but Brea ignored him. The magical bond that lived inside her now didn't care for her indifference, but she deadened the pain with more wine. Alona kept her cup filled, and Brea only ate the food her friend brought her. When it came time for the bride and groom to cut the cake, Brea was surprised by how human the act was. She refused to eat the cake, but she made a show of offering a piece to Griffin before she smeared it all across his face. Silence fell all around them as Griff wiped the icing off his face. A warm fuzzy feeling enveloped her, and she giggled. "It's a tradition where I come from."

Griffin smirked, grabbing a piece of cake from her plate he returned the favor, careful not to get any in her mouth.

"To the bride and Groom!" Regan raised her glass high.

"Here, here," the crowd cried.

"It brings me great joy to see the two people I love most in this world happily married." Regan came to stand between them. "This union of my niece and my ward represents the future of Fargelsi." She turned to Griffin. "My boy." She squeezed his hand. "You've been the son of my heart, but through marriage, you are now my truest family." She turned back to the crowd of noble men and women hanging on her every word. "I present to you all, Prince Griffin O'Rourke. My heir and future king of Fargelsi. When we are blessed with a child, that child will become my blood heir, strengthening me and my reign as your queen for many years to come." The crowd cheered as if on cue, but Brea could see it in their faces, the last thing they wanted was more Regan.

"Sadly, I must also announce the defeat of our dear friend, Callum O'Shea. For years, we worked together, uniting Fargelsi and

Iskalt, but alas, Iskalt has a new king. The Eldurian queen has signed a treaty with this new Iskalt king. We cannot allow that. As Fargelsi grows stronger by the day, our enemies think they can threaten us. But they will rue the day they came against the might of Fargelsi. We will stand united and victorious!"

Brea's knees threatened to give out beneath her, but Griffin held her up. *A new King of Iskalt? A treaty?* "He did it," she murmured. Lochlan took his throne, and he was working with her mother to repair the years of damage Callum wrought in Iskalt. Perhaps all was not lost yet. With Brea and Alona on the inside and Faolan and Lochlan working together on the outside, they could destroy Regan once and for all.

Brea's chest seared with the heat of her marriage bond. It would be the death of her, but she would fight it. She was strong, she could endure the pain of seeking her freedom, seeking Lochlan, when all the magic wanted was to hold on to Griff.

Chapter 5

BREA

In the dark, Brea could almost imagine the day never happened. She closed her eyes, willing a different future into her mind, one where she wouldn't remain a prisoner in this palace, this marriage. The bond between her and Griff tightened around her heart at the thought. He'd told her the pain would lessen in time, that one day she'd realize it no longer hurt to love him.

Brea tried to think of before. Before she returned to Fargelsi. Before she walked down that aisle, choosing one O'Shea brother over another. It had only been hours, and the yearning for Lochlan faded with each moment. She was happy for him. He would be a great king, the kind talked of in storybooks long after they're gone.

And one day, he'd find a queen to stand at his side, one who could love him fully.

She turned onto her side in the large bed, and her eyes drifted to the small couch in front of the fireplace she'd made Griff sleep on. They would be expected to share rooms now, and Regan insisted he move into Brea's—probably because she was already listening to any word spoken in here.

The fire in the hearth simmered to a low glow, no longer warming the room. With a sigh, Brea kicked off her blankets and padded across the room. Crouching down in front of the dwindling fire, she muttered a soft "Dóiteán." Flames licked up the logs, slowing spreading until heat warmed her face. She smiled, satisfied she could at least do something right.

Casting a look over her shoulder, she took in Griff's sleeping form. The flickering light highlighted his auburn hair as it stuck up against the pillow. His limbs bent at awkward angles, trying to fit his tall frame onto the small surface.

Turning, she sat on the floor, her eyes never leaving him. The magic inside her cried out to be closer. It wanted her to stop resisting the ties that would now forever exist between them. His face, relaxed in sleep, had shown so much guilt during their wedding celebration.

But guilt didn't erase his weakness. And that weakness? Regan.

"Why do you follow her?" she whispered, trying to find answers in the slow breath parting his lips, the arms hugged across his chest.

Griff made no sense. He did bad things even when he didn't want to, all in the name of loyalty to the woman who raised him. Brea too was raised by a heinous woman, and she'd more likely push her mom off a cliff than follow her orders to do that to someone else.

Griff had family. He only had to see it. Lochlan now sat on their parents' throne. It wouldn't happen right away, but he'd forgive his brother for everything if Griff asked for it.

And Brea? What did she forgive? She was beyond the lies and manipulations of many months before. If it was only that, she could move past it and maybe even see Griff as a friend. But Myles? Alona? He'd abducted both of them, subjecting them to Regan's whims.

That was going to take longer.

Pain speared through her heart at the thought. The magic wanted forgiveness for Griff, it wanted love.

With a sigh, she pushed herself up and ambled toward the bed.

She'd laid her head on the pillow when Griff's low voice cut through the dark. "She has given me everything. She's my mother."

Brea didn't answer for a long moment. "No. She killed your mother." Brea looked to the ceiling, knowing Regan could hear every word.

"My mother died on a mission into the human realm. Regan took me in, raising me as her own. I am her heir."

"It all comes down to power, doesn't it?"

He sat up, his eyes glowing violet. "Is that what you think of me?"

She ignored him, staring at the canopy over her bed. Griff's footsteps sounded against the floor as he walked toward the bed. He lifted a hand and drew his fingers in toward his palm.

"What are you doing?" His magic buzzed in the air, and she didn't know whether to be scared or entranced.

"Blocking Regan from listening to us. From now on, we can speak freely within this room at night." He looked down on her. "I do not want you to hide your feelings from me, Brea."

"How?" Most of the people inside this palace couldn't use more than basic magic because of the Gelsi berries in the food.

"She trusts me." His eyes burned into Brea. "The question is, do you?"

She lifted her chin, trying to keep her voice from wobbling. "I don't trust anyone in Fargelsi. Least of all a man who has done nothing but lie to me."

His lips twitched. "That's number nine."

"Number nine what?" But she knew. He'd begun his list of reasons he loved her back when she believed the words leaving his mouth.

"I love you for how quickly you learn." One corner of his mouth curved into a smile. "There is no such thing as trust in the fae realm."

"Do you really believe that?" What a sad life he lived without a single person he trusted. "You could have everything I did. Lochlan, my moms, Myles, Alona, Finn. They could be your family too if you let them."

"They aren't your family, not anymore." He straightened and walked back to the couch. "I am. We are married, Brea, and that is not something you can escape."

His voice faded away and for a moment, she thought he'd gone to sleep. This man, her... husband, she didn't understand anything about him. But she wanted to. Her heart ached for him, wanting to let him in, even if it wasn't real.

Tears hung in her lashes as she blinked them away. She wouldn't cry for herself, not when she lay in an ornate bed with every luxury afforded her. Alona resided in the dungeons. Lochlan had to fix a broken kingdom. And her mother prepared for war.

What right did she have to feel sorry for herself?

When Griff spoke again, his words were so soft she almost missed them. "I will protect you, Brea. That I promise you."

She shut her eyes against the oncoming tears. Griff's promises meant nothing. "Except when it suits my aunt, right? She always comes first."

Silence stretched between them, punctuated only by the sound of their breathing. "That's the problem, Brea. When it comes to you, I break all other vows of loyalty."

"I wish I could believe that."

"It's always been you, Brea. One day, you'll see that."

Her head told her it was another one of his lies, but in her heart, she hoped he spoke true.

Sobs wracked Brea's body as she jolted awake.

She'd tried to keep the tears at bay, but it was all too much. Too much loss. Too much feeling. The binds around her heart threatened to make it stop beating altogether, and she struggled to breathe through her sobs.

Lochlan's face swam through her mind, but all emotion related to him unspooled. She tried to grasp the remaining threads but found only emptiness instead. Every minute they spent together became emotionless moments in time. She could feel the spaces where the love once filled her, now voids, chasms inside her filling with the tears of a bleak future.

She thrashed in her bed as memories assaulted her.

She needed someone… her best friend. Myles would have known what to do. He'd have held her, keeping her together as she tried to fall apart.

"Myles," she cried. "I need you." It had been months since his release, and she didn't know where he was, if he was okay.

A hand rubbed down her arm, and for a moment, she thought her wishes conjured him, but as she turned, she came face to face with Griff, her husband.

"Shhh, Brea." He wiped a thumb under her eye, drying a tear before more poured down her face.

"I don't have a right to cry." She hiccupped a sob. "Not when Alona is in the dungeons."

"Everyone has the right to cry." He climbed onto the bed and lay down beside her.

"What are you doing?" Her eyes widened.

"Holding you." He wound his arms around her and pulled her against his firm chest.

She stiffened for a moment before relaxing against him. As much as she wanted to fight, this felt right, like his arms were meant for her. The magic hummed its approval, and for the moment, Brea couldn't bring herself to care that it was just an illusion.

Her tears soaked into his shirt, but he didn't pull away. She slid an arm around his back and curled the fingers of her other hand in the soft linen shirt.

"Brea," he whispered into her hair. "You and me, we're in this together now."

She nodded against him, because she knew. This magic between them, this marriage bond, wouldn't let them betray each other. It meant that maybe she was wrong. Griff was the only

Fargelsian she could trust, because he had no choice but to be true to her.

The thought brought a strange sense of comfort. She wasn't alone here. Alona took care of her, and Griff would be there for her. She let the remaining threads holding her to her old life, her old family, in Eldur spin away from her.

There was no use pining after what she could never have again.

Now, all she could do was stay alive.

She held onto Griff tighter, and he kissed the top of her head.

"You and me," he whispered again. "We may not have had a choice in this, but we have a choice in what we make of it."

Her sobs lessened as she embraced this new life of hers. "You know I won't stop fighting, right? I will never be loyal to Regan."

"I've known that since the moment I met you. You're not like me. You're good."

"You could be too." She pulled back to look up at him.

His eyes flashed violet as he smiled. "You hated me until the marriage ceremony tied us together. How do you have such faith?"

"I believe people are good. They have to choose not to be."

"Ah, that's where you make your mistake. 'People' is a human term, Brea. We are not human. We are fae, and some of us make no choices at all."

"One day, Griff, I'm going to prove how wrong you are. One day, you'll do something so selfless, even you will have to call the action good."

He pulled her closer. "And on that day, maybe you won't need the magic to love me."

She didn't respond to the hope in his voice.

"Wakey wake, eggs and bakey." Alona pushed open the door with her shoulder as she carried a silver tray. "Myles said that to me one time, and I always wanted to try it." She giggled as if this was just a normal morning, and one prisoner princess of Eldur wasn't serving another prisoner princess of Eldur.

Brea groaned as she opened her eyes and noticed a weight across her waist. Griff's arm. Her eyes went wide as they met Alona's. The maid-princess stood stock still as she stared at Griffin in Brea's bed.

"What is he doing there?" she mouthed, trying not to make a sound.

Brea pushed Griff's arm off and sat up. "I don't know," she whispered. Sunlight streamed through her windows as wind whistled against the building, chasing the shadows away—which meant Griff's Iskalt magic wasn't working anymore and Regan would be able to hear them speaking until night fell again. Unless... Brea found a way to block all sound with her own magic. She pulled on the Eldur strands, feeling the power rise.

"Push it into each corner of the room." Griff's whisper surprised her. It was barely audible, but she held onto the words, doing as he asked.

"Did it work?" She strained to hear anything but even the wind didn't penetrate the magic.

Alona set the tray on the table by the bed and tried to carry on with the conversation she'd started when she opened the door. "You know, when Myles woke me up like that, all we had for breakfast was some stale bread. It's funny this morning because I actually brought you eggs and bacon." She removed a silver lid to reveal a plate piled high with steaming eggs and greasy bacon. Brea's mouth watered.

Alona poured her some tea and handed her the cup. She'd have given anything for some Eldur Brew right about now. Glancing over her shoulder, she saw Griff sitting up. Her face heated as she shifted her eyes away. They hadn't done the usual marriage night activities, but just sleeping in a bed with him felt intimate in a way she wasn't ready for, even if the magic begged for it.

"Morning." He yawned.

Brea clenched her jaw, not wanting Griff to speak to Alona. When he did, did he think of how he'd abducted her from her family?

Alona grunted and turned away from him.

"Did you know Alona, and I were sort of friends once." Griff reached across Brea, stealing her tea.

"We were never friends," Alona scoffed.

"Sure we were. I took you to the human realm."

Brea jerked in surprise at that, though it shouldn't have shocked her. When she met Alona those years ago, someone had to open a portal, and Lochlan wouldn't have done it.

Griff reached for the plate, and Alona slapped his hand away. "This is Brea's. If you'd like breakfast, I suggest you go to the hall before they finish serving it."

Griff pouted. "I'm starving. We worked up quite the appetite last night."

"No—"

Griff cut off her protest by nudging her with a grin.

"Oh, yes." She rolled her eyes at Alona. "Griff is the best lover I've ever had. Truly a magnificent beast of a man."

Even Alona cracked a smile at that.

Griff's brow creased. "Surely the only lover—"

"Don't even finish that misogynistic sentence."

"I do not know that term, but..." His jaw tightened. "Who? I will fight for your honor."

Brea lifted her eyes to the ceiling and sighed. "Fae men are so strange. Go ahead. See if you can best your brother in a fight. I dare you."

It was like all life was snuffed out of the room. Brea didn't know why she'd said it. Maybe she'd wanted to hurt him, to prove he couldn't control her. Or maybe some part of her wanted to feel more for that night with Lochlan. She wanted to experience everything she'd felt for him again and instead was being drawn to his brother.

Alona normally stuck around while Brea ate, but she backed out of the room, probably wanting to get away from Griff. Great, now she'd left Brea with an angry O'Shea. She knew how well that usually went.

Picking up a piece of bacon, she turned and slid the tip of it through his lips. His eyes snapped to hers. "Bacon makes everything better." She slid the plate over, wishing she could take back her earlier revelation. "We can share. Alona brought plenty." She held out the fork like some sort of peace offering.

Griff stared at it for a moment before taking it. "What is it with you and eating in bed?"

"Get used to it." She nudged him. "Because I'm lazy."

That brought out his smile she knew so well.

"You know." She took a bite. "If you have my back, I'm going to insist you have Alona's too."

"Why do you care so much about her?"

"Because I'm not a robot," she snapped. "Because from the moment I met her in the human realm when I was sixteen, it was like we understood each other. We're sisters."

"But not really."

"In all the ways that matter, we are."

He nodded. "I've never felt that way about anyone."

"I'm sorry." She offered him another bite, and he took it.

"Do you..." He sighed. "I can't believe I'm asking this, but do you want to know what's happening in Iskalt?"

The fork froze halfway to her mouth. "You'd tell me?"

He nodded. "Lochlan... there was a battle. He led an army of Eldur militia and Iskalt villagers to the Iskalt palace."

She smiled. The army she helped him gather. "Go on."

"They defeated Callum, and Lochlan took the throne. Our sources inside tell us the Eldur queen traveled to Iskalt to sign a magically-binding treaty, tying the kingdoms together in their fight against us."

"More," she whispered. "Please, is there any other news?" She needed to hear of the people she loved, the ones she'd left behind.

"Myles is in Iskalt as part of the Eldur delegation. His name was on the list we received."

She closed her eyes. Myles was okay, alive, and with her mom. Faolan would take care of him. "And Neeve?"

"She's there too."

Brea reached for Griff's hand, intertwining her fingers with his. "Thank you." Her lips twitched into a smile. "I needed to feel some kind of hope today."

He released her hand and resumed eating, refusing to look at her.

It would take a long time for her to come to terms with this new reality, but Griff had a long journey ahead of him as well. Brea wasn't the same girl he'd fallen in love with when she first arrived in the fae world. She wasn't the girl who'd believed his lies and thought he could make her happy.

Now, she was stronger, harder. She'd fought grown men and survived, traversed the wilds of the Vatlands multiple times and held a future king as his people lay dead around him.

Each moment, each day in this world changed her, forcing her to become more than she'd ever thought possible. More powerful. More determined.

More herself than she'd ever been.

A marriage couldn't change that.

Chapter 6

LOCHLAN

"Your Majesty, the delegation from Fargelsi arrived last night, they have been waiting to meet with you. What should I tell them?" Lord Donnal rarely sought to speak with Lochlan. The young nobleman must have drawn the short stick today.

"You can tell them whatever you like. I have more important matters to deal with." Lochlan sifted through the mountain of reports on his desk in the throne room. Everyone and everything in Iskalt needed his immediate attention.

"Lochlan," Faolan chastised. "No matter what they've come to say, they've come as a peace delegation. You must meet with them."

"To what end? There will be no peace with Fargelsi as long as Regan sits on the throne that belongs to her brother." Lochlan was grateful for Faolan's continued presence since the treaty signing. With Tierney ruling Eldur in her absence, Lochlan leaned on the woman who raised him as he struggled to find his footing as king.

"They've no doubt come to spew more lies. But like it or not, you are King of Iskalt, and it is your job to hear them out."

"Very well. Donnal, I will meet them in council chambers in twenty minutes."

"In one hour," Faolan interrupted. "Lochlan, you need to clean up first if you want to look the part of a king."

"I suppose I could do with a shave." Lochlan rubbed his prickly jaw.

"Very good, sire. And will there be... be a... a ball, your Majesty?" Lord Donnal seemed to lose his nerve at the look on Lochlan's face.

"A ball? For what?"

"To honor the Fargelsian delegation, your Majesty."

"Honor? They have no honor. No, there will not be a ball."

"You must throw them a farewell banquet at the very least," Faolan insisted. "I'm afraid it's the name of the game, Lochlan dear. Some of the greatest strides in diplomacy have happened at these very events."

"Not this time." Lochlan turned to leave his study. "I would be pleased if you would join me for these *peace* talks, Faolan."

"I would be honored." Faolan rose to follow him. "But it feels odd to have you use my given name."

"It wouldn't do for me to continue calling you Majesty."

"No, I was thinking something more like Mother." She took his hand in hers. "I am just so proud of you, my son."

"It would please me more than you could know to call you Mother." Lochlan squeezed her hand when he really wanted to fall into her arms and lean on her shoulder like he did when he was a scared young prince in a foreign kingdom.

"Are you ready?" Faolan asked him when Lochlan came to join her outside council chambers. "Now that you look like a king?"

Lochlan ran a hand down the smooth brocade jacket of silver and blue. A simple gold crown sat on his head. He still wasn't accustomed to its weight. "Ready as I'll ever be." He nodded to the guardsmen standing by the double doors. An ancient tree adorned the doors, intricate carving with inlaid silver. He remembered those doors from his childhood. He'd spent hours waiting outside for a chance to see his father. And now he was the king, though he still felt like that little boy, hoping to catch a glimpse of his father.

"Ladies and gentlemen, King Lochlan of Iskalt and Queen Faolan of Eldur," a royal page announced their arrival.

"Come, Mother, let's see what lies they've traveled all this way to tell us." Lochlan led Faolan into the chamber where he offered her his mother's throne at the apex of the room. Lochlan took his father's seat—he still couldn't bring himself to call it his own.

A long narrow table ran the length of the room where all the Gelsi nobles stood upon the king's entrance.

Lochlan raised his hand. "Please be seated." Several men and women took their seats, leaving their mouthpiece to stand before Lochlan.

"My Lord." The man bowed. "I am Lord Tadleigh Bainebridge of northern Fargelsi. My vast estates border Loch Villandi, which makes me your closest Fargelsian neighbor." The man dressed as flashy as a one would expect from a Fargelsian nobleman with his gilt-encrusted green coat and tailored breeches of the same color. His fake smile radiated confidence, and his bearing oozed wealth and privilege. Privilege built on the back of Gelsi prisoners.

"And what brings you here today, good Sirs and Ladies?" He was already bored with the courtly flair the Fargelsians brought with them. In Iskalt, he hoped to maintain less formality. Much less.

"We bring her Majesty's good wishes for your reign as King of Iskalt. Queen Regan begs you to know that she holds no ill will for the imprisonment of your predecessor."

"Is that so?" Lochlan sat back on his throne. "Wasn't she allied with my uncle?"

"Yes, my Lord, but their friendship was... troubled. Her Majesty would like to move on to a brighter future where Eldur, Iskalt, and Fargelsi can coexist peacefully."

"For that to happen, your queen must be willing to make concessions."

"A discussion for another time, my Lord." Bainebridge proceeded without missing a beat. "We have brought happy news with us today. It pleases Queen Regan to announce the successful union between her niece, Princess Breanna Louise O'Rourke and her adopted son—your own brother—Prince Griffin O'Rourke of Iskalt and Fargelsi—"

"Fargelsi?" Queen Faolan interrupted.

"Yes, Madame." Lord Bainebridge beamed at her before turning back to Lochlan. "Upon his union with our princess, your brother has become the heir to Fargelsi. He will be our next king, my Lord."

"That is not her name." Lochlan's hands gripped the arms of his throne, his nails digging into the polished aged wood.

"Pardon, my Lord?" Bainebridge asked.

"Your princess. That is not her name. She is Brea Robinson, daughter of Queen Faolan and heir to the Eldur throne."

"Our queen has given her niece her own name. It is a great honor for Princess Breanne, daughter of our late King Brandon."

"Her name is Brea." Lochlan slammed his fist against the armrest, his heart thundering in his chest. She really did it. She entered into a marriage bond with his brother. She willingly said the words that would bind him to her forever. Somewhere deep inside he'd thought there was no way she'd actually go through with it.

Already she was forgetting everything they'd shared as the magic of the marriage bond took root in her heart.

"Are we to believe you have simply brought us this 'happy' news of my daughter so we may celebrate with you?" Faolan asked.

"Of course, Madame. It is a time of joy. Princess Breanne and Prince Griffin with their ties to Iskalt and Eldur will unite us all."

"Griffin has no ties to Iskalt," Lochlan muttered.

"You mean their child will strengthen your queen so she may reign for many years to come." Faolan's jaw ticked.

The thought of Brea bearing Griff's child was like a hot dagger through Lochlan's heart.

"Their child will be Regan's blood heir." Faolan went on. "O'Rourke blood will flow through that child's veins, strengthening your queen in a way her grown niece cannot, given that Brea is already my blood heir. This union is not about uniting the fae realms, it's about giving more power to a queen who will never be satisfied with what she has."

"I'm afraid we've gotten off track." Bainebridge cast a nervous glance over his shoulder to the other delegates.

"No, we have not." Lochlan stood and everyone seated at the table rose with him. "We are done here. Pack your bags and return to your queen." He and Faolan crossed the room to the double doors.

"Will you have a message you would like us to deliver?"

"Yes." Lochlan turned. "You may tell your queen until she lowers that barrier of hers and releases every man, woman, and child held in bondage behind it—including a certain man she'd like us all to believe dead—there will be no peace with Iskalt."

"Or with Eldur," Faolan added before they marched out of the room.

Without a word, Lochlan headed for his quarters. He needed to be alone.

"Loch, she must have had no other choice," Faolan called after him.

But the Brea he knew would never marry someone she didn't love, and she had loathed Griffin. Could she have forgiven him during her time in Fargelsi? She'd loved him once. Could she truly love him again after all he had done to her and those she loved?

"Grumpy Loch?" Myles knocked on the doors of Lochlan's chamber. "People are worried. There's a stench coming from your rooms, so we just need to know if you're dead in there."

Lochlan snatched the door open. "It does not smell in here. I let the servants in to clean daily."

"When was the last time you had a bath?" Myles stepped into the room.

"This morning." Lochlan returned to his small study where he'd spent the last week running the kingdom with few interruptions from his court. He was thinking of making it a permanent arrangement.

Myles flopped onto the chair in front of Loch's desk. "Faolan is heading back to Eldur in a few days."

"And?" Loch returned to his work. "That is where she belongs."

"We have some planning to do before we leave."

"What planning?" Lochlan scribbled his signature on a document that would provide food for a village in dire need far to the north.

"What planning? Do you hear yourself, man?" Myles leaned forward, his elbow on his knees. "We have to get her out of there."

"We can't. Brea has made her choice."

"I don't care what that Gelsi peacock said, there is no way Brea wasn't under duress."

"But she wasn't, Myles. The way a fae marriage bond works, both parties have to willingly speak the words of magic or the bond will fail. It's over."

"It's not over until we hear the words out of her own mouth." Myles shot to his feet. "Something isn't right with this, Loch. You know it, and I know it."

Lochlan leaned back in his chair, brushing a weary hand over his brow. "I don't know how to get to her."

"Then we need to focus on another problem."

"That's what I'm trying to do, human." Lochlan gestured to the piles of paperwork on his desk.

"Someone else can take care of doling food out to the villages. There's another king out there, dude. The rightful king of Gelsi is rotting in a cramped cell right under your nose. Get him, kill Regan, and park Brea's dad on the throne. Then we can get Brea back and figure out what to do from there. Maybe she's bound to your brother forever. I don't care. I just can't go back to my world knowing she's trapped there with that awful woman. You say you love her? Then make sure she's okay. I'm just a human. I can't make these things happen, but you can. So get out of this funk you're in and do your job."

"I could have you drawn and quartered for speaking to me like that."

"But you won't." He grinned. "Because you know I'm right." Myles sat back down and propped his foot on his knee. "You got any good books in here?" He browsed the spines along the bookshelf behind him. "Your palace library leaves something to be desired." He flipped through a book on Fae nobility.

Lochlan took the book from him and returned it to the shelf. "You can find what you're looking for on the shelves in my bedroom. You've likely read all the human books, but there are many fae books in there you will enjoy."

"So, about that planning?" Myles stood at the door with his arms folded across his chest.

"I will work on it." The human boy was right. No matter what happened with Griff and Brea, Loch would never rest until he knew for certain she was okay. And she would never be okay as long as Regan was in power. It was time to make a serious move against Fargelsi.

"Lochlan?" A knock came at the door, but it wasn't Myles.

"Finn?" Lochlan looked up in surprise. He hesitated for a moment. The last time he saw his best friend, Finn had abandoned him along with Brea. Shaking his head, Lochlan rid himself of the negative thought and crossed the room. "It's good to see you, Finn." Lochlan embraced his friend. "What news have you brought?" He helped a travel weary Finn to the seat Myles had just occupied.

"Good news, I think." Finn groaned as he sat back against the chair. "We managed to create a rift in the barrier for a short time before it collapsed. Just long enough for us to get a man through to the other side."

"Who?"

"I tried to go, but my father wouldn't hear of it. He went instead."

Lochlan didn't like the idea of Eamon all alone on enemy territory. "Can we communicate with him?"

"It's not likely, but he is going to scout ahead. When we meet again, he will fill us in on what's really going on in Gelsi."

"I'm glad to have you back, though I know you will need to return to the border soon."

"I'm sorry I abandoned you when you needed me, but it looks like you've done well on your own, your Majesty."

"Don't call me that," Lochlan grumbled. "It sounds mocking when it comes from you."

"Good, I meant to mock you."

Lochlan grinned. He'd missed his best friend—the only one who treated him like a normal person.

"What news do you have for me? Much has happened since we last spoke." Finn leaned forward.

"I have a lot to tell you."

CHAPTER 7

BREA

Every morning, Brea woke up with a sense of happiness in her chest that didn't feel quite right. It took her a few moments to remember everything that had happened. She was a prisoner, married to a man she didn't want... yet, she did. She couldn't explain it. Her mind fought an attachment to Griff with everything she had, but her heart, her body wanted him, and she didn't know how much longer she could keep battling.

The days were the same, bleeding together in a monotonous haze of breakfasts with Alona after Griff rushed off to Regan's side, citing royal duties. They hadn't given her any duties, claiming her only job as the future queen was to relax, read books, learn to sew, and have lots of babies.

Screw that.

She looked over her shoulder as she ran across the bridge, half expecting to see an entire troop of soldiers following her. But now, only the single guard Regan assigned for her "protection" hustled after her. It was hard not to resent Blaine, the young man who never took his eyes off her for fear of repercussions from Regan. He couldn't have been older than fifteen, and the armor covering his small frame was too big for him.

He reported her every movement to Regan, but it wasn't out of malice. Like most of the people in Gelsi, he too was a prisoner behind the border magic. He'd had no choice of his lot in life, just like her.

Tearing her eyes from the guard, she continued across the bridge, letting the sounds from the crashing waterfalls drown out the constant noise in her mind. She picked up her pace as she reached the other side and could practically smell the hay of the barn. It was a familiar scent reminding her of the Merrick farm, but also of Eldur.

The sliding door stood open, and stable boys led giant war horses in and out of the barn. A smile tilted her lips as she thought of her ponies. Dawn and Dusk wouldn't remember her if she ever got to see them again, but she'd never forget them.

Being around animals beat hanging out in the stifling palace where no one knew quite what to say to her. Maids ducked their heads in her presence, all too aware of her status as both prisoner and princess. They pitied her but also feared angering the queen.

Except for Alona, the girl whose name she couldn't speak aloud where Regan listened. She knew now why Regan forbid her from knowing her maid's name. That knowledge held a power in it, a hope.

Because it meant Brea wasn't alone.

Brea didn't know the horses in this barn, but that didn't matter. She'd only needed to feel like the girl she was months ago before the marriage bond, before her second imprisonment. That girl fought for everything. She didn't give up.

She choked back tears and her magic burned within her, but she couldn't let it out, not yet. If she used her magic, she worried what Regan would do to Alona. Would she use her to keep Brea in line?

Wiping the back of her hand against her eyes, she rubbed the nose of a large stallion with a shiny black coat. "What am I to do, buddy?" There was nothing to do, not anymore.

The horse snorted as if agreeing with that thought.

Brea scowled at him. "But to accept that would be giving up. We can't have that, can we?"

She stayed in the barn as long as she possibly could without the hands getting annoyed by her presence. After too many scowls and grumbled words about princesses being in the way of their work, Brea trudged back toward the palace, feeling more like herself than she had in days. Blaine followed close behind, and she held her head high, nodding to passing guards and servants. They averted their eyes.

As she reached her room, she caught sight of Alona hurrying down the hall with a tea tray. Turning to Blaine, she pasted on a smile. "Thank you for your company, Blaine. I will take tea in my rooms."

"Yes, yy-er Highness. I'll be out here." He pressed his back against the wall next to her door and stood taller.

Brea sighed as she opened her door. Alona rushed in after her.

"Tea is early." Brea shed her lightweight cloak and left it on the floor before toeing off her boots.

Alona set the tray down. "I'm sorry, my Lady. There is a lot of work to be done in the kitchens." She flicked her eyes to a folded paper in the center of the tray. "I will be down there after I leave you."

"Good to know." Brea reached for the paper as Alona poured her tea.

I must speak with you but cannot be seen to stay in here too long. Come to the kitchens, and we will find a way.

Brea stood and walked to the cold hearth. "Dóiteán," she whispered. Flames danced to life, and she tossed the note into them, watching it shrivel and blacken until it disappeared.

Once satisfied, she returned to the tray and lifted her teacup. "You may leave."

Alona left without another word.

Even if she managed to block Regan from listening to this room, she still couldn't speak to Alona for long, not with the guards watching the comings and goings in the hall.

Brea sipped her tea, still not used to how much tea these people drank. It was strange. Have a problem? Call for tea. Need a morning break after only working for a short time? Teatime! Want to sit and have awkward conversations with an aunt you detest? How hard was it to slip some poison in?

That made her smile. Man, this fae world was twisting her.

Brea poured herself another cup. She slid the small glass lid off the sugar bowl and froze. It was empty. Who brings a tea tray with no sugar?

Someone who needed to give Brea a reason to rage—as if she didn't have enough already.

Raging over sugar wasn't exactly a Brea thing to do, so she closed her eyes, channeling her inner princess. When she opened them, she let out a scream.

The door to her room burst open, and Blaine ran in. "Are you okay, your Highness?"

"Am I okay?" Brea fumed. "Am I okay?!" She shot to her feet and paced the length of the room, empty bowl in hand. She shoved it in his face. "What do you see?"

"Uh, nothing?"

"Exactly. My dolt of a maid brought a tea tray with no sugar." She sucked in a breath. "The disrespect." Her fists clenched at her sides. "That girl is insolent. I am a princess! One day I will be the queen, and she will see who lacks sugar then." It took everything in her not to laugh. "I'm going to find her and make sure she never makes such a grave error again."

Stomping from the room, she whirled when she heard Blaine following her. "No. You will stay here. I won't have anyone pulling me back from that horrid maid."

"But, your Highness—"

"Fine, if you must come, you will wait outside the kitchen while I find that maid!" Her voice echoed off the high ceilings, winding through the hall. Fae stopped to watch her storm past.

By the time she made it to the kitchens, her chest was heaving.

She pushed through the door, entering the bustling space, thankful Blaine was too scared of her now to follow her in. Cooks yelled to each other as servants left with trays. This was the heartbeat of the palace, and Brea felt it pulsing through her just like she had once before.

Memories of another secret meeting assaulted her. Neeve risked a lot getting her out of Fargelsi only to have her return again.

Brea scanned the long countertops and the fae working behind them, searching for a familiar face.

"Brea." Alona's voice came from the doorway of the same storeroom Brea once met Neeve in.

She hurried toward her and shut the door behind them before whirling to face the other girl. "I just threw an epic tantrum over sugar. That was fun."

Alona rolled her eyes. "You could have just said you wanted to fetch it yourself."

Brea shrugged.

"Listen, we haven't gotten a chance to talk privately since your marriage, but now things are different. You're tied to Griff in a way Regan wouldn't allow me to warn you of. That's only going to make it harder for us to get out of here."

"I don't care how hard it is." Brea sat on a stack of rice sacks, rummaging through the shelves lining the walls with jars of spices and dry goods. There had to be something here that was edible and not tainted. "We'll get out."

Alona sighed. "I don't think you grasp just how screwed we are."

Brea unleashed a grin and sat forward, resting her elbows on her knees.

"Why are you smiling?" Alona frowned. "Stop it. It's not right."

"Sorry, it's just, you said 'screwed'. That's a human sentiment. Was Myles teaching you how to talk like a human?"

"No," she scoffed. Leaning back on a shelf, she crossed her arms. "Okay, maybe. But it works, doesn't it? We are screwed. We need time to figure this out, and knowing you, you're going to end up right alongside me in the dungeons."

"Hey!" Brea feigned offense. "I know how to keep out of trouble. Plus, my aunt needs me to make her a blood heir baby. She'd never put me in the dungeons."

"She only needs you if you're doing what she wants. She doesn't need an insolent niece who refuses to eat in the hall with the nobles or attend balls. What she wanted was a happy couple, an heir who looked like she was on the verge of producing another heir."

"I…" Brea knew she was right. "I'm messing everything up, aren't I?" She'd kept to her rooms except to make trips to the stables. She was only allowed out of the queen's quarters with Blaine as her escort —and even then, she could only visit certain places.

"You can fix it. Play nice with Regan. Act the happy couple with Griff, like you've given into the magic and are hopelessly in love and can't believe your good luck."

Brea buried her face in her hands, wondering how she was supposed to make this work. It was true, she didn't hate Griff anymore, but that was only the magic.

Alona walked forward and crouched down in front of Brea, her pale pink dress fanning around her legs. "Brea."

Brea lifted her gaze to meet that of this girl she still barely knew, yet understood completely. They were exchanged at birth and had lived each other's lives. Their futures were intertwined, and Brea would do whatever she had to do to make sure Alona returned to Eldur, to their mothers, and to Finn.

"We can think of another way," Alona whispered.

Brea shook her head. Earning Regan's love, her trust, was their only path. If Brea had to become a part of the queen's family, a part of this court, she had to be honest with herself. "No." A tear leaked from the corner of her eye. "I can love him."

Because that was what it would take.

Nothing fake.

No playing at anything.

Brea had to let the magic continue to pull her too Griff. She had to let herself fall in love with him.

Another O'Shea's face faded further from her mind as it had every day since the ceremony. Marriage magic allowed those involved to only love one other. There was no longer room in her heart for missing what she couldn't have.

Alona leaned forward, wrapping her arms around Brea. Brea expected her to issue words of comfort, but none came. Instead, Alona hugged her tighter, her voice only a whisper in Brea's ear. "I need to tell you something else."

Brea pulled back, not liking the ominous words. In this world, it was never good when secrets came to light. "What is it?"

"Your father." She swallowed. "He's alive."

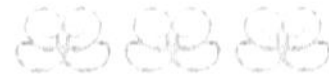

Brea drummed her fingers on the table in front of her, letting the opulence distract her from the chaos in her head.

"Your father. He's alive."

She thought she'd misheard Alona or imagined those words coming from her lips. But there was no denying the truth in her nervous babbling. As Alona talked fervently, Brea's mind had only picked up on small nuggets of information.

Brandon O'Rourke was in the dungeons, had been for eighteen years.

Brandon O'Rourke, her father and the rightful king of Fargelsi, lived.

He lived!

Tap. Tap. Tap. Brea's fingers didn't stop moving as she watched the servants enter with silver serving dishes.

Tap.

A dish was presented to the queen.

Tap.

Griffin nodded his appreciation for the food.

Tap.

Brea stared at the coated duck held down for her to see. "I'm not eating that." Tap.

Alona's voice entered her mind again. She had to play the part. Tonight, this grand dinner only had three diners—the queen and the happy couple. The food wouldn't have Gelsi berries in it.

A hand pressed down on hers, stopping her tapping. "Brea, darling." Regan's grip tightened.

Brea looked up, her eyes clearing of the haze she'd been under. "I'm sorry. What I meant is I'm not eating that first. You must serve the queen."

Regan smiled in approval. "Tonight, niece, I am overjoyed you have joined us. We are celebrating our family, so my title does not matter. Not when it is just us."

Griff's smile was warm as she reached over to take his hand as well. The two of them were a family in the same way his brother fit into the queen of Eldur's family. But where did that leave her? A stranger to both.

Not that she wanted to be part of the Fargelsian royal family, not when her father, the queen's own brother, was locked away.

Servants leaned between them to fill their plates, and Brea reached for her wine goblet, taking a long drink.

"Auntie." She set the cup down.

"Yes, dear?"

Brea hesitated for only a moment. "Can you tell me about my father?" When Regan only stared at her, she went on. "It's just, my human father—the man who raised me—was quite cruel. I never knew a father's love. I would have very much liked to meet my real father."

Regan's hand clenched around her fork, the only sign that the question bothered her.

Griff, on the other hand, looked excited at the question. "Yes, I've heard stories of his heroics. I too would love to know more about him."

That answered that question. Griff didn't know her father was alive.

Regan's hand relaxed as she set her fork down. "He was a good man."

"A good man?" Brea tried to keep the irritation from her voice. "Is that all? You can't give me anything else?"

"Darling." Regan sighed. "Speaking of my brother brings me great sadness. Why don't we change the subject? Tell us what you did today? I'm sure that will bring forth a more riveting conversation."

Brea busied herself eating, unable to stop. It was delicious, better than any of the food Alona had been making her. Roasted duck and crisped potatoes sat on a bed of greens with a poached egg drizzled in some kind of savory non-Gelsi-berry-sauce.

With each bite, she checked to make sure Regan was also eating. It was the only way to be sure she didn't ingest the wrong thing.

Regan dabbed her mouth with her napkin. "Blaine tells me you went to the stables."

Of course, he did. Brea forced a smile. "Yes. In Eldur I was an apprentice helping with the horses." Her smile turned genuine at the memory. "I helped birth two ponies."

Regan's lip curled in disgust. "What a ghastly pursuit for a young princess."

Brea shrugged. It hadn't been ghastly at all. Sometimes, she'd thought it was the only thing keeping her sane.

Regan went on. "And you had some difficulty with your maid?"

Griff's eyes snapped to hers. Only he knew Brea was aware of her maid's true identity.

Brea took another bite. "Just a sugar misunderstanding."

"Hmm." Regan pursed her lips but didn't press the issue. She continued chatting like they were a family who ate together every night. Brea learned of the Fargelsian peace delegation that was in

Iskalt, and the new crop of rebels they'd arrested from one of the villages. It seemed Regan and Griff had been busy.

As they finished their meal, three fae entered carrying stringed instruments and bowed to the queen.

"Ah." Regan clapped her hands together. "The entertainment is here." She nodded to them. "Please, begin."

They took their seats in the corner of the room on stools that had been set up. The fae sitting in front held an instrument that looked like a cello, but also not. It had an extra string, and the bow was curved and hard.

The other two played violin lookalikes.

A sweet melody wound through the room, unlike anything Brea had ever heard. Once her place was cleared, she found herself leaning forward, wanting, needing more.

"You look mesmerized, Brea." Griff's smile reached his eyes.

"Maybe it's my proximity to you." She winked.

Regan laughed as if it was the grandest joke in the world.

Griff raised a brow. "Then I must insist upon a dance." He scooted his chair back and stood before offering a hand to Brea.

She looked from his hand to his eyes. "How can I resist?" The moment their skin touched, something clicked inside her. The magic rejoiced at their nearness.

Brea swallowed as he led her onto the dance floor, trying to remind herself what she felt wasn't real. This was the man who'd lied and abducted Myles. He'd made her believe she was a murderer.

But as he pulled her closer, she melted against him. His arm snaked around her waist, each touch making her want more.

"Brea," he whispered into her hair.

She expected him to confess his feelings like he'd done many times before.

"Why are you being nice tonight?"

She pulled back to get some distance. "I'm always nice."

He yanked her against his chest. "Stay here if you do not wish your aunt to hear us."

"I don't care what she hears. I will obey her wishes. I've decided it's time to stop fighting this life, Griff." Her hand skimmed up his chest of its own accord. It seemed her body obeyed the marriage magic on its own.

He caught her hand in his. "I wish I could believe that. I truly do."

She had to prove it to him, to make him think she had turned over a new leaf. At least, that was the reason she gave herself for why she stretched up on her toes, fitting her mouth over his. At first, he didn't kiss her back, but then it was like his body called out to hers, molding every curve, every plane together, and he sighed into her mouth, taking everything she was willing to give.

Their kiss felt right and also so, so wrong. The magic made her love Griffin O'Shea, but her heart ached with the emptiness once filled by another man.

Regan's clapping broke their moment. She stood, rounding the table to get to them. "I am happy to see the two of you so in love." She sighed. "It is good to fill this palace with joy. Now, I am off to bed. I suggest you two go back to your rooms and get started on that heir I wish for." She winked before waving a hand to the musicians. The music cut off, and as the queen left, Brea and Griff stared at each other.

"Did she just tell us to…?" Brea couldn't voice it.

"Yes." Griff dipped his head, capturing her lips once more.

As he led her back to their rooms, something inside Brea broke. She might break free of this palace one day, of her aunt, but these feelings she now had for her enemy, it was a magic that would haunt her the rest of her life.

And yet, when Griff kissed her again, the magic filled her mind, erasing every worry, every doubt.

She wasn't only a prisoner in Fargelsi, but in her own head as well.

Her dad was alive, but a part of her never would be again.

Chapter 8

LOCHLAN

"Your Majesty, Iskalt is still reeling from the change in power with a new king. We cannot afford to become involved with the doings of Fargelsi. Not now. Maybe in a year."

"A year will be too late," Lochlan said, trying to keep his tone civil. "The borders are vulnerable now." He was doing this whether the Iskalt Lords and Ladies of his council approved or not. "The time to strike against Fargelsi is now, while we have a man on the inside."

"With all due respect, your Majesty, *we* do not have a man on the inside," Lord Hughes said. "Queen Faolan of Eldur has a man on the inside. Let her make the effort to free her daughters."

"That's not how our treaty works." Lochlan massaged his temples, wishing Faolan was still here to help him manage his council. She'd left for Eldur only days ago, and he already missed her calming presence. This constant bickering over the issues gave him a headache. "And this issue isn't just about her daughters. It's about all the men, women, and children enslaved behind that barrier. Eldur is our ally now. We will come to their aid in this matter and together. We will defeat the Gelsi Queen."

"But, sire, surely you don't have to be the one to travel to the border?" Lady Burke said. "There are other matters here that need your attention. Iskalt matters. Your coronation happened on the battlefield. It is time we have a proper celebration now that you've established your reign. After all, you are a young king. You should be spending your free time meeting the eligible ladies of the court."

Something inside Lochlan's chest shriveled and died at her mention of his marriage. He couldn't fathom moving on from Brea after so many years of loving her from a distance only to lose her to his brother. "On that matter, Lady Burke, we shall have to agree to disagree. Marriage is the furthest thing from my mind when our world is poised on such a precarious edge. By doing nothing, we are telling Regan O'Rourke that we don't care what she does. It is only a matter of time before she pushes us too far. I mean to strike before that happens, and I would like to do so with my council's approval, but I will do it without, if I must."

"Who will rule in your stead while you are away?" Lord Hughes asked. "Your reign has only just begun, Majesty. We must take the time to focus on Iskalt. There are protocols to enact."

"Protocol?" Lochlan slammed his fist down on the table where he sat at the head. "This is a time of war. We do not have time for luxuries like protocol."

"If you insist on traveling to the border, then you must name one of us as regent before you go," Lord Hughes said. "In the event you are killed in this venture, Iskalt must have a ruler to take your place. Since you do not have an heir, it should be someone from your council." He held his head high and preened before his council peers, obviously thinking Lochlan would no doubt choose him.

"I've already named a regent."

The men and women of his council exchanged glances. "Who, sire?"

Lochlan nodded to the page waiting by the doors. "Please bring him in, Master Stewart."

"Yes, your Majesty." The young boy bowed and opened the doors to announce their guest. "Please welcome, Lord Brennan Cormac, retired General of Iskalt and the new Lord of Isvasi estate and all its surrounding properties to the north."

"Isvasi?" The council murmured as the retired general stepped into the room, still looking like he'd just left the battlefield. But Brennan was the only man in Iskalt Lochlan fully trusted.

"Please join us, Lord Cormac." Lochlan held out a chair for the man.

"Thank you, your Majesty."

"Pardon, sire, but the Isvasi lands belonged to your uncle. Such vast holdings should go to a senior nobleman."

"Cormac served my father, and he was the only person in this room who came to my aide when I made the move to claim my throne. He is the most noble man among us. And he will serve as regent while I am gone."

"Your Majesty, we must discuss this—"

"The matter is closed. I will not leave Iskalt in the hands of any other, and I'll not hear another protest. I leave for the Gelsi border tomorrow."

"Please, sir. Wait a few days longer so we may make the proper preparations for your absence," Lord Hughes said, clearly realizing he wasn't going to sway Lochlan on this matter. "We must also discuss the goals of this endeavor at the border."

"Brandon O'Rourke is alive," Lochlan announced. The room fell silent at the mention of the rightful king of Fargelsi. "He has spent the last eighteen years in the dungeons far below the Vindur palace. Captain Donovan of the Eldur queen's guard has crossed the border when we were able to open the barrier for a short time. The point of this venture is to put a king back on his throne and end the tyranny of a queen who would have us all believe Brandon dead by her own hand. We have the men in place to make that happen, but we need the strongest magicians in our world to work together to bring down the barrier. With Callum's imprisonment, I am Iskalt's strongest wielder of night magic. It is my duty to go. Queen Consort Tierney of Eldur will meet me there, and we will lay waste to that barrier once and for all."

"Of course, your Majesty," Lord Cormac said. "And I will do my part here at home to see all of Iskalt continues to recover from years of Callum O'Shea's neglect."

"Which is why I chose you." Lochlan nodded.

"Surely Iskalt doesn't have to interfere in this misunderstanding with King O'Rourke?" Hughes said. "It can't be the only reason you feel so strongly about this matter."

"Princess Brea of Eldur has married my brother."

Gasps rang out around the room. Since the delegation arrived to bring him the news, Lochlan hadn't shared it with his council yet. For days he'd thought of nothing else but Brea's betrayal. Once he'd gotten over the shock of it, he realized one thing the delegates hadn't said.

"Regan has named Griffin her heir and has given him her name. Any child they have will be her blood heir as well as heir to all *three* kingdoms. Regan is setting herself up for a long reign and ultimate rule over us all—whether through herself or through the offspring of her heirs. Potential heirs with the magic of all three realms."

"We cannot allow that." Lady Burke's tone changed from her usual courtly simpering to that of a shrewd woman. "Iskalt must intercede before a child is conceived."

She might not be a total loss after all.

"I will leave tomorrow."

"Who will go with you, my Lord?" Lord Hughes asked. "You must take a delegation with you."

"I will take soldiers. That is all that is needed for a siege."

"I would be honored to attend you on this journey," Hughes offered.

"Attend me? What does that mean?"

"I will care for your person, my Lord. See to your clothes and your tent. Oversee your meals and make sure your needs are met."

Lochlan snorted. "I have never had much need for a valet at home much less at war. I would have you stay here. I can care for my own person. Thank you. You are all dismissed."

Lochlan remained seated as the nobles cleared the room, murmuring amongst themselves.

"You are a good king, Lochlan. Your father would be proud." Cormac clapped him on the shoulder before taking his leave.

"Uncle Bren?" Lochlan called him back.

"Yes, sire?"

"Whip them into shape while I'm gone. I can't abide their courtly drama any longer. Teach them to be more like my father's council. And make it clear I will be making further changes when I return."

"Consider it done." Lord Cormac left Lochlan alone in his council chambers.

"Hey, Loch, you about done in here?" Myles stuck his head inside the room.

"You have no sense of self preservation, human." Lochlan poured over a ledger of Iskalt's finances. Once he'd dealt with Regan O'Rourke and restored Brandon to his rightful throne, he had a lot of frivolous spending to curtail within his court. He would not allow such waste under his rule.

"You're just grouchy because I'm the only one in this world who doesn't have to bow and scrape to you royals." Myles sat in the seat beside Lochlan and put his feet up on the table, his finger stuck inside a book to mark his page. The boy had insisted on staying in Iskalt after Faolan returned to Eldur so Tierney could join him at the border.

"Have you just come to irritate me, or do you have something to say?" Lochlan tried to hide his smirk. He was almost certain Myles thought he'd have better luck getting Lochlan to take him to the border than Tierney.

"I'm coming with you to the border. Neeve too."

"It's not necessary," Lochlan said, knowing Myles would just follow him, anyway. It was what he would do in the boy's shoes.

"She's my family, Loch. I'm coming. I promise to stay out of the way, but I will be there when she is freed."

Lochlan understood Myles' need to be there for Brea. He wished he could be the one she would lean on when she was delivered out of Gelsi. With her marriage to Griff, he could no longer be that person for her. But Myles could. He was right, he needed to be there for her.

"Very well." He nodded. "We leave tomorrow. Bring your girlfriend with you if you must."

"Girlfriend? Neeve?" Myles laughed. "I'm sure she'd have something snarky to say about that."

Myles stood to leave. "I'm going to go raid your bookshelf for a few books to keep me entertained while you do all the hard work at the border. See ya."

CHAPTER 9

BREA

"I'm hopeless." Brea blew the hair out of her eyes and tried to focus on the cup of tea in front of her. But it wasn't working. She narrowed her eyes, letting the word sit on her tongue before whispering, "*hita*." Waiting a moment, she dipped her finger into the tea and growled. "Cold." She had half a mind to throw the cup against the palace wall.

A low chuckle came from the other side of the high balcony she sat on. "You're not hopeless, Brea."

She lifted her eyes to her husband—ugh—and clenched her jaw. "Nothing is happening."

He pushed away from the ivy-covered wall and sauntered toward her. She hated how good looking he was because that was the one nice thought about him that wasn't caused by the magic.

A gust of warm air ruffled his auburn hair, revealing vibrant green eyes she couldn't look away from. At least they couldn't flash violet in the day. That was when Griffin O'Shea became something else, something dangerous, and not in the physical sense.

You don't love him, she reminded herself. Her Eldurian magic churned within her, sparking at her fingertips as if telling her what a liar she was. But the magic loved him, not her. She hadn't realized she'd stopped breathing until he lowered himself to the tiled floor at her side.

They'd opted for magic practice on a balcony shrouded in flowering vines. There was less to break out here. Brea held the cup in the palm of her hand and concentrated on her emotions, the contentment she'd felt over the last few days, and also the fear. She didn't want to be content. Not with Griff and not in this place. It felt like a betrayal of her moms, of Loch. Of everyone in this kingdom kept prisoner by Regan's magic.

She extended the cup to Griff. "See? Warm." She'd been trying to heat the tea for the last half hour.

He sighed. "Brea, you're not supposed to use your Eldurian magic. The point of today is to learn the other side of your power."

Her shoulders slumped. "I know. But I'm not getting it. The words don't work."

"They do. What about the fires you're able to start with Fargelsian magic?"

"That's just a fluke. Fire likes me for some reason. Tea does not."

His lips curved up, and he reached out to tip her chin. "Inanimate objects do not have preferences."

"Are you sure?" She sat back against the stone half-wall encircling the balcony and picked at a pale pink flower that had fallen onto her simple shift dress. "Because I'm starting to think tea has gotten wind of my preference for Eldur Brew. It's holding a grudge against me."

He leaned forward, pressing a kiss to her cheek, his breath warm on her skin. "I love you."

She nodded, unable to say it back. For the past week, they'd dined together for every meal—many with Regan—shared a bed, and even been... intimate, but the one thing the magic hadn't been able to affect were her words. Just like the words used for Fargelsian magic, love had a power the moment it rolled down someone's tongue. That was the same whether one lived in the human realm or the fae realm.

This life she'd been living, it wasn't real. It was an illusion of fae magic, and one day she'd break the picture of the perfect Fargelsian royal family.

Griff never seemed to notice when she didn't respond to his sentiment. Instead, he pulled back. "This isn't working."

"That's what I've been saying!" Brea threw her hands in the air. "I'm not meant to have Fargelsian magic."

"Don't be an idiot, Brea. We both know you're not. You are a Fargelsian royal. In this kingdom, you will use Gelsi magic." He put his hands on his knees and pushed to his feet. "What I meant is that it's not working with me as your teacher."

"What?" She stood to face him. "Why not?" The idea of letting any other Fargelsian near her curled her stomach, at least ones who were loyal to Regan.

"Because I don't have Fargelsi magic." He sighed. "And the sun's out, so I can't even use my Iskalt magic to guide you. You need a teacher."

Her shoulders slumped. "Probably. You and I are hopeless together."

He frowned, sadness entering his gaze. She'd meant hopeless with this kind of magic, but by the way he turned his back on her, he knew it was more than that. One day, they'd be torn apart by the coming war. They both knew it. The only person who seemed to think this story had a happy ending was Regan.

But what was happy? For Brea, it wasn't a marriage she hadn't chosen.

"I'm going to find you a teacher." Griff walked back into the palace, passing Blaine who stood guard at the door.

Brea lowered herself once more, pulling her legs up under her as she tried again. "*Hita.*"

Still cold.

Maybe it was a sign. The only side of Brea's heritage that

mattered was her Eldurian lineage. But even as she had the thought, her mind went to her father—a man she'd never met, a man who the world thought dead. And each night, he slept only a few floors below her.

If her mother considered him friend enough to have a child with him, he must be a good man. Eldur wasn't the only kingdom that mattered to her, not anymore. Fargelsi was in her blood, these people were in her blood. They weren't the enemy. Regan was.

She was going to save her father and everyone else under Regan's power.

She had to.

The door opened again, and one of the triplets walked through, curtsying when she stopped. "Highness."

"Um." Brea pushed her hair over her shoulder. "Can I help you?"

"Oh no." A smile lit her face. "I'm here to help you. Prince Griffin said you had need of my assistance."

It was strange to see any of the triplets without the others. Their mindless chatter didn't fill the space. Instead, this one only stared at Brea expectantly.

"You're my teacher." She pursed her lips. It could be worse. Griff could have sent all three of them. "Do you know where my husband is?"

She nodded. "He said he had duties to attend to, but that I shouldn't let you burn the palace down."

Brea suppressed a smile. If things were different, she'd have wanted to be friends with Griff. In a way, he reminded her of Myles. "Okay... well first, I need to know what your name is."

"Cait, your Highness. It's just me today. Neither of my sisters have magic, so they are of no use in this."

Shame washed through Brea. She'd paid such little attention to the triplets that she hadn't bothered to learn their names. "Well, Cait, would you like to sit?" She gestured to the open space in front of her.

Cait's eyes widened. "In your presence, Highness? I couldn't."

"Well, I won't have you hovering." She smiled. "Please sit. I promise I don't bite."

"If you wish to bite me, that is your right as princess."

Brea laughed for the first time all morning, letting the tension of her lessons with Griff fade away. "All right, just sit. And for these lessons, you won't say 'Highness' every sentence. Just be cool, dude."

Cait sat, her expression perplexed. It would take a year to explain human slang to this girl.

"Okay." She pointed to the teacup. "Griff couldn't tell me why I suck at this. He just kept being his insufferable self."

A smile tilted Cait's lips before she managed to suppress it. Were these servants and guards not even allowed to joke with royalty? "I very much doubt you... suck."

The word sounded strange coming from the fae girl's lips. "Oh, you haven't seen me try to heat this tea yet." She glared at the cup. "*Hita.*" She lifted her eyes to Cait's and sighed. "Go on. Test it."

Cait lowered a finger into the tea. "Tell me what you were feeling just now."

"Anger. Annoyance. Resignation."

"All right, none of that means anything."

"What?"

Cait lifted the cup. "You were trying to use Fargelsian magic as if it was the same as Eldurian or Iskaltian. It's not. There is nothing emotional about our power. What we feel when using it does not matter, our intent does."

"Intent?"

She nodded. "Why did you want to heat the tea?"

Brea ran a hand through her hair. "Because Griff told me to. To show I can use magic. I've done it before. I can light fires."

"And why did you want to light those fires?"

Brea thought on each time she'd done it. First, to keep the troops from freezing in Iskalt, then to warm Griff, and finally to destroy a note from Alona. "Warmth."

"A worthy intent. The word of power obeyed you because you believed in your goal."

"But then... why are people able to do evil things with the power?" She didn't mention her aunt by name, but if Fargelsian power had to believe in the intent, it didn't make sense.

"Magic has no sense of right or wrong. When someone uses it, that fae believes whatever they are doing is right for them. It doesn't matter what their motives are, only their belief."

Why couldn't Griff explain all this? Brea had no desire to heat tea. "So, you're saying the way to learn my magic is to practice with skills I have use for."

"Exactly. Well done, Princess." Cait smiled again, and this time didn't try to hide it. "The most important rule of Fargelsian magic is to take care. Too much at once can be exhausting and cause a sickness where one succumbs to intense dizziness."

Brea nodded and studied her, wondering if the girl could keep a secret. Probably not. "Cait, whatever we do out here, whatever you teach me... are you reporting this to anyone?"

"Only Prince Griffin. He wants kept abreast of your progress and says he will keep the queen updated himself."

But how much did Brea trust Griffin? Enough to risk imprisonment? Did she have a choice? "Okay." She scooted forward. "I know how we can practice intentional magic."

"Good. Then let's begin. What would you like to try?"

Brea was quiet for a long moment before speaking again. "Teach me how to unlock a door."

It was a simple request, but one that could change everything.

Chapter 10

BREA

Brea counted down the minutes, waiting to hear Griff's breathing slow into the even patterns of sleep. But he kept speaking even as his voice grew tired.

"I just don't understand why you had to send for Alona so late. She's probably exhausted."

Brea leaned back in the bed, keeping a distance between them like she'd been doing since the one night they grew closer. "Do I have to have a reason? Griff, I'm a princess, if I can't call for tea at any time of the night, then what's the point?" She smirked at him.

He seemed to get the joke, knowing princess privileges meant nothing to Brea. "Fine, I get it. You don't have to tell me." He rolled onto his side to face her.

Brea sighed. "Okay, sometimes I get... lonely in this place." She looked to the ceiling.

He reached for her hand. "You're not alone."

She resisted the urge to roll her eyes. This was not a conversation she'd wanted to have, not when she and Alona had set a plan in motion that hinged on him going to sleep. "Alona is an ally, you know? She reminds me of my moms."

He went quiet, and she worried she'd said the wrong thing. Finally, he squeezed her hand. "You miss them, don't you?"

Tears built in her eyes, but she didn't let them fall. Of course, she missed her moms. She missed everything outside these palace walls. Training with Cait over the last week opened her eyes to the kind of power Fargelsians could have if Regan didn't suppress it. "I'm not talking about this with you."

"Why not? I'm your husband."

"Not by choice." The words were out of her mouth before she could call them back.

Griff froze beside her, his eyes flashing violet. "I am well aware. I just thought..."

"What, Griff? What did you possibly think? That I didn't know every feeling I have for you is the result of magic coursing through my veins?" There was no stopping the word vomit now. "That somehow I moved beyond the lies and the awful things you've done?" She pointed to her chest. "This feels something for you, but my head will never forget what you are."

He rolled away from her, his back tight with tension, and she fought the urge to reach for him, to tell him she didn't mean anything she'd said and let him hold her all night. But that part of her wasn't Brea Robinson, that was Breanna O'Rourke, a girl who didn't exist.

Silence choked the air until Griff spoke one last time. "I know what this is between us, Brea. I've always known. Just... I am sorry. I hope you believe that. I'm sorry you're here with me instead of with him."

They both knew who he spoke of, but Brea couldn't call on her feelings for Lochlan. They no longer lived inside her. Instead, the magic smothered that love, snuffing it out like a candle in the wind.

The silence stretched between them, and after a while, Griff's breathing evened as he fell asleep.

Brea slipped from the bed and changed out of her sleeping gown into riding pants and a soft tunic. Strapping a leather knife sheath at her waist, she paced the room, waiting. And waiting.

Moonlight danced across the floor, casting shadows in her wake.

When she started to think Alona would never come, the door creaked open, revealing the other princess. Brea rushed toward her and pulled her into a hug.

Alona hugged her back just as tightly. "Are you ready?"

Brea nodded as she pulled back. "I have to do this." She'd sent Blaine to fetch her maid and then told him to find his bed. No one stood guard while Griff was in the room with her. So, when the two girls stepped into the hall, no one was there.

At this time of night, the only guards would be stationed outside the palace, letting those inside roam. Walking through a sleeping castle was a lot like traipsing through a dragon's lair—at least she assumed it was. One wrong move, one noise too loud, and it could wake the beast.

Alona nodded to a servant they passed as if they had an understanding. "She's from the dungeons as well. We servants do not report each other to Regan."

Brea smiled at the knowledge that there was even a tiny resistance inside the palace.

Alona pushed open a door. "We must go down through the kitchens first. We are less likely to be seen this way. Only the bakers are awake at this hour."

They hurried through the labyrinth of kitchens, past a burly man taking bread out of an oven. Beyond the pantry, a hallway lead to a dead end where bookshelves lined the walls from floor to ceiling.

"It's locked," Alona whispered.

"It wasn't when Neeve took me through here the night we escaped." But this was what Brea had been preparing for. She closed her eyes, focusing on her intent and how much she needed to get through that secret door. "*Opna.*" Something clicked. "Try the door again."

Alona pushed against the shelf, and it opened. Her eyes widened as she turned to Brea. "Here I am with no magic, and you have two ancient powers inside you."

Lochlan would tell Brea pride was a useless emotion, but she wasn't ashamed at how proud she was of herself. Yet, this was only the first step. They entered the long hallway, following it as it wound down, the floor tilting.

Dampness coated the air, sinking into Brea's skin as a chill raced up her spine. Water seeped down the walls the farther down they went into the darkness. "*Ljos*," she whispered. A shimmering light appeared in her hand, illuminating the hall.

"There will be guards outside the doors." Alona held out a hand to stop Brea as they reached another door.

Brea met her gaze. "You forget, they've been eating Gelsi berries as has everyone in this palace, everyone except Regan, Griffin, and me. I don't have full knowledge of my Fargelsian power, and my Eldurian power only seems to work at night randomly—which it's not supposed to do, but I still have more magic in me than them." She put a hand to the door. "*Opna*." Yanking it open, she darted inside, not giving anyone a chance to reach for their weapons before saying, "*Sofa*." Armor crashed against the stone floor as the four guards passed out.

Alona stood frozen on the threshold. "I think I love you."

Brea threw her a grin. "Don't tell Finn." She bent over one of the guards to make sure he was really sleeping. His eyes twitched beneath his eyelids.

Straightening, she looked too Alona. "Where is he?"

"Down one level in the farthest corner of the dungeons." Alona gestured to an open doorway.

Brea ran toward it and thundered down the steps before bursting into a hall-filled chamber with rows and rows of prison cells. Prisoners yelled to her, but she couldn't hear them over the beating of her own heart.

He was here, only steps away.

Alona called directions to her from behind, and Brea ran around the corner, stopping as a single cell came into view.

She'd never seen a picture of her father and knew hardly anything about him, but there he was. She'd still have recognized him anywhere. Maybe it was the kind eyes staring through the bars or the way her magic pulled her forward as if wanting to be closer to his.

But she just knew.

The man standing before her was Brandon O'Rourke. Alona caught up to her, and the man smiled. "Alona." His voice was hoarse, probably from lack of use. "How did you get back here?"

"We have to get him out," Brea whispered to no one in particular. "We have to." She rushed forward, one hand outstretched. "*Opna.*" Nothing happened. Louder this time. "*Opna.*"

There was no telltale click, no door swinging open. She grabbed the metal bars and yanked but they didn't budge. "*Opna.*"

"Brea." Alona put a hand on her arm. "I thought you'd have known. The cells are sealed by magic and can't be opened by simple spells. Most have keys, but this one is different. Only Regan can unlock it."

"The magic recognizes her." Brea could feel it in the buzz in the air. Regan used a complex spell of her own making to keep her brother in his cell.

Alona nodded. "She only lets him out for an occasional bath in the river."

Brandon rubbed his scraggly beard, his eyes never leaving Brea. "I know you."

A tear slipped down Brea's cheek and she closed her palm, cutting off the light in hopes it hid her desperation. That voice... she'd never known to dream of hearing it, but now she couldn't just let him go.

"How do I know you?"

Brea swallowed back her tears. "Because I'm your daughter."

The world stopped turning as the words left her mouth. Brandon released a strangled cry and stumbled back away from the bars.

"My... my..." His eyes met hers once more. "Show me your face again."

"*Ljos*." Light appeared in her hand, and she held it below her chin.

"It's true." A sob wracked his body. "Oh, my girl. I would know you anywhere. You look so like your mother." He inched forward, but his face darkened. "You shouldn't be here. It's not safe."

"We made it into the dungeons without being seen."

He shook his head, a crazed look in his eyes. "Fargelsi. It's not the place for you. Evil happens here."

"I didn't have a choice." She hiccupped back a sob. "And now I am married to Regan's heir, Griffin O'Shea. Our child will one day rule Fargelsi."

"O'Shea?" His eyes snapped up. "No. That can't happen." He tried to reach through the bars, but pain flashed across his face, and he pulled back. "Any child of yours is dangerous in the wrong hands. The union of my daughter and an O'Shea?" He scrubbed a hand across his face. "Regan is trying to control all three kingdoms."

It hit her then—what she hadn't considered before. Lochlan was the king of Iskalt now, but he had no heir. She was the heir of Eldur—and Fargelsi, depending on who you asked. Griff was Regan's current heir. Any child of theirs could rule any of the three kingdoms. "Or all of them," she whispered.

Suddenly, all Regan's motivations became clear. Her interest wasn't in the power of Brea's combined magic, only her bloodlines.

"But I am the weapon." She wiped her tears away, hardening herself against a father she'd never met. "That's why I was conceived. I don't know what it means, but only I can defeat Regan. Maybe I need to be in Fargelsi."

"What is your name?" Brandon's face softened. "At least give me that."

"Brea Robinson."

"Robinson?" His brow creased. "You are a Cahill, dear. I don't know where your mother is or what is happening in the world, but I do hope you have had a safe life with her."

It was on the tip of her tongue to tell him the truth. He didn't know she'd been exchanged at birth or raised by cruel parents in the human realm.

But it wasn't in her to further break an already broken man.

"Did you ever want me?" The question was out before she could call it back.

He didn't answer for a long moment. "Brea, all I ever wanted was another child. You are more than a weapon against my sister. You were loved before you were even born."

Brea almost missed the last part of what he said because her mind snagged on the earlier words. *Another* child. "I have a sibling?"

Fear shone in his eyes as if he'd said something he shouldn't have. "Regan can't know. Brea, I don't know you, but my magic does, my... heart does. You're my daughter, and I'm trusting you with my other daughter's life."

Brea swallowed, reaching for Alona's hand. "A sister?"

He nodded. "I loved her mother, but she died when sickness swept through the villages. My girl was three when I brought her to be raised by a maid in the palace. That was only months before Regan imprisoned me. I do not know what has happened to her." His eyes lit up. "But you can find her. If she's still out there, search for her. Please."

Brea tried to even her breathing, to not let this man's secrets drag her into the darkness. "You want me to find the daughter you cared for?" She nodded as if it all made perfect sense. "I'm just the science experiment, the weapon created for a purpose."

"I do not know what that means, but you have to believe me when I tell you I cared for you. I did not know you, yet I have spent the last eighteen years sitting here wondering what you looked like, if you got your mother's sharp mind instead of mine. But you were raised in a palace with a family. Your sister had no one to protect her. You can be that protection now."

"How? I can't even help myself."

"You'll find a way. Promise me you will look."

The tears Brea had been holding back broke free. He was right. If she had a sister, Brea had to find her. "What can you tell me about her?"

His expression softened as he recognized her acceptance. "Her name is Neeve."

"Neeve." Brea gasped, and Alona went still beside her. "Neeve is your daughter?"

"You know her?" His hopeful gaze cut through her.

"She helped me escape. But she isn't here."

"Where is she?" His eyes implored her for the truth.

"Eldur." Brea breathed a relieved sigh. Some good news at least. "Regan must not know her true parentage because she released her to Eldur."

"Thank the heavens." Brandon sat down on his makeshift bed of rags. "At least one of my girls is safe."

Brea backed away from the cell, needing space from her father, from this entire messed-up situation. "I need to go." She turned on her heel and ran back through the halls, not seeing anything she passed.

Neeve was her older sister, her blood, and another potential heir to Fargelsi.

And Brea would get to her again.

She sprinted through the palace, almost knocking over a servant. Alona didn't follow, but she wasn't who Brea needed to see.

Slamming into her rooms, Brea marched over to the bed and shook Griff's arm. He rubbed his eyes.

"What? Brea? You okay?"

"Tomorrow, tell Cait I need to see her. It's time I learned the full extent of my magic."

Griff gave her a strange look and nodded before he fell asleep again.

But Brea didn't care. Plans rolled through her mind. It no longer mattered that she was tied to Griff, or that she might die trying to get out.

If she was as powerful as her parents planned when they conceived her, she could do this.

It was time to escape Fargelsi—again—and rejoin the right side of this war, her mothers' side.

Her sister's side.

CHAPTER II

LOCHLAN

"Are we there yet?" Myles asked, returning his book to his saddlebag. Lochlan had never seen anyone read a book while riding horseback. He was itching to try it next time he traveled. When the human wasn't with him, of course.

"Actually, your incessant questions are about to pay off," Lochlan nodded across the bleak plains. "See how the grass is greener in the distance? That means we're nearing the Gelsi border. We'll arrive before sunset."

"Thank god, my butt is saddle sore, and I'm frying like a burger in this heat." Myles shifted on his mount.

"Human, there are some things you should just keep to yourself."

"I feel like you've said that before."

"I have. You are like Brea. You don't listen."

"We tend to just be us." Myles shrugged, shielding his eyes in the blazing Eldur sun. "Can we see the barrier?"

"No. But even you will feel its power."

"Will we be able to bring it down? And by we, I mean you and that army behind us." He gestured back at the Iskalt troops he'd brought with him.

"Between Tierney, myself, and all of Eldur and Iskalt's greatest magic wielders, we finally have enough skill to bring it down. That barrier doesn't have a chance now that Callum is no longer Regan's greatest ally."

"Now you're talking like a human, Lochy my boy. No plan and a lot of arrogance." Myles eased his mount into a canter.

"You're going the wrong way, human."

"Then lead the way, my liege. I'm tired, thirsty, and sunburned. And I have sand stuck in some not-so-nice places. I'd like a hot meal, a bath, and some sleep, not necessarily in that order."

"You do realize we aren't going to another castle?" Lochlan picked up his pace, eager as Myles was to reach their destination.

"At least there will be tents with beds and hot meals, right?" Myles gave him a horrified look when Lochlan didn't immediately answer.

"My tent will have a bed, and a hot meal. Yours, probably a cot or a bedroll and some sort of hard tack and dried meats. Probably fleas too."

"I'm moving in with you, you know that, right?" Myles followed.

He wouldn't shake Myles so easily and for some reason, Lochlan was really starting to like the human. He reminded him of Brea in all the best ways.

"You know, you read the books and you see the movies, but I don't think anything can prepare you for the stench of an army camp preparing for battle." Myles covered his nose with the sleeve of his shirt.

"This isn't an army camp, and we aren't preparing for battle." Lochlan led them through the throng of smaller tents to the larger one Finn had prepared for him.

"It looks like one, and we are preparing for battle with the barrier. Let me live vicariously. In my memoirs, this will be an epic battle."

"Loch!" Finn called them over to the tent he'd just left. "You're just in time."

"Just in time for what?" Myles asked.

"We're about to make another go at the barrier once dusk settles. We have Eldurians, but your Iskaltian magicians might be just what we need."

"Has Tierney arrived?" Lochlan left his things with an attendant and followed Finn through the maze of tents.

"Not yet, but we could use your help if you're up to it."

"That's why I'm here. Any news from your father?"

"No, we haven't been able to breach the barrier since he left."

"Let's see if we can get someone through tonight." Lochlan rolled up his sleeves and joined the others at the invisible wall keeping Brea from him. If will alone was enough, he'd have this wall down by dark.

A line of men and women formed up where the brown and green Eldur grasslands met up with the lush green grasslands bordering Loch Villandi in the distance beyond the invisible barrier. Once they broke Regan's spell, they would make their way through the Southern Vatlands. From there, they would meet with the rest of Faolan's army and Lochlan's own troops he'd brought with him from Iskalt. Together, they would make a move against Regan.

As the sun sank along the horizon, Lochlan's magic awoke to join the Eldurian's during the one part of the day when they were both powerful.

"Your Majesty," Finn called him forward. "Please lead us tonight." Finn and the others fanned out behind Lochlan, giving him space to make the first strike.

Lochlan closed his eyes, drawing on the emotions that always simmered just under the surface of his calm facade. Grasping hold of his anger, fear, and confusion, the magic swelled up inside him, burning like ice in his veins. Blue sparks skimmed over the surface of his body.

"For Brea," he murmured. Raising his hand, he guided his magic toward the invisible barrier that stood between so many and their freedom. A steady stream of his light crashed against the wall, joined by the others around him. The reds, oranges, and yellows of the Eldurian's magic united with his in a rainbow of warmth and light. Greens, blues, and violets of other Iskaltians joined as well, tempering the Eldurian's heat with their ice. As the most powerful of the magic wielders present, Lochlan drew strength from their magic, calling it to him and guiding it toward the wall.

He could see the artistry of Regan's spell work. The intricate weaves of magic that allowed her to create this impenetrable wall. She'd placed it here, brick by brick, pulling each strain of her magic together to create a single structure. Like a corporeal stone wall that no wind or storm could ever knock down. Except Lochlan was willing to stand here all night, picking it apart, thread by thread, until it lay in shambles at his feet.

Focusing on a single piece of the wall, Lochlan began to reverse one of the thousands of spells that made it. Pulling at the threads of Regan's magic, the spell began to unravel. He hoped all it would take to collapse the wall was reversing this one spell, but he knew that would be asking for too much.

"You've got it," Finn's voice echoed over his shoulder, but Lochlan ignored him. "Keep going, Loch. The first one is leading into the second. We'll be here with you until our magic fails."

He was right, as Lochlan collapsed the first spell, taking a brick from the wall, he picked up a loose thread of the next spell. Unraveling it like a sweater, he removed a second and third brick from the wall.

Sweating under the last rays of sunlight, he realized this job was going to take both Eldurian and Iskaltian magicians working together day and night to bring this wall down.

As the first of the Eldurian magicians stepped away when their magic faded with the sun, Lochlan's focus slipped, but he managed to recover, taking another chunk of the wall down. The Iskalt magicians flanked his sides as he worked his way down from the top of the wall to the ground. If he could finish this one section tonight, there was a chance it wouldn't close, and they could get another person through to rendezvous with Eamon Donovan on the other side and bring them an update.

"Careful, Loch," Finn whispered. "I'm stepping out now." His powerful friend had held on longer than all the other Eldurians, but it was nearly dark, and Finn's magic faded with the last of the light.

The moment Finn stepped away, the magic faltered. Lochlan fixated on the Iskalt soldiers, guiding their magic into his. Pulling another brick from the wall, he trembled. Only a few bricks remained, and soon he would have an opening.

"Hold the line!" He demanded, tugging on the thread that would lead him into the next spell, releasing the next brick. But it was too much for the handful of magic wielders left.

A loud crack sounded from the wall, like it might collapse right here and now.

"Loch!" Finn shouted a warning.

"We almost have it! Stay focused." He shouted orders to his magicians, pushing them to their limits.

Ice flooded Lochlan's veins, and his arms trembled from the effort. He stumbled to his knees, fighting to hold the magic steady. "Just a few more." He tugged at the thread again, begging it to give way like all the others had, but the magic pushed back into him. His teeth chattered, and his heartbeat slowed as a stream of blood poured from his nose.

"Brea," he whispered her name through frozen lips. Violet, green, and blue lights shattered around him as the wall trembled and shook. He couldn't hold it. Each spell that he'd reversed collapsed in a loud blast that echoed across their camp. The force of the explosion knocked Lochlan on his back. The magic rushed back into him and each of his wielders.

"Loch? Are you hurt?" Finn slid to the ground next to him.

Lochlan slammed a fist into the dry Eldurian dirt. "No, I'm not hurt." As he gazed back up at the invisible barrier, his heart plummeted to his stomach. It was just as solid as it was the moment he arrived.

"It's okay, we will try again tomorrow. You almost had it. We just need more magic wielders. Lots more."

"And we will have them once Tierney arrives." Loch took Finn's hand and pulled himself up. "Was anyone hurt?"

A scream had them both running toward the camp.

"Finn!" Neeve rushed up to them, a stricken look on her face.

"What is it?"

"It's Myles," she gasped. "He got too close. The blast."

"Take me to him," Lochlan said, grasping her hand and running across the grassy plains at her side, fearing the worst.

"Myles, talk to me." Lochlan dropped to his knees beside Brea's best friend, taking his limp hand in his.

"He just collapsed when the blast hit us. Most of us didn't really feel more than a jolt, but Myles..."

"Is human." He cursed himself for not seeing to Myles' safety. He shouldn't have let him anywhere near the barrier tonight.

"I don't think he's breathing," Neeve cried. "We have to do something."

"Myles, stay with me." Lochlan checked his pulse and listened for a breath. "You do not get to die." He slapped the boy's face, trying to get a response.

"What do we do? Will our healers even know how to help a human?" Neeve sobbed. "Please, Myles."

"Run to the healer's tent," Lochlan ordered. "Go! Bring anyone you can find." He needed to get Neeve out of his way.

Brea would kill him if he left anything happen to Myles. Lochlan placed his hands on Myles' chest, just below his breastbone. He'd seen this on television once. Not that he would ever admit to anyone he enjoyed watching Netflix documentaries as a means to study humans.

Pressing down on Myles' chest in three rapid pumps, he moved to tilt his head back, listening for any sign of a breath. Nothing.

"You have not annoyed me enough, human. You do not get to die yet." He puffed two quick breaths into Myles's lungs.

Murmurs rose up around him as a crowd gathered.

"Loch, what are you doing?" Finn crouched beside him. "Can I help?"

"One, two, three." Lochlan pumped his chest, moving to breathe into his mouth. "It's called CPR. I don't know if I'm doing it right, but it's what humans do when someone isn't breathing." Lochlan pressed his ear up against Myles' chest, searching for the faintest heartbeat. Still nothing.

"Come on, Myles." He pumped his chest again, harder this time. Finn took over breathing into Myles' mouth, but it wasn't working.

"Do not leave her, you hear me, Myles! You cannot leave her here alone. She needs you!" Lochlan slammed his fist down on Myles' chest and something cracked.

"He's fragile, Loch. Be careful," Finn said. "I don't think this is working."

Lochlan grabbed Myles' shirt and ripped it down the middle, exposing the makings of a bruise. Placing his hands against his sternum and right ribcage, Lochlan let his fear call on his magic. Blue sparks crackled against Myles' pale skin as Lochlan's magic jolted through him.

"You're going to kill him," Finn cried.

"I have to shock his heart." He sent another jolt through him, harder this time.

Myles trembled and took a deep shuddering breath as he came up swinging. His fist cracked against Lochlan's jaw before his eyes even fluttered open.

A gasp rang through the crowd, but Lochlan pulled the human up, wrapping his arms around him. "You're okay?" He held Myles at arm's length, examining his breathing before he hugged him close again.

"You jerk. You broke my ribs." Myles coughed. "And you're choking me."

"Move aside." A healer shoved through the onlookers. Neeve following behind.

"Myles." She darted past the healer. "Are you okay?" She slid to her knees beside him.

"I-I don't know. What happened? Dude, did you just give me mouth to mouth?" He stared at Lochlan.

"I did CPR. You weren't breathing."

"Thank you." Myles winced. "I knew you loved me, you big brute."

"Let's get you back to my tent, young man." The healer leaned down and looked into Myles' eyes while he checked his pulse.

"Will he be okay?" Lochlan asked, scooping Myles up into his arms.

"I can tend his broken ribs, but we need to give him a careful examination, your Majesty. Humans are terribly fragile creatures, so we will need to check him for internal bleeding. Please follow me."

Lochlan charged after the healer with Myles in his arms.

"Awe, look who's a big ol' softy." Myles attempted a teasing tone but coughed instead.

"Quiet, human. I just saved your life, so you will not risk it again. I don't want you anywhere near this barrier."

"Yes, oh great ice king." Myles coughed again.

"She would never forgive me if I let anything happen to you."

"No, she wouldn't. She likes me better than you." Myles laid his head on Lochlan's shoulder.

Lochlan didn't like his color. "You with me, Myles?"

"I don't feel so good."

"We're nearly there. The healer will make sure you're comfortable very soon."

"Don't leave me."

"I won't. I'll stay with you until I know you're okay. She did that for me once. It's time I returned the favor."

Chapter 12

BREA

"Knock, knock." Cait stuck her head into Brea's room just after breakfast.

"Come in, Cait." Brea flashed a smile at the young maid. After working with her closely over the past few weeks, Brea found she had a real soft spot for the pleasant girl. She was always happy and cheerful, despite her role as a servant to the demanding queen. Cait found the good in everything.

"I brought you something, your Highness." Cait bobbed a curtsey and handed Brea a thick leather-bound book. "It's a book of spells. I found it for you in the palace library."

"This is perfect, Cait, thank you." Brea flipped through the delicate pages of the old textbook. It was exactly what she'd been looking for.

"It has three sections." Cait leaned over her shoulder. "You should stick to the first part, which is basic Fargelsian magic. You'll find the proper words of magic for most simple tasks in here. The next two sections you'll need to work up to. Intermediate magic will teach you how to perform more complex spells by combining words of power through your intent, and in the final section, you'll learn how to construct your own spells. I thought it would be good reading for you in between our lessons. Though, you're learning so quickly, I'm sure you'll fly right past me in no time."

"Don't tell your sisters, but you're my favorite." Brea leaned in to hug the girl.

"Oh, no your Majesty, it wouldn't be proper." She moved out of Brea's reach.

"And when have I ever been proper?" Brea smiled, squeezing the girl's hand. "Thank you, Cait. You have no idea how much this means to me."

"You're welcome, Highness." Cait blushed and dropped another curtsy before she left.

The moment the door closed behind her, Alona and Brea crouched on the bed together, flipping through the book. They only had a few minutes before Alona would have to leave for appearance's sake.

"You know what this means, don't you?" Brea whispered.

"You'll master Gelsi magic in no time, my Lady," Alona said for the benefit of their magical listeners.

Brea didn't block all sound from the room every day, only when it was absolutely necessary. She didn't want Regan to think she was in here plotting rebellion.

"Cait has been a huge help, but with this book, she's probably right, I'll outpace her in no time." Brea gave Alona a pointed look, hoping she would read between the lines.

"So you'll be needing a new teacher soon, won't you?" Alona busied herself with folding a stack of clean linens, eyeing the book like it was made of gold.

"Perhaps. And perhaps I can just learn from this book. For a while at least." Brea scribbled on a piece of paper and held it up for Alona.

We leave tonight. Her lessons with Cait were the only reason

Brea hadn't attempted escape before now. With the spell book in her arsenal, she was ready to continue her lessons on her own. She'd scoured the library for books on magic and never found anything on teaching Gelsi magic. This book couldn't have come from the palace library, meaning Cait—and likely her sisters too—were much more perceptive than they'd have the queen believe.

Alona gave her a fearful look as she moved to burn the paper in the fireplace. Shaking her head, she let Brea know she didn't think her plan was a good idea. "This *awful rash* on my hands is bothersome. I hope my Lady isn't repulsed by my *red hands*."

Brea smiled at Alona's worries. It *was* rash, but they needed to take advantage of this opportunity. "There are some gloves in my closet you may borrow to protect your hands." Brea crossed the room to her large walk-in closet. They were fairly certain no one was listening in on them in the closet—closets were for maids, not princesses—still, they didn't often risk it.

"Where are the riding clothes Griffin ordered for me? He promised to take me riding soon." Brea took down a bag from the top shelf and started stuffing her essential belongings inside.

"I'll do that for you, my Lady." Alona took the bag from her, slipping the book of spells inside. "You have other things to attend to, I'm sure."

Brea nodded, grateful Alona was on board. Brea just needed to make sure Griffin and the queen were distracted this evening. Regan had arranged for a private concert at dinner tonight and had invited a few guests. It was the first entertaining the queen had planned since the wedding.

Brea needed to come down with something this afternoon. Perhaps a good case of morning sickness and a little fainting spell would get the queen in high spirits and off Brea's back for one night.

"Brea, darling, how are you feeling today?" Regan made a fuss over her every morning, just dying to see the first signs that Brea might be pregnant. If Brea didn't know any better, she'd think Regan cared about her, but she knew all Regan wanted was Brea's child. She wanted it more than anything, but Brea would die before she'd have a child with Griffin, much less hand it over to Regan to corrupt.

"I'm very tired, Auntie." Brea sat across from Regan for their afternoon tea. She was so sick of these teas she could vomit.

"Make sure you get plenty of rest today, darling. You won't want to miss the concert this evening. It's going to be grand." Her eyes sparkled with the excitement only entertaining gave her.

"I'm looking forward to it." Brea offered her aunt a convincing smile.

"Girls." The queen rang a bell for the triplets. "We will have our tea now. I had the kitchens make something special for us today. Smoked fish sandwiches with pickle and quail egg. Please say you'll join me?"

Sometimes the food in Fargelsi left much to be desired. "Sounds delicious." Brea forced another smile. She hated fish. Hated the smell of it. It always made her nauseous, and smoked fish was the worst. It was perfect. She rarely ate anything from Regan's table, much to her aunt's dismay.

The triplets rushed in with covered dishes from the kitchen. The fishy smell already made her nauseous.

Cait placed a plate in front of Brea and lifted the cover. The smell hit her, making her stomach heave. "Oh, no." Brea leapt from her chair and ran to the balcony railing, letting her hair fall around her face. She stuck a finger down her throat and achieved the desired effect. Coughing, she threw up the meager contents of her stomach.

"Brea, darling, are you okay?"

Brea stood up, her hands trembling from the effort of forcing herself to vomit.

"I'm so sorry." Brea clutched her aunt's hand. "I feel faint." She swooned into Regan's arms.

"Don't be, Brea. These things happen." Regan guided her back to her seat. "Have you been feeling ill lately?" She pressed a cool glass of water into Brea's hands, dabbing at her brow with a linen napkin.

"Just the last few days. I must have a slight bug."

"Of course. We will call for the healer immediately. There's a chance you could be pregnant, darling. Isn't that wonderful?" Her smile gave Brea chills.

"Oh, please don't call for the doctor. Not today, Aunt Regan. I just need to rest. I don't want to get my hopes up too early. If I still don't feel well in a few days, I'll see the healer."

"All right, dear." She turned back to the waiting triplets. "Help the princess back to her rooms and see to it she's not disturbed. Brea, darling, I want you to rest today and stay off your feet. We will miss you at the concert tonight, but I think it's for the best."

"Thank you, Auntie. I appreciate how well you take care of me." Brea turned toward her rooms, trying to hide the triumphant smile on her face.

"It's almost dinner time, my Lady. Are you sure you're not feeling up to attending the concert?" Alona asked.

That was code for, "are you ready to escape this hell hole now?"

"No, I think I'll just take it easy tonight and finish this book. Please take the evening off. I won't be needing you." Brea closed the spell book and slipped it back into her bag. She was already dressed to leave but threw her dressing gown over her riding clothes.

"Goodnight, my Lady." Alona closed the door with a wink. They had plans to meet in their secret room downstairs in just a few minutes. Brea would give Alona time to gather her things before she left. From there Brea just had one more thing to do before they could leave this place forever.

Pacing the room, Brea thought of Griff. Her heart ached at the thought of leaving him like this. Sometimes she couldn't tell if it was still just the magic making her feel things, or if some of her feelings were real. He was a good man when he wanted to be, but his loyalty to Regan would be his downfall. Part of her wished she could talk him into going with her.

A soft knock at the door had her leaping under the covers. Brea snatched her book from the bedside table just before Griffin entered their bedroom.

"Hi," she said, willing her heart rate to slow down.

"You feeling okay?" He frowned as he sat on the bed beside her. Cupping her face in his palm, the touch sent fake warm fuzzies to her stomach. Stupid confusing magic.

"Yeah, I'm just a little tired."

"Regan said you were ill at tea this morning."

"It was the fish. I've never liked fish, and I hate the smell. It's not what she thinks."

"Oh." His shoulders slumped, and she hated to disappoint him. Griffin very much wanted to be a father, and Brea could sense his motives were pure. He didn't yet realize what it would mean for them to have a child together. Their child would be a pawn, not just in Fargelsi, but in each of the fae realms.

"It makes her happy to think there might be a little one soon. I didn't want to burst her bubble, and you know how I hate her elaborate events."

"I know." He leaned forward and pressed a kiss to her forehead. "Enjoy your night off. I'll sleep in my old rooms tonight so I don't disturb you."

"Thank you." She squeezed his hand. She could barely breathe, her heart hurt so much at the thought of this as their final goodbye. "See you in the morning."

"I'll bring you breakfast in bed." He smiled, turning to leave. He paused at the door. "We're happy, aren't we, Brea?"

She choked back her tears. "We are." She managed a tight smile.

With a smile he closed the door. She could have loved him so easily if he'd ever learned to make better choices, but Griffin would always choose Regan. He would never understand that Brea couldn't be happy when she felt like a prisoner in their marriage.

She waited several minutes before flinging the covers off and shedding her dressing gown. She didn't give herself time to think before she grabbed her pack and shoved her feet into her boots. She left without a backward glance, confident she would never see this room again.

"What took you so long?" Alona snapped the moment Brea walked into the boarded-up room they'd used more frequently before her marriage to Griffin.

"Griff came for a visit. I had to wait until I was sure he was gone." Brea watched Alona's furious pacing. "Hey, relax." Brea pulled Alona into her arms. "It's going to be okay."

"I know." Alona took a deep breath. "But I won't feel good about this until we get out of this stupid palace." She kicked a pile of soot-stained sheets that had once covered the furniture Brea and Alona used when they came here.

"We have one thing we have to do before we leave."

"What?" Alona gave her a wary look.

"We have to go get my dad."

"You want to break out the rightful King of Fargelsi? The man everyone thinks is dead? The man locked behind Regan's own spellwork?"

"Yes. Don't worry, I have a plan. I found a spell that might work, and I also have my Eldur magic for a few more hours, so we have to hurry."

"We're so getting caught." Alona rushed to follow her.

"Whatever, it's better than your plan of going out the front door."

"My plan involves stealing horses to get us to the border faster."

"So we'll walk. It'll be fine." Brea followed Alona down to the kitchen, keeping her head down in case they ran into anyone who might recognize her out of her usual attire of the simple dresses her aunt despised.

"Everyone is focused on the queen's concert tonight." Alona looked over her shoulder as they scurried past the kitchens. No one gave them a second look.

Alona slipped through the concealed door to the dungeons, and Brea followed close behind, murmuring the words to close the door behind them. With Cait's guidance, Brea found Gelsi magic much easier to use than her Eldur magic.

Just like last time, Brea barged into the underground prison. "*Hunsa*," she whispered. The guards looked right past her and Alona like they weren't even there. She got away with just knocking them out last time, but this time she needed to leave as little evidence behind her as possible.

Tiptoeing past the guards, they made their way into the depths of the dungeon to her father's cell.

"Who's there?" Brandon's voice cracked from disuse.

"It's Brea."

"Why can't I see you?"

"We're breaking you out," Alona whispered.

Brea focused on her fear, controlling it and allowing the fire of her Eldur magic to spark along her skin. She would need all of her power to manage this spell, and it still might not work. "*Mölbrotna*," Brea said the word that should shatter the spell holding her father in his cell.

Nothing happened.

"Brea, please." Her father begged. "Leave me. I've grown accustomed to my fate. I will only hinder you. Please, save yourselves."

"We're not leaving without you."

"I'll never make it through the Vatlands."

"You let us worry about that." Brea had a plan to help him once they were away from the palace. "Stand back, Lona, I don't want to hurt you."

This time Brea called on her Eldur power first, sending a shaft of yellow light to crash against the spell locking Brandon on the inside. The spell work was intricate—and so much more than her fire magic could handle. But Brea was a weapon with more in her arsenal than any other fae ever born. "*Mölbrotna*," she said the word louder this time, letting her Gelsi magic color her voice so it no longer sounded like her.

The bars to Brandon's cell shuddered as the spell shattered.

"You did it." Brandon's jaw dropped. "But... you're still just a child."

"A child with a how-to book and no idea what she's doing." Brea's Eldur magic began to fade as she whispered, "*Opna*," to unlock the cell door. Brandon shuffled out on unsteady feet. "Get his other side." Brea draped Brandon's arm around her shoulder. With Alona on his other side, they shuffled back to the main prison chamber.

"*Hunsa*," Brea uttered the powerful word that made the guards ignore them as if they were invisible.

Together, they hurried through the chamber, past rows upon rows of prisoners in cells. Brea vowed she would never forget them. She would come back for them. All of them.

As soon as they entered the tunnel behind the waterfall, Brandon stumbled.

"I can't slow you down. Girls, you need to leave me."

"Not happening." Brea hefted his weight onto her shoulders. "*Lána Styrkur*." She'd just learned the words this morning for empowering another. Brandon's weight eased off her shoulders as he stood on his own. A wave of fatigue hit her, but she'd prepared for that.

"What was that? I've never heard that spell."

"I found it in a book."

"And you've never practiced it? Brea, that's dangerous."

"Do you feel stronger?"

"I do."

"Then let's chat about it later. We have to get out of here." Brea led the way through the tunnel. Last time she had Neeve to guide her, and horses waiting for them on the outside. This time she had to be the guide, and they were on foot. She didn't even have Neeve's smelly oils to keep the swamp creatures away. Tonight was going to be an adventure for sure. But this time she had magic on her side.

"Brea, you can't keep giving me your strength." Brandon slogged along behind her. "You need to terminate the spell."

"I don't really know how to do that." Brea lifted her foot from the thick mud and took another step. Exhaustion made her limbs heavy.

"You're going to harm yourself trying to save me. Magic like that always has a cost, and this might be far too much for you to handle."

"I will either carry you through this swamp on my back, or I will use my magic so you have the strength to do this on your own. Either way, we're making it through the Vatlands. All of us. Together."

"And then what?" Brandon asked. "The Eldur desert awaits us on the other side."

"Once we're out of Regan's reach, we can rest and make a plan to get to Raudur City," Brea said. "We just have to find our friends." But she wasn't so sure Lochlan or even Finn would call her friend after she'd married the enemy. Maybe Alona's safety would be enough to buy her some good will once she was home.

"We have to stop for a rest," Alona said. "We've nearly reached the barrier, but I can't go another step without a break." After they fled the palace, they ran, putting as much distance behind them as they could. They'd walked throughout the night until they reached the marshy grasslands at the border of Fargelsi and the Southern Vatlands.

They still had to get across the barrier. As a human, Alona could walk right through, but Brea still needed to figure out how to get herself and her father through without calling Regan down on them.

"There's high ground just ahead." Brea led them across the muddy plains to a patch of solid ground among a grove of trees.

They all three dropped to the ground, exhausted.

"We aren't going to make it, Brea." Alona wiped a sweaty hand over her face. "If you strain your magic any further, you're going to push yourself too far. I think I need to go get help."

"We're sticking together if it kills me." Brea shook her head. "I just need to rest my eyes for a moment." Brea leaned back against a tree trunk. "We'll head for the barrier in just a few minutes." Her eyes drooped.

"Brea, wake up!" The familiar voice shook Brea from her stupor.

"What? No." Brea fumbled to sit up. She'd fallen asleep, and from the looks of it, the others had too.

"Brea, you need to sever the spell." Griffin scrambled to her side. "It could kill you."

"No, why are you here?" She tried to pull away from him, but she was too exhausted.

"Speak the words, Brea. *Skera.*"

"*Skera,*" Brea muttered the powerful word.

"Focus your intent." Griff shook her. "You need to sever the spell connecting you with this man."

"*Skera,*" Brea said it louder this time. The fog rolled back from her mind, and she realized what was happening. "Griff. No, please don't take us back." Tears of frustration filled her eyes, and she thought she might be sick for real. "I can't go back. I won't."

"Brea?" Brandon stirred from his rest. "You broke the spell, thank the heavens." His eyes widened when they fell on Griffin in the moonlight.

"Brea?" Alona shot up to her feet the instant her eyes fluttered open. "I'm so sorry, I was supposed to keep watch." Alona moved between Brea and Griffin.

"Relax everyone. I am not the enemy." Griffin took Brea's flask and made her drink from it. "Believe what you must, but I don't want any of you imprisoned. Now tell me what you hope to accomplish."

"We just want out," Brea said. "We want our freedom. Is that so hard to believe?"

"No." The look on his face gutted her.

"You are my husband, but I will never know if it's the magic that makes me love you or if some part of it could be real. I won't live like that, Griff."

"Who is this man?" He gestured at Brandon.

"My father," Brea said. "Brandon O'Rourke, rightful King of Fargelsi."

He stumbled back, shaking his head. "That's impossible. He was killed when Regan was just a princess."

"My little sister could never bring herself to kill me." Brandon rubbed a tired hand across his face. "She tried several times through the years, but somewhere deep inside, Regan still loves me. I've lived in a cell deep under the castle for more than eighteen years. But I will go back if you will please let my daughter and Alona go."

"It's a lie." Griffin shook his head again.

"Just look at him, Griff," Brea said softly. He looked just like her. Blond hair and blue eyes, full lips and only slightly taller than his sister.

Griff stood and paced back to his horse.

"Should we run?" Alona asked.

"Give him a minute." Brea frowned, watching Griffin's back as he grappled with indecision. This time she hoped he made the right one.

Brea flinched when Griffin cried out into the night, a mournful wail that shattered something inside her. She started to go to him when he lifted his saddle bag from his mount and slapped her rear to send her back across toward the grassy plains.

Griffin stared after her for a moment before turning to join them. "Let's go."

"Go?" Brea followed him toward the barrier.

Griffin didn't speak as he approached the invisible barrier that held all Fargelsian's prisoners. She recognized the violet light of his magic as he reached out with a delicate hand and parted the barrier for them.

"Go." His voice was a harsh rasp in the night.

Brea's heart thundered in her chest as she realized he meant to help them.

Alona and Brandon rushed through, but Brea paused.

"Thank you." The words were inadequate as she looked up at her husband, unable to fathom what he was thinking. Brea stepped across the barrier and turned to face him.

"Come with us."

"I can't. There is nothing for me outside Fargelsi."

"There could be." She held her hand out for him, willing him to take it. "I can never truly be your wife, Griffin, but I'd like to be your friend."

A shudder ran through his body as he reached out and took her hand. Stepping through the barrier, he let his magic wink out, closing it behind them. "I choose you, Brea." He squeezed her hand.

Her heart ached with love for him, and she knew she couldn't contribute all of her feelings to the marriage magic. For once, Griffin did what was right. Brea wrapped her arms around his waist and pressed her cheek against his chest.

"We'd better hurry. It won't be long before she knows we're gone." Griffin took her hand and led them into the Vatlands.

"What spell did you use to help Brandon?" Griffin asked. "You should never link yourself like that with magic."

"I tried to lend him strength," Brea explained.

"Try *Lána Skogur Styrkur,*" Griffin said.

"What does that mean?"

"Lend strength from the land." Griffin gestured at the swamp lands teeming with life all around them. "You can ask the land to lend him the strength he needs to make this journey."

Brea paused to settle her intent in her mind before she tried the spell. "*Lána Skogur Styrkur.*" The words left her mouth, and she could almost taste the power in them.

Brandon stood taller, taking in a deep breath. "Thank you. Thank you both." He took Brea's hand. "My daughter." He smiled, shaking his head. "You are extraordinary. That was a complicated spell, yet you accomplished it on the first try as if the words themselves held the power."

"Don't they?" She moved to follow Alona into the swamp with Griffin at her side.

"Yes and no." Brandon squeezed her hand as they walked. "Fargelsi magic begins here." He tapped her forehead. "In the mind as you focus your intent on the words you speak. A person must have perfect control of their thoughts as well as their intent, and for most, that takes practice before conquering a new spell. The more complex the spell, the harder it is to focus your intent. But you're a natural. Once you have the proper training... you will be a formidable woman, my dear."

"That's great, but can we continue this little magic lesson on the other side of this swamp. I'd really like to see my mothers again soon," Alona urged them on.

"Mothers?" Brandon looked at Brea.

"It's a long story." Brea followed her sister, trying not to think about how happy her marriage bond was to have Griffin with her.

"Almost there." Brea clasped Alona's hand. Her human sister was exhausted, and Brea's magic couldn't help her.

"I've got her." Griffin swept Alona up in his arms to carry her the rest of the way.

The muddy waters of the Vatlands began to dry up as they entered the rolling hills of the Eldurian border.

"We're nearly home, Lona." Brea couldn't hide her smile. She'd once thought she might never see Eldur again. This place was in her blood. It made her come alive.

"Halt right there!" A row of soldiers on horseback aimed their weapons at Brea and her weary companions.

Brea beamed up at the soldiers she'd expected to see wearing her mother's colors. "We made it! Please take us to the border camp, I must speak with whoever's in charge." But as she took another look, she realized these men and women wore Iskalt colors.

"Silence!" The leader moved to strike her, and Griffin charged forward.

"Wait!" Brea held him back. "You don't understand."

"I said silence, woman." The soldier dismounted his horse.

"Okay, then, I guess we're doing this the hard way." Brea and Griffin stood united between the soldiers and Brandon and Alona.

"On your knees, you filthy cowards." The soldier drew his weapon and held it at Griffin's throat.

Brea held her hands up as she and the others sank to their knees in the mud. This was not the reception she'd hoped for.

Chapter 13

BREA

"Let us go." Brea bucked and kicked against the soldier lifting her down from the back of his horse. "Your king will hear about this." If Lochlan still cared after everything that happened. She glanced back at her unconscious father, wondering if she should reveal his identity. They'd knocked him out when he'd tried to explain the situation.

No. She wouldn't tell anyone but Lochlan.

The guards looked to each other and chuckled. "Callum O'Shea is no longer our king, little girl. He will not be able to save Fargelsian nobles."

"Fargelsian." Brea stomped on his foot. "Take that back!"

"It's no use," Griff muttered. "The minute they saw you with me, any trust you might have had was gone. And your father looks like a Fargelsian through and through."

Griff didn't even try fighting the guards. He just released a resigned sigh, and Brea wanted to take his hand, to tell him she wouldn't let anything bad happen to him. He'd left the Fargelsian palace, a place where he was safe and revered, to protect her on her journey through the swamps and to get her through Regan's spelled border.

He'd done it all for her.

Any remaining ill will she felt for him faded the moment he'd told her he chose her and helped her father.

"Griff." A tear tracked down her cheek. What would Lochlan do to him? They'd realized the moment the guards found them they were Iskaltian and not Eldurian like she'd hoped. She might have had a chance of convincing her mother not to imprison Griff. "I love you," she whispered. She hadn't said it before, and it wasn't real, but in that moment, it didn't matter if the magic forced the feeling into her. It was what he needed to hear.

A smile tilted his lips, and he nodded, straightening his spine as if the words gave him strength.

Through all this, Alona remained silent, her eyes scanning over the sea of tents before them.

"Come on." A guard shoved Griff forward, and Brea and Alona followed without protest. Two others carried Brandon behind them.

A familiar man ducked out of a nearby tent and froze. "What is..." His eyes went past Griff and widened. "Brea?" Finn took a step forward before his entire body went rigid with shock, his eyes locking on the bedraggled girl beside Brea. His lips formed her name, but he couldn't voice it.

Tears shone in Alona's eyes.

Orange flashed across Finn's irises, his magic responding to the emotions Brea could only imagine he was feeling. He took one step and then another before breaking into a run, pushing past the guards and yanking Alona into his arms, his back shaking with sobs. "Alona," he whispered.

She gripped him like she would never let go, and Brea couldn't tear her eyes away. The guards shifted, and the one holding her loosened his grip as if realizing she might not be who they'd thought she was.

After a long moment, Finn pulled back, framing Alona's tear-streaked face with his hands. He didn't look at the guards as he spoke to them. "Do you know who it is you lay hands on?" His voice darkened. "These are the princesses of Eldur."

Alona laughed through her tears like she couldn't quite believe they were standing here. When they'd escaped, they'd assumed it would be a long journey to Eldur. They never imagined safety would come so close to danger.

The guards backed away from the girls. "And what of Griffin O'Shea and the other Fargelsian?"

Finn's face darkened as he turned to glare at Griff. "Take him to the king. The Fargelsian looks like he needs a healer. I will escort the princesses to where they can get some food and rest."

Finn wrapped an arm around Alona and held a hand out for Brea. Her eyes shifted from the hand to Griff's back as it got farther and farther away. It would be so easy to go with Finn and try to forget this entire nightmare, but something inside her couldn't let Griff face Lochlan alone.

She took Finn's hand and squeezed once before releasing him. "It's good to see you, Finn. Take care of Maid-Girl. She's been through a lot." As Brea hurried away, she heard Finn asking about the nickname.

"It's a long story," Alona said.

Soldiers looked up from their tasks as Brea ran past them, trailing after Griff and his escort. She saw the men carrying her father, but he'd be in better hands with the healer than Griff would be with Lochlan.

The men and women wore Iskaltian colors with only a few Eldurians mixed in.

The guards entered a large tent at the end of the row, its size the only thing differentiating it from the others. Brea hovered outside, garnering a few stares from those nearby, but no one stopped her.

"Griffin," Lochlan's rough voice drifted out, a voice Brea hadn't known she'd ever hear again. She closed her eyes to stop the oncoming tears.

"Lochlan," Griff responded.

"Is that all you have to say to me, brother?" Lochlan paused for a moment. "Everyone else out."

Brea ducked around the corner as the guards filtered out of the tent.

Griff's voice was just as dark as his brother's. "What would you like me to say, your Majesty." He spit the title out like a curse. "Enjoying sitting on our father's throne and allying yourself with the kingdom that got him killed?"

Brea held her breath, waiting for Lochlan's response. "Fargelsi killed our parents."

"No, they were on a mission for Eldur."

"Yes, protecting the woman that is now your wife!"

Brea flinched.

Griff's laughter echoed in Brea's mind. "That's what this is about, isn't it? Brea."

"No, it is not about a girl. You have betrayed everything our parents stood for, using our family's portal magic to abduct humans, following a queen who would keep her own people prisoner within her borders. And for what, Griff? What purpose does any of it serve?"

"She was all I had!" Griff's voice trailed off. "She's my family. And now, so is Brea."

"Well, I hope you're glad you came here for Brea, because you are now my prisoner."

Brea couldn't listen anymore. She burst into the tent, coming face to face with Lochlan for the first time since she'd left him sleeping the morning she put Eldur behind her.

And what a face it was. Half shaven and even more defined than she remembered. He stood before her shirtless, with a small blade in his hand and a bowl of water on the table by his side. He must have been shaving when Griff arrived.

His dark blue eyes bore into hers, waiting for her to speak.

"Please don't punish Griff." She couldn't believe the words coming out of her mouth. Darting a look over her shoulder at the man in question, she sucked in a breath and continued. "He helped me and Alona escape."

Lochlan's eyes widened. "Alona is here?"

Brea nodded. "She's with Finn. Please, Lochlan." It hurt to ask it of him, seeing the pain flash in his eyes. "Griff… he's your brother and my…"

"I know what he is to you." Lochlan turned away to grab his shirt. "I will decide what is to be done. I am a king now, Princess. My word is law." He pulled a blue shirt over his head. "Do not enter this tent again without permission." Turning back to her, sympathy entered his gaze, but it was gone just as quickly. "We are glad you are safe. Eldur will rejoice. I have a prisoner to attend to. Please leave."

Her shoulders dropping, Brea turned, but she stopped halfway to the door. "He helped us get my father out of Fargelsi. The rightful king."

Lochlan's eyes widened. "Brandon O'Rourke is free?"

He showed no signs of surprise that the man was alive.

Brea crossed her arms. "He's with the healer. He wasn't exactly conscious when we brought him in."

Lochlan looked from her to Griff, his eyes calculating. "One good act does not negate all the bad. Please leave, Brea."

On her way to the door, she put a hand on Griff's shoulder. "I won't let anything happen to you."

He offered her a sad smile because they both knew she'd have no say in his fate.

Unable to face Lochlan again, she stepped out into the sun. The foreign camp closed in around her, and she didn't know where to go. These weren't the people she'd known, the ones she'd come to love.

Except for one. A tall girl she'd recognize anywhere argued with a soldier, her arms crossed over her chest.

Brea broke into a run, barreling into her friend and almost knocking her over. "Neeve."

"Princess... oh, what the hell, proper schmoper." She hugged Brea back just as tightly. They'd both been on their own journeys since they saw each other last, but Brea never stopped worrying over her friend, the one who got herself thrown in the dungeons to help Brea escape.

The girl she now knew was so much more than a friend.

Her father's words came back to her. Neeve was her sister. There was a reason she'd felt a connection to her from the moment she met her.

"I heard you were here." Neeve pulled back. "But none of these incompetent soldiers could tell me where."

"You were searching for me?" That thought warmed her.

"Not just for me. He needs you, Brea. He won't admit it, but I can see it in his eyes every time he looks at that border."

"He who?"

"Myles."

Brea's heart froze. "He's here?" Her lip quivered as she barely held herself together. After everything that had happened, was she steps away from reuniting with her best friend?

Neeve nodded. "We came with the Iskalt regiments, but Tierney and the Eldurians are expected to arrive tomorrow."

Brea barely heard anything else Neeve said as her mind turned over and over. "Where is he?"

"The healer's tent at the Eastern edge of camp."

Brea started running before she realized her legs were moving. She needed to see him, to hear his voice and know this was real. She was free. He was alive. They were in this together.

Neeve matched her pace, leading Brea through the collection of tents and supply wagons. Brea couldn't think, could hardly breathe.

This was the moment she'd dreamed of since that awful day at school when she thought she'd killed him.

Neeve slowed to a jog before stopping outside a tent that looked no different from any others with its nondescript white canvas. "I'll wait out here."

Brea braced herself before entering. She hadn't thought to ask about his injury or how severe it was. Pushing aside the flap, she found the tent empty except for a sleeping man—her father —on a cot on one side, and one man standing at the back, bending over a tray of food and shoving bites into his mouth.

One side of her mouth curved up. "Some things never change."

His back went rigid before he straightened and lifted his eyes to her. Bread crumbs fell from his lips. "And sometimes the crazy farm girl becomes a princess." He spoke through his food, the words coming out jumbled. Swallowing, he grinned, and it was like Brea's entire world shifted upright once more.

They stared at each other for a moment longer before both rushing across the tent, colliding in a massive hug. Brea wrapped her arms around his torso, feeling safe for the first time since coming through the portal. That was what Myles was to her. Safety. Family. A sob shook her, and she buried her face in his shoulder.

It took her a moment to realize he was crying as well. Big, strong Myles who tamed horses and played on the football team was crying.

"I thought I'd killed you," she whispered.

"Is that why you traded yourself for me?" He pulled back and wiped the tears from her face with his thumbs. "Because Brea Robinson, that was just about the stupidest thing I've ever heard of."

"I was being noble, not stupid."

"Is there a difference?"

She pinched him, and he grinned, pulling her back against his chest. "This hurts right now because your boyfriend blew up my ribs and then kissed me, but I'm not letting you go."

A laugh burst out of her. "Dude, you can't just say something like that and not explain. We'll circle back around to Lochlan kissing you. You're hurt?"

He pulled away from her with a sigh. "It's music to my ears to hear someone say dude." He shot her a wink. "And don't think I didn't notice you knew who I meant when I said boyfriend. I thought you were supposed to have a husband somewhere. Totally weird, by the way."

"Tell me about it." She gestured to her unconscious father. "Not as weird as that man being my dad."

Myles jaw fell open. "Your dad?"

A smile tugged at the corners of her mouth, and she pointed to the empty cot. "If you're injured, sit. We'll talk about me later. Tell me what happened."

He obeyed, lowering himself to the bed and patting the spot beside him. She rolled her eyes as she sat.

Myles sighed. "I won't forget to make you explain the dad thing. There I was all innocent sleeping soundly after helping with the border magic when Lochlan knelt at my side and laid one on me while feeling up my chest."

Brea laughed. "So, what you're saying is you were being useless and got yourself blasted by magic. Lochlan rushed to your aid and tried to perform CPR like he'd probably read in some human book. Am I missing anything?"

"Did your tiara sap all jokes from the great Brea Robinson?"

She bumped his shoulder. "You know I'm still me, right?"

"Gosh, I hope not."

"What is that supposed to mean?"

"Brea." He turned to look at her. "Human world Brea Robinson grew up believing the lies people said about her. That she was crazy, unworthy of love."

"You always loved me."

He nodded. "Because that version of you, the one you saw in the mirror, didn't come close to the one I saw when I looked at you. They talk about you, you know."

"Who?"

"Everyone. The people at the palace in Eldur, in the city. Finn. Neeve. I'm sure this dad you have to tell me about feels the same. There's a reverence in their words, but also a deep affection. Here, in this world of magic where the two of us simple farm kids are surrounded by royalty, the girl I saw and the one you saw have sort of melted together like one giant pile of goo."

"I'm this goo?" She couldn't help smiling at his comparison.

"The gooiest." His arm slid around her shoulders. "But you were my goo before theirs. Just don't forget that."

She hid her smile against his shoulder. She was exhausted from her travels and starving from months of eating too little, but it would take a forklift to move her from Myles' side.

"Now." His brow scrunched. "Tell me why the heck you would marry Griff."

"That's a long story."

"Then it's a good thing neither of us are going anywhere. I think you broke poor Lochlan's heart, and as grumpy as he can be, I kind of like the guy. We're bros now."

Oh no. Lochlan and Myles were friends? Brea sighed. She could only imagine how insufferable they were together.

With a laugh, she shook her head and told Myles everything, holding nothing back about her months in the fae world.

Brea stayed with Myles until the healer came in and forced him to take a sleeping drought, saying it would speed up the healing process. He'd fought it at first, claiming he didn't want to sleep when he'd just gotten Brea back.

But as he drifted off to sleep, she kissed his forehead, checked on her father as he started to wake, and slipped from the tent in search of something to eat. Her stomach rumbled, reminding her just how long it had been. She'd contemplated falling asleep with Myles, but her hunger had won out.

The sun had almost faded away, and with it, the Eldurian magic in her veins went dormant, leaving only Fargelsian power in its wake.

But she was too tired to do the spells even if she could recall the words when her mind was so hazy.

She found Finn and Alona sitting beside a fire with wooden bowls in their laps. They dipped hunks of bread into stew that smelled heavenly.

"Hi." She didn't know why she suddenly felt so out of place among these people. Maybe it was the Iskaltians taking up most of camp, or the fact she knew what they all must think of her for marrying Griff.

But not Finn. Good, happy Finn never let her down with his smiles. He glanced up at her, his eyes sparkling. "Brea." His smile stretched all the way across his face. "Want something to eat? You look far too thin. Did they not feed you in Gelsi?"

"Yes, please. Let's just say I never trusted the food in Gelsi."

He set his bowl aside and jumped to his feet. "I'll be back."

Brea watched him go before sitting beside Alona. It felt strange to be so openly equal with her. In Fargelsi, they'd always had to act like princess and servant, but here, they were both princesses.

"I'm glad to see you two together." She elbowed her sister.

Alona's face reddened. "Oh, we're not together. Not like that. Finn is my friend. Kind of like Myles is yours."

Brea snorted. "Myles and I are not like you and Finn. For one, Myles isn't in love with me."

"Finn's not... we can't... it isn't..."

Brea grinned. "Stop worrying so much about the future, Lona. What do you want right now in this moment?"

Alona chewed on her lip. "I don't know."

"Well, now you're just lying."

She released her lip. "You're right. We don't know what will happen when we get into Fargelsi. All we have is now."

"Preach, girl."

Alona handed her bowl to Brea and got to her feet, brushing a hand down her dress before marching to where Finn walked back toward them, bowl in hand. She stopped in front of him, waiting only a beat before rising up on her toes and pressing her lips to his.

Finn went still for a moment before the bowl fell from his hands, splattering Brea's dinner across the ground. He wound his arms around Alona's back and pulled her closer.

Soldiers hooted and hollered, but Brea looked away. She was happy for them, and also jealous of how simple it seemed to be.

Every time Brea thought of Lochlan, her heart squeezed like a thread corded around it, keeping it from letting anyone else in. The magic meant she could love no one but Griff, but then how did she explain how much it hurt to see Lochlan's pain?

How much she wanted to wipe all his worries away?

She had to see him.

Forgetting her hunger altogether, she stood and looked to a nearby soldier. "Is the king in his tent?"

"Not at this time of night. He'll be working on the border wall." The soldier pointed toward a path that led from camp.

Brea nodded in thanks and took off through the dark. The magic inside her begged her to stop, to turn around and look for where Griffin was being held instead. It took everything she had to ignore its call.

Each step toward Lochlan and away from Griff was harder than the one before, but she didn't stop, not until she saw them, the Iskalt soldiers standing shoulder to shoulder with their king as they focused all their power on the impenetrable wall of magic before them.

Brea had never seen anything so beautiful. Multicolored magic combined in a rainbow of effects, directed by the icy blue power coming from the strongest among them. Brea had known Lochlan as a general, a lost prince, but never a king. But she had always seen what he could be. It was what had drawn her to him. Among the ice and anger inside him was a true king waiting to be given a chance.

He called orders to his soldiers with authority, and they obeyed without question.

She didn't know how long she stood watching this dance with

Regan's magic, but it occurred to her this could be what she'd been conceived for. A weapon crafted by Faolan of Eldur and Brandon of Fargelsi.

"Let me help." The words came out as no more than a whisper, so she cleared her throat and said a quick "*hátt*" to increase the volume of her words. "Let me help."

The magic fell, crashing to the ground as more than a few soldiers turned to look at her. Lochlan continued to stare at the Fargelsian border, his back rigid. "Go get some rest, Brea."

"I can help. I'm the weapon, right?" She was beyond resenting her purpose if it could help.

Lochlan ripped his eyes from the border and surveyed his tired men and women. "That's enough for tonight. The Eldurians will arrive tomorrow to aid us." The soldiers dispersed, heading back to camp, leaving only Lochlan and Brea standing underneath a thousand stars with magic buzzing in the air around them. "We don't know what you are, Brea." He looked at her, his eyes pained.

"We know I'm powerful. I healed you all those months ago—at night, no less. Have you forgotten that already?"

"And have you done it since then?" He raised a brow.

"Well... no."

He grunted and crossed the distance between them. "That is because you still don't have enough control over your powers." He gestured to a nearby moss-covered boulder.

Brea pulled herself up to sit. "I have control."

He sat beside her. "Of each individual power. But, Brea, you must learn to combine your Eldurian magic and your Fargelsian power, funnel one into the other. That is what will make you truly powerful."

Her shoulders slumped, and she didn't respond.

"You must be exhausted."

She shook her head. Yes, a part of her could sleep for a year, but the other part had so much it needed to say to the people she'd only been reunited with hours ago. "I'm okay."

"Are you? You've been in Regan's palace for months." His voice lowered. "You look half-starved. What did she do to you?"

Nothing. Brea had to marry Griff, but she did that for Alona more than herself. She'd been given elaborate rooms and was allowed to have Alona prepare what little food she could gather. No punishments, no true hardships. But how did she say that to the man beside her?

She needed to change the subject. "So... King, huh?"

"Yes." He rubbed the back of his neck. "It still doesn't feel real."

"It suits you." She paused. "I'm proud of you."

Lochlan seemed to need a subject change as much as her. "Tell me about your father. Has he been in the dungeons all this time?"

She nodded. "I think... I mean, I don't know him well yet, but I think he's a good man."

He took her hand and flipped it over, tracing something on her palm. "This changes many things. Once the Fargelsian people know he lives, they might rise up and join us. We just have to get across the border. How is he? Will he be okay?"

She shrugged. "He was starting to wake. I think his body is just weak from captivity, and the journey took a lot out of him."

It still seemed like a dream to her that he was alive but sharing it with Lochlan made it more real.

"I always knew you'd save us all." He smiled sadly. "Even when I fought with you, I knew. And saving Brandon O'Rourke might be the key."

All the feelings Brea thought had vanished the moment the marriage magic took hold rushed into her in a single moment. Lochlan. It had always been Lochlan. Pain wound through her chest, and she cried out, ripping her hand from his and clutching her shirt.

"What's wrong?" Lochlan turned to her, worry in his deep gaze. "Are you okay? Brea, talk to me."

As quickly as it came, the pain was gone. Tears hung in Brea's lashes. Was that what it would feel like every time she let herself feel something for Lochlan? "I never wanted to hurt you," she whispered.

It was the last thing she'd wanted. Hurting Lochlan was like hurting herself. She felt his pain on a different level, one that wasn't supposed to be possible when she was married to Griffin.

He didn't respond for a long moment. "You married my brother. I don't think there is a greater pain I could have experienced."

"Loch—"

"No, I need to get this out. I know there's no going back now. The marriage magic will never release you from your vows. I know you probably... love him." He looked away. "But that morning I woke to find you gone. I wanted to go after you, to give up the fight for my people for just one more day with you."

"But you didn't."

"No, because that is not who I am. I have been in love with you for too long, Brea, since before you knew me. I watched you overcome so much in your human life. You're the strongest fae I have ever known, but also the most honest and brave. When I am near you, I want to be closer." His finger skimmed her arm.

She sobbed as the pain returned, twisting her heart.

"And when I am away from you, I want to hate you."

She sucked in a breath. "Loch—"

He wasn't done. "But hating Brea Robinson is as impossible as melting the ice of Iskalt. I'm not wrong, am I? You love Griff?"

"It's not me, Loch. I can't control it."

"But it will never go away and neither will the pain you feel because of it." He ran a hand through his long hair. "I never wanted to cause you pain. And that is why I must let you go."

"Loch—"

"I was meant to find you, Brea, to watch over you in the human realm. But maybe I was meant to lose you too."

"No. That can't be true." She'd never imagined returning to the people she cared about would be harder than remaining a prisoner.

"I need to stop loving you. For me and for you." He slid off the boulder. "You will be the queen of Eldur one day, and we will be the greatest of allies. Maybe even friends."

"I don't want to be your friend, Lochlan."

He sighed. "That is your choice as well." He walked away without another word, leaving Brea alone on the boulder. The pain intensified as her feelings broke through, washing over her like a wave.

"Brea?"

The pain lessened at the sound of Griff's voice coming out of the dark. He approached her cautiously. She let out a cry and jumped from the boulder to sink against him. His arms wrapped around her, and the pain disappeared with his touch, the magic rejoicing.

"Wait." She pulled back. "How are you here?"

"Lochlan decided he doesn't care if I stay or not. He knows I won't help with the border magic. It's the one thing I can't make myself do, so he has no use for me. I don't think he believes I'll leave while you're here, and he doesn't think I'm strong enough to abduct you again now that you know your magic."

She fell into his embrace once more. "You heard everything, didn't you?"

He winced. "You told me once you'd had something with Lochlan, but I didn't know he was in love with you. My brother doesn't love anything."

"I don't think you know him like you think you do."

Griff sighed, smoothing her hair back away from her face. "You love him too. Even with the marriage magic, you're in love with my brother."

Tears returned to her eyes. "I can't be." She buried her face in his chest. "I don't want to feel like this, Griff."

He didn't respond except to drop a kiss on the top of her head. No matter what anyone said about Griff, he'd risked a lot to help her and Alona get across the border. Even without the magic, she thought he'd love her.

"I'm sorry," she whispered.

Chapter 14

LOCHLAN

Lochlan sat on a boulder near the barrier long after his soldiers and the Eldurians had retired for the night. Another day and another failed attempt at bringing the wall down. He was a failure. He'd left his kingdom weeks ago, hoping this would be a quick endeavor so he could get back to the business of transforming Iskalt. He still didn't have a firm foothold in his kingdom, and he needed to get back soon, but they were no closer to destroying Regan's wall than when he first arrived.

It was nearly a full moon, and Lochlan was at his strongest. He should be able to do this with Tierney at his side. Together they were a powerful force. More powerful than this wall. Lochlan cast his icy blue magic against the barrier. It was like throwing a pebble at a mountain. But he needed to study the wall. If he could understand its construction, he could find its weakness. That was the key to destroying Regan's spell work.

A flicker of violet light caught his attention. It could only belong to one person.

"Griffin," he uttered his brother's name like a curse. The coward was stealing away in the night. Lochlan recalled his magic, charging across the grassy plains to follow his brother. "Running home to your queen, brother?"

Griffin turned to face him in the moonlight. Brea's husband. He still couldn't fathom how she'd gone through with the marriage bond. He wanted to hate his brother for stealing the woman he loved. Part of him did, but there was another part of him that always saw the two-year-old Griffin when he looked at him. He recalled the day they learned their parents had died and their uncle was going to separate them. That part of Lochlan would always love his little brother.

"Not that it's any of your business," Griffin said, "But I have my reasons for returning to Regan." Griffin cast his eyes down at his feet, unable to look Lochlan in the eye. "You said you didn't care if I stayed or went, so what's it to you if I leave?"

"She loves you, and you're just going to leave her?" Lochlan crossed his arms over his chest. "You don't deserve her."

"No, I don't." Griffin sighed, running a hand through his hair. "I've made so many mistakes with Brea. She doesn't love me. She never did."

"She married you."

"She didn't know what she was getting into. I didn't find that out until after. Then it was too late."

"What didn't she know?"

"Take care of her, Loch. Not that she needs it. She's going to make an amazing queen someday. I was a fool to think she could be satisfied as queen consort of Fargelsi."

"Queen consort?" Lochlan snorted.

"I will be king of Fargelsi someday. She was to be my queen. When I have taken the throne, I will make things right. You'll see. I'm not the puppet you think I am. I know Regan doesn't always make the right decisions. She's had a hard life."

"We've all had a hard life. That doesn't give her an excuse to enslave her people."

"It will be different when I am king. I will free my people."

"You are a fool if you think Regan will ever let that happen. You are of Iskalt, brother. The Fargelsians will not accept you as their king. They have never been your people."

"She's named me her heir, Loch. It's done."

"That woman will never allow you or anyone else to take her throne."

"She can't live forever."

"And when you have young heirs that carry her blood? What will happen then?"

Griffin refused to look at him.

"It will make Regan stronger than ever once she has a blood heir. That's what all this was about. She doesn't love Brea. She just wants her child to give her ties to all three realms."

"I will make sure that never happens." Griff turned to leave.

"You're a coward." Lochlan was ashamed of the man his brother had become. It would have killed their parents to see him like this.

"She is all I've ever had, Loch. You had two mothers. A sister. A best friend. They became your family. Well, I had Regan. She was my whole world. All I've ever known. I have to go back."

"You can't save her, you know that, right? We will have to kill her to end this."

"I know." Griffin's shoulders fell. "I know she's gone too far, but I can't leave her alone."

"Then go. I won't stop you because I love Brea, and she would want you to make your own choices. She would never stoop to making decisions for you."

"I love her too. I always have."

"But you're leaving because you've never loved her enough. She thinks you finally made the right choice. She's been advocating for you since the moment you stepped foot in my camp. Once you walk away this time, you won't be able to come back from all you've done. You think you can make amends once you become king, but Gelsi was never yours. You were never meant to sit on a throne. That thirst for power will be your end, brother. I hope for Brea's sake, you figure that out before it's too late."

"I will make this right, Loch. For Brea, I will make it right. That's why I have to go back."

"Well, give your queen a message from me. I'm coming for her. All of us, together and united, we will make her pay for all she's done. To Brea. To Alona and Neeve, Myles and all of Fargelsi."

"Brea is the key," Griffin said. "She is the key to bringing this barrier down. Her magic is strong. Both sides of it, despite Regan's attempts to keep her weak. But she needs to learn how to pull her magic together. You will teach her, but she will need your help, Tierney's too, to bring the barrier down." Griffin stepped up to the barrier and cast his magic against the invisible wall. An opening parted the wall, allowing Griffin to step through.

Lochlan rushed up behind him, casting his magic into the breach. If he could hold it open after Griffin was gone, they could get some of their troops through.

"Don't bother. The barrier recognizes my magic," Griffin said. "Once I'm through, it will close behind me."

Lochlan took another step closer, studying the inside. Griffin's violet magic lit the tunnel, and Lochlan could see every brick, every web of spells interlocking. The sight of it crushed something inside him. The wall was much thicker than he anticipated. All of their efforts thus far had barely scratched the surface.

"Maybe next time I see you will be different," Griffin said as he reached the other side. "Until then, don't take it out on Brea. This is all my fault, and I'm going to try like hell to fix it."

Lochlan jumped back as the tunnel closed, and the barrier sealed him out. Even with all the might of Eldur and Iskalt combined, he was no longer certain it would be enough to conquer this wall.

"It's not entirely his fault, you know?" A strange voice sounded behind him. "My sister can be quite beguiling, and he is just a boy. Your brother is no match for Regan O'Rourke."

"Your sister? Who are you?" A chill ran down Lochlan's spine as he took in the rather broken looking man with the green eyes.

"Brandon O'Rourke. That brother of yours risked everything to get us here. Regan will know what he's done by the time he returns."

"Us?" Lochlan couldn't seem to get his mind to work.

"My daughter rescued me from the Gelsi dungeons and brought me here. She refused to leave without me." Brandon smiled, looking up at the stars. "I never thought I would see the stars again." He turned his gaze back to Lochlan. "Or that I'd see both the Iskalt Princes in love with my Brea."

"I am king," Lochlan said.

"Ah, yes, I did hear about your recent coup against your uncle. Well done, you. Callum O'Shea and Regan were a diabolical pair."

"You should be king of Fargelsi. You're the key." Lochlan took a step toward the man who was the answer to all their problems.

"Me? I'm afraid not. I will never be king. I am no longer strong enough."

"Fargelsi needs a ruler, and it can't be Brea. She's not ready, and she's too much like her mother to rule her father's kingdom. She will be Eldur's greatest queen someday. When she's ready. No one will force her into it before then."

Brandon moved to sit on a boulder, patting the space beside him.

"I was king once. Briefly before my sister usurped me." Lochlan sat beside him. "I understand sibling rivalry among royals, son. I hate everything my sister has done to my people and our kingdom, but she is still my sister. I love her as much as I hate her actions. She must be stopped, but I can't be the one to do it. When I look at her, I will always see my angelic baby sister. She knows that is my weakness."

"How can you forgive her for stealing your life as well as your throne?"

"I can't forgive her, son. But I still love her. With age comes perspective. I've had time to come to terms with my life. Now that I am free... I don't know what my future holds, but I do know one thing. Whatever time I have left I want to spend it getting to know my daughters."

"Daughters?"

Chapter 15

BREA

"Keep going!" Lochlan walked behind the line of Eldurian and Iskaltian soldiers as they all directed their magic at the same section of the barrier. The early light of dawn rose on the horizon, allowing them all to work together for a short time. His Iskaltians had been at it all night, but as soon as the full light of day came, the Eldurians would take over.

Brea watched as Lochlan stepped up beside Tierney, his chest heaving with exhaustion. She could see it, the magic draining from him.

Tierney clenched her teeth, and her silver magic directed the multitude of colors coming from everyone else. Brea pushed her yellow power into Tierney's.

Brea and Tierney shared a look, and Brea stepped away, gesturing for Lochlan to follow her. With his waning power, he had little to add anyway, so she knew he'd follow her.

Finn waited for them near the path back to camp. Brea and Finn were both worried about their friend.

"You need rest, Loch." Finn crossed his arms.

Lochlan sighed. "What we need is to bring the barrier down."

Brea pursed her lips. "Have you been sleeping during the day?" She'd seen him watching the Eldurians while his men and women slept to prepare for another night of magic wielding and pulling the barrier apart thread by thread.

Lochlan shrugged. "I'm fine."

"You're not fine." Finn put a hand on his shoulder and shoved him back.

Lochlan stumbled, his legs unsteady beneath him.

Brea speared him with a glare. "You'll be no good to us when we break this magic if you can't even stand." She pointed to the road. "Call in your Iskaltians. Their magic is done for the day. You all need rest."

Lochlan shook his head, looking to the sky, and for a moment, she thought he was going to argue with her just to argue. She wished he would. That was the Lochlan she once knew. Instead, he turned. "Iskaltians, we're done for the day."

Without another look, he marched down the path, his soldiers stumbling behind him.

Finn wrapped an arm around her shoulders. "He'll be okay."

She sank into his embrace. "But will we? Will he ever look at me again without pain in his eyes?" She lifted her gaze to Finn's. "It's worse than hatred, Finn."

"Lochlan is stubborn."

"No." She shrugged off his arm. "This is more than that. He wants nothing to do with me. It's like..." She sucked in a breath. "He's never going to forgive me, is he?"

"Brea, you know I love you, but did you really think you'd return married to Griff and things would go back to the way they were?"

"I didn't have a choice." She ran a hand through her sweaty hair. "You know that, right?"

"Yes, but knowing something doesn't make it feel any better.

Lochlan lets very few people into his life. He doesn't allow anyone to see who he really is. But he let you. You need to recognize how much it hurts whether you meant to cause that pain or not."

A sigh rattled through her chest, and she found herself missing Griff and his easy ways. The magic inside her wanted to reach across the border spell to find him. At the same time, she realized it should have hurt a lot more than it did when he left. Instead, she'd been unsurprised, unaffected.

An arm slipped through hers, and she smiled weakly at Neeve. She'd stopped worrying about proprieties since Brea returned, instead treating her as a friend.

"Finnegan," Tierney called. "Get over here."

Finn bowed to the women with his trademark grin. "Duty calls."

Neeve giggled after him. "He's kind of ridiculous, isn't he?"

"Always." She pulled Neeve closer into her side as her eyes found a man sitting on the ground near the barrier, his body swaying from exhaustion. "He's been out here since yesterday." With his Fargelsi magic, Brea's father could work on the barrier night or day. Brea pulled Neeve in that direction.

Neeve yanked her back. "I can't."

"Why on earth not?" Brea glanced from Neeve to their father, her eyes widening. He hadn't told her yet.

"He is the king."

"So is Lochlan, but you don't run from him."

Neeve pushed out a breath. "Yes, but Lochlan is the king of Iskalt. Brandon O'Rourke is the lost Fargelsian king. My king."

"And he doesn't bite." Brea laughed. "Come on."

They stopped next to him, but he didn't seem to notice their presence. Brea cleared her throat. "Um, your Majesty." That didn't seem right. "Brandon." Nope. "I don't really know what to call you."

He looked up, opening his mouth to answer her before his eyes rolled into the back of his head, and he fell to the side. Neeve yelped as she jumped toward him, her instinct kicking in.

Brea screamed for help as her father's body started convulsing. Tierney yanked in her magic and ran toward them, dropping to the ground at his side. "Brandon." She shook him before looking to Brea. "Magical poisoning."

"What?" Panic bloomed through her.

With Tierney's magic not directing the others, soldiers reined their own power in and ran toward them.

"He's been sitting here since yesterday, muttering non-stop spells."

Brea remembered what Cait had told her about the first rule of Fargelsian magic. Take care with how much you use at once.

Tierney looked to Brea. "He's used too much. I don't know what we can do for him."

"You mean he's going to die?"

"I don't know." Tears gathered in her eyes. "Probably not, but I don't know!"

"No." Brea kneeled on his opposite side. "My father has survived too much to die now." She leaned down. "Do you hear me, Dad? I don't know you, but you're the only father I have who is worth anything. If you die now, I'll never forgive you." Power coursed through her veins. She'd healed Lochlan once. She could do this now.

Feeling for a pulse, she found none. "This is not your day." She put her hands on his chest, directing her magic straight through his veins.

His body jerked, but his eyes didn't open.

She did it again.

His eyes shot open, and a cry left his lips.

Brea pulled her hands back and stared at her palms. What had she just done? Neeve watched her with wide eyes as if she didn't know her at all.

Tierney sat back on her heels. "He needs rest. We all do." She looked up at the invisible barrier. "This is coming down tomorrow. I can feel it. And we must be at our strongest when it does."

Brea scanned the tired faces of the soldiers who'd spent the past few days doing nothing but using their magic. Tierney was right. They all needed rest.

Brea gestured to Finn and another Eldurian man. "The Fargelsian king needs to get to the healer."

They nodded and lifted him, starting down the path.

Brea's entire body shook as she stood. Neeve wrapped an arm around her waist while Tierney looped their arms together. "You're special, Brea."

"No, I'm not."

"You just saved a king," Neeve whispered.

Brea sighed. "Not the first and probably won't be the last with the way these kings behave."

"Well—" Tierney smiled. "—At least you're modest."

Brea hovered over her father's bed while he slept. Tierney tried to convince her she needed rest, but she couldn't shut her eyes until she knew he was okay.

"Brea?" Neeve's voice came from outside the tent.

"Come in." She looked up as Neeve entered carrying two bowls of beans and salted pork. "You brought us dinner?" Brea had forgotten to eat lunch, and her stomach rumbled at the smell.

Neeve handed her a bowl. "I brought one for his Majesty as well, but—"

"Is that my girl?" Brandon muttered. "My daughter."

"I'm here." Brea reached for his hand.

Brandon's eyes slid open, but they still looked foggy from sleep. "Both of you together." A smile curved his lips.

Neeve froze. "I'm just a palace maid, sire. No one special."

His head thrashed from side to side. "So special."

"We must check his mental state," Neeve whispered.

Brea nodded in agreement, but she knew exactly what her father was trying to say. There would never be a good time for this discussion, but tomorrow they'd venture back into Fargelsi, and no one knew what would happen there. "Neeve, you should sit." Brea patted a spot beside her on the small bench.

Neeve put the bowl in her hands on a table beside the bed and lowered herself next to Brea, a question in her eyes.

Brea took her hand, intertwining their fingers together. "Neeve, what do you know of your parents?"

Her brow furrowed. "My mother died when I was young, but my father is a mystery to me. I was raised at the palace."

Brandon pushed himself up, struggling to sit and meet Neeve's gaze. "I never meant to abandon you."

Neeve went still, not a muscle moving.

Brea squeezed her hand to let her know she was there.

Brandon went on. "I used to visit your mother after you were born. When she died, I made sure you'd be taken care of at the palace. But no one could know your parentage. My sister had grown dangerous. And then she imprisoned me, taking me from you completely."

"You're..." Neeve looked from Brandon to Brea, tears building in her eyes.

"See." Brea nudged her. "You're not just a servant." She smiled. If there was one person who knew what it was like to go from a life of drudgery to the status of a princess in a heartbeat, it was Brea. "We're sisters."

When Brea was young, she'd begged her parents for siblings. They always told her one was enough problems for them.

"Sisters," Neeve whispered, her hand tightening around Brea's. Tears flowed down her face now, and Brea had to wipe her own away.

Brandon's glistening eyes matched theirs. The three of them had been through so much, yet here they sat safe and together with no more lies between them.

"Neeve, you're the Fargelsian heir," Brea whispered.

Neeve shook her head. "I c-can't be."

"But you are." Hadn't Brea fought the same thing? She didn't want to be the queen of Eldur, but she couldn't escape the title of heir.

Brandon sank back on the bed, his strength waning.

Brea wrapped an arm around her sister. "He needs to rest if we are to cross the border tomorrow."

Neeve sniffled and nodded. "Thank you." She directed the words to Brandon. "You... I've had no one in this life. Now..."

He smiled. "I haven't not always known both my girls, but I have always loved them."

Brea wiped the back of her hand over her face as they left the tent behind. Neeve didn't follow her, instead staying behind to watch over their father like Brea had done most of the day.

She wasn't watching where she was going when she ran into a hard chest and stumbled back. Strong hands gripped her arms. Hands she'd know the feel of anywhere.

"Are you okay?" Lochlan asked.

She dried her face and stepped away. "These are happy tears, I promise."

"Brea." Myles bounced toward them, breaking the tension between Brea and Lochlan. He pulled her into a crushing hug. "There there. Whatever Lochlan has done now can't be all that bad."

She pushed him away with a laugh. "It wasn't Loch. Just my father." That felt weird to say, but she liked how it felt on her tongue.

Myles grinned. No one had been happier for her than him. "I like that Gelsi king dude. Much better than this Iskaltian grump."

"Iskaltian king right here," Lochlan grumbled.

Brea hid her smile behind a cough. "Did you get some sleep today?"

"Oh, yes." Myles answered for him. "I made him snuggle me. He slept like a baby."

Lochlan's jaw tensed. "That didn't happen."

Myles shrugged. "We're coming up with battle plans for once we cross the border. Loch came to me for my extensive knowledge."

Lochlan didn't dignify that with a response.

Brea's brow arched. "Oh yeah?"

He nodded. "We'll be fighting with magic, right?" He tapped the side of his head. "I have all the Harry Potter tricks stored right here."

Lochlan grunted. "We won't be fighting in the department of mysteries. Think more north of the wall."

Myles eyes lit up. "Even better."

Brea crossed her arms. "Too bad you won't be there."

All laughter faded from Myles' eyes. "If you're going, so am I."

"Myles, you're human."

"And what? That's a bad thing now?"

Brea sighed. "No, but you don't have magic. This isn't a fight for you."

Myles started to say something else, but Lochlan cut him off. "The boy comes." The glare he shot Brea should have frozen her, instead it sent fire blazing through her. Who did he think he was?

"Myles isn't your friend." She narrowed her eyes. "His safety is my responsibility."

"The boy comes," he repeated before turning on his heel and walking away. Myles followed him without a word.

Brea rubbed the back of her neck as she watched them walk side by side.

"I think we've been replaced." Finn stepped up to her side, laughter in his voice.

"Well, if I could choose me or Myles to be friends with, I'd definitely choose Myles. But I don't know why he's so attached to Loch."

Finn laughed. "Yes, you do."

"Fine, I do." Lochlan was broody, sure, but his intensity was like a forcefield drawing people to him.

"You look weary."

"I am." She rubbed her eyes. She'd meant to sleep, but the opportunity hadn't come. Her exhaustion was the least of her issues. The last few months had left her with a bone-deep weariness. Nothing was ever easy. There were people to impress, others to save. Secrets to unravel, others to bury. "Will this ever truly be over?"

"I hope so." He bumped her shoulder. "But then you will become queen one day. With Lochlan as king of Iskalt, we just need to find a Fargelsian ruler to keep peace."

"Being queen sounds exhausting. Is it wrong of me to want to find a cottage somewhere and live alone for the rest of my days?" She thought of Griff's idyllic cottage and what kind of life could be created there.

"Not wrong to dream of it, but you were not born to disappear. Some people have a greater destiny."

That was what she was afraid of. Destiny. Fate. Whatever fae liked to call her lack of choice, it was coming for her, and she wouldn't be able to escape it. Well, unless she died in the coming battles. Then she'd escape it all. A laugh bubbled out of her, and she couldn't stop it. And then another followed.

Finn gave her a wry smile as Alona joined them. "What's so funny?" she asked.

"Just death." Brea couldn't get any other words out through her totally inappropriate laughter.

Alona stared at her in shock. "I have never been more thankful for the switch so I didn't have to grow up in the human realm. Is everyone there this strange?"

"I doubt it," Finn said. "Brea is probably odd even there."

Brea nodded, wheezing as she tried to catch her breath. How did she explain her thoughts that led to the laughter? Fear. That's what it was. She was terrified of the coming days. But she was a princess and heir. She had to put on a brave face. Straightening, she breathed deeply. "We're going to survive this." She hoped.

Finn wrapped an arm around Alona, dropping a kiss on the top of her head, but he didn't respond. Saying the words made the danger real, turning the fear of the unknown into reality.

There was no work on the barrier magic that evening. They were close, Brea could feel it. Now that Tierney's people had been here a few days, and Lochlan's were rested, nothing could stop them.

At least, that was what Brea hoped.

Brea surveyed the fires spread across camp in the waning light. She sat with Alona, Tierney, Neeve, and Brandon—who'd recovered enough to leave the tent. This was her family, the one she didn't know she'd been searching for her entire life. Her other mother wasn't here, needing to be in Eldur for their people, but Brea felt her presence in the love surrounding her.

Myles sat with Finn and Lochlan around a nearby fire, the three of them rolling with laughter. It was the first time Brea had seen Lochlan smile since returning. Myles had that effect on people.

"Faolan won't believe her eyes." Tierney smiled at Brandon. "I don't think a day passes she doesn't think of you."

He stared into the flames. "Faolan Cahill was the best friend I ever had. I should like to see her again." Brandon was her mom's Myles—except Brea couldn't imagine having a kid with Myles.

"Once we defeat Regan, the realms will have peace for the first time in a long time." Tierney gripped Alona's hand on one side and Brea's on the other.

"I wish you'd stay behind once the barrier is down." Brea shot both Tierney and Alona looks. Tierney had the power to fight in the battles, but she was too important to Brea to lose.

And Alona... she was human like Myles.

Tierney's lips tipped into a sad smile. "It is my duty to fight."

"And mine." Alona leaned forward against her knees. "I'm not useless, you know."

"We know that." Brea would never think Alona was useless. "But you and Myles don't have magic."

"I've already argued with Finn about this, and he couldn't change my mind, so neither can you. I might be human, but this realm is just as much mine as anyone's. Don't I deserve to fight for it as much as you?" Brea heard the true meaning in her words. As much as a girl who didn't grow up here.

She started to say something else, but Neeve cut in. "Yes, you do." She met Brea's gaze. "You do not get to make decisions for others on what their lives are worth. If Alona wants to risk hers for the world she loves, then it is her choice. And Myles, he isn't fighting for this world, but for the people in it. You've been in Fargelsi for months, Brea, and he has spent all that time forming bonds. That is just as important as a connection to the land. If they want the right to fight for those they love, you need to let them."

Beside her, Brandon smiled. "Spoken like a princess."

Neeve shrank back into herself as if embarrassed at the praise.

Brea didn't respond for a long moment as she considered her sister's words. Her shoulders deflated. "Neeve is right. Our choices matter, and I have no right to take yours away."

Alona nodded. "Or Myles'."

Brea sighed. "I won't stop trying to protect you both, but my..." she smiled. "... sister speaks of everything I once believed in." She paused, her gaze falling on Alona. "You're my sister too, you know that, right?"

Alona reached across Tierney to grip Brea's arm. "And you know I believe in you, right?"

Neeve nodded. "We both do. You are going to lead us, Brea. Give us hope." She gestured to the tired troops huddling around the flames. "They need it."

She was right. Tomorrow, when a new day dawned, they'd work once again to bring the barrier down and eventually cross into a land they didn't know if they'd ever leave. If they didn't defeat Regan, she'd trap them within her borders like she had her people.

Brea stood and brushed the dust off her pants. Reaching a hand down to Neeve, she smiled. "We must show a united fae realm. You are the rightful Fargelsian heir."

Neeve took her hand and pulled herself up before looking down at her father. Brandon shook his head. "I'll let the young people of our future be the inspiration. They don't need old men and women like us." He looked to Tierney, and she laughed, also waving off a hand from Brea.

Brea moved around Tierney, looking down at Alona.

Alona's eyes widened. "I'm only a princess until this is over and I become a servant."

Brea leaned down. "Not on my watch." She pulled on Alona's arm until she stood.

Neeve and Alona followed Brea to the clearing in the center of the fires. "Lochlan," she called as she passed. "Get over here."

He jogged to catch up with her, his ever-present scowl flitting across his face. "What are we doing?"

"Giving our people a reason to fight."

Brea stopped in front of the mass of soldiers, Iskaltian on one side and Eldurian on the other. For a moment, no words came to her. She closed her eyes, drawing on the strength she'd gathered through months in captivity.

Opening her eyes, she knew exactly what she had to do.

All chatter died down as she lifted a hand, pointing in the direction of the border. "My husband is across that border sitting in a palace surrounded by finery that has been gathered on the backs of trapped Fargelsian citizens." She had their rapt attention. "There will be no secrets between me and you. For the Iskaltians who might not know, I am Breanna O'Rourke Cahill." She embraced the name, choosing to honor both her parents, shedding once and for all her Robinson past. "Heir to the Eldurian throne. My husband is Griffin O'Shea."

Muttering surrounded her, but she couldn't hear their words.

"I tell you this because I love him, but I did not choose to love him." She chanced a glance at Lochlan whose jaw was tense. "Just like the Fargelsian people did not choose to remain trapped within their borders. It is our duty to free them."

A few soldiers cheered.

"It will not come without cost. Not all of us will make it out alive, and we could very well end up trapped alongside the Fargelsians. Yet, we go anyway because that is who we are." She pounded a single hand against her chest. "It is not who I am. I know what you've heard about me, the princess raised as a human, but there is one thing inside me that is very much fae. I will not give up."

More cheers.

"I will fight for you."

Louder this time.

"Just like I know you will fight for me when we break through that wall."

She waited for the cheers to die down and stepped back between Lochlan and Neeve, taking their hands in hers. Lochlan held Alona's hand on the other side.

Brea grinned as she looked down the line at her friends and turned back to the soldiers who'd go into battle with them. "This is the future of the fae." They lifted their hands. "Not Regan and her barrier spells keeping people out, keeping us separated. The kingdoms are meant to help each other, to rely on each other. We will bring about that future."

They kept their arms raised as the crowd of soldiers cheered, probably imagining peace coming to the fae.

A peace they'd fight for.

A peace Brea would make sure they won.

Lochlan released her hand and walked away, past the fires illuminating the night.

As the soldiers went back to their chatter, much more joyous than before, Brea followed Lochlan to the barrier and the boulder they'd spoken on the week before.

He stopped with his back to her. "I saw Griff when he left."

She sucked in a breath, not wanting to let him into her mind any more than she already had. "And you..."

"I let him go."

"Why?"

He kept his back to her. "Because he didn't love you enough to stay."

No, Lochlan had that wrong. Griff loved her so much he chose her over Regan when he helped her escape. He just didn't love *himself* enough to stay.

And Lochlan... "He knew the magic wasn't enough."

Lochlan turned, eying her like one would eye a predator—with distrust. She expected him to ask her what she meant, and she was prepared to tell him. No matter how much it hurt, or how impossible it was supposed to be, the marriage magic couldn't stop her feelings for Lochlan.

But he didn't ask for the words. Instead, he got to her in two long strides and crashed his lips against hers, stealing everything she'd wanted to say.

Pain throbbed through her, intensifying with each moment, but she kissed him back with everything she had. "I thought you were letting go of me," she whispered.

"And I thought you didn't want to be a queen."

"I don't."

He brushed her hair back from her face. "That's a shame. When you spoke tonight, I wanted to follow you. No matter what else I felt, no matter how much pain, you are my queen."

"You're a king. You aren't supposed to follow anyone."

"Ask me if I care." He kissed her again, this time slower and more deliberate, savoring the moment they both knew might never come again.

The pain laced through her heart until she cried out and stumbled back. "Loch." It magnified, threatening to break her in two. "W-we can't."

"I know." He stepped further away from her as if distance would lessen the pain. "I just had to know what it felt like one last time."

"What?" She breathed through the pain.

"Hope."

Tears flooded her eyes as she watched him walk away. He was right. They might defeat Regan and make it out of this alive, but there could never be hope for them.

Not as long as the magic tied her to Griff.

Chapter 16

BREA

"You almost had it that time, Brea," Tierney said. "Try it one more time before we give the wall another go."

"The two sides of my magic are so different, Mom, I just don't know how to bring them together. One is all about emotions, and the other is all about intent. In my head they're entirely separate things. I don't know how to think of them as one."

"Brandon, are we asking too much of her?" Tierney turned to Brea's father.

"It's difficult for us to know what she needs. In theory, it sounds easy, but in practice, our girl is all on her own, I'm afraid. All we can do is guide her the best we can."

"Take a deep breath, Brea," Alona said. "You've got this."

"Emotion and intent." Brea shook out her hands and stretched to loosen her tense muscles. "Just bring them together. Like peanut butter and jelly."

"Does she ever make sense?" Brandon asked, looking to Neeve for advice.

"No." Neeve, Alona, and Tierney said together before dissolving into a fit of giggles.

"I can hear you, you know." Brea couldn't help her smile. She loved her growing family. Even the ones she didn't know well yet.

"Ignore your sisters," Tierney said. "Focus, and just let your instincts guide you this time. Trust your magic. It knows what to do."

"Try closing your eyes," Neeve offered. "That has always helped me."

Brea took a deep breath and closed her eyes. wrapping her fist around the rock in her hand. She was supposed to crush it using both sides of her magic at the same time. But her human brain wanted to use one or the other to accomplish the simple task.

Calling on her emotions using her Eldur magic didn't help because she was indifferent about the rock. "The rock is Loch," she muttered gripping the stone tighter in her hand. He had barely talked to her since the kiss. Heat scorched her body at the memory of his lips on hers, and the pain it caused. The hopelessness of it all crashed over her again.

Yellow sparks crackled beneath her skin as her fire magic responded to her emotions. Focusing, she held onto the magic, keeping her emotions focused on the overwhelming sense of loss she felt losing both O'Shea's in one fell swoop.

She imagined the rock represented the sadness she felt. And then she imagined how it would free her if that sadness was destroyed. "*Springa*," she uttered the spell her father taught her, sending all her fear and sadness into the stone in her hand.

Energy surged within her, and Brea's eyes popped opened. Instinct took over, and she tossed the rock into the air. Golden yellow light burst from the rock, shattering it into powdery sand that rained down on them.

"You did it." Tierney beamed with pride, pulling her into her arms. "That's my girl."

Brea slumped against her mom.

"Are you all right, darling?" Tierney gave her a worried look.

"Yeah. I'm good." Brea tried to stand on shaky legs. "That took it out of me." She gazed out toward the wall where the Eldurians and Iskalt soldiers waited for her to make the final push that was supposed to get them through the wall today. But a tiny rock just kicked her butt.

"Hey, look at me, Brea." Tierney tilted her chin up. "No one expects you to go out there and be perfect. And you won't be alone. We're all right here with you."

Brea took a deep breath and nodded. "But what do I do?" Brea turned to her mother, hoping she would have the answers. "I know nothing about magic compared to you, yet somehow I'm supposed to be the key to bringing this barrier down?"

"All you can do is try. Go out there and do exactly what you just did. That wall is just a bigger rock. We will follow your lead, and our magic will strengthen yours so it will not cost you as much. And if it does prove to be too much, so be it. We'll move on to plan B."

"What's plan B?"

"I don't know yet, but we'll cross that bridge when we get there."

"I'm glad you're here, Mom." Brea clutched Tierney's hand, grasping for her father's with the other. "I wish Mother was here, too." She cast a look back at Alona and Neeve.

"Faolan is so proud of you, Brea." She gave her hand a gentle squeeze. "No matter what happens, we are all proud of you." They marched toward the wall where every magic wielder in camp waited in the early dawn light.

Lochlan and Finn were already busy studying the wall. With Brandon, Tierney, and Lochlan at her side, she likely had the most powerful magic wielders in all the fae realms, barring Regan herself.

"You can do this, Brea." Myles called from the hillside as they passed. She gave him a watery smile, grateful the healers would watch over him this time. They were prepared to cast a shield over Myles and Alona if they had a repeat mishap with the magic again.

"All right, everyone. Let's do this." Brea clapped her hands and moved to stand beside Lochlan with Neeve beside her.

"You were right, you know," Lochlan said.

"Which time? I get confused with all the other times I've been right." Her mouth twitched into a rueful smile as Lochlan maintained his composure. Mostly. He didn't always smile with his mouth. Sometimes she could see his amusement reflected in the depths of his dark blue eyes.

"You, me, Alona, and now Neeve, we are the future of our world. Let's make it a good one."

"I can get on board with that plan." Brea shielded her eyes, trying to see past the spelled border to catch a glimpse of Loch Villandi in the distance. "What about you, sis?" She turned to Neeve.

"Your Majesties, I'm just a servant. That's all I've ever been. I am not fit to be a princess of anything."

"I should introduce you to past me from like six months ago," Brea said. "She was so where you are right now. But here I am, present me, about to go remove a queen from her throne."

"You say the oddest things." Neeve laughed. "But somehow you manage to say all the right things when it really matters. I'll never be like that."

"Neeve, you will make a fine princess," Lochlan said. "You risked your life to help your sister escape even before you knew you were sisters."

"And you worked for years right under Regan's nose, helping so many people escape while you stayed behind. That sounds like a princess to me. One who puts her people above herself. And besides, you'll have Dad to help show you the ropes. And Lona."

"And you?" Neeve took her hand.

"Oh, I'm no role model." Brea chuckled. "Everyone keeps telling me I'm a princess and heir to kingdoms, but I still don't feel like a princess."

"Here's a secret, girls." Tierney leaned in to whisper. "You never will."

"It's time," Finn said. "The Eldurians are ready." The faintest light illuminated the horizon. Now was the time to strike when everyone present was in possession of their magic.

Brea, Lochlan, and Tierney stepped toward the barrier, their magic sparking and crackling at their fingertips.

"You first, darling. Just like we practiced." Tierney nudged her to continue.

Brea's emotions were all over the place, but like before, she focused on her warring feelings for Lochlan. Casting her yellow magic at the wall, it bounced and sparkled in the darkness as it shimmered over the barrier's surface. Envisioning the barrier as she had the rock, she visualized her intent. The two sides of her magic burned within her.

Brea nodded to Lochlan, and he cast his magic toward the invisible wall, his blue light dancing with her yellow. In so many ways they were opposites, yet somehow together they made a beautiful display of magic. Tierney's silver magic joined them next as hundreds of soldiers followed their lead. Each thread of magic united with hers, making Brea feel stronger than ever. Working together as a community they could do this. They could conquer Regan and her wall.

Brea looked to her father and her sister and counted down. "Three, two, one. *Springa,*" they each spoke the word of power in a strong, clear voice. The Magic of Eldur, Iskalt, and Fargelsi came together as one. Brea held their magic, guiding it with her own. She could feel the vibrations of it as she worked together with Lochlan to unravel Regan's massive spell.

Sweat rolled down Brea's face as the sky grew lighter with each passing moment. The magic burned her from the inside out, but she held on, focusing on controlling her emotions and her intent, visualizing them as two sides of the same coin. She couldn't hold on to it much longer. It was too much magic for one person.

Closing her eyes, Brea took a deep breath and pushed through the blazing heat, guiding her combined magic toward the barrier. Golden yellow light burst from her somewhere deep inside, crashing against the invisible barrier. The ground shook from the impact, and a clap of thunder echoed across the sky.

"Hold the line!" Lochlan called to their soldiers. "Steady, Brea."

Lines of yellow light sparked across her hands, and her legs trembled from the weight of so much magic. A rainbow of colors illuminated the boundary spell with lines of light crisscrossing like a billion tiny threads. Each of those threads snapped like rubber bands stretched too thin.

The wall fought back, refusing to fall.

"I can't hold on much longer." Brea's teeth rattled with the effort of speaking. The magic was pulling her apart. She was going to snap apart just like one of those whispy threads of magic.

"Hold on, Brea," Lochlan said. "Just a moment longer."

Too many emotions swelled inside her, and there was no room for them. She couldn't breathe.

Dawn broke over the horizon, and the sun shed its light on the trembling wall. A surge of strength rushed through Brea, and all the Eldurians around her. She gave one final shove, thrusting the magic toward the wall. As she let go, Brea fell to the ground.

Staring at the wall, for one horrible moment she thought she failed, but in the next instant, the barrier spell exploded in a thousand colors of light before it vanished, and the crystal clear waters of Loch Villandi shone in the distance. Like a chain of dominos, the entire barrier spell failed, sending an explosion of light along the border of Fargelsi. In no time, the whole kingdom would know they were free.

Brea screamed in triumph, slamming her fist against the ground. She rocked back on her knees, unable to stand.

"You did it." Lochlan crouched down beside her, but Brea shook her head.

"No, Loch. We did it. All of us, together."

Brea was exhausted, they all were, but they had to move quickly before Regan had a chance to react. Following Queen Tierney, their bone-weary army made their way into Fargelsi on horseback.

Brea wanted to cry when they reached the shores of Loch Villandi only to find they either had to traverse the beautiful, yet dangerous waters of the lake, or make their way across the swampy plains of the Vatlands. Again. It was slow going, but the trip across was shorter here where the Southern Vatlands gave way to the fertile rolling hills of Fargelsi.

"I hope I never lay eyes on that swamp again." Brea urged her horse forward. The Eldurian and Iskaltian soldiers were awestruck by the beauty of Fargelsi. Most had never seen it.

"I didn't have much of a view from my prison cell," Myles said, "but this place is gorgeous. Look at these flowers." He turned toward Brea, but she smacked his hands forcing him to drop the vibrant purple flowers. "Ow! What was that for?"

"Touch nothing. It's like Australia here, everything's trying to kill you."

"Not quite everything." Neeve took Myles' hand, checking for any signs of irritation from the deadly flower. "But the general rule here is the more beautiful a thing is, the more deadly it likely is. So, you probably shouldn't touch anything without making sure it's safe first."

"Same goes for you, Lona." Brea turned worried eyes on her human sister.

"We will be fine, Brea. You can't worry about everyone, or you'll never have another moment's peace."

"Just, please be careful. Both of you. All of you." Her emotions bubbled up to the surface, and she thought she might burst into tears right here. "I can't bear to lose any of you." She returned to her horse and pulled herself up into the saddle. "I'm going to see what's going on at the front."

A sea of horses and soldiers fanned out around her. Many more than there should be. Brea shielded her eyes, but she couldn't see who Loch, her mom, and Finn were talking to. Easing her horse into a canter, she rode ahead.

"Captain Donavan?" Brea slid from her mount when she realized what his presence meant. "I'm happy to see you've brought reinforcements, but how?" She scanned the unfamiliar faces of his militia. Hundreds of them.

Tierney turned toward her with a smile. "Our Captain of the guard has been very busy recruiting among the villages and towns of Fargelsi. It seems there is much unrest in the farthest reaches of Gelsi. We've spread word that their king is alive, and that he has two heirs to strengthen him. Your people are eager to stand with you, and your father and sister."

Brandon and Neeve made their way through the crowd. Men and women bent their knees, bowing their heads for their rightful king and his heir. There was something so natural, so right about the scene before her.

"She will make an amazing queen someday." Brea smiled through her tears, watching her sister greet their people. "Captain Donovan, do you have a map of Fargelsi?"

"No, your Majesty, but I have come to know this area quite well recently. The militia have taught me how to move across the kingdom without the queen's notice."

"I believe we should be just a few hours march to the Dragur Forest. Regan will know by now what we've done, and she's going to come for us. We don't want to meet her inside the forest."

"My thoughts exactly." He gave her a courtly nod. "I am familiar with Dragur. The main road just south of here will lead us directly there."

"After a short rest to regroup, we will head out." Lochlan turned to rejoin his soldiers.

Brea's shoulders fell as she watched him go. She had too much on her mind to be worried about him not speaking to her. Not at a time like this. They were about to march into battle. She had more important things to consider. But like always, as he walked away, he took a piece of her with him.

Brea and her sisters rode with Tierney and Finn at the head of the Eldur army. Lochlan and his troops led the way, and the Fargelsi militia brought up the rear with Captain Donovan and Brandon.

"This place is nothing but hills and valleys. It all looks the same," Myles muttered as they crested yet another lush green hill along the road to the Dragur Forest. But it was all too familiar scenery to Brea. She couldn't fathom how much had happened in the months since she'd arrived in the fae world. Not too long ago, she'd traveled this very road with Griffin, off to meet her aunt, the Queen of exotic Fargelsi. That Brea no longer existed. The human girl who had no idea what life had in store for her. She supposed she would always feel like a human girl, but now she was more fae than human. Stronger and much more capable than the girl who hadn't believed in herself.

Brea looked down into the valley below, not surprised to see Regan and her army waiting for them at the mouth of the forest. Her troops stood in perfect rows, battle ready and well rested. But far too few for the numbers they had on their side. Mercifully, dusk was upon them, breathing new life into the Iskaltians and giving the Eldurians a final surge of strength in the fading light of the evening sun.

Without a word, Brea moved her horse though the haphazard rows of weary Eldur and Iskalt soldiers to Lochlan's side. Tierney followed, leaving Neeve with Myles and Alona.

"Careful daughter, she will try to bait you." Tierney's eyes danced with the silver light of her immeasurable power.

Brea nodded, not sure what their next move would be.

"Brea." Lochlan moved beside her. "Don't look." He tried to block her view of the commotion below.

"What?" She craned her neck to see around him. He tried to shield her from it, but it was too late. All the color drained from her face as she laid eyes on her husband. Griff kneeled in front of Regan, not forty feet from where she stood now.

"Griff?" Her mind tried to reconcile what her eyes saw. His beautiful face was bloodied and bruised, and his hair hung limp around his slumped shoulders.

"Brea, my dear, you have something that belongs to me," Regan's voice reached them across the valley, magically amplified by her formidable power, but there was something off in her tone. "Several somethings, in fact."

"Brea, she's goading you," Lochlan warned, trying to tear her attention away from her tortured husband. "She knows the marriage bond will make you go to him. I need you to fight it, Brea. You're stronger than she knows."

Brea ignored him, nudging her horse forward another step.

"Escort the prisoner you stole from my dungeons back to me now, and Griffin will not be harmed further." Her voice grew louder, like it spiraled out of her control. "I'll even make you a deal, Brea darling. Come home with me now and send your... friends back where they belong. Come home and let me care for you. You shouldn't be out in here in your condition. It's not good for the baby."

Brea felt Lochlan flinch at her side, but she only had eyes for Griffin. He met her gaze with a nod. He was still with her.

She cocked her head, the menacing set of her mouth betraying the calm she forced into her tone. "Come home, and when you deliver my heir, you may leave Fargelsi and never return. You can go home to your mothers and your Iskalt lover. Or... you can try to defeat me right here, right now, but you will never win, Brea." She laughed, sounding like every insane evil queen Brea had seen in movies. "You are just a child, playing with magic you don't understand. I am the most powerful queen our world has ever known. You cannot hope to best me, even with your numbers."

Green fire swirled in her hands as Regan chanted a spell Brea couldn't hear. As she laid her hands on Griffin's shoulders, her magic shot through him. Griffin's tortured screams lit a fire inside Brea, like an echo of his pain.

Lochlan tried to talk her down, but she couldn't hear him over Griffin and the tug of their marriage bond inside her. Her husband needed her.

Snatching the dagger from Lochlan's hip, Brea screamed a battle cry and charged across the valley, Tierney and Finn followed with the might of the Eldur army behind them.

CHAPTER 17

LOCHLAN

Lochlan stared after Brea for a moment before sending his men to follow her. He charged down the hillside, terror lodged in his throat as he followed the woman he loved into the fray of battle. She was too brave for her own good. Too noble. Always fighting for those she loved to the detriment of her own well being. She didn't know how to use the blade in her hand, but she lashed out with her magic, taking care of herself as she pursued her enemy with single-minded focus. Lochlan no longer cared if she was married to his brother. He needed this woman in his life. Whether as a lover, wife, or friend, it didn't matter as long as she counted him among the people she would go to battle for.

He would not let her face Regan alone.

"*Svero!*" Brea shouted, striking with her magic and landing her blow like a sword in Regan's side.

Regan screamed, cursing a string of spells in retaliation.

Brea braced for the impact, but Lochlan threw a shield up

between Brea and her crazed aunt. The spells bounced off his shield like raindrops.

"*Blaedir,*" Brea countered, landing her spell before Regan threw up a shield of her own.

Ribbons of Brea's Eldur magic wrapped around Regan a moment before blood seeped through her white dress where the two sides of Brea's magic touched her.

"Who taught you the language of power?" Regan snarled. "My worthless ward?" She lashed out at Griffin, still chained and on his knees as the battle raged around them. Regan couldn't have expected them to arrive with such a force. She would lose this battle, and if they played their cards right, Brea's father would sit on the Fargelsi throne again before sundown.

Griffin slumped over into the grass, passed out from whatever torture Regan put him through.

"You've always underestimated me, Regan." Brea circled her aunt, putting herself between Griffin and the queen. "I am far more capable than you know."

Tierney and Finn moved in to circle behind Regan, each ready to strike when needed. But Regan stood between them and Brea.

The queen's soldiers closed in on Brea as she had her back to the melee. Urging his horse forward, Lochlan put himself between the Gelsi soldier's and their spells, and Brea, refusing to let their war magic touch her. There were six of them. Lochlan clashed swords with the nearest soldier, gliding his blade across the man's neck. Turning to face the other five, he found seven inching their way closer.

"Loch," Griffin groaned. "Get me out of these chains."

Lochlan ignored him. Pressing his Iskalt magic against his circling enemies, holding them back so they couldn't reach Brea.

"When the barrier came down, all those spells crashed back into Regan, all that magic. She's lost her mind, Loch. I didn't think she'd hurt Brea before—or me—but this isn't the same woman. Brea needs help."

"She's never needed help a day in her life," Lochlan snarled at his brother as he lunged with his sword, separating one of the queen's men from the herd. The man pulled Lochlan from his horse, putting them on an even playing field for a moment before Lochlan crushed his spine with a sweep of his magic. "That's the difference between you and me. You coddle her, thinking she's too soft for this world." Loch heaved another bloodied soldier off his back. "I always saw her. The real Brea. And she's stronger than you know."

She was pregnant. The pain of that knowledge raced through him, fueling his magic as he grappled with his opponent. Lochlan's blue magic covered him in a sheen of light, the swords and daggers of his enemies glancing off him before they could land their blows.

"Let me fight, Loch!" Griffin screamed, kicking out at a soldier raining down sizzling hot bolts of magic on him.

With a roar of frustration, Lochlan brought down his sword against the chains holding his brother, hacking away at the spell that strengthened them, but Gelsi spells were no match for his ice magic.

Griffin rolled to his knees, too weak to fight but too stubborn to walk away. Lochlan tossed his brother a dagger, and together they swept the queen's guard into a retreat—none of them loyal enough to sacrifice their lives for hers.

"She's *my* wife, Loch."

Lochlan cursed, whirling around, he slammed his fist into his brother's already bruised and swollen face. Griffin fell to the ground, scrambling to get away from Loch. "She was never yours, brother. You lost her with the first lie you uttered."

"I lied to protect her. She knows that." Griffin lunged at Lochlan, grabbing him around the middle and tackling him to the ground. "She doesn't need you making her feel guilty for the choices she made." Griffin grappled with Lochlan and landed a punch to his jaw.

Lochlan hurled Griffin off of him, letting him land with a thud on the hard ground. Lochlan stood, spitting blood on the ground beside his brother's head. "I know her better than you do. She's never loved you, and she never will love you. The bond you share with her is a twisted perversion of what love is supposed to be—and it will never be enough for her." Lochlan left him to fend for himself. It was up to Griffin which side he would ultimately choose.

With a groan, Lochlan turned to find a sea of blood and magic as soldiers battled on all sides. They were driving Regan's army back into the forest. They were winning, but scanning through the chaos, he couldn't find Brea anywhere.

Lunging back into the fray, he cursed himself for letting Griffin distract him from what was important. He hacked his way through the battle, pleased to see Regan's men losing at every turn.

As he charged toward the Dragur Forest, Lochlan caught sight of Brea. He was relieved and proud to see her holding her own against Regan, but Regan was toying with her. It was only a matter of time before the cornered queen made a desperate move.

Two Fargelsian soldiers wearing Regan's colors blocked his view of Brea. Raising his sword, Lochlan channeled his magic, striking out against his foes. He could take two at once, and they would regret ever daring to stand between him and the woman he loved.

Chapter 18

BREA

"Brea!"

Brea whirled around to find Griff pushing himself to his feet. Blood ran from a gash on his cheek, a river of life flowing down his beautiful skin.

The magic inside of her wanted to go to him, to save him. But none of this would end if she didn't stop her aunt.

An Iskaltian soldier ran at Griff, and Brea sent a wave of her waning Eldurian magic toward him. He flew through the air, landing on the ground with a thud.

"You get *one*, Griff!" She couldn't let his fate distract her from saving all the fae realm. Husband or not, he hadn't been on their side until Regan turned on him. Her eyes scanned the fight, looking for the people who'd been in this with her since the moment she was put into that jail cell in the human realm.

Lochlan grappled with two Fargelsian soldiers at once, their magic pounding against each other.

Myles and Alona held their swords aloft, but Finn focused his energy on shielding them from the magic they couldn't match.

Neeve rushed through the battle with their father at her side and Fargelsian villagers at their back, hacking their way to Regan.

"Brea, watch out!" Captain Donovan called just in time for her to see a Fargelsian noble she recognized from the Beltane festival during her first captivity. Lord Bainebridge ran for her, his sword held above his head as his lips muttered the words that would draw his magic forth. A spiral of light encompassed Brea, swirling around her until it was all she could see.

Her mind turned over, trying to find a word to help her escape Bainebridge's power, but she was trapped, and he hadn't stopped running.

Bending her knees, she readied the sword that still felt too heavy in her hands. "You can do this, Brea. You aren't a Robinson, a worthless coward. You were born of the house of Cahill, a fae." She'd grown out of the habit of talking to herself, but in the brief moments she waited for her attacker, seeing nothing but a bright light, she was all she had.

She closed her eyes to block out the light. "*Heyra*," she whispered, opening her ears to the sounds around her. The footsteps running toward her sounded like an elephant clomping through the forest.

Wind rustled through the trees, whistling past the magic in her eyes.

And the sun... it was like she could hear it sinking on the horizon, taking the Eldurian's magic with it.

Bits of her power faded away, leaving only the Fargelsian part behind. It tried to grab onto her Eldurian power, but there was no time. For now, it would have to be enough.

The steps grew closer and still, she didn't open her eyes. As he swung his sword in a giant arc, she heard it swish through the air and tilted her body out of the way. The sword cut through the light encompassing her, shattering the magic.

The battle crashed in around her, and her eyes sprang open just in time to find the large man preparing to strike again. She heard every move he made in advance, every shuffle of his feet, every time his grip shifted on the sword.

He swiped at her legs, muttering another spell. This time, she jumped, avoiding both the magic and the sword. Her movement threw him off balance, and she advanced, pulling in all her power.

The Eldurian magic that she thought had disappeared with the sun flooded her veins, brought back to life by her Fargelsian side. She twisted it, intertwining the strands around each other until the magic was one. Emotion and intent.

"*Haust*," she said. Fall. Bainebridge cried out as his legs collapsed beneath him.

She prepared another spell, one she couldn't take back. The helpless Fargelsian noble stared up at her, fear entering his gaze. Before she uttered another word, he jerked, and his head bent to an unnatural angle before he went still.

Anger burned through Brea as she looked to Lochlan who stood nearby looking at the same man. "He was mine."

There was nothing smug about his expression like she'd have expected from Griff or even Finn, nothing excited. Lochlan didn't thrive on battle, he didn't want to fight. The blood splattered across his jacket was as much a burden as anything else.

His strained eyes met hers, a thousand emotions in their depths. "I did it so you didn't have to."

Griff stumbled toward them, his eyes flicking from Brea to Lochlan. But this wasn't the time for obnoxious love triangles or brothers who couldn't see eye to eye. For the first time, they were all on the same side.

Griff wiped a hand across his bloodied face, his eyes widening at what he saw in the distance. He took off running, well half-running and half-stumbling. Brea didn't see what had him so scared until she caught sight of Myles and Alona standing back to back, no magic shield protecting them. Two humans among a sea of fae.

Finn fought to get to them, but his magic left with the sun.

Fargelsians closed in around them, and Brea let the magic inside her rise, bubbling to her fingertips. Before she could release it, Griff barreled into two Fargelsian soldiers, knocking them to the ground. He rolled off them and jumped to his feet with surprising agility in his state. Now, only Griff stood between the Fargelsians and the humans.

He brandished his sword as he released Iskaltian magic the Fargelsians batted away.

Brea let her anger reach its breaking point, and her Eldurian magic returned, pulled from the darkness by the other side of her power. It poured out of her, searing into every enemy soldier circling her best friend and sister. Today was not the day she'd lose them. Not after everything they'd been through.

The soldiers dropped to the ground like bowling pins, and Brea's chest heaved as Griff fell to his knees.

Alona and Myles helped him to his feet, and Brea couldn't tear her eyes from them.

"Fargelsians!" Neeve's voice boomed over the remaining soldiers, sounding more like a princess than the servant she claimed she was. "Your rightful king has returned! Drop your weapons. I am King Brandon's heir, and together we will protect you."

Brea's gaze found her sister, amazed that she could embrace her duty after only days when Brea herself still didn't want her throne.

"Where's Regan?" She said to no one in particular. They'd been separated in the fight, but she couldn't have gotten far.

Around her, Fargelsian soldiers who'd been fighting them only moments ago dropped their weapons and lowered themselves to their knees.

Neeve continued speaking, using a Fargelsian spell to amplify her voice, letting it wrap around the soldiers captivated by her every word. "Your queen has kept you prisoner, forced you to fight for her, and claimed Eldur and Iskalt are the enemy. She has lied to you! This battle need not continue."

Brea could barely hear her as she ran through the remains of the battle, jumping over a body sprawled out on the ground. Regan wasn't here. "Where is she?"

Lochlan sprinted after her, gripped her arm to make her stop moving. "She lost the battle."

"But she's still alive. I know it." Brea turned hard eyes on Lochlan. "This won't be over until I face her." She yanked her arm out of his grasp as Griff reached them and bent over, his breath wheezing out of him. "I saw her take the road to the palace. She was injured."

"On foot?"

He nodded.

That was all Brea needed to hear. Her tired legs ached as she stumbled around dead fae of every race. Today, they were all the same. This battle hadn't needed to happen.

She was terrified of staying and learning who hadn't made it but even more terrified of what would happen if they didn't end this. So, she ran with no care if anyone accompanied her. She ran, not thinking of what would happen when she faced the aunt who had done so much wrong to the people she loved.

Brea sprinted around a bend in the path, her legs threatening to give out beneath her. Darkness covered the forest, and the trees stood as shadows against the night, blocking out the moon.

Still, she kept moving.

When she spotted her aunt, it was all she could do to remain upright. "Regan!" she screamed.

Regan didn't stop. Instead, she pulled a dark hood up to cover her head and veered off the path into the thicket of trees, her steps stumbling.

"*End*," Brea whispered, directing her magic to make Regan still.

It struck a tree, barreling back at her and giving her only a second to lunge out of the way, rolling to the ground. She crashed onto a patch of moss, but it wasn't enough to soften the blow as pain snaked up her arm.

"Regan!" She pushed herself up. "Get back here and face me." Stumbling over tree roots, she found Regan again in the distance. "Coward!"

Regan's crazed laughter echoed through the trees. "The only reason you have lived this long is for that heir in your belly, girl."

Brea put a hand on her stomach. She'd slept with Griff once a couple weeks ago, but Regan somehow thought she was pregnant and far enough along she'd know already? She couldn't have just heard this before the battle. Brea's eyes widened as she thought of the freedoms she'd started to gain at the Fargelsian palace almost as soon as she was married, the extra luxuries. Regan hadn't even fought her on the food she ate.

"Griff told you I was pregnant right after the wedding." As if they'd been intimate beforehand.

Regan's back went rigid, and she turned, letting Brea close the distance between them. "It was a lie." Her eyes lit with sudden understanding before they narrowed. "Griffin has been such a disappointment, but no one could let me down quite as much as my dear niece." Brea could have imagined it, but she thought she heard sadness in Regan's voice.

Regan's eyes darted around the clearing like she couldn't keep them focused.

Brea advanced. "I was abducted." Another step. "My friends were imprisoned." Closer. "My father has been in the dungeons my entire life." She reached Regan, a sneer on her lips. "I married a man I didn't love because I was scared of you, of what you could do to the people I love." Her eyes searched Regan's in the dark, and her lips twitched. "I don't fear you anymore. You are nothing to me." Saying the words aloud set something free inside Brea.

Blood didn't matter. Families weren't built on lines of succession.

Her family were the people she loved. Some of them shared her blood, others only shared her heart.

But this woman, she was nothing.

Brea needed to make a move, to prepare to fight, but exhaustion spread through her, holding back the threads of her power. She felt the magic building in the air around her before she could stop it.

Brea stumbled back, holding her sword in front of her. It would be no match for Regan's power, but she refused to run.

"*Skjöldur*," she said, trying to throw up a shield around her, but nothing happened. She tried to pull on the Eldur magic that had returned to her despite the moon hanging over head, but it too lay dormant inside her.

She backed away as Regan advanced, lifting a hand. "I am sorry, niece. We could have led Fargelsi to greatness together."

"A queen isn't what makes a kingdom great or worthy." Brea lifted her chin, refusing to cower. "The people do."

Regan's lips curled into a smile. "You are a noble child. Long ago I held such ideals, but once you taste power, you will see everything in a new light."

"I will never be like you," Brea spat.

"No." She frowned. "Sadly, you won't get the chance."

She muttered a word Brea couldn't make out, and pain seared down Brea's sides. She dropped to her knees, clutching at herself. "What are you doing?"

Regan's lip curled. "Returning every wound I suffered in that battle to you."

Brea screamed as the magic flooded her every cell, draining them of energy. Blood dribbled from the corners of her lips, and she couldn't breathe. "Regan!"

Regan's lips moved, but each word was so quiet Brea couldn't hear them over the beating of her heart. The pounding in her ears lessened as the beat slowed, and agony pierced her chest.

"You broke my heart, dear niece." Regan leaned down. "Now I will break yours."

An incantation started on her lips, but as the final word filtered into the air, someone slammed into Brea, knocking her to the ground and collapsing on her like an immovable weight.

Soldiers rushed through the forest calling Brea's name, but she couldn't move. Whoever saved her remained still.

She lifted her eyes to Regan, but the woman was already gone.

"Brea!" Lochlan's voice echoing through the forest brought her back to her senses, and she rolled the body off her.

It took her a moment to register the sight before her as her heart splintered, fracturing into a million pieces. Regan was right. She'd succeeded in breaking Brea's heart.

Because the person who saved her, the one now lying still, the only movement her lashes fluttering against her cheeks, was Tierney.

"No!" Alona's wail reached her moments before the girl dropped to her knees at Tierney's side. Brea sat up, her head not registering what her heart already knew.

"S-she saved me." Tears gathered in Brea's eyes, matching the ones already glistening on Alona's cheeks. Regan had been right there, ready to give Brea her final farewell.

Alona pulled Tierney's head into her lap as Tierney's eyes opened, a silver film—the same color of her magic—clouded them.

Her lips moved, but no sound came out.

"I can save her," Brea whispered. The healing power. What purpose did it have if not for this? "I can save her."

Hope lit in Alona's eyes, and she nodded. Neither girl paid attention to the people crowding around them. This moment was for them, their family.

Brea leaned forward, putting her hands on Tierney's chest. Her desperation pulled every thread of her magic to the surface. She pulsed it into Tierney, sending it straight into her heart.

Tierney's body convulsed, and blood seeped through her shirt.

"Brea." Her father's voice sounded like it was under water. "You need to stop."

She didn't. Each wave of her magic brought no results, and her desperation grew. The pain from Regan's attack faded away as all she could feel was a gut-wrenching agony that had nothing to do with any wound.

"Brea." It was Lochlan this time. He stood nearby with Griff's arm slung over his shoulders. Even that sight wasn't enough to distract her. "That's enough."

"Again," Alona whispered.

In this, they were together just the two of them.

Tierney tried to lift a hand, but it dropped. Brea reached for it and folded it between hers. "Stop," Tierney whispered. "Please."

Those words broke Brea, and she bent forward, tears dripping down her face. A hand landed on her shoulder, but she didn't know whose it was as she shook it off.

Tierney tried to say something else, so Brea and Alona leaned forward.

"Take care of each other." Her words shook. "And your mother... tell her I tried to return to her."

Brea wiped the tears from her eyes, but more replaced them. "I love you, Mom." She bent forward, placing her forehead on Tierney's shoulder as she sobbed. "So much." Tierney was the first person in this world who'd been honest with her, the first one who'd made her feel wanted, loved. She couldn't imagine walking into the Eldurian palace without her.

"Mama." Alona's entire body shook. "I love you."

A smile tilted the corners of Tierney's mouth as her eyes slid shut one final time.

No one spoke, and the only sounds were muffled sobs. Brea scooted around Tierney to pull Alona into her arms. In that moment, they didn't care how many people watched their hearts break. All Brea could think about was how they'd never be whole again.

CHAPTER 19

BREA

"Dóiteán." Brea clutched Alona's hand as their mother's pyre went up in flames. She should feel something. Anything but this cold black emptiness inside. She was still too numb from the battle to process Tierney's death. How would she ever tell Faolan her wife was gone?

Alona's sobs reached her ears, and she turned, pulling her sister into her arms, offering her whatever comfort she needed.

She was gone. The mother Brea was just beginning to know and love would never return to Eldur again. Tierney sacrificed her life for nothing. She'd saved Brea from Regan's magic, but Regan got away, and they were right back where they started. What was the point? Alona held on to Brea as they paid their last respects.

What was the point of any of it if Regan still won? Brea was born to be the weapon that would end Regan's reign, but she'd failed. Again. She'd failed everyone.

"Alona?" Finn stepped up behind them, and Alona turned away

from Brea and flung herself into Finn's arms, crying the tears Brea didn't seem to have in her.

"I'm so sorry, Alona," Brea whispered before she left them to each other. She felt like she had no right to mourn the fallen queen. Tierney had been Brea's mom for only a few months, but she'd been Alona's mom her whole life.

Brea wandered back toward camp where the more experienced soldiers were putting things to right again after the chaos of battle. The dead had their own pyres burning on the opposite side of camp, and the healers were busy treating the injured. The camp worked like a well-oiled machine. Brea didn't know how she was supposed to do that. Pick up the pieces and move on to whatever was next.

All of this was her fault, and the burden weighed on her now.

"Brea? I'm so sorry about your mother."

She looked up from her aimless wandering to find Griffin standing in her path. Beaten and bruised, he looked nothing like the handsome stranger that had whisked her away to another world so many months ago.

"It's *your* fault," she whispered, anger surging like a fire inside her. "It all started with you." She shoved him, pain snaking down her sides at the action. "Why couldn't you just leave me with Loch that day?" She shoved him again. "He was going to take me home to my mothers! Everything would have been fine if you'd stayed out of my life." She beat her fists against his chest. "We would have fallen in love and been happy. And Tierney—" her voice broke, and the fight went out of her. Scalding hot tears rolled down her face, and she couldn't breathe.

"I'm so sorry, Brea." Griffin pulled her into his arms, but she shoved him back. Not even the marriage bond could make her feel anything for him now.

"You destroy everything you touch!"

"I will make this right, Brea. I promise."

"Right?" She stared at him, unable to stop the tears now that they'd started. "She's dead! My mom is dead because of you." She whirled around, needing to put some space between her and Griff before she did something she'd regret, and she ran right into Lochlan.

His familiar arms slid around her, bringing the comfort she wanted from the man she loved. "Brea, love, I'm so sorry. She was a mother to me too." Brea clutched his shirt in her fist as she cried.

"Brother, I suggest you stop being so familiar with my wife." Griffin's voice grew dark just as Lochlan's body grew tense.

"And I suggest you give her some space to grieve." Lochlan cupped the back of her head against his chest. Part of her wanted to stay right there forever. But the other part of her wanted Griff. The magic that bonded her with him burned hot in her veins, reminding her that her lingering feelings for Lochlan were wrong.

"Enough." Brea pushed away from the comfort of Loch's arms. "I can't handle this constant tug between you both. I'm going to find Myles." Brea left them bickering behind her and headed to the main camp to creep into Myles' room like she used to do before the fae interrupted their perfectly boring lives.

"Brea, wait." Lochlan stopped her at the edge of camp. "How could—" He paced back along the trail, turning to face her again. "I have to know. How could you marry him, Brea?"

Brea kept walking. "I've told you. I didn't have a choice."

Lochlan grabbed her arm to stop her. "No one can force you into a fae marriage, Brea. That's not how the bond works. You have to say the words. You have to be willing to bind yourself to the other person for life. I just... help me understand what you were thinking? How could you give up on us so easily?"

"Easy? You think what I did was easy? I. Didn't. Have a choice. I was drunk."

"Drunk?" Lochlan frowned.

"It was the only way I could get through it, Loch. Lona brought me wine, and we got drunk. I walked down the aisle and said what I was supposed to say. But I wasn't there, Loch. I didn't know about the marriage magic until it was too late."

"No one ever told you?" A dark cloud crossed his face.

"Griffin told me that night. But it was done." She shrugged. "And there's nothing you can do about it."

Lochlan set off down the path that led to Tierney's funeral pyre where she'd left Griffin moments ago.

"Loch," she called after him. "Loch, stop." Fear lurched through her, and she ran after him into the darkness. She heard them before she found them.

"Loch, no!" she screamed as his fist slammed into her husband's jaw, sending Griff sprawling onto the ground.

"You didn't tell her?" Loch raged. "You tricked her?" He grabbed Griffin by his hair and lifted him back to his feet. "You're a coward." His eyes glittered with the blue light of his power.

"Loch, please calm down. Don't hurt him!" The marriage bond feared Lochlan might kill him.

"I didn't know!" Griffin shouted, the violet light of his power sparked at his fingertips.

"You as good as raped her, you arrogant, selfish bastard!" A streak of light lashed out like a whip, striking Griff across the face. Blood ran down his chin as Lochlan struck him again and again.

"I didn't know until after. I swear." Griffin stumbled to the ground, and Loch stalked him like a lion about to kill his injured prey.

"Stop!" Brea put herself between them. "None of it matters. It's done. We can't change the past. Loch, please leave. You've done enough damage for one night."

His chest heaved with his ragged breath, and his eyes flashed with barely-controlled anger. Without another word, he left her alone with Griff.

"I'll take you to the healers." Brea hefted Griff's arm around her shoulder and helped him stand. She stumbled under his weight. Regan's spells didn't cause flesh wounds, but she could practically feel the burns inside her.

"I didn't know, Brea. I thought you knew. She told me she explained it all to you."

"Of course, she did, Griff. All the woman does is lie and manipulate." They made their way into the camp and along the path to the healer's tents.

"One day, I will make it right, Brea. I promise."

She nodded, leaving him with the healer. But unless Griff could find a way to undo the past, he could never make it right.

Brea wandered through the camp until she found Myles sitting by the fire with Neeve. She watched as he said something that made her laugh, and he brushed a stray curl from her face. Brea felt weird about interrupting their moment. She envied them, envied Neeve. She'd lost her girlfriend Moira and was able to walk into the future with no regrets. Maybe it was because Moira died for something they believed in. She'd have known the risks, and no amount of guilt from Brea or Neeve would bring her back.

Turning, she walked among the rows of tents until it occurred to her that she didn't know if she even had a tent of her own. Brea had never felt so defeated and alone. Her mother was dead. Regan escaped. She was married to a man she did not and would never love. She'd lost Lochlan, the one man she truly loved, but the bond with Griffin had suppressed those feelings until she didn't trust her own emotions anymore. Brea just wanted to go home, but she wasn't sure where that was anymore.

Exhausted and chilled, she found an empty seat on a log by one of the many fires dotting the camp. As she warmed herself by the fire, she watched the men and women seated near her. Some were Iskalt soldiers. Some were of Eldur, and a few were Fargelsi soldiers. The same soldiers they'd fought only a few hours ago.

"Have some stew, your Highness." Someone shoved a bowl and a hunk of bread into her hands.

"Thank you, I'm starving." Brea shoveled a bite into her mouth.

"To Princess Brea, the Wall Breaker!" an Eldur soldier shouted, and the others cheered.

"Drink up, Princess." A grizzly Iskalt soldier poured her a mug of ale. "It's bad luck not to drink with your soldiers after winning a battle."

Brea took a long gulp of the warm ale. "Winning?"

"Aye, we won. Though we are all sorry to hear about your sweet mother. She was a fine lady." He lifted his glass, shouting, "A toast for the fallen Queen Tierney!"

Her mother's name echoed through the camp, and Brea smiled despite her sadness. She hadn't considered today a win, but clearly the soldiers did.

"The name's Ailbhe, Princess." The Iskalt man sat beside her, refiling her mug. "It was a hard day, Highness, but we sent that dark witch running for her castle. She's got nothing left. Her army is scattered or dead. More than half of them turned against her when they realized their king was back from the dead—with an heir to boot." He lifted his mug to the Fargelsi soldiers dining with them. "And thanks to you, her wall is gone. When you brought that barrier down, you told all of Fargelsi they were free. They won't let her take back control now she's lost her biggest weapon. You did good, Highness. Before this is over, you'll put a king back on his throne." He lifted his mug, and Brea tapped hers against his.

"But now what?" Brea's shoulders slumped. She couldn't see what her next steps should be. She'd felt like it was over. That she couldn't possibly defeat Regan now.

"Now we chase the witch," Ailbhe said with a hearty laugh. "She's running scared. She won't have anyone to turn to with her lackey boy, Griffin gone. Er, sorry, Highness. No offense to your husband."

"None taken." Brea sighed.

"When an animal is injured, they run home scared. They lick their wounds. That's when the hunter goes in for the kill. You don't want to give her a chance to put that wall back up. She's weak after today. And scared. Make your move, Highness. And we'll all be there to back you up."

He was right. She couldn't sit here faltering while Regan put herself back together.

"Ailbhe, you're officially my favorite person today." She leaned over and kissed his cheek.

The big mountain of a man turned bright red beneath his bushy beard.

"Thank you." Brea shot to her feet. She had to find her father and Captain Donovan. They had some scheming to do.

Chapter 20

BREA

The first time Brea rode toward the palace of Fargelsi, it filled her with a sense of wonder with its twin waterfalls, high bridges, and twisted spires that kissed the sky. The second time, she arrived with a feeling of resignation. She'd had no choice if she wanted to save Myles. The crashing of waterfalls became the song of her captivity, the bridges representing her dreams of escape.

And now?

The stone arches and walls covered in beautiful ivy weren't what they seemed at all because she knew the truth. That beauty hid the rot inside Regan's soul, the darkness she filled her palace with. Gleaming marble halls no longer covered up the pain living within those walls.

Brea sat atop her horse, her gaze lifted to the twin waterfalls. Captain Donovan rode to her left, and Lochlan sat on her right. They'd spent the last day planning a full assault on the palace. The plan was to clear out the grounds, section by section, before getting to the palace itself.

But as they'd ridden through the forest city of Vindur, they'd found it eerily quiet without a fae in sight.

Finn galloped toward them, pulling up on the reins as he neared. "The stables are empty. I couldn't even find a servant. They've all fled now that the barrier is down."

Brea's brow creased. "She wouldn't have let them go so easily."

Griff nudged his horse forward. It was the first Brea had seen of him since his fight with Lochlan. As soon as Lochlan learned Brea hadn't known of the marriage magic before agreeing to it, he'd put measures in place to make sure Griff couldn't get anywhere near Brea. Her magic missed him, tugging her toward him even now, but the rest of her was grateful Lochlan kept him away.

"She'll have gathered her remaining people inside the palace." Griff rubbed the back of his neck. "That way—"

"We'll have to fight through them to get to her." Lochlan cursed.

Brea's eyes widened. "But they're prisoners. At least, most of them are. We can't fight them."

"If we want to get to Regan, we may not have a choice." Lochlan looked toward the dark sky like he was cursing the heavens.

Despite the mid-day hour, the sun had yet to make an appearance through angry storm clouds. It meant the Eldurian powers were still there, but weak. If they were smart, they'd wait for the storms to pass to take on Regan so Brea had an entire army at her back.

But Brea didn't want the army fighting Regan. She didn't want more people to die at her aunt's hands. If she was as powerful as her parents hoped when they conceived her, it was time to be the weapon she was meant to be.

Brea slid down from her horse and walked toward the bridge, her combined Eldurian and Fargelsian magic buzzing at her fingertips. There was no place in all the worlds she hated more than the palace before her. It represented everything that was evil in this world.

"Go back to where the army is stationed in the forest and lead them here," Lochlan said, probably to Captain Donovan. But Brea didn't turn to look at him. She barely registered his words.

Crouching down, she brushed a hand over the massive vines that created the bridge, images flashing through her mind.

Falling for Griff the first time because of his and Regan's lies.

Her heart squeezed.

Sitting safe in Eldur and learning Myles had been taken prisoner.

The pain of it still felt fresh.

Returning to Fargelsi only to marry a man she despised.

The images tumbled through her mind faster than before.

Magic forcing her to love him, making her want to sleep with him.

Her father standing in his cell, weak and confused from his years underground.

Tierney.

Anger burned through her, swirling around the pain in her chest until she wasn't sure which was new, and which was a remnant of everything she'd suffered, everything her friends and family suffered.

"This isn't a fight for an army," she whispered.

A fresh wave of grief washed over her, and she closed her eyes, seeing Regan in the moment before Tierney dropped to the ground, never to rise again.

Her fingers clawed at the vines, and she forgot the people standing behind her or the ones trapped inside the palace. All that existed was the struggle between her and Regan. "We're going to end this."

Her Eldurian magic burned down her arms, springing to life as it latched onto the hatred flowing through her like a river, uncontrollable.

"You're not my family, Regan." Brea used her Eldurian power to amplify her voice, letting it permeate the air and wrap around the palace. "But you'll pay for what you did to it."

"Brea, what's happening?" Her father shook her as the skies opened and a torrent of rain tumbled toward the ground, pinging off armor and soaking the stone and dirt underneath their feet.

"*Pruma*," Brea whispered seconds before thunder shook the

world. Her sopping hair stuck to her face as she leaned forward like she wanted to kiss the bridge. "*Brot.*" She touched a vine, and it snapped in two. A smile curved her lips.

"Brea," Lochlan yelled over the rain. "What are you doing?"

Brea ignored him as she stood from her crouch and stepped onto the bridge. Lochlan ran after her, but she threw a hand out behind her, letting her Eldurian magic amplify the Fargelsian power as she yelled, "*Molna!*" The bridge behind her crumbled into dust. The bridge should have collapsed the moment the vines broke, but she held it in place with the Eldurian power.

"There are still prisoners in there," Lochlan yelled behind her.

His words flitted through her mind, trying to take hold, to pull her back, but she was past stopping now. The emotions controlled her, her heart warring with her head.

And her heart won.

Because it knew none of them would be safe until Regan died.

"Where's Griff?" Lochlan yelled.

"He ran for the entrance under the falls," Finn called back. "He said she couldn't die like this."

Betrayal amplified the already dark emotions inside Brea. Even after everything, Griff still wanted to save Regan. But there was no saving her now. Her eyes shifted to the falls where she knew an entrance to the dungeons and the rest of the palace hid beneath crashing water. If she collapsed it, Griff wouldn't be able to get out and neither could Regan.

Not even her marriage magic was enough to stop her.

She lifted a hand, the word on the tip of her tongue, but movement caught her eye as three people slipped behind the falls.

Neeve looked back over her shoulder at Alona and Myles, beckoning them forward.

"Brea," Lochlan yelled again. "They've gone to save the prisoners. You need to get control."

Control. The word refused to take hold inside her, but for just a moment, her heart left its mission of revenge as it wanted to protect her true family. Myles and her sisters.

Not the man she'd married.

Not the aunt who'd claimed her.

The people who'd fought for her.

Her anger abated, and with it, the rain. By the time the rain ceased, not an inch of her was dry. But she didn't feel it. She didn't feel anything.

The sun peeked through the clouds as the sounds of horses reached her. She threw a look over her shoulder at her army, the army made up of soldiers from the three kingdoms. Her Eldurian power rejoiced with the sliver of sunlight, and yellow light exploded from her every pore.

She cried out, falling to her knees.

Fae called to her. Lochlan. Her father. Finn.

But she couldn't get to them as she slammed into the vines, and the entire bridge shook from the impact of her magic. It was too much, too real.

Her grief threatened to swallow her whole as the power overwhelmed her, filling every empty space with its wrath. The Eldurian magic strengthened the Fargelsian power, and the Fargelsian magic darkened that of Eldur. It was a cycle she couldn't break free of as pain shot through her, and the bridge trembled, trying to fall into the water below.

"I can't hold it in," she cried. Myles, Alona, and Neeve would die because of her. Tears streamed down her face as she curled her fingers into fists and planted one foot on the ground, pushing herself from her knees.

When she stood, she looked up at the beautiful palace, the wondrous prison.

So much pain. So many lies.

Was this what it meant to be the weapon? Had Brandon and Faolan created her as nothing more than a nuclear bomb? And she'd come here now, ready to explode.

One person wasn't supposed to hold two kingdom's powers inside them.

"Brea Robinson is a lie," she whispered, walking to the center of the bridge.

Because she wasn't Brea Robinson, the crazy human girl raised on a failing farm by drunken parents. She never had been.

Brea of Eldur, Brea of Fargelsi was only meant for this purpose, this fate.

She gritted her teeth, trying to hold the magic in until the people she loved were safe, but it escaped her, striking the palace walls like spears of lightning. The stone spires shook and began to crumble.

She yanked her hand back, hoping it would pull the magic. Instead, a section of the roof sailed toward her. She ducked, and it flew past the bridge, tumbling into the crashing water below. Stone by stone, vine by vine, her magic started pulling the palace apart just like it had with the barrier wall.

There was no magic to tear down here, only stone. And all stone could break.

Her heart mirrored the palace she destroyed, cold, hard, and in danger of crumbling into dust.

The only sound she heard was her magic rushing in her ears like wind during a storm. She didn't know if anyone still tried to reach her, but she threw a hand back. "*Hindrun.*" Her Fargelsian magic created a barrier preventing anyone from stopping her even if they managed to get across the broken vines of the bridge.

This wasn't their fight.

It was hers.

Chapter 21

LOCHLAN

"We have to stop her." It was not the first time Brandon had voiced those exact words as he watched his daughter succumb to the magic inside her.

And Lochlan couldn't hear it anymore. Fear coursed through him, but not for the fight they'd prepared for. That would never come to pass, he knew that now. No, the dread building in his heart was for the girl standing in the middle of a broken bridge that should have fallen if not for her magic. Her wet hair stuck to her reddened cheeks.

Yellow sparks sizzled along her arms, singing the clothes and burning away her sleeves to reveal unmarred skin. All bruises from the battle the day before had faded away under the power of her magic.

Even as she lost control, she was the most beautiful fae he'd ever seen. The fire in her eyes blazed bright with conviction that only amplified the Fargelsian side of her magic. She believed in what she was doing.

Stones broke away from the palace until the entire front facade collapsed, revealing the inner sanctum of a feared palace.

Lochlan jumped forward at the sight before them. Crowded into the entryway were Fargelsian servants, stables boys, cooks. They stood as a shield, a distraction.

Was Griff helping Regan escape right this moment?

"Brea," Lochlan yelled. "Remember they're innocent!"

He hoped the girl he knew was still in there, still controlling her actions.

"Finn." He looked behind him to his friend who hadn't said a word since they learned Alona sneaked into the palace with only another human and Neeve for protection. "Take twenty men and climb down to base of the falls. Those people can't cross the bridge, and we need to get them out of there."

He nodded and went to gather his men.

"Hold on, Brea." Lochlan breathed a sigh of relief when it seemed she wouldn't target the servants.

Instead, she focused her efforts on another part of the palace, uttering Fargelsian words to pull the stones and vines free. By the time she was done, the palace would be nothing but dust.

"Focus on the barrier keeping us from her." Lochlan directed four of the Eldurian sorcerers to the invisible wall Brea had created between them and her.

If she didn't stop, she was going to kill herself.

Dust rained down on them as another part of the palace crashed inward. Lochlan spared a glance for Finn and his men where they helped fae climb down from the bridge to the riverbed below, clearing out of the entryway.

The moment the last servant was out of the way, yellow magic funneled into the great hall, blasting it apart and sending a shower of rocks onto the soldiers down below.

There was still no sign of Neeve, Alona, and Myles, and Griff had yet to reappear.

For just a short time, Lochlan wondered if his brother had chosen the right side. He'd fought for them, bled for them and turned against the woman he called mother.

Like Faolan was for Lochlan. He'd fight for Faolan, die for her.

On some level, he understood his brother. But he would have to pay for his choice.

"Pull the threads of magic," Lochlan yelled to the sorcerers. "Don't let go." One moment, they couldn't break past it, and another the barrier crashed down around them, sending a wave of power toward Brea as her body pulled it back in. It slammed into her, and she stumbled, teetering on the edge of the bridge. "Keep the bridge from falling," he yelled to his soldiers.

Lochlan didn't hesitate before backing up and sprinting forward, using his arms to propel him across the gap. His feet slammed into the bridge as Brea disappeared over the side. Heart lodged in his throat, he dropped to his knees, a wave of relief rushing over him when he found Brea hanging onto the edge by the tips of her fingers.

His hands clamped around her wrists. "I've got you." He pulled her up, and she collapsed into his chest for only a moment before pushing him away and getting to her feet.

"I'm not done."

"Brea, the palace is almost in ruins. She couldn't have survived this."

Brea shook her head, magic sparking in her fingers. "I'm not done."

Two figures appeared in the crumbling entryway.

"Griff," she whispered.

Lochlan's jaw clenched at the affection in her voice even as Griff held her enemy upright. Regan no longer looked like the regal queen who ruled Fargelsi through intimidation and power. Her red dress was ripped and covered in dust from her crumbling palace. The same dust streaking through her once elegant hair. Blood ran from her hairline, trickling down past her ear. Rivulets of red dripped down her arms, but her face showed no weakness, only a crazed glee.

Griff had been right. The barrier breaking turned Regan from cold and calculating to insane and maniacal.

Griff walked forward, bringing her with him. He lifted one hand in surrender.

Brea stared at them, her chest heaving.

"Brea." Griff took a tentative step toward her. "You've won. Fargelsi is yours."

"You betrayed me." Her voice held a deep timbre, unlike the pleasant sound he'd grown used to. "Again."

"She's my mother, Brea. What would you have done to save Tierney?"

Lochlan felt like he'd never seen his brother before. The man who'd been hurt by this woman and forced to do evil things... he protected her.

"Do not speak that name to me." Brea's hands clenched at her sides, the words tearing from her mouth like shards of glass.

Even under the circumstances, Regan's face was calm, collected. "Niece, I am your prisoner."

"Prisoner?" Brea looked from Regan to Griff.

Regan was too far gone to sit in a dungeon somewhere.

Griff shifted to lend her more of his strength. "She's dying, Brea. Let her leave for the prison realm. She won't last long."

Regan coughed, but Lochlan couldn't tell if this was true or only more lies.

A growl ripped from Brea's throat. "You think sending you to the prison realm to be forgotten is winning?" She took another step forward. "No one will ever forget what has happened here. My mother will know who killed the woman she loved. My father will know it was his own sister who imprisoned him. No, Regan, you have left a mark on the fae world that will never wash away. We will move on, have no doubt about that. But the memory of evil, of you, will keep us from letting it happen again."

"Brea—"

Yellow light shot from Brea, striking Regan in the chest. "*Skreppa.*"

Lochlan could feel it, the Fargelsian power joining its Eldurian counterpart, intention intertwining with emotion.

Regan clutched her chest, falling back and away from Griff. "No." The skin of her face wrinkled, stealing all youth from her appearance. Brea twisted her hand, letting the yellow light settle over Regan, swirling around her as her body shriveled. "Niece," she wheezed. "I am your family."

Brea stepped forward, her face hard. "No, you killed my family." Another step. "You imprisoned my family." She turned her hand. "You are nothing to me." Yanking her hand back, she snapped all of her magic back into her.

Regan's body jerked forward, her mouth falling open as her hair turned gray. She remained suspended in time for a moment longer before falling back, her head cracking against the bridge and her eyes staring at the sky above.

The queen of Fargelsi was dead.

Lochlan tried to wrap an arm around Brea, but she pushed him away, power enveloping her once again, swirling around her like an angry tornado.

Stones flew from the remaining tower of the palace faster than before, dissolving into dust midair with a single word from Brea.

Her entire body shook.

"She's going to kill herself." Griff looked up from where he knelt beside Regan's still form, his eyes rimmed red.

He was right.

Lochlan stepped forward, pushing back against Brea's magic like he was pushing into a storm, using his strength to break through the winds. It was still hours before dusk, and his own power lay dormant. But when it came to Brea, he didn't need magic.

He kept going when her magic sent spears of pain through him. He didn't stop when it threatened to blow him right off the bridge.

"Brea," he yelled moments before lunging toward her and throwing his arms around her to stop the magic. "You have to stop."

Power exploded out of her, striking him along his entire body. His arms lost their grip, and he sailed through the air before slamming into the road across the broken bridge.

For a moment, it was like everything stopped. All sound. All commotion.

And then there was nothing left to fight for as the world went dark.

"Lochlan?"

A drop of water struck his face, and he waited for more rain that never came.

When his eyes slid open, he realized it had been a tear from the girl hovering over him. Was this real, or had they both died?

Brea brushed the hair back from his forehead. "I thought I killed you."

"You're..." He lifted a weak hand to put it on her thigh. "Are we alive?"

She nodded and wiped away another tear. "I'm so sorry." Bending forward, she put her forehead to his chest, her back shaking with sobs. "I couldn't control it."

"But you did. You pulled it back in."

"Only because I thought you were dead." She lifted her head to look at him, shifting her ebony hair over one shoulder. "You're not allowed to die, Loch. Not ever."

"That's going to be a very hard promise to keep when I get old."

"I don't care." She gave him a watery smile. "I can't lose you."

"What happened?" He looked at the fae surrounding them. Finn, his own eyes rimmed red. Captain Donovan laid a comforting hand on his son's shoulder.

Brandon, looking just as tired as the rest of them, stood in front of where the vines once connected this road to the palace. The bridge no longer spanned the distance.

And then there was Griff.

Lochlan tried to sit up as soon as he saw his brother. "Arrest him," he tried to shout, but his voice hoarse. "Griff, I'm going to stick you in a cell in Iskalt where you'll never again see the light of day. You are under arrest for treason against Iskalt." Captain Donovan used his Eldur magic to bind Griff's wrists but didn't lead him away.

Brea spared one sad glance for Griff before she leaned forward again, wrapping her arms around Lochlan. "I think I almost died today."

He hugged her tighter against him. "I thought you were going to."

"I'm so tired, Loch. Of fighting. Of losing people I love. Of this magic."

One of those stuck in his mind, and he searched the faces for the people he didn't see. "Where are they?"

Brea knew who he meant without him voicing the names. "They never returned from the dungeons." He saw the moment realization dawned in her eyes. She'd destroyed the entire palace with her best friend and sisters inside.

Finn turned his back on them and walked away.

Fresh tears appeared in Brea's eyes.

"How is this possible?" Griff asked.

Brea lifted weary eyes to him, but Lochlan kept his gaze on Brea. "What?"

"You're in love with him. The marriage magic should prevent that."

Brea put a hand to her chest. "It hurts, Griff. Every time I think of him, pain spears my heart." She met Lochlan's eyes. "But this is magic I can't control. Stronger than the bonds Regan tricked me into with you, bolder than any lies. Because for once in my life, I know what is true."

"And what is this truth?" Lochlan asked.

"The only thing that could pull my magic back, the only feeling more overwhelming than the anger and hatred I felt was loving you and thinking I'd killed you."

Lochlan reached up to brush his thumb over her cheek. "Brea, I have loved you for so long I don't remember what not loving you feels like." Even as he said the words, he knew how hopeless they were. Brea had to return to Eldur, to rule her mother's kingdom, and Lochlan's place was in Iskalt. They did not belong together no matter how hard they tried.

Griff met his eyes, and a strange understanding passed between them. This wasn't magic making Lochlan love Brea, it was life. Loving Brea had brought both brothers pain.

Captain Donovan led Griff away. They would deal with him later. The crowd dispersed, and Brea helped Lochlan to his feet. They held each other up as they stumbled through the camp their armies had started setting up.

"I need to go search for Myles," Brea said.

Lochlan hugged her closer to his side. "You can barely stand. Let Finn and his men go."

Before she could agree, commotion wound through the soldiers, and they parted to let three haggard-looking figures—two human and one fae—lead a stream of prisoners into camp.

A sob escaped Brea's throat as she dropped Lochlan's arm and half ran, half staggered toward them. Myles caught her before she fell, and her sisters joined the embrace.

Finn sprinted toward them, pulling Alona away and kissing her like he'd thought he'd never see her again. Lochlan envied the easy way they gave themselves to one another. Even as a future servant and guard, their future together held more hope than his with Brea.

The palace now lay in ruins, Regan was dead, and they'd survived. He should have been relieved it was over, but now he'd return home without the people he cared about most, without Brea.

Lochlan joined the celebration as he directed his men to care for the freed prisoners.

Tonight, the moon brought the promise that this day was done. And tomorrow, the sun would rise on a new day.

Peace had come for the fae realm.

Yet a storm continued to brew within the Iskalt king.

Chapter 22

BREA

Brea sat in the palace gardens—what was left of them—watching her husband stack wood to make a pyre for his surrogate mother. The only family he thought he'd ever had. A ring of soldiers stood guard over the prisoner, but Brea wasn't sure they could hold him if Griffin really wanted to escape.

The marriage bond wanted to free him, but the logical side of her mind knew his crimes were too great. He would have to pay for his ambition. His treason. But it still made her sad to think of him locked in a cold dark cell in Iskalt when he could have been so much more if he'd chosen his true family over the woman who'd lied and manipulated him his whole life.

Griffin laid his mother across the pyre, his face white with the shock of her death.

Brea felt an odd sense of sadness for her aunt. She was power hungry and evil to the core, but she was also Brea's family. Brea had loved Regan when she first arrived at the palace. But she felt nothing for the fallen queen now—nothing beyond a sad ache in her heart for what might have been.

Griffin stared down at his mother, his shoulders shaking with grief.

"Despite everything she did, he is just a son grieving for his mother." Brandon came to stand behind her, draping a blanket over her shoulders. "Just as I am a brother grieving for a sister." He walked past her down to the pyre.

Brea watched as her father rested a hand on her husband's shoulder, and Griff turned to him, overcome with his loss. A loss Brea could never truly understand.

"Dóiteán." Brandon's voice reached her where she sat on the cold hard ground. Flames as red as Regan's dress spread around her body. Brea intended to watch until there was nothing left of her. Only then would she feel like this was finally over.

Brandon left Griff to mourn in peace, making his way back toward Brea. Folding his long limbs, he sat beside her. "You did what was necessary, Brea."

"It was what I was born for, after all." Brea was numb with a bone-deep weariness she couldn't shake. The magic took everything she had, leaving her an empty shell, hollow, like a fired weapon.

"Yes," Brandon agreed. "Your mother and I hoped for a child strong enough to do what we could not. But that was not the only reason you were born. Faolan wanted a child more than anything, and we loved each other. She was my best friend. She could have had any powerful man's child. She was the queen of Eldur and could have surrounded herself with dozens of children. But we wanted *you*, Brea. We wanted a child who was not only strong and powerful, but the best of us both. And you exceeded all our expectations."

A tear slipped down Brea's cheek, and she wiped it away. "Is it pathetic that the one thing I want more than anything in this or any world right now is my mother? I miss her so much. We were just getting to know each other when I left."

"You will see her again soon." Brandon draped an arm around her shoulders, pulling her to his side. "But will a loving father do for now?"

Brea rested her head on his shoulder.

"I'm scared, Dad. I have to tell my mother I got her wife killed." Above all else, she feared what Faolan would say when she knew how Tierney died.

"She will not blame you, Brea. Tierney died doing what a mother does, protecting her daughter. Faolan will understand because if the situation were reversed, she would have made the same choice as her wife. If I had been there, I wouldn't have hesitated to protect you or your sister with my life. It's what parents do for their children."

"Thank you, Dad." Brea gave him a weak smile. "I am glad you are here with me now, but Fargelsi is going to need their king, and I have to return to Eldur soon." She wondered if she'd ever get a chance to truly know him.

"I am not the one Fargelsi needs. My time has passed. I am weakened from my time in the dungeons. This is a new world, and new worlds are for the young. You would be a wonderful queen of this realm. The people already love you, and Gelsi is in your blood." He took her hand in his. "One day, you will make a great queen, but not of Fargelsi. You are so much like Faolan with the fire of Eldur in your veins. You are needed there. There is another who will stand for Fargelsi."

"Neeve." Brea nodded. "She is exactly what Gelsi needs."

"Shall we go crown your sister?"

"Now?"

"Many kings and queens have been crowned on the battlefield. I believe your Lochlan was crowned just after a recent battle."

"He's not my anything." Brea sighed. "Let's do it. We need to end this day on a happy note." Brea stood, gathering her blanket around her shoulders like a shawl. Everything hurt, and she felt a thousand years old as she followed her father across the broken grounds of Regan's home.

They found Neeve directing servants and soldiers to repair the bridge so it was safe to cross.

"In the coming weeks, we will clear the rubble, and our king will rebuild his castle on the ashes of the old one, just as Fargelsi will rise from the ashes."

"She's already a queen. She just needs a crown," Brea said.

"I went searching through the rubble earlier." Brandon reached into his coat pocket. "I found the crown jewels of our family. Most were damaged, but I've secured them for Neeve." He pulled a simple circlet of golden vines from his coat.

"It's beautiful."

"It belonged to your grandmother, Queen Reanna."

"It's perfect for my sister."

Brandon stepped forward, calling for the activity to stop. "My good people of Fargelsi, join me to thank our guests of Eldur and Iskalt for their help in overthrowing my sister, Regan. It saddens me to see how her ambition ruled her life. And it saddens me to see her gone, never to be redeemed. But we are on the precipice of a new day. One I am not fit to lead us into."

Many of the Fargelsians groaned and shared concerned looks, probably wondering who would lead them if not their rightful king.

"After eighteen years in a prison cell, my magic fails me. I do not have the strength to rule, and I will not put my people through another reign fueled by ambition."

"Who will rule us?" someone shouted from the crowd.

"My daughter. You already love her as she is one of you. Neeve, will you come stand with me?"

Shocked murmurs spread through the crowd. Not everyone knew of Neeve's relationship to their king.

Neeve dropped a handful of debris she'd collected from the ruins, her face smeared with dust and sweat as she moved to join their father.

"Neeve, you've had a difficult life as a servant. But your mother was a strong Fargelsi woman, and your father a king." He held their grandmother's crown before her. "Do you accept your duty as the most capable royal of this realm?"

Neeve took a deep breath, glancing at all her people watching on with bated breath. "I don't feel like a queen, Father. But I love Fargelsi and its people. I will do my best to serve them well."

"I, King Brandon O'Rourke of Fargelsi, abdicate my crown to my daughter, Queen Neeve O'Rourke. Long may she live." He placed the simple crown on her head.

Brea was certain she cheered the loudest for her sister. This was what she'd worked so hard to achieve. A lightness entered Brea's heart where she thought only darkness remained. It was a new day here in Fargelsi, perhaps she would get a fresh start too.

Brea made her way through the war camp long after the soldiers finished celebrating with the last of the ale. She couldn't sleep with so much on her mind.

"Princess Brea," a soldier greeted her near the stables where they were keeping the prisoners—those loyal to Regan who'd survived the battle.

"I'd like to see my husband, please."

"Of course, your Majesty." Another soldier came to escort her to Griffin's temporary cell.

"Can't sleep either?" She leaned against the stall door. Iskalt magic pulsed around the stall, keeping Griffin and all the other prisoners in their makeshift cells.

"I have a lot on my mind." Griff leaned against the wall behind him. "I figured you'd be with Loch tonight."

"I am married to you."

"Against your will. I know whatever you feel for me is just the marriage magic. I convinced myself you would grow to love me again in time."

"I'm not sure what is real and what is the result of the magic when it comes to us. It's not so black and white anymore."

Griffin met her eyes, and she saw so much pain there. So much regret.

"If you were free, what would you do now, Griff?"

Heaving a deep sigh, he stared into her eyes. "I haven't done what I've wanted in so long, I wouldn't know where to begin."

"Convince me you deserve a full pardon, and I'll make it happen." She wanted to give him one last chance. "If you could walk away now, what would you do?"

"I'd try to make amends with my brother. You. Everyone I've hurt through my actions. I'd go back to my cottage and try to figure out where I belong. I am of Iskalt, but I've always lived here in Fargelsi. It is my home, but I doubt they want me here as a reminder. Honestly, I can't see a future for myself. I don't deserve one. I am from Iskalt, Brea. I have to answer to my king."

"Why?" She peered down at him from her vantage point. "Why did you serve her with so much loyalty even to the end?"

"She was my mother." He threw his hands up. "For all her faults, she was always there for me. Always."

"Until she turned on you."

"I betrayed her first. For you. I love you, Brea. When I came after you in the Vatlands, I was going to bring you home. But when you told me about Brandon—when I saw him with my own eyes—I couldn't justify her actions any longer. That was a turning point for me. I sacrificed her ambitions—her vision for the future—for you. Because you were miserable, and I wanted to give you the one thing you wanted. Your freedom."

"But you still betrayed us when you skulked off in the night to return to her side. You knew it had to end with her death, but you still tried to save her."

"I wasn't trying to save her, Brea. I went back to try to convince her to put an end to her single-minded pursuits. That was when she turned on me and tortured me to get to you. I knew Regan would die today. I went to her again because I didn't want her to die alone. I needed her to know I still loved her despite all her actions."

"I will fight for you, Griff, but you have to promise me your ambitions are over."

He shook his head. "I don't want you to fight for me. It's over. I have asked to go to the prison realm rather than face a cell in Iskalt."

"No, you don't have to do that." Brea's eyes burned with unshed tears. She was so tired of crying, but she didn't want to forget Griffin O'Shea. She couldn't imagine a world where he no longer existed.

"It won't be so bad. I can make a new life there."

"As a prisoner?"

"It's not quite like the prisons of the human realm. I'll have certain freedoms there I won't have in Iskalt."

"He's already agreed to send you there, hasn't he?" Anger burned hot inside her at the thought of Lochlan making such decisions that would affect her life without even speaking to her about it.

"It was my idea, Brea. My brother didn't want this either. But I leave in the morning. Soon you will forget all about me. Our marriage will be nullified, and you can get on with your life without anything holding you back. I owe you that much. You were right. This is all my fault. Had I stood up to Regan that first day and let Lochlan take you home to your mothers, none of this would have happened."

"What if I don't want to forget you?" Hot tears rolled down her face. "Don't I get a say?"

He smiled sadly, his voice dropping. "Number ten." His eyes glassed over. "There are so many reasons I have loved you, but once upon a time I promised ten."

"Griff."

"Number ten," he said again. "Even after everything I've done, you still see hope for me. You refuse to give up on me. I don't think you'll ever know what that means."

"There's always hope."

"Please, let me do this for you, Brea. A clean break. It's for the best. I let Regan's vision of the future cloud my judgment. She convinced me we needed you on our side, and I am not afraid to admit I wanted the future she dreamed for us. I wanted to be king."

"You know it was all lies, Griff."

"I think I always suspected." He took a deep breath. "But I didn't want to believe the woman who raised me with so much love and kindness could be so conniving. I was blinded by my love for her." He smiled. "And I was blinded by my love for you."

"That's it then? You're just going to leave? Take my memories without my permission? Divorce me?"

Griffin moved from his seat on the ground, crossing the stall to stand in front of her. "Brea, whatever you feel for me is the marriage bond. You don't want to be married to me. I know that. When the bond is gone, you'll feel differently. You'll finally be able to trust your feelings again."

"So, this is goodbye?" She held her hand up to the magical barrier keeping him inside. He pressed his hand against hers.

"I will miss you, Brea O'Rourke Cahill." He gave her a sad smile. "Go find your happiness. Turn this world on its head, and make a new life for yourself and whoever you choose to love."

"I love you, Griff." She wiped the tears from her face. "And I wish you nothing but good things wherever you are going."

Brea finished packing her things, preparing for her journey home to Eldur tomorrow. She would be back to visit Neeve in the coming months as Eldur helped the new queen rebuild Fargelsi to fit her vision of the future. Alona and Brea had promised to return with the first delegation. She had a feeling the three sisters would see each other often, but right now, Brea had one more goodbye to say, and this one was going to hurt more than any other goodbye she'd ever said.

She made her way across the repaired bridge and into the gardens behind the pile of rubble that had once been a beautiful palace. Myles waited in the moonlight with Neeve and Lochlan.

"I can't convince you to stay?" Brea could already feel the threat of tears tighten in her throat. "Just a few more weeks? Come back to Eldur with us."

Myles shook his head sadly. "I have to get back to my family, Brea. They'll be so worried."

"Of course." She nodded, sniffing back her tears. She understood his need to return to the human realm.

"I have high school to finish and then college. The farm. I have to check on the new colt. Captain America will be freaking out by now I've been gone so long."

Brea pressed her hand over his mouth. "You're babbling." She wrapped her arms around his waist and held onto him for as long as she could.

"I can come back for a visit. My buddy douchey Loch can come get me anytime when I'm not in school. Or working the farm."

"Yeah, sure." Brea smiled. She knew she'd likely never see him again. "Wait, you've been calling him douchey Loch?" The corner of her mouth lifted into a smile.

"Of course. You weren't there and someone had to bring him down a peg or two."

"I know what that means now." Lochlan stood behind them with arms crossed over his chest. "Don't think to flatter me with such human slang any more."

"You'll come up with something good." Myles winked, turning to Neeve.

"Give us a second?" Myles asked.

"Of course." Brea left him to say goodbye to her sister. She'd never know what they'd gone through together. From prison cells to Eldur and Iskalt and back again only to discover she was the queen of Fargelsi.

"He'll be happier in his own world," Lochlan said softly.

"You'll watch over him?"

"Of course. I'll check on him from time to time."

"Like as often as you did for me? And then you'll tell me everything?"

"Let's not get crazy here, I am a king now, not a seventeen-year-old boy with a crush."

Brea avoided his intense look. Since Griffin left earlier that day, she couldn't think about anything other than the looming hour when she would forget him from one moment to the next.

"I think I'm ready," Myles said, a heartbroken look on his face.

"I wish we could FaceTime." Brea wrapped her arms around her best friend in all the worlds.

"Me too, but you have this wonderful huge new life to get on with, and I have a human life to get back to."

"I know."

"I love you."

"I know." She smiled.

"You love me too." He crushed her to him.

"I know," she murmured against his chest.

"Ready?" Lochlan asked.

Myles nodded, giving Neeve one last look.

Lochlan's blue magic lit up the night as he opened a portal back to the human world.

"Live your best life, Myles." Brea smiled through her tears, taking her sister's hand with a gentle squeeze.

"Love you." He said one last time, and Brea wasn't sure which of them he was talking to.

Chapter 23

BREA

"We're almost home." Alona rode beside Brea along the Eastern road into the Raudur City canyon. "I've missed this wonderful place. And I can't wait to finally see mother again."

"Me too," Brea murmured. She just wondered what kind of reception she would receive. News of Queen Tierney's death would have reached the queen more than a week ago.

"And Rowena." Alona smiled. "I've missed that dear sweet woman."

"I'll fight you for her," Brea said.

"Rowena would die before she'd let anyone else care for either of us."

"That sounds like her." It was odd returning home to Eldur with the princess that had haunted the palace in her absence. Would there be room for Brea now that their beloved Alona had returned?

Finn and his father rode ahead with Brea's father who had

decided to visit Eldur to see the queen and spend time with Brea before returning to Fargelsi.

"So much has changed, Brea." Alona sighed. "I'm scared we can't go back to the way it used to be."

"Probably not, but that's nothing to be scared of. It's a whole new world now. We get to create a new normal."

"I am eighteen now," Alona said sadly. "I will have to join the serving class soon. I'm supposed to move to Sandur along the coast to the north to serve Lady Driscoll."

"That rule doesn't make any sense. Why should a princess have to have magic? It's ridiculous. Besides, it doesn't apply to you anymore, sister."

"What?" She frowned. "Oh! You're right!" Alona shifted in her saddle. "I hadn't thought of it like that. I keep forgetting I am human."

"And adopted human daughters of queens don't have to have magic." Brea beamed a smile at her sister. "So you never have to leave. You'll stay in Eldur and serve as its princess."

"One of them." She smiled.

"One of them," Brea agreed.

"You seem so sad, Brea. What's on your mind?"

"I don't know, actually. There's just this feeling like I've lost something important."

"Lochlan?"

"Yes and no." The Iskalt king had returned to his palace. Brea would always miss him, but there was something more to her pensive mood today. Something she couldn't place, like she'd forgotten something important. "I guess it's just the aftermath of everything. It's almost like a letdown, you know?"

"Kind of like none of us really know where to go from here."

"Exactly."

Crossing the bridge into the palace courtyard was bittersweet. Part of her expected to see Lochlan there, waiting for their daily lesson. Instead, her mother paced at the palace entrance.

"Girls!" Faolan rushed across the cobblestone courtyard.

"Mother!" Alona flew into her mother's arms. Faolan kissed her daughter's cheeks, holding on to her like she'd never let go.

Brea slid down from her horse, approaching her mother hesitantly.

"Brea." Faolan pulled her in, wrapping her arms around both of her daughters. "I've missed my girls so much." A tear slid down her face.

"I'm so sorry." Brea burst into tears. "It was my fault."

"Oh, my darling, no, it wasn't your fault. You saved us all from a tyrant. Yes, my beloved Tierney was lost to us, but she died saving you." Faolan hugged her tight. "I will come to terms with her death, my sweet girl, but I could never blame you. She made the sacrifice any mother would have, and she sent my girls home to me. My Tierney wouldn't have it any other way." The queen linked her arms through her daughters' and guided them into the palace. "I grieve for my wife, and we will all miss her effortless laugh and the beautiful way she saw the world, but she would want us to focus on what's ahead and never look back."

"Faolan?" Brandon followed close behind them.

The queen turned, all the color draining from her face. "Brandon?" She flung herself into his arms. "They told me you lived, but I couldn't let myself believe it until I laid eyes on you."

"I've missed you, old friend." He kissed the top of her head.

"I can't believe it's really you."

Brea smiled as she watched her parents together at last. Clearly, they loved each other in the way lifelong best friends do.

"Come, let's get you all settled." Faolan grasped Brandon's hand and headed toward the private residence. "I know you're all tired, but I want to hear everything."

"Some of it's a little fuzzy for me still," Brea said. She couldn't seem to recall all the details of what transpired between her and Regan on the battlefield.

"I imagine so, darling. You've all been through such an ordeal. I want my girls to get lots of rest. Rowena is itching to take care of you both."

Brea was eager for a nice long soak in her enormous bathtub.

"Wait, where is your room?" She asked her sister.

"Right across from yours," Faolan answered with a smile. "I designed it that way, hoping one day you'd both be here, together, and that you'd love each other like sisters."

"I think your wishes came true, Mother." Alona nudged Brea.

"I get Rowena first." Brea charged toward her room.

"No way, I've been gone the longest. I get her first." Alona took off to her rooms on the opposite side of the naked man fountain Brea had claimed as her own. It was good to be home.

"They're adorable." Alona sat in the grass watching the young ponies play together. Their mother, Raven munched on grass as she watched over her children.

"Dawn is yours, and Dusk is mine." Brea sat down beside her sister. "I laid claim to them for us when they were born."

"I can't believe you helped deliver them—in a ball gown—with Lochlan O'Shea." Alona laughed. "And Mother really sent you to work in the stables with Master Arturo?"

"I was bored out of my mind, and she realized I needed something to do. I've always loved horses, but I think Mother intended me to learn about horse breeding and not actually get my hands dirty. I'm eager to get back to my apprenticeship soon."

"I told her Majesty I'd find you two up here." Finn called to them from his perch on the paddock fence. "Your mother would like to see you both in the throne room. You should probably dress the part. All the nobles are in attendance today."

"Oh my." Alona smoothed a hand over her perfectly proper dress. Brea was dressed in her typical trousers and tunic.

"We'd better get back and change." Brea dusted the grass off her rear. "Bye, babies." She waved to the ponies. "We'll be back to see you soon."

"She's mad about those horses, isn't she?" Finn walked beside Alona, standing a little closer than princess and royal guard probably should.

"She brought them into the world. She gets to love them like a proud mama."

"Make sure they get enough to eat," Brea called to the stable boy.

"Yes, your Majesty. I'll give them extra myself."

"What do you think Mother wants?" Brea followed Finn and Alona back down through the orchard to the palace courtyard.

"We will find out."

Brea joined her sister after a mad dash through her closet, leaving a harrowed-looking Rowena fanning herself on the couch. Looking slightly more princess-like in her proper throne room attire, Brea followed Alona through the palace.

"I'm nervous." Brea took Alona's hand.

"Don't be. I think this will be good news." Alona gave her a knowing smile like she already knew why their mother had summoned them.

"Please welcome Princess Alona and Princess Brea," Faolan announced their arrival.

Men and women of the court stood to greet the princesses.

Brea had never seen the throne room so crowded.

"It's a full house," Alona murmured. "She's called in the nobles from all across Eldur."

"Please be seated." Faolan directed her court to return to their seats, guiding Alona and Brea to take the smaller thrones to her left. Tierney's throne still sat where it always had to her right.

"I've called the full court of Eldur today to fill them in on the goings on of late. And also to announce my retirement. With the death of my wife, I find I no longer have the heart to rule. I've presided over Eldur for more than one hundred years. It is time for a new generation to step forward and take the helm now.

"Brea, darling, I know this may come as a shock to you, but you are ready to take my place. You are my blood heir, but I will not force this on you. I've come here today to ask if you will be my successor. Will you rule Eldur as is your birthright?"

"What about Lona?" Brea blurted, reaching out to clutch her sister's hand. She didn't want this. She never wanted a crown. She thought her mother had finally understood that.

"Alona is a princess of Eldur as my adopted daughter, but she is human and lacks magic. She cannot rule."

"Why?"

"It's okay, Brea," Alona whispered.

"No, it's not," Brea insisted. "Please, Mother. Your Majesty, why can't she rule? My sister has grown up in the Eldur court. She knows our people, and they love her. It seems only natural that she follow in your footsteps."

"It is the law, Brea. A queen must have fire magic to rule Eldur. It's as simple as that."

"With all due respect, aren't you the queen? Change the law."

Faolan gave her an indulgent smile. "I cannot change thousands of years of Eldur tradition. Not without the court's unanimous approval and a dozen ratifications to the law."

"So? Do it. Alona Cahill is as much of Eldur as anyone. More than me. She knows this land and its people. She can rule. She should rule. It's not fair to pass her over for me. Yes, I am the queen's blood heir, but I've lived in Eldur for what, a few months?" Brea turned toward the court. "It would be my greatest honor to be your queen, if I were the best person for the job. But that is not me. It will never be me. That role belongs to my sister." She turned to Alona seated beside her. "Would you rule Eldur as our mother's successor?"

"It is up to the court and our lawmakers, but if they were to choose me as successor then it would be my honor to serve." Alona sat on her throne like the queen she should be.

"Will you consider her?" Brea addressed the court.

Faolan shook her head with a perplexed smile. "You are an

extraordinary young woman, Brea O'Rourke Cahill." She turned toward the court. "I would know your thoughts on the matter."

The lords and ladies of the court exchanged glances and hesitant smiles before the head Lord-guy stood to address the queen. "Your Majesty, the court would not be opposed to exploring the proposition young Princess Brea has brought to us. Though, our biggest concern would be how to protect our human queen in this scenario. Princess Alona would need someone to act as the magic behind the queen."

"I volunteer!" Brea stood. "I have no desire to rule, but I do have magic. Lots of it. If that is all that would stand between Alona and her rule, then I will be her protector and her greatest ally. I will stand in for her whenever my magic is needed. Eldur is my home, and I will protect it and its queen with my dying breath."

"I believe that would please the court, your Majesty, and the people. We love and greatly admire both your daughters. If Princess Alona will be your successor, we have much work to do to amend the laws. And a proper vote needs to be held so that all members of the Eldur court have an equal say in the matter."

"Very well, then." Faolan nodded. "We shall begin proceedings to decide if Alona Cahill can serve as our next queen."

"Oh, I have another suggestion," Brea said with a little too much excitement.

Faolan chuckled. "And what is your suggestion, darling?"

Brea stood and schooled her features, trying to mimic her sister's decorum. "Captain Eamon Donovan and his son, Finn Donovan went above and beyond their duties to serve Eldur and their queen. During our siege at the Fargelsi border, both men sacrificed their own well being to see the tyrant Regan O'Rourke brought to her knees. We would not have emerged victorious if not for Captain Donovan's selfless acts and his guidance. I believe both men should be honored for their service, your Majesty. Perhaps a raise in status? A duke?"

Behind her Alona gasped as she realized what that could mean for her and Finn.

"An earl? Do we have earls?" She turned to ask her sister.

"Yes, Brea. We have earls. But we need to have some lessons about how to behave at court."

"We've tried," Faolan whispered. "It didn't take."

"Is that a possibility, your Majesty? Or have I overstepped again?"

"I will take your very wise suggestions and confer with my advisors on that matter. We have much to discuss in the coming weeks. It's a new day for Eldur, and I for one am excited to see where our young princesses will lead us. It is clear they are a force to be reckoned with and will no doubt stand together as a united front. May we all survive their enthusiasm."

CHAPTER 24

BREA

Sunlight heated the stones under Brea's bare feet as she entered the courtyard, her courtyard. The naked-dude fountain smiled at her like it had missed her—but that was her weary eyes playing tricks on her.

"Did you guys miss me?" It was a question she'd asked them over and over, waiting for an answer like a crazy person. She smiled up at the guys, her eyes roaming past the sculpted butts that couldn't have been a real interpretation. She'd seen a real male butt now, and they definitely didn't look like that. A laugh bubbled out of her, and she took a seat on the edge of the fountain, swirling one hand into the crystal water.

Nausea rose in her, but she held it back. She'd had a lingering sickness over the weeks since returning to Eldur.

Pulling a coin from a pouch at her waist, she flipped it into the air. It hit the water before sinking into the depths just like every wish before it. "I want them all back," she whispered. She spent too much of her time missing people. Tierney, Myles, Neeve, and now her father after his departure several days ago. It turned out she was a total daddy's girl when that daddy actually gave a crap.

And Lochlan. He'd been on her mind each day as Eldur received more news from Iskalt about villages being repaired and trade being opened between all three kingdoms. She could picture him sitting on his throne with a cold expression on his face. Would he let the people of his court see behind the mask? Would he let them in?

She hated the thought of him living his life as the man of stone she'd once believed him to be.

Her heart ached with remembrance, but there was a piece of their story missing. For weeks she'd gone over their every interaction, replaying conversations about some barrier that sat between them, something more than just their obligations to their kingdoms.

She dug into her pouch for another coin. "I wish to remember." The coin hit the water with a tiny splash. Brea had long since stopped believing in the power of her wishes, yet she didn't stop voicing them aloud. The fountain held no magic, but if she kept her desires in her thoughts, maybe they would come to be.

"You're letting me down, you know that?" She stood and put a hand on the statue, patting the smooth stone.

"Are we interrupting something?" Finn's laughter came from one of the archways, and Brea looked up to find Alona at his side.

"No." She didn't remove her hand. "I just needed to think."

"Is that all you were doing?" His smile widened.

Brea caught sight of her hand resting casually on a certain part of the statue's anatomy and yanked it away, her cheeks growing hot. "Erm..." She started to say something else, but she lost the battle with her stomach and sprinted toward a flowering bush across the courtyard, barely making it before her breakfast spewed out of her.

Alona ran toward her and pulled her hair back. "Are you okay?"

Brea sucked in a deep breath and wiped her mouth. "Fine."

Alona's brow creased. "You've been sick since we returned. Have you been to the healer?"

"She's probably pregnant," Finn joked.

Brea froze. It had been quite a while since the single night she'd spent with Lochlan. She counted back in her head. She'd gained weight, but she assumed it was because of the lavish food her mother had been foisting on them as they ate through their grief.

"Nah." Brea laughed. It was ridiculous. "I probably just got sick from all the, you know, saving your butts." She matched his grin. "It was very taxing."

"Okay, you two." Alona wrapped an arm around Brea's waist and led her to sit on the edge of the fountain once more. "I wanted to talk to you."

"That's my signal to leave." Finn flashed her one final grin before sauntering away, a whistle on his lips.

Brea didn't get a lot of alone time with her sister. Alona spent her days learning the ins and outs of running a kingdom and her nights surrounded by nobles, and Finn, of course. In a way, it felt like it had when Brea first arrived. There wasn't much for her to do here. Only this time, there was no Lochlan to distract her.

Alona folded her hands in her lap and peeked a look over her shoulder at the fountain. "I never used to spend much time in this courtyard."

Brea laughed. "Why, sister, do naked men scare you?"

Alona's entire face went red. She was about as proper as one could be and way too easy to tease.

Brea took Alona's hand in hers. "You're the one who took the time out of your too-busy-for-your-sister schedule to come talk to me. What's up?"

Alona lifted her eyes to the sky. "I'm guessing the right answer to that is not the sky or the clouds or the sun."

"You're catching on. I'll make a human of you yet." Brea didn't miss the irony of that statement. The fae teaching the human what it was like to be human.

"I do not wish to be human if it means groping stone statues."

"Dude, that was an accident, and you know it."

Alona shrugged. "Okay, fine, I did seek you out for a reason. I've been watching you these weeks."

"Creepy, but go on."

"Can you shut up for one moment?"

Brea froze in shock before a slow smile spread across her face. She'd taught Finn the phrase shut up, and he'd thought it was hilarious. Apparently, he shared his glee with Alona.

Brea suppressed her smile and nodded for Alona to continue.

"You seem distant. Not just with me, but with everything. Well, except Dusk. That pony gets the best of your attention."

Alona wasn't wrong. It had been hard for Brea to find the joy in anything since their return. She enjoyed being with her family, but part of her was missing—something she'd barely been able to admit to herself. "I'm sorry, Alona. I've been trying to figure out where in this new world I fit."

Alona squeezed her hand. "I don't need you."

"What?" Brea pulled her hand away.

"My nobles want magic behind my throne, but Eldur itself is magic. This palace is full of those with immense power who can protect me. And... I hope to marry a man with magic and make him king consort."

Brea nudged her. "A certain son of a newly-minted earl?"

Alona ignored the question. She was on a mission, it seemed. "I'm trying to give you your freedom here, Brea."

"Freedom?" She wasn't sure she knew the meaning of the word. She'd never had choices in her life and had resigned herself to the fact that as a princess, she'd forever do the noble thing, not what made her happy.

"You never wanted the duties of the crown, and that is exactly what we've saddled you with in tying you to my throne, in keeping you here."

Brea couldn't breathe as panic wound through her chest, latching onto the magic she hadn't had much use for since returning. "But... what am I to do if I don't serve you?"

Alona stood and smiled down at her. "That is for you to decide. Isn't that the point of freedom? You can stay if you wish, but you can also go."

Brea jumped to her feet and pulled Alona into a crushing hug. "I love you, you know that, right?"

"If you love me, why are you trying to kill me?" Alona's laugh vibrated through them both.

Brea released her. "I am your sister. Wherever I am, however old we grow, I will always come when you need me."

Alona cupped her cheek. "Brea, I have known you were special since I met you in the human realm all those years ago. Something drew us together even then, and I have no doubt our lives are forever intertwined. But I am not your destiny."

Brea squeezed her eyes shut, and tears broke through. When she opened them, she saw her sister in a new light. Alona Cahill was the queen Eldur had always needed. And it was time Brea let her fly on her own.

Chapter 25

LOCHLAN

After everything that happened, a battle with Fargelsi, a king who tore the kingdom apart, hunger and desperation, the Iskalt people stood strong. Lochlan's amazement would never cease. He stood on the balcony off the throne room, gazing out across the fields that had been planted with winter crops—beans and root vegetables—the hard land only allowing certain things to grow.

To the west, he could see the ice cliffs dropping off into the frigid sea. Shipbuilders bundled themselves in furs as they worked to rebuild the trading vessels Callum had neglected.

In the villages, fae worked together to construct homes where once structures had been turned to rubble.

There was a defiance in this Iskaltian fae, a strength of will. They refused to bow their heads in defeat. Instead, they worked and struggled to bring about this better world their new king promised them.

Lord Brennan stepped onto the balcony. He'd served Iskalt well while Lochlan was away with the army, and Lochlan rewarded him by making him a top advisor among his nobles. "It is time."

Lochlan nodded, leaning against the low stone wall around the balcony. "Have you ever wondered what makes Iskalt so strong?"

Brennan shook his head. "I do not have to wonder, your Majesty. It is just who we are."

"My father used to say we had ice in our veins, but what about our hearts? Surely not ice." He'd seen how vehemently his soldiers fought to free the Fargelsians. Fae with icy hearts didn't fight for foreign kingdoms.

"Wisdom, sire."

"Wisdom?" Lochlan turned toward him and raised a brow.

"Yes, Iskalt is the wisest of the three kingdoms." His lips curved up, signaling the joke.

Lochlan shook his head with a low chuckle. Iskaltians were known for being brutes, not scholars. It fit the icy plains. "Well." Lochlan clapped his advisor on the shoulder. "Let's go be wise."

They walked into the throne room where two hearths sat with fires blazing. Lochlan shed his coat and handed it to a servant with a nod of thanks. The throne room was empty save for Brennan and the servant, but soon it would buzz with life.

Since he returned from Fargelsi, Lochlan had taken to meeting with his people every day when the sun sat highest in the sky. He'd seen his father do the very thing, listening as fae described their troubles and brought tributes to their king. Niall O'Shea was beloved, and he loved his kingdom in return.

Lochlan only hoped to be half the king his father was, and this was a start. He'd grown up in Eldur, so his fae didn't know him. It was time for that to change.

He let a cool mask settle over his features as he stepped up to the velvet-covered throne and lowered himself. After a life spent wondering if he'd ever wear his father's crown, this felt right. Reaching up, he adjusted the simple golden circlet atop his head.

Soon, fae would crowd the room, clamoring for their king's attention. And he'd listen, truly wanting to fix their problems, but also scared to let himself feel for them. Emotions only led to pain.

He'd learned that recently. Nothing came good from letting people in.

Maybe his father was wrong. Ice wasn't in his veins. It had entered his heart as well.

"Are you ready, your Majesty?" A guard poked his head in. "You have quite the crowd today."

"Let them in." He folded his hands in his lap and straightened his spine.

He was the king now. There were no more adventures with Finn or afternoons in the library with Alona. Faolan wasn't here to hold his hand. Tierney would never again brush away a boy's tears.

And Brea... She belonged in Eldur with the family he missed dearly.

Pushing thoughts of everyone he'd left behind from his mind, he nodded to the first fae who approached his throne. Each parishioner was accompanied down the long aisle by a guard.

"Sire." She bowed, keeping her eyes on the ground.

"Rise." Lochlan gestured to her.

She still didn't meet his gaze. "I live in a village near the mountain Vatlands, your Majesty. For months, our cattle have been picked off by bandits."

"Bandits?" He leaned forward.

She nodded. "We think they are escaped prisoners from the prison realm. Your uncle and Queen Regan released them in hopes they'd fight for Iskalt. But when you took the throne, they disappeared into the mountains."

The prison realm struck dread in the hearts of most fae, but Lochlan only felt an immense sadness he couldn't understand. Part of him wondered if someone he cared about had been sent there to be forgotten by everyone they knew.

He shook off the feeling. "I will send soldiers to the village. Give any detail you can remember to my scribe." He met her gaze. "I promise we will help you."

Relief flooded her face. "Thank you, your Majesty. Thank you." She practically ran toward the scribe to give him the information.

Lochlan waited for the next fae to come forward.

He didn't know how long he sat on that throne listening to both complaints and praise. The kingdom's resources were already stretched thin, but he'd do what he could for everyone in need.

He rubbed his temples, giving himself a short break before the next fae approached.

"Your Majesty." Lochlan's heart stopped. He would know that voice anywhere, but for a moment he wondered if he'd imagined it. "I've come a long way to beg a favor."

He lifted his eyes slowly, drinking in the sight of the girl he'd let go of, the one who should be in Eldur where she belonged. "What is this favor?" He choked out the words.

She wiped her palms on her pants—having not bothered with a dress when coming to his court. He looked around, realizing how little she fit in with the ladies around him. And it was the best sight.

One side of her mouth curved up. "Well, a little birdie told me the O'Shea's have the power to go to the human realm."

Murmuring wound through the room, and Lochlan almost laughed when he heard someone say, "Birds don't talk."

"Do you wish to return home?" Just the thought of her leaving this world altogether sent a pang through his chest.

She nodded. "I do."

His shoulders sank. Brea had come to Iskalt for his portal magic, nothing else.

She went on. "There's a boy there. He's sort of my best friend. And I need to talk to him."

"Myles left just a few weeks ago. Surely you want to give it more time."

She shook her head, her eyes glassing over. "You see, Myles and I tell each other everything. When he left, I was headed home to Eldur as my mother's heir, but he knew I wasn't happy. He always knew. So, now I need to tell him I'm okay, that he doesn't have to worry about me. It seems my family has finally realized they shouldn't give me a throne I don't want. But I need to tell Myles I think I finally found what I do want."

Lochlan didn't know when he'd stood or how he'd forced his legs to move as he walked down the steps. "You won't be queen of Eldur?"

She shook her head. "Once she's ready, they're going to crown Alona. And that blasted sister of mine set me free. Can you believe that? She told me she didn't need me."

Lochlan was only vaguely aware of their audience as he stopped in front of Brea. It took every bit of strength not to reach for her. "And with this freedom, you wish to go to the human realm?"

She nodded.

She'd also said she knew what she wanted. He leaned down to meet her gaze. "And what is it you want, Brea?"

"You." She breathed out the word. "I want y—"

He crushed his lips to hers, breathing her in like she was the air he needed to live. Brea hummed in the back of her throat as she deepened the kiss.

He tugged her shirt, pulling her further into his arms, never wanting to let her go again. He fell in love with Brea Robinson when he was a teenager sent to watch over her. His feelings had grown every time she fought him, every time they fought what lived between them.

Because this emotion, it was a living, breathing thing.

"Brea," he whispered against her lips, ignoring the murmuring of their audience. "Iskalt is not your kingdom." He needed her to be sure, because if she let him, he'd keep her with him forever.

"I never wanted the Eldur throne. Now I know why. There's one thing Eldur doesn't have that I need as much as I need my next breath."

"What?"

"A certain grumpy Iskaltian king."

He kissed her again, more slowly this time, savoring all the moments that would make up their future. "I love you."

A few nobles cleared their throats, and Lochlan vaguely heard Brennan forcing the crowd to leave. Fae grumbled, and when the doors shut, leaving him alone with Brea, all he could see was her.

She put a hand against his cheek and looked up at him. "I will love you under three conditions."

He laughed. "Of course, you have conditions."

Brea glanced around them as if noticing they weren't alone for the first time. She shrugged as if it didn't bother her. "I'm not fancy. I don't want big dresses. I'll do ruley things and help our fae, but if you force me to actually wear the crown, I'll just use it as a Frisbee."

He had no idea what a Frisbee was, but he didn't care. In that moment, he'd have given her anything. She crossed her arms. "Okay, the next one is more serious. I really need you to take me to the human realm to tell Myles the news."

"What news?"

"That's condition number three. I want to marry you, Lochlan O'Shea. We've been through so much and lost a lot. I don't want to waste any more time. I want to be tied to you, magically, non-magically. In every way possible."

He only stared at her for a moment before pulling her against his chest, a genuine smile parting his lips. A laugh broke free of him, and he lifted his eyes to the empty room, knowing the fae who'd seen them would spread this gossip about their king far and wide. "Iskalt is going to love you." Just like Eldur did. Brea was always meant to be a queen whether she'd wanted the title or not.

He rested his chin on her shoulder, listening to her shallow breath and letting it remind him this was real.

He'd been wrong before. Lochlan O'Shea might have had ice in his veins, but his heart... that was full of fire.

Of Brea.

What about Brea's wedding? Check out the bonus chapters after the epilogue.

EPILOGUE
GRIFFIN O'SHEA

SIX WEEKS AGO

“This is where we leave you.” The Iskalt guards stood in a line behind Gri n. “Whatever magic ties you to our world will be destroyed the moment you cross through the archway, including your restraints.”

Gri n’s hands were magically bound behind his back as he gazed up at the massive archway between the stones flanking the road. He’d never traveled this far north into the mountainous Vatlands bordering Iskalt.

“Everyone forgets once I’m on the other side?” Gri n took a step forward, not sure he could go through with it.

“We can do this the easy way or the hard way. Your choice.” Gri n nodded, not sure he wanted to experience the hard way.“I can do this,” he murmured to himself. It was his decision to come here. To free Brea from their farce of a marriage. It killed him that she would soon forget the sacrifice he was about to make for her.

“What’s on the other side?” He asked the guards.

"No idea." A guard draped a supply pack across his shoulders. "Best of luck to you, Prince Griffin O'Shea."

His shoulders fell as he realized that was likely the last time anyone would ever call him by his full name and title. A title he'd given up in pursuit of another. He deserved this. With a deep breath and a nod to his countrymen, Griffin took the final steps toward his destiny.

He expected to feel the momentous change from one moment to the next. Glancing behind him, the guards had vanished, like he'd stepped through a portal. With his hands free, Griffin surveyed his surroundings. Nothing but snow-capped mountains and wilderness greeted him. It was a vast and beautiful place, this prison world.

A crushing weight of realization hit him, and he stumbled to his knees. Everyone he'd ever known. Everyone he'd loved had forgotten he ever existed. Memories flashed through his mind of him and Lochlan as children. Of Brea on their wedding day. For them it was all gone. Vanished in an instant. He hadn't expected it to hit him so hard.

"The first day is the worst." The unfamiliar voice sounded behind him.

Griffin scrambled back to his feet, unsure of what to expect from the other prisoners. She was covered in furs and weapons, but something about her felt unthreatening.

"What did you do?" She rested her hand on the sword at her hip.

He didn't see any sense in trying to hide it. "I betrayed my brother, king of Iskalt and supported Queen Regan of Fargelsi. I was to be her heir."

"So you're a royal." Her lip curled up into a sneer. "If you want to survive here, you'd best keep that to yourself. Most of us are here because of Regan O'Rourke. She dead?"

"Yes."

"Good. Follow me."

"How do I know I can trust you?" Griffin stood his ground.

"You don't." She shrugged. "But you don't want to risk anyone else finding you."

Gri n took a step toward her. "Where are we going?"

"Somewhere safe. At least for now. You coming?" She turned back toward him.

"I suppose you're my best option." He followed her up the pathway into the mountains.

"I'm your only option. Welcome to Myrkur. Otherwise known as the prison realm."

It's not over yet! The story continues in Fae's Prisoner: Queens of the Fae BookFour Available Now!

But first, keep reading to check out the Bonus Wedding Chapters at the end of the book!

Bonus Chapter I

BREA

Pain exploded through Brea's stomach, and she shot up in bed. She'd taken to napping during the day, and today was the biggest day of all. She needed her rest.

But someone else wasn't having it.

"Kicking isn't nice." She put a hand on her stomach, a smile flitting over her tired face.

The door to the room opened, and Brea sprang from the bed. "Myles!" She rushed for her friend, laughing as her growing belly got in the way.

"Um, Brea." His eyes widened. "I think you have a growth."

"So funny, Myles. You should take up comedy."

He laughed and pulled her into another hug. She hadn't seen him for months—since visiting the human realm to tell him the news. Lochlan had met every condition she set for him.

"I have a present for you, but it's kind of mean since you can't enjoy it until after the baby is born." He slid the bag off his shoulder and opened it to reveal packages and packages of her favorite coffee grounds.

"That's the best present ever." She snatched the bag. "Assuming I can teach people here to brew it for me."

"I'm guessing they'd do just about anything for you." He walked farther into the room, whistling at the sight. High stone arches reached up to the domed ceiling. Three hearths kept the room warm in the cold kingdom. "You ready for today?"

She smiled. "Yes." She'd never been more ready for anything. Living in Iskalt was very different from Eldur, but she loved it just the same. And Lochlan... neither of them were perfect. They both had tempers, and she loved nothing more than to annoy him, but they were perfect together. "I love him, Myles."

"I know." He smiled. "I've known you loved him since the moment I met him."

"That makes no sense. I wasn't even there."

"But I saw how much he loved you, and I knew there was no way it wasn't returned. It was always meant to be him. Even when you were with Griff, Lochlan was in your heart."

Brea's brow scrunched, and she cocked her head. "Griff?"

Myles flopped onto her bed. "I mean, you never really loved the guy."

"I don't know what you're talking about, Myles."

"Right. You probably don't want to talk about Lochlan's brother on the day of your wedding."

Lochlan didn't have a brother. "Seriously, Myles, nothing you're saying makes sense."

Myles sat up. "He was on his way to the prison realm when I went back to the human realm. I felt kind of bad for him. He never stood a chance with you."

The prison realm? Brea's blood went cold. For months, she'd felt like a memory was missing, an important one.

She sat in front of her looking glass and stared at herself, the circles under her eyes, the puffiness of her cheeks. Myles was right, today wasn't the day to think of anything but her wedding. "I wish Lochlan would have let us wait until after the baby was born for the wedding. I look like a whale."

"You look beautiful." Lochlan's voice came from the doorway where he leaned against the frame. They'd decided to forget propriety and had shared these rooms since she came to Iskalt. She'd never get used to waking up next to him.

Myles stood and crossed the room to hold his fist out. Lochlan bumped it with his own. They must have been practicing because Myles nodded in approval. "I'll leave you to be all gross and stuff." He winked. "I heard a certain Fargelsian queen has arrived, and I'm off to do some wooing of my own."

When he was gone, Brea laughed. "Myles and Neeve?"

"He does know he lives in an entirely different world, right?" Lochlan shook his head.

"Talk about long-distance relationships."

Lochlan crossed the room and leaned down to drop a kiss on her neck. "There's no going back after today."

"Do you want to go back?" She held her breath waiting for the answer.

"Never."

Brea stood and threaded her arms around his neck. "There's no escaping me now."

He kissed along her jawline until he reached her ear. "You're the one who is trapped in my kingdom."

"Whoa." She laughed, pulling away. "Too soon, dude. Too soon."

He reached for another kiss, but she dodged him with a laugh. "Can I ask you a question?"

"Of course."

"Do you have a brother I don't know about?"

He raised an eyebrow. "Looking for a better option?"

"No, it was just something Myles said."

"I was an only child. My parents died before they could give me siblings." He cocked his head. "A fact you already knew."

She pursed her lips. "Yeah, okay." She walked toward the uber comfy couch in front of one of the fireplaces and sank into it. "My feet hurt."

He laughed. "Do I need to carry you down the aisle?"

"That would be nice."

A folded piece of paper sat on the table. She hadn't seen it before, but it looked worn, like it had been through a journey. "What's this?" She lifted it.

Lochlan sat on the arm of the couch. "I found it in my saddle bags when I cleaned them out yesterday. Part of me wondered if it was a note from Finn to Alona."

She unfolded it and scanned the words.

NUMBER 7: I love that none of this scares you.

I miss you.

-G

"Who is G?"

Lochlan took the paper. "A fake name Finn used maybe? Before Alona was taken, writing something like this to her could get him in trouble."

"Yeah, maybe."

G... Griff. That was the man Myles mentioned. Why was it numbered? Were there more? And how did it come to be in Lochlan's saddle bag?

Asking questions Brea would never get answers to had no purpose. Pining after memories she no longer had would only hinder the future she sought. With a sigh, she hefted herself to her feet.

"What are you doing?" Lochlan asked.

"Letting go of the past." Whatever that past was. She approached the blazing fire and let the note fall from her fingers. The edges curled in moments before it disappeared.

She didn't know what secrets the note held or what memories had been erased, but the prison realm only held darkness. Whoever it was that had been sent there must not deserve to be remembered.

She curled back onto the couch, pulling Lochlan down onto the seat. His arms wrapped around her, tugging her back against his chest where she belonged.

After all the evil they'd endured, Brea O'Rourke Cahill—soon to be O'Shea —deserved a little good.

Bonus Chapter 2

BREA

"This is really a human tradition?" Brandon looked down at Brea in her white dress and fur cape. "You're not just trying to include your old dad in the wedding?"

"No, it's like *the* human tradition. It's your job to walk me down the aisle and dance with me at my wedding." Brea tucked her hand into the crook of his arm.

"Are you nervous?"

"No." She smiled up at her father. "It feels like I've been waiting on this day forever. I'm about to get my happily ever after." She rested her free hand over her growing baby bump, eager to see her almost-husband.

"You deserve all the happiness life brings you, and I'm so excited about being a grandfather. I warn you, I will spoil that baby if it's the last thing I do."

"Between you and Mother, I'm starting to wonder if I'll even get to hold my baby."

"It's our first grandchild, and we missed out on your childhood."

"We're all here together now. That's all that matters."

"It's time." Neeve stepped into the antechamber where Brea and their father waited. "You look beautiful."

"Thank you. I'm so glad you're here."

"I wouldn't miss it." Neeve handed Brea a bouquet of white winter blossoms and left to make her way down the aisle with Myles. Alona and Finn followed. She'd planned a small wedding with all the human and fae traditions melding together.

As she walked with her father across the ballroom where their wedding celebration would take place, the growing sense of deja vu overwhelmed her. Pausing, she rubbed her pregnant belly.

"Everything okay? Do you need to sit down?" Her father frowned at her pale face.

"It's nothing. Just the excitement." She pushed her confusing thoughts away and braced herself on the threshold to the winter garden. Several rows of seating fanned out around the alter under a canopy of vines. Twinkling lights flickered among the vines, casting an ethereal glow over the small crowd of happy faces there to celebrate with Brea and Lochlan. Everyone she loved was here. Her parents, sisters, and closest friends as well as some newer friends among the Iskalt court she'd grown to love in her short time here.

Brea smiled as she walked down the aisle with her father, but she couldn't shake the feeling that something was missing. The moment she laid eyes on her husband to be, all thoughts of forgotten things vanished from her mind. He was so handsome in his winter white jacket, trimmed in silver with his shiny blond hair tied back from his face.

Brandon took each of their hands and linked them together in the tradition of the fae, leaving them at the alter to sit with Brea's mother.

Brea was nervous about this next part. She was thrilled to be marrying Lochlan, but the magic of the marriage bond that would unite them for life worried her for some reason.

Lochlan's intense blue eyes washed over her, calming her as he spoke the words that would bind him to her.

"I am Lochlan O'Shea, King of Iskalt." His voice rang out around them, confident and proud. "Today, I come to you with my whole heart bared for you, Brea O'Rourke Cahill. If you will have me, I am yours, for always. I enter into our marriage with nothing to hide and without hesitation. I bind myself to you. Everything I have is yours. I willingly vow to never love another." His eyes shone with the light of his magic. Blue bands flowed around their hands, binding them together.

It was her turn now.

"I am Brea O'Rourke Cahill, Princess of Fargelsi and Eldur." Her heart was so full she couldn't stem the flow of words that once scared her when she first heard what she had to say to invoke their fae marriage. "I come to you with everything I have." Her free hand rested over the swell of their child inside her. "Lochlan O'Shea, you are my love and my life, you carry my heart with you wherever you go. I take you, gladly, and with my whole heart. I am yours, for always. I enter into our marriage with nothing to hide and without hesitation. I bind myself to you and our growing family. I willingly vow to never love another." The yellow light of her fire magic snaked around their hands. Ice and fire, united forever.

"Can the best friend cut in?" Myles approached Brea and Lochlan on the dance floor inside the ballroom.

"Cut in?" Lochlan frowned at his human friend. "She is my wife. I get to dance with her on our wedding day."

"He meant to say, yes, Myles, my friend, you can have the rest of this dance."

Lochlan grunted, stepping aside with a twitch of his lips. "I will be back."

"Bring some snacks," Brea called after him, taking Myles' hand in hers.

"Congratulations, Brea. Married with a baby on the way and barely nineteen. How very rural Ohio of you."

"You can take the girl out of Ohio, but you can't take Ohio out of the girl." She rested her head on her best friend's shoulder. "I'm so glad you got to be here today. Can you stay for a while? I miss you so much."

"I can stay for a few days, but—"

"That's not good enough. I need you for at least a week before the humans can have you back. And you have to promise to come back when the baby is born. Uncle Myles has to be here to step in with the whole lamaze thing when I threaten to kill Lochlan."

"I have a thing I have to—"

"Put it on hold," Brea insisted.

"Will you shut up for two seconds?" Myles rolled his eyes.

"Fine, what excuses do you have for leaving me in my time of need?"

"Your time of need? You just got married, Brea. This is the happiest I've ever seen you. You deserve it, you know." He whirled her around the dance floor. "I want you to promise me you'll always be this happy. Fargelsi is a long way from Iskalt, so I won't get to see you as often—"

Brea stopped dancing. "What did you just say?"

"I can't live without her, Brea. I've tried, and it sucks."

Brea squealed and clapped her hands. "You're staying?"

"I don't think I have a choice, actually." He glanced back at Neeve with a brilliant smile. "She's decided to make me her king consort."

Brea burst into tears, and Lochlan came charging across the room. "No, no. Don't kill him, Loch. I'm just so freaking happy." She threw her arms around her best friend. "You're going to be my brother for real. But what about your family?" She leaned back to look him in the eye.

"I love them, but I've said my goodbyes. And besides, I have my good buddy Loch here to take me home whenever I want."

"Does anyone in this family realize I am a king?" Lochlan rolled his eyes. "I'm a little busy these days."

"Is she okay?" Neeve crept up beside Myles.

"Neeve!" She fell into her sister's arms. "I'm only ugly crying because I'm really pregnant and really, really happy." Lochlan came up behind her and pressed a lace handkerchief into her hand, pulling her back against his chest.

"We are so happy for you both, and we can't wait to dance at your wedding," Lochlan said.

"Oh, when is it? Please say after the baby, I don't want to feel like a dancing cow at another wedding."

"Myles has this human thing he wants," Neeve said with a grin. "It's sweet."

"What?" Brea dabbed at her eyes, hoping she didn't look like a puffy eyed wreck.

"I want my niece or nephew to be the ring bearer."

Brea started crying all over again.

"Myles, stop making my wife cry," Lochlan said, turning to Brea. "And stop referring to yourself as a cow. You are beautiful, Brea."

"It's... o-kay." Brea sniffed. "I'm all good now." She dabbed at her eyes again, smiling through her tears. "I couldn't be happier if I tried." She stared around the room at all her family, dancing and celebrating with her. It was a far cry from the family she grew up in, but she'd go through it all over again to arrive in this moment for her very own fairytale come true.

If you're ready to meet Brea and Loch's children, download Fae's Prisoner now!

What's Next

A traitor in search of redemption. A king's champion on a mission.

He wants to free his people, but she's determined he'll never succeed.

The moment Griffin crossed into the prison realm, every fae he'd ever known forgot he existed. Left with nothing—not even his magic—he's had to survive in a land of eternal darkness where a ruthless king terrorizes his subjects.

Now, he must return to his homeland with one purpose—destroy the magic binding the Dark Fae to the prison realm—or suffer the consequences.

But he isn't alone. Riona, a devoted supporter of the Dark King, watches his every move, forcing him to remain focused on their mission, even when facing a brother who does not recognize him, a former love who doesn't know him, and two children who could be the key to everything.

This time, Griffin will have to decide if becoming a traitor—again—will lead to the redemption he seeks.

Fae's Prisoner: Queens of the Fae Book Four
Available Now!

Fae's Prisoner Preview

GRIFFIN

Ten years of cruel darkness and starvation.

Ten years of scraping by in a prison realm, of bowing before a king who liked nothing more than seeing his people on their knees.

But Griffin O'Shea had no delusions. He deserved his fate, deserved the punishment that sent him across the powerful barrier surrounding the fae prison realm, to have everyone outside that barrier forget he ever existed.

He tried to forget too, tried to put his brother from his mind, to forget the woman he'd married—not that she'd wanted to marry him. He'd felt it all those years ago, the moment their marriage bond shattered the day he left his old life behind.

There were only two ways to get out of a fae marriage.

Death.

Or a fate worse than death. The prison realm.

Griffin's anger had long since subsided over the fate his brother and his wife allowed him to choose, the one they'd accepted without a fight. There was no time for hatred anymore, no time to do anything but survive.

Which was what Griffin tried to do.

The cheers from the gathering crowd reached him where he leaned against the cold stone wall of the tunnel beneath the castle. For ten years, he'd managed to avoid the notice of King Egan Byrne, but that wasn't possible anymore, not when the people he'd grown to care about were in danger.

But he'd failed them.

Failed to infiltrate the castle, failed to save the little girl who looked to him with so much trust.

He pushed off the wall and paced the length of the tunnel.

He didn't deserve Nessa's trust. When Nessa's sister, Shauna, found him on his first day here, he hadn't deserved her kindness or her friendship. She'd saved his life that day.

But he deserved this day, now.

The crowd, come to watch the newest battle, would assume Griffin had betrayed King Egan. He supposed he had, but that wasn't why Griffin wanted this, why a fight for his life was long overdue.

If they knew the true reason he was here in the prison realm, he'd lose their trust.

He'd been an ally of Queen Regan O'Rourke, the now dead sorceress of Fargelsi. If word got out, not even Nessa would look to him with trust.

Because the queen he'd spent most of his life in service to sent a good many of them here—to a realm the rest of the fae world forgot existed. The fourth kingdom of Myrkur. The realm of the Dark Fae, where it was always night and Griffin O'Shea held no magic.

If he died today, he would die still feeling like a traitor.

Light footsteps echoed through the tunnel behind him, and he lifted his head to find Gulliver, an orphaned kid Griffin found about a year after joining Shauna's village. They'd been together ever since.

But he shouldn't be here. "Gullie, what in the name of all the realms do you think you're doing here?"

Gulliver narrowed his cat-like eyes. His tail curled around his middle. He wasn't the first Dark Fae Griffin had met with such features. Before crossing the prison barrier, he hadn't thought fae like him existed.

But they did. Here in Myrkur some fae had tails or tusks, others had horns or wings. They were the Dark Fae, exiled to this realm generations ago.

"I came to see you." Gulliver crossed his arms, trying to project strength like he always did when he thought he was in trouble.

Griffin sighed. He didn't want his last words to his twelve-year-old charge to be a chastisement. "If the king or his men catch you here—"

"I know. I know. They'll take me as an indentured servant to work in the mines." He flashed Griffin a grin. "Good thing they never catch me."

"Yet," Griffin grumbled. "They haven't caught you *yet*." Gulliver was a thief. A good one. He had the ability to move around unseen, unheard. And his tail was lightning quick, shoving his stolen bounty away faster than a blink. It came in handy. "Were you trying to sneak up on me?"

"No. That would be useless. You always seem to know I'm there." Gulliver kicked at a rock on the ground before lifting his vulnerable eyes to Griffin "The crowd says you're going to fight the king's greatest warrior."

"Gullie, I'm going to be okay."

"Do you promise?"

Griffin sighed but didn't respond. They both knew it was a promise he wasn't sure he could keep. "You've never seen me fight." He'd had many chances to wield a sword over the years but mostly to protect their secret village from other Dark Fae. There was a difference between that kind of fight and single combat with a trained swordsman. "Have you seen my competitor yet?"

Gulliver shook his head. "Do you think it'll be a Dark Fae?" His eyes narrowed to slits. "Or Tuatha De Dannon?"

"Probably Dark Fae." The king only took Dark Fae into his employ. Light Fae, those like Griffin, were more likely to be indentured servants, and the Tuatha De Dannon were land fae, like Gulliver. An ancient race of fae born here in Myrkur but enslaved all the same.

"What if it's a mountain ogre? Or a Slyph with great bat wings?"

Griffin planted a hand on each of Gulliver's shoulders and dipped his head to look him in the eye. "I don't want you watching this fight."

"But—"

"When you leave here, find Shauna and get as far away from the castle as you can."

Gulliver's bottom lip quivered. "What about Nessa? The king still has her."

"Practice patience. I will do my best for Nessa but I don't want my fate to be yours. You're a good man, Gulliver, but I need to know you'll be safe."

He puffed up his chest even as he fought back tears. Griffin yanked him into a hug, not wanting to let go.

Since entering the prison realm, Griffin had found what he'd sought his whole life, what he'd once deluded himself into thinking he'd found with Regan—the queen who raised him.

A family.

He had to fight for them now, to honor them until his last breath.

Which could very well be today.

Releasing Gulliver, Griffin pushed him back the way he'd come. "Go before someone sees you."

Gulliver took a strengthening breath, giving Griffin one last look, before running down the tunnel, leaving Griffin alone once more.

He'd never been strong in his convictions. At least, not until coming here. He'd had a tendency to let people down, never being who they wanted or needed him to be. The day he'd found the three-year-old Gulliver sleeping on the street, he'd made a vow to himself. He would always be there for him, and he'd try to be better, to do better. For the kid.

But now, it was time to break that vow.

It was time to say goodbye to the best friend he'd ever had, Shauna. Time to leave Gulliver as he promised he never would.

Time to give up on saving the young Nessa, who'd only had eight years of freedom and would spend the rest of her life in captivity.

He'd failed them all. Because he wasn't going to win this fight.

The crowd outside grew louder, their stomps over the tunnel making dirt rain down on him. They came to see a battle, to see blood.

Footsteps echoed through the tunnel from the arena ahead, and Griffin turned to see the king himself approaching, the short tusks protruding through his beard made his smile seem even darker.

Griffin didn't bow, instead he straightened his shoulders and narrowed his eyes.

A loud clang echoed as King Egan threw a sword at Griffin's feet. He bent to pick it up, examining the rusted blade and cracked hilt.

"The great Griffin O'Shea." The king crossed his arms.

Griffin didn't make a habit of sharing his last name, but something told him he didn't want to find out how the king knew it. Yet... "You don't get to speak my full name."

"Your little Nessa has been a great wealth of information."

Griffin lunged for him, slamming the king against the stone wall. "What did you do to her?" Even as a kid, Nessa wouldn't have given information freely to this man, information only Shauna was supposed to know.

The king smiled. "The child is strong in her convictions. I quite like that. She wouldn't give me information to save herself. But to save you..."

Griffin cursed. Nessa must have thought telling the king Griffin was of royal blood would earn him a place of power. She was wrong about one thing. Griffin didn't want that power.

The king pushed Griffin away and righted himself. "It doesn't have to come to this. Join me now and this all goes away. I could use a soldier with the royal blood of Iskalt running through his veins."

Royal blood. The blood of Iskalt, one of the other three fae realms where his brother now held the throne. But Griffin had never honored his blood. He hadn't chosen Iskalt in the war that brought him here. He'd served the Fargelsi Queen all his life, fighting against both Iskalt and Eldur.

"I will never join you." Griffin spat.

King Egan's lips ticked up into a pleased smile behind his unkempt beard. "Let's make this interesting, shall we? I don't believe you will win, but if you do, the girl's contract is yours, and you're free to take her home."

"The girl... you'd give Nessa to me?"

His smile widened. "Of course. Though, she could have value as an indentured. She's beautiful. A bit young and weak, but perhaps she'll prove useful in many ways."

Griffin gripped the hilt of his sword tighter, wishing he could drive the rusted blade straight through Egan's belly. But it was no secret the paranoid king surrounded himself with loyal servants who wouldn't let Griffin take his next breath if he slayed the king where he stood.

Griffin stepped closer to Egan, dropping his voice. "One day, I'm going to kill you."

A booming laugh echoed against the stone. "Well, my boy, you must win this day first. I'll see you in the arena."

When he was gone, Griffin leaned his head back against the wall, finding a new strength in himself. If he won today, maybe he wouldn't fail Nessa after all.

This was for her and every other fae who'd made Griffin one of their own.

He ran a hand through his long auburn hair, adjusting the ribbon that held it away from his face.

Ogres were big and dangerous but also slow. He could use that to his advantage. A Slyph however, with their powerful wings, they were fast and difficult to catch.

A key rattled in the lock at the end of the tunnel that led into the arena. A bald man dressed in the king's colors stepped in. Black ragged wings protruded from his back. "It is time." The Slyph spoke with a gravelly voice that matched his countenance.

Griffin was ready. He would save Nessa or die trying.

He stepped away from the wall and followed the man through the opening. Rough stone turned to fine sand beneath his feet.

He couldn't make out the faces of the crowd in the inky darkness, but that wasn't unusual. The sun never rose in Myrkur. It was one of the harshest things about this broken and cruel realm. Griffin had almost forgotten what it felt like to have sunlight warm his skin.

Or magic sparking at his fingertips.

Upon entry into the prison realm, all magic vanished from those who could wield it. Griffin hadn't been able to call forth his own magic in more than a decade.

Torches lined the arena and the platform on which the king sat, creating a circle of light. Griffin wiped a sweaty palm on his linen pants before tearing his white shirt off over his head and tossing it to the ground.

The crowd chanted and cheered along with the rhythm of a heavy drumbeat coming from somewhere behind the king.

The king stood, and the crowd quieted, straining to hear his every word. "My fae friends, thank you for coming today." Egan turned to the crowd, raising his hands at their applause.

Griffin wondered if the crowd was full of only Dark Fae, the ones who were loyal to their king. Or had they forced others to attend these macabre fights?

The king continued. "This morning, the young man before you was given a choice. Serve me or face his own mortality."

The crowd booed and hissed at Griffin.

But he wouldn't let himself become an indentured servant to a corrupt king. He'd faithfully served Regan despite knowing it was wrong.

Never again.

"And he has chosen death!"

The crowd roared with anger at Griffin's audacity to deny their king.

Griffin refused to look at the fae calling for his demise.

The king held up a hand to quiet the cheers. "Now, I am not a heartless fool. On the chance Griffin manages to defeat my best warrior, he will win the contract of my newest servant, Nessa." His eyes drifted to Griffin. "The rules are simple. Fight to the death by any means necessary."

If Griffin managed to kill an ogre, he'd have no regrets. He'd take Nessa home, and they'd tell stories of tonight for years to come.

The thick metal grate blocking the entrance to another tunnel lifted. Griffin braced himself, ready for whatever fae beast came for him.

Out of the shadows came a warrior.

Not an ogre.

And not someone Griffin wanted to kill.

AVAILABLE NOW!

Fae's Prisoner: Queens of the Fae Book Four

Don't miss the FREE prequel,
Fae's Dilemma
Grab your copy at
https://BookHip.com/VJMXVGD

ABOUT MELISSA

Melissa A. Craven is an Amazon bestselling author of Young Adult Contemporary Fiction and YA Fantasy (her Contemporary fans will know her as Ann Maree Craven). Her books focus on strong female protagonists who aren't always perfect, but they find their inner strength along the way. Melissa's novels appeal to audiences of all ages and fans of almost any genre. She believes in stories that make you think and she loves playing with foreshadowing, leaving clues and hints for the careful reader.

Melissa draws inspiration from her background in architecture and interior design to help her with the small details in world building and scene settings. (Her degree in fine art also comes in handy.) She is a diehard introvert with a wicked sense of humor and a tendency for hermit-like behavior. (Seriously, she gets cranky if she has to put on anything other than yoga pants and t-shirts!)

Melissa enjoys editing almost as much as she enjoys writing, which makes her an absolute weirdo among her peers. Her favorite pastime is sitting on her porch when the weather is nice with her two dogs, Fynlee and Nahla, reading from her massive TBR pile and dreaming up new stories.

Visit Melissa at Melissaacraven.com for more information about her newest series and discover exclusive content.

Want to see more books by Melissa A. Craven? You can view them here

https://books2read.com/ap/ng5y22/Melissa-A-Craven

Join Melissa and Michelle's Facebook Group: @Fantasy Book Warriors

Follow Michelle and Melissa on TikTok

@ATaleOfTwoAuthors

facebook.com/MelissaACravenAuthor

instagram.com/melissaacraven

amazon.com/Melissa-A.-Craven/e/B00VSPF86W

ABOUT M. LYNN

Michelle MacQueen is a USA Today bestselling author of love. Yes, love. Whether it be YA romance, NA romance, or fantasy romance (Under M. Lynn), she loves to make readers swoon.

The great loves of her life to this point are two tiny blond creatures who call her "aunt" and proclaim her books to be "boring books" for their lack of pictures. Yet, somehow, she still manages to love them more than chocolate.

When she's not sharing her inexhaustible wisdom with her niece and nephew, Michelle is usually lounging in her ridiculously large bean bag chair creating worlds and characters that remind her to smile every day - even when a feisty five-year-old is telling her just how much she doesn't know.

See more from M. Lynn and sign up
to receive updates and deals!
michellelynnauthor.com

Join Melissa and Michelle's Facebook Group:
@Fantasy Book Warriors

Follow Michelle and Melissa on TikTok

@ATaleOfTwoAuthors

Want to see more books by Michelle?
You can view them here

https://books2read.com/ap/R5my46/M-Lynn

www.ingramcontent.com/pod-product-compliance
Lightning Source LLC
Chambersburg PA
CBHW020244030826
48979CB00030B/2543/J
9781970052176